WEREWOLF
AUGUST 1945

WEREWOLF
August 1945

By the same author

Scarecrow

Matthew PRITCHARD

WEREWOLF
August 1945

SALT

CROMER

PUBLISHED BY SALT

12 Norwich Road, Cromer, Norfolk NR27 0AX United Kingdom

Printed in Great Britain by Clays Ltd, St Ives plc

Typeset in Sabon 10/13

ISBN 978 1 907773 80 8 paperback

1 3 5 7 9 8 6 4 2

'Do not rejoice in his defeat, you men. For though the world has stood up and stopped the bastard, the bitch that bore him is in heat again.'

— BERTOLT BRECHT

PART ONE

I

August 1945
Occupied Germany, British Zone

Safe now within the shadows of the trees, Little Otto pulled the mask from his face and peered back towards the house.

British soldiers in berets and leather jerkins lounged by the wrecked kitchen door, smoking cigarettes and chatting as a shaven-headed sergeant dragged Little Otto's suitcases out of the kitchen and smashed the locks from them with a rifle butt. One by one the soldiers yanked articles of clothing from the suitcases and began comparing and trying them against themselves.

'Blasphemous pricks,' Little Otto hissed, as he saw his trophies defiled. That clothing was his. It was meant to be savoured and enjoyed. Caressed. Touched. Smelt.

Little Otto's fingertips fluttered across the surface of his Mask of Many, seeking reassurance in the rasp of its leathery surface. He buried his face in the mask's rigid folds, sucking in its soothing aroma – glue and the tang of cured flesh. His breathing slowed and his heart stilled; anger and hatred faded. He ran his fingers across the loops of twine that bound the mask's lips as he considered his position.

The soldiers would head down into the cellar soon. That was when the real fun would begin: he'd left all his tools down there. But it was what he'd left at the top of the house that most concerned him. His eyes went towards the garret window, the room he'd been in when the soldiers had arrived and begun bashing at the door with their boots. Otto had had to escape through the hole in the roof.

He fingered the heavy key in his pocket. Should he move his treasures? No. There were too many of them. Where would he put them all? He would just have to wait it out.

A cry sounded within the bowels of the house, followed by shouts and sudden flustered activity. A young soldier ran outside, rested his rifle against the side of the house and sprinted in the direction of the town, his face pale.

Little Otto watched the soldier go then tucked the Mask of Many inside his coat and loped towards the deeper dark at the centre of the wood.

A small matter. He had been interrupted before. He knew what to expect.

But he wouldn't let anyone stop him this time, though.

4

2

DETECTIVE INSPECTOR SILAS Payne took the Brunswick road north-east out of Eichenrode. He followed the pitted strip of tarmac for a half-mile then turned his utility onto a dirt road. A soldier in British uniform appeared from between the trees and waved for him to stop.

'Are you the gentleman from Scotland Yard, sir?' the young private said, as he bent beside the car window. 'HQ said you were coming.'

Payne handed him his identity papers. As the private turned to examine them, Payne noticed the man seemed to have an article of clothing stuffed down the front of his battle blouse: the end of a white woollen sleeve was dangling above the private's belt buckle.

'How many bodies are there?' Payne said, taking back his identity papers.

'Two. Least that's what I heard.'

'You've not seen them?'

The private adjusted the strap of his rifle and shook his head. 'I've seen enough of dead bodies for one life, sir, what with all the fighting I've done. The house is just around the corner. Ask for Sergeant Beagley.'

Payne drove away, thinking how glad he was that the war was finally won; the private looked barely old enough to vote.

The house was set back from the road behind a row of oaks. It would have been an impressive dwelling once – three stories of half-timber built in the rural German style with bay windows on the lower floor – but the walls were peppered with bullet holes and a mortar had ripped a massive hole in the crow-stepped roof. The shell had obviously exploded inside the house, as the unkempt garden was strewn with glass and household items.

A group of soldiers stood beneath the shade of an oak. When Payne pulled up next to them, they waved for him to go round to the back where a burly sergeant with close-cropped hair stood leaning against the jamb of the back door, hands in the pockets of his leather jerkin.

'Who wants to know?' he said when Payne asked if he was Sergeant Beagley.

'Detective Inspector Payne, Scotland Yard. Major Norris of Public Safety Branch has asked me to look into this matter.'

The sergeant looked him up and down, as if to check Payne was real. Then, he said, 'You're a bit off your usual beat, aren't you, Detective Inspector?'

Payne smiled politely. He'd been in Germany only four days, but he'd already heard that particular quip more times than he cared to remember.

Beagley led him inside.

'The corpses are in the cellar,' he said, indicating a low door in the wall beside the fireplace. He crossed the kitchen and started down the cellar steps, but paused when Payne did not follow him.

The crime scene was a shambles from a procedural point of view, but nineteen years' service with the Metropolitan police had taught Payne the benefit of taking the time to notice the small things. He stood in the centre of the room and slowly turned a full circle.

There were no chairs or tables in the kitchen, but there was a sink in the far corner and the shelves above it were lined with tins of British army rations. Payne turned back towards the door. The wood on the inside of the frame was splintered. He crossed the room and bent to examine the door handle.

The wood around the latch bolt was cracked and the escutcheon plate was crumpled inwards. It looked like the door had been kicked open from outside. The damage looked recent, too. Had Beagley stood in the doorway to hide that fact? Payne decided that he had: Payne's examination of the door had caused Beagley to frown.

Payne straightened and traced his finger over the words chalked on the exterior face of the door: '*Requisitioned by 21st Army Group*'. Those hadn't been written recently, though, the chalk was too faded and smudged. That meant the house had likely been requisitioned by combat troops when they occupied the area back in May. The occupation force was called the BAOR now, the British Army of the Rhine.

'Are British personnel billeted here?' Payne said.

Beagley motioned towards the tins on the shelf. 'Looks that way, doesn't it?'

Payne picked up a tin of bully beef and wiped a fingertip through the light covering of dust on its top. There was dust on nearly all the horizontal surfaces in the kitchen, now that he came to look. No, Payne thought, no-one had lived there for at least a month, maybe longer.

The air in the cellar was moist and cool. Cobwebs dangled

from the rough-hewn beams in the ceiling and the wooden steps creaked as Silas Payne followed Beagley's torch-light down into the darkness.

The male corpse lay on a heavy table in the centre of the cellar. The woman lay on the earth floor. Both were naked but for pieces of sacking that covered the woman's breasts and both their groins.

'Did you put that sacking there, Sergeant?' Payne said.

Beagley shook his head. 'That's how we found them. My boys didn't touch a thing.'

Payne turned on his own torch and touched the back of his fingers to the man's naked arm. The corpse was ice cold and rigid, the skin a whitish-blue colour. The woman's was the same. Blood had pooled in the lower half of both corpses, in the buttocks and the backs of the calves. That told Payne they'd been lying like that when they died, or had been placed in that position soon afterwards.

Payne shone his torch on the horizontal bruise that circled the man's neck just below the Adam's Apple. It looked like someone had wrapped a ligature around his neck then twisted it tight, but there were no other injuries on the man's body: no cuts, bruises or scrapes; no damage to the fingernails. That was uncommon in a strangling: the violence of the victim's death throes was normally terrible.

The woman's body had the same horizontal bruise across the neck. However, unlike the man, she seemed to have struggled. Two of her fingernails were broken and she had a bruise on the side of her face. Her upper lip was slightly swollen, too.

That still wasn't much damage if she'd been strangled,

though, Payne thought. Perhaps the killer had knocked her unconscious first.

'That's the creepy bit,' Beagley said, motioning towards a small table at the far end of the cellar.

The table was covered with surgical instruments. There were four scalpels, a hacksaw and a length of serrated wire ending in wooden handles. Beside them were a long, curved sewing needle and a roll of catgut; beyond those, various glass vials filled with liquid and a syringe. A leather apron hung from a hook in the wall and Payne saw there was a bundled tarpaulin beneath it.

'That there's a surgeon's needle,' Beagley said. 'I've seen medics stitch wounds with 'em.'

Payne crossed the uneven soil floor to take a closer look. A neat rectangle of felt covered the table top and the scalpels and hacksaw were set out upon it perfectly parallel to one another.

Payne studied the labels on the vials. Avahxim. Goloqta. They sounded like brand names. The list of chemical compounds was written in German. Payne could understand the words, but they meant nothing to him.

'Do you think someone was going to operate on 'em?' Beagley said. 'Before they were strangled, I mean.'

'I've no idea,' Payne said, as the beam of his torch glinted on scalpel blades and curved glass. The same thought had occurred to him, but operate for what?

'What were your men doing out here?' Payne said. 'It's quite a long way from the town.'

'We were doing a sweep through this area. We still do them even though the war's over. Keeps the lads sharp. We'd not patrolled this area before and . . . well, we saw this house had been requisitioned so we came to see if we could scrounge a cuppa. Nobody was home, so we came inside and this is what we found.'

Payne nodded. Beagley wasn't lying, but he hadn't told Payne the whole truth, either: the sergeant's answers had been preceded by momentary pauses, as if assessing how best to answer to his own advantage. You didn't get far in the Met without learning to spot that.

Payne returned to the bodies. The dead man looked to be about Payne's own age, early forties, but the woman was younger, perhaps as young as twenty-five.

'What's this tattoo here, sergeant?' Payne said, indicating small Gothic letters tattooed on the inside of the man's upper arm.

'Lord, I didn't notice that,' Beagley said, bending to examine it. He blew air. 'It's his blood group. That means he was Waffen SS. We've been briefed to watch for that among the refugees. Some of these bastards are trying to skip the country now they're facing trials for war crimes.'

Payne pushed the brim of his hat upwards. That complicated things. He needed to speak to Major Norris.

'Looks like the bastard got what he deserved, anyway,' Beagley said with a sneer.

Payne ignored the comment. From what he'd seen of conditions in the British Zone of Occupation, the line between proper justice and arbitrary vengeance had become badly blurred.

'Men from the RAMC should be coming here soon to take the bodies away for an autopsy,' Payne said. 'Can you and your men guard the house until then?'

Beagley agreed. The two men went back upstairs to the kitchen. Payne began to examine the rest of the house.

Some of the ground floor rooms were furnished, but the air in them smelt stale. Payne's shoes stirred dust as he walked across the rugs.

There was nothing of any worth in the rooms upstairs. The furniture had all been broken up and burnt; charred scraps of chair legs and bed frames littered the fireplaces. It confirmed the impression Payne had formed in the kitchen: no-one had lived there for weeks.

At the rear of the first storey was a small staircase that led to the second storey garret. Payne climbed the steep, uneven steps with a wary eye on the ceiling above him: the mortar blast had cracked the roof beams and they sagged in a downward V directly above his head.

The door at the top of the stairs was heavy and old. Payne turned the handle. The door wouldn't budge, but Payne couldn't decide whether it was simply locked or blocked by rubble on the other side. He tried shoving the door with his shoulder but stopped when the roof beams creaked and dust and rubble poured onto the brim of his hat.

He went downstairs and out into the back garden. Cushions, scraps of paper and fabric lay mouldering in the unkempt grass. The sun was below the horizon now and the shadows between the trees were deepening into darkness. Thick clouds raced westwards, like puffs of dirty smoke.

The branches of a tall oak shaded a bower at the back of the garden. The bower held a broken child's swing and a circular well-head made of red brick that rose a yard or so above the ground. Moss grew between the pitted bricks of the well and its wooden cover was gnarled with age.

Two hessian sacks rested against the bole of the oak. Payne toed the sacks and sniffed the air. Just for a moment, he fancied the wind carried with it a faint chemical tang. He tried to lift the cover from the well, but it was held in place by shiny padlocks, one on either side. He bent to examine the padlocks, but paused when a dull explosion sounded somewhere to the west of him. Payne took his binoculars and walked through the trees to where he could look out across the whole valley.

Engineers were clearing anti-personnel mines from the western approaches to Eichenrode; the fields around the town were still strewn with thousands of the wretched things. From here, Payne could see the sandbag revetments of the German trenches that the mines had been placed to defend. He watched as a plume of dirt rose briefly against the horizon and another dull pop sounded.

He went back to the front of the house and saw the RAMC ambulance had arrived. Payne put on his gloves and went downstairs to collect the surgical tools and vials as evidence. Then he took a camera from his utility and photographed the dead bodies.

'All set, Inspector?' Sergeant Beagley said when he'd finished.

'Just a few more questions before I go, if I may. How would I find out which unit requisitioned this building? And whether anyone is billeted here now?'

Beagley shrugged. 'The first units through here, back in May, requisitioned practically every building that was standing. Normal procedure was to give the German owners a chit and eight hours to sling their hooks. But a lot of those troops have gone back home, now. I suppose you could try Housing Branch, see if they've got records, though I doubt it. They were drowning in requisition chits and receipts last time I went there.'

Payne nodded, made a note of it. Then he looked Beagley full in the face.

'Do you know where the victims' clothes are, Sergeant?'

'Clothes?'

'Both bodies are naked. I presume they were clothed when they came here.'

Beagley's frown returned. 'They might have been killed somewhere else and brought here.'

'Not according to the marks left by livor mortis. You see, when the heart stops pumping, the blood sinks in a downward direction. In this case, the blood has pooled in the back, buttocks and calves, which means they died in a horizontal position, lying face upwards – most likely right where they are now. So, tell me, Sergeant, did your men find any clothing inside the house?'

Beagley's big face had become hard and aggressive. Payne thought he was seeing the real man for the first time.

'No.'

'Are you sure? Because I fancied that young private out by the road had a white jumper shoved down his battle blouse. And that kitchen door has been recently kicked in, which means your men were likely hoping to find more than a cup of tea inside. So, I'll ask one last time: Did your men –'

'Questions, questions,' Beagley said, dropping his voice. 'It's always the same with coppers, isn't it? Well, I've got news for you. Whether that door was kicked in or not ain't your concern, and I'll tell you why: me and my lads were out here spilling our blood and guts while you were back home checking blackout curtains. So you can take your questions and shove 'em where the sun don't shine. If I'm going to be questioned by anyone, it'll be the redcaps. Clear?'

Payne held Beagley's eyes. Then he turned and walked back to his utility.

'You're way off your turf, copper,' Beagley called, as Payne drove away. The other soldiers laughed.

Payne thought about what Beagley had said as he headed back to town. He'd been chancing his arm, trying to strong arm a man like Beagley. After all, Payne had no jurisdiction over army personnel out here. Truth be told, he wasn't sure he had jurisdiction over anyone.

But he was damn sure about one thing: Sergeant Beagley was hiding something.

3

THE NEXT DAY dawned, overcast and grey. As was his habit, Captain James Booth rose early and took a walk through the streets of Eichenrode.

The fighting in this part of town had been especially fierce and hardly anything man-made was left standing: the odd chimney stack, a brick facade. They reminded Booth of the monastery ruins in the dell beyond his old school's rugby field. *Perhaps this is how history's footfalls always look*, he decided, *scraps of architecture rising from mounds of pulverized stone.*

The Germans queuing beside the standpipe at the end of the road looked as bleak and broken as their town. Opposite the standpipe, the trunk of a huge oak formed an unofficial notice-board for the German populace. Hundreds of papers fluttered from the tree's bullet-scarred bark, and all began with the same words, *Ich suche,* and then the name of the missing family member that was sought.

Booth paused in his customary spot opposite the oak and lit a cigarette. Six months ago, the thought of standing on German soil and looking out over biblical desolation would have thrilled him, but now that victory had arrived it didn't seem quite as pristine as he'd always imagined it. One of Booth's friends in Bomber Command had assured him that by the end of the war the RAF could deliver more tonnage of bombs in a single weekend than the Germans dropped on London during the whole of the Blitz. Booth had assumed the man was exaggerating. Now he wasn't so sure. The bombed areas of London were mere purgatories compared to the hell of some of Germany's urban areas. The scale of the destruction was beyond imagining.

When Booth returned to the billets of his field intelligence unit, the duty sergeant gestured towards a man in a cheap grey flannel suit standing opposite the door to Booth's office.

'My name is Detective Inspector Silas Payne,' the man said, shaking Booth's hand. 'I hear you're the man to speak to about werewolves.'

Booth closed the door to his office, checking his watch as he did so. 'So, you've been seconded to the Control Council for Germany, Detective Inspector? Should I call you that, by the way, or just Mr Payne? Or should I use your CCG rank?'

'I'd prefer Detective Inspector. But it's your decision.'

Yes, you would prefer that, wouldn't you? Booth thought. You could tell this Silas Payne was a policeman. It was the way he stood, with his hands thrust in his pockets, rocking on the balls of his feet as he took everything in. And that long, bony nose of his, it was just right for sniffing around in other people's affairs.

'What brings you to our part of Germany, then, Detective Inspector?' Booth said, inviting Payne to sit.

'I'm to run a training centre for German policemen here in Eichenrode.'

'A training centre? I wasn't aware there was one.'

'There isn't. That's the problem.'

'Oh, dear. Been a bit of a stuff up back in Blighty has there?'

'I've got the building. What I don't have are students. They've all been interned.'

'I'm afraid I'm partly to blame for that,' Booth said, wondering why Payne's thin, austere face seemed so familiar. 'The Colonel in charge of this area ordered us to arrest all the German policemen a few weeks back.'

'Was that wise?'

'Colonel Bassett – that's our commanding officer – is typical of these Blimp types the military government are wrenching out of retirement and turning into ad hoc proconsuls: still wet with the mud of Flanders fields, and with no interest in seeking *rapprochement* with the 'damned Jerries', if you catch my drift. The good colonel has a tendency to conflate all Germans with Nazis, and once he got his hands on a list of names and addresses, he had us round all the local police up. I think he's convinced they're all ex-Gestapo agents. But do tell, Detective Inspector, what is your interest in the werewolf insurgency?'

'There was a double murder here yesterday. The dead man was Waffen SS. Major Norris of Public Safety Branch has asked me to look into things. It's been suggested these Nazi partisans, the werewolves, were involved.'

'I say, this isn't something to do with that clandestine field hospital they found out by the Brunswick road, is it?'

Payne frowned. 'Who told you it was a field hospital?'

'Well, that was the rumour doing the rounds in the officers' mess last night. I presume the soldiers that found your dead bodies must have reported it that way. But I can see from your face you don't agree.'

Payne shrugged. 'I found surgical tools and vials of medicine there. But I still think it was something else.'

'Something else . . . how?'

'That's the problem. I don't know. It's just a feeling. But I know a murder scene when I see one.'

Booth sighed. 'Well, I'm afraid supposition and hunches won't get you very far with Colonel Bassett. If it's been reported to him as a field hospital, that is what it will be *in perpetuum,* no matter how eloquently you argue the contrary.'

Payne had a notebook out now. 'What can you tell me about the werewolves, captain?'

'It seems they were the brainchild of Himmler, back in late '44, but the whole thing was always very hush-hush, for obvious reasons. The fact that the Nazi hierarchy were preparing partisan-style resistance in areas the Allies were poised to conquer constituted an open admission that the war wasn't going quite as well as the propaganda ministry would have had people believe.

'The German code name for it was *Operation Werwolf.* According to a training manual I translated in October, these partisan cells were to have access to arms dumps and explosives and were to "*fall upon the Allied lines of communication like werewolves.*" That said, we've not had many problems with them in this sector: just the odd cut telephone wire, pit traps, that sort of thing. I think the werewolves' main impact has been psychological, principally due to the name. It's so terribly evocative, isn't it?'

'I've heard the British advance guard found bodies strung

up from lampposts when they moved into Eichenrode. I've been told they were Germans executed by the werewolves.'

'Ah, yes. Didn't actually see it myself so I can't say. But it's more probable that those people were killed by SS or Wehrmacht units engaging in a last minute spasm of hate.'

'Wasn't there one of those elite Napola boarding schools in this region? The children at those were bred to be fanatics.'

'Agreed. But it's important to realise that children is what they still are, even now. Or, rather, young adolescents.'

Payne tapped pencil against notepad for a moment, then took a cardboard file from his satchel. 'Do you think adolescents did this?' he said, handing Booth a series of photographs.

In the first, a naked male body lay on a wooden table. The second showed a woman lying on a dirt floor, her breasts and crotch covered with sackcloth. Thick bruises ringed each of their necks. A third photo showed surgical implements on a table. *No, he's right*, Booth thought as he looked at the photos, *this was not carried out by a teenager.*

'In each case, the victim was strangled,' Payne said. 'As you can see in the photos, there is a furrow in the flesh of the neck that indicates a ligature of some sort was used. An army medical officer performed an autopsy last night and he suggested that, given the bruises found on the backs of the necks, some form of tourniquet was applied and used to gradually tighten the ligature until strangulation occurred.' Payne gestured towards the photos. 'Have you seen anything like this before, Captain?'

'Well, if it were something to do with the werewolf insurgency, it would suggest a level of organisation we've not seen before. But anything's possible, I suppose. It does look like some type of medical operation was about to be carried out, doesn't it?'

'What about British soldiers murdering Germans? Have there been many incidents?'

Booth shifted in his seat. He blew air and gestured towards the photos. 'Surely you're not suggesting British soldiers did this?'

'I'm not suggesting anything, Captain. But I can't discount the possibility at the moment. And it seems to me that blaming it on werewolves could be a convenient smoke screen. Have there been any incidents of British troops committing murder?'

'Murder is such an emotive word, isn't it? But if you're talking about summary justice being dispensed, well, yes, I'm afraid there have been some incidents, mainly involving combat troops. Some of the fellows we had here at the beginning of the occupation were real tough old 30 Corps veterans. They'd seen more fighting than you or I could imagine, and they'd all lost someone dear to them. You never know how a chap will react when he's put under that sort of pressure. Suffice it to say that 99 per cent of those incidents were limited to the weeks directly following the German collapse. It was all a bit chaotic back then. But I really don't think this' – he motioned towards the photos of the corpses – 'could have had anything to do with British soldiers.'

Payne made notes then said, 'You mentioned that you used a list to arrest the local Nazis. How come this Waffen SS man hadn't been caught and interned already?'

The faint note of reproach made Booth look up from the paperwork he was sorting, but Payne's expression was neutral.

I know who you look like, Booth thought: Old Crippley, a schoolmaster he'd had, a former cleric; Payne had that same air about him, horsehair shirts and self-denial.

'Arresting Nazis is not a clear-cut business, Detective Inspector. Men hide out in the woods. They lie about who they are, mix themselves in with the DPs, the displaced persons. Don't forget, a lot of these chaps will be facing prosecution for war crimes. The prospect of the hangman's noose does tend to give a chap pause before handing himself in.'

If Payne noted the irritation in Booth's voice, he chose to ignore it, so Booth went over to the attack. 'Actually, talking of Germans, I suppose you'll need to interview some sooner or later. I don't mean to be rude, but do you actually speak any German?'

Booth repeated the question in German for good measure, but the smile on his lips faltered when Payne replied in rapid and flawless German, saying that, yes, he thought he knew enough to manage.

Booth needed a moment to overcome his surprise.

'Well, I must congratulate you on your German, Detective Inspector. It's as good as mine, I'd say, and I was top of my class at Oxford.'

'I've been told you have access to files on SS men,' Payne said, ignoring the compliment. The policeman possessed a deep inner calm that was really quite annoying, Booth thought.

'Yes. A unit of our advance guard captured a load of files from *RuSha*.'

'And what is that?'

'*RuSha*? The SS Race and Settlement Main Office. It was originally established to safeguard the racial purity of the SS, but it ended up organising most of the mass deportations that occurred in the conquered territories.'

'What do the files consist of?'

'Before joining the SS, a man had to obtain a licence from *RuSha* to prove the purity of his bloodline – a little like a pedigree for a dog, really. Part of that process involved supplying lots of photographs – something which has proved very useful to chaps like myself who are trying to find former Nazis.'

Payne nodded towards the photo of the dead man's face. 'Is there any way we could use the files to find out who this man was? I can't really move my investigation forward until I know who the victims were.'

Booth laughed when he saw that Payne was serious.

'Detective Inspector, there are tens of thousands of files. It would take weeks – months – to check every single photo.'

'We have his blood group, though. I checked with the surgeon, he's AB negative. Less than one person in a hundred has that type of blood. Surely that should whittle it down?'

'It's impossible, Detective Inspector. Absolutely impossible,' Booth said, rising to show Payne the conversation was over. 'Now, unfortunately, I've got to head off somewhere. Call me if you need anything else, though. Always happy to help.'

And even happier to refuse you, again, Booth thought as he closed the door on the policeman, then wondered why he'd taken against the man so. *Must be the resemblance to Old Crippley*, he decided.

4

*T*HIS REALLY IS *too much*, Ilse Drechsler thought, as she hovered beside the bed.

Cousin Ursula's breathing was deep and regular now and the irritating mucus-rattle barely audible, but it had taken four hours to get her to sleep.

Four *hours*.

Each time Ursula seemed on the verge of drifting off, she had begun to writhe and fight with unseen attackers, gritting her teeth so hard it seemed the tendons in her neck would snap. Part of Ilse had longed to go downstairs and leave Ursula to it, but she couldn't risk her cousin crying out and attracting attention.

No-one must know Ursula was there.

Ilse took a corner of the bed sheet and lifted the covers to inspect Ursula's injuries. The whole of her lower half, from the breasts down, was covered in bruises, and the sheets beneath Ursula's posterior were damp with blood.

That was the problem: whatever wounds she had were *inside*. Ilse had tried to examine the damage, but whenever she went to part Ursula's thighs, the woman became hysterical. Whatever it was, the wound smelt bad now. It smelt of rot. Ilse should call a doctor, but there were so few left in Eichenrode and those that had stayed couldn't be trusted; they all worked for the Tommies now.

There was no way round it, she realised, Cousin Ursula must stay hidden until she got better and then she must go somewhere else: there couldn't be *two* women called Ursula Drechsler living in Eichenrode . . .

Ilse's troubles had begun months earlier, out east in the Warthegau. The Russian breakthrough had come so suddenly. In the morning, the radio had said the front was stable; by lunchtime, the Russians were everywhere, like a ravening swarm of rats, biblical in their savagery. When a friend in the German High Command had phoned to warn Ilse, she had barely had time to bundle together a bag of possessions before the shells began to fall. There'd been no time to warn anyone else. Cousin Ursula had been away shopping in the town at the time. Ilse had taken Ursula's identity papers, hoping to find her cousin on the road later.

But when Ilse stopped running that first evening, the horizon in the east was a solid mass of smoke and flame, and the rumble of tanks and artillery was all that could be heard.

Weeks of hell followed.

Ilse went to her Berlin house first, thinking she would be safe there, and then managed to escape the capital before the Russians encircled it. After that, what was left? Her parents' house in Eichenrode was the only place she had to go.

It took a week to drive there, each day more chaotic than the last as the Reich fell apart. When German soldiers took the car from her at gunpoint, she had to walk the last leg of her odyssey, more than thirty-six hours across country, dragging her suitcases behind her.

She didn't glimpse her conquerors until the third day of peace, when English soldiers knocked at the house and asked to see her papers.

And that was when Ursula's identity documents had become so useful.

Dear dizzy, dim little Cousin Ursula, with her plaited hair and dirndl skirts. Oh, she'd danced with her share of SS officers and rattled collection tins for the *Winterhilfswerk* fund – but she'd never joined the Party. That fact was worth its weight in gold, now. The Tommies were arresting Party members and locking them up. Torturing them, some said. Ilse was damned if she would go to prison just because she'd done what millions of other Germans had done and hitched her horse to the Nazi wagon.

After pretending to be Cousin Ursula a number of times, it was relatively simple to actually *become* her. There was a man in the town who had attached Ilse's photographs to Ursula's documents and the switch was made.

Ilse had wondered at first whether posing as her cousin might be too obvious, but she was glad of her decision when she came to fill in the *Fragebogen*, the huge questionnaire the Tommies were making all Germans complete. There were more than a hundred sections, detailing membership of political parties and churches and Nazi organisations ranging from the SS and the Gestapo to the Kameradschaft USA; other sections enquired about speeches given, articles written, rallies and parades attended and all sorts of other personal questions about scars and census results and relatives who belonged to the Party. You couldn't possibly hope to invent an identity; the questions were far too complex.

But Cousin Ursula had spent so much time wittering on about her life that Ilse actually found it easy to think herself into Ursula's shoes and the Tommies had swallowed her story. As far as they were concerned, she was Ursula Drechsler, aged thirty-four and unmarried. The fact that Ilse hadn't returned to Eichenrode since her parents had died meant that the chances of anyone from the town recognising her were minimal. The set up was perfect . . .

. . . until two days ago, when the old man in the cart had arrived, calling out at the door, speaking with a thick Prussian accent. Ilse had told him to leave without opening it, but then the old man had pulled back the covers of the cart and Ilse had realised that the bloodied, bruised thing that lay within was her cousin.

'Men at the frontier,' the old man had said, as if that explained everything.

The only words Ursula had spoken in all the days that had followed were to ask for a bundle of letters from her bag. When Ilse fetched them she'd managed to read only the first line of the top one – 'My darling Ursula' – before Ursula had snatched them away and clutched them to her bosom. They were still there now, a crumpled mass tied together with blue ribbon, rising and falling softly as Ursula slept.

Ilse rose, tiptoed away from the bed and went downstairs, taking the crooked steps one at a time. The farmhouse was a ruin. A heavy explosion had reduced the front rooms to a pile of rubble and soldiers had slept in the still habitable part at the rear: soldiers from both sides, to judge by the cans and ammunition crates dumped around the place. That wasn't all they'd left, either: the pigs had pissed and shat all over.

She stopped by the kitchen window to examine her reflection in the cracked glass, then looked down at the dowdy frock she wore, the woollen stockings, the heavy shoes. *God, I look like an old washerwoman*, Ilse thought. Small wonder people found no difficulty in mistaking her for Cousin Ursula.

Still, I must possess something men want, Ilse thought with a faint smile, thinking now of the Englishman she had taken as her lover at the end of May.

Ilse's Tommy had arranged things with the military government so that the farmhouse would not be requisitioned. That was something at least. Half a roof over her head was better than nothing. After all, where else could she go? Since the Tommies invaded, there was no running water, no electricity, no post, no buses or trains, no coal or milk. In the town, people queued at a standpipe for hours to get water and they lived like troglodytes, crowded together in cellars.

Besides, even if she had had somewhere else to go, how would she have got there? Germans weren't allowed to go anywhere unless they had permits from the military authorities or the Red Cross – and it was damned risky even then. It was not a good time for Germans to be wandering the roads. Ilse had already been set upon once by a vengeful horde. That was how she had met the Tommy. He'd fired his pistol in the air and scared the bastards away. If it hadn't been for him, she would probably have been killed. Or, worse, they could have left her like Cousin Ursula.

No, this shattered hovel was the best she could hope for at the moment. She couldn't imagine how other people were managing. Even with the food the Tommy brought her, she was still famished. The hunger was always there, in the pit of her stomach, sucking at her well-being from within. And at least her arrangement with the Tommy had the semblance of a relationship. She had seen the way many German women were surviving now, whoring themselves in bombed out buildings for tins of peaches and cigarettes.

The floorboards above creaked and Cousin Ursula cried out; her groans echoed through the cracks in the house. She was having another of her attacks. Ilse rose wearily. She needed medicine, but where could she get it? And what sort of medicine? She had no idea what Cousin Ursula needed.

She was about to go upstairs when she heard a vehicle coming towards the house. She peered through the window, ducking back when she saw her Tommy parking his jeep.

She mustn't let him inside: he might hear Cousin Ursula's moans. It would raise too many questions.

Ilse took a moment to arrange her hair in her reflection in the window, then slipped through the kitchen door and went round to meet the Tommy at the front of the house.

'*Liebling*, what a lovely surprise,' Ilse said, throwing her arms wide and beaming at him.

'Hello, my darling Ursula,' Captain James Booth said.

5

Silas Payne parked his utility outside the *Rathaus*, the town hall building which was now home to the British military government in Eichenrode.

He wasn't overly fond of young Captain Booth, Payne decided. Perhaps it was the big words he had used: rapprochement, conflate. Payne had always mistrusted men who felt the need to show their learning so obviously. Or perhaps it was because Payne had met so many Captain Booths back in London, earnest young men fresh from university for whom 'The War' had been little more than an extended jolly.

Look at the street names in Eichenrode. The first thing the Military Government had done on occupying the town was to remove all the street names with connections to the Nazi regime, but a competition had then begun among the junior officers to see who could find the replacement that would prove most irksome to the Germans: Churchill Platz, Eisenhower Straße; the former high street was now 'El Allee Main'.

But then Silas Payne had always disliked the Army, disliked anything that encouraged people to subsume themselves in a greater whole. No good ever came of mass emotion. He'd learned the truth of that when policing football matches as a young copper. Wasn't the current state of the world proof that he was right?

The *Rathaus* building was still dressed for war, with sandbags piled against the exterior wall and crosses of tape on the windows. Payne showed his ID to the guard at the door, then headed upstairs to Major Norris's office.

Norris led the CCG's Public Safety Branch for the administrative district to the west of the city of Brunswick. As such, his duties and responsibilities were many and arduous; too arduous, to judge from the harassed, sleepless look of the man.

Norris was in his early fifties, but had the air of a man with whom old age had caught up quickly and unexpectedly. When Payne walked upstairs to his office, he found the major trying to unravel some dispute between German civilians – not an easy task, given that Norris obviously spoke no German. He was followed wherever he went by an officious young German woman with a clipboard and pencil who translated for him. If it weren't for Norris's uniform, a casual observer would have thought the translator had been the person in charge.

As Payne listened he realised that most of the time what she translated was not precisely what Norris had said; sometimes she would even add her own information. When Norris mentioned that Payne spoke German, though, she looked at him sharply and blushed. Her translations were scrupulously correct afterwards.

How these men were supposed to govern the country without speaking German was beyond Payne, but that seemed to be the story of the occupation so far. If the war had demonstrated one thing about the British, it was the immense depth of their trust in muddling through somehow.

It was twenty minutes before Norris had finished with the

German civilians. Late afternoon sun filled the room as he invited Payne into his office.

'Here we are, Detective Inspector, take a seat and tell me what you've managed to ascertain about this wretched business out by the Brunswick Road. They're saying in the officers' mess it was some sort of ad hoc field hospital.'

Norris frowned when Payne failed to reply, then realised that the policeman was looking at his translator. 'We shan't be needing you for this, thank you, Fräulein Seiler.'

The woman's eyes met Payne's for the briefest of moments. Then she smiled and left the room.

'Indispensable,' Norris said when she'd left. 'And her father, too.'

'What does he do?'

'Doctor. He's taken charge of the medical care at the civilian internment camp near town. We can't have the chaps we lock up falling ill, can we? That wouldn't be very civilised, would it? No, we've got to work on rebuilding the world, now, get things back to how they were before all this bloody mess started.'

Norris sucked a Bismuth tablet as he listened to Payne's report, one hand on his stomach.

'So, Captain Booth agreed with your assessment?' he said when Payne had finished.

'Yes. He seemed to think the field hospital theory very unlikely. He thought the same about the involvement of werewolves.'

'But what were the drugs you found?'

'I'm still trying to ascertain that.'

'Surely that lends credence to the field hospital theory?'

'It's a strange kind of hospital that strangles its patients.'

Norris thought about that, staring at the window. 'Do you think this Beagley chap and his boys might have been dispensing a bit of summary justice? Found out this chap was SS and did him in?'

Payne shook his head. 'Beagley seemed genuinely surprised when I spotted the SS tattoo. And, if they had killed them, why would they report it? But I can't rule out the possibility that other British personnel were involved. And I'm certain that Sergeant Beagley was hiding something – the theft of the victims' belongings, most likely. That's why I asked if you could speak to Beagley's commanding officer.'

'Yes, I got your message about that and we're in luck. Turns out the CO is a friend of my bridge partner.'

'And?'

'Well, as you can understand, I couldn't very well just weigh in and start accusing people of theft – Sergeant Beagley has an impeccable war record, after all. But I did mention the matter and the CO applied some pressure in the right quarters.'

Norris rose, walked to a corner cupboard and withdrew a large brown paper parcel tied with string, which he placed on the desk.

'It seems some of the victims' clothing had gone walkabout. This is what has been sent over.'

Payne cut the string with his penknife and unfolded the paper. Inside was a selection of sturdy, practical clothing, both male and female: trousers, vests, skirts. The only remarkable item was a long ebony dress in a tailor's box. As Payne opened the tissue paper in which the dress was wrapped, a waft of apples and pears rose to greet him. The dress was made of silk;

silver embroidered butterflies fluttered down from one shoulder strap and across the bodice.

'Is this all of it?' Payne said. 'It doesn't seem very much. And this clothing must have been inside something. Were there any bags or suitcases?'

The pained look returned to Norris's face; he cradled his belly protectively. 'It's all we're going to get. I've stepped on enough toes as it is getting you that.'

'With all due respect, Major, two people have been murdered. And if the world is ever going to 'get back to normal', the concept of murder has to start meaning something again sooner or later.'

Norris looked at Payne as if trying to decide whether he were serious. When he realised he was, he said, 'Oh yes, well of course, you're perfectly right. Couldn't agree more. What was it Churchill said at the beginning of the war? You know, the thing about us having to win the war so the world could move forward into *something-or-other*.'

'Broad uplit sunlands.'

'Precisely, Detective Inspector. Broad uplit sunlands. Let's go forward and find them, eh? Show the world the efficiency of British justice. But let's do so without upsetting any apple carts. No murky diversions. No fuss.'

'Fuss?'

Norris winced, as if Payne's failure to understand caused him genuine pain. 'What I mean, to put it into words of one syllable, is that if you intimate that British soldiers have been murdering Germans, you're going to get yourself into hot water. And when the *supposed* murder victim is ex-Waffen SS, then said water is going to get very hot, very, very quickly.

Do I make myself clear? You're not going to make yourself any friends out here if you're seen to be taking the Germans' side.'

'Police work is not conducive to popularity as a rule, Major.'

'Well, just tread easily. These regular army chaps are already looking down their noses at the CCG. Let's not give them anything to crow about, eh?'

When Payne reached the door, Norris said suddenly, 'I'm not going to regret putting you in charge of this, am I, Detective Inspector Payne?' – as if he'd spent the whole conversation putting off asking that one question.

Payne paused in the doorway. 'That depends on whether you want to know the truth or not, sir.'

Norris reached for another Bismuth tablet. That did not seem to be the answer he'd hoped for.

Payne took the package of clothing and went downstairs. On his way out of the *Rathaus*, he passed a room where three women in ATS uniforms were working. Payne paused as he listened to the clack of their typewriters. Then he went back and knocked on the door.

'Excuse me, ladies. I don't suppose you could spare me a minute, could you?'

The three women crowded round when Payne put the tailor's box on the table and withdrew the long silk dress.

'Lord, look at that, Angie,' the youngest of the ATS women said. 'What an absolute beauty. Look at the embroidery. I haven't seen anything like this since before the war.'

'And even then, it was only with your nose pressed up against a shop window.'

'Too right. I'll bet this cost 10 guineas. Where on earth did you find it, Detective Inspector? Is it for sale?'

Payne smiled and shook his head. 'It's part of an investigation actually. I'd just like a woman's opinion on it, if you ladies wouldn't mind. I'm a bit out of my depth when it comes to dresses.'

'Well, for starters, this isn't a 'dress', it's an evening gown.'

'Where might you buy it?'

'You wouldn't buy it; you'd have it made especially.'

'Do you mean to say this is a one off?'

'Of course, it is,' Angie said. 'You don't think any woman able to afford something like this would risk having someone else turn up wearing the same dress, do you? This will be the fellow who made it, I imagine,' she said, pointing to an address on the inside of the box lid for which Payne had not even thought to look. 'Maurice Petiot, Rue La Salle, Paris. Ooh, doesn't that sound posh?'

Payne thanked the women and went back upstairs to Norris's office, feeling pleased with himself. It was one of the basic rules of good police investigation: if you knew nothing about a subject, always ask someone who did.

'Do you have a French dictionary and a telephone I can borrow?' he said to Norris.

'What on earth for?'

'I need to call someone in Paris.'

It took Payne an hour to get the Paris telephone number

for the tailor and another hour to get connected. Payne's French was of schoolboy standard, but he had a French-speaking intelligence officer provide him with a detailed description of the dress and the other vocabulary he would need.

The line crackled as the phone rang, then a man's voice answered.

'Yes, I am Monsieur Petiot,' the tobacco-hoarse voice said in response to Payne's query.

Payne began to explain who he was in faltering French, but Petiot said, 'Yes, yes, but what do you want?'

'An evening gown you made. If I describe it to you, might you remember it?'

'*Might* I remember it, Monsieur? Each article of clothing I produce is unique. I burn the patterns once each one is completed.'

Payne had ten lines of French describing the material and style of the dress. Petiot interrupted him halfway through the third.

'A full-length evening gown in black silk with a halter neck and a bow brooch at the back? Butterflies in silver lace? I began to make it April 3rd, 1943. I finished it on the evening of the 5th. And that was only because a supplier failed to get me the taffeta I needed.'

'Do you remember who you made it for?'

'Of course.'

Payne waited but Petiot began a muffled argument with someone beside him.

'– I will not shut up, woman.' The line became louder. 'I made it for a German SS officer. Konrad Jaeger. He was a

Haupt-something or other. He said it was for his wife but I didn't believe him. No man buys such a dress for a wife.'

Payne went to ask more but the line became muffled again. He heard Petiot's voice rise in irritation.

'Take your hand from my arm. What I say is true. I'm not ashamed of whom I do business with. The Germans have gone but what do we have now instead? Communists and social –'

The phone went dead.

Afterwards, Payne phoned to Corps HQ, where the captured SS personnel files Booth had mentioned were kept.

'This must be him, sir,' the clerk said an hour later by telephone, reading from the *RuSha* file. 'Konrad Jaeger, from Hamburg. Joined the Nazi party in 1929, the SS in 1934. Rose to the rank of *SS-Hauptscharführer*. That's the equivalent of Battalion Sergeant Major. Saw service in France, Yugoslavia and Italy, then transferred back to France. Of good solid Aryan stock and . . . oh, look at this,' the clerk said. 'He's got a pink chit in with his file.'

'What does that mean?' Payne said.

'It means the lawyers in Nuremburg are looking for him, sir. It seems your *SS-Hauptscharführer* Konrad Jaeger is a war criminal.'

6

CAPTAIN JAMES BOOTH was in a foul mood. What the hell was Ursula playing at?

He'd been to her farmhouse three times in the last two days, and on each occasion Ursula had found some excuse not to invite him inside. He'd convinced himself he was imagining things after the first two visits, but now he was not so sure. It was especially galling because without Booth Ursula wouldn't even have a damned house: if he hadn't sorted things with Housing Branch – at a great deal of personal risk and expense – the house would have been requisitioned long ago and she'd have been left to fend for herself. Didn't she realise he'd risked his bloody commission doing that?

For the umpteenth time that morning, Booth found himself on the verge of becoming genuinely angry; then he remembered who it was he was thinking about and the emotion faded. He could never get truly angry with his dear little Ursula.

He had met her back in May, when his detachment first arrived in Eichenrode. Booth had been driving back along the Brunswick road when he'd seen a group of ragged men pointing and prodding a young woman. Christ, he went cold when he thought about how close he'd come to driving past. Ursula had been holding her ground, but there was no doubt it would have ended badly: physical violence, almost certainly, rape or murder quite possibly. In those early days of peace, German civilians were fair game and most British troops did little to prevent the Nazis' former slaves from venting their anger.

But Booth *had* stopped and set himself between Ursula and the vengeful horde with only his uniform and sidearm to deter them. It had been enough.

Just.

Afterwards, he'd meant to drive Ursula to a safe distance further down the road, then ask her to get out. After all, the non-fraternisation order was rigidly enforced back then; he wasn't even supposed to talk to Germans, let alone give them lifts. But as they drove and chatted and Ursula calmed and began to smile, he found himself inventing excuses to keep her with him while they drove through the summer evening. When she shivered, he let her wrap his greatcoat around her shoulders, and suddenly it seemed that the evening air had never smelt so fresh or clear . . .

Part of him knew it was foolish to get so dippy over *any* woman, let alone a German one, but when it came to his feelings for Ursula, the voice of reason was shouting into the wind. One heard about this love-at-first-sight rot, but nothing had prepared him for how overwhelming it would be when it came. Like a flash flood, within minutes of setting eyes on her he was trapped upon a strip of high land staring down at a world consumed by surging torrents.

Of course, he'd been scrupulous about checking her background. He'd had a patrol drop one of the *Fragebogen* questionnaires into her house the day after he'd realised he had feelings for her. The one hundred and twenty-four questions were designed to pinpoint how deeply a person had been involved with the Nazi party, and were so baffling in their depth and complexity it was very difficult for that person to lie without being caught out. The answers were then checked against the German records the Allies had seized and the person was graded from I to V, with I being a known war criminal and V an ordinary civilian.

Ursula Drechsler was a category V, which meant she was considered to be almost completely innocent. The only blots on her copybook were a cousin in the Waffen-SS and her former role as a leader in the *League of German Maidens*. That wasn't really anything to worry about in the greater scheme of things. After twelve years of dictatorship, there were few Germans who didn't have some connection with the Nazi regime. Besides, the idea of Ursula teaching German girls to cook and sew was risible: the poor thing could barely peel a potato.

No, Booth felt no compunction about his romance with her. Quite the opposite, in fact. If the Allies were ever going to get Germany back on its feet, they would need people like Ursula. In some ways, it was his *duty* to protect the decent Germans. And part of Booth felt he was owed some happiness. He was tired of obeying orders. He'd done nothing else now for years – years when he should have been living it up at university. The constant bustle and activity of the war had hidden the fact that life had become an enervated, sterile thing, more of an existence than a life, really. It was time to feel human again and that was precisely what Ursula had given to him. God, the last two months had been bliss. It was as if before meeting her he'd been emotionally colour blind.

So, why won't she let me in her bloody house?

The thought came to him in a sudden jag of petulance and

he found himself drifting towards anger again. He lit a cigarette from the butt of the one he'd just smoked and brooded.

Had he done something wrong?

That was the most likely explanation, but he was damned if he could think of what it was he might have done. But then women were always so damned difficult to read . . .

Although Booth would have been loath to admit it, he'd not had much experience with the fairer sex. When had there been time? He was only twenty when the war began and he'd been called up in '42. He'd walked out with girls, naturally, but girls were all they had been. Ursula was thirty-four. She was a fully-fledged woman of the world. He'd realised that the first time their relationship became physical: unlike for him, it obviously hadn't been Ursula's first time.

He chewed his lip. That thought did nothing to improve his mood, so he went back to considering why she would not allow him inside.

Was it the state of the house? Did she feel ashamed of living in a ruin?

No, it couldn't be that, either. She'd let him inside dozens of times before without any problem. Besides, after all the cleaning and repairs Booth had done around the place, it was a palace in comparison to how it had been when he first met her. No, this problem was recent. It had only really cropped up in the last two or three days.

He smoked his cigarette and calmed himself. Anger faded again and was replaced by a deep yearning to see her, but Booth knew that wouldn't be possible until the evening: Ursula had to work at the transit camp today. Booth had considered trying to wangle her an exemption from that – God knows, she'd dropped enough hints – but he'd decided it was best not to tempt fate. Besides, after the business with her house, he couldn't really afford another bribe.

He would get Ursula a present, he decided, a crate of victuals. That always got him into her good books – like most of the Germans in the town, Ursula found decent food hard to come by. Booth finished his cigarette and drove across town to the supply depot, where he asked to speak to the regimental quartermaster sergeant, Suttpen.

Jacob Suttpen had first come to Booth's attention when their division had crossed the Rhine and the really serious looting began. Legend had it that one of the combat units spent a whole morning fighting their way into a German town, only to find that Suttpen and his helpers had already been there an hour and had filled two lorries with furniture, paintings and mirrors. Booth had no idea whether the story was true, but he could well believe it. Since then, Suttpen had established himself as the nexus for every shady deal that happened within a dozen miles of Eichenrode.

It was Suttpen that had ensured Ursula's farmhouse was kept off the requisition list. Apparently, he had a contact in Housing Branch that could arrange things like that. Booth was not surprised. Suttpen seemed to possess the innate ability of divining which palms needed greasing and of determining exactly how much it would cost.

A storeman carrying a wooden crate told Booth that Suttpen was at the back of the depot. When Booth got there, he found Suttpen talking with a short, ferrety German man in civilian clothes whom Booth recognised from somewhere. The German was frowning as he listened to Suttpen and he occasionally cupped a hand to his mouth to whisper something in the quartermaster sergeant's ear. The two men carried on talking, but when Suttpen saw Booth, he hissed something and the little German bolted.

'Not interrupting anything, am I? Booth said.

'What? Oh, that? That was nothing, sir.'

'That man seemed quite worried about something.'

'Nothing I can't handle, sir.'

'Isn't that fellow the German doctor that treats Colonel Bassett?' Booth said, realising where he'd seen the man before. 'Doctor Seiler, isn't it?'

Quartermaster Sergeant Suttpen forced his spiv's smile even wider than usual. 'That's right, sir.'

'You know you're not supposed to speak with German civilians, don't you? The non-fraternisation order is still in effect.'

'That was business, though, sir. I slip Doctor Seiler some supplies when I can. Medicine, bandages, that sort of thing.'

'Well, don't let the other ranks see you chatting with him out in the open. It gives the wrong impression.'

They walked as they talked, Suttpen leading Booth into his office at the rear of the building. When they were inside with the door closed, some of Suttpen's servile manner disappeared as he reached below his desk and pulled out a box covered with a cloth. This he lifted to allow Booth to examine the merchandise within: onions, potatoes and leeks on one side, apples and pears on the other, with an assortment of tins and jars down the centre.

Booth nodded. 'How much do I owe you for this? The usual?'

Suttpen's smile became especially oily and complicit. 'Oh, you can have these on the house, this week, sir.'

Booth frowned. 'That's suspiciously generous of you. Why do I get the feeling you're going to ask me for a favour?'

Suttpen beamed. 'You're a sharp one, sir. You really are.'

'Go on then.'

'This business with the house out by the Brunswick road. They say some policeman chap's been looking into it. Is that right, sir?'

'Yes. His name is Detective Inspector Payne. Of Scotland Yard, no less.'

For a moment, Suttpen's smile faltered and was replaced by a hard, thoughtful look. Booth lifted the box of vegetables. 'I'm afraid I can't say anything more than that, though,' he said, enjoying the disappointment on Suttpen's face. 'It's all a bit hush-hush. But thanks for the victuals. I'll make sure they find a good home.'

Suttpen didn't seem to hear him, though. Outside, Booth fell to chatting with a lieutenant from the signals. He was still there talking when Suttpen left his office carrying a bottle of whiskey, a loaf of bread and a length of sausage.

It took Booth a moment to realise what it was about Suttpen's appearance that had drawn his attention. It wasn't the food he was carrying: it was the holstered sidearm he now wore at his belt.

7

ILSE HAD TO do three days' work for the Tommies each week.

She'd had no say in the matter. Back in May, English soldiers had simply turned up at her house one day, kicked at the door and manhandled her into a lorry, along with a dozen other terrified German women. At first, she'd thought that someone had denounced her and she was being taken away to prison, but no, they'd simply wanted her to work.

For the first two weeks, she was made to clear rubble from streets in the centre of Eichenrode; once that was done, they put her to work at a transit camp the International Red Cross had set up at the local fertilizer factory.

She woke early and checked on Cousin Ursula. Ilse was taking a chance by leaving Ursula alone all day, but what choice did she have? She put an apple, two slices of stale bread and a glass of water on the table beside Ursula's bed, then explained where she was going and when she would be back. Ursula just stared at the ceiling and clutched her letters.

It was a forty-minute walk to the transit camp. Ilse hated the place.

O'Donnell, the Irishman that ran the camp administration, was a drunkard and a gambler. Rumour had it he had lost a fortune at poker to an English soldier, the one who ran the supply depot. Worse than that, though, he was a lecher. Only just the other day he had tried to grope her, but Ilse had scraped her booted foot down the front of his shin and left the leering jackass writhing and cursing on the floor.

Then there were the actual inhabitants of the camp: Poles, Ukrainians, Greeks, Czechs, Italians, Yugoslavs. God, the way they looked at Germans, nowadays, it was like being locked up with a bunch of wild animals. Ilse had lost count of how many times they had insulted or spat at her.

Still, she should give thanks for small mercies. The first week in July, a Polish man had accused another of being a Gestapo informer. Within seconds, a crowd had started kicking and punching the man as he rolled in the dust. Then men and women came with sticks and beat the man to death while the Tommy soldiers just watched. The man's body had lain there for an hour afterwards, the blood leaking from his cracked head.

A Tommy officer had come to the camp after that and bawled at the inmates. They mostly left the Germans alone, now, and that suited Ilse fine. She didn't want to go near those shabby, tattered, lice-ridden people anyway. The first thing the Red Cross nurses had to do each morning was line the camp's inhabitants up and pump clouds of white powder up their shirt sleeves and down the front of their trousers and skirts to stop typhus from spreading. That said everything you needed to know about the quality of the people in the camp.

The German women Ilse worked with were not much better. Most of them were peasants that spent all their time bemoaning the fate of the sons and brothers and husbands they'd lost in the war. And they were all so craven. That irritated Ilse more than anything else.

When the Tommies first came to Eichenrode, they had set up boards in the square outside the *Rathaus* and forced the Germans to walk in single file past them. The photographs pinned to the boards supposedly showed what had been happening in concentration camps in Germany – the words YOUR FAULT! were written at the top of each board – but Ilse didn't pay them much attention. The English and Americans had their propaganda, the same as anyone else. She felt no guilt. Why should she? She'd never hurt anyone. That was why Ilse always made a point of walking with her head held high. She was not ashamed of being German and she wouldn't let anyone bully her into feeling that way. Besides, the English had no claim to the moral high ground, not after the way they had firebombed Germany's cities.

It was mid-morning now and Ilse was making her way through the centre of the camp towards the brick outhouse where the camp's supplies were kept. She knew there were medical kits inside, little bundles with bandages and plasters and syrettes of morphine. She had no idea what she would do with the kit once she had it, but she had to do something for Cousin Ursula. Ilse needed to make her well and then get rid of her. She couldn't keep turning Booth away when he came to her house.

The soldier guarding the hut recognised Ilse and waved her inside. The medical supplies were stacked in wooden crates next to huge tins of the white typhus powder. Ilse fished inside one of the crates and removed a canvas package. It was a little larger than a bag of sugar and had the words *Field Medical Kit* printed across the top of it in English.

Should she take the whole thing? Or would it be better to open it and take what she needed?

As she debated the matter, she realised the soldier outside was talking to someone. Ilse hurried to the opposite side of the room, stuffing the medical kit down the front of her dress as she did so.

'And what are you doing in here, might I ask, Fräulein?' a man said in broken German.

Ilse turned and felt her heart plunge when she recognised the figure in the doorway: it was O'Donnell, the one that had tried to grope her.

He was a slender man with a ready smile, although close up you noticed that his eyes were small and dark and his cheeks patched with rosacea. He seemed to shave only every other day and he smelled like he slept in his clothes.

O'Donnell passed a hand through his lank hair and smiled as he walked towards her.

'If you touch me, I'll claw your eyes out,' Ilse said in English.

He held a hand up in mollification. 'Don't worry. I just want to talk.' He reached behind him, brought out a bottle of whisky, some bread and a length of cured sausage. Ilse's stomach did a queasy flip at the sight of so much food.

O'Donnell laid them atop a crate then backed away, hands still raised. He motioned for her to take them.

'Where did you get it?' she said.

'I've got friends in the army. Same as you.'

'What's that supposed to mean?'

O'Donnell said nothing, but he smiled now, showing his yellowed teeth.

'What do you want in exchange?' she said, fighting the temptation to throw herself on the food.

'There's a policeman here,' O'Donnell said, his voice low but clear, as if he were used to speaking in half-tones. 'His name is Detective Inspector Payne. I need to know why he's so interested in that house out by the Brunswick road.'

'What could I possibly know about that?' she said.

'Your captain knows something. I want you to find out from him.'

Ilse's hand froze an inch from the food. 'Captain? What captain?'

O'Donnell's wide mouth twisted into a lecherous smile.

'Captain James Booth. The same Captain Booth that recently paid to keep a certain ruined farmhouse off the list of requisitioned properties. Christ, you don't think I don't know, do you? Eoin O'Donnell don't miss a trick, remember that. Not a single one.'

Ilse's hand hovered above the food. O'Donnell knew about Booth; there was no point in denying it. What mattered now was what he would do with the information.

Ilse scooped up the food. Then she said, 'I'll take this for now. But you must bring me more when I find something out. Cheese. And some eggs.'

O'Donnell folded his arms. 'Quite the little business woman, ain't ya? How's about this? You take that lot there and I won't mention the medical kit you've got stuffed down the front of your dress.'

He laughed when he saw the panic on Ilse's face.

'Go on, get out of here,' he said. 'And I'll want some answers soon.'

As Ilse passed him, he said, 'Course, you're way too much woman for the young captain, aren't you, Ursula? But I guess he'll find that out the hard way.'

Then he pinched her bottom.

'Pig!' she said and slapped his hand away.

O'Donnell's laughter followed her as she hurried from the building.

8

SILAS PAYNE WAS billeted in Eichenrode's police station. Since he'd taken residence there, Germans had knocked at the door on a number of occasions. Was he the new face of authority, they had asked. Did they report crimes to him now? He'd even had one comical exchange with a heavily-disguised woman offering to denounce her neighbours 'as she used to do' in exchange for food and tobacco.

He was standing in the window of the police station now, still in his pyjamas, enjoying the bright morning sunlight and watching German children playing football in the street with a tin can.

The file on the Waffen SS man, Konrad Jaeger, lay on the table behind him. He'd had the clerk at Corps HQ send it over to him by courier the previous evening. The file contained two photos of Jaeger. Payne had compared the photos with those he'd taken of the murder victim and there was no doubt it was the same man. The clerk had also included a handwritten note on the war crimes for which Jaeger was wanted: *It seems Herr Jaeger had a predilection for shooting French civilians. He's wanted on four counts of that. He's also accused of torturing two women suspected of resistance involvement.*

Payne had considered what that might mean. The French Zone of Occupation was in the south-west of Germany but there were plenty of French soldiers and personnel passing through this area all the time. Could that have something to do with Jaeger's murder? It was possible, he decided, but unlikely. An act of random violence still seemed the most likely explanation – and yet nothing about the crime seemed random to Payne.

He sipped coffee and wondered what it was about the killings that had given him the hair-at-the-back-of-the-throat sensation he always got when he was missing something. It was the surgical instruments. It wasn't just their presence, it was the way they had been set out: it went beyond the mere orderliness of the professional. Their arrangement had the fussy precision associated with a ritual or obsession. That was it, Payne realised. It wasn't what had happened that had bothered him, it was what had been *about* to happen. The killing of the man and woman had been only the first stage in something larger and more sinister – Beagley and his men had *interrupted* something, he was sure of it.

Payne had converted his bedroom from a small office at the back of the police station. He went there now and put on a clean suit. Returning to the front of the police station, he heard the clatter of horses' hooves on the asphalt of the street outside.

Colonel Bassett's adjutant, Captain Fredrickson, had been out hunting with some of the other officers. A pair of bloodied fox tails hung from the pommel of Fredrickson's saddle. A private soldier walked behind the mounted men, holding the leashes of five beagles. Rumour had it Fredrickson's father was something big in the city and that the hounds had been shipped out to Germany especially.

When Fredrickson reached the German children and their

tin can he rode his horse straight at them, causing them to scatter. Fredrickson said something over his shoulder as he rode past and the officers behind him laughed.

Payne finished his coffee, thinking about something Major Norris had said the day before, something about getting the world back to normal. Norris was wrong: the world would never be the same again. Not now. Buildings and bodies weren't the only things the war had damaged. It had skewed men's morals, too, and let the wilder side of human nature run free. Some of the British soldiers Payne had seen in Germany wore expressions you normally only saw in the hard, lawless parts of the East End, and three months of occupation had shown that the members of Eisenhower's Great Crusade were prone to succumb to their baser instincts, too. Payne had heard stories about the wild days at the end of the war – the shootings, the beatings, the rapes. And now there were stories of lorries full of loot being bussed out to Holland and of cargo planes taking off loaded with antique German furniture.

When he had been a young copper, Payne's first sergeant had summed up good police-work for him. 'When a crime's been committed, there's only two types of people, Silas: victims and villains. Comfort the former, catch the latter and don't pay no heed to whether you likes or dislikes either one of 'em. Remember that and you'll do all right.'

Payne *had* remembered it; had made it the cornerstone of his whole career, in fact. That was what this murder case represented to Payne. Britain had fought the war for a cause higher than the individual and it was time to put the morality underpinning that cause into practice, to stop basking in the VE-day sunshine. If the war was going to have meant anything at all, then all this lawlessness had to stop. The British people owed it to themselves to govern Germany well.

At nine o'clock, Payne took his utility and drove across town to what was left of the local hospital. This was the place where the Royal Army Medical Corps had set itself up. The soldiers on guard outside recognised Payne and waved him through. He crossed the waiting room and headed downstairs to the laboratory.

Captain Shelley was the GDMO – General Duties Medical Officer – for Eichenrode. He was a cheery, good-natured sort who had performed the autopsy on Jaeger's body and had offered to take a look at the vials of medicine Payne had found at the murder house.

When Payne knocked at the lab door, Shelley answered it, wearing a white lab coat over his uniform and drying his hands on a towel.

'I'm glad you came over, Detective Inspector,' he said scratching at his long nose. 'You've saved me a trip.'

'Have you found something?'

Inside the laboratory, a small German man was removing the lab coat he wore. Test tubes containing coloured liquids stood in racks on the table.

'This is Doctor Seiler,' Shelley said, introducing the man. 'His daughter works as an interpreter over at the *Rathaus*. He's been helping me out. He's a far better chemist than I am.'

'Oh, you're embarrassing me, Captain,' Seiler said brightly, extending his soft, moist hand for Payne to shake. 'But I'm always glad to help the British. You can't imagine what a relief it is to be finally free of that Austrian monster and his Brownshirts.'

So far, Silas Payne had met three types of German: the first were those that were too tired and broken even to notice the occupation; the second resented it bitterly and were suspicious and surly; the third were like Doctor Seiler, Germans that had recognised which way the wind now blew and were determined to fill their wings with it.

Payne shook the proffered hand, thinking that Seiler reminded him of a theatrical agent he'd interrogated once: the easy smile, weak chin and unctuous manner were all uncannily similar. Like his daughter, Seiler spoke good English and, like his daughter, Seiler seemed intent on lingering to hear what Payne had to say.

'Yes, Detective Inspector, a truly fascinating case,' he said, turning to the test tubes on the table. 'But, as I said to Captain Shelley, I might be able to provide more information were I to know specifically where these items were found and what the case entails . . .'

Seiler's raised eyebrows invited Payne to comment. Payne said nothing.

'Oh, well, I'll be going,' Seiler said, once the silence had become uncomfortable. Still, Payne said nothing. Seiler gave a weak smile and headed towards the door.

'Close it behind you,' Payne said.

'We could have talked in front of Doctor Seiler,' Shelley said when the German had gone. 'Most of what I'm about to tell you is his information, anyway.'

'Better safe than sorry. Besides, I have managed to identify the male victim and I'd rather Seiler didn't know.'

Payne explained who Konrad Jaeger was, then asked Shelley what he had found.

Shelley indicated the vials on the table, the ones Payne had taken from the cellar of the murder house.

'These are all fairly standard vaccines. According to Seiler, these particular brands were used by the Wehrmacht for troops who were fighting abroad. North Africa, places like that.'

'Are they difficult to get hold of?'

Shelley shrugged. 'Under normal circumstances I would say 'yes', but who can say nowadays, with so much military equipment left lying around everywhere? Someone could easily have stumbled across a crate of medical supplies.'

'What are they vaccines for?'

Shelley indicated each of the vials in turn. 'Hepatitis A. Tetanus. Tuberculosis. Typhus. But, as I mentioned last night, this is the one that interested me,' he said, tapping one of the vials with a pencil. 'I've used this myself, before the war, and I've never seen it that colour. So we ran some tests.'

'And it's not a vaccine?'

'Far from it. It's some form of barbiturate.'

'What effect would that have if it was injected? Could it be used to kill?'

'Depends on the dose. At this level of concentration, I would say it was more likely to induce unconsciousness.'

'Why would someone store a potentially lethal drug in a wrongly-labelled vial?'

Shelley shrugged. 'Human error. Or perhaps the original receptacle was broken and they were trying to salvage what they could.'

'Or someone was pretending to inject a vaccine when in fact they wanted to render the person unconscious before strangling them.'

Shelley smiled. 'That's the policemen in you talking, Detective Inspector. But, yes, it's perfectly possible. And it would explain why Jaeger's body does not bear any cuts or scratches, despite his having been strangled. He could have been sedated first.'

'How quickly would this barbiturate take effect if it was injected?'

'In a matter of seconds. Why?'

'I think it explains the minor injuries the woman suffered, too. I think the killer injected Jaeger first. But as Jaeger wilted, the woman smelt a rat and panicked, forcing the killer to subdue her physically before he could inject her and put her out of the picture, too. Can you check the bodies for needle marks?'

Shelley shook his head. 'I'm afraid the bodies have been burnt. Colonel Bassett's orders. We have only limited capacity for storing bodies here.'

'What about the scalpels and the knives? Do you have any theories about them?'

'That was the other thing I wanted to talk to you about,' Shelley said, his face serious now. He led Payne across the room to a table where the tools found in the cellar had been laid out.

'You were quite correct in assuming that these are surgical tools. Of course, the scalpels and the saw could theoretically be used for other purposes, but this is the real clincher,' he said, indicating the length of serrated wire with the wooden handles. 'In the trade, this is known as a Gigli wire saw. It's used in surgery for bone-cutting – amputations, that sort of thing. It's such a specialist tool, I can't really imagine it being used for anything else.'

'What are you saying? That the killer *was* intending to operate on the victims at some point?'

Shelley shook his head. 'Not an operation, Detective Inspector. I think he was planning on performing a dissection.'

At midday Payne drove to the centre of town and parked outside the offices of Housing Branch, the administrative organisation that dealt with the requisition and allocation of housing in the area. Shelley's information worried him. That was why he wanted to know precisely who had requisitioned the murder house and which unit had been billeted there.

The Housing Branch clerk rolled his eyes when he saw Payne and said, no, he still hadn't had time to determine which British unit had requisitioned the house by the Brunswick Road. Nor would he find it any time soon, to judge by the man's languid tone of voice.

'It's imperative you find the details,' Payne said. 'Can't you have a look now? Or at least show me where to look?'

'Listen, chummy,' the clerk said, putting his pencil down, 'nearly thirty per cent of the thousand or so addresses on the German records in this town don't exist anymore. And most of what *is* left has been requisitioned by us. We've got boxes and boxes of ruddy chits and receipts.' By way of illustration, he pointed towards a pile of cardboard boxes that leaked paperwork. 'There's only four of us work here, you know. And if you think I'm going to let you loose on them, you've another thing coming. It's taken me weeks to sort that lot out.'

'Isn't there some central office that keeps copies of the requisition chits?'

'That would be in Brunswick. You'd have to fill in a form. Or you could go to Brunswick.'

Payne asked who was in charge.

'That'll be Mr Lockwood.'

'Let me speak to him, then, please.'

Mr Lockwood was a nervy little mole of a man with the face of a born bureaucrat, small and pinched beneath hair that was lacquered and swept severely across his forehead. The belt of his CCG uniform served only to accentuate the extent to which his belly protruded beneath it. He emerged from the gloom of his back office and peered at Payne through thick glasses.

'Yes. Yes. What is it? Do I know you?'

He blinked three times very quickly when Payne told him he was a British policeman. When Payne explained a double murder had occurred in a requisitioned house, Lockwood said, 'What house? It's nothing to do with me. I mean us. Whatever it is.'

'It's a house on the Brunswick Road, about half-a-mile beyond the town. Big one, three stories, with a hole in the roof. Perhaps you know it?'

Lockwood did. As Payne described the house, the colour drained from the man's face and, for a moment, he seemed somewhere else entirely, his myopic eyes unblinking now.

'Dead bodies?' he said, making a visible effort to hide his distress. 'Nasty business. Very nasty.'

'You can appreciate why it's so important to know who

requisitioned the house, then. And who is currently billeted there.'

'Well, you'll have to fill out a form requesting the information,' Lockwood said and bolted for the safety of his office, but Payne called out his name before he could close the door.

'It really is very important. There could be very serious repercussions for anyone involved. Especially if they try to keep information from the police.'

Lockwood's face was the colour of wet ashes now.

Payne filled in a form requesting the name of the unit that had been billeted at the murder house. Then he went outside and walked to a point across the square from which he could see the steps of the Housing Branch office. Lockwood knew something about the murder house, Payne would stake his pension on it.

The question now was whether Lockwood would sit and stew or run to someone else for advice. Payne's bet was on the latter. Experience had taught him to spot that certain light in a man's eye that preceded panicked flight.

The morning wind was sharp, a reminder that September was just around the corner. Silas Payne pulled the collar of his coat up and leant against the wall, his eyes fixed on the door of Housing Branch. He would wait as long as it took.

When the European war had ended back in May, the invading armies had simply stopped wherever they were and established military governments. Germany was divided into four zones: British, Russian, American and French. Now, in August, members of the Control Council for Germany – the CCG for short – were moving in to take over local administration in the British zone.

It was a vast and complex task. The policy of denazification – by which all trace of Nazism would be purged from the country – meant Germany's entire bureaucratic structure had to be rebuilt from the bottom up. The task for the British was especially difficult, as their north-western zone contained most of Germany's big cities – cities the Allies had spent years systematically destroying. Payne had heard Major Norris comment on it: 'The Yanks got the scenery, the French the wine. All we got were bloody ruins.'

It wasn't an exaggeration. The situation in the British Zone was chaotic: no water, no electricity, no gas, no schools, no doctors. Roads and bridges had been bombed, train tracks destroyed. Millions were homeless, millions starving.

From what Payne had seen, the arrival of hordes of CCG bureaucrats would do nothing to alleviate the problem. Payne had rubbed shoulders with all sorts of misfits at the 'training' session they'd been given before being sent out to Germany: drain inspectors, retired officers, failed businessmen and civil servants from every far flung corner of the Empire. Some Army wags were already saying CCG stood for Charlie Chaplin's Grenadiers or Complete Chaos Guaranteed.

As a fluent German speaker, Payne had been seconded from Scotland Yard to come and run a training school for German policemen, but the most productive thing he'd done during his first seventy-two hours in Germany was to sweep the floor of the police station. It was bloody frustrating, given the state of the country. That was why he'd jumped at the chance to look into this murder. The one thing Silas Payne truly feared was inactivity and he would do –

The door to Housing Branch opened and Payne withdrew to a spot around the corner that was out of view, but only the clerk taking paperwork over to the *Rathaus* emerged. Payne resumed his vigil.

He wondered how the German police would have handled a situation like this and decided he knew the answer. He'd seen the windowless cell deep in the basement of Eichenrode's police station, the cell with the metal chair bolted to the ground and porcelain tiles on floor, walls and ceiling.

Tiles: they were easier to sponge down afterwards. Look carefully and you could still see the brown-red stains on the grouting.

That was no way to police a country and that was the whole point of his coming to Eichenrode. Germany's national police force had been more or less forged by the Nazis and German policemen needed to learn what it meant to police society within a democracy. No more midnight knocks. No more *Nacht und Nebel*. No more tiled cells. The German police were to be public servants, nothing more. It was important the new Germany got that part right. How a society chose to police itself was a measure of how civilised it was. From what Payne had seen of Germany so far it had a long, long way to go.

A few minutes later, the clerk returned. Payne withdrew around the corner again and watched as the man headed up the stairs, opened the door . . .

. . . and Lockwood pushed past him down the stairs and set off along the road, walking with small, rapid strides.

Payne gave him a twenty-yard head start, then set off after him.

Wherever he was going, Lockwood was in a hurry. He didn't want to be recognised, either: the little man wore a civilian coat over his CCG uniform and he walked with the brim of his hat pulled down.

They crossed town for half-a-mile, heading towards Eichenrode's eastern edge. The damage here was less severe and many of the British personnel had been stationed in houses there. Payne wondered whether Lockwood was headed back to his billet, but when he saw the man turn left and stop at a sandbag revetment manned by British soldiers, Payne realised Lockwood was making for the supply depot.

The depot was the centre of life in Eichenrode, the only place you could get anything at the moment: food, clothing, blankets, chocolate, cigarettes, alcohol. During the war, Payne had heard soldiers laugh about the quality of the goods at the army stores, but, in the bleak economy of post-war Germany, with its boarded-up, bombed-out shops, the depot seemed a veritable Aladdin's cave of wonders.

The supply depot in Eichenrode occupied three warehouses. The canteen and kitchens were situated in the largest of the buildings, while the two other buildings held the stores. The whole area had been surrounded with barbed wire fences. Guards with rifles and Bren guns patrolled the perimeter.

Lockwood headed for the larger of the two stores.

Payne waited before following him inside the building, considering what to do. It was possible Lockwood was only here on some trivial errand. If he followed him inside, Lockwood would be alerted – something Payne wanted to avoid doing until he had some idea of what it was he was on to. However, it was also possible that Lockwood had come here because he wanted to speak to someone.

He would take a chance and follow Lockwood inside, Payne decided. The little man's attitude had been so hurried and furtive that Payne was convinced that his visit to the depot had some connection with the questions Payne had been asking about the murder house.

Payne showed his ID papers to the guard on the door and walked inside, to a small room with a wooden counter. Half-a-dozen people in CCG uniforms were queuing before the counter, waiting to hand their requisition chits to the storemen. Long green curtains hung behind the counter and obscured the stores from view.

Mr Lockwood was nowhere to be seen.

Payne walked to the head of the queue, ignoring the grumbles behind him, and said to the storeman on duty: 'A little man with glasses just came in. Did you see where he went?'

The storeman pointed behind him with his thumb. 'He's round the back with the quartermaster sergeant. You can't come through this way, though,' he said when Payne went to lift a section of the wooden counter. 'That's for authorised personnel. Go outside and walk round the back.'

Payne went outside and walked to the back of the building, wondering how it was that Mr Lockwood of Housing Branch had come to be considered 'authorised personnel' at an army supply depot.

The ground at the back of the warehouse had been churned into thick mud by the passing of hundreds of vehicles. It was here that the lorries, trucks and utilities of the British Army came to collect their provisions. A dozen storemen in green shirts and braces carried boxes and crates out onto a ramp. Here soldiers loaded the goods into the back of their vehicles.

Payne asked a storeman where the quartermaster sergeant was and the soldier pointed away to the left, towards a concrete outhouse. Payne walked between two of the lorries queuing to receive supplies, and followed the blind side of the vehicles to get closer to the outhouse.

The regimental quartermaster sergeant was a stocky man with slicked back hair; he was about Payne's age. He was listening to Lockwood speak, and, as he did so, a sneer appeared on his face. Lockwood was speaking with rapid, nervous hand movements, but he froze when the quartermaster sergeant stepped closer and grabbed his forearm.

The man was trouble, Payne realised. He'd crossed swords with far too many cheap thugs and con men in his life not to recognise the expression on the quartermaster sergeant's face as he wagged a finger at Lockwood. Bullying came easily to him; violence, too, most likely. Payne frowned when he noticed that the backs of the quartermaster sergeant's trousers were stained with soot-like black marks.

He watched as the two men continued to talk and Lockwood's air of perturbation increased. Then the driver of the lorry which shielded Payne gave a long toot on the horn and shouted something at Payne from the cab. Both Lockwood and the quartermaster sergeant looked up, but Payne had already withdrawn. Payne crossed behind the vehicle's tailgate and saw Lockwood hurrying away.

Payne headed towards the front of the supply depot, thinking about the expression on Lockwood's pale face. Payne recognised that, too: whatever it was that Lockwood had gotten into, he was in way over his head.

9

WHEN CAPTAIN JAMES Booth looked at his wristwatch for the third time in as many minutes, Chaplain Clifford said, 'Am I keeping you from something, Captain?'

Booth smiled and pulled the sleeve of his battle-blouse down. He'd been hoping to slip out and see Ursula this evening, but the chaplain's visit had scotched that: curfew would begin in an hour and Booth couldn't keep inventing excuses about why he needed to pass through checkpoints and sentry posts after dark. Besides, he didn't want the chaplain to think him rude. Ursula's present would have to wait until tomorrow.

They chatted while the Polish boy, Piotr, prepared them tea. When Piotr leant over to pour, the chaplain tried not to stare at the boy's face, but it was difficult not to: the upward twist of Piotr's hare lip nearly reached his nose, revealing snaggled teeth and a moist patch of pinky-coloured gum.

Piotr set the teapot on the table and extended a grimy hand. Booth handed him a packet of cigarettes.

'He's a trifle young to smoke, isn't he?' the chaplain said, when Piotr had left the room.

'The cigarettes aren't for him. Tobacco is the currency around here now. He uses them to buy food and firewood.'

'How old is he?'

'I've never been able to establish that. About thirteen, I

would guess, from the looks of him, though I'm not sure what his mental age would be. Truth be told, I don't think he's really all there, but you won't meet a simpler, more helpful soul.'

'Where on earth did you find him?'

'I took him under my wing in Holland and he's been with me ever since. The Nazis had him working in a factory there.'

'He sounds fortunate to be alive.'

'Yes. But the luck didn't extend to his family. From what I've been able to ascertain, they're all dead. But Piotr's my good luck charm. I made a sort of covenant when I found him. I promised God I'd look after Piotr, no matter what, as long as nothing bad happened to me. Rather selfish, I know, but Piotr delivered admirably on his end of the bargain.'

'Your concern for his welfare is admirable, captain, very admirable indeed.' The chaplain blew on his tea and rested the cup in the saucer. 'Actually, Piotr's welfare is the reason I stopped by.'

'Really?'

'One of my congregation mentioned you were looking after a Polish orphan. It just so happens, a friend of mine back in Hampshire has established a home for Polish children in a little Hampshire town called Fleet. I could speak to her if you liked, see if she had room for Piotr.'

Booth shifted in his seat. 'I don't know if I'd want to send him off with strangers, padre.'

'I understand that completely, but you have my personal assurance of the quality of this woman's credentials. She is half-Polish herself, on her father's side.' He sipped his tea. 'Also, there is the question of the suitability of the boy's current environment: no schools, no family, the somewhat lax moral atmosphere that unfortunately prevails in Germany at the moment. It would be easy to imagine the boy falling in with a bad crowd, given the amount of time you are forced to dedicate to your duties.'

Yes, there is that, Booth thought as he offered the chaplain a cigarette. 'Can you tell me a bit more about this woman?'

Ten minutes later, Chaplain Clifford finished his tea and rose. 'I see I have piqued your interest, captain. Please feel free to consider the matter for a few days and let me know your decision.'

Booth showed the chaplain to the front door and smoked a cigarette on the steps, looking out across the ruins of Eichenrode. Across the street, Piotr was playing some form of tag with a group of German children.

Booth was only half joking about the covenant he'd made. When Booth had found Piotr, the boy had been little more than a tangle of pale skin and protuberant bones, sleeping beneath the machine he tended in a filthy Dutch factory – and yet, when Booth had wept at the boy's pitiable condition, Piotr had smiled and hugged him and tried to wipe the tears from Booth's face. That was the thing about Piotr, Booth had realised: despite all the horrors that had befallen him, he had never lost hope. That was why Booth had taken it upon himself to care for him. There was something pure and essential about the boy. If anything happened to Piotr, the world would be a worse place for it.

His cigarette finished, Booth jumped into his jeep and drove west through the town. If he couldn't see Ursula tonight, he might as well get on with some work and he had a new batch of information films to sort. They were making lots of these back in England now, short films and documentaries designed to be played to the occupation troops. The general idea was to outline what the purpose of the British occupation of north-west Germany was going to be, but no-one back home seemed to be controlling the output and the films often contradicted each other. When you watched the films back-to-back, as Booth did, it gave a depressingly composite view of the lack of direction behind the occupation: rather like a man groping his way through a darkened room trying not to bump into things.

A church in the centre of Eichenrode had been rigged as a makeshift cinema, although the structure was less than perfect: the exterior walls were cracked and pitted and there were numerous holes in the roof. The evening air in this part of town was still heavy with the smells of war, gasoline, brick-dust, cooking fires and damp tarpaulin. Booth parked outside the cinema and headed towards the back door, but paused as a sudden peal of laughter drifted from within the building, the sort of laughter men make when they tell each other dirty jokes.

The door to the cinema was locked. Booth rattled the handle then rapped loudly on it. The sound of hurried, furtive movements came from the other side. Then the bolt was drawn and Sergeant Hoyle's face appeared in the crack.

Hoyle was regular army and had a particular way of snapping out a parade-perfect salute when he had something to hide. Booth did not bother to return the salute. He pushed straight past Hoyle and said, 'What the devil are you up to in here, sergeant?'

A group of men was gathered inside. All stood to attention when they saw Booth's insignia. Although the men were older than Booth, there was a curiously schoolboy air to them as they exchanged glances and hung their heads. They looked guilty as hell.

Booth saw that the projector was set up with a roll of film and the huge white blanket that served as a screen was unrolled.

'What are you watching? Don't bother denying it; you've obviously just turned the projector off.'

'Begging your pardon, sir, but it won't be of any interest to –'

'I'll be the judge of that, sergeant. Now show me the damned film.'

Hoyle looked sheepishly at the other men, then put the film on.

The projector whirred and the film flickered into life, showing a black and white image of a bedroom. It took Booth's eyes a moment to separate the grainy black and white images into two naked bodies copulating, the woman's pale buttocks raised high as she knelt forward on the satin sheets, the man crouched behind her. Booth's jaw dropped as he took in further details – the candles beside the bed, the huge mirror on the wall – then he said, 'What the devil is this filth? Turn it off, sergeant. Turn it off, now.'

Hoyle hurried to remove the film from the projector. Booth told the other men to leave.

'Well, sergeant, you've some explaining to do,' he said when they were alone.

Hoyle was standing rigidly to attention again. He said nothing.

'Where did you get this from?'

'A patrol brought some canisters of film in when we were first billeted here.'

'How many canisters of film are there?'

'Four, sir.'

'You'd better let me see them.'

Hoyle took a box from under the table. Inside, there were four circular metal film canisters. In the centre of each lid was a piece of paper. TO BE USED WITH was printed on it in German, followed by a vertical list of German surnames. Nearly all of the surnames had been crossed through, although Booth noticed some of the surnames were repeated on different canisters.

Booth opened one of the tins. The circular label stuck to the inside had a strange oval shaped design on it – a vertical sword circled by a loop of ribbon, the whole surrounded by runic designs – and the words *Wehrwissenschaftliche Zweckforschung* printed below it. Booth frowned when he saw that: it meant Military Scientific Research.

'How long have these private viewings been going on, sergeant?'

'Not long, sir.'

Booth gestured towards the film canisters.

'Is the content of all four films sexual in nature?'

'That one is. The other two are something different.' Hoyle's face clouded. 'It's not very pleasant stuff, sir.'

'Let's take a look.'

Each film ran for about two minutes. The films were all silent, the images blurred and grainy.

The first film showed groups of five men in civilian clothes being made to run from a point behind the camera down into a gully. Away to the right and left of the image, German soldiers stood with rifles, chatting amongst themselves and smoking. At a signal, they lifted their rifles and fired down into the pit. Another five men were then run forward and the process was repeated. A German soldier chewing a hunk of bread walked in front of the camera and smiled. The image faded.

In the second film, naked women stood in single file, arms wrapped around sagging breasts in an attempt at modesty. Some stared at the ground, others had their mouths open, as if wailing. One among them stared openly towards the camera, shouting at the cameraman.

'Oh Lord, don't you dare!' Booth said when a German soldier appeared from the left of the image, threw the woman to the ground and shot her twice in the head with a pistol. The camera lingered on the blood pooling beneath her hair; then the image flickered and faded to be replaced by a vast tangle of limbs.

Hundreds of dead bodies were piled on top of each other in a concrete chamber. Men wearing leather aprons and equipped with metal tie tongs dragged the bodies on to carts. The floor was covered in a dark pool of effluent.

The film finished. The loose end of the reel whickered within the projector as Booth and Hoyle stared towards the now empty screen. Booth could say nothing. His mouth hung open.

'I said it wasn't very pleasant viewing, sir.'

'You know what this is, don't you, sergeant? This is evidence of war crimes. When the hell were you planning on showing this to me?'

Hoyle said nothing. He clearly hadn't been planning on showing Booth anything.

'Box those films up and bring them to my office. And don't tell anyone else about this.'

It was evening, now. Booth walked outside, enjoying the sensation of cleanliness the limpid air imparted. The sunset tinged the horizon red and backlit the town's ragged skyline. When Sergeant Hoyle came out with the box of films, Booth said: 'Now, sergeant, I think you'd better tell me exactly how these films came into your possession.'

ILSE SPENT THE afternoon working in the transit camp's laundry.

She normally tried to avoid this duty, as it was hard work, but there was a particular German woman, a bony old hag with a witchy nose and warts, who never took her eyes from Ilse. When the Tommies divided the women into working parties, Ilse always made sure she wasn't in the hag's group. The woman wasn't mentally stable.

The laundry was set up in a large concrete chamber to one side of the main body of the camp. Ilse was one of six German women working there today, but they were forbidden from talking among themselves. A Tommy with a rifle and a Red Cross nurse watched over them as they stirred huge cauldrons of boiling clothes and hefted sopping baskets through to the drying room.

Ilse thought about Captain Booth as she worked.

Poor Booth had fallen head over heels in love with her, but there was nothing Ilse could do about that. She'd felt a little sorry at having to turn him away *again* the previous evening. She had come to enjoy his company. It was nice to have at least one Englishman look at her with something other than contempt or indifference, even if he did think her name was Ursula. Physically, Booth was young and fit, two words that could never have been applied to Rüdiger towards the end of their marriage.

But O'Donnell knew about Booth. Would that be a problem? No, Ilse decided, not as long as she did what O'Donnell wanted. But who was this policeman he'd mentioned? And why was O'Donnell so worried about him?

Ilse had heard rumours about the two dead bodies that had been found in the cellar of a house out by the Brunswick Road. Lots of Germans were whispering about it. Rumour had it they'd been murdered by the Tommies. Did O'Donnell have something to do with that? It wouldn't have surprised Ilse if he did. O'Donnell had that look about him, the look of a man who would smile as he picked your pocket. *Say what you like about the Nazis, they knew how to deal with people like that*, she thought.

How the hell had O'Donnell found out about her and Booth, though? Ilse thought about this and decided the Tommy soldier called Suttpen must have told O'Donnell. Everyone knew Suttpen and O'Donnell played cards together; and Booth had had to bribe Suttpen to stop Ilse's farmhouse from being requisitioned.

By late afternoon, the soldier that watched over the laundry had begun to chat with the Red Cross nurse. When he invited her outside for a smoke, Ilse hissed at the woman next to her, a big-hipped Bavarian with ruddy cheeks and her hair sweat-plastered to her forehead.

'What is it?' the woman said when Ilse hissed again. 'We're not supposed to talk.'

Ilse stole a glance over her shoulder then moved closer.

'Have you heard about the murders on the Brunswick Road?'

Murder: it was strange the power that word had. Millions had been 'killed' in the last five years and nobody seemed to pay a blind bit of notice. But use that word, murder, and the world still caught its breath.

'They say it was the Tommies,' the Bavarian woman said, dropping her voice to a whisper, 'and I believe them. My neighbour works at the *Rathaus* and she says the man they killed was in the SS.'

'What about this English policeman who is investigating?'

The woman waved her hand dismissively. 'I don't believe they *are* investigating. What do the Tommies care if Germans die?'

Ilse went to say more but the Red Cross woman shouted something at them and the Bavarian woman blushed and hurried away.

Ilse had to fight not to lose her temper. She wasn't a school-girl to be shushed like that. What the hell were they punishing her for, anyway? What had Ilse ever done? She'd never killed anyone. She'd always been very fair to the Polish girls that served her in the Warthegau. This was so humiliating, being forced to soak and scrub other people's filthy clothing. *But that's the whole point, isn't it?* she thought. It wasn't enough that the Tommies had won the war: they wanted the German people to *know* they'd been beaten. They were going to rub their noses in it. Still, it could be worse, she thought. God, if things were like this with the English in control, what the hell must things be like under the Russians? Then she remembered Cousin Ursula. *That* was how things were under the Russians.

The sun was sinking low in the sky when the Red Cross woman let them leave. Ilse hurried across the camp to the place where she'd hidden the medical kit and the food O'Donnell had given her. She almost cried with relief when she saw that they were still there. She took a nibble of the bread and sausage after making sure she wasn't watched, then stuffed the whole lot down the front of her dress and headed for the gates.

As always, there was a huge queue outside the factory's admin building. This was where people queued to obtain the identity documents and travel permits they needed to get home. It always made Ilse happy to see how crowded it was. That was good. The more of them received their wretched documents, the more of them would leave and the faster Germany could get back to normal again.

Close to the gate now, she heard the rumble of a lorry behind her and the tooting of its horn. When she turned and saw the Red Cross symbol painted on the roof, she stole away into the bushes by the side of the road.

So, he was back, was he?

The man who drove the lorry was named Joost. He was a strange fellow, practically the only man in the camp that didn't ogle the women. In fact, he didn't really seem to notice anyone; he seemed to look through people. He said he was South African, but Ilse had discovered he wasn't actually one of the official Red Cross workers. Still, the war had thrown up all types of refugees. There were hundreds like Joost in every transit camp, people willing to help out in order to improve their own status a little. Joost was often gone for days at a time, picking up supplies and dropping people off at different transit camps. He'd given Ilse a lift, once, but he'd begun to take a very roundabout way to get to her house. When she'd asked him where he was going, he wouldn't reply. In the end, a British patrol had stopped them and made Ilse get out because she didn't have the right documents. Ilse remembered feeling quite relieved.

When the lorry had passed, Ilse emerged from the bushes. She was nearly at the gates when someone in front of her called her name.

It was the hag woman, the mad one, standing by the gates. Ilse tried to hurry past, but the woman blocked her path, hissing at Ilse as she did so.

'Who are you?' Ilse said, pushing the woman away and quickening her step. 'Leave me alone.'

Ilse ran now, heart racing, but when she reached the bend in the road, she could not resist looking behind her.

The hag stood in the middle of the road, staring straight towards her.

Ilse continued to run. Panic gripped her, but it wasn't until she was halfway home that she realised why: the hag had called her by name – but not Ursula, the one everyone in the camp knew her by.

She had called her Ilse.

11

Silas Payne woke early and busied himself preparing
coffee and bacon over the potbellied stove in the police station. As he ate, he considered how to move his investigation
forward. He had spoken to Major Norris the previous evening and told him that he thought Mr Lockwood and Quartermaster Sergeant Suttpen knew something about the murder
house.

'Lockwood?' Norris had said. 'Little fellow with jam jar
specs? You can't surely think he's capable of killing someone?'

'Experience has taught me that anyone is capable of anything, given the right circumstances, major,' Payne had replied.
'But I didn't say I necessarily thought they were responsible for
the murders. They know something, though, I'm sure of it.'

Norris sighed. 'Well, Quartermaster Sergeant Suttpen
would sell his own mother if he thought there was profit in
it, there's no denying that. They had problems with him back
in England, apparently. And in Holland. But I'm afraid men
like Suttpen and his motley crew are in the ascendant at the
moment, given the current moral climate.'

Payne had wanted to bring Suttpen in for questioning, but
Norris had shaken his head. 'I'm afraid you don't have any
jurisdiction over army personnel and Suttpen's got the backing
of Colonel Bassett. I'd be more inclined to pursue this Housing

Branch fellow first, Lockwood. He's CCG, so we've some leverage with him.'

Payne had agreed, but reluctantly.

After breakfast, Payne washed, shaved, dressed in his suit and went outside – and saw that all four of the tyres on his utility had been slashed.

Payne walked around the vehicle. With its deflated wheels, the car looked like it was sinking into the ground. There was no way to repair the tyres. The vandal had made sure of that, carving ragged slits six inches long in the rubber walls.

Being without a vehicle would severely hamper his investigation. Payne wondered about the timing of the vandalism.

A soldier came over and stood beside Payne, shaking his head. 'You can't get tyres for love nor money at the moment. And you need all four.'

Payne wondered whether the soldier had had something to do with the vandalism and was taunting him but decided that, on balance, his irritating sympathy was too artless to be anything other than genuine. Payne went back to the police station and phoned Norris to see if he could get him a new vehicle, but there was no answer.

When Payne returned to the utility, Colonel Bassett was standing in front of it, regarding the slashed tyres with an attitude of suppressed fury. The translator, Fräulein Seiler, stood beside him, jotting down notes as Bassett dictated.

'. . . Germans perpetrating acts of sabotage will be summarily shot, regardless of age or sex. Regardless, Miss Seiler, do you hear? *Regardless*. I want that word stressed. The same goes for curfew breakers.'

With his swagger stick and stentorian voice, Colonel

Bassett was a ruddy-faced caricature of the retired military type. There were hundreds like Bassett in Germany now, old men that had leapt at the chance to command again as part of the military government of Germany. His staff seemed to regard him as an amiable eccentric, but Payne disliked the man. Beneath his shaggy unkempt eyebrows, Bassett's eyes were hard and dark, the way stubborn, unimaginative men's often were.

'Don't worry, Detective Inspector,' he said when he saw Payne, 'we'll clear this matter up for you. And we'll make the Jerries responsible rue the day.'

'Do you think a German did this?'

'Who the hell else would it have been? We've been plagued with cut telephone lines and smashed windows now for months. Well, not any more, do you hear? They'll stop this, right now, or I'll personally see to it that the civilian population is ridden hard and put away wet. It's the only thing these bloody people seem to understand.'

Payne hitched a ride to the far side of town with some soldiers and had them drop him by the offices of Housing Branch.

A different clerk was on duty. Mr Lockwood wasn't there, though.

'No, I don't know where he is, sir,' the Housing Branch clerk said, irritably. 'He should have been here an hour ago.'

'Is it like him to be late for work?'

'No.'

'I don't suppose the information I requested has arrived yet?'

'That'll be another 'no'.'

Afterwards, Payne left and walked to Lockwood's billet,

a semi-derelict townhouse that Lockwood shared with six other CCG men. He knocked at the door of the house and was shown in by a bare-chested man with a pencil moustache.

'Nope, I haven't seen old Lockwood since last night,' he said, when Payne asked.

Lockwood shared his room, which was upstairs, with a young man who was still asleep. Payne shook him awake and the man turned bleary, hungover eyes towards him.

'No, I haven't seen Lockwood,' he said, moistening gummy lips. 'But then I was out all night at a party.'

'Was he here when you got home? Did you hear him leave this morning?'

'Sorry, old man, I was a bit blotto.'

'Do you have any idea where he might have gone?' Payne said, looking towards the immaculately-smoothed sheets on Lockwood's bed. It had either been freshly made that morning or it hadn't been slept in at all.

'Absolutely no idea. But then old Lockwood isn't the chattiest of fellows.'

The man with the pencil moustache was shaving in front of a cracked half of mirror resting on the bedroom's mantelpiece. He wiped lather from the razor, then paused. 'Now that I think about it, someone came to see Lockwood last night. They spoke outside.'

'Who was he?' Payne said.

'You can't expect me to recognise him, old man. I've only been here a week. He was a tall fellow, I think. Heavy set.'

'Was it the quartermaster sergeant, Suttpen?'

The man laughed. 'No, it wasn't old Jacob. I'd have recognised him, don't you worry.'

Payne looked through Lockwood's possessions, but there was nothing of interest. He thanked the men and left.

Outside, Payne stood in the shadow of a broken building. Should he be worried about Lockwood? It was too early to say.

Perhaps Suttpen would know something. Payne had checked the duty roster at the *Rathaus* the night before and he knew Suttpen was off duty today. He thought about what Norris had said about not bothering Suttpen. Payne decided he didn't care.

He began walking across town.

He had no idea what he'd say to Suttpen, but that didn't really matter. Payne only wanted a chance to take stock of his opponent. In a perfect world, Payne would have let another officer do the talking while he watched from the sidelines. Often you could learn far more from watching a person's reactions than by talking to them.

It wasn't a perfect world, though. He was on his own out here. He would have to do the best he could.

Suttpen and his men were billeted in a beautiful property on the edge of Eichenrode, a place where the urban area began to merge with farms and fields. Outside the house, lines of clothing flapped in the breeze and empty wine bottles, tins and leftover food were littered across the table. As Payne approached, he saw a cat picking through some chicken bones.

A soldier wearing American sunglasses lay on the grass outside the house, sunning himself. When Payne asked where Suttpen was, the soldier pointed towards a pathway that led to a barn.

The barn door opened inwards. Inside, dust motes danced

in the shafts of sunlight that came through the gaps between the wall-boards. Goods of every type – lamps, artwork, clothing, silverware, crockery, even a pair of skis and a sledge – were arranged around the walls and floor of the barn. They weren't stacked or dumped, either. The goods had obviously been set out with a view to impressing prospective buyers.

Jacob Suttpen sat at the back of the barn, eating tinned jam with a spoon. He stopped when he saw Payne and his eyes narrowed. He set the tin on the table and rubbed his hands on his battle-blouse. 'Can I help you, sir?' he said in a tone that made it clear helping Payne was the last thing on his mind.

'My name is Detective Inspector Payne. Of Public Safety Branch.'

'Pleased to meet you, Detective Inspector. But I think you must have taken a wrong turn somewhere. This here ain't a *public* place, it's a private residence. And it's totally safe. I make sure of that personally.'

In a single fluid motion, Suttpen swept up a scoped rifle from behind the desk and hefted it in his hand. His smile became broader as he clicked the rifle bolt and put a round in the chamber.

Payne did not move, but he met Suttpen's gaze and held it.

'How would I go about getting new tyres for my utility?' Payne said.

Suttpen drew his breath. 'Why? Has something happened to it?'

Again, the two men looked at each other in silence.

It was him that slashed my tyres, Payne thought. *He wants me to know it was him, too.*

'It's quite an impressive collection you've got,' Payne said.

'Not bad, is it? To the victor the spoils. And I for one intend to spoil myself rotten. The Jerries owe me for six years of my life. To say nothing of being bloody shelled in France in the last lot. Did you serve? In the Great War, I mean.'

'No.'

Suttpen nodded as if some previously-formed opinion had been confirmed.

'Are you a friend of Mr Lockwood?' Payne said.

'Mr Lockwood?'

'Short man, about our age, wears glasses. He works at Housing Branch.'

'Oh, yes. I call him Theo. That's why I didn't twig.'

'How do you know him?'

Suttpen had put the rifle down and now played with a pencil. 'If I were a rude man, Detective Inspector, I'd ask you what bloody business of yours it was. Lucky for you, though, I'm not.' He smiled. 'I know everyone. It's one of the perks of being regimental quartermaster sergeant. Especially in a situation like this.'

'A situation like what?'

The pencil twirled in the air. 'This. Eichenrode. Germany. You might not have noticed, but the creature comforts are a little hard to come by at the moment. That's why people want to get pally with me.'

'And did Mr Lockwood?'

'You could say so. He got me these digs. That's no secret.'

'You have a reputation as a man that can get things. If I wanted something, could you get it for me?'

Suttpen's eyes became wary. 'Depends whether you were

asking me as a copper or not. There's rules against entrapment, aren't there?'

'Say I wanted medicines. Vials of vaccine, for example. Could you get me those?'

The momentary confusion on Suttpen's face seemed genuine. 'Probably. But you'd have to tell me first what the hell you wanted with it.'

'What about barbiturate? Can you get that?'

Suttpen laid his hands flat on the table and leant towards Payne. 'Want to know what I think, Detective Inspector? I think you're testing me. You're not asking me about medicines because you want some. You're asking me to see how I react. So let me tell you, nice and clear, that I don't have the foggiest idea what you're going on about. I've bought and sold just about everything you can imagine in my time, but I've never sold vaccines. And if you find who is selling barbiturate, send 'em my way. We can do some business. Now, if it's all the same to you, I'd rather you went now and let me enjoy my day off.'

Payne turned. There was no point in staying. As he reached the door, Suttpen called out to him.

'You're going to be watching me, I know that, Payne. But I'll be watching you, too. This here is mine, do you understand? I earned it.'

Afterwards, Payne walked back to Housing Branch. There was still no sign of Lockwood, so Payne did what any good policeman would have done. He began knocking on doors and stopping people in the street, describing Lockwood to them. He worked methodically along each side of the roads closest to Lockwood's billet, speaking to Army and CCG personnel, DPs and German civilians. Someone always knew something. That was the thing to focus on as the hours of tedium slid past and the endlessly repeated words seemed to be wearing a groove on your tongue.

Persistence paid off. Yes, people did remember the little man with the glasses from Number 26 hurrying along the street the previous evening. People had noticed him because he looked so self-conscious.

Over the course of the afternoon, Payne pieced together Lockwood's movements. Two people had seen Lockwood heading out of town by the north road, hurrying along as if he were late to meet someone, but that was where the trail went dry.

Payne followed the road to the last place anyone had seen Lockwood, then walked a hundred yards out into the country-side. It was nice to breathe air that was free from brick dust, to see the rills the wind blew across the rainwater in the roadside ditches.

Payne paused by an oak tree, looked out across the fields and watched the haze growing within the dells as evening drew in. Then he turned and started to walk back towards the town. As he did so, the cloud cover shifted and the day's last sharp sunlight lit the road.

Payne paused as he walked, wondering what it was that had caught his attention. And then he saw it, a pair of thick-rimmed glasses that lay at the bottom of a ditch, sunlight glinting on the one remaining lens.

12

THAT MORNING, BOOTH took his jeep and drove east out of Eichenrode for fifteen miles, until he saw the divisional signs for Wolffslust prison.

It had taken him thirty minutes of cajoling the previous night to discover where Sergeant Hoyle had obtained the films. Hoyle initially claimed to have forgotten who had brought in the film canisters so Booth had the sergeant begin the laborious process of searching through all the receipt stubs for the information the Field Intelligence unit had received. Curiously, it then took Hoyle only ten minutes to find the correct stub.

'I remember now, sir,' Hoyle had said, brandishing the paperwork. 'It was a corporal from the Devonshires brought us the films, Corporal Peaver. He's part of the forces looking after Wolffslust prison.'

Booth hated Wolffslust. The map listed it as a castle and the first time Booth had gone there, he'd expected a picturesque Schloß. What he found instead was a brick bastion built in a blunt and ugly style that rose from the damp tangle of forest that surrounded it like a toad's head from mud. The wartime watchtowers and wire did nothing to improve its aspect. Much of the prison was below ground and the cell doors opened off stone corridors filled with moss and watery echoes.

Booth read the official report on the occupation of the prison as he drove, balancing the document on the steering wheel. The British advance guard had overrun the prison in late April and found it to be seriously overcrowded – the German authorities had been using Wolffslust to house prisoners from other institutions that had been damaged in air raids. The prison governor and most of the gaolers had fled the day before the British troops arrived, leaving the whole institution in chaos. Many of the prisoners in the overcrowded medical ward had been suffering from malnutrition and some had died. Most of the prisoners belonging to Allied nations had been immediately released, and now the remaining prisoners at Wolffslust were nearly all Germans.

The report was incomplete, though. There was no information on which unit had first found the prison and the report lacked an officer's signature.

Ten minutes later, Booth drew up outside the prison. The British soldiers on duty at the gate were sitting inside the guardhouse drinking tea and smoking. They waved Booth through without looking at his papers. Inside, groups of prisoners lazed in the prison courtyard, playing cards and smoking. One group was cooking a pine marten over a campfire while British soldiers joked with them.

Booth found Corporal Peaver in the mess hall, hands wrapped around a steaming mug of tea. It was clear Sergeant Hoyle had spoken some word of warning to the corporal, as the man began with an apology.

'If I'd known what those films were, sir, I'd have turned 'em straight in to an officer. I didn't realise they were so important.'

'That's quite all right, corporal. I've checked the records. You've done nothing wrong.'

Corporal Peaver was a big, rosy-cheeked man with a Hampshire accent, probably a good fifteen years older than Booth. Booth told him to stand easy, then said, 'What I really wanted to ask is how you found these films. And where. I don't know if you saw the inside of the canisters, but it said something in German about military research. Given the subject matter of the films, it could be important evidence for the lawyers at Nuremburg.'

Corporal Peaver scratched his cheek. 'Where I found them? That's going to be difficult, sir. It was a terrible mess when we got here. The German guards had scarpered and there were prisoners wandering loose all over the place. By the time I got here, they'd ripped most of the admin wing apart and thrown the filing cabinets out of the window. And my unit wasn't the first British one to get here. There'd been other units here before us.'

'How had so many prisoners got free of their cells?'

'Well, some of them were Allied POWS, British and French. Plus, there were a lot of the Germans' forced labourers in here, too, locked up for petty stuff. Apparently, the first British officer on the scene ordered the POWs and the workers released. They in turn went round letting all the others out.'

'Who was this officer?'

'I've no idea, sir. He was long gone by the time I arrived. It was all a bit chaotic back then.'

Booth frowned. 'Do you mean to say this officer released prisoners without first checking what their crime was?'

'I suppose so. Is that a problem, sir?'

'Of course it's a problem, corporal. There might have been serious criminals inside the prison.'

'I hadn't thought of it like that before, sir. But if they were locked up by the Nazis, that sort of makes 'em on our side, doesn't it?'

'Criminals are on nobody's side but their own, corporal. You'd do well to remember that. Logic dictates Nazi Germany must have had its murderers and rapists, the same as any other society.'

'I thought most of them were in the SS, sir.'

Booth ignored the quip. He was thinking of something else. 'If the prison was thrown open, why didn't all the prisoners escape?'

'To be honest, sir, some of 'em did, but most came back when they saw what things were like outside. I think most of the German lads were sharp enough to realise they were far safer inside a prison than they were out wandering the streets. They're not a bad bunch, actually. I've found they're pretty well behaved as long as they get three meals a day and we don't shout at 'em too much.'

Booth lit a cigarette. Something about the situation worried him, though he couldn't put his finger on it.

'Let's get back to the films. Try and think where it was that you found them. It could be important.'

Peaver nodded. 'Come to think of it, sir, it could well have been down in the cellar, in one of the corridors leading up to the dungeon.'

'Dungeon?'

'Sorry, sir, that's what me and the lads have named it on account of it looking like a dungeon.'

The corporal was right: it did look like a dungeon. The corridor was obviously from the original 17th century Schloß. Bulbous stones protruded from the walls and the floor was patched with puddles; electric lights flickered in brackets on the wall. The corridor ended in an enormous slab of a door studded with iron bands.

Booth dropped his cigarette in a puddle of water and placed his hand on the gnarled wood.

'What's on the other side of this?'

'No idea, sir. It can't be opened.'

'Good God, man, do you mean to say this door hasn't been opened since May?'

'Begging your pardon, but it's a prison door, sir. It's not meant to be picked. Or opened, for that matter, once it's closed.'

'But there could be prisoners on the other side.'

'With respect, sir, if there were prisoners in there, there won't be none left now,' Peaver said without any hint of sarcasm. 'Plus, I don't think there are any cells down there. Not according to the prison blueprints. I checked that when I realised we didn't have the key.'

'I want this door opened, corporal. If you can't open it yourselves, get a detachment of engineers up here and blow the damned thing off its hinges.'

The engineer detachment promised to be up at Wolffslust by the afternoon. There was no point driving back to Eichen-rode, so Booth ate lunch in the mess then spent a few hours trying to impose some semblance of order on the prison.

The first thing he organised was a roll-call of the prisoners. It took forty minutes to establish that there were 314 men currently at the prison but the count had to be redone twice when Booth noticed prisoners who had been outside in the forest sneaking back in. However, even a cursory look at the fragmented documentation that had survived the prison's liberation showed 314 was fewer than half the amount of men the prison had held in April.

Booth told Corporal Peaver to gather up all the prison's remaining paperwork, which actually consisted of a dozen postal bags stuffed with crumpled files, ledgers and ripped, dirty pieces of paper. Booth emptied the first postal bag onto a table.

'Right,' he said, looking at the mess in front of him. 'First of all, I want to know exactly who was in this prison and why. Once we've done that, we can start on the most important part.'

'What's that, sir?' Peaver said.

'Finding out whether the blighters are still here.'

13

LITTLE OTTO TOOK the ring of keys from his pocket and rattled the big silver key into the lock. The door creaked as it opened and stale, dusty air wafted out to greet him.

This was Otto's other house, the one he had kept back for emergencies. It did not please him as much as the property on the Brunswick Road – Otto loved to sit in that house's garret, playing with his treasures as the moonlight shone through the hole in the roof – but it would have to do.

Otto put the key ring back in his pocket and rested the packet of quicklime on the kitchen floor. Then he went back outside to where the little man lay on the ground. He checked the bindings that held the man's ankles and wrists together were still tight. Then he took him by the ankles, dragged him inside and sat down to wait for Mr Lockwood to awake.

Otto donned his Mask of Many while Lockwood was still unconscious and made sure that the first thing Lockwood saw as he came round was Otto pushing his masked face towards him and running his fingertips across the loops of twine that bound the lips together. Otto wanted to show the bastard exactly what it was that he valued most in others: silence and compliance.

Lockwood didn't understand. He began whimpering and crying almost immediately, the sound quickly rising to a hysterical crescendo, despite the gag. Otto kicked his head until the man quietened down. He was standing over Lockwood now, staring down at the man's smooth skin that had become streaked with grime and tears.

Should he add him to the mask?

No, Otto had another idea. Lockwood had lost his nerve. He would give the game away. It was only fair that he help to hide Little Otto.

Otto crossed the room. Behind him, Lockwood continued to snivel and weep. Otto took the black pennant from his pocket and rolled it into a blindfold.

Then he reached for the quicklime.

14

EARLY IN THE night, Cousin Ursula began screaming. The sound wrenched Ilse from sleep. She lit the paraffin lamp and went to her cousin's bedroom. Ursula's body was totally rigid as she loosed her banshee wails into the darkness. Only her mouth moved, opening so wide it seemed hinged far behind her jaws.

The medicine had served only to make Ursula worse. Ilse had started off applying ointment to some of the cuts and bruises on her cousin's arms and legs, but Ursula had begun to writhe and gasp as if she were lying on hot coals. In the end, poor Ursula had seemed to be suffering so much that Ilse had injected her in the thigh with a syrette of morphine, following the instructions inside the medical kit. That had seemed to quieten her, although Ilse still hadn't been able to part her cousin's legs and examine the damage.

Ilse crossed the room, making soothing noises. Ursula calmed a little when Ilse sat next to her, but she wouldn't stop trembling and her eyes bulged.

Ilse opened the medical kit, took another of the syrettes of morphine and jabbed the needle into Ursula's upper arm. The prick of the needle made Ursula jolt upright, but then she let out a long slow breath and sank back onto the bed, her crumpled love letters clasped between her hands.

Ilse sat stroking Urulsa's hair until she fell asleep again, but the sound of the mucous rattle in her chest seemed to have doubled in volume. It was as if something had worked itself loose and was banging around inside her. Ilse held the lamp up and took a good look at Ursula's clammy, jaundiced skin.

Ursula wasn't going to get better, Ilse realised suddenly. She was going to linger there on the cusp of death forever, rattling and shrieking and stinking.

Ilse stood up, trembling herself now. She couldn't take any more. She'd done her best with the medical supplies, but how could you help someone who became hysterical every time you touched her? This whole situation was so unfair. Why did bloody Ursula have to come here of all . . .

Ilse turned away from the bed, swept by sudden shame. How could she have thought such selfish thoughts? It must be because she lacked food.

She was exhausted, yet she knew there was no way she would get back to sleep again. She went downstairs to the kitchen, poured herself a tot of O'Donnell's whisky and lit a cigarette. She drank the whisky, then poured another, larger this time, and leant against the wall, allowing her thoughts to drift towards happier times, back when they had first moved to Berlin . . .

She and Rüdiger had hosted such wonderful parties. All the best people had attended. Magda Goebbels had even come one night and stayed two whole hours. For a moment, it seemed to Ilse that she could smell the perfumed scent of those wonderful evenings again, see chandelier light dance on silverware, hear the purr of the conversation. The men had looked so smart in their uniforms. And the flags, red, white and black, fluttering against the walls. Give the Nazis their due, no-one in history had known how to create pageantry quite like they could.

Of course, she'd never taken them too seriously. There had been a brief moment when she'd felt the stirrings of genuine devotion – who hadn't in those heady early days of the war? – but the Nazis were only ever a means to an end for Ilse. After all, it was all such a lot of garbled nonsense. Anyone that took a moment to look behind the uniforms and histrionic speeches could see that, surely?

Trust an idiot like Rüdiger to take it all so seriously. She could picture him now, sitting in bed, trying to learn the words to his SS oath like some huge idiot child preparing for catechism. And to think that she'd had to exert all her influence at one point to stop him joining the SA. He'd have been in his element there, shoulder to shoulder with all the other bullies and bores. Anyone with any intelligence could see those knuckle-draggers' goose was cooked the moment Hitler took power.

But that was the problem: Rüdiger was not intelligent. That was how they'd ended up in the Warthegau, as the Nazis had named the southern portion of the territory reclaimed from the Poles.

What the hell had Rüdiger known about coal mining? He'd studied Law. But once one of his damned SS chums had filled his head with nonsense, he'd accepted charge of that wretched mine quicker than you could say *Lebensraum* and forced them both to move to some rural hellhole close to Posen. Ilse had made a point of never even visiting the mine the whole time she'd lived there.

She finished her whisky and went upstairs to get a blanket. It was the first time since summer she'd felt the need for a blanket at night. It wouldn't be long now before the cold weather came. God, how was she going to survive the winter?

As she pulled the blanket free from the cupboard, a small wooden box fell to the floor with a thud, spewing photographs across the floorboards. Ilse crouched to pick them up and smiled when she saw they were her mother's photos.

Here was Rüdiger before they married, slim and smart in his Party uniform. And little Johannes in shorts, practising his stiff-armed salute out in the garden.

Ilse held the photograph up to the light.

Dear little Johannes. Ten years her junior, he'd been more like a son than a brother. She thought of how he would snuggle into her bed after bathing, and paused, surprised by the sudden clarity of the memories. She thought of the smell of his damp hair, the scent of his skin. Children always smelt so warm and clean at bedtime.

Johannes had been such an ardent little Nazi. He'd been chomping at the bit to join the *Deutsches Jungvolk* when he turned ten and was let into the Hitler Youth a year early. She smiled when she thought of him on that first day, standing in his pristine uniform in the centre of the kitchen, his hands on his hips.

Of course, there had been trouble. There always was with Johannes. On one evening march, Johannes had beaten a boy from the town with a horsewhip. No-one knew exactly what had happened, but the boy had been left blind in one eye. And two of the youngest members of his Hitler Youth group had returned from a weekend camping trip with pneumonia. They said Johannes had made them stand in the chest-deep waters of a stream for nearly an hour as a punishment.

Johannes was the only one of her relatives Ilse had mentioned on the *Fragebogen* questionnaire. It was Question 101: *Have you any relatives who have held office, rank or post of authority in any of the Nazi organisations listed above?*

What should she have put? Cousin Ursula had three relatives who matched the criteria, but the link between Cousin Ursula and Rüdiger was Ilse. What was the point of pretending to be someone else if she was only going to draw the Tommies' attention to that?

To put nothing, though, had seemed like tempting fate. Better to give them something to look into, to draw their attention. So she'd put Johannes's name down, and listed his full career. *Deutsches Jungvolk* and Hitler Youth, then, later, full membership of the NSDAP and enlistment in the 3rd Division of the Waffen SS, the *Totenkopf*.

There were more photos, but she put them back into the box and closed it, suddenly wearied by the weight of so many memories. A terrible sensation of solitude welled within her. She had no-one now. Rüdiger was dead, killed by partisans in June of '44. And she'd heard nothing from Johannes for two years. Ursula was the only relative she had left.

She went upstairs and sat in the chair beside Ursula's bed, warmed by the whisky. Before she knew it, her head was lolling in time to Ursula's breathing . . .

It seemed she'd only slept a few minutes, but when she woke silver-white moonlight was filtering through the window. Ilse woke slowly, rubbing her eyes and remembering the sound of a distant boom that had woken her, before she noticed that something was wrong in the room. It took her a moment to understand what it was: the wax and wane of Ursula's breathing could no longer be heard.

She reached for her cousin's arm; she screamed when her fingers found flesh that was cold and stiff.

Her first reaction was to run from the room, desperate to wash her hands. What if Ursula had died from some disease? She spent the next ten minutes scrubbing her hands. She felt dirty all over. Then she went back upstairs, hoping against hope that she was wrong and that Ursula wasn't dead, but, when she stood in the bedroom doorway, she realised there could be no mistaking the horrible twist of Ursula's lips. No live person's face looked like that .

Strangely, she felt nothing. She was too tired, she realised. She went and poured herself another tot of whisky. Instantly, practical considerations crowded in to destroy the release that she had hoped the warmth of the liquor would give her. Ursula was dead. What would she do with the body? She couldn't leave it inside the house: it would rot and smell, and there would be flies. But if she contacted a funeral director – if there was one in the town – the Tommies were bound to come round asking questions. She could lie, say she had no idea who Ursula was, but it would attract suspicion.

No, she would have to bury Ursula herself. There was no alternative.

When she returned to the bedroom her cousin's legs were already stiff, but her arms flapped heavily like stockings packed with sand as Ilse dragged her down the staircase, bumping Ursula's head against the steep steps as she went.

It was cold outside and the birch trees shone silver in the

moonlight. She dragged Ursula's body to a patch of ground twenty yards from the house. Then Ilse took a spade from the garden shed and began to dig.

15

WHEN THE MUFFLED explosion sounded in the dead of night, Silas Payne awoke instantly.

He lay there, staring into the darkness, wondering whether he'd dreamt the noise rather than heard it. A few minutes later a jeep screeched to a halt in the street outside and someone began knocking at a door across the street. Silas knew that it belonged to the house where an infantry lieutenant was billeted. Running feet sounded on the cobblestones and men's voices began shouting.

Something was wrong.

Payne looked at his watch as he dressed: 03:50.

He reached for one of his civilian suits, but quickly decided his CCG uniform would be more appropriate. Outside, he asked a soldier what was going on.

'We think a mine's gone off in that stretch of field out by the canal.'

'Do you mean it went off alone? Or that someone set it off?'

'No idea.'

When the young lieutenant emerged from the house opposite, Payne asked if he could accompany him.

'I don't know about that, Detective Inspector. This is a military matter.'

'Not if it's a civilian in the minefield. Then it's my business, too.'

That seemed to throw the lieutenant. Or perhaps it was simply too complex a problem for such an early hour. He waved assent that Payne might accompany him.

They climbed into the lieutenant's jeep and drove through the ruined ramparts of the town's gates and out into the countryside. Mist rose from the fields and the moon rode high and full, lining the clouds with silver light.

'What's the situation, sergeant?' the lieutenant said, after they had crossed the Bailey bridge that led over the canal and pulled off the road.

The sergeant nodded towards a nearby fence. 'There was someone out there in the minefield, sir.'

'Do you know who it was?'

'No idea, sir. When we heard the explosion, we came running straight away. Then we fancied we heard someone crying and calling for help. Lucky for us we realised where we were, else one of the lads might have hopped the fence and gone to find the poor sod.'

'And you definitely heard someone cry out?'

'Yes, sir. We think he's still alive.'

'Is that possible if he's stepped on a mine?' Payne said.

The lieutenant nodded. 'Depends what he stepped on. The Jerries used to rig some mines to maim rather than kill.'

He was going to elaborate when the wind shifted slightly and the sound of a low moan was carried on the breeze.

Each man there froze momentarily. Then they concentrated their torches on the darkness, trying to locate the source of the sound. Now they could hear a man's voice, calling out for help. He was speaking in English.

'For God's sake, man, it's away there, over to the right,' the lieutenant said as a private stood on the lowest bar of the fence and shone his torch into the darkness.

'HELP!' the voice screamed, louder now and touched with a genuine sense of terror, as if the man had only just become aware of his predicament. The field seemed to be filled with moving shapes as the clouds above scudded across the face of the moon.

'MY EYES! MY GOD, MY EYES! HELP!' Hysteria distorted the man's voice, but that wasn't what had made the hairs on Payne's neck stand up. Was it his imagination or did he recognise the voice?

'Stay still, you stupid bastard,' a young private said, as sounds of thrashing and other frenzied motions came from the field. One of the privates had a megaphone. 'Stay still. You are in a minefield. Remain where you are and . . .'

The soldiers were obviously from a fighting unit: when the mine detonated, they all dropped flat to the ground, whereas Payne merely flinched as earth showered around him. The explosion seemed so close it took Payne's breath away; he felt it like a blow in the pit of his stomach and he heard dirt pitter-patter on the brim of his hat. Then something heavy and organic landed with a wet thud on the bonnet of a jeep. One of the soldiers cursed and Payne caught sight of a dark smear that ran across the front of the vehicle before he looked away.

The engineers waited until daylight before going into the mine-field to collect the body.

Once the sun began to rise Payne could see clearly where the explosion had taken place, as there was a circle of scorched earth about 20 yards from the fence. Crows hopped and fluttered in this area, pecking at a dark and ragged shape that lay away to the right of the crater caused by the explosion.

While the engineers edged forward towards the body, Payne walked the edge of the minefield, trying to find where the dead man had entered it. Around a hundred yards from the canal, the ground on the other side of the fence had been churned up, as if someone had been kicking and thrashing their legs. Muddy holes showed where the man had stumbled away from the fence, heading deeper into the minefield.

The engineers had reached the remains and gathered them up and were making their way back with them on a stretcher.

Payne went and stood beside the ambulance. As the engineers carried the stretcher past him, he lifted the tarpaulin that covered it. The lieutenant grabbed his arm and asked him what the hell he was doing, but Payne shook himself free. He had to be sure. He bent closer to the corpse's head.

The face was smeared with mud and the eye sockets were red and blistered, but there could be no doubt. Payne was right: he *had* recognised the voice.

The stretcher harboured what was left of Mr Lockwood.

16

CAPTAIN BOOTH WAS drinking tea and considering what to have for breakfast when a jeep screeched to a halt outside his billet and Colonel Bassett's adjutant, Captain Fredrickson, got out and ran up the steps.

Booth's nose wrinkled. If Booth merely disliked Colonel Bassett, he actively hated Captain Fredrickson. With his thick black hair, prop-forward's build and abrasively upper-class accent, Freddy was the sort you just knew had been a bully at school. It was oafs like 'Freddy' Fredrickson that would give the occupation a bad name, boorish drunks acting like the overlords of some new European Raj.

Booth's problems with the man had begun back in Holland. That was when Freddy had still been a lieutenant. He'd been serving under Booth in Field Intelligence. They'd been working as part of the division's advance guard, engaged in a sweeping-up operation that involved interrogating men and women suspected of being members of the Dutch fascist party who were therefore also suspected of collaboration with the Germans.

A couple of days after some arrests had been made, Booth had collected the detachment's laundry from a local washer-woman. She was profuse in her apologies: she'd tried everything but she just couldn't get the red speckles out of Lieutenant Fredrickson's shirt cuffs. Was it beetroot, perhaps? Or wine?

Booth discovered what it was that same night, when he walked in on Freddy with his pistol rammed into the mouth of a terrified Dutchman. A second man sat crying on the floor, blood pouring from his mouth.

Booth had taken the matter straight to Division and then on to Corps. Nothing was done. Lieutenant Fredrickson had an impeccable record. It was war. Officers in the field had free rein to use whatever tactics they saw fit.

Instead of being punished, Freddy had been promoted to captain and now served on Colonel Bassett's staff. It was no secret that he had Bassett's ear and had used his influence on a number of occasions to ensure Booth's unit was given irksome duties.

Booth stayed in his office, listening to the low rumble of the duty sergeant's voice in the corridor outside. When he heard Freddy leave, Booth got up and opened the door.

'What was that about, sergeant?' he said.

'It seems there was a bit of a flap early this morning in one of the minefields out by the canal. Someone's been hurt. Colonel Bassett wants you to meet him at the RAMC barracks right away.'

Booth tossed the remains of his tea away, put his mackintosh on and walked to his jeep, chewing his lip.

He'd planned to go back to Wolffslust today. He'd wasted the whole of yesterday afternoon waiting in vain for the engineers' detachment to come and blow open the wretched door. When he had got back to Eichenrode in the evening, he'd had strong words with one of the engineers' NCOs and they'd promised to send someone that morning.

He looked at his watch. With any luck, this business with Colonel Bassett wouldn't take too long.

The RAMC had occupied the remains of the local hospital. When Booth arrived, he saw Detective Inspector Payne walking down the main staircase deep in thought. Booth thought the man's usually calm face looked somewhat perturbed.

'Where's he off to?' Booth asked one of the guards outside the hospital, as Payne pulled the collar of his coat up and walked away into the wind.

'He and Colonel Bassett have had words,' the guard said. 'The colonel bawled him out for bothering Quartermaster Sergeant Suttpen. Then, when the Detective Inspector said he wanted to attend the autopsy, the colonel said it was a military matter and turfed him out.'

'Autopsy? What on earth's been going on?'

'I don't rightly know, sir. But it seems there was some bother in that minefield down by the canal.'

When Booth went downstairs to the tiled corridor that led to the hospital's morgue, he found Colonel Bassett stalking up and down in front of his staff officers, in serious danger of breaking the swagger stick gripped behind his back. He seemed to have been waiting for Booth's arrival. As soon as he saw Booth, Bassett began to speak.

'I'm sure you have all heard what happened this morning in the minefield. If anyone hasn't, I can tell you that one of our men has been killed. But before we look into it, there's something that I want to make abundantly clear.

'When I arrived this morning, that wretched Scotland Yard

fellow was here. I've previously held my tongue on this matter, but now I want to spell it out for you all. I don't like policemen. Never have. And I don't want this Payne fellow snooping around in army business any longer, is that perfectly clear? And I don't want a word of today's casualty getting out, understood?'

Bassett regarded each man in turn as Captain Fredrickson whispered something in his ear.

'Thanks to Captain Fredrickson, we know who the dead man was. It seems he worked for Housing Branch, a Mr Lockwood. Now, this just proves why we have to keep an eye on these CCG people. It seems any Tom, Dick or Harry can get a CCG job as long as he's got a passport from an Allied country and is willing to work, but they're not proper soldiers, remember that.' Bassett turned towards Fredrickson. 'What do we know about this Lockwood fellow? Was he a drinker?'

'Not that we know of, sir,' Freddy said.

'Then what the hell was he doing wandering through a bloody minefield in the middle of the night? And why on earth wouldn't the blighter stay still and wait for someone to rescue him? I want answers, gentlemen. This sort of business makes us look damned stupid in front of Jerry and that is something I won't have. Do I make myself –'

The door to the morgue opened. Shelley, the medical officer, appeared.

'I think you'd better come and have a look at this, gentlemen.'

Mr Lockwood lay under a blanket, although Booth noticed there was a huge dip where the man's waist should have been and his left leg was missing. Shelley angled the lamp towards

Lockwood's face then pulled a corner of the blanket back.

Men winced and drew their breath.

'What the devil's wrong with his eyes?' Bassett said.

'That's what I wanted to show you,' Shelley said.

They moved closer. Lockwood's eyes were closed but the sockets around them were red raw and blistered, as if they had been burnt, although there was no sign of charring. The wounds had an unpleasant yellowy colour to them. Shelley motioned towards a metal tray on which a piece of black fabric lay, rolled up and tied into a ring.

'That was found on the ground near the body. It was blown free in the blast, I would imagine.'

'Blown free from where?' Bassett said.

'From his eyes. I think Mr Lockwood went into the mine-field blindfolded.'

'You mean someone tied that around his head then set him loose in a minefield?'

Shelley nodded. He lifted the tray and pointed towards two blotches of discoloured cloth on the inner surface of the blind-fold. 'And that same someone also poured some type of caustic powder into his eyes. I think that explains why he wouldn't stay still. The pain must have been excruciating.

'I've questioned the engineer detachment and they've found a line of muddy footprints crossing the field. My guess is that Mr Lockwood was set free and stumbled into the centre of the minefield. The first explosion must have injured him without killing him. He then lay stunned for a while. But when he came to again, the pain would have caused him to start moving. I think he crawled across the second mine.'

'Why didn't he just pull the wretched blindfold off?' Bassett said.

'I think his hands were tied behind him,' Shelley said. 'It's difficult to tell, given the extent of his injuries, but there seem to be some scraps of twine embedded in the wounds close to the wrist.'

'Is it my imagination, or is there some sort of design on the blindfold?' Booth said.

Shelley donned rubber gloves and carefully spread the fabric out, to reveal a black pennant. A crude runic design was stitched in its centre, a capital Z, the diagonal crossed with two horizontal lines.

Each man there stared at it. 'Bastards,' Freddy said, then whispered something to the colonel.

Bassett's eyebrows bristled; his eyes narrowed. 'Am I correct in surmising, Captain Booth, that the symbol on that pennant is the one used by those wretched werewolf partisans?'

Booth nodded. 'It's the *Wolfsangel*, sir, The Wolf's Hook. During the advance across Germany, the Nazi regime encouraged civilians to scrawl this on the doors of people collaborating . . . or, rather, helping us, the Allies. But it's strange that the werewolves would announce their presence so –'

'Am I also correct in recollecting that your assessment of the werewolf threat in this sector was 'negligible'?'

'With respect, sir, I don't think this incident proves –'

'What in God's name does it prove then, captain?' Bassett said, his voice rising to a roar. 'I'll tell you what this incident proves. It's a challenge. They've murdered one of our men and they want us to know it was them. Well, by God, if these blighters want to play it rough, I will give it to 'em rough. I want to know how this happened. And I want those responsible caught and punished. If Jerry hasn't realised yet he's lost this war, we will just have to show him, won't we? And if you ain't up to the job, Captain Booth, I'll damned well find someone who is.'

With that, Bassett stalked from the room. Freddy lingered a moment, long enough for his eyes to meet Booth's and a faint smile to flicker across his lips.

'You'd best get cracking, Captain,' he said. 'You've some werewolves to catch.'

PART TWO

I

A LITTLE AFTER DAWN, Little Otto walked out to the house on the Brunswick Road. He carried with him his big heavy killing knife and a torch. He kept to the paths through the woods as the roads were alive with military activity. That was good, though, it was what Otto had hoped for when he set Lockwood loose among the mines. It would keep them distracted, keep them from looking for Little Otto.

When he arrived at the house, he hid for twenty minutes among the trees, watching the kitchen door, just to be sure. He was aching to return and take possession of his treasures, but he knew he must be cautious.

Finally, when he could take it no longer, he stole across the lawn and entered the house. Inside the kitchen, he closed all the shutters. He didn't want anyone peering in. Then he reached inside his jacket and withdrew the Mask of Many, his skin tingling with anticipation. He sucked in its sweet aromas as he raised the mask to his face and tied it into place. Then he walked across the room and headed upstairs, fingering the key to the garret door and thinking about his Papa . . .

Back when Little Otto was a boy, his Papa had always called the people they kept in the cellar 'guests'. 'I'm going to see to our latest guest,' he would say to Mutti as he dabbed his mouth and rose heavily from the dinner table. Sometimes, Little Otto would secretly watch through the keyhole as Papa scrubbed his hands with carbolic, tied the leather apron around his wide waist and pulled on the gloves and face mask. When Papa opened the cellar door, Otto could smell the cold air and chemicals that wafted up from below.

The other people who came to the house – the ones that were not taken straight to the metal table in the cellar – had serious faces and uniforms. The women who came wore black and cried into their handkerchiefs.

Little Otto was ten the first time Papa took him down into the cellar.

'This is what I do, Otto,' he'd said, 'what puts food on our table. One day, you will do the same.'

That was the first time he had helped Papa with one of the guests – *their* guests, now – setting the modesty cloth over the body's sticky, stinky parts and bending and flexing the stiffness from the rigid joints.

The guest's skin had been ice cold and blue-white. Little Otto had never seen anything so beautiful. People were hot, noisy, smelly creatures, but the cellar guests were different: death had made them quiet and cold and perfect. He lay awake that night, imagining the spirit of the cellar-guest flitting like a bat beneath the eaves of the house.

Year by year, he learned more of Papa's trade. Papa always worked with a photo of the guest beside the big metal table. First, he used a curved needle and ligature to seal the mouth; then he set the eye caps to keep the lids closed. If the guest was a man, he would shave the stubble.

Then the injections began and Little Otto would watch the big white ghost of Papa's reflection slide on and off the curved silver surface of the tank which held the embalming fluid.

One Sunday morning Little Otto feigned stomach ache. Papa wanted to force him to go to church, but Little Otto could always get Mutti on his side. 'Let the boy sleep,' she'd said, stroking his hair, while Little Otto nuzzled his face into her soft bosom and sucked in her hot, swampy smells. He had watched from his bedroom window as they walked away, down the street towards the church. Then he went straight to the cellar.

The new guest was a young peasant girl from the village. Something heavy had fallen on her and cracked her neck. Little Otto pulled the sheet down to admire the perfection of her. Mutti would have looked this way once, he thought, blond and plump. The girl's hair smelt of soap and flowers. Otto had pressed his face against her cold white flesh, wishing somehow he could dive within her skin and know what it was like to be a different person, to see out through a different pair of eyes.

That was the first time he felt it, that awesome sense of serenity, as if the quiet calm of cathedral cloisters had filled every particle of his being. There was nothing sexual about the feeling, despite what they told him later in life. He never felt so chaste as when he was with one of his guests, the master and the mastered, the god with his disciple.

He feigned illness again the next week and went down to the cellar. The third Sunday was when Papa caught him, the pristine intimacy of the cellar sucked away by the sudden swish of the door opening and Papa's podgy silhouette framed by the hall light.

'My God, boy, what are you doing?' ...

2

IT WAS MIDDAY now and the streets outside the police station were alive with the sounds of military activity: jeeps, lorries, marching boots, shouting voices.

Silas Payne drank tea and watched the soldiers come and go from the window. As with most military activity, the emphasis seemed to be on looking and sounding busy rather than actually getting anything done.

Captain Booth had been right about one thing: this Colonel Bassett fellow was an idiot. Not because he'd embarrassed Payne earlier by insisting he leave Lockwood's autopsy – such petty insults meant nothing to Silas Payne. No, Bassett was an idiot because he mistook knee-jerk impulse for decisive action. If he'd taken five minutes to listen to Payne, he would have seen that all the check points and searches that he was implementing were a waste of time. Mr Lockwood's death had nothing to do with the werewolf insurgency; Payne had been certain of that even before he had caught Shelley, the medical officer, outside the *Rathaus* and asked him for the details of the autopsy.

He sipped his tea as he pondered the matter. The obvious suspect was the quartermaster sergeant, Suttpen, but he had an alibi; Payne had checked. Suttpen had been playing poker the night before with no less than seven men from different units. The game had begun in the early evening and did not end until four in the morning. Suttpen had not left the game at any point.

Back home, Payne would have brought Suttpen in for questioning anyway; given him a good, long session. It was the only way with men like Suttpen: you had to show them you were possessed of limitless reserves of patience as you walked them through the same series of events once, twice, three, four, five times – as many as it took for them to talk themselves into knots. Suttpen might not have set Lockwood free in the minefield, but he knew something about the incident, of that Payne was certain. But Suttpen had the backing of both his CO and Colonel Bassett. Payne would have to wait before he approached the man again.

So, who had killed Lockwood?

Payne sat on his trestle bed with notepad and pencil and began to write down what he knew.

His first contact with Lockwood had prompted the little man to run straight to Suttpen. Payne thought about the conversation he had witnessed between the two men, of the panic on Lockwood's face and Suttpen's contemptuous reaction. The two men were up to something together, that much was clear, although Lockwood seemed to have been regretting his involvement. That same afternoon, an unidentified man had visited Lockwood's billets. Later that evening, Lockwood had walked to the edge of town and disappeared.

Payne thought about the pair of spectacles he'd found. It was clear Lockwood had been abducted, but he hadn't been killed straight away. Instead, the killer had waited approximately thirty hours, then set Lockwood free in a minefield.

That meant the killer obviously had access to a place where he had held Lockwood captive. But why choose such a public way of killing him? Why not kill the man and bury him? And why use a werewolf pennant as a blindfold?

There was only one answer, Payne decided: the action had been so blatantly visible that it had to be a ruse to divert attention from something else. What that something might be, though, still eluded Payne. Once again, he had the feeling he was only seeing one small part of a far larger whole.

Payne was still pondering the matter when someone knocked at the door of the police station. He opened the door and found a man in a long, tatty overcoat standing outside. He addressed Payne in German.

'Are you the English policeman? My name is Schaeffer. I have information I need to give you.'

From the man's furtive behaviour Payne deduced that he did not want to impart the information on the stairs of the station, so he invited him in. He stirred the embers of the stove and warmed tea for them both.

Wherever it was that Schaeffer had come from, he had clearly been walking for a long time. The lower edges of his serge coat were spattered with mud and one of his military boots was held together with a twist of ripped fabric. But despite his dishevelled appearance there was a neatness and precision to his manner.

'I shall be brief,' he said. 'There have been murders here recently, have there not? In a house. With surgical implements found.'

Payne's mug stopped halfway to his mouth. 'What do you know about that?'

'It is my belief that certain very dangerous individuals are at large among the civilian population. And it is not what *I* know that should interest you.'

'What do you mean?'

'I was formerly an officer in the Wehrmacht. Until yesterday, I was held prisoner at an internment camp ten miles from here. In this camp there is an ex-Gestapo man. He claims to know who is responsible for these murders.'

'How did he know about the murders if he was interned?'

Schaeffer laughed mirthlessly. 'What else do interned men have to do but gossip with the guards? And men get moved from one facility to another. Somehow or other this Gestapo man has found something out.'

'Tell me about him,' Payne said.

'His name is Toth, Amon Toth. He was a *Kriminalkommisar* in the Gestapo. A few days ago I overheard him talking about this house here in Eichenrode, about the bodies that were found in the cellar. He was laughing, saying that the Tommies did not know what they were up against. He claimed that this murderer had already killed more than a dozen people in Germany during the war and that now the Tommies had set him loose.'

Payne was watching the man carefully now. 'Why do you set such store by what this Gestapo man says? He could have been making it up out of boredom.'

Schaeffer sipped his tea. 'My brother-in-law was a military policeman. When I was last home on leave he told me his unit had been sent to a prison near here, Wolffslust Prison, on two occasions, with orders to execute prisoners. These men were not part of the usual prison population. They were part of a special research programme, run by a doctor. He said they had been transferred from a medical institute in Brunswick after the city was bombed. These men who were brought for the doctor's programme had been serving on the eastern front. They were murderers and rapists.'

'Why are you telling me this?'

'Because it is my duty. *One does evil enough when one does nothing good*,' Schaeffer said. 'Recent German history is surely proof of that. If what this Gestapo man says is true, people could be in danger. I have been to the prison and the security there is very lax.'

But Payne was thinking of something else, of the old woman who had knocked on the door of the police station the day Payne had arrived in Eichenrode. He'd paid her little attention at the time, but now memory of her words sent a chill through his body. 'I've seen him,' she had said. 'The man that raped my daughter. They put him in Wolffslust Prison, but I saw him this morning, walking the streets, free as a bird!'

Payne went straight to Major Norris and said he wanted to question the Gestapo man, Toth.

Norris wasn't keen on the idea, but relented when Payne persisted. 'You won't get into an internment camp alone, though,' Norris said. 'I'll have to ask someone from Field Intel to go with you.'

Payne had instructed Schaeffer to wait for him while he spoke with Norris, but when he went back to the police station, Schaeffer had disappeared.

Small matter. Payne had the feeling that Schaeffer had told him all he knew, in any case.

An hour later Payne was on his way to the internment camp in a jeep driven by a lieutenant named Taylor from Booth's Field Intelligence unit.

Outside Eichenrode, the countryside still bore signs of war. Burned-out vehicles sat beside the road and the grass verges were littered with scraps of clothing, broken pieces of ordnance and discarded army crates, all empty and smashed apart. People moved along the edges of the road, in both directions. Others lived in the woods. As they drove past, Payne could see fires flickering beneath ragged awnings and smoke drifting between the trees.

'What a ruddy mess,' Payne said, looking behind him as a man on the roadside swung a punch at a smaller man.

If Taylor heard him, he did not react.

Payne had been initially happy about going with Lieutenant Taylor – the prospect of a long drive with Captain Booth had not thrilled him – but as they drove in silence and Payne watched the man out of the corner of his eye, Payne realised the man was deeply troubled. Payne knew that nearly everyone called Lieutenant Taylor by his nickname, Tubbs, but whoever had given him the moniker obviously hadn't seen him recently. Taylor now had the sallow skin of a man who had lost a lot of weight quickly. Payne had heard that Taylor had witnessed the clearing of a concentration camp and that he'd not been the same since.

Payne could believe it. Taylor's eyes were bloodshot and he had a nervy, brittle edge to him as if, emotionally, he were staggering forward on his last reserves of energy. It happened to men, sometimes. On the outside they seemed fine but, like the lead of a dropped pencil, they were all broken apart inside.

The internment camp was set up within the grounds of a country manor that had formerly belonged to a German industrialist. The house itself seemed medieval in its size and splendour, but its magnificence was tarnished by a sort of shanty town that had grown up on the lawns beside it. As they drew closer, Payne saw that an area of perhaps the size of a football pitch had been enclosed within barbed wire. Inside, the ground was covered with all manner of makeshift shelters made from blankets, scraps of wood and holes dug in the ground. Watchtowers equipped with machine guns had been erected at each corner of the camp. Groups of British soldiers stood along the perimeter, chatting among themselves and smoking cigarettes.

Payne knew there were camps like this all over Germany now. In the final days of the war the Wehrmacht had begun to surrender in such massive numbers it was impossible to care for them all to the standards demanded by the Geneva Convention. To circumvent this, a new category of prisoner had been invented: DEFs, Disarmed Enemy Forces. Soldiers assigned to this category were not classified as POWs and therefore didn't have to be looked after to the same standards. Payne had heard that there were still hundreds of thousands of Germans locked away in these camps.

'It's quite a contrast, isn't it?' Payne said.

For the first time in an hour, Taylor spoke. 'Oh, I see what you mean,' he said, looking out across the grounds towards the mansion house and the camp beside it. He sneered. 'It won't do German soldiers any harm to see the sort of luxury they were fighting to preserve. I expect most of that mansion was paid for with Nazi war contracts.'

'What'll happen when autumn comes?'

'They'll get cold and wet,' Taylor said in a way that made Payne feel the lieutenant would like the Germans to suffer far worse inconveniences.

As they approached the barbed wire perimeter of the camp, hundreds of eyes turned to meet them, staring from emaciated, dirty faces. The German soldiers wore every conceivable type of filthy and torn uniform and some men still had grubby bandages wrapped around their hands and heads.

Taylor spoke to an officer and explained what they were doing there. A call was put out for the former Gestapo man, Amon Toth. Ten minutes later, Toth arrived at the gates to the camp. He was painfully thin and shabbily dressed in a plain soldier's camouflage uniform. Despite this, he displayed an innate hauteur.

Speaking through the wire, Taylor addressed him in German.

'We've been told you know something about a murder that occurred close to the town of Eichenrode.'

Toth's face became sly. 'Yes, that is true. I fear a beast is loose among you. There could be more deaths. Many more. But I can help to prevent them.'

'And how do you propose to do that?'

For the first time, the German smiled, an ironic curl of the lip, revealing sharp white teeth. His dark eyes sparkled.

'I can tell you who this beast is and how he hunts. And, more importantly, I can tell you how to catch him.'

3

At lunchtime Booth returned to Wolffslust Prison.

He was taking a chance by going back there, as Colonel Bassett had instructed him to prepare a briefing on the dangers of werewolf activity in the area, but Booth wanted to find out what was behind the 'dungeon' door, for the simple reason that if he didn't, no-one else would.

The overcast day gave the hulking brick prison a sinister air. As he pulled up in the courtyard, he saw the promised engineer detachment was already there, unloading equipment from a lorry. Booth went downstairs to the dungeon door and found the sergeant in charge of the engineers bending to examine the lock.

'It's pretty jammed up in there, sir,' he said.

'I know, sergeant,' Booth said. 'That's why I called you.'

The sergeant had a slow West Country accent. He continued as if Booth had not replied. 'Wouldn't be surprised to find someone snapped the key off inside the lock,' he said, poking in the keyhole with a screwdriver. He straightened and banged his fist against the door. 'Mighty fine piece of wood, though.'

'Can you open it?'

'We can dynamite it. But that would ruin the door.'

'Do what you have to do, sergeant.'

Booth left the engineers to it and went back to sorting paperwork. The sound of drilling and banging echoed up through the stone walls of the prison. An hour later one of the sappers came to say they were ready.

'You'll want to take cover over there,' the engineer sergeant said, as he attached electrical cables to a plunger. Booth had the soldiers clear the underground passages and return all the prisoners to their cells. All around the prison courtyard, faces were pressed to the barred windows, watching. Booth took cover and waved to the engineer sergeant, who twisted the plunger and pressed it down.

There was a split second pause, as if the world had caught its breath, then smoke and dust billowed from the corridor, driven forth on a roaring wave of sound. Booth gritted his teeth and put his fingers in his ears. There was a metallic creak, followed by the sound of falling rubble, then the force created by the huge impact shuddered through the roots of the building.

It took two minutes for the dust to clear. When it was safe to descend the stairs once more, Booth saw that the door had been blown clear of its hinges and fallen forwards.

'Right, let's see what we can find through here,' he said, clicking on his torch.

Dust spiralled in the beam of light as Booth crept forward across the shattered door. The air was thick with the smell of explosive. It was pitch dark in the room beyond; Booth searched until he found a light-switch. When he clicked it on, a strip light in the ceiling flickered into life.

Each man there drew his breath.

'What the hell is all this?' someone said.

Booth looked around him. The walls of the large room

were of rough ancient stone, worn and stained by centuries of dripping water. In the centre of the chamber was a metal chair with leather restraints for head, wrists and ankles. Beside it was a wheeled metal trolley, also equipped with restraints. A machine with wires, cables and electrometers stood beside the trolley. Metal tools dangled from a rack on the wall.

Booth motioned for the men behind him to stay where they were and moved towards the chair at the chamber's centre. As he got closer, he saw that the metal chair was attached to some form of ratchet and could be tipped backwards with a lever. A square hole was dug in the ground behind the chair. When Booth shone his torch into the darkness of the hole, he saw it was filled nearly to the top with liquid.

He bent to sniff it. It smelt of brackish water.

Booth looked around the room. There were dozens of packing crates and boxes piled against the walls. Booth had the impression that the equipment in the room had been moved from a larger facility and never properly unpacked. Metal filing cabinets in one corner leaked thousands of documents. Beside them were piles of cardboard boxes, also filled with documents. Thousands more sheets of paper were strewn across the floor.

One pile of packing crates had swastikas burnt into the surface of the wood and the words 'Institute of Racial Hygiene' printed below. Some of the crates also bore the strange symbol Booth had seen inside the lid of the film canisters, the sword and ribbon surrounded by runic symbols. *This must be where the films came from*, he thought.

He motioned for the other soldiers to come into the room. Together they began searching the boxes.

Booth took a handful of papers from one of the crates and flicked through them. They were written in neatly-typed German and looked like film scripts. As Booth read them he realised that in reality they were transcripts of conversations held between a doctor named Wiegand and various patients. The patients' names were not given; instead, each one was identified by a number.

He opened another of the cardboard boxes and recoiled when he realised it was filled with human skulls, more than a dozen of them, packed together in the box like bleached eggs.

When he had recovered from his shock, he began to remove the skulls from the box. Each was carefully labelled with a German man's full name. Lines had been scratched into the bone of each skull, forming grids on which various sections had been labelled with words in Latin that Booth could not understand.

Beneath the skulls were a number of neatly folded charts and diagrams. Each chart referred to a different man's skull and was filled with measurements and algebraic calculations of which Booth could make little sense.

As he looked at the names, he paused, wondering why they seemed so familiar. Then he remembered. These were the same surnames that he had read on the insides of the film canisters. He looked at the skulls. No wonder the names had been crossed through.

Booth tried to lift a swastika-marked packing crate down from the top of a pile, but stopped when he realised how much it weighed. He pulled a chair over and stood on it to peer down at the two glass jars that were inside. Both jars measured roughly a foot in width and height and were filled with clear liquid: formaldehyde, by the smell of it. Booth signalled for the engineer sergeant to help him and together they lifted the box down from the shelf.

'Oh Lord, is that what I think it is?' the sergeant said, hurrying to put the jar down on a desk. 'Oh God, it is, isn't it?'

A human brain bobbed within the liquid.

Booth looked at the name on the front of the jar: Tjaden, Albrecht.

He'd seen that same name on one of the skulls. What the hell had been going on down here?

One of the other soldiers had found a box containing hundreds of documents relating to births, marriages and baptisms, together with family trees and genealogical tables. The documents all bore the official stamp of the *Rassenforschungsamt*, the Nazi Race Investigation Office, and all of them related to the names on the skulls.

'They seemed very interested in the racial lines of whoever these people were,' Booth said, as he flicked through the pages. 'There's one here whose family tree goes back to the times of Martin Luther.'

All the documents were originals. The edges of some pages showed signs of having been razored out of books. That explained the wonderful smell of antique paper, but it didn't explain why dozens of parish records had been ruined. Whoever these people were, they must have been important in some way.

'What the hell is this?' someone said, putting a calliper rule down on the desk and withdrawing another tool from a box. It was a curious angle of metal with screws and straps attached to it.

'I think it's a craniometer. For taking measurements of people's heads,' Booth said.

'What for?'

'Anthropometry, I would guess,' Booth said, 'given the nature of these documents. It's a sort of pseudo-science, by which a person's intelligence can supposedly be calculated by taking precise measurements of his or her body.'

On the far side of the room, a door led into a long rectangular chamber. A film screen hung at the far end of the room and there was a film projector to the side of the door. Wires ran across the walls and were hooked up to speakers in each corner. Apart from that, the room was entirely empty, save for another metal chair with restraints set in the centre of the room. Booth noticed that this one was bolted to the floor.

'I could get this working, if you liked, captain, ' the engineer sergeant said, fiddling with wires and switches in the dais beneath the film projector. 'It doesn't look too complicated. If we just plug this thing in –'

The speakers erupted into a burst of static, followed by a deafening blast of sound. So sudden and tremendous was the cacophony that Booth fell backwards with his hands to his ears.

Then he noticed the images on the screen. Naked women stood in a line, some holding children. German soldiers with dogs and whips prowled beside them. The sound was so loud that Booth felt it almost as a tangible thing. Screams. Shouts. Shots. Dogs barking. A wailing wall of noise, a perfect distillation of human suffering, as if a thousand voices were raised in an agony of supplication.

Booth gestured frantically towards the engineer sergeant,

who lunged for a lever below the dais. The sound and images died.

'What in God's name was that?' one of the soldiers hissed.

Booth was dusting off his trousers. 'That is precisely what I intend to find out,' he said.

4

FOR THE FIRST time in what seemed an age, Ilse slept late.

For one glorious moment when she awoke and pulled her hair from her eyes, she had no idea where she was. Then the wind stirred and blew through the cracks in the wall and she remembered everything.

Cousin Ursula was dead.

Her last family member was gone.

Ilse walked to the window and looked down at the messy grave she'd dug in a corner of the garden, a long, ragged scar of freshly turned earth. How anyone was supposed to dig a grave six feet deep was beyond her. In the end, all she'd managed to create was a trench perhaps a little over three feet deep in which to lay Cousin Ursula's body – and that had taken her all night. Her palms and fingers were one mass of blisters. She hoped the layer of rocks and rubble she had placed on top of Ursula's body would be enough to deter animals from scratching and scrabbling at the remains.

The enormity of the situation hit her suddenly and she burst into tears. Then sudden fear gripped her and she ran to the other side of the room and looked through the window, towards the rose bush by the path.

No, you couldn't see the other hole, she realised, the hole Ilse had dug when she had first come to the house two months before. The grass had grown back and only the faintest outline of it was visible, a rectangular hole, two feet by twelve inches.

That was good: Cousin Ursula was not the only one of Ilse's secrets buried in the garden.

It was cold when she went downstairs. After days of wishing to be free of Cousin Ursula, Ilse now found the house felt strangely empty. Having two people inside it had given an illusion that the place was still a dwelling; now she was alone again, the house was revealed for what it really was, a battered box of brick and beam without any water or electricity.

Ilse built the fire up and ate some of O'Donnell's bread for breakfast. Then she remembered the wretch would be expecting information about the policeman from her when she went back to work at the transit camp. Well, O'Donnell would have to wait. It wasn't her fault she hadn't seen Booth.

She warmed her toes by the fire and admired the dancing flame as she prepared tea.

When she went back into the pantry she spotted the bundle of letters on the floor. They were Cousin Ursula's, the ones she'd held clutched to her chest all though the long agony of her death. They must have fallen from her hands when Ilse carried the body outside. Ilse went back to the fire with the letters.

Really, she should burn them. They had obviously been important to Ursula; they were private. Yet they were almost the only memento that remained of Ilse's family. She looked at the top letter and the words that were written there: *Liebling Ursula*.

No-one would ever know, she decided, then saw that her

fingers were already unpicking the blue ribbon that held the letters together.

Her eyes strayed across the first page. The letter contained precisely what she expected to find, cloying promises of love and undying devotion from some soldier, someone who had served on the eastern front. Ilse frowned when she spotted an allusion to 'playing together as children'. Her frown deepened when she saw the letter was signed 'Johannes D'.

As she skimmed through more of the letters, she realised her suspicion was correct: her brother, Johannes, had written them. There were so many references to childhood incidents and mutual relations, it had to have been him. Ilse frowned even more as she read the sugary protestations of love and promises of marriage that her brother had sent back from Russia.

How could that be? Johannes had always despised Cousin Ursula. He had bullied and taunted her as a child, even though Ursula was eight years older than he. Ilse's expression grew yet more serious as she read on. The later letters were filled with talk of the glory of the Final Victory and how Johannes's unit had imposed 'German culture' on the Slavs.

'*Good news, my dearest, sweet darling! I have achieved the posting of my dreams. Fortune has smiled upon me and I have been transferred to an elite unit, the SS-Sturmbrigade 'Dirlewanger'. They really are the crème de la crème of our Führer's boys. You should see how their boots and buttons sparkle when they are on parade. We're very popular with the local Slavs. Whenever we visit one of their villages, all the women and men come crowding out into the street and head for the local church to sing our praises. We always give them a warm reception.'*

Ilse looked at the letter. It was written in pencil on grubby, torn paper. There was certainly nothing about the scrawls that suggested an elite unit. And the whole tone of the letter was wrong: the Johannes she'd known would never have been capable of such saccharine sentimentality.

She looked at the date on the letter. That, too, did not dovetail with her memories of Johannes. It was dated November 1943. That meant the letter had been written a few months after Johannes's final fateful visit to the Warthegau.

The last time Ilse had seen her brother he had been a changed man. Not only did he have that lean, hard look most of the fighting men from the east had, the cruel spiteful side of his character had come fully to the fore.

Of course, Johannes was the centre of attention at the party Ilse had organised in his honour – how could he not be? But every person who went to congratulate him on the prowess of the German Army walked away from him disturbed. They whispered that he was voicing all sorts of unwise opinions about the Party and the war.

It was inevitable Johannes should fall out with Rüdiger. 'No, *you* don't understand, Herr Hoffman,' Johannes had shouted across the dinner table, after drinking a whole bottle of hock with the entrée. 'We *have* to win this fucking war now, because if the Ivans ever come here and do to us even a fraction of what we've done to them, within a year there won't be any Germans left.'

The dinner party had ended hours earlier than anticipated,

by which time Johannes had been lying unconscious before the scullery fire for some time.

Ilse sipped her tea. What had Johannes been doing, exchanging letters with Cousin Ursula? Had he changed? It was possible – sometimes the thought of coming home to a simple plain woman like Ursula was what a soldier needed to keep him going – but somehow it didn't fit her brother's character. If the sentiment wasn't genuine, what had provoked his expression of it? Had Johannes been poking fun at Ursula?

Yes, that was more like it, she realised. Johannes had always possessed an odd sense of humour, the type that enjoyed laughing *at* rather than *with* other people. And who was this *Sturmbrigade Dirlewanger*? As far as she knew Johannes had always served with the 3rd Division, the *Totenkopf*.

What did it all mean?

She sipped tea, staring at the fire. And then it suddenly occurred to her in a spike of emotion just how pointless all this wondering and theorising was: they were all dead. All of them. Ursula. Johannes. Rüdiger. She had nothing, now, and no-one.

Ilse looked at her blistered hands, then rose and went to the pantry for the whisky bottle, trying to ignore the tears that had clouded her eyes.

5

Amon Toth sat in the centre of the interrogation room with a booted foot resting on the knee of his left leg. When Payne pulled aside the slat that covered the peephole and peered through, the German raised his hand and wiggled the tips of his fingers towards the door in a dainty wave.

Toth was in his early thirties and good-looking in a chisel-jawed Teutonic way. His hair was platinum blond and exceptionally fine, but his eyes were unusually dark and surrounded by darker lashes. Most SS men Payne had seen were unimpressive without their uniforms, but Toth had presence; there was something of the fallen angel about him, radiant and yet perverse.

Payne pulled the slat closed and said to the duty sergeant, 'What can you tell me about him?'

The sergeant had taken an age to find the right file. 'His name is *Kriminalkommisar* Amon Toth. Not that he told us his real name first time around. According to the file, we picked him up right after the surrender. He tried to pass himself off as a normal soldier when he was first questioned, but one of the inquisitors flagged him as being suspect, so he was sent back to the cage. Then a German soldier told us who he really was: Toth is ex-SS and ex-Gestapo. He was quite high up in Department C.'

'Department C? That was Administration and Party Affairs, wasn't it?' Lieutenant Taylor said.

'Yes. And that's the problem. We know he was linked to the Einsatzgruppen that were going round shooting civilians when the Jerries invaded Poland and Russia, but we can't find any trace of it. Toth's a crafty sod. Most likely he destroyed all of his own records. I know the inquisitors at the interrogation centre in Bad Nenndorf are keen to have a crack at him, but I think they're still gathering the information they need.'

When Taylor and Payne entered the interrogation room, Toth pointed at Payne's civilian clothes. 'Who are you? Why do you not wear a uniform?'

The German smiled when he received no answer. 'I know what you are doing. You are trying to intimidate me with your silence. I, too, have been trained in interrogation techniques.'

Toth spoke good English, but pronounced it with an air of amused contempt, like an adolescent forced to play with children's toys. 'I wish to smoke also,' he said when Taylor lit a cigarette.

'Is that your way of asking?'

'Our conversation will be mutually beneficial, I assure you.'

Taylor handed him a cigarette. Payne could see the lieutenant looked nervous and uncomfortable. That wasn't a good frame of mind in which to start an interrogation, Payne thought.

He was right.

Taylor was a disaster.

Payne had learned that the worst thing you could do when questioning intelligent, voluble men like Toth was to enter into a verbal joust with them, but that was precisely what Taylor did.

'That's *Lieutenant* Taylor, to you,' he said when Toth kept referring to him as Mister.

Toth shook his head. 'I can tell you are not a professional soldier, Mr Taylor. You are like most of your army, a civilian in uniform, a dilettante.'

'Dilettantes that won.'

Toth waved his hand. 'It was the Russians' inexhaustible contempt for human life that broke the Wehrmacht, not your cosseted soldiers. Were it not for the eastern front, your armies would have learned of what the German soldier was truly capable.'

Payne said nothing. The only way to make things worse would have been to interrupt Taylor and undermine the miniscule amount of authority he had managed to establish. Payne awaited his opportunity. Eventually, Lieutenant Taylor said, 'Detective Inspector Payne has some questions to put to you.'

'*Detective Inspector* Payne,' Toth said, pretending to be impressed. 'After the chisel comes the scalpel. Where do you serve? Are you from the famous –'

'I'll ask the questions, Herr Toth.'

Toth smiled at the interruption. 'The voice of authority. At last,' he added, nodding his head contemptuously towards Taylor. 'What is it you need to – ?'

Payne made a point of looking at his watch. 'What do you know about the murders in Eichenrode? Get straight to the point, or you're going back outside to the cage.'

Toth made himself comfortable in his seat.

'It has come to my attention that certain crimes were recently committed in a house outside the town of Eichenrode. A man and a woman were found murdered in the cellar, I believe. I am in a position to help you.'

'How?'

'I know who the murderer is.'

'If you know this man so well, tell me what I found at the crime scene in Eichenrode.'

'Oh, I imagine there would have been some scalpels, yes? And some form of sewing implement? And vaccines that perhaps were not all they appeared to be.'

Payne tried hard to hide his reaction, but Toth was good. He watched Payne's face carefully as he spoke and smiled when he saw the evident interest there.

'And what does he do with these scalpels?' Payne said.

'Oh, it's far more fun if you find that out for yourself. And you will do, soon, that I can promise. I imagine your security forces have yet to realise the extreme danger the individual responsible for these crimes poses. If this man has been living free among you since the end of the war there will be more than two victims, I can assure you. You just haven't found the others yet.'

'And who is he?'

'He is what the doctors call a psychopath, a man with no conscience, no morals and no qualms – a monster, if you will, whose only concern is following the dictates of his twisted pathology. He led the Reich's security forces a merry dance for nearly eighteen months before we caught him. And he was extremely active during that period. He managed to kill a total of thirteen men and women.'

Payne was making notes as Toth spoke.

'Tell me how you became involved in this case.'

'My involvement began in Berlin, in July 1943. There had been a particularly heavy air raid and the rescue teams were searching the cellars of damaged buildings for the dead. In the cellar of one building they found the remains of six men and women.

'There was no question of their having been killed in the air raid, as each person's remains had been very carefully butchered and the body parts stored in lime. The matter was first reported to the Kripo criminal police, but when it became apparent three of the dead men were soldiers who had previously gone AWOL, the matter came to the attention of the Gestapo.'

'I suppose you'll tell me these murders were all hushed up and that there's no way of corroborating them?'

'On the contrary, they were widely reported. Especially when more houses with more bodies began to appear across the Reich. They were attributed to English air crews at first. It was a way of stirring up a little extra hate, I suppose. Any of the national newspapers should have coverage of the murders.'

Payne looked at Toth's face. Was he bluffing? No, Toth was too good for that. He must know Payne would check up on what he was saying.

Toth smiled, as if reading Payne's thoughts. 'Although, I must warn you, the newspaper reports do contain one very important factual error.'

'Which is?'

Toth smiled, said nothing.

'You mentioned that this man was caught,' Payne said. 'If that's so, how is it he is free now? Surely he would have been executed.'

Toth smiled and wagged a finger playfully. 'No, Mr Payne. I have no intention of telling you that.'

'And how was it he was able to possess so many houses?'

'Nor that.'

'So, what precisely are you offering us?'

'I can provide a detailed description of your man, both physically and psychologically, perhaps even provide you with photos if I am granted access to the correct files. I can tell you how he hunts, the profile of his victims. I can tell you enough to ensure his swift and easy capture.'

'And what is your price for supplying us with this information?'

'I want safe passage out of Allied Europe. You will take me to some point close to the Spanish border – Perpignan, for example – and supply me with all the necessary documentation. I will then divulge all I know about the nature of your problem.'

When Taylor laughed, Toth sneered at him.

'Do you think it is not already happening? I'll wager if I had been working at Peenemünde on the V-weapon project I would already be in America or England, living like a lord. I know of men with questionable backgrounds – far more questionable than my own – who have successfully bought their way out. There are upwards of 5,000 men in this camp alone. It would be simplicity itself for one man to disappear.'

Taylor had been shifting on his seat while Toth spoke. Now he stood up suddenly and began berating the man in a voice made shrill by emotion.

'You're wanted for war crimes, you bastard. You won't be allowed to wriggle off the hook.'

Toth waved his hand dismissively. 'War crimes? Human history is a litany of massacre. In the last war, the Turks slaughtered the Armenians; the Greeks slaughtered the Turks. What answer would you receive from a Boer, were you to mention concentration camps? Or talk of the civility of British government to an Irishman? Or an Indian? Colonial government is never easy. History will either absolve the Germans or it will accuse all empires of these 'war crimes'.'

Taylor's face was bright red. Payne saw tears had formed in his eyes.

'Why don't you go and get a glass of water, Lieutenant?' he said.

Taylor left the room, his hands shaking.

'How did you catch him?' Payne said, when the door had closed. 'It will be very difficult to go to my superiors with details of your proposal if I have nothing to offer them.'

Toth blew smoke rings towards the light bulb as he considered this. 'Very well. Check the newspapers and you will readily discover the discrepancy in the official version of the story. And look for details on the military operation code-named *Greif*. It was that which finally allowed us to capture him. When you have done this, return here with details of when and where I am to be released and we will talk further.'

'Greif? What was that?' Payne said. The word meant gryphon in German.

'I will say no more. But from that you will discover a detail that will be particularly useful if you wish to catch this man. And particularly dangerous, given the current circumstances in Germany.'

When Payne left the interrogation room, he found Taylor

outside, leaning against a wall, smoking a cigarette.

'I'm sorry about that,' Taylor said in a flat voice. 'I just . . . hate them all.'

'Do you think there's any truth to what he says? About Nazis escaping, I mean?'

Taylor waved his hand dismissively. 'One hears rumours, naturally, but I don't believe them. If there were organised routes of escape, why did we manage to capture people like Göring and Himmler? They would have been the first to use these so-called ratlines, don't you think? You don't look convinced, Detective Inspector.'

Payne wasn't. Men were fallible. And greedy. There was always a way.

Taylor put out his cigarette. 'Surely, you don't put any faith in what he said, do you? Didn't you get the impression he was a flim-flam operator of the highest order?'

Payne thought about that as they walked back to Taylor's jeep. He didn't like Toth; that had been his first, overriding impression. There was something oily and unpleasant about the man. Then Payne realised there was one other impression he'd formed while interrogating Toth: he was damned glad their situations had not been reversed.

6

THAT EVENING, CAPTAIN Booth attended a drinks party hosted by Colonel Bassett's staff.

Military Government social events were the bane of Booth's life: it was bad enough having to serve alongside these idiots, but socialising with them off-duty was torture. Colonel Bassett was the sort of crusty old imperialist Booth would have walked a mile to avoid back in civvy street and the rest of the occupation forces stationed at Eichenrode were just as bad: braggarts, blusterers and blunderers, the lot of them. Most had never seen a shot fired in anger and yet they strutted around before the German civilians like they'd stormed the Normandy beaches single-handed. And this werewolf scare had got them all lathered up. You could see it in their faces: they were excited at the prospect of seeing some 'action', especially now the chances of sustaining a serious injury were minimal.

Booth went to stand beside a window. Outside, the streets were filled with military activity. Bassett had ordered numerous roadblocks and extra guard posts to be established on all the major thoroughfares in the town and the night patrols had been doubled.

Across the room, Booth could see Lieutenant Taylor standing by the drinks table, getting quietly sloshed in the same way

Tubbs seemed to do five nights out of every seven these days. Booth sipped his own drink, lost in thought.

In his heart of hearts, Booth knew that what had happened to Tubbs Taylor wasn't really his fault, but he had never really been able to shift his sense of guilt. It had all happened so quickly.

Back in April, a call had come through that a group of SS men had approached 2nd Army's lines to warn them of a typhus outbreak and said that they were offering to surrender. Could someone from Field Intel go up there and help with the arrests? Booth had been all set to go, but Tubbs had said, 'I don't mind popping over there, Jimmy. I've just filled the utility up. What's this place called?'

Booth looked at his notes. 'Bergen-Belsen.'

Tubbs returned two days later, a changed man. He'd never really spoken about what he saw there, but his usual nervy introspection had been replaced by something else, something raw and vulnerable, as if he were a tree stripped of its bark.

That first night after his return Tubbs had wet the bed. He had tried to hide it, rising early and removing the bedding and turning his mattress, but after ten years being educated at boarding schools Booth could read the signs of what had happened.

That was why Booth had ensured that, since his visit to Belsen, Tubbs had been given the lightest of duties: mostly paperwork, carrying out background checks on suspected Nazis, liaising with officers from the Public Safety Branch and vetting the *Fragebogen* questionnaires. Booth and the sergeants handled most of the hands-on stuff now.

That was why it irked him so much that Detective Inspector Payne had taken Tubbs off to interrogate this Gestapo man earlier in the day. Tubbs simply wasn't up to it.

When Booth had asked how the interrogation had gone, Tubbs was non-committal. That almost certainly meant it had gone badly. Booth had sat in on some of Tubbs's interrogations and he could picture what had happened. Tubbs just couldn't avoid getting genuinely angry. Let the prisoner realise that, and the battle was pretty much lost before you'd even begun.

To make matters worse, Colonel Bassett had bawled Booth out for it.

'I hear that policeman has been out hobnobbing with the bloody Gestapo today, Captain Booth,' Bassett had said as soon as Booth had arrived. 'With the *Gestapo*. And to cap it all, one of your officers went with him to facilitate the process. Did I not make myself clear? I do not want this wretched Peeler interfering with army business.'

Booth had tried to defend himself. 'I'm sorry, sir, but Detective Inspector Payne is investigating crimes that –'

'A bloody Waffen SS officer and his floozy get their just desserts and you call it a crime? Do you know what this Gestapo bastard said to the policeman? He wants to cut himself a deal in exchange for giving us information. That's the real crime. Well, I've pulled the rug from under his feet. I've had him shipped off to the high-level interrogation centre at Bad Nenndorf. They'll know how to look after him there. There'll be no deals cut with any of these bastards, not while I'm in charge.'

A roar of laughter drew Booth's attention back to the party. He lit a cigarette and began mingling again.

Guest of honour at tonight's bash was Professor Svoboda,

a small Czech man from the World Medical Association whose surname nobody had been able to pronounce correctly even before the serious drinking began. Accompanied by an escorting officer, Svoboda was touring Germany and Austria to gather evidence on the human experimentation that had taken place in the concentration camps. Svoboda's presence was the reason Booth had agreed to attend the drinks party. He needed to speak to the man.

All of the documents Booth had found at Wolffslust were here in Eichenrode now. Booth had organised a work detail from among the prisoners and had had them load all of the boxes and crates aboard a lorry. The offices of Booth's field intelligence unit were now crammed with them.

Since coming back from the prison, he'd had a cursory look at the documentation and had quickly realised it was so far beyond his field of experience that he would have to seek outside help. All he'd established so far was that there were medical records for more than forty patients, all of whom had German sounding surnames, and that, according to the Nazis' warped racial criteria, their bloodlines were faultlessly Aryan.

Except one.

This man, Patient 14, had a half-Jewish ancestor on his mother's side from three generations back. The word *Mischling* – mixed-blood – had been written at the top of this patient's records in red ink. The word had been underlined and was followed by three exclamation marks. Booth thought there was an almost triumphant flourish in the way the word had been highlighted, as if this was what the investigators had been seeking all along.

That was Booth's sole find of any real interest. Much of the documentation consisted of endless transcripts of conversations that had taken place between the chief doctor, Wiegand, and the patients. The transcripts covered all manner of subjects: childhoods, sexual fantasies, relationships with their parents.

The prisoners at Wolffslust knew very little about what had gone on in the cellars of the prison. Some remembered that in the autumn of '44 soldiers with construction equipment had come to begin work in the cellar. Lorries filled with SS men and civilian workers had arrived with crates of equipment. Then had come a number of vehicles that had arrived in the dead of night. They contained men in white overalls and 'special' prisoners who were kept apart from the others.

One prisoner remembered helping to drag huge blocks of ice to the door of the cellar. Another mentioned seeing a man in ankle and wrist chains being walked from one of the cells on the lower floor down into the cellar.

Booth poured himself another pink gin and hovered by Svoboda's side, waiting for an opportunity to get the man's attention.

'I say Professor, I was wondering if this symbol meant anything to you?' Booth said, drawing the professor aside and showing him a sheet of paper on which he had copied the sword-and-ribbon symbol found on the film canisters and the crates at Wolffslust.

'It's the symbol of the *Ahnenerbe*,' Svoboda said, his interest immediate. 'It was an intellectual society formed by high-ranking Nazis who were dedicated to 'proving' the historical superiority of Aryan culture. Himmler was its principal patron.'

'You know of it, then?'

Svoboda nodded. 'Despite its lofty intellectual trappings, the *Ahnenerbe* was guilty of engaging in all sorts of pseudo-science. In fact, it commissioned a great deal of the medical experimentation on human beings that the WMA is investigating.' The professor's saturnine face became animated and his voice rose. 'Some of what they got up to beggars belief: immersing victims in freezing water, undertaking muscle and bone transplants without anaesthesia, deliberately exposing patients to mustard gas and phosphorus. And don't think I'm exaggerating. I've seen the photographic evidence and I didn't eat for days afterwards. They've got two dozen Nazi doctors in Camp Ashcan, now. They're going to be tried at Nuremburg right alongside Göring and Speer and all the others.'

'Would you mind if I showed you something?' Booth said.

Twenty minutes later they were at the makeshift cinema in Eichenrode. Svoboda sipped his drink as Booth set up the projector and played the films found at Wolffslust.

Svoboda sneered when Booth played him the film containing the pornographic images, but his interest returned when he saw the footage of the mass killings.

'What do you think it means?' Booth said afterwards.

'Judging by the names on the canisters, it would seem these films served some purpose beyond mere titillation. I would suggest the surnames listed here were those of the patients or test subjects each film was designed to be used with.'

'But why?'

'We'll likely never know. Perhaps they were used to see how patients would react to certain visual stimuli.'

'And what is it that we are seeing? What do the killings and the dead bodies signify, I mean.'

Svoboda's gaze remained fixed on the blanket-screen, as if still contemplating the images. 'The level of the Germans' barbarity – especially in the east – has been an open secret for years. What is not generally known is the extent. The scale of it is quite . . . staggering. According to depositions taken from high-ranking Nazis and Wehrmacht personnel, there was an organised policy of extermination operative in the east from the very earliest days of the war. At first these killings were undertaken by mixed SS and police units known as *Einsatzgruppen*, men who simply marched their victims into the countryside and shot them beside open graves.

'However, this policy was deemed unnecessarily *stressful*' – here, Svoboda's voice dripped with scorn – 'for the killers. Many of them suffered severe psychological traumas due to their experiences and so a new policy was introduced: secret camps were established in Poland and a policy of industrialised slaughter initiated, using gas chambers and crematoria. Some estimates put the number of victims in the millions.

'I think these films document those processes. The first film shows mass executions by rifle. I think the second shows one of the gas chambers being cleared. Those naked women we saw were probably queuing outside a gas chamber. They used to disguise them as showers.'

Neither man said anything for a long while after that, but as they walked outside Booth thought of the dozens of crates of documents he had taken from Eichenrode.

'Are you going to be in this area for long, professor?' he said. 'Because there's something for which I could really use your help.'

7

NEXT MORNING ILSE rose early and washed herself using a bucket as best as she could. It was Thursday morning and Captain Booth was coming to see her.

She was downstairs, drinking tea and smoking, when she heard the crunch of his tyres on the gravel outside. She fixed a smile on her face, went outside to greet him . . .

. . . and stopped dead.

Sitting beside the Tommy in the jeep was a young boy with the worst hare lip she'd ever seen. *What the devil is he doing, bringing people like that to the house?* Ilse thought.

Booth must have seen her smile falter, because when he got out of the jeep he put an arm around the boy and said, 'Ursula, this is my friend, Piotr.'

Piotr stuck his bony hand out. Ilse hesitated before grasping the mangy fingers, but forced a smile when she saw Booth frown. Then he said, 'I've brought you some victuals,' and lifted a box of vegetables, fruit and tins from the jeep's rear seat. 'There's fat and potatoes in here. I thought we could fry them. Can I come inside the house?'

Thank God I can say yes, Ilse thought, as she motioned for him to come inside. The suspicion in Booth's eyes had been evident this time. Now she no longer needed to provoke his mistrust.

She led him into the kitchen and made tea, which they drank sitting at the rickety kitchen table. Booth's pensive air continued, though. There was something else on his mind, she realised. He looked tired and nervous, but he wouldn't say what the matter was, so Ilse stopped asking and they drank in silence. Why was it that men always thought they were protecting women when they refused to tell them what the hell was going on?

They smoked cigarettes as Booth began cooking; soon the kitchen was filled with the smell of frying potatoes. God, she nearly fainted when she breathed it in. For a moment, it was as if the hollow in her stomach had become a real thing and she'd felt herself folding in half.

When the food was ready, Booth took the Polack a plateful. The boy set about it with his filthy fingers, seated on the grass. Ilse and Booth sat down together at the table inside.

'Have you heard about the murders that happened a few days ago?' he said, after a long silence.

'Of course. People in the town are talking about them.'

'I don't think you should be alone out here, but I'm going to be very busy for while, so I've asked Piotr to come and look in on you each day. I promise he won't be too much bother. He can chop wood and fix things for you, do some odd jobs. I think you'll find he's very handy to have around. I hope that's not a terrible imposition.'

Ilse did her best to smile. *Imposition*? As far as Ilse was concerned, the Polack was precisely the sort of person she should be locking doors and windows against. Who knew what sort of raddled nonsense went through a head like that?

'Well, if he's to come here, I want him to wash,' she said. 'He smells like a pigsty.'

Booth nodded in agreement. They continued to eat in silence.

'Have you ever heard of the *Sturmbrigade Dirlewanger*?' she said after a while. 'They were part of the Waffen SS, I think. Were they an elite unit?'

Booth scoffed. 'Elite? They were the worst of the worst. Thieves and murderers, for the most part. I think they were originally made up of poachers, the idea being that they would hunt down partisans in the woods. In the end, though, they let all sorts of criminals join.

'The Poles are very keen to get their hands on ex-members, that's how I know about them. According to intelligence reports, the Dirlewangers single-handedly destroyed an entire quarter during that bloody mess in Warsaw last year. The list of crimes attributed to them beggars belief: rape, torture, murder, mutilation. But why do you ask?'

'Oh, nothing, just curiosity. A woman at the camp mentioned something about her son.'

They ate in silence as Ilse considered the information. Thieves and murderers? That couldn't be true, Ilse thought. That was the wretched Polacks spreading lies. And yet Ilse had heard men talking in Berlin about what had happened in Warsaw when the SS had gone to quell the rebellion. There had been little room for mercy so late in the war. Terrible things had happened. Could Johannes have been involved?

They had finished eating now. As they cleared away the plates, Ilse remembered O'Donnell. God, she was supposed to be asking Booth about this wretched policeman. She'd already missed one opportunity to turn the conversation to the subject, so she sat next to Booth and snuggled her head into his neck.

'Actually, darling, talking of the women at the camp, one of them mentioned a curious thing the other day,' Ilse said. 'She claims there is an English policeman here. From Scotland Yard.'

The cigarette paused on the way to Booth's mouth. 'What an extraordinary thing for one of your friends to know,' he said, after a moment's consideration.

'Is it true? Is there a Scotland Yard man here?'

'Quite true, yes. He's not here in an official capacity, though. He's supposed to be training German policemen – his mother was Swiss-German, apparently, so he's a fluent German speaker – but they've all been interned, so he's at a bit of a loose end. He's been looking into this murder business.'

'Is he a good policeman?'

'Do you mean good as in competent? Or good as in a good man?'

'The first one.'

'Yes, he seems very thorough. Hard-working, too. He's a bit of a cold-fish, though. Not an easy man to like.'

'Has he discovered much?'

'He was out interrogating a Gestapo man yesterday. But I haven't had much to do with him, really.'

'What actually happened out at the house on the Brunswick Road? I've heard so many rumours.'

'It's really quite a strange affair. They found a man and a woman strangled to death. The man was Waffen SS, but we've no idea who the woman was – his girlfriend, probably, given the age difference. But it sounds like someone was planning on chopping them up. Apparently there were all sorts of scalpels and surgical instruments there and some –'

An involuntary shiver shook Ilse. Booth looked at her.

'Are you all right, darling?'

'Oh, let's not talk about such horrid things, please,' Ilse said, and meant it.

He placed a hand on her shoulder.

'What's the matter, Ursula? Why do you look so scared all of a sudden?'

'I'm fine. It's just . . . all that talk of scalpels and strangled bodies. You make me think the *Flickschuster* is loose again.'

She felt the change in him immediately. Booth's body tensed.

'The *Flickschuster*? Who was that?'

'Oh, it's just a story mothers used to scare children,' she said, trying to play the matter down. 'I'm sure what they said about him was exaggerated.'

Booth was gazing at her intently now. 'Do you mean to tell me something like this has occurred before? Look at me, Ursula, this is important.'

Ilse sighed, realising she would have to explain herself now.

'There were murders a few years ago, here in the Reich. They called the killer the *Flickschuster*. But they caught him, a Dutchman. He was executed. I read it in the newspaper. So forget all about it, please. People got so hysterical about the whole thing, he became a stupid story, like the Bogeyman or Jack the Ripper.'

Booth was quiet for a long while. Then he said, 'Jack the Ripper was real,' as he stared at the window, lost in thought.

8

Silas Payne was born in 1901. He was thirteen years old when the Great War began.

The question of his mother's Swiss-German nationality wasn't a problem at first. But, by October 1914, when the British had suffered their first serious reverses and the newspaper stories of German atrocities had done their work, business began to tail off at the grocery shop his parents ran.

His mother tacked signs to the inside of the display windows – This is <u>not</u> a German business – but it did no good. Payne's father came home one night with a bloodied lip and buttons missing from his shirt; the next day, a group of girls spat at Silas as he walked home from school.

Silas was in bed on the night of November 2nd, the night the mob came. There were only a few of them at first, hurling insults up at his parents' bedroom window, but within minutes others began spilling out of the local pubs and a crowd began to form.

Silas had gone into his parents' room as the insults grew in volume and severity.

Hun bitch.

Fuck off back to Germany.

Hang the spy.

Then someone threw a stone and glass smashed downstairs; the crowd's restraint broke with it. They were all over the shop in seconds, dragging the goods from the window. Payne remembered them standing in the street, afterwards, chatting and laughing as they munched apples and sausage and bits of cheese.

Payne's father had been all set to go outside with a walking stick, but his mother had thrown herself on his legs and begged him to stay. They had sat there, the three of them, huddled together on the edge of his parents' bed, listening to the sound of their livelihood being torn apart.

And then the whistle had sounded, a single three-beat blast that had silenced the crowd immediately.

When Payne peered from the upstairs window he saw the local police sergeant standing between the crowd and the shop window, taking his tunic off and flexing his big fists open and closed.

'You all know me,' he said in a low, calm voice, 'and I know most of you. So believe me when I say that the next one of you blighters to take something from this shop is going to have to go through me to get to it. Is that perfectly clear?'

The crowd wavered and men began whispering. The quiet seemed to last forever but when no-one made a move, the police sergeant cracked his knuckles and smiled, the master now of the situation. 'It's a mighty cold night, lads, so either we get straight to it or we all go home. What's it to be?'

That had broken the spell. Some laughed at the sergeant's temerity, others pulled their caps down to hide their faces and slunk towards the shadows. As quickly as the crowd had formed, it was gone.

'Don't you worry, Mrs Payne,' the sergeant had said afterwards, as Payne and his parents began salvaging what they could from the wreckage, 'I'll see those animals don't trouble you again.'

He'd been true to his word, too, prowling up and down their street each hour, on the hour, for the next two weeks, whistling tunelessly and swinging his truncheon. And, as Silas had watched the man, feeling the calming aura of strength and safety he exuded, he had realised one person *could* make a difference – it was all a question of persistence and determination. From then on, Silas Payne had known precisely what it was he wanted to do with his life . . .

Payne blinked eyes that were gummy with sleep. He sat up on the creaky trestle bed in the police station and pressed a hand to his chest. His heart was hammering, the way it always did when he dreamt of that night back in 1914. Even now, more than thirty years later, Payne remembered the hysterical terror and confusion of the experience with total clarity; during the whole of his career in the police force, nothing had ever come close to it. He rose, made coffee and got straight to work. He knew from experience that the best antidote was to occupy his mind.

As soon as it was light, Payne went to the *Rathaus*. He kept going over what the Gestapo man, Toth, had told him. Was there any truth to his claims? There was only one way to find out, Payne decided.

The cellars of the *Rathaus* were extensive. A veritable warren of corridors connected dozens of vaulted stone chambers, some of which must have been over five hundred years old. There was a chaotic lack of orderliness in most of these chambers: Eichenrode had been bombed by mistake back in '44 and most of the books and paperwork salvaged from the town's library had been stored haphazardly in the cellars.

Payne picked his way through piles of cardboard boxes towards a desk that stood at the back of the main chamber.

'Am I right in thinking there are some boxes of German newspapers down here?' Payne said to the soldier on duty, steadying himself by placing a hand on the wall as he stepped over a box.

'How do you say newspaper in German, sir?' the man asked.

'*Zeitung.*' Payne wrote the word down for the man.

'Ah, yes, I recognise that word. Down that corridor, turn right, chamber on the right. You'll find all the *zai-tongs* you could want in there, sir. But I don't think they've been sorted.'

He was right. There were boxes and boxes of newspapers but they were all jumbled together. Once Payne had located all the relevant boxes, he took them to a desk in a side chamber and began the laborious process of sorting the newspapers by title and date. First, he divided them into their relevant editions. The boxes contained copies of three newspapers: *Der Stürmer, Völkischer Beobachter* and *Das Reich.*

An hour later, Payne leant back in his chair and sighed. He'd become totally sidetracked, he realised, massaging his temples. His head was swimming and not just from the effects of staring at newsprint under the dim light. He had never realised quite how cynically perverse the minds that had controlled Germany had been.

Within the pages of these newspapers, every single event of the last ten years of European history had been turned about-face, upside down and inside out: British aggression had started the war, Stalingrad was a great feat of German arms, the Russians were Asiatic barbarians who had launched a war of extermination against the virtuous and peace-loving German people and the Jews and Bolsheviks were responsible for everything . . .

Payne could pinpoint the moment when the war had begun to turn against the Germans: the smug tone common to all the publications was replaced by an ever more histrionic incitation to 'resist', 'punish traitors' and 'hold on until the Final Victory'.

The closer the publication date to the end of the war, the more the newspapers shrank in size. They provided a graphic depiction of the melting of the Reich's power and of the delusional nature of those final months. The *Völkischer Beobachter* had still promised Final Victory even when it had diminished to a single sheet of paper.

Payne took a moment to regain his concentration. Then he set to work.

He examined the copies of *Der Stürmer* first.

So, this was Julius Streicher's infamous Jew-baiters' bible. Owing to its worldwide infamy Payne had always imagined *Der Stürmer* as a great tome of a publication, but it was really little more than a pamphlet. It was quite gratifying to see Streicher's tripe limited to so few pages. The pre-war issues had sixteen pages. By the 'forties, though, it had been reduced to a mere four pages.

What it lacked in size, it made up for in offensiveness.

Payne paused to examine the cover of one issue on which a fat-lipped man in Hassidic garb and ringlets was feeding an Aryan child into a sausage machine with pound and dollar signs on the barrel.

An issue of *Der Stürmer* dated September 1942 was the first to report anything that might corroborate Amon Toth's claims. The headline read 'New Jew Horror' and described the discovery of a Brunswick house at which 'Jew blood rituals' had been practised, killing 'more than four good Aryans'.

It described in graphic detail how the victims were slowly bled and tortured by Jews still hiding in the Reich. The article claimed the 'Jew killers' went on to mutilate their victims' corpses, although in what way was not specified.

That was hardly surprising, Payne decided. The article – if that was the correct word for it – was short on any real details as to what had happened. It ended with hysterical warnings to 'watch for the Jew among us' and never to hesitate in denouncing 'race-traitors' who might be hiding 'murdering Jewboys'.

Payne threw the copy of *Der Stürmer* back into the box with the others, glad to be done with it. Still, the article had served one purpose: it had given Payne a date he could use as a reference point when searching the other newspapers.

Payne then turned to the copies of the *Volkischer Beobachter* and Goebbels's own personal newspaper, *Das Reich*.

Both covered the series of murders. This time they were attributed to a new terror weapon being employed by – depending on which newspaper you read – English spies parachuted into the Reich for the purpose or enemy aircrews that had bailed out over Germany. According to the articles, these 'murder squads' lured Germans into secluded places and killed them before mutilating the bodies. Goebbels had even written a brief editorial on the subject in *Das Reich:*

But London is mistaken if it believes it can by terror break German morale. We have said it a hundred times before and will say it a hundred times again: today's German people has nothing in common with the German people of 1918. Our morale breakdown then was a one-time exception, not the rule.

Proof of their desperation has seen them turn to the cruellest of methods. Even when shot from the skies by the steel ring of defences that surrounds the capital, the English aircrews fall among us and behave like animals, murdering and mutilating. This latest outrage shows to what lengths they are prepared to go: a young soldier, home on leave, murdered alongside his fiancée, their bodies mutilated in the most horrific ways imaginable.

By early 1943, though, both newspapers had begun speaking of a single killer, a man they took to calling the *Flickschuster*. Payne paused. How could he best render that name in English? Translated literally, it meant a person that cobbled or patched something together, like a shoemaker, but Payne sensed the word was used more figuratively in relation to the killer: the Patchwork Man might be a more accurate translation.

The reports in the newspapers mentioned the discovery of a cellar full of dismembered body parts after an air raid on Brunswick. Some of the body parts had been buried under the floor of the cellar; others had been shoved into a furnace and burnt. The newspapers said the remains of six people had been found in the cellar, although bone and tooth fragments found in the stove indicated there might have been more.

Payne read on, cross-referencing each news story.

Another 'House of Horror' was discovered in Berlin in July 1943. This was the crime Toth had mentioned investigating. Again, the bodies were discovered in the cellar of the house. This time, though, witnesses spoke of a tall, well-built man who had been seen leaving the house on a number of occasions.

According to the newspapers, a Dutch worker named Wilhelmus van Rijn was arrested in May, 1944 and charged with the murders. The captions that accompanied the grainy photos of van Rijn surrounded by Gestapo agents highlighted his bulbous eyes and 'Jewish features'. A large amount of coverage was given to the show trial and subsequent execution.

Payne stopped. Execution?

He checked his notes. Toth said they had caught the murderer but had mentioned nothing about the man being executed. What did it mean? Clearly, Toth knew something the newspapers had not reported.

The Dutchman was probably innocent, Payne decided. If not, why would Toth have deliberately steered Payne towards looking in newspapers, knowing the stories published there would undermine his claims? Is that what he had meant when he said the newspaper reports contained an 'important error'?

Payne massaged the back of his neck. He was tired. And hungry, he realised. It was nearly eleven and he hadn't had any breakfast.

He rose from the desk. Then he stopped and frowned.

A familiar voice was echoing off the walls of the cellar.

It took Payne a moment to place it: Captain Booth. He leant against the door frame and listened to the captain's voice.

'. . . looking for German newspapers. Anything really, the more populist the better. Why? I'm looking for details on a series of murders that happened here in Germany during the war, sergeant.'

Payne frowned. How the hell had Booth discovered the same line of enquiry? It was too much of a coincidence. He would have to speak to the man. He rose and stepped out into the corridor.

'Hello again, Captain Booth,' he said, hands in his pockets. 'Do you know, I think I might be able to save you a lot of time and effort.'

9

Later that afternoon, the two men sat opposite each other in Booth's office, the relevant German newspapers piled on the table between them.

They had spoken for half an hour in the cellar of the *Rathaus*. Payne had shown Booth everything he'd found in the newspapers about the *Flickschuster* series of murders. Then he had told Booth about the claims made by the Gestapo man, Toth.

It was very strange. Booth had spoken to Tubbs at length about the interrogation, but the lieutenant had mentioned nothing about a series of murders that had already taken place in Germany. Then again, though, Tubbs was all over the place emotionally.

'Your theories are all very well and good, Detective Inspector,' Booth said, 'but I think there's one serious problem: according to the Jerry newspapers, they caught the killer. Guillotined him in June last year.'

Payne shook his head. 'They got the wrong man. At least, that's what I think Toth was intimating. He claimed more killings occurred after the Dutchman's execution. Killings that weren't reported.'

'But Toth is looking to save his neck. I've seen his files. Even though the evidence is incomplete, it seems likely he'll be indicted for war crimes. He'd say anything to get out of that.'

Payne nodded. 'That's very true and we'll have to bear it in mind. But it doesn't mean we can discount everything he's told us. Didn't you once mention to me that you had a list of German policemen?'

'That's correct. Why do you ask?'

Payne indicated the newspapers. 'According to these reports, there was a man from the Kripo criminal police in this area that headed up the investigation into the house they found in Brunswick, a policeman by the name of Metzger. It would be useful to find him. Perhaps he could tell us more.'

Booth nodded and promised to dig out the relevant files. Payne continued to look at his notes.

'Do you know anything about this Operation Greif? Toth mentioned that, too; said it was relevant.'

'Yes, I remember it very well. It was the German codename for a false flag operation the Jerries ran last year – *their* soldiers in *our* uniforms up to mischief behind the lines.'

Booth rose, rummaged through a filing cabinet and withdrew a file.

'Here it is. According to this, Operation Greif was a false flag operation organised by an SS man, Otto Skorzeny, the same man that organised Mussolini's rescue in Italy. In October 1944, Skorzeny got the green light to gather together a special unit of SS personnel that could speak English. The troops were trained in Grafenwöhr, in Bavaria, then moved to Münstereifel in Westphalia for the beginning of operations. During the December '44 Ardennes offensive, Skorzeny's men donned American uniforms and wrought havoc behind the

Allied lines. Many of the men involved are now being sought in connection with war crimes.'

Payne frowned. 'What possible connection could it have to what I am investigating?'

'Perhaps Toth used it as window dressing. You know, a little bit of truth to sweeten the odour of an otherwise entirely rotten barrel of fish. I can look into it, though, if you like.'

Payne nodded almost imperceptibly and murmured 'thanks' as he pored over his notes. Booth sat back in his chair and watched Payne work.

What he'd previously mistaken in the policeman for haughtiness was actually concentration, Booth realised. That was why Payne gave the impression of being such a cold fish. Little that was outside the immediate focus of his attention seemed to really register. Booth wondered if it was an inevitable consequence of a life spent trying to catch others out.

Booth had the desk sergeant run over to the mess and bring them a round of sandwiches and a flask of tea. As Booth tucked in, he told Payne of what he had found in the basement of Wolffslust prison.

'Do you think it could be related to what you are investigating?' Booth said when he'd finished.

'It's possible. And even if it's not related, the possibility that hundreds of serious criminals were released is something that needs to be looked into. We need to ascertain who this British officer at Wolfsslust was,' Payne said, 'the one who went in with the advance guard and oversaw the sacking of the prison. Perhaps he might know something.'

'I've looked into that already,' Booth said. 'I'm afraid there don't seem to be any records as to precisely which unit overran the prison. It was all very chaotic back then. But I've got Lieutenant Taylor investigating. Tubbs is a bit of a wiz when it comes to unravelling army red tape. If anyone can discover who this officer chap was, it will be Tubbs. And I wouldn't like to be in that officer's shoes if we do find him. Christ, if Toth is right and this idiot has released a mass murderer, it's going to make the British look bloody stupid,' Booth said.

'Have you had time to examine the medical documents you found at the prison?' Payne said.

'No. Since the business with Mr Lockwood in the minefield, Colonel Bassett has had me working overtime investigating this alleged werewolf cell. I've got a Czech professor looking at the documentation, though. Hopefully, he'll get back to me soon. But I have done some digging elsewhere.

'From a Nazi perspective, every one of the men in this medical programme seemed to possess faultless bloodlines, so I phoned their names through to Corps HQ. That's where they store the *RuSha* files, the ones we captured from the SS Race and Settlement Main Office. I'll phone now and see if the archivist up there has had time to cross-reference the names with the lists they've got.'

'Hello Killy,' Booth said when he'd been connected. 'Had any luck?'

Corporal Kilminster was the chief archivist at Corps HQ. 'Hello, sir,' he said. 'I'm not sure whether it constitutes luck or not, but out of the forty-odd names you gave me, thirty-one appear in our files.'

'So the others weren't SS?'

'Not necessarily. It could be that the others are in the files somewhere and I just haven't found them yet.'

'What have you got on the men you have found then?'

'All of them were SS officers with equivalent ranks of lieutenant and above. But that's beside the point. The interesting thing is where these men served. Out of the thirty-one I've found records for, seventeen served as concentration camp guards and the others all served in *Einsatzgruppen* in Poland and Russia.'

'So, all of these men are potential war criminals?'

'They would be if they weren't all dead.'

'Dead?'

'Yes, sir. Every one of them was killed in action, sir.'

'Are you sure? Because I got their names from the records of a medical programme they were all part of.'

Booth wrote the dates of death down. He and Payne then cross-referenced the names with the data Booth had taken from the medical files. Five minutes later, Booth was back on the phone to Killy.

'Are you absolutely certain about those dates you gave me?'

'Of course.' Killy sounded slightly peeved at the inference they might not be. 'Why?'

Booth didn't answer that. He was too busy tapping a pencil against his teeth and wondering why, according to Killy's official files, every single man on the list had supposedly died a week before they entered Doctor Wiegand's medical programme.

10

THAT SAME DAY, Ilse had to work at the transit camp.

As she pulled on her woollen stockings a sudden thought occurred to her. What with one thing and another, she'd forgotten what was, potentially, her biggest problem: the hag woman that knew her real name.

She thought about her problem as she walked to the camp. It was obvious the woman intended to blackmail her. If not, she would already have gone to the Tommies and denounced her.

The best thing to do was avoid her, Ilse decided. If they didn't see each other, the woman wouldn't be able to make her demands. Ilse hurried her pace and arrived at the camp twenty minutes early, before the other German women had got there. She volunteered to work in the laundry room again.

I'll have to get a transfer to work somewhere else, Ilse thought as she tipped piles of dirty clothing into the vats of boiling water. Yes, that was the best idea. She would have to speak to Booth about that. Not that Booth had paid her much attention the day before. After Ilse had mentioned the *Flickschuster* murders, Booth had become so pensive she could hardly get a word out of him.

At midday Ilse volunteered to walk across the camp with a wheelbarrow and fetch a fresh crate of detergent from the stores. She wanted an excuse to see O'Donnell and tell him what she had learned about the murders. She steered the rickety wheelbarrow along the camp's main road, but when she was out of sight of the laundry she turned to the right and headed towards the admin building.

As usual, it was chaos outside that building. Hundreds of people had formed into straggling, swaying queues, all of which converged on a single doorway. Ragged children danced between the legs of the adults and the air was filled with a dozen unintelligible languages.

When Ilse asked the guard on the door where O'Donnell was he pointed across the way to a gap between two buildings.

O'Donnell was talking with the soldier, Suttpen.

The two men seemed to be arguing. As Ilse watched, Suttpen raised his fist at the Irishman, who shook his head and began explaining something. Suttpen looked at his watch. Then he nodded, turned and stalked away.

When O'Donnell walked back towards the admin building, his face was furious. Ilse turned away. Nothing would induce her to speak to him now. She hurried back across the camp towards the storehouse.

The rest of the day passed in the usual fug of monotony. Ilse thought about what she had witnessed. What were those two up to? Because it was clear they were up to something. She knew that the soldier, Suttpen, was even worse than O'Donnell. Rumour had it he exchanged food with German women for sexual favours. What connection could he have to O'Donnell, though? The men gambled together, she knew that, but what she'd witnessed had seemed something far more serious than a simple argument over money.

As well as being angry, both men had looked worried about something.

At five o'clock the Red Cross woman signalled that Ilse could go. She took her coat from the peg, trying to flex some feeling back into her raw, swollen fingers. She returned to the admin building and asked for O'Donnell, but he wasn't there.

Her route home took her near to a field where some of the camp inmates slept in tents. She was close to the camp gates when a sudden series of screams erupted amid the rows of tents.

Ilse's first reaction was to flinch; then she realised the screams were of happiness.

An old Jew wearing a ridiculously small fur coat stood with his hands clasped towards heaven in an attitude of profound gratitude, tears flooding his cheeks as a young woman knelt in the dirt, hugging his legs and kissing his knees.

Ilse had never seen two people happier to see each other. All around people stared and the air was suddenly heavy with raw emotion. Some smiled. Others cried. The Jews were hugging and kissing now, touching fingers to each other's faces as if to ensure the flesh each felt was real. The young woman trembled all over and kept making small steps on the spot, as if the ground burnt her feet.

Ilse hurried past, surprised to find her own eyes moist with half-formed tears. Then she felt a hand grab her arm. She spun round, expecting to see O'Donnell.

It wasn't him, though. It was the hag.

'If you run away this time, I'll tell the Tommies who you are,' the old woman hissed.

'I don't know what you're talking about,' Ilse said, but her voice quavered as she spoke.

'Your name is Ilse Drechsler. You were married to Herr Hoffman's son, Rüdiger.'

'Let me go.'

The woman's grip increased.

'Not so high and mighty now, are you? Where's your car and driver? Where's your precious Party, Ilse?'

The soldiers at the gate had begun looking towards them. Ilse pulled the woman out of their sight.

'What do you want from me? Money? Food? I have neither.'

The hag sneered. 'I'm not going to blackmail you, don't worry.'

'Then what do you want?'

'I want you to come with me, to my home. I want to show you something.'

'Don't be so ridiculous.'

'Ridiculous?' The woman's voice rose as she spoke. 'You dare to call me ridiculous, Frau Hoffman?'

She enunciated the last two words with exaggerated clarity. Ilse hissed for her to be quiet. The hag smiled triumphantly.

'If you want me to be quiet, come with me. If not, I will go straight to the Tommies and tell them who you really are.'

Ilse had no choice but to comply. They left the camp and walked in silence along country lanes, back towards the edge of the town, then turned into a street where the buildings were little more than brick boxes filled with rubble and broken wood. Dazed, dusty women sat in the street, half-heartedly trying to scrub clothes in makeshift tubs, while tattered children played.

The hag took Ilse to a set of steps that led down from street level to a cellar door.

'In here,' she said.

The dark room smelt of cabbage and damp brick. There was little in the room apart from a few sticks of furniture and what seemed to be half of a sideboard, its splintered edge pushed up against the wall. A child, wrapped in blankets, lay on a makeshift bed in a corner of the room. The child moaned and whimpered softly as the hag approached. She made soothing noises, then turned and motioned for Ilse to approach.

'This is what you must see,' the woman said and flung back the covers.

Ilse stifled a cry as she saw the wretched, twitching thing beneath the blankets was not a child, but a young man. His legs ended in puckered stumps a foot below his hips and his face was missing an eye and most of the teeth. The remaining orb rolled and darted beneath the scarred lid like that of a frightened horse. Saliva dripped from the jabbering lips and gums.

'There,' the woman said. 'That is all I have left of three sons. No, look at him, you heartless bitch,' she said, when Ilse tried to turn. 'My eldest was killed in Africa. My second died in Italy. And this . . . this is how my youngest came back from the fighting in Normandy. I had everything I wanted in life. Then you Nazis came and turned the world upside down and now I have nothing. Less than nothing. What argument did I ever have with the English or the Americans? Or the Russians? Or even the damned Jews?'

Ilse wanted to flee, but she found herself paralysed by the woman's cold fury.

'What do you want from me?' Ilse said. Her voice trembled as she spoke: she was genuinely afraid of hearing the reply.

The woman looked at Ilse and as she did so the blaze of hatred in her eyes, which had been suppressed before, flared up; her lip curled. 'You were a Nazi, Frau Hoffman. For years you strutted around in front of the ordinary people, making out you Nazis were something special when in reality you were selfish, arrogant shits, the whole lot of you. So, I want you to say sorry. I want you to look at my son, I want you to hold his hand and I want you to apologise.' She came so close now that Ilse could smell her breath, which was rank with acorn coffee. 'You people, you Nazis, you filled their heads with drums and dreams of glory. But this is where you led them. That is why I want you to kneel beside his bed and ask his forgiveness. This is your fault and you must admit it. Then I will decide whether to tell the Tommies who you really are.'

Ilse could not move. It seemed to her that a hundred possible courses of action were flashing through her mind as she stared down at the crippled soldier, but she could not decide which one to take. When the hag put a hand on her shoulder and pushed her down, Ilse's knees buckled. She knelt beside the bed.

The man's scarred hand was hot and dry when she held it. She opened her lips but no words emerged. The woman prodded her.

'I'm sorry,' Ilse whispered.

'Again.'

'I'm sorry.'

The woman knelt beside her.

'Kiss his brow and tell . . . don't you dare try to run, you bitch!'

But Ilse was up now and stumbling towards the door.

'Come back,' the woman hissed. Behind her, the lump on the bed began to rock and cry, flapping his stumps impotently against the wooden board in an effort to rise.

'I'm sorry. I'M SORRY!' Ilse cried, then turned and ran for the door. She fell and grazed her knee on the stairs outside, but she got up again quickly and did not stop running. Children stopped and watched her as she fled along the street, weeping hysterically, but their dead eyes showed no emotion. They had seen far worse things.

11

CAPTAIN BOOTH'S INTEREST in the *Flickschuster* case had confirmed Payne's suspicions. This business with the dead bodies and Lockwood had nothing to do with Nazi partisans. There were no werewolves. Something else was going on, Payne was certain of it. That was why at midday he walked out to the murder house on the Brunswick Road, carrying a canvas sack filled with tools.

It was always good to return to a crime scene. Payne found it helped focus his mind on the facts that had been learned in the intervening period. And he nearly always spotted something new, some tiny detail he had previously overlooked . . . and it was the tiny details that usually made the difference between success and failure in a criminal investigation.

There was a lot of military traffic on the roads today, so Payne walked along the grass verge, the sack thrown over his shoulder. Before he reached the murder house, he walked to a property that was on the hillside opposite, the only one that overlooked the crime scene. Really he should have done this when he first began investigating the matter, but he'd been distracted.

There had been a fence outside the house once: lines of torn earth showed where the fence posts had been ripped out. The house's shutters were all gone and the lower floor windows were boarded up from the inside.

Payne knocked at the ruined front door. When no-one answered, he peered through the chinks in the window boards. An elderly woman's face appeared at a second-storey window.

'*Wie kann ich Ihnen helfen?*' she said.

'Could you come down, please?' Payne said in German. 'I need to ask you something.'

'Are you a soldier?' she said. 'When will you people go back to your homes and leave us in peace?'

Payne thought about showing her his CCG identity card, but thought better of it: telling her he was a policeman might not calm her, given the reputation that the first wave of Allied soldiers to reach Germany had acquired. 'Come down and speak to me; then I will leave you in peace.'

It took the woman a while to remove whatever it was that was holding the front door closed. When she did so, it fell inwards. The old woman was wrapped in a ratty dressing gown. She was trembling, Payne noticed, although the day was not cold.

'How long have you lived here?' Payne said.

'All my life.'

'Who owns that house over there?' he said, pointing towards the murder house.

'Herr Tauber.'

'Where is he?'

She shrugged. 'Someone in the village said he was killed fighting with the *Volkssturm*. I've not seen him since November.'

'Did you ever see anyone come to the house? In the last few months, I mean.'

The old woman thought about this. 'There were some English soldiers, but that was back in May. They only stayed a few weeks. Then people came in a lorry sometimes.'

'A lorry?'

'Yes, a big one, painted green.'

'Who were they?'

'Travellers.'

'Why do you say that?'

'They had suitcases with them. And they were always gone the next day. I think they only ever spent single nights there.'

'How many people did you see?'

'I don't know. Four, maybe five couples. And lights. I saw lights in the house at night sometimes.'

'When?'

'I'm seventy-three. I can't remember things like that. Every few weeks or so.'

'When was the last time?'

'Last night.'

Payne froze.

'Last night? Are you sure?'

The woman nodded.

'Which windows did you see the light in?'

'That one, at the top,' she said and pointed her stick towards the garret window.

When Payne got to the murder house, he went straight to the

well in the garden and prised the top off it with a crowbar. This was something else he should have done when he first began investigating.

It took a bit of brute strength to break the wood free from the padlocks, but he managed it in the end. Payne tossed the wooden cover to one side and put his hand to his nose. The chemical smell he had detected on his first visit was stronger now; there was no doubt it was coming from the bottom of the well.

Covering his mouth with a handkerchief, he shone his torch down into the dark cylinder of the well shaft. The red bricks seemed peppered with white powder, as if someone had thrown sacks of flour down into the darkness. The chemical smell rising from the well was unpleasantly strong and caught in his throat.

Payne rested his hands on the edge of the well-head and dropped a stone into the darkness. The faint thud that sounded a few seconds later told him the well was deep and dry. Payne was unsure whether it was his imagination, but his nostrils seemed for a moment to detect the faint whiff of decay amid the chemical stench. He replaced the crowbar in the sack and headed towards the house. The kitchen door was closed but not locked. It creaked as he pushed it open.

It was pitch black inside the kitchen; the blacked-out windows were all closed.

Had the soldiers left it like that? Payne closed his eyes, trying to picture the kitchen as he'd left it. No, the windows were definitely open then: he remembered shafts of dusky evening sunlight that had crossed the kitchen and shone on the enamel surface of the sink.

Payne used his torch to guide him to the nearest window and fumbled the latch open. Gloom disappeared as summer sunlight flooded the room. He crossed to the other pair of windows and opened those, too. The hatch to the cellar was closed. He opened it and went halfway down the stairs.

It was just as he'd left it.

He returned to the kitchen and headed for the stairs that led to the upper stories, but stopped when he had only reached halfway across the room. The muddy footprints Sergeant Beagley's men had left on the kitchen floor had dried to dust and were still perfectly visible – except in one place near the door, where the dust had been scuffed. It looked as if someone had dragged something across it.

Payne cursed himself for not being more careful. He couldn't be sure whether he'd done it himself while crossing the kitchen to open the window.

'Hello?' he called up the stairs. 'Is anyone there?'

No answer.

He said the same in German and French.

The only response was a faint creak.

Payne crept upstairs a single step at a time, one hand on the wall to steady himself, neck craned upward. His heart was racing. This was not something he'd considered properly. He had always made a habit of returning to murder scenes, but never alone. There was something about places where violent death had occurred, he realised now: some echo or scent to which the animal in human instinct responded.

He paused at the top of the stairs. Sunlight flooded through the shattered windows. He checked each room, but there was no sign of anyone having been there. In the smallest bedroom, he paused and stared at the ceiling. Motes of dust were falling from a crack in the plaster. As he watched them, the beam above him creaked very slightly.

He tiptoed up the stairs to the garret, to find that the solid door at the top was closed. Payne turned the handle and leant his weight against it. The door would not budge. He ran his hand across the rough surface of the door. There was no way he could force it, even if he could get a run at it. He tried the handle again, rattling the door in frustration, then walked back downstairs. The house was utterly quiet now, although it seemed to Payne's jangled nerves the silence was more that of a breath being held.

When a window shutter banged in the wind he nearly jumped out of his skin. Then he was running helter-skelter downstairs, out through the kitchen and on into the daylight in the garden.

He stood in a shaft of sunlight, one hand pressed to his chest, and let the warmth calm him. It had been years since he'd had such a bad case of the heebie-jeebies.

Then he went out and stood on the side of the road. He knew that an army vehicle would be along soon.

Twenty minutes later, two soldiers in a jeep that Payne had managed to flag down returned with a long wooden ladder balanced along the length of their vehicle.

Payne had originally hoped to get some engineers to open the garret door but they were all too busy working on the minefields outside the town, so he had been forced to resort to Plan B. If they couldn't get into the garret via the door, they would have to use the hole in the roof.

The two soldiers shouldered the ladder and followed Payne across the grass towards the back of the house. The sun shone bright and strong; its light glinted on the thousands of tiny fragments of shattered window that lay among the grass.

'That's where I want to get to,' Payne said, indicating the ragged hole in the building's crow-stepped roof.

The elder of the two soldiers was called Bill Ainsley. He scratched his cheek and shook his head like a builder assessing a tricky piece of work. 'Are you sure it's safe up there? Look at those roof beams, they're all cracked. It could be a death-trap.'

'I've been up to the garret on the inside,' Payne said. 'It seems structurally sound.'

The ladder was just long enough to reach the edge of the collapsed roof.

'There you go, sir,' the younger soldier said, when the ladder was in place. 'Do you want me to foot it for you?'

Payne looked up at the ladder. This was one practicality he hadn't considered. It was a long way up. Christ, how high was it? Eight yards? If he fell from that height he'd break his neck.

The young private beside him smiled when he saw the doubt on Payne's face.

'Do you want me to go up there, sir? I used to be a window cleaner, so heights don't bother me.'

'If you wouldn't mind, son. Just see if there's a way to open the door from the inside.'

The young soldier climbed the ladder. He paused at the very top and examined the splintered brickwork around the edge of the hole.

'Seems solid enough,' he said as he pulled himself up onto a roof beam, swung his legs over into the hole and dropped down. A few seconds later, his blond head appeared amid the cracked roof tiles.

'It's a bit of a mess up here,' he said, 'but it seems solid enough.'

'What can you see?' Payne said.

'Well, there's a ruddy great hole just behind where I am standing. But the other half of the room seems fine. There's a load of clothes up here. And suitcases.'

'Suitcases? How many?'

The head disappeared for a moment.

'I can see seven. But there might be more.'

'Can you see if the door opens from the inside? It might be bolted.'

'Will do, sir.'

'And you watch your footing up there, Charlie,' Ainsley said. 'You've come a long bloody way if it's only to go and break your neck now.'

Charlie grinned. 'Don't worry, Bill, it's fine up here. I think the mortar went through and –'

The young soldier's head snapped downward so suddenly, both Ainsley and Payne cried out. It was as if the floor beneath him had collapsed but there was no sound. Then a hand flailed in the opening and Payne heard a muffled scream before the sound was cut short. A faint gurgle followed, then silence.

Ainsley continued to shout the soldier's name as Payne began to climb the ladder, taking the rungs two at a time. The ladder wobbled and jerked beneath him as he neared the top; roof tiles slid away and smashed on the ground below. Payne ignored them as he took hold of the jagged masonry on either side of the hole in the roof and lowered himself down into the garret.

'Charlie?' Payne said. He saw a pair of boots poking from the rubble. There was no answer.

The garret was little more than a triangular crawl space formed by the peak of the roof but there was enough space to walk upright at its centre.

Charlie lay on the floor, totally still. A huge puddle of blood had pooled beneath his head and throat. Payne knelt beside him, felt for a pulse. There was none. Then Payne lifted the boy's chin, and drew his breath when he saw the horizontal rent in his throat that had severed both carotid artery and windpipe.

How the hell had that happened? Had he slipped and impaled himself on something? Payne stood . . .

. . . and the figure pounced, rising up from behind a pile of rubble with a terrible cry.

Payne caught a momentary glimpse of motion through the fallen beams, then cried out as he realised the face rushing at him was formed of patches of leathery skin, the lips sewn shut with thick loops of twine; animal eyes blazed from the ragged eyeholes and then the man-thing was upon him, pushing him backwards as it hissed and wailed, a shrill German voice that screamed *'BlasphemouscuntI'llkeepyouawakewhileIcutyou!'*

Payne put his hands up to protect himself, but the thing swung the rock it was clutching and struck Payne on the side of the head. He stumbled backwards, fell, and landed on his buttocks with a thud. His teeth rang with the impact of the rock and he tasted blood; his head swam and his vision blurred.

The thing came at him now with a huge knife, slashing at the air, but Payne managed to kick out and catch it a painful blow on the shin. He heard a piercing scream of pain and then the creature was gone. Payne heard a key rattle and a door open and close. Footsteps sounded on the wooden stairs.

Payne's head swam as he stumbled to the breach in the roof and shouted down.

'Bill, get your rifle and go round to the front. He's getting away.'

Payne tried to lift himself up through the hole in the roof, but his hands slipped on the jagged edge of the breach and he cried out as he cut a gash in the fleshy part of his palm. He heard three shots ring out and another of those terrible, high-pitched screams.

Then his head swam, his knees buckled and everything became dark . . .

12

Booth spent the morning helping Professor Svoboda sort through the medical documents he had found at Wolffslust. At midday, he went to get some lunch. On the way back he stopped in on Tubbs Taylor.

'Have you made any headway in ascertaining which unit overran Wolffslust prison, yet?' Booth said. 'Or who this benighted officer was that set everyone free?'

'I'm still collating, actually, Jimmy.'

'Well, I don't want to press you, Tubbs, but I'm going to need something soon. Do you want me to give you a hand?'

'No. I work better alone.'

It was the second time in as many days Booth had asked Tubbs about his progress and for the second time he went away with the impression that Tubbs was dragging his feet. Booth returned to his office and lit a cigarette as he considered the problem. He'd no evidence, of course, so there wasn't really anything he could do about it. The last thing he wanted to do was to confront Tubbs about it. Still, it was a damned nuisance. If there was one thing Tubbs Taylor was good at in life, it was sorting through paperwork, and yet, after two days of ferreting, Tubbs still had nothing for him.

When Booth returned to Professor Svoboda the man's face was clouded with worry.

'I've had a chance to peruse some of these documents now, captain,' he said. 'They are absolutely fascinating. And highly incriminating of the medical staff involved.

'As we feared, this medical project was indeed commissioned by the *Ahnenerbe*, under the auspices of a psychiatrist, one Doctor Hans Wiegand. The project began sometime in 1940 at the Institute of Racial Hygiene in Brunswick. However, as a result of the damage caused by the October 14th air attack on the city last year the project was then moved to the cellar of Wolffslust prison.'

Booth looked at the documents Svoboda handed him. 'What was this Wiegand up to then?'

'It seems the original thrust of his research was to determine where the psychological breaking points were in a sample of men, with a view to finding out how much strain combat troops could stand. I suppose the fundamental purpose was to discover how much horror a man could take before he ceased to function psychologically.

'However, as the war progressed, the thrust of the research changed. It seems that from 1942 this Doctor Wiegand began to concentrate solely on SS men who had broken down as a result of their duties. That is why you found so many men who had belonged to the Einsatzgruppen or were concentration camp guards. It was these experiences that had caused them to break. And the SS hierarchy wanted to know whether this 'weakness' was due to hereditary or genetic factors. Could it be assessed and measured? Could it be isolated? Could it be stopped? That is why the genealogy of the patients was studied in such obsessive detail. After all, in their view, the Einsatzgruppen were only killing animals, *Lebensunwertes*

Leben. Do you know what that means? Life unworthy of life. That is the classification that was applied to those deemed racially unsound by the Nazi regime.'

'So, The *Ahnenerbe* wanted to know why their racial thoroughbreds had become so skittish?'

'Precisely.' Svoboda handed Booth another sheaf of paper. 'As you can see, the patients' breakdowns took a variety of forms. Some showed signs of hysteria – crying, nightmares, bed-wetting, insomnia – while others were deemed to have enjoyed the killing duties too much. They became, in the words of the report, *'demi-human predators'* given to extremes of violence deemed unsuitable even by their SS overlords. We must not forget how prudish Herr Himmler was. By his own warped standards he considered himself a civilised man. His SS butchers were expected to spend their days killing but then return to their families in the evening as if nothing had happened.'

'So what happened to these men?'

'It seems Wiegand's 'patients' were subjected to the most extreme forms of psychiatric stimuli: electric shocks, immersion in iced water, the film images that first alerted you that something was going on. Some were given lobotomies, others were sterilised via radium injections in the testicles. Their responses were then studied.'

'But how could this Doctor Wiegand get away with it if these men all belonged to the SS?'

'You mentioned you had discovered a discrepancy in the dates of the men's deaths. These men, once brought into the project, were not to survive it. That is why the officially recorded dates of their deaths precede the dates on the medical records by a few days or weeks. They faked the actual death dates.'

'Could they do that?'

'You may have noticed that many of these documents were stamped by the SS *und Polizeigericht zur besonderen Verwendung*. The Extraordinary SS and Police Court was a secret tribunal convened to deal only with highly sensitive issues which were desired to be kept secret even from the SS itself. Basically, it could do whatever it wanted.'

Svoboda handed Booth the last of the files.

'According to the records, the patients were liquidated once they were no longer useful to the programme. However, it seems Wiegand had between two and four subjects being tested at any one time and that his work continued right up until the end of April 1945.'

'Which means one or more of these men could have been at Wolffslust when the British overran the prison?'

Svoboda nodded.

Booth blew air as he sorted through the paperwork, his eyes lingering on the words *demi-human predators*.

He needed to warn Ursula.

Svoboda began to speak again when both men became aware of shouting and a commotion outside. A jeep shot past Booth's window, beeping its horn. He opened the window and called to a soldier.

'What the devil is going on, Private?'

The soldier's expression betrayed a mixture of excitement and anger.

'Werewolves, sir. They've killed another one of our lads. Slit his throat by all accounts.'

PART THREE

I

LITTLE OTTO SNUCK in by the coal chute. Then he went upstairs to wait for Suttpen.

He had lost it all: the house, the clothes and jewellery, the suitcases, the travel documents: ten weeks of work gone, just like that. He touched his fingertips to the scratch on his face, to the place where the Mask of Many had been ripped away. That was the bitterest loss. The mask had required months of patient work, slicing and drying and stitching.

It had all happened so quickly. He'd killed the first blasphemer that had entered his sanctuary, high up in the rafters of the house. But when the second came Little Otto had known the game was up and fled down the stairs, out through the kitchen door and across the lawn.

How he had wailed when the edge of the mask caught on a branch and he felt it tear from his face. He'd been running so fast that he was several steps past it before he could stop and turn back. Then bullets had begun to snick the ground beside his feet and the air had filled with the whipcrack report of rifle fire, forcing him to flee, wailing and screaming as he did so . . .

Little Otto had first killed as a young man, but it had been a noisy, messy affair that had given him no pleasure. He knew it was wrong but when the urge came, it gave him no rest until it was satisfied, so he preyed upon drunks and tramps and whores, the human refuse of Germany's industrial cities. He had longed to spend time with them afterwards, to press his face to theirs and feel the heat slowly fade from them, but it was too risky. It was impossible to obtain the privacy he needed in order to enjoy the experience fully. The police were always sniffing around.

That was after the first war, when Germany had become a republic. When the Nazis arrived on the scene, he was initially dismissive of them. How could he not be? In the early days, they were nothing but brown-shirted thugs, brawling and breaking bones with their hobnail boots. But when Otto had first seen men from the SS on parade, resplendent in their ebony and silver plumage, he knew he had found his place within the new order.

When war came they had trained him as a medical orderly and sent him to the eastern front, but not to take part in the war. Little Otto was part of one of the special commands charged with cleansing the conquered territories of Jews. It had been a crude and ugly business, the spirit of Nazism made manifest. Like the other men, Little Otto had dulled himself with alcohol and got on with it as best he could, but the Jews always seemed to sense what awaited them and they filled the air with their crying and religious whimpers as they were made to dig the pits.

The experience had inflamed the unquiet voices in Little Otto's head and when the urge to kill returned, it was a hundred times stronger. He could no more stop it now than he could stop himself from breathing . . .

Otto tensed when he heard the rumble of a vehicle approaching.

He could start a new mask by killing Suttpen, he thought, but then decided against it. Suttpen was big and strong. Otto would have to slice him quickly and he never liked working with bodies that were messy with blood.

No, killing Suttpen was a necessity, nothing more: the bastard could ruin everything. Suttpen had been out at the camp that morning, arguing with the Irishman. And he'd confronted Otto, hissing in his cheap pimp's voice that he knew what Otto had been up to and that he wanted his cut.

No, Otto would not wear anything made from Suttpen. Besides, Seiler had more travellers for him. He would start his new mask with them. Then he would deal with the doctor and move on.

Headlights flashed across the window. A vehicle stopped outside. Otto wrapped his big fingers around the handle of his killing knife. So Suttpen wanted his cut, did he?

Otto would give the bastard that all right.

2

I<small>T RAINED THAT</small> night. Ilse hardly noticed. She was exhausted. The experience with the woman and her crippled son had drained her last reserves. She built the fire up when she came home, wrapped herself in blankets and drank tea and whisky, but she continued to tremble all over. It was one thing for the Tommies to despise her, but how could a German woman hate her so?

She drank far more whisky than she should have. Eventually, she slipped into unconsciousness and was released from her troubled thoughts.

At daybreak, she woke suddenly with her head swimming and her mouth filled with saliva. She rushed to the kitchen door, stumbled outside and vomited. That calmed her nausea, although her mouth was foul with the taste of whisky and tobacco. She leant against the wall.

People were moving on the road that passed the end of Ilse's garden, some going eastwards, some towards the west. The grass sparkled as the sunlight picked out droplets of water. The wind smelt clean and fresh.

She laughed as a thought occurred to her: she would probably be better off if she set up a tent and slept in the garden. The air inside the farmhouse was thick with the cloying smell of mould and damp rubble. She turned and headed back towards the house.

That was when she saw that the muddy ground outside the kitchen door was covered with fresh footprints, the kind a man wearing boots would make.

She caught her breath in fear as she saw now that the trail of footprints led from the woodland straight up to the kitchen door and then back again. A half-remembered dream came to her of someone knocking at the door during the night. She shivered as she realised it wasn't a dream.

Could it have been Booth? No, he had been on duty. Who was it, then?

It was probably only some refugee seeking shelter from the rain, she told herself. People saw the building and assumed no-one lived there. After all, it was a ruin. She examined the boot prints. It looked as if only one man had come. Still, that was bad enough. He might come back.

Ilse went inside and sharpened the largest of the kitchen knives. Then she checked that the locks on all the windows and doors were sound.

She was actually glad when the Polack arrived. He came earlier than usual, dragging a huge bundle of firewood behind him. He accepted Ilse's greeting, then set to work stripping the branches of twigs, carefully collecting them in a wicker basket that Ilse gave him.

Later that morning, she found the Polack dragging a huge water butt round to the front of the house. She asked him what he was doing, but his response was incomprehensible. At the front of the property the house had collapsed in such a way that the rubble formed a steep slope that ran up to the undamaged portion of the roof. The Polack rolled the empty butt up this slope. Ilse noticed he had a length of rope coiled around his shoulder and a hammer and nails tucked into his belt. Once more she asked him what he was doing, but this time the Polack did not seem to hear her, so intent was he on trying to balance the water butt upon a ledge of relatively flat rubble.

She left him to it and went inside to make herself tea. The rest of the morning was filled with the sound of hammering and sawing and the crunch of the Polack's boots on the rubble slope.

At midday, Ilse heard a new sound, the clanking of metal. She went outside and saw that the Polack had managed to secure the water butt close to the edge of the flattened ledge with lengths of shattered roof beam. He had also taken pieces of metal pipe from the house's ruined plumbing and strapped them together. One end of the pipeline was attached to the water butt; the other ended in a shower nozzle.

The Polack had stripped to the waist and was carrying buckets of water from the stream at the bottom of the garden. When he saw Ilse staring at his contraption he became agitated and, even though Ilse could not understand a word he was saying, she got the distinct impression he was telling her she had spoiled a surprise.

For another hour, Piotr trudged back and forth, carrying brimming buckets from the stream, one in each hand. Finally, his mangled face appeared at the window and he beckoned for Ilse to come with him.

She went outside. Piotr was hopping from foot to foot in excitement. She saw that the final section of the pipe had a lever attached to it, close to the shower nozzle. He motioned for her to open the lever.

When she did, there was a faint gurgle – and then water began to spurt from the shower head.

It was a ramshackle contraption – water leaked from a dozen fissures along the length of pipe and the spray that emerged from the shower-head was little more than a trickle – but it worked. Ilse could not help smiling as she held her hand beneath the water, angling the shower-head back and forth.

Piotr made motions for her to undress.

'You're mad if you think I'm going to undress in front of you,' she said, but her irritation faded when Piotr greeted her refusal with such a look of such wide-eyed bemusement she realised there had been nothing salacious about his sugges-tion. Even so, Ilse waited for the boy to leave before she began searching for the lump of scented soap she had brought with her from Berlin.

She started to undress next to the shower, but felt horri-bly exposed, so she waited until the sun had set and dark-ness had come before she went back to it and stripped naked. The ground was warm beneath her bare feet and the moon-light shone silver on her pale skin as she opened the lever and stepped beneath the stream of water.

The water was freezing cold and emerged in a dribble – but that feeble jet of water seemed to Ilse a luxury the like of which she had not felt for an age. She allowed the water to play across her whole body, then shut off the tap and soaped herself, covering her skin in a wonderful lather of scented suds. She stood for a while enjoying the smell, then washed the soap off and wrapped herself in a bathrobe.

Clean, at last. How long had it been since she could say that? She'd forgotten what it felt like. She felt lighter somehow. *Now* Booth could say she was beautiful. She was a woman again.

The evening air was pleasantly warm, so Ilse smoked a cigarette outside, still wrapped only in a towel, watching clouds scud across the silver face of the moon. Then she dressed and walked barefoot back across the grass to the house.

And stopped.

The kitchen door was open.

Wide open.

She was sure she'd shut it before she went to shower. Her heart raced as she went closer and saw fresh boot prints in the earth by the kitchen step.

'Who is it? Who's there?' she said, cursing her own stupidity.

'Come in and you'll find out, won't you,' a man said in German. Ilse felt her knees weaken as fear gripped her. She'd left the knife inside.

She heard a chair scrape and footsteps sounded on the kitchen floor. A man's figure stepped into the doorway, a burly man in ill-fitting peasant clothing, silhouetted against the flickering light of the fire.

Ilse took two steps back and bent to pick up a rock. The man laughed. The sound stopped Ilse dead.

She recognised that sound.

'Hello, my little *Gräfin*,' Johannes Drechsler said. 'Don't you have a kiss for your own dear brother?'

3

'A<small>H, GOOD</small>, I see you're awake.'

The voice came to Payne through clammy cobwebs of consciousness. His head was full of fuzzy dreams. He blinked and smacked gummy lips, wondering where he was and why he was lying in a bed.

'You've had quite a shock, Detective Inspector,' Captain Booth said.

Payne jerked as memory returned. A terrible sensation of panic filled him, but he could not remember what had caused it. Payne swung his legs over the edge of the bed, gasping. His head ached.

'What happened to me?' he said, touching the lump on the side of this head.

'We were rather hoping you'd tell us, Detective Inspector. We've spoken to the soldier who was with you when the attack occurred, but his report was rather garbled. Do you remember anything about your assailant?'

Assailant? Yes, Payne remembered something now, but the memory seemed fragmented and unreal, like some half-recalled nightmare. Payne struggled to concentrate on the facts, to winnow out the false information fear and surprise had caused him to register.

'There was a man in the garret of the house,' he said

slowly, speaking for his own benefit as well as Booth's. 'He must have been there when I arrived at the house and was therefore trapped by my presence. I sent a soldier up into the garret. Whoever was there attacked him, slit his throat. When I followed the young soldier up, the same man attacked me. He hit me with a stone. I must have passed out.'

'What did this man look like?'

That was the bit Payne was trying to focus on. The only images he had were grotesque and distorted. 'He wore a mask, I think. A mask made of leather.' Payne stretched. 'How long have I been unconscious?'

'They brought you in yesterday evening. It's the afternoon of the next day now. Here, let me get that for you,' Booth said, when Payne reached a tremulous hand towards the water pitcher beside the bed. 'You've missed all the excitement in the interim.'

'Excitement?'

'Colonel Bassett is convinced you were attacked by werewolves. He's turned the whole district upside down. Random searches, roadblocks, patrols. And the curfew's been brought forward by two hours. Some of the men are joking it's the most work they've had to do since D-Day.'

Payne sipped water as he listened. His head hurt. 'You don't agree about it being werewolves, though, do you, Captain Booth?'

'No. No, I don't,' Booth said, after chewing his lip. 'I'm convinced now that there is a maniac on the loose, a man from Wolffslust prison. That's why I wanted to come here and speak to you. Why are you investigating Quartermaster Sergeant Suttpen?'

Payne shrugged. 'I've said all along that I suspect he is involved somehow. Whether he has anything to do with the killings is another matter, but I should have brought him in for questioning a long time ago. If Colonel Bassett won't let me speak to him, perhaps you could have the MPs pick him up?'

Booth scratched his cheek. 'There's the rub, Detective Inspector. Quartermaster Sergeant Suttpen has gone AWOL.'

'AWOL? When?'

'No-one knows precisely. I spoke to the MPs and mentioned your suspicions. That was yesterday evening. They went out to speak to Suttpen this morning, but no-one can find him.'

'They waited a whole night before trying to bring him in?'

'To be fair to the MPs, they didn't have a great deal of choice, what with Colonel Bassett blustering and bullying about his wretched werewolves.'

'What happened at the house?' Payne said. 'After I was attacked, I mean.'

Booth's face became serious. 'As you mentioned, young Smith was presumably killed by your assailant. The other soldier, Private Ainsley, managed to loose a few shots as the man ran from the house. Then he ran out to the road and flagged an Army lorry down. After that, practically the whole ruddy garrison was put on alert. It's been bedlam these last twenty hours or so. Most of us have been up all night.'

'What did you do with the suitcases and clothes? And did you notice the well?'

It was only now that Payne realised how strained Booth looked. The captain's face was sallow and grey.

'That's another reason I wanted to speak to you. There's

going to be a conference later on to discuss what we've found at the house. It's really quite an . . . extraordinary situation. You were right to look in the well. I suppose it was you that prised the top off?'

'Yes.'

'By the time I arrived, they'd got you and the dead man out of the garret and taken you off to hospital. Everyone was rushing around, promising vengeance on the Jerries and not really taking a blind bit of notice of anything else. But then I spotted that the well had been opened.

'Well, I took one sniff and knew something was amiss. Dry wells are not supposed to smell like that. Anyway, once the white powder inside the well was identified as quicklime, I sent for a team of engineers. They established that the well was around ten metres deep and dry. Then they sent a man down.'

'What did he find?'

Booth went to speak but words failed him. He ran his fingers through his hair.

'I think it's simpler if you come downstairs to the mortuary and see for yourself.'

When the RAMC medical officer, Shelley, emerged from the mortuary thirty minutes later he was pale and his hands shook. Silas Payne followed him out. He removed his face mask and rubbed away the smear of Vaseline beneath his nose.

Captain Booth had waited for them outside.

'Tell me something, Detective Inspector,' he said, extinguishing his cigarette, 'have you ever seen anything like this before?'

Payne's eyes flickered towards the door to the mortuary. The metal tables with their blanket-covered mounds were visible through the door's rounded window. He shook his head.

'That's what I thought,' Booth said. 'I saw the aftermath of plenty a battle during the war and I've not seen anything that gruesome since Falaise.'

Payne turned to Shelley.

'What are your conclusions?'

Shelley rubbed his long chin. 'You'll understand that as an army doctor I've not really had much experience with autopsies,' he said. 'But we did do a little theory work at Med. school. I've arranged the body parts that were found at the bottom of the well as best I can. Each cadaver has been dissected, post mortem. The dissection follows a similar pattern in each case, with saw cuts made below the knee, at the top of the thigh and below the chin. There are seven bodies in total, four men and three women. Each is complete bar one omission. There are no heads. Not a single one.'

'What does that mean?' Payne said.

'I don't know.'

'How long have they been dead?'

'It's not possible to say with any degree of precision, owing to the effects of the quicklime. That stuff sucks all the moisture out of flesh, causes it to mummify. I would guess two of them died fairly recently, probably within the last three weeks. The other five died before that, although I can't really be specific.

We had a hell of a time cleaning the lime from the body parts: water makes the ruddy stuff caustic.'

Payne had his notebook and pencil out. 'How did they die?' he said.

'Again, I can't say with total certainty. But given that the first two victims – the Waffen SS man and his girlfriend that you found in the cellar of the house – had been strangled, I made a detailed examination of the neck stumps and found indications that the seven victims in the well also died from strangulation.'

'So, our killer drugs his victims, then strangles them. Then he cuts them into little pieces and throws them into the well,' Booth said. 'What possible purpose does it serve?'

Payne shrugged. 'Who can say? Look at the Jack the Ripper crimes. What explanation is there for what he did to those women? And yet, in the killer's mind, the savagery served some purpose. But that's presuming the crimes are related.'

'Surely they must be,' Booth said.

'I agree. But it's dangerous to make assumptions until we have concrete proof.' He turned to Shelley. 'Do any of the bodies have the SS blood group tattoo?'

Shelley shook his head.

'But that doesn't necessarily mean they weren't SS,' Booth said. 'Only fighting troops tended to have the tattoo. Also, the Germans seemed to have used the tattoo less and less as the war went on.' Booth looked at his watch. 'It's nearly time for the conference. We need to tell people what we've found. Do you think it is the same man, Detective Inspector? Is it the *Flickschuster*?'

'It's either the same man or someone who knows of his crimes.'

Shelley lit a cigarette. 'There's something else I'd like to show you before we go to the conference,' he said.

Booth and Shelley followed him upstairs to his office.

Payne shuddered when he saw the leather mask that lay face upwards on a sheet of brown paper in the centre of Shelley's desk. It was the one his assailant had worn.

The mask depicted a human face in a rough sort of a way. The surface of the mask was creased and crumpled as if made of different layers, like papier-mâché. Crude stitching formed a seam along the line of the lips. Payne found himself unable to examine the thing for long: there was something unwholesome about the mask, something that made him shy away from too detailed an examination.

Booth leant down to examine the mask more closely.

'Is that leather?'

Shelley extinguished his cigarette and took a sip of water. 'No. It's human skin.'

Booth jerked upright. 'Surely you're joking?'

Shelley shook his head. 'What you are looking at there is called in dissection a facial mask. An incision is made across the hairline, down along the jaw and across under the chin; the skin is then peeled away downwards from the scalp.'

'But why would anyone create such a thing?' Booth said. 'Have you ever heard of anything like this, Inspector?'

Payne nodded. 'There was a series of murders just before the war. Three prostitutes were beaten to death in the space of a week. They were really savage attacks and in each case some of the victim's fingernails had been pulled out post-mortem.

Then we noticed the girls' hair had been snipped, too. And that was how we caught him, in the end. He had the nails and the hair in an envelope underneath his pillow.'

'But why?'

'It was a type of trophy, a keepsake. These people kill as part of some strange ritual only they understand.'

The three men stood in silence, regarding the mask.

'If it's human skin, why is it so thick?' Payne said after a while.

'Yes, that puzzled me at first, too.' Shelley leant on the table edge and began indicating parts of the mask with the tip of his pencil. 'If you look, there are parts where the mask appears not to coincide. And the eye holes are an odd shape. It took me a while to realise why: there is more than one facial mask here. It's quite possible there are four or five of them, placed one within the other and glued together.'

'Are you saying our man is a doctor?'

'No. But I would say that whoever did this had rudimentary medical knowledge. That's another reason the edges are so ragged.'

Payne thought about the surgical tools he had found beside Konrad Jaeger's body. 'Presumably the killer was about to operate on the two original victims but was interrupted?' Payne said.

'That must be the case,' Shelley said, 'I'm certain of it.'

'I'll tell you something else we can be certain of,' Payne said, looking at his notes. 'Given the ritualistic nature of the crimes, I think our man already has a real taste for killing. He won't ever stop. Not unless we catch him.'

4

THE CONFERENCE WAS held that evening in the main room of the *Rathaus*. All the heads of the military government in Eichenrode were there. The mood inside the room was sombre.

The members of Colonel Bassett's staff had gathered at one end of the large conference table, whispering among themselves. When Booth entered the room, Freddy looked up and for a moment his eyes burned with hostility. Then Freddy began speaking again with Bassett, who was clenching his big fists and nodding as he listened.

Seven suitcases of all shapes and sizes had been placed on the table, together with a mass of male and female clothing. The mask lay next to them on a sheet of brown paper.

'We all know why we're here, so I won't bore you with preliminaries,' Bassett said. 'Another one of my men was killed yesterday. Had his throat slit with a knife. Now, it's perfectly clear to me that this was the work of werewolves. And it's my fault. I want you all to know that. I've been far too lenient.

'Our problems in this area began with cut wires and vandalism and I did nothing. After that, we had pit traps and still I did nothing. Then a CCG man was blindfolded and set loose in a minefield. Only then did I react, but it was already too late. The rot had set in.

'We've been too soft on the Jerries. But I want every man in this room to know that it's going to stop now. I didn't lead my men halfway across Europe only for them to have their throats slit by masked maniacs months after the bloody war ended. We're going to catch this killer in short order. Do I make myself clear?'

Every pair of eyes in the room was fixed on the table. Bassett hadn't led his 'men' anywhere: he'd been appointed by the military government a week after peace was declared.

'Another thing: I don't want a word of this to get out to the Jerries. Not the soldier's death. Not the suitcases. Not the bodies in the well. We can't have them gloating about this.

'Now, I've spoken to the soldier that survived, this Ainsley fellow, and managed to get precious little sense out of him,' Bassett continued. 'I've allowed you to attend this meeting, Detective Inspector, in the hope that you can shed some light on the incident.'

Payne had been staring at the table while Bassett spoke. He began to explain what had happened at the murder house in clear, concise words, but Colonel Bassett interrupted him.

'You say you saw *someone* in the garret of the house. Please be more specific.'

'It was a man. He was wearing a mask. That one there, on the table.'

Each person at the table looked at the leather mask. Bassett was the only one able to fix it with his gaze for any length of time. He turned to Shelley.

'You've given this the once over, Captain Shelley. What are your thoughts?'

Shelley explained what the mask was. A few men at the table winced as he spoke. Colonel Bassett looked at the mask again, and his moustache began to tremble. His cheeks flushed red.

'Disgusting,' he murmured, then repeated the word twice more.

'I've consulted with Captain Booth and Detective Inspector Payne,' Shelley said. 'We do not concur with the opinion that this was the work of werewolves. We feel we are dealing with a deeply disturbed individual, a psychopath.'

Colonel Bassett gave a rumble of displeasure. 'Individual? What the devil are you two talking about, man? There were seven bodies chopped to pieces and stuffed down a well and you think it was one person? This is clearly the work of an organisation.'

Silas Payne shifted in his seat. 'I think it would be foolish to jump to any conclusions until we know the identities of the victims in the well.'

Captain Fredrickson was sitting next to Bassett. He smoothed his dark hair down, looking very smug.

'I think I can shed some light on that, Detective Inspector,' he said. Freddy stood up, opened a file and threw a handful of Red Cross travel permits on to the table. 'We found these among the victims' belongings.'

'So these people were DPs?' Payne said, examining the documents.

'That's the way it looks. Three Poles, two Czechs, a Frenchman and a Dutch woman. Precisely the sort of people werewolves would prey upon.'

'But it makes no sense,' Payne said. 'The other two victims

were Germans. These people could have been, too, travelling on false papers.'

'Or they might have been capos in concentration camps,' Freddy said. 'Or informers. Or spies. Or just unlucky. Thousands of people were killed in the weeks after the war ended. I understand you're used to peacetime policing, Detective Inspector Payne, but I'm afraid this werewolf attack is a little beyond your experience. And, if you'll forgive me, your capabilities. What we have here is clearly the sort of terror tactics the werewolf insurgency was trained to engage in. They exist to promote confusion and dissension and generally do everything they can to ensure the occupation is as problematic as possible. They want to intimidate us. I spoke with a Russian officer when I was in Berlin and you wouldn't believe the things the Jerries got up to out there.'

Colonel Bassett was nodding his head.

'With all due respect, Colonel, ' Booth said, 'Detective Inspector Payne has informed me of the results of his investigation and I, too, have grave doubts as to whether this business represents action by the Werewolf insurgency.'

'Informed you, has he?' Bassett said. 'Well, that just proves this matter would have been better handled by the military from the get-go.'

Payne took a deep breath. 'Perhaps I could continue to pursue my own investigations in parallel with the military response. I believe the army currently has a number of German police personnel in custody. Men from the Kripo criminal police and other security forces. Perhaps –'

'Men from the Kripo *and other security forces*,' Colonel Bassett interrupted. 'You know what the Detective Inspector means by that, don't you, gentlemen? The bloody Gestapo is what he means.'

Bassett rose and rested his meaty knuckles upon the table.

'We all know you've gone cap in hand to the Huns once, Payne. I won't let it happen again, do you understand? As far as I'm concerned, your involvement with this matter is over. Now, I'd like you to leave, if you don't mind. We've army business to discuss.'

The conference rumbled on for another twenty minutes while Bassett and Freddy outlined the military response to the situation. An interrogation centre was to be set up in the centre of town and every German male within a five mile radius to be brought in for questioning.

After the conference, Booth went to find Payne.

'I'm afraid this was always going to happen,' he said. 'There's just no talking to Bassett once he's got an idea into his head.'

'Can we speak to Toth again?'

Booth shook his head. 'Not if he's at Bad Nenndorf. The security there is very tight. Added to that, Colonel Bassett has muddied the waters for us. I'm afraid it's absolutely impossible.'

'What about the policeman, Metzger, the one we read about in the newspaper reports? Can we find him? He ran the original *Flickschuster* investigation.'

'Yes, that's a possibility. If he's in one of the civilian internment camps, the security won't be anywhere near as tight.'

'I'll head out to the Red Cross camp tomorrow and see if I can discover anything about these travel permits. But we need to find out where Captain Fredrickson found them in the first place.'

'There's something else we need to know about Fredrickson, Detective Inspector,' Booth said. 'We need to understand why the hell he is bending the Colonel's ear. It's him that's pushing this werewolf idea, I'm sure of it.'

5

ILSE AND JOHANNES sat opposite each other at the kitchen table, sister and brother together again. For ten minutes, Ilse was genuinely glad to see him. Then she began to notice how different Johannes was now from how she remembered him.

First, there were the scars: a starburst of livid tissue that crossed his jaw-line and another, thick and red, on the back of his hand. They were only the most noticeable blemishes, though; the whole of his being seemed nicked and notched now, like an old ham bone. And his demeanour was different. He had been sly and cheeky as a boy, but what had once been merely a mischievous air had an undercurrent of genuine malevolence to it, now.

The conversation came in spits and spurts. They spoke about their experiences at the end of the war. Johannes said he had deserted at the end of April and had been living in the woods ever since. He did not mention where he had been serving or with which unit.

'You look older, sister,' he said. 'And you're thinner. There's grey in your hair. Just here.' He reached across the table and brushed dirty fingernails through the hair at Ilse's temples. She resisted a momentary impulse to flinch. Something about her little brother scared her now, she realised.

Johannes finished his tea. 'Haven't you got anything

stronger, my *Gräfin*?' he said as he finished his tea.

Ilse shook her head. She was damned if she would share her whisky with him. It irritated her that he kept calling her *Gräfin*, duchess: it had been their father's pet name for Ilse.

Johannes looked at her, eyes hooded. 'Are you sure you don't have any liquor, *Gräfin*?'

'Oh, certainly, what would you like? Shall I open the bar? And stop calling me that. I'm not your *Gräfin*.'

'What would you prefer I call you, then? Ilse Hoffman?'

He laughed at the way the sound of her real name made her flinch. 'Yes, I'm sure the English solider you're fucking would love to know all about Rüdiger. Who did you tell him you were?'

Ilse ignored the question. 'What do you know about that?'

'You don't think I would just saunter up to the house and knock, do you? I've been watching you for days, waiting for the right moment. And don't worry, I won't harm your Englishman. I've enough problems as it is. You've done well to get one so quickly, though. You were always a little sharp for most men's tastes. What was it father used to say about you – 'All thorns and no rose'?'

'He never said such a thing.'

Johannes shrugged. 'Believe what you like.'

More silence. Then Ilse said, 'Do you know anything about Cousin Ursula?' as she watched Johannes's reaction carefully.

'I know quite a bit about her, actually. She used to write to me when I was in Russia. And I used to write back. That was one part of the week the boys really looked forward to, listening to Cousin Ursula's love letters. They used to help me compose the responses. I think the dumb bitch thought I was going to marry her.' He laughed, a harsh bark of a sound.

'That was wicked of you, Johannes, to taunt poor Ursula like that. She came here. To this house, I mean. Men at the frontier had raped and beaten her. She died of her injuries a few days ago.'

If the information meant anything to Johannes, he did not show it. He picked food from between his teeth with a finger-nail.

'Where will you stay tonight, Johannes?'

Again the crooked smile. 'Do you mean to say I can't stay here?'

'Of course not. There's no room.'

'But this is my house, too, now. And I intend to sleep here.'

Ilse said nothing. Johannes watched her then said, 'Don't worry. I've no intention of staying here for long. Or in Germany for that matter.'

'Where will you go?'

'Spain. Then on to South America. The Tommies are hanging SS men like me.'

'Well, you would do well not to hang around too close to Eichenrode. Someone might recognise you. And the Tommies are searching houses. They think there are partisans here con-tinuing to fight. People have been murdered.'

Johannes nodded, as if the information pleased him. 'I can get going tomorrow. If you're prepared to help me, that is.'

'Help you? What can I do?'

'There are people here that can get me the documents I need: ID papers and travel permits.'

'And you want me to speak to these people? I have no influence with –'

'I want you to pay. I need some of your money.'

Ilse laughed. 'And what makes you think I have any money?' Her laughter grew as she waved towards the cracks in the wall, the piles of rubble, the fractured roof beam. 'Oh, that really is wonderful, Johannes. Money? Yes, you're right, how much would you like? Did you not hear? I really am a *Gräfin* now and this is my castle.'

Johannes peeled the skin from another potato and watched her in silence until her laughter faltered. For a moment, fear gripped Ilse. Did he know about the box buried in the garden?

No, he was bluffing. He must be.

'You can't really believe I have any money, Johannes,' she said when the silence became uncomfortable. 'It was all I could do to get out of the Warthegau with the clothes I wore. You've no idea what it was like for civilians when the Russians broke through. It was chaos. I had to run for my life, literally.'

Johannes held the strips of potato skin in the palm of his scarred hand, crushed them into a single mass and swallowed them. 'But you didn't run straight here, though, did you? You said yourself you went to Berlin.'

Ilse felt her face blush. 'What of it?'

'Remember when I visited you in the Warthegau? Rüdiger told me about his deposit box at the bank. His escape plan, he called it. Of course, back then he was thinking about what would happen if he ever fell out of favour with the Party, wasn't he? But I bet that was the first thing you went to collect when you got to Berlin. In fact, I'm willing to bet that was the whole reason you went there in the first place.'

'I don't know what you're talking about, Johannes.'

'Yes, you do. Don't think I can't spot when you're

lying, sister. And don't try to hide your face by looking out of the window. You know we could always read each other.'

He laughed when she refused to turn.

'What do you need with travel permits, anyway?' she said, more to fill the silence than anything. 'You can go cross country. Travel at night. You're a soldier. Live off the land.'

Johannes laughed. 'It's amazing how quickly those words come to the lips of those who've never tried it. Live off the land? Live off what, precisely, when every turnip from here to the Pyrenees is probably already dug up. There are millions of people on the road, now. You must have seen them. They are like ants, everywhere at once, on the roads, in the woods, crossing fields, on the riverbanks. There is no land left to live off.'

After that pronouncement, Johannes took firewood – more than Ilse would have used for a whole week – and built the fire up to a roaring blaze. Then he took a tattered blanket from his gunny sack, spread it out before the hearth and lay down and slept. Just like that. He had no pillow, but within seconds his breathing slowed and he was deeply asleep.

The flames cast flickering light onto the gaunt angles of her brother's face. Ilse watched him sleep, then went to stand on the porch. The moon was nearly full and bathed the country-side with silver-white light. To the east, lights shone amid the dark bulk of the town, serving only to highlight its cracked and irregular skyline.

Winter was around the corner, the harsh, unforgiving winter of northern Germany. Lord, how would she survive then? She had Booth, but what would happen if he was recalled to England? Would Booth look after her? Marry her? Take her with him?

That was about the best she could hope for, but what would that be like? If the English here hated Germans, what would they be like in the towns and cities that had been bombed?

No, there was no future with Booth. He was a pleasant young man. In other circumstances, she could have loved him. But not here, not now. She would not be dependent on a man's goodwill for her own happiness.

She stood and smoked a cigarette, weighing the pros and cons of the situation.

Johannes was right. She *had* gone to Berlin to get Rüdiger's box from the bank vault.

She'd been lucky to get all this way without having the box stolen. When the soldiers took her car at gunpoint she'd thought she would lose the box, but they'd never thought to check her luggage. Ilse had seen in their eyes that all they were thinking of was saving their miserable hides and so she had unloaded her suitcases from the boot, then handed them the keys. It had given her a secret thrill to think of the riches that were right under their noses. All told, she had eight thousand dollars and some jewellery.

But Johannes knew. She could be sure of that; they *could* read each other. He knew she had the money here, hidden, just as she knew Johannes would stay until he got his own way. And there was that something more to her brother, now, a part that was deep, dark and different, the part that said, *This time I am asking. Next time, I will simply take.*

She looked out at the darkness for a moment longer, then turned and headed inside.

She sat on the stool beside the fire and shook Johannes. He emerged from sleep with such a sudden jolt that Ilse jumped back, stifling a scream: for a moment, there was no recognition in his eyes, only a leer of bestial aggression.

'It's me, Johannes. Ilse. Your sister.'

Johannes's hand fell from the hilt of his hunter's knife, but his eyes remained narrowed.

'Don't ever wake me like that again. What do you want?'

'You can have your money, Johannes. But I have one condition.'

Johannes yawned. Then he smiled. 'I would expect nothing less, my *Gräfin*. Name your price.'

'I want to go with you.'

6

PAYNE COULDN'T SLEEP. Each time he closed his eyes he saw the young soldier's face emerging from the hole in the roof, waving cheerfully and then disappearing from view. By now, the boy's commanding officer would have written the letter home. Payne could imagine the mother, hair-scarf tied above her head, scrubbing at a washboard, nattering across the fence in the back garden about what she would do when her little Charlie came home.

He'd had men die before – three of the officers at Payne's station had been killed during the war – but this was different. Deaths in peacetime held meaning again. In some ways that was a thing good, he supposed. For six years, death had been a mere statistic. Now, when someone died, once again whole communities would grieve, whole countries. A murder would become front page news once more.

Payne sat in his pyjamas, feeding wood into the potbellied stove, a blanket wrapped around his shoulders, listening to the patter of rain outside. It was times like this, in the deep, lonely reaches of the night, that he was best able to think.

Colonel Bassett's emergency council had confirmed Payne's worst fears. Bluster and bullying was all very well in the barrack house, but it was fatal to a police investigation. With his checkpoints and house searches and random interrogations, Bassett was about as subtle as a drunken elephant.

There was no arguing with the man, though. He'd had two full companies of men mobilised. They were sweeping the woods and countryside around the murder house, knocking on doors, waking Germans, watching roads and generally making a nuisance of themselves everywhere within a five-mile radius of Eichenrode. Tomorrow, they would be rounding up German civilians in order to question them.

But that was beside the point. There was a killer on the loose, a man who killed to satisfy his own strange needs.

Payne considered what he knew of the killer's *modus operandi*.

He kept trophies: that was the key. Not just the mask, but the suitcases and clothes, too. But why had the victims been carrying full suitcases in the first place? That was crucial to understanding what had taken place in the murder house.

Payne thought about the Red Cross travel permits. The old woman in the house across the way had mentioned a lorry arriving and seeing people with suitcases. The victims must have been expecting to travel somewhere, somewhere beyond Europe most likely: that would explain why the killer was able to give them vaccination shots. The travel documents were the key, Payne realised. He needed to discover if Konrad Jaeger, a known war criminal, had also been travelling with Red Cross permits. And he needed to look into Suttpen's disappearance as well, to determine whether the man had bolted or been silenced.

Eventually Payne dozed in his chair. The sun woke him, creeping above the horizon, casting the bright, golden light that often follows a night of rain. A little after eight, a soldier knocked at the door with a message from Major Norris: Payne's new tyres had arrived, sent straight from Army HQ.

Miracles would never cease.

Payne borrowed a jack from the army unit billeted across the way and changed the tyres. Then he drove out to the Red Cross transit camp.

From a distance it looked a little like a military camp; up close, though, you started to notice the people were not soldiers.

Some sat listlessly by the roadside; others wandered in the shade beneath the trees. There were men, young and old, and women of all ages. Children played on the dust esplanade at the centre of the camp, kicking stones. Everyone was dressed in a curious motley of garments. Some wore suits and shirts and long coats, while others still wore the striped pyjamas that they had been issued in the concentration camp. White DDT powder leaked from trouser legs and shirt sleeves as they walked. A Belgian nurse attended him when he arrived at the camp gates and offered to show him around. Payne said nothing about the travel documents found at the murder house. He wanted to find out how the camp was run before revealing his hand.

'We've got all sorts here, Detective Inspector,' the nurse said. 'Armenians, Poles, Latvians, Lithuanians, Estonians, Yugoslavs, Greeks, Ukrainians, Czechoslovaks. The first thing we do when they arrive is to register them. Then we classify them according to their pre-war nationality and sort out whether they are able to return to their own countries. We also check them for signs of disease and malnourishment. Then we try to find information on missing relatives. It's all very complex and chaotic at the moment. I don't think humanity has ever had to try and sort out a mess on this sort of scale before.'

'What do you do after you register them?'

'We shower them, dust them down with DDT and try to get them some decent clothing.'

'What about travel permits? Who can get those?'

'That depends on each case. Many of these people were brought to Germany against their will and don't have any documentation. Others have only the identity papers given to them by the Nazis, which obviously no-one wants to use anymore.'

'But when are these travel permits issued?'

'We try to encourage people to stay put, simply to keep them off the roads. But obviously, people are looking for relatives, so when they've tried one camp, they head on to the next. And people of certain nationalities try to stay together. Certain camps get a reputation for having large populations of one ethnic group and then more of the same people arrive at them. They need some form of ID to get them past the checkpoints and across the new internal borders in Germany.'

They were in the centre of the camp now. Here were neat rows of marquee tents distributing food and outdoor showers. Nurses and volunteers stood behind trestle tables upon which sat steaming vats of porridge.

Payne paused as something caught his eye. Behind the tables, there was a pile of hessian sacks. Some bore the Red Cross symbol. Others had British Army markings. He walked closer and examined one of the sacks. It bore the markings of the Army depot in Eichenrode.

'Do you know a man called Suttpen?' Payne said. 'Jacob

Suttpen? He's quartermaster sergeant here.'

'Yes, of course,' the nurse said. 'We get some of our supplies from him.'

Payne nodded. He'd found his link between Suttpen and the camp. He needed to find the quartermaster sergeant. He was certain the man was at the centre of this whole business.

'Could you show me where the travel permits are issued?'

'Of course. You can speak to Mr O'Donnell as well. He runs the camp.'

The admin office of the International Committee of the Red Cross was like Bedlam: there was no other way to describe it. Hundreds of people crowded the building and every one of them seemed to Payne to speak a different language. The whole spectrum of human emotion was visible within a few feet of the door: anger, despair, joy, apathy.

A man with a lilting southern Irish accent was in charge. He introduced himself as Mr O'Donnell, but any trace of affability disappeared when Payne said he was a British policeman.

'What is it you want exactly, Mr Payne?' he said, interrupting Payne's attempt to explain precisely that. *He made a point of calling me Mister, as well*, Payne thought. The man had been drinking, Payne was certain. As a teetotaller, the smell of spirits on another's breath always hit him like a slap in the face.

'I'd like to know how a person goes about obtaining a Red Cross travel permit.'

O'Donnell's lips pursed. 'It's a complicated process. But as you can see we are rigorous in checking each applicant before the documents are actually issued.'

Yes, Payne could see that. The chaotic line outside fed into perhaps half-a-dozen smaller lines inside the building. At the end of each one Red Cross personnel sat behind desks with translators whose function seemed to be to question the refugees and check that each person was actually a native speaker of the language they claimed as his or her own.

Payne had arranged for a list of the seven names found on the travel documents at the murder house to be sent to the camp. He asked O'Donnell about it.

The Irishman shook his head. 'We've no record of issuing travel permits to any of those people.'

'Are you sure?'

'Didn't you just hear me? I had one of my nurses look through the records, then I double-checked it myself personally. Those people were not issued travel permits at this camp.'

The Belgian nurse was still with them. At mention of the travel documents, she had looked away suddenly.

'And yet the permits exist,' Payne said, dividing his attention between O'Donnell and the nurse now. 'And they've got the official stamp. I've seen them myself.'

'What you have or haven't seen, Detective Inspector, is beside the point. There is no record of these people having passed through this camp.'

O'Donnell made it clear that he considered their business concluded and began walking away, but Payne was far from finished. He caught O'Donnell up in a couple of strides and kept pace beside him.

'Is it possible there could have been some mistake? Perhaps the documents were issued in another camp but stamped here? Or could you have lost the relevant records?'

'I have neither the time nor the inclination to explain the intricacies of Red Cross procedure to you, Mister Payne. There are millions of people currently without any form of valid documentation.'

'How would someone obtain them illicitly?'

O'Donnell stopped. His bloodshot eyes blazed. 'What the devil are you insinuating?'

'Is there a register?'

'Yes, there's a register, but I'm damned if I'll let you look at it.' O'Donnell's face flushed a yet deeper shade of carmine. 'I know all about the British police, Mr Payne. You and your fucking G-men and Black and Tans. They smashed some of my brother's teeth out. So if you think I'll tell you anything, you're wrong. As far as I'm concerned, you're not much better than the Nazis.'

With that, O'Donnell turned and stormed away, waving a hand in the air and shouting curses in Gaelic.

The nurse held Payne's eyes for a moment until O'Donnell turned and shouted for her to follow him.

She hurried away.

7

THAT DAY HAD turned into a nightmare for Captain James Booth.

During the morning, Colonel Bassett's patrols began to round up German civilians and bring them to a temporary interrogation facility that that wretch Freddy had set up. As there were only three fluent German speakers on the whole of the staff of the British Military Government in Eichenrode, most of the interrogators had to use German translators which, as far as Booth was concerned, defeated the whole object of the exercise. It was bad enough having to do it in the first place, without knowing the whole thing was a complete waste of time.

The more Booth thought about it, the stranger it seemed that Freddy would be such an enthusiastic adherent to this werewolf idea. A galumphing bully Freddy might be, but he wasn't stupid; yet by promoting the idea so forcefully Freddy had actually created an enormous amount of work for himself, something that he would normally have assiduously avoided.

Booth conducted more than a dozen interrogations during that morning. At lunchtime, he took a break and motioned for Tubbs to follow him out of the interrogation building.

'Have you had any luck finding that officer's name, yet, Tubbs? The one at Wolffslust?'

For a brief moment, Tubbs looked guilty. Then he shook his head.

Booth stepped closer and dropped his voice. 'What's going on, Tubbs? I just don't understand it. I can't help feeling you're dragging your feet on this one.'

Tubbs had a way of twisting his wedding ring when he became nervous or upset. He was doing it now.

'Come on, Tubbs, out with it. I know something's up. You should have found that information for me days ago.'

Tubbs sighed. Then he said, 'The truth is I've known all along who the officer was at Wolffslust. And actually, it was *officers*. There were two of us.'

It took Booth a moment to realise the implications of what Tubbs was saying. 'Do you mean to say you were there?'

Tubbs nodded. 'Freddy and I went into Eichenrode with the advance guard. I think Freddy wanted to make sure he got decent billets. When we reached the town some combat troops radioed in about the prison, so we went there to take charge of the situation.'

'You mean to say you had a hand in causing all that chaos?'

Tubbs shrugged. 'Most of the prisoners were already free when we arrived there. Anyway, the looting and vandalism were already going on.'

'Why didn't Freddy stop it?'

'I think the situation went to Freddy's head a little, especially when we found some of the Allied prisoners in the medical ward. They were terribly thin. Freddy went wild after that and ordered all the prisoners to be released. He even organised a little ceremony. He had the men of each nationality march through the prison gates singing their national anthem, led by a flag bearer: first the Russians, then the Dutch, the Belgians, the Poles and the French.'

Booth was thinking aloud now. It all suddenly made sense.

'And presumably that is why Freddy is so hell bent on convincing Colonel Bassett that we have a werewolf problem here? Because it's just possible that Freddy has released a bloody maniac?'

Tubbs shook his head. 'No, that isn't it. I don't think Freddy believes in your killer theory at all.'

'Then what on earth is the problem?'

The wedding ring was turned full circle. Tubbs's gaze returned to the floorboards. He seemed to be fighting some internal battle. When he sighed, it was a sigh of capitulation. He looked up.

'Freddy doesn't want attention focused on Wolffslust, because he shot two of the German guards.'

'What?'

'When we got to the prison, there were still two German guards locked in a room. Freddy stood by as the prisoners pelted the men with stones. Then he marched the guards round to the back of the prison and shot them both in the head. They're buried in the woods, somewhere close to the walls. That's why he fudged the report. He realised there might be consequences.'

'Why on earth didn't you say something before, Tubbs?'

Taylor looked towards the window. His eyes were wet with tears now.

'Do you know what Freddy and I found when we came into Eichenrode? The bodies of three young German boys, hanging from the trees on the main street, tongues poking out, blue in the face. They couldn't have been more than ten or eleven years old. They'd tried to contact the Allies and tell them the best way to enter the town to prevent any more killing, so the town commandant had them executed. The war was hours from ending and yet he still killed three children.

'I made a note of the bastard's name: Glasisch. He walked into captivity a few days later. I had to interrogate him. Do you know what he said to me? *Endlich ist mein Krieg vorbei.* At last, my war is over. He even tried to shake my hand.'

Tubbs stared at his right hand, turning it from side to side as if it were now forever sullied. Tubbs gave a great gulp and his voice became ragged. The tic in his eye trembled a few times, the way Booth had noticed it did when Tubbs was really upset.

'Why didn't you tell someone about Freddy?'

'Do you think I was going to dob Freddy in just because he shot a couple of Jerries? Do you know what I saw at Belsen when I first got there? The Germans deserve to be punished, Jimmy.'

Tubbs was going to say more, but stopped mid-word. He looked upwards and the light reflected the tears in his eyes. Then he began weeping. It happened so suddenly it took Booth a moment to react. He stood and put a hand on Tubbs's shoulder and the man seemed to unravel before his eyes.

'You're all done in, aren't you, old man? It's OK.' Booth fetched whisky and poured Tubbs a stiff measure. Tubbs drank it down before he got up and dried his eyes.

'I'm sorry,' he said. 'I shouldn't have told you that. About Freddy I mean. I'm going back to the interrogations, Jimmy. Do what you have to about Wolffslust. I just don't care anymore.'

'Tell me one thing, Tubbs. Where did Freddy find those travel permits? The ones at the murder house.'

'They were stitched inside the linings of the suitcases.'

Booth went back to his office. He wouldn't waste any more time on the interrogations. He knew what he would say to Freddy if the bastard tried to make any trouble.

He sighed as he considered what he should do about Tubbs's admission. If he went by the book he should report the matter straight away. But what if Tubbs withdrew his statement? He would be accusing a fellow officer of murder. That wasn't something you could do lightly. He would have to think it through.

A lorry rumbled past outside, bringing more German civilians in for questioning. Booth suddenly felt very tired. He was sick of the Army and everything that went with it. All he wanted now was to find a home for Piotr and then settle down in a quiet part of the English countryside with Ursula. Somerset, perhaps, or Gloucestershire.

At midday he went to the police station and told Detective Inspector Payne about the Red Cross permits.

'We need to find Jaeger's suitcases,' he said, when he'd listened to Booth's explanation.

'How would we do that?'

'Beagley, the sergeant who reported the finding of the first two bodies. We need to find him.'

'Can you be sure he has the suitcases?'

'Someone does, I'm certain of it. Jaeger and his woman had plenty of clothes with them and I'll wager they weren't carrying them in their arms.'

They found Sergeant Beagley standing by the door of a

wooden barrack hut, supervising an entire company of men as they packed belongings and equipment into duffel bags and stripped bedding from bunks. Beagley rolled his eyes when he saw Payne.

'You've a damned nerve to come out here, copper. I've said everything I have to say to you.'

'That's enough in that tone of voice, sergeant,' Booth said, stepping into the barrack hut behind Payne. 'You're to answer Detective Inspector Payne's questions as if you were speaking to an officer. That's an order, sergeant. And stand to attention when you address us.'

Beagley gave Booth a grudging salute.

'Begging your pardon, sir, but my CO spoke with Colonel Bassett and he said I was to go to him if the Inspector came round bothering me.'

Payne stood his ground. Some policemen enjoyed the argy-bargy of police work, but Payne prided himself on getting what he wanted without ever raising voice or hand. 'I hear your unit is being taken back to England, sergeant.'

'Yes. So?'

Payne moved until he was standing shoulder to shoulder with the sergeant. Then he turned his head and said in a low voice, 'Because earlier in the week you lied to me, sergeant, and I mean to know why. You can either tell me now or you can do it when you're back in England. It's your choice, but I'll tell you one thing: as soon as you step off that gangplank in Dover, you *will* be on my turf. I'll have officers waiting for you at the port and they'll take you in for questioning as soon as you leave the ship. This is a major investigation now. What's it to be?'

Payne felt the man bristle. Then Beagley sighed in the deep, weary way people do when preparing to unburden themselves of a secret.

'What do you want to know?' he said.

'Why did you break into the house?'

'We went inside to see if there was anything we could nab. In case you hadn't noticed, the whole of Germany has become one vast Tom Tiddler's ground. Everyone else is going home with their pockets stuffed and yet me and my boys, we've always missed out – mainly because we were too busy fighting.'

'And I presume you found something?'

'Suitcases. There were two suitcases on the floor of the kitchen. They were nice ones, brown leather with big chunky locks. And filled with clothes.'

'So your men removed evidence from a crime scene?'

'They didn't know it was a crime scene. It was just another bombed-out house, like dozens they'd seen before. Most of these lads came into the forces as teenagers and they've had five solid years of war. If they've learned to grab what they can when they can, you can hardly blame them.'

'What did you do with the suitcases?'

'We cracked 'em open and started divvying up the clothing that was inside. Some of it was real nice stuff. Then someone went down into the cellar and . . . well, you know what we found down there.'

'Where are the suitcases now?' Payne said.

It took only a couple of minutes to locate the suitcases; Beagley had been planning to take them back to England with him.

Payne stood the larger of the two suitcases on a table, opened it and examined the silk lining. He saw that at the top right hand corner about four inches of the seam had been carefully unpicked and then re-stitched.

Payne used his penknife to cut the lining open, then turned the suitcase on one end and shook it. A Red Cross travel pass dropped out onto the floor.

'Bingo,' Booth said.

They checked the other suitcase. That, too, contained a travel permit, hidden within the lining of the suitcase.

Payne held the permits up to the light to examine better the passport-sized photos in each.

They were undoubtedly of Konrad Jaeger and the woman whose body had been found in the cellar of the house. Jaeger's travel pass identified him as Tomáš Novák; his nationality was listed as Czechoslovakian. The woman was also described as Czech.

Payne handed the documents to Booth. 'We have our proof. We know now for certain that a man wanted for war crimes has somehow obtained a Red Cross travel pass that could have got him out of the country. I'll bet he had to pay handsomely to get it, too. We also know that Suttpen has links with the Red Cross camp. I think we really need to find out who requisitioned the murder house. I'm willing to bet that Lockwood and Suttpen had something to do with it.'

They drove to the offices of Housing Branch. The clerk was none too pleased to see Payne, but when he saw Booth's uniform his attitude changed. Booth told the man to find the boxes containing the relevant requisition chits. Booth and Payne sat down and began sorting through them.

'Here it is,' Booth said an hour later, handing Payne a file.

According to the file, the murder house was first requisitioned on May 5th 1945 by a combat unit of 30 Corps that had been moving in to occupy the area. That unit had left the house on May 14th. It had then been requisitioned for 'Army Stores' by Regimental Quartermaster Sergeant J. Suttpen on May 19th. The receipt stub was signed by Mr T. Lockwood.

That was the link between the two men, as Payne had suspected all along. He showed the file to the clerk and said, 'I need to see the details of all the houses requisitioned as army stores and signed for by Mr Lockwood.'

The clerk grumbled, but he did as Payne asked. When Payne offered to come back for the paperwork later, the clerk said, 'No, I want you to see how much bloody work it is trying to find this nonsense.'

It took him another hour to find the relevant documents.

There were four properties in total. Each one had been requisitioned as an 'army store' and each had been signed for by Suttpen and Lockwood.

Payne thought about what that meant: Suttpen had probably been paying Lockwood to requisition specific properties, he decided. Yes, that made sense. It explained why Lockwood had looked so panicky when Payne first mentioned the matter to him: Lockwood's name had been on the requisition receipts but he had no idea what was behind them. Did Suttpen? That was the burning question.

'I think this Lockwood chap was accepting bribes to keep certain properties aside,' Payne said. Booth nodded and looked away sharply, his face flushed.

'Do you know something that you think you should tell me, Captain Booth?'

Booth sighed. 'I don't really want to go into details, Inspector. But I can tell you that, yes, you are entirely correct in your supposition.'

Payne indicated the list of addresses. 'In that case, I think we should drive out to each of these properties and take a look at them.'

The requisitioned properties were all in secluded locations, well beyond the outskirts of the town. First on the list was the house by the Brunswick Road. The next two houses had been locked up. Payne pressed his hands to the windows at each of them, trying to see in.

'For storerooms, they look mighty empty inside,' he said.

Booth nodded. "It's as I said before, Detective Inspector. The very idea of having army stores in such a secluded location – and unguarded – is ludicrous. I suppose Mr Lockwood had to put something down though, didn't he?'

The fourth property was the furthest from the town, an isolated two storey farmhouse hidden behind a copse of silver birch. A wooden placard was nailed to a tree at the end of the driveway. It said, 'DANGER, TYPHUS', in English, German, French and Polish. Similar messages had been daubed across the exterior walls of the house, and the windows and doors in the lower storey had been boarded shut.

'We must have made a mistake,' Booth said, indicating the signs. 'No-one's been here for weeks.'

Payne said nothing. He began checking the boards on the windows one by one, to see if any were loose, but they were all firmly nailed shut.

Booth was looking at the warnings daubed on the walls. 'That message about typhus could be genuine, you know.'

'I'm willing to take the risk and enter if it means we'll get some idea of where Suttpen has gone. He's the key to all of this,' Payne said, walking round to the back of the house. The windows and doors were boarded up here, too. Payne stood with his hands in his pockets, looking up at the second storey windows. They were free of boards but they were all fastened shut; the glass in all of the windows was intact.

Booth lit a cigarette. He was thinking aloud. 'As we know that Suttpen was able to get houses requisitioned on the sly, I suppose it's possible he might also have had entrées into other bureaucratic channels.'

'What do you mean?'

'I'm thinking about the travel documents we found in the suitcases. Supposing they are false, they would had to have come from somewhere, wouldn't they? Do you think Suttpen might have had something to do with it?'

'It's possible,' Payne said, as he completed his circuit of the house. 'It'll certainly be one of the first questions I ask him. I know he was supplying the Red Cross with army foodstuffs, which means he had a few favours to call in. And there's definitely a market for false travel documents. Mr Suttpen doesn't seem a man that would pass up on a good business opportunity.'

'But how does that tie in with these people being killed? Who would go to the trouble of obtaining these travel documents if they just wanted to kill the people for whom they were intended?'

Payne shrugged. 'I admit that part of the equation doesn't add up.'

They had reached the far side of the house now. The door here was boarded up. Then Payne saw other doors close to the ground.

He pulled the doors open, revealing a short metal chute leading down into darkness. The chute was black with coal dust but scuff marks were clearly visible on its surface. Payne knelt to examine it. It was wide and high enough for a man to slide down and a rope had been tied to the top of the chute. He thought about the first time he'd seen Suttpen and the black marks on the seat of his trousers. This must have been how he'd got in and out.

With only a brief moment's hesitation, Payne climbed inside the chute and slid down it.

He found himself inside a small, square chamber. Payne crossed the room, climbed the stairs on the far side of it and tried the handle on the door. It was not locked.

The door opened into the kitchen. Payne pushed it open a crack and looked inside. Gloomy daylight filtered through the boards on the windows. Payne sniffed the air. It was rank with the smell of death. He covered his mouth with his handkerchief.

'Lord, what's that smell?' Booth said when he also came down the chute but then relapsed into silence: he already knew the answer.

As they climbed the steps to the upper storey the low buzz of flies became audible, the smell stronger.

They found Suttpen on the floor of the front bedroom, lying at the centre of a huge pool of dried blood, his throat cut wide open. Payne shone his torch on Suttpen's face. The skin was marbled blue with decay.

'How long has he been dead?' Booth said.

'It's difficult to say. I'd guess at least a day.'

'Why was he killed?'

'That's the real question, isn't it? We know Lockwood procured these requisitioned properties and we know Suttpen was involved. Why did they want these houses in the first place? And for whom did they want them?'

Booth began searching the other rooms while Payne examined Suttpen's pockets. They were completely empty.

'Have you found something?' Payne called, when he heard Booth swearing in the other room.

'You'd better see this, Detective Inspector. Whatever the murderer's motive was,' he added, when Payne entered the bedroom, 'I think we can rule out robbery.'

Booth gestured towards a hole in the floor on the far side of the room where two of the boards had been prised up. Payne shone his torch at the hole. The light reflected on jewelled surfaces and brightly shining metals.

'Lord, look at this,' Booth said, kneeling beside the hole and holding up an ornate silver plate. 'This must have come from a church.'

They levered up a third floorboard and found rolls of canvas. The tattered edges suggested that they were paintings that had been torn from their frames. Booth unrolled one of the canvases and revealed a portrait of a nobleman in doublet and breastplate. 'This must be hundreds of years old. Where the hell did Suttpen get all of this stuff?'

'You told me Suttpen had been looting right across Germany.'

'Yes, but we've never came across anything like this before. Look at this stuff. This must have come from a cathedral or a museum,' Booth said, fishing out an ornate candle snuffer.

'It doesn't look German, either, does it?' Payne said, examining a square religious icon. Cyrillic lettering was imprinted in the silver lametta that covered its edges. There were more icons among the booty and an ornate Bible written in a language that he thought was probably Polish.

They took Suttpen's loot and loaded it into the boot of Payne's utility. Booth said he knew of a unit that was specifically charged with tracking down cultural items looted by the Nazis and returning them to their rightful owners. They would take care of any objects handed over to them.

They left Suttpen's body where it was. When they returned to the town Payne and Booth drove to the RAMC barracks and arranged for it to be collected by an ambulance.

'I don't think Suttpen did loot all that stuff,' Booth said as they drove back towards his billet. 'I think that stuff was looted by the Germans when they reached the east.'

Payne nodded. 'If Suttpen was involved in helping get war criminals out of Germany, the loot could have been part of his payment.'

'But why were these people killed?'

Payne shrugged. 'At least we have a good idea *how* they were killed. They had suitcases and travel documents. They clearly expected to go somewhere. However, at some point in the proceedings they were given a vaccination which contained a barbiturate. Then they were strangled.'

'Well, I've heard about these organisations that are supposedly helping Germans to escape the country. Ratlines, some of the chaps are calling them.'

'Except that if we're correct about this, it's not a ratline that's operating here,' Payne said. 'It's a rat trap.'

8

THE FIRST THING Johannes told Ilse to do was meet a man named Eugen. Johannes said he'd already contacted the man through a go-between, a young boy from the town, but that Ilse would have to take over negotiations for the travel permits now.

After she had agreed to do as he asked Ilse made Johannes leave the house and promise not to come back until evening. Piotr would be there soon and she couldn't risk his seeing Johannes. And she needed time to dig up the box.

When she told Johannes to leave he gave her that sardonic smile of his and picked up his gunney sack and sauntered out of the house and away across the fields towards the copse of trees that stood beside the stream.

When he had disappeared from view, she took the shovel and dug the metal box up. She carried it through to the kitchen table and removed from it the money and the jewellery. She took half the money and hid it inside one of the cracks in the wall. The other half she stuffed inside her knickers. Then she headed towards the town.

There were more checkpoints on the roads than usual. The Tommy soldiers were more suspicious than she'd experienced before: enough to make Ilse wonder what on earth was going on. She made sure she took her accustomed route into town, the way that she walked when she was going to the transit camp. The soldiers on the checkpoints knew her and once they'd looked at her papers they simply waved her through. As she walked along the road she saw lorries rumbling past filled with German prisoners.

Johannes said he had arranged to meet Eugen in the centre of the town at 10 o'clock. Ilse arrived fifteen minutes earlier and waited in the agreed place, hovering in the queue by the standpipe.

She recognised the man long before he sidled over to her. He was a small ferrety-looking fellow who was loitering in the shadows of a ruined building and observing the queue with sharp eyes. When their eyes met, the man nodded and walked around the perimeter of the square, twice. Finally, he walked towards the queue, passed close to Ilse and whispered, 'This way.'

Ilse followed him out of the square, through the ruins of a building and on to a café, one of the few in the town that was still open for business. Eugen led her to a booth at the back of the café.

She recognised him, Ilse realised when they sat down and she had the chance to look at him properly. His name wasn't Eugen. He was one of the doctors from the town that was collaborating with the Tommies. What was his real name? Seiler, that was it, Doctor Seiler.

Seiler sat with the fingers of his small hands folded into each other. As he spoke, his thumbs beat together. His attitude was all mock civility and regret but his eyes glittered greedily.

'How many are you?' he said.

'Two. Myself and a man.'

'And where do you want to go?'

'To Spain.'

Seiler hissed. 'That means travelling through France. You will not find many friends along that road. It is far safer to head south, through Bavaria and on into Austria and Italy. There are people along that route sympathetic to Germans. But the route you choose . . .' He hissed again and shook his head.

'Are you saying it is impossible?'

'No, of course not. Anything is possible. For the right price. Regrettably, though, there has been a change of circumstance since last I communicated with your friend,' he said. 'Just as the transport of certain goods requires greater precautions – and a corresponding increase in cost – the same is true of our little network. I'm afraid things have become very complicated in the last few days. The British are watching the roads. And for that we must ask more.'

'How much more?'

'The price will now be two thousand American dollars. Per person. Plus another thousand for sundry expenses.'

Ilse swallowed. Five thousand? That was more than half she had.

'And what does that price include?'

'Everything. Documentation. Road transport to within a few miles of the German border. Vaccinations.'

'Vaccinations?'

'If you plan to travel abroad it is advisable. Certain diseases long since controlled in Europe are still rampant in South America. Plus, given the current state of the world, infection is a constant danger. Look what happened after the Great War: the Spanish influenza ravaged the continent.'

'Five thousand dollars seems an exorbitant price.'

'Please understand that I am a mere go-between. It is an associate of mine that actually runs the network, so there is no point in trying to haggle with me. And if his price seems expensive, you are welcome to shop around.'

Seiler stood to leave. Ilse put a hand on his arm.

'Don't be hasty, sir,' she said, 'I was merely checking.'

Seiler smiled and sat back down.

'A wise decision, Fräulein.'

'When do we pay?'

'I want three thousand now. The other two thousand you will pay when my associate collects you.'

Ilse went into the toilet and counted the money out, then returned to their table and slid the money to Seiler under her hand. Seiler counted the money beneath the tabletop, folded the bills and popped them into his top pocket.

He said he could have the travel documents ready for the next evening but that he would need photographs. Johannes already had four passport-sized photos, but Ilse had used all hers when she'd had Ursula's documents changed. Seiler said he could get her some for one hundred dollars and told her to meet him that evening at a property on the outskirts of the town.

Ilse went home and sat beside the fire, watching the clock. At six, she left to meet Seiler again. She had thought about reburying the box, but decided simply to carry what remained of her stash with her. It was the only way she could be sure it was safe.

As she walked across the fields behind her house, she fancied she saw someone moving among the trees opposite. She called out Johannes's name, but there was no answer. It was so gloomy beneath the trees that she got nothing more than a glimpse, but nevertheless she drew her scarf tight around her head and hurried across the fields.

Seiler was waiting for her outside the house he had named, tapping his watch. He took her into an outhouse. A white sheet had been hung from the wall. A stool was placed before it and a box camera stood on a tripod. Seiler took the photos using an old camera and a magnesium flash, then hurried her back outside. The flash made dots swim before Ilse's eyes.

'What happens now?' she said.

Seiler handed her a piece of paper and a key. 'You must go to this address tomorrow evening. There is a door at the back of the house that leads into a cellar. Wait there. My associate will come to meet you, bringing your travel documents. He will also vaccinate you. Then he will drive you to your destination. You should pack a single suitcase each.'

It was dark when she began to walk home. The Tommies were patrolling the main roads with jeeps and lorries, so she took the back roads home, smoking a cigarette as she walked.

It was over. She was going. There was no alternative. She had already parted with more than half her money.

A twig cracked somewhere in the darkness. Ilse quickened her step, looking behind her as she walked through the gloom.

She didn't see the men until it was too late. They emerged from the trees and surrounded her before she'd even realised they were there, four of them, all raggedly dressed.

'Who are you? What do you want?' Ilse said in English,

although she already knew the answer as the men grinned and fanned out around her. There was no mistaking the hungry malice in their eyes. They wanted her bag. Then they would beat her. After that, who knew what they might do?

Ilse moved backwards a few steps as the men advanced, seeking the moment to strike. She picked up a thick stick from the ground and waved it at one of them, but the man to her right side stepped forward and punched her hard on the side of the head. The blow sent her tumbling to the ground and made her ears ring.

All four of the men leapt forward, shouting in a foreign language. Ilse kicked out as one tried to pull the bag away from her and another began to paw at her legs. She felt a hand go up her skirt. One of the men laughed. Ilse could smell his foul breath.

She was now lying on the ground and still trying to keep hold of her bag when she saw a shadow sweep in from the right, coming silently and swiftly towards the men from behind.

Two of them fell in an instant as a blade rose, glinting in the moonlight. Then the shadow struck at the third man and there was a horrid cracking noise as the man fell back, screaming and gurgling. The fourth man tried to run as the sinister new presence turned and threw something. The man fell to the ground.

The clouds moved and Ilse saw that it was her brother pulling his hunter's knife from the man's back. The third man lay writhing on the ground, clutching at his face, sobbing and gurgling. Johannes Drechsler strode up to him, raised his boot and twice stamped the heel of it on the man's throat. There was a horrible silence.

'Get up,' he said, staring at Ilse, his expression unnaturally composed.

'Thank God you were following me,' said Ilse, panting.

'I wasn't following you. I was following our money. Now help me get this shit off the road,' Johannes said, grabbing the ankles of a corpse and dragging it towards the bushes.

Ilse and Johannes returned to the house. It was now completely dark. Ilse was trembling. Despite all those years of war and all those millions of deaths, she'd never before actually seen anyone killed.

Johannes took bread from the pantry and ate in silence. Afterwards, he lit a cigarette.

'What?' he sneered across the table when Ilse's gaze fell upon a red stain on the outside of the cigarette packet.

'Did you take that from one of the dead men?'

'They're fuck all use to him, now, aren't they?' Johannes said. Then he laughed mirthlessly. 'Why do you look so shocked, sister? What was it you thought I was doing all those years in the east? Learning to play the balalaika?'

'I know where you were sent to serve at the end of the war. You were in a penal battalion, weren't you? The Dirlewangers.'

Johannes mimed silent applause.

'They say your unit murdered civilians. Is it true?'

Johannes laughed. 'Murder? On the eastern front? You might as well ask a man tossed into the sea why he becomes wet. Murder, you say?' His laughter increased in volume.

'What was it you people thought your precious little Fuhrer wanted his troops to do in Russia?'

'What happened to you, Johannes?'

It was the wrong thing to say. His expression, already surly, became angry.

'What happened? You and your fucking husband happened. You filled my mind with all that Nazi shit. Do you remember? We were to be the first among nations, the chosen people. And little Adolf was to lead us there. I believed you. Do you hear me? I believed every fucking word about destiny and honour and the new order. I believed it all, right up until the war started to go wrong.'

His lip curled. 'Do you know how many good men I saw chewed up on the Russian front? And while our men froze to death for lack of winter clothes, the newspapers spoke of strategic retreats and well-fed pigs like your dear Rüdiger in his pristine party uniform urged us on to make the supreme sacrifice for the Fatherland. But what happened when the shelling came close? We, the *Frontkämpfer* in our shabby uniforms, bore the brunt of it, while the party men were running for their miserable lives. And then, when I dared to criticise the way the war was being fought and brought it to the attention of your dear husband, I was sent to a penal battalion.'

'What do you mean?'

Johannes's smile was back. 'It was Rüdiger who had me thrown out of the *Totenkopf* division. One of his SS chums was friends with my commanding officer. After that visit to the Warthegau, Rüdiger had him watching me. They got me on some trumped-up charge and threw me out. I had two choices: a concentration camp or the *Dirlewangers*. Do you know, in a funny sort of a way, I felt far more at home with them. At least they dispensed with all the moralistic bullshit, all the pageantry. You and Rüdiger would have loved some of my boys.'

'I don't know what you mean.'

'Don't you?' That hint of darkness within her brother flashed across Johannes's face and the effect was like deepening cloud on a showery day: the chill of it filled the kitchen. 'Without Nazis like *you,* Ilse, there would never have been Nazis like *me.* Remember that.'

'That's a lie.'

Johannes was working himself up to a crescendo now. 'Do you want to see what it was like? What the east was really like?'

He fumbled in his pocket, withdrew a crumpled photo, folded in half. Five soldiers were surrounding an old man, forcing him to kneel while they pinioned his hands behind his back. One of the soldiers had grasped a clump of the man's hair, pulling it upwards. Two of the others, grinning for the camera, held either end of a woodsman's saw, the teeth of the blade resting on the old man's neck.

'What you can't see is what the rest of the lads were doing to his wife,' Johannes said in a low voice. 'They made a real mess of her.'

Ilse stared at the photo. She began to tremble again. She pushed the photo away.

'Enough of this, Johannes. Please, I can't stand anymore.'

Johannes looked at her for a moment and began to laugh, pounding the table with the flat of his hand.

'Do you know what's so funny now, my Gräfin,' he said suddenly, and the humour fell from his face, quick as a slammed door. He stubbed a finger at the photo. 'That's *exactly* what that old bastard was saying when I took that photo.'

That night Johannes found the bottle of whisky. It happened before Ilse realised what was going on. One moment, Johannes was fumbling around in the pantry in search of more food; the next he was swigging from the neck of the bottle. The dark light in his eyes grew as he drank.

When he had finished the whisky, he rummaged in his gunny sack and withdrew a bottle of Korn, which he began swigging like a bottle of beer. Ilse tried to chide him for drinking like a brigand, but when he turned towards her his raw eyes were wet with tears and he did not seem to recognise her. She locked the door when she went to bed. She could hear Johannes fumbling and crashing around downstairs long into the night.

Next morning she found him lying fully clothed in the pantry, surrounded by broken glass. She sighed heavily, hands on hips. The floor was sprayed with vomit.

She sat in the kitchen, staring at the embers of the fire. Then she took out the piece of paper Seiler had given her containing the address. She recognised the name of the street: it was on the other side of the town, one of the country roads lined with farms and summer houses. She picked up the bottle of Korn and realised there was still some left. She went to pour herself a glass but put the bottle down when she noticed the bloodied fingerprints on the label.

God, how could she travel anywhere with her brother? It

was like being locked in a cage with a wild animal. But she'd spent so much money, three thousand dollars. She was trapped with him, now. Her mind raced, weighing pros and cons as she played with the piece of paper. She would have to go with him as far as Spain. It was too dangerous to stay in Germany. She'd already been recognised once. It could happen again and perhaps the next time the person would want more than a simple apology. But it would be impossible for her to go to South America with Johannes. She wanted to get away from her brother as quickly as she could.

Groans sounded from the pantry as Johannes emerged, hair unkempt, eyes bloodshot. He walked straight to the table, picked up the bottle of Korn and sucked at it greedily. 'What's that?' he said, nodding towards the paper Ilse held.

She handed it to him as she said, 'Go outside and wash. You smell like a brewery. There's soap on the mantelpiece.'

Johannes said nothing. He chewed a piece of stale bread, his expression contemplative as he stared at the address. Then he slid the paper under the bottom of the bottle, took the soap and walked outside.

Ilse went upstairs to pack. From her bedroom window she could see Johannes on the far side of the yard. He pulled off his ragged tunic, revealing his broad chest and pale, grubby skin, but left his trousers and boots on. Thick tendrils of scar tissue ran across one breast; his shoulder bore the signs of old burn-marks.

Ilse watched as he soaped and lathered his upper body beneath the makeshift shower. As he lifted his arms and tilted his head back to let the water fall onto his face, she saw that he was smiling in the same way that he had sometimes smiled as a boy. From this distance it was almost possible to believe he was still the young man she had once known.

That photo of the men with the saw – it must have been a fake. He was kidding her. He'd always been such a liar when he was a boy. Yes, that was it. It was probably just one of his stupid jokes. Surely he couldn't really have done –

Ilse froze when she saw Johannes spin round and lower his arms slowly. The change in his attitude was so precipitate that it made Ilse catch her breath. Johannes resembled a hound catching scent of prey.

Ilse shivered as she followed his line of sight and saw Piotr standing nearby clutching a bundle of firewood, ready for his day's work, his mangled mouth trying to smile as he caught Johannes' eye.

She banged on the window but Johannes was already loping towards the trees, waving for the boy to come closer while the fingers of his other hand sought the handle of his hunting knife, tucked into the back of his trousers.

9

Dᴇᴛᴇᴄᴛɪᴠᴇ Iɴsᴘᴇᴄᴛᴏʀ Pᴀʏɴᴇ woke before dawn and put on his CCG uniform.

Booth had sent him a note the previous evening saying he had found where the policeman, Metzger, the man who had investigated the early *Flickschuster* murders, was being held. It read: *Former Eichenrode police chief held at Civilian Internment Camp 42. Inmates not regarded as serious security risk, so do not foresee any problems about you speaking to him (touch wood). Make sure you don't go in civvies, though. Colonel Bassett has made it clear he doesn't want you speaking to Germans, but I think you'll be OK as long as you flash your CCG papers and get in and out quickly.*

Civilian Internment Camp 42 was twenty miles outside the town. It consisted of four block houses made of brick and wood, surrounded by barbed wire. It was here that the men and women from the Eichenrode district who were suspected of being minor Nazis – bureaucrats, Hitler Youth leaders, Gestapo informants – were interned. The fence posts and barbed wire that surrounded the camp were the only items that looked new. Paint was peeling from the wooden walls; the windows of the blockhouses were cracked and dirty.

The soldier on the gate looked at Payne's ID and wandered away without saying anything. When he returned a few minutes later, accompanied by a rotund army officer, Payne thought the game was up. However, the man introduced himself as the camp commandant. He listened as Payne explained what he wanted, nodding occasionally.

'That shouldn't be a problem, Inspector,' he said, after examining the chit Booth had filled out for him. 'Step this way, I'll show you where Herr Metzger is.'

German men in civilian clothing stood in groups outside the block houses. As Payne and the commandant approached, they stopped talking and turned thin, nervous faces towards them.

'I hate the way they look at me,' the commandant said. 'They remind me of stray dogs. I never know whether to make them salute me or not.'

They stepped into the chill, gloomy interior of one of the blockhouses. Men stirred on banks of wooden bunks, then looked away. Some smoked; others merely stared at the roof. There were no bunks at the far end of the blockhouse, where the prisoners slept on straw palliasses.

'We don't actually have any facilities for interrogation here, Detective Inspector,' the commandant said. 'For all the heavy stuff, the prisoners get taken over to the larger facility.'

'It doesn't matter. I only want to speak to him.'

'He's down there at the end. I'll leave you to get on with it. Let me know if you need anything.'

The police chief, Metzger, was in his early fifties. He was sitting on the floor in his shirtsleeves, hair unkempt, pot-belly pressing against the front of his shirt. Payne greeted the man in German. Metzger's eyes flickered slightly, as if showing interest.

'What do you want of me?' he said.

Payne handed him the photos of the two bodies he had found in the cellar. Then he handed the man black and white shots of the body parts taken from the well. He let Metzger examine them. Then he said, 'Do you remember a killer called the *Flickschuster*?'

Metzger's eyes became guarded. He was clearly registering something, but didn't want to show his hand.

'I might do.'

'I need your help.'

Metzger gave a short, bitter laugh.

'You must think me a fool, Herr Detective Inspector. First, you take my gun and my badge. Then, you take my belt and boots and give me straw to sleep on and just two bowls of soup each day. You do everything you can to take my dignity from me. And yet you come here to ask my help? I suppose you're going to make me an offer, tell me you can get me released? Or get me reinstated in my job?'

Payne shook his head. 'No. I don't think you'll ever work at that again.'

Metzger was taken aback for a moment. Payne's honesty had unsettled him. 'Then why should I help you?'

'Because you were a policeman once and you helped hunt this man. People are dying. And if you ever took any pride in your uniform, you'll tell me what I need to know, so that I can catch this monster before he kills again.'

Metzger thought about this. Then he stood up.

'Let us take the air together, Detective Inspector. Tell me what you know.'

Payne told him everything. Metzger listened in quiet concentration. When Payne had finished, Metzger said, 'You are right to suspect that the Dutchman they executed had nothing to do with it.

'As you have seen from the newspapers, the first set of *Flickschuster* crimes was discovered in the autumn of 1942, in Brunswick. We found bodies in the cellar and more buried in the garden, and a bath tub filled with quicklime. I don't think they ever found out how many victims there were. Then other houses containing bodies were found. There was one in Regensburg. And another in Berlin.

'The more victims were discovered, the more the political pressure increased. I knew the arrest of the Dutchman was mistaken. The authorities had a way of rushing things through when they were trying to please their political masters.

'Anyway, there was a 'trial', the Dutchman was found guilty and they guillotined him. Then they found the house in Würtemburg. For the first time, there was no official announcement of the crimes. We heard about them, though, through a Gestapo man who worked from our office. He just couldn't resist boasting whenever he knew something the rest of us didn't, especially when he had a few beers inside him.

'After that, there were more murders at Grafenwöhr, in Bavaria. That was in October '44. And others were uncovered at Münstereifel in Westphalia last December.'

'Why do you think they kept the subsequent killings secret? Was it to avoid embarrassment over the false arrest?'

Metzger drew closer and dropped his voice. 'Part of it might have been that. But I think it was mainly for a different reason. I think the authorities had realised by then that the killer was an SS man.'

'An SS man?'

'Think about it. How was it the killer was able to get access to so many houses? Well, a Kripo man I knew named Gohrum found out the answer. In each case, they were houses the SS authorities had confiscated from Jews. They were supposed to be given to the families of SS men or turned into offices, but someone had fudged the books and so they lay empty. And when the killer began using them, nobody dared ask who he was.

'But the real proof was when those bastards from the SS special court began sniffing around. That was when we knew it had to be something serious because it took a lot to get them to leave Berlin.'

'SS court?'

'It was a special tribunal that looked into crimes committed by SS personnel. Basically they could write their own rules. Dangerous bastards.'

Payne told Metzger about the Red Cross travel documents. 'Did you see anything like this during the *Flickschuster* case?'

Metzger smiled. 'That was the most interesting part. The killer was cunning. Do you know how the Gestapo became involved in this crime? They were investigating something else, what seemed like a totally separate incident at the time, a clandestine organisation that could supposedly help get enemies of the regime out of Europe: deserters, Jews, communists. They had managed to infiltrate this group with a Gestapo man posing as a Jew. But then the Gestapo man disappeared. Do you know where they found his body?'

'At one of the killer's houses?'

'Exactly. He had an unusual birthmark on his chest, so

they knew it was him. Plus they found his clothes and wedding ring and ID papers in the attic. And that was when the authorities realised what was really happening. The killer was like a spider and the false escape network was his web. These people went to the killer expecting to escape Germany. Instead they were murdered. And, of course, when they disappeared, no-one was looking for them as they were *supposed* to disappear. It was a fiendishly inventive plot.'

Metzger had been going to say more when the camp commandant appeared, looking perturbed.

'I say, Detective Inspector, I've just been on the phone to HQ and they don't know anything about this interrogation of yours. I'm afraid I'll have to ask you to leave.'

There was no point in arguing. Payne walked back to his car, thinking about the suitcases in the attic, the travel documents. Christ, it had all happened before.

He stopped by his car and looked at his notes. Those names, Grafenwöhr and Münstereifel, he'd heard them before, too.

He searched through his notebook. When he came to one particular page, he ran back towards the camp and knocked on the door to the guardhouse.

'Can I borrow that?' Payne said, pointing at the telephone. 'It's important.'

10

CAPTAIN BOOTH WOKE an hour before dawn and made himself a thermos of hot, strong tea. Then he went to the building where the boxes of documents he had found in the cellar of Wolfflust prison were stored. He pulled a desk and chair close to the stove, sat down and poured himself a cup of tea. Then he opened the first box, withdrew the pile of papers from within it and set to work. Somewhere among the files, documents and transcripts of conversations was the killer's identity, Booth was sure of it.

He worked for three hours before he realised the task he had set himself was near impossible. Nearly fifty SS men had gone through Doctor Wiegand's programme between 1941 and the end of the war, and each patient's case had produced hundreds of pieces of paper.

He looked at the piles of cardboard boxes. He needed to find some way of narrowing the parameters of the search. He and Payne had discussed the possibilities the day before. Because of the dates of the *Flickschuster* crimes, they could be fairly certain that their man had not entered Wiegand's programme until mid-1944 at the very earliest. That still didn't help very much, as some of the patient records were fragmentary and others lacked dates.

Booth spent the morning trying to put some order to the

mass of notes. At lunchtime, Payne phoned and told Booth what the German police chief had said.

'The killer used the lure of a false escape network to reel his victims in. I think he's doing the same here. And it definitely wasn't the Dutchman,' Payne said. 'There were more *Flickschuster* crimes committed after the Dutchman was caught and executed.'

'When and where were these other crimes committed?'

Payne opened his notebook. 'In Würtemburg. And then in Grafenwöhr in Bavaria. That was in October '44. And Münstereifel in Westphalia, in December. Do you recognise those names, Captain?'

Booth tapped his pencil against his teeth. He did recognise the names but he couldn't remember from where.

'It was Operation Greif,' Payne said. 'The men of the SS unit trained in Grafenwöhr during the autumn of 1944. Then they began operations out of Münstereifel in December. That's what Toth meant when he said Greif was of special significance. Our man was part of Operation Greif. That was how they found him. The fact he had murdered in those places meant they could pin him down to specific areas at specific times. He'd created a trail they could follow: the murders coincided with his movements as part of Operation Greif. And that means our man might not have entered the programme until January 1945.'

Booth was nodding. 'If you're right, it means something else. It means our man can speak English. He may even be fluent.'

'Yes. That was what Toth meant about him being especially dangerous. He can blend in. But that might be to our advantage. If he is fluent, he must have some link to an English speaking country. Keep looking through the files. I am going to follow up on the travel documents. I need to speak to one of the nurses from the Red Cross camp. I think she knows something about O'Donnell.'

Booth set to work again, searching through the paperwork. Hours passed. Outside, it began to rain. Army lorries rolled past, their tyres spattering mud against the windows of the building. At three, hunger got the better of him, so he stopped for an hour and went in search of lunch.

He had to force himself to go back to the paperwork. His eyes were hurting from sifting through type-written documents all day.

He sat down, opened up a new box and lit a cigarette . . . and there it was, the information he had spent all day hoping he would find.

Patient 43. His parents were Germans but he had been born in South Africa, where he had learned English and Afrikaans. *Christ, this is him*, Booth thought as he read through the details and saw the date Patient 43 had entered the programme: January 22nd, 1945.

Booth put all the other paperwork aside and concentrated on the details of Patient 43.

Twenty minutes later, Booth had telephoned the archivist at Corps HQ. 'Killy? I need you to pull the *RuSha* files on a man named *Scharführer* Otto Flense. Joined the SS early 1936. Served as a medical orderly with the Order Police in Poland and Russia, attached to the 14th Army as part Einsatzgruppen I. Can you check if you have his personnel files? Would you mind dropping whatever it is you're working on and doing it right now? I'll take the flak.'

Booth put the phone down. His hands were shaking as he reread Doctor Wiegand's notes on Patient 43, this man named Otto Flense.

A variety of visual stimuli were shown to the patient. He experienced severe reactions to film reels A, B, D, E and F. He proved indifferent to reels C and G.

Patient 43's pathology is founded upon the tangle of contradictions that form the very centre of his being. He considers himself a witty, sophisticated and intelligent man, but his conversation is actually dull and repetitive. There is no more substance to his personality than there is to the wooden hoardings on a film set. The epicentre of his being is a monstrous and overwhelming selfishness, if that word can be applied to a patient whose psyche understands only the concept of self; beyond that, there is only vacuum. He is torn between an infantile self-absorption and a deep-seated loathing of his own mediocrity. Just as the coprophile is drawn to his or her own feculence, patient 43 seems obsessed by the evil within himself.

He values others only in as much as he can dominate and use them. Many aspects of the patient's case are typical: the restrictive, religious father, the doting, permissive mother; the adolescent patterns of petty crime and cruelty to animals. Indeed, his first description of the sensation of 'empowerment' associated with his crimes comes from his killing of cats and dogs as an adolescent, although, interestingly, his experiments with burning and hanging the animals were discontinued as 'they squawked too much'.

The unusual post-mortem treatment of his victim is, I feel, fully explained by his father's working as a mortician. Patient 43 grew up in an environment where death was a common-place and, crucially, divorced from any sense of tragedy or pain. The patient described first helping his father with the dressing of corpses at the age of ten but was not allowed to speak with the relatives of the deceased until well into adoles-cence.

Interestingly, it is this familiarity with death which seems to be the fulcrum upon which his pathology rests, as the trauma of his experiences on the east front, particularly the liquidations en masse of Jews as part of Einsatzgruppen I, are paramount in understanding the deviant reasoning behind his crimes. The unrestrained displays of suffering he witnessed there seem to have clashed violently with his preconceptions of death; indeed, to have shattered them utterly.

In conversations with me, he has described the eastern front killings as 'crude and brutish' and seems to regard them as having offended his aesthetic sensibilities. He talks of making his victims 'perfect' through his ritual and re-serves the highest praise for the 'silent and painless' way in which he dispatches his victims. However, again we see the contradictions at the root of this case, as Patient 43 admits to having killed a number of times long before he was sent to the eastern front and has also proved to be a savage and opportunistic predator, quite capable of acts of extreme violence should he feel his secret to be threatened. He is a –

Booth jumped when the phone rang. His hand trembled as he reached for the receiver.

'You're in luck,' Killy said. 'I've got him here. Otto Flense, born 1906. Ugly-looking brute.'

'Killy, take the whole file, put it in a briefcase and get the first dispatch rider you can find to bring it to me right now. I can't stress how important this is.'

The file arrived an hour later, the soldier on his motorcycle skidding to a halt outside Booth's billet.

Booth opened the file and removed the single photo inside, a head and shoulders photo of Flense in SS uniform, staring into the camera.

Killy was right: Flense was an ugly bugger. His nose was big and bulbous, his eyes small, crafty and cruel. His fair hair was shaved into a severe line just below the crown of his head. Booth had hoped that he might recognise the man, but he was disappointed. Flense looked like a hundred other SS men.

And yet . . .

There *was* something. Booth angled the photo towards the light. Was it his imagination or was there something familiar about the man's face, the arrogant set of his jaw-line? Had he seen the man before?

He was still examining the photo when a knock sounded at the door and Sergeant Hoyle's face appeared, pale with worry.

'What is it, sergeant?'

'There's a bit of a problem at the interrogation centre, sir.'

'Problem? What sort of a problem?'

'With Captain Fredrickson, sir. I think you'd better get over there right away.'

Booth jogged from his jeep to the building where the makeshift interrogation centre had been set up and followed Hoyle towards the steps that led to the cellar. As they descended them, Booth noticed a smear of blood on one of the steps.

There was more inside the door, a trail of red droplets that led along the corridor and towards a room at the back of the cellar. Booth heard shouts coming from the room. He hastened towards the door and flung it open.

Freddy was standing with his back to the door, bellowing at a youth who was sitting on a chair.

'What the devil's going on, Captain Fredrickson?'

Freddy turned. His face was red and sweat covered his forehead. 'Oh, it's you, Booth.'

'Yes, it is me. Now answer my damned question. What are you doing?'

'This little shit,' Freddy said, twisting the boy's head round to face Booth, 'is the root of our werewolf problem. A patrol picked him up last night. He was trying to cut some telephone lines. Got him bang to rights. He had wire cutters, pliers and a knife on him.' Freddy gestured towards the tools and weapon which lay on a table beside him.

'What's his name?' Booth said.

'Putzi.'

'Do we have anything on him?'

'He was a student at the Napola Academy close to here. And that's enough for me.'

Booth wasn't listening. He was looking at the boy's bruised and bloodied face. 'Have you struck him, Captain Fredrickson?'

Freddy snorted. 'I might have tapped the little bastard a

couple of times, just to keep him on his toes. But there's no permanent damage, I've made sure of that. I want him to be awake when they shoot him.'

Booth motioned to Hoyle to leave the room. Then he said, 'Christ, Freddy, how much longer are you going to continue with this charade?'

Freddy flexed his fists. 'Charade? What the devil are talking about?'

'This. The boy. The interrogations. I know why you're doing it. I know what happened at Wolffslust. About the German guards.'

'What about the German guards?'

'You killed two of them.'

Freddy's eyes narrowed. 'You've been chatting with that weasel, Tubbs, haven't you? That's absolute rot about the guards. You want to get your facts straight before you make accusations like that, Captain. As it is, you're for the high jump anyway when Colonel Bassett finds out what this chap has told me,' Freddy said, gesturing towards the boy slumped on the chair.

'And what's that?'

'This one is just the tip of the iceberg. He's got a Waffen SS accomplice hiding out in the woods, something you would have been aware of if you hadn't been chasing your tail with nonsense about murderers. That's why I'm trying to sweat some answers out of the little swine.'

'How could you possibly know he has a Waffen SS accomplice?'

'Two days ago a local woman, a friend of young Putzi's mother, came here to denounce a known Nazi, someone she recognised from before the war. Apparently, she saw young Putzi acting suspiciously in town and decided to follow him, whereupon said woman saw Putzi speaking to this SS fellow.'

'And how did she know he was SS?'

'Because she got a damned good look at the bugger and she recognised him as a local man. That's his *RuSha* file over there. Ex-Waffen SS. And wanted for about every war crime you can possibly imagine. But do you know the really interesting bit? This SS bastard is planning on getting himself some false travel documents.'

'How?'

'That's what I'm trying to get out of our friend here. He spoke to someone in the town about it. Apparently this SS fellow is going to have to pay 2,000 dollars for his documents. But little Putzi won't tell us who the contact is.'

'How can you be so certain this woman recognised the man?'

'Oh, if you'd seen the hatred in her eyes when she said his name, you'd have had no doubt. It seems this fellow ran the local Hitler Youth before the war. The woman claims this Drechsler fellow blinded her son. Beat him with a horsewhip.'

But Booth wasn't listening. A local man named Drechsler?

He walked across the room, opened the SS man's file and withdrew the photos within.

The bottom fell from his world.

11

FOR THE SECOND time in a week, Ilse found herself digging a grave in the garden. She cried as she dug. The tears welled up suddenly from somewhere deep within her and she could no more stop them than she could have stopped water seeping from a leaking pail.

She had been too late to stop Johannes. It had taken her all of twenty seconds to get outside and into the garden, screaming Johannes's name as she went, but by the time she could run to the spot where she had seen Piotr emerge from the trees, Johannes was already walking back from the woods, wiping the blood from his knife blade with a leaf.

Ilse had rushed past him, hands trembling. Piotr lay where he'd fallen, face up, his hare lip splayed. Blood welled from a horizontal slit in his chest just above his heart.

That was for whom she was digging the grave. The blisters on her hands bled as she scratched at the earth with the shovel, but she paid no mind to the pain.

She stopped as she sensed her brother behind her.

Johannes nodded towards the grave. 'That hole's nowhere near deep enough, you know,' he said, as Ilse grasped Piotr's ankles and dragged him towards the narrow trench.

'Leave me alone, Johannes. Go back to the house. Or go to hell, for all I care. But leave me be. I've had enough of you.'

Johannes came close and stood in front of her. 'Are you crying, sister?' he said, mumbling through a mouthful of apple. 'Whatever for? Those tears can't possibly be for that, can they?' he said, gesturing towards Piotr's corpse. 'A filthy Polack. And a diseased one, too. What was that phrase Rüdiger always used? You know, when he was pontificating from the end of the dinner table. *Untermensch*. That was it. God, I can see him now, waving that huge cigar around and patting his fat belly.'

'Why did you kill him? He meant no harm.'

'He saw my tattoo.' Still bare-chested, Johannes raised his left arm and pointed to the small gothic letters tattooed on the underside of his arm. 'I saw his eyes. He knew what it was. They are hunting Germans with these tattoos.'

'You had no right to kill him.'

'No right?' Johannes laughed. 'If you'd ever bothered to take a walk down to your husband's fucking mine, you would have seen a dozen corpses like that every day, I promise you that. But you didn't, did you, Ilse? You stayed in your house and pretended the world was still a fresh and innocent place.' Johannes spat on the floor and his eyes dripped with contempt. 'Take a good look at the boy's body, Ilse. That's your fucking *Lebensraum* right there.'

He waited for Ilse to respond. When she said nothing, he tossed his apple core into Piotr's grave and went.

Ilse did the best she could with the grave, but it was a poor effort. It was obvious to anyone what the rectangle of freshly dug earth represented. And Johannes was right. It wasn't deep enough. She was hampered by the blisters on her hands.

She didn't go back inside the house afterwards. She sat

beside the grave and dried her tears while she considered her predicament.

Her brother was mad. She believed the worst now. That photo of him with the saw, it wasn't a fake. The money didn't matter anymore, Ilse decided. She would take her chances in Germany.

She sat there in the garden for the rest of the day. When the sun began to set, Johannes came outside.

'You need to get ready.'

'I'm not going.'

'What?'

'I don't want to go anywhere with you, Johannes.'

Johannes took a step forward. His scarred hand grasped her arm. The pain made Ilse cry out.

'The travel documents are for a husband and wife, so you have got to come. You're coming as far as the Spanish border, at least. After that, you can do whatever the fuck you want.'

'I won't go. Do you hear? I won't –'

Johannes struck her across the face, knocking her to the ground. A second later, she felt the blade of Johannes's knife pressing into her throat.

'You are coming, Ilse. If you don't, I will kill you.'

Ilse said nothing. One look at Johanne's eyes and she knew he was in deadly earnest.

He stood over her as she packed her belongings, his knife tucked into his belt again, but with his fingers resting on the handle.

They left an hour after sundown. When Ilse went to lock the door of the farmhouse, Johannes began laughing.

'Even if you were to come back here, what is there inside to steal? Leave it open,' he said when she continued to work the key inside the stiff lock.

She left it open in the end. She didn't want to arouse his suspicion. She had already decided how she would get away from him. She would claim she needed to pee, then she would run away into the darkness and hide herself. She would wait until it was daylight and make her way back to the house. Johannes would not be able to hang around for long.

When they set off, Johannes insisted she walked in front. He was using her as bait, she realised. If there were attackers lurking in the darkness, Ilse would meet them first. And then Johannes would deal with them.

They crossed the silent fields and woodland paths, with only the silvery light of the moon to guide them. That didn't matter. They both knew these tracks.

When they arrived at the address, Ilse withdrew the key Doctor Seiler had given them.

'No,' Johannes said, looking around him at the darkness, his scarred hand wrapped around the hilt of his knife. 'We will wait outside, sister.'

'We were told to wait in the cellar.'

'And leave myself trapped? Do you think me so stupid?'

Johannes took her by the arm and pulled her towards the bushes.

12

IT WAS MID-AFTERNOON when Payne drove out to the townhouse where the Red Cross nurses were billeted. He had to ask directions of soldiers a couple of times and they gave him sly grins when they heard his destination.

When he arrived, he asked to speak to the Belgian nurse. The women on the porch frowned, but when Payne said he was a policeman one of them went inside and returned a few minutes later with the Belgian woman, who was wearing a man's dressing gown and towelling her wet hair. When she saw Payne, she smiled at her workmates to show them it was fine and drew Payne away towards his car. She seemed to suspect why he was there.

'The other day, at the camp, when I spoke to O'Donnell about the travel permits,' Payne said. 'Was he telling me the truth? It's important.'

The nurse looked over her shoulder before answering. She shook her head.

'Not all the documents are properly processed. There is a man, a German man. He has come to Mr O'Donnell three times now. Each time O'Donnell has had the documents drawn up but there has been no record made of them. He does everything in private. I only came across him doing it one night when I was looking for something in his office.'

'Did you not think it suspicious?'

'I assumed it was only people bribing their way to the head of the queue. There's normally quite a wait for travel permits. You don't think these people have done anything wrong, do you?'

'And who is this German man?'

'The doctor, Seiler I think his name is. He was at the camp today and I saw O'Donnell give him something.'

'That happened today?'

She nodded.

Payne thanked the nurse before he ran back to his car to drive to the Red Cross camp. It was dark now and the camp was preparing itself for bed. The light was still on in O'Donnell's office. Payne knocked before he pushed the door open. O'Donnell's face fell when he saw who his visitor was.

'What the hell do you want?'

'On my last visit I asked whether you ran background checks on everyone to whom you issue travel documents. I want to ask you that question again.'

O'Donnell folded his arms. 'You've obviously heard something or other, Detective Inspector. So out with it.'

Payne pulled the photo of Konrad Jaeger from his pocket. 'Do you remember doing the documents for this fellow? He's wanted for war crimes. And you helped secure him the documents. Now, you may be right if you say that I have no jurisdiction here. But I'm sure the lawyers working down in Nuremburg will be interested when I tell them a Red Cross official is helping war criminals to escape. And they *do* have jurisdiction.'

'That's a lie.' O'Donnell spoke with genuine anger but

there was a trace of uncertainty to his bluster now. He kept licking his lips and blinking.

'When did you last do travel documents for Seiler? Come on, man. People could die.'

O'Donnell bit his lip. 'Today.'

'Did you give them to Seiler?'

He nodded his head. 'He brought me the photos yesterday. But he told me they were for a man and woman that needed medical treatment abroad. He's the one that's been helping war criminals, not me. You remember that.'

'And where did Suttpen fit into all of this?'

'He supplied the houses. These people needed places to meet and sort out their business.'

Payne drove to the *Rathaus* and found out where Seiler lived. When he pulled up outside the townhouse, he saw the earth in front of the building had been churned by deep tyre tracks, as if a heavy vehicle had driven across it recently.

He jumped out of his utility and rushed up the steps. He knocked on the door, but there was no answer, although lights blazed within the house.

He knocked again then kicked at the lock of the door. On his fourth try, the wood around the lock splintered and the door opened.

Seiler lay on the floor of the living room in a pool of blood, his throat slit from ear to ear. Payne stepped around the mess of blood. The daughter lay dead in the kitchen. Her throat was cut, too.

The killer was tidying up all the loose ends. He was preparing to move on. Payne had to catch him now. Payne knew he would be using one of the houses Suttpen and Lockwood had secured for the man. He would drive to each in turn until he found which one.

Payne ran back to his car.

13

BOOTH WAS IN his jeep, driving out of town. His face felt numb, but it had nothing to do with the wind that was driving against it.

He knew the truth now: Ursula wasn't who she'd said she was. He muttered her real name as he drove towards the house: Ilse Hoffman.

He'd known something was wrong as soon as he saw the photograph inside the file on the SS man Freddy was hunting, that Johannes Drechsler. The black-and-white image that stared up from the page was the spitting image of Ursu . . . of this Ilse bitch. The queasy feeling of dread growing in the pit of Booth's stomach had increased when he read details of Drechsler's service record. He'd been in the 3rd SS Division, the Totenkopf, one of the Waffen-SS's elite units. And then his career had been crushed by disciplinary problems. One moment he'd been the top of the pile. The next he was transferred to the SS-Sturmbrigade 'Dirlewanger'.

Dirlewanger.

For a split second Booth had wondered why the name was so familiar. Then he remembered Ilse asking him about them, in the kitchen, the day he'd taken Piotr to the house.

It was the account of Drechsler's service in the Dirlewangers that occupied most of the document. Drechsler's unit had machine-gunned women and children. They had locked civilians in barns and burned them alive. Throats had been slit, heads crushed, limbs lopped off. They had been pitiless rapists. The Poles had found dozens of mass graves amid the ruins of Warsaw in the sector where the Dirlewangers had been operative.

A separate file contained details of Drechsler's Nazi affiliations and his family connections. His brother-in-law, Rüdiger Hoffman, had been a known Nazi and 'coordinator' of a mine in conquered Polish territory. He had married Drechsler's sister.

That was when Booth had realised there were more photos beneath the documents. With a trembling hand, Booth had pulled out a photo of Ilse Hoffman, dressed in furs, gripping the arm of her husband on the stairs of some huge building against a spot-lit background of swastika banners. She stared directly at the camera, hips angled to display the curves of her body to best effect. She was instantly recognisable but utterly alien at the same time: her eyes had a dark shine to them; her face was a mask of hauteur.

That was why Booth was driving out to her house now, the house of lies. His anger was cold and hard; he focused on it alone.

As the jeep advanced through the darkness, Booth considered how he would greet her, this changeling bitch. First of all he had thought he would strike her in the face, but he decided against that. That would be what a Nazi would do. There was no reason to behave so brutally. He would look her in the face and spit in her eye. He would let her see the contempt he felt for her. Then he would arrest her.

He drove his jeep right up to the house, beeping the horn.

In the trees, two wild dogs were worrying at something on the ground. They growled when Booth got out of the car. Booth shouted at them, feeling suddenly furious. He kicked the kitchen door, expecting it to be locked, but it flew open.

He realised why when he examined the interior of the house. Everything was gone. All the food. All her clothes. The two battered suitcases.

The bitch had done a runner.

Then he noticed the boot marks on the flagstones, the muddy prints that belonged to a man's feet. The brother. It had to be. But where would they go? They would never get past the roadblocks, the patrols.

Then he noticed the bottle of Korn on the table and the sheet of paper beneath it. He looked at the address written on it in pencil. He saw that it belonged to a rural property. Perhaps they had journeyed across country. That meant there was still time to catch them.

When Booth went back outside he noticed the dogs were fighting. He jumped into his jeep and turned on the headlights.

And stopped.

The beams of light had revealed a pale shape protruding from the ground. That seemed to be what the dogs were fighting over.

Booth took a flashlight and walked towards the two animals.

One of them fled. The other, the larger one, stood its ground. It growled at Booth as he approached and stared at him with feral eyes. Booth made calming noises but the dog's stance did not change. It lowered its head, teeth bared.

But Booth hardly noticed now. He was staring at the thin

pale arm the dog had been gnawing, the bulge of freshly-dug earth. Someone was buried here. The animals had gnawed the flesh from the fingers.

Booth unbuttoned the pouch that held his sidearm and shot the animal in the face. The sound sent birds flapping from the tops of the trees.

Booth scraped away the earth. His fingers increased in speed when he saw the face that was emerging, saw how the dark earth had filled the mouth and now revealed the huge black rent in the centre of the corpse's features, just below the nose.

Captain Booth realised that he was staring down at Piotr.

He screamed and fell to his knees.

It took Booth ten minutes to recover. He considered digging up Piotr's body to rescue it from further indignities, but he realised he didn't have time. He wanted to find Ilse Hoffman. She had killed Piotr and left him as carrion for wild animals. He would give Piotr the burial he deserved later on. At the moment he needed to ensure that justice was done.

The first thing he did was walk to the edge of the wood where the other dog still lurked and shot it. Now there were two animal corpses for any new predators to chew on.

Then he drove out to the road and headed towards the address he'd seen on the paper.

14

ILSE AND JOHANNES were crouching in the bushes opposite the house, waiting, until they saw the vehicle arrive. The
lorry's headlights formed twin pools of white light as they
swept across the front of the building.

The driver jumped out of his cab and Ilse realised she knew
him. It was that wretched driver from the Red Cross camp,
Joost. So he was in on it. Yes, that made sense. He knew all the
Tommies that guarded the road. They were used to him rumbling back and forth picking up supplies and taking people from
one transit camp to the next. What could be more natural than
for him to offer a couple heading in the same direction a lift?

Joost went inside the house. Johannes waited for at least
five minutes, anxiously peering into the darkness. Once Ilse
fancied she saw someone else moving amid the trees. Then Johannes dragged her to her feet and pushed her towards the
cellar door.

Joost turned when they pushed the door open. He looked
at them from behind his glasses in that curious way he had
of looking at people, almost as if he saw straight through
them. He didn't smile. He licked his dry lips twice and nodded
towards the Red Cross travel permits on the table. Johannes
scooped his up and tucked it deep within his tunic. Ilse put hers
in the bodice of her dress.

Joost was unwrapping a leather pouch from which he extracted glass vials and some hypodermic syringes.

'What the hell do you think you're doing?' Johannes said.

'Don't you want your vaccinations?' Joost said, and for the first time Ilse realised his German was perfect. He spoke with a slight accent, was from Hamburg, maybe. He was no more South African than she was, she realised.

'Vaccinations?' Johannes said.

'I believe Doctor Seiler mentioned them to your companion. You are travelling to South America. Doctor Seiler told me to give you shots for Hepatitis, Diptheria, Typhoid, Tuberculosis and Rabies. It would be a shame to have survived so terrible a war only to fall victim to a fatal and yet easily preventable disease. And you have paid a great deal of money for them.'

Johannes shook his head irritably and began to roll his sleeve up. 'Who are you to be administering vaccinations?' he said. 'Are you a doctor, too?'

'Something like that.'

The light swung from the ceiling, glinting in the glass of the bottle.

15

W HEN SILAS PAYNE drew up in front of the house and saw the Red Cross lorry outside he knew he'd found the right property. Pale light shone from around the edges of the cellar door.

He parked and began to creep towards the door. He wanted to find some window, some vantage point where –

A figure moved out of the darkness. Payne jumped before he saw that it was Captain Booth. His face seemed different somehow, lit as it was from below by the orange light of his cigarette.

'He's inside. The man you are looking for. Your killer. His victims are with him,' Booth said, with a curious lack of inflection in his tone.

'What the hell are you doing out here, then?'

'Because I want the people inside to die. I know who they are. I know the killer's name, by the way. It's Otto Flense. I stood over there in the trees and watched his victims go down the steps there with him. He's probably wrapping his ligature round their necks right now.'

Payne began to walk towards the cellar door.

Booth stepped into his way, blocking his path.

'What are you doing? Let me pass.'

'Isn't that what you want? Justice. Then let the bastard alone. Those people in there deserve to die.'

'That's not your decision to make, damn you.'

Payne moved forward. Booth fumbled the sidearm from his holster and pointed it at the policeman.

Payne stood very still, watching Booth, seeking eye contact.

'You don't want to do this, Captain Booth.'

The barrel of the pistol trembled.

'They have killed my friend. So what better way to repay them than to let that psychopath have his way with them? We're going to stand out here and let Flense finish. Then you can arrest him.'

'Captain Booth, I am not going to stand aside and allow these people to be murdered, even if they are murderers themselves. So you're going to have to shoot me or get out of my way.'

Payne took one measured step forward, then another. Booth hesitated. The pistol barrel trembled.

'Stay where you are, Payne.'

'No.'

Payne took another step forward and Booth cried out, 'Damn you!', lowered the pistol and threw himself at Payne, trying to push him back.

The two men struggled and then the pistol suddenly bucked in Booth's hand and Payne's ears rang and he fell back onto his buttocks.

Silas Payne groaned and sat up. Then he saw that Captain Booth lay on the floor, gasping, with his hands clasped over his stomach, trying to staunch the flow of blood welling through his fingers.

Payne knelt beside Booth and tried to unbutton his battle-blouse. Booth was shaking and his face was already pale.

'I've blown a bloody hole in my guts,' he said, wincing.

Payne took his coat and rolled it up, placing it beneath Booth's head.

And then the cellar door rattled.

Payne froze. Someone inside was trying to open it. The handle moved, the door rattled again and blows began to sound on the wood.

Payne rose and looked at the door. A tremendous blow shook it and the wood around the lock began to break and splinter. More blows sounded. Payne picked up the pistol from the ground.

The door opened. Dim light within outlined a man's figure.

'Stay where you are, Flense, or I'll shoot,' Payne said, positioning himself at the top of the stairs and raising the pistol.

'What the fuck are you saying?' the man said in German.

'I know you speak English. I saw the records.'

Flense still spoke in German. 'Do you know, I've just about had enough of this fucking nonsense for one night. Get out of my way or I swear I will cut your eyes out.'

As the man spoke he began to shuffle up the stairs towards Payne.

Payne brandished the revolver. 'I won't let you –'

Something heavy flew up the stairs and hit Payne on the shoulder. He stumbled backwards and the man charged at him.

'Stop!' Payne shouted, knowing the warning was pointless, as the moonlight caught the wild, murderous look in his attacker's eyes. The knife blade rose and . . .

The pistol barked in Payne's hand and the man seemed to

hit an invisible wall. The bullet stopped him dead and he collapsed.

Payne rose and walked towards him, keeping the pistol trained on his head.

The bullet had caught the man in the centre of his chest, right above the sternum.

He made weak movements as blood poured from his wound, but his eyes held Payne's as he whispered low curses, teeth bared in his gaunt face so that he seemed more animal than man. Hatred and rage flared for a moment and then the light faded from his eyes. A hideous rattle sounded in his throat: he was gone.

Payne raced down the stairs to the cellar.

A woman lay face up on a table. She was breathing, but her skin was pale. A single droplet of blood was meandering across the inside of her bared forearm.

A man was lying on the floor beside her, face down. The hair on the back of his head was matted with blood and there was blood on the floor beside him. It looked as if there'd been a struggle in the cellar: a chair was overturned and another had been smashed.

Payne checked their vital signs and found that both their hearts were beating strongly. He ran towards the road and began waving his flashlight in the direction of the nearest army checkpoint, flashing a single repeated message: SOS.

After he had done this for several minutes, he returned to the place where Booth was lying, caught hold of his hand and held it. Stomach wound, he thought. It was the worst place to get hit. Booth was losing a lot of blood. Several times he had tried to speak, but it caused him too much pain to continue.

It took ten minutes for the soldiers to arrive and another ten before the ambulance drew up. By then Booth was unconscious.

The ambulance took Booth and the two people from the cellar away on stretchers. Payne called out to one of the stretcher bearers, 'Make sure those two are placed under guard. They might try to escape.'

Afterwards he stood outside the house, staring up at the moon. He was trembling. He'd made a point of avoiding physical confrontation throughout his career and now within the space of thirty seconds he had separately shot two men.

Shooting Captain Booth had been an accident. It was one of the few times Payne had been unable to put his reasoning skills to good use. This failure would plague him; he knew that already. His hand was still trembling, a sense memory of the recoil as the pistol fired.

The killer lay on the floor where Payne had shot him. The soldiers had covered him with a tarpaulin. Payne lifted it and examined his face. It had been a lucky shot: a quick, clean death. The man's face still held an expression of surprise, the features frozen in the precise moment when the bullet had struck and for that one split second his brain had registered that the shot was mortal.

How old was he? It was difficult to tell, he was so battered and scarred. Payne examined the starburst scar on the man's jaw and wondered what had caused it. He stayed at the crime scene for two hours, overseeing the collection of evidence and trying to piece together what had happened.

There had definitely been a fight in the room. That must have been between the killer and the male captive. The woman did not have a mark on her.

Payne tried to reconstruct the scene in his mind.

Flense would have injected the woman first. That stood to reason. And then what? The woman would have passed out. Did the male victim become suspicious? Had he attacked Flense? Yes, that must have been what had happened. The male had been beaten unconscious. Payne returned to the police station, brewed tea and drank it slowly, staring at the embers of the flame.

An hour later a soldier knocked at the door.

'Pardon me, sir. Captain Shelley, the medical officer, asked me to bring these over to you. When they were putting the young lady to bed at the hospital they found these tucked inside her clothes. There was another one on the dead man.'

Payne recognised the cardboard documents: they were Red Cross travel permits.

He thanked the soldier. Then he said, 'You've made sure the two casualties are under guard, haven't you?'

The soldier nodded.

Payne went inside and opened the first travel document. The woman's face stared back at him. Payne wondered who she was, what it was she was trying to run from. He held the photo up to the window and tried to detect something in the woman's features that might betray why she needed to escape.

There was nothing: she looked utterly nondescript, pretty even, in a worn, weary kind of way.

Perhaps the man's photo would show more.

Payne opened the document . . .

. . . and ran across the room towards the door, waving his hands at the soldier who was turning his jeep around.

'Is there a problem, sir?' the driver said, halting his jeep with a squeal of brakes.

'The male victim, where did you take him?'

'To the hospital, sir. But what on earth's the matter?'

'The man on this card, the man that was trying to escape Germany. *This* is the man I shot.'

They drove straight to the hospital, but when Payne saw there was no guard in the corridor outside the male prisoner's room he was certain of what he would find when he opened the door. He pushed at it, found it blocked from the inside. He had to find someone to help to break it down.

Only the guard was inside, lying stretched out on the floor. A thin trickle of blood ran down his forehead. The cord from the window blind was wrapped tightly around his neck. His eyes and tongue bulged horribly. His battle-dress blouse and trousers were missing.

The window was open.

16

ILSE AWOKE IN a hospital bed. For a moment she lay completely still, enjoying the luxurious sensation of the clean linen against her skin. Then she began to remember what had happened and wonder where she was and how she came to be there. She remembered that Johannes had been arguing with Joost, the lorry driver, in the cellar of a house. Joost wanted to vaccinate Johannes but Johannes had become suspicious. He had insisted that Joost inject Ilse first. He had threatened the man with a knife. Ilse remembered allowing Joost to roll up her sleeve, the prick of the needle. And then . . .

. . . nothing. She couldn't remember a thing after that. It was all a blank.

She sat up in bed and realised a man in a civilian suit was sitting on the chair beside the bed. The man poured her a glass of water. Ilse drank it, handed back the glass.

'Who are you?' she said, looking up at his long, angular face.

'My name is Payne. I'm a British policeman. What happened in that cellar?'

'My name is Ilse. Ilse Hoffman, née Drechsler.'

'I know. That isn't what I asked you.'

'The man from the Red Cross, the lorry driver. He was going to vaccinate me. He wanted to inject my brother first but Johannes wouldn't let him. He made the man inject me instead.'

She trembled as the mention of her brother's name brought her memories crashing back. 'My God. Johannes. He killed the boy. The Polish boy.'

The policeman knew that, too. His expression did not change, but he nodded. 'He's been buried now. Did you know a man named Captain Booth?'

Ilse nodded.

'I'm afraid he's been flown back to England. He suffered an accident.'

'Accident?'

'He was shot. In the stomach.'

'Did my brother do it?'

The policeman looked towards the window. 'No. Your brother is dead. I shot him.'

Ilse felt nothing initially. Then relief swept through her.

'Will Captain Booth survive?'

Payne hesitated before answering and his eyes became briefly distant. 'Yes, he'll live. He might not recover completely, though.'

On the next day, Ilse was woken by a military nurse with a cold, abrupt manner. The nurse bullied her out of bed, gave her a plain shift to wear and clumpy boots with no laces.

'Where am I going?' Ilse said.

'To an internment camp. At first. They'll decide what to do with you when you get there.'

Ilse followed the nurse outside towards the waiting lorry, watching her laceless boots stir dust as she walked past the British soldiers, her head bowed.

EPILOGUE

Little Otto was nearing the end of the winding path now. His feet ached, but the mountain air was so crisp and pure he felt he could walk all day. He turned and looked back at the green plains of southern France. This would be one of his last opportunities to see them before the path wound down into a valley. But his spirits were soaring. He was looking forward to seeing Spain.

Two hours later he paused to eat some cheese and salt beef. He had made sure that he was well-provisioned.

Evening came as Little Otto spotted the huntsman's cabin at the far end of the valley. A light snapped on in the window.

Little Otto paused and watched it twinkling as shadows crept down the foothills. He wouldn't be alone tonight. That was lucky. It had been a while now.

He rummaged in the bottom of his bag, looking for his scalpels.

THE END

ACKNOWLEDGEMENTS

I WOULD LIKE TO thank the following people:

Chris, Jen, Linda and Jim from Salt Publishing for their continuing support.

Peter and Rosie from Ampersand for believing in me.

My family and friends for . . . everything, really.

Ian Wickes and Domyan Shalloy, who both read early drafts of the book and helped sharpen the storyline.

Hugh 'Basset' Winter, who served in occupied Germany after the war and was the first person of my acquaintance to mention the word 'werewolf' in connection with German soldiers. Although I am certain most of the stories he told me were either wildly exaggerated or entirely apocryphal, they did pique my interest enough that in later life I began to investigate the subject further.

The historian, Dr Christopher Knowles. Not only did his blog provide me with fascinating details of day-to-day life in the British Zone of Occupation, he was also deeply generous in giving me both his time and opinions as I sought to make the book as historically accurate as possible.

I used about thirty different books while researching Werewolf. Rather than list them all, I will only mention those that I found particularly helpful or inspiring.

The Last Nazis – SS Werewolf Guerrilla Resistance in

Europe 1944–1947 by Perry Biddiscombe and Christian In-grao's *The SS Dirlewanger: The History of the Black Hunters* were both obvious sources of inspiration. *A Strange Enemy People: Germans Under the British, 1945–50* by Patricia Meehan was an excellent source of information on British policy during the occupation, while Richard Bessel's *Germany 1945 – From War to Peace* painted a vivid picture of just how chaotic the situation was in Germany in the months after the German capitulation. My father also gave me an original copy of a booklet entitled *Why We Are Here* that was distributed among the soldiers of 30 Corps when the occupation began and which was invaluable as a tool to think myself into the mindset of British troops back then.

Finally, I must mention *Death in the City of Light* by David King, which tells the real life story of Marcel Petiot, a serial killer who terrorised Paris during and after the German occupation of the city. It was never my intention to write a second novel with a serial killer as the principal antagonist (in fact early drafts of *Werewolf* had a totally different focus) but I found Petiot so horrifying that, without realising at first, my baddie began to morph into something quite different from what I had originally intended. Now, much of Otto Flense's modus operandi (such as the mask of human skin, the use of a false escape line to lure victims and the treasure trove of suit-cases) is based directly on Petiot's.

MATTHEW PRITCHARD worked as a journalist in Spain for ten years, writing mainly for the ex-pat press and UK nationals. He grew up in a house filled with gas masks, military helmets, swords and rifles and has possessed a passionate interest in WWII ever since. Together with his father and uncle, he has amassed a sizeable collection of memoirs and memorabilia contemporary to the period.

EXCERPT FROM *Scarecrow* (2013)

I

Mamá was fast, considering her size: Tommy never saw the blow coming.

'¡Imbécil! I told you to go downstairs.'

His face stung as the cellar door slammed and he peered into sudden darkness. He felt for the wall, tried to remember what he'd overheard his sister telling her friend: four steps forward, duck, two more steps and bend, then feel for the loose board in the wall.

He stumbled once, feared he'd lost his place. But the torch was exactly where it was supposed to be; spare batteries, too. She was smart, his sister.

Little bitch.

The torch lit mildewed walls, cobwebs, musty furniture covered with sheets. Spiralling motes of dust fell through the beam of light as Mamá moved across the floorboards above. Tommy heard a gruff voice, then Mamá answering with her funny English: 'It's true I pissed off. Someone stealed my cat.' A pause. 'You pay now.' The voices faded as they headed upstairs.

Now he was safe. He shone the torch into the hole,

*exploring the treasures his sister had hidden there, picking
them out one by one.*

Doll.

Lipstick.

Mascara.

*The doll's hair was matted. Lipstick and mascara filled the
creases of the face where it had been applied, then wiped off.
So this was what she did down here: it was she Mamá normally
locked in the cellar. Mamá hated the slut.*

*Something behind the board in the wall stank. Tommy
knelt, played the torch beam over a carrier bag at the back of
the hole. It took him a moment to realise what it was; the red
smears on the see-through plastic had dried to a dark brown
mess but patches of ginger fur were still visible.*

*It was funny: after all the hissing and clawing, Mamá's cat
was so stiff and still now. That had been fun, fun to slice and
peel the animal into silence. He didn't care that it was* her *idea.*
HE had done the real work.

*A rhythmic thudding began somewhere far above. Tommy
swung his legs in time as he took the plastic doll's head and
began to smear it with make-up. He cradled the doll, traced a
finger from breast to belly, then moved onward to the smooth
plastic between the legs. He frowned. That wasn't right.*

Little girls weren't like that.

*Tommy yanked the legs apart, fished in his pocket for the
knife.*

2

Nineteen years later

He pulled the duvet cover to the top of the stairs with a final heave and toed the mass that lay within with the point of his shoe; a muffled whimper emerged, but nothing stirred.

Good. The sedative was still working. Like the rest of the house, the stairway was half-finished, a zig-zag of concrete rectangles in the centre of the building site. He'd never used this house before. The old place was no good; not since they'd built above it. Caution and patience: that was how he'd avoided capture all these years.

He walked to a windowless hole in the exterior wall and checked that he had not been followed.

Nothing. Wind rustled the palm trees; somewhere a dog barked. Lights – distant and stationary – sparkled against the mountain foothills.

Time to work.

He'd wanted to be rid of the thing ever since it lost its nerve: blubbering about nightmares, sticky red hands that clutched at its throat. He'd needed to exert all his influence to make it comply the last time. Best to be rid of it.

As always, he'd built the first half of the wall the week before. He put his hand atop the waist-high row of bricks and *wobbled it. Solid as a rock. He unpeeled the duvet cover and stared at the pale expanse of naked goose-flesh curled within, knelt for a moment, and cupped the cold-shrivelled genitals in his hand. There was a knife in his tool kit.*

Tempting.

But no. The thing did not deserve the honour. He could wait. Caution and patience. The dark did not scare him.

Not anymore.

He used the winch to raise the thing from the ground. Once suspended, he bent the legs backward from the knee, fed them into the tiny space between the interior and exterior walls. As he did so, the thing moved, barked its shin on the edge of the bricks. Sentience returned and with it a groggy presentiment of danger. It began to struggle feebly as it dangled above the wall. He traced a finger over the tight black mask that covered the thing's head. 'You've displeased me. You things always do. Now it's time for us to part.'

He watched, expressionless, as the thing raised a feeble arm; then he released a handle on the winch. The thing slumped, disappeared into the foot wide gap between the walls.

He turned to the pile of loose bricks, looking for his trowel.

Scarecrow
by Matthew Pritchard
ISBN 9781907773600
Available now

NINTH HOLE

Up in the World   80

TENTH HOLE

Golf, TV and Me   92

ELEVENTH HOLE

Home and Away   107

TWELFTH HOLE

Preparation and Practice   123

THIRTEENTH HOLE

I'm Enjoying It, Honest ...   136

FOURTEENTH HOLE

Golf? What is Golf?   149

FIFTEENTH HOLE

It Works For Me!   159

SIXTEENTH HOLE

The Shot That Got Away   175

SEVENTEENTH HOLE

Celebs and Showbiz Partners   186

EIGHTEENTH HOLE

Around with O'Connor   200

NINETEENTH HOLE

Golfers' Heaven   212

PROLOGUE

Teeing Off

GOLF IS the best of games, golf is the worst of games.

On a bad day, golf has a fury that would frighten Lucifer himself.

On a good day, golf has a serenity seemingly bestowed by the angels.

It has heights of ecstasy and lows of despair, and extreme swings of temperament such as are unknown to any other sport.

Golf is the last bastion of sportsmanship, fair play and competitiveness.

Golf is also wide open to abuse, score manipulation and law-breaking.

It has a language and a humour all its own – 'He's the type of golfer who shouts "Fore!", shoots six and puts down five on his card . . .'

'He's the only person I know with three balls in play and none is a provisional . . .'

Golf is played by using virtually every muscle and fibre in the body, but is governed by the six inches of grey matter between the ears. If you feel well, you play well, and the art of golf lies in preparing yourself to feel well – no matter what.

I have played well. I have played badly. And I've heard myself saying, 'Never again!' or 'What am I doing?' or maybe 'That's a worker!' – and similar choice phrases – time and again.

I have had pars and bogeys, eagles and birdies. I have broken 80, I've parred a course, but I've never reached the 'holy grail' of a hole in one (which, according to my mate Paul is only a 'fluke shot' anyway)!

In golf, if I can't claim to have been there and back, I reckon, like most incurable fanatics, to have been some of the way and enjoyed it.

Join me as I wander the course again, and remember . . .

My thanks to Mizuno, Stylo and Veldon Engineering for their unstinting support.

FIRST HOLE

When the Bug Bites

'WHEN THE bug bites, you never get free.' How true were the words of my first road manager Tommy, an ex-footballer, a great snooker player and a steady golfer. He used to tell me, 'I'm not very good, boss, but I'm hard to beat' – and he was!

In the summer of 1977 a wonderful man called George Willard told me, 'Remember, the golf club is a pendulum. She moves in a circle . . . remember our old friend the circle.'

George had in his time helped Val Doonican to become a single-figure golfer and given first lessons to a number of celebrities doing summer season. He also had limitless patience for the job.

And I was a wet-nosed comic from Liverpool,

3

appearing twice nightly at the ABC Theatre in Great Yarmouth – and spending all day doing nothing, much to the chagrin of Tommy the Roadie.

'Boss,' he urged, 'come on! The sun is shining, the day is free. Just give it a try . . .' And like a school-kid taking his first drag on a surreptitious Woodbine behind the bike shed, I was led to the golf course – the ex-teacher going back to school.

How lucky I was that the teacher prepared to give me my introduction to golf was George Willard, a gentleman, a pro and a stickler on the etiquette of the game.

An hour of chat and indifferent practice swings, not a little frustration and contemplation, and a good deal of listening and learning, culminated in my hitting a seven-iron shot that seemed never to come down – as a little old lady once said to me, 'It's the second best feeling in the whole world!'

George made me quit after that good shot. 'Remember, son,' he told me, 'it's the good one that brings you back.' And he was so right – the bug had bitten! I was never to be the same man again.

I bought my first clubs, with a bag and a trolley, and golf balls which retailed at 30p each – oh, how times have changed!

4

After three days of lessons, I was led to the tee for the first of six actual golf holes played. 'Just play the loop,' George suggested, 'where you won't be in anyone's way'.

A par on the third hole – two seven-irons and a 20 ft putt – and the world was my oyster.

A happy summer followed with more pars and surprisingly few disasters, with good habits taught by George and bad habits picked up from fellow golfers. Isn't it funny how you remember bad advice longer than good advice? . . .

On a long dog-leg hole, George would tell me, 'You'll take two shots to the green anyway, so hit a four-iron down the fairway and a five-iron to the green.' This worked more often than not and kept the blood pressure at a normal level.

At the same hole in the company of a fellow hacker, I heard: 'A big feller like you can open his shoulders and lamp one over the corner. You'll only be a wedge away from the green . . .' I swear that 'lamping' a ball over the corner of a dog-leg has cost me more balls than you'd need to furnish a driving range – but so what? When the bug bites, all sense disappears.

I have seen late nights pale into very early mornings, I have seen practice grounds with dew still on the grass, I have suffered blistered hands and shoulders sore from 'golfers' shoulder strap'.

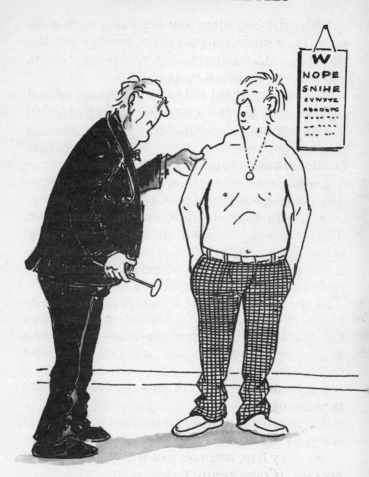

Golfer's shoulder

When the bug bites you become a sucker for every little invention and gimmick on sale in the pro-shop: 'All-in-one tool for cleaning clubs, balls, shoes, trolley wheels – £7.50'.

'Pro tees, guaranteed never to break, cannot be lost – 50p for five' (but who would ever need more than one!).

'Golf bag accessories – towel, score card holder, drinks container . . .'

There are special shoes, socks, gloves, different designs for dry weather, wet weather . . . balls of different consistency – low trajectory, high trajectory . . . 'What the heck – get a dozen of each!'

After four weeks of practice, performance and post-mortem, you're ready for new clubs . . . 'These are all right for beginners but the way you're hitting them you need the new Sevvy Ballesteros set, like me!' So speaks a bloke who's been playing for 20 years and still can't beat me . . .

But he must be right because he knows all the terminology . . .

'I was two under fives for the first nine.' (What is he talking about?)

'We play five, five and five with oozalems and presses.' (Come again?)

Actually this is an accumulator game when you are playing for money and counting birdies –

7

a deadly 'double or quits' cocktail which can be a surefire way to lose your mind – and a lot of money. I saw a man lose a Merc that way once – and, believe me – I definitely don't want to know!

Yet it is true that just when you think that golf is about playing for pleasure, about putting a small ball into a small hole, you are stunned to discover that the only sure test of skill lies in what you say.

How often have we stood on a tee and watched a player completely duff a shot, then heard ourselves say, 'That's a worker!' – just to rub it in. Nobody ever says, 'I'm going to hit a worker here.' Every shot tends to be a surprise – you're dumbfounded if it goes right, you're mortified if it goes astray.

I've seen a man hit a ball out of sand so fiercely that it cleared the green at a height of 60 feet and rising while his partner cried, 'Sit!!'

Perhaps my favourite all-time golf expression came from a pro-friend of mine, Alan Egford, who said, 'I've got this new driver – persimmon head, graphite shaft, 12 degree loft. It goes ten yards further than any other club I've ever thrown!'

Ah yes – the golf bug has many insidious symptoms and manifests itself by filling your head with dreams of greatness – 'If I'd only started younger, I'd be another Faldo . . .' It also

covers your hands with calluses and fills your house with accoutrements you'd never heard of last year, and will probably never need next year.

The bug even affects the way you celebrate Christmas, miraculously changing all Yuletide presents from ties, hankies and socks to balls, tees, hip flasks, all kinds of golfing gimmicks . . .

The bug bit me in 1977 and I have not been the same man since. Despite everything, I reckon I have a lot to be thankful for.

SECOND HOLE

Keep Taking the Lessons

'REMEMBER son, that golf, particularly the swing, is very much an individual thing . . .'

Nobody needs to show you how to drink a pint of lager – it's natural. But just try to explain in words the exact movements your body makes in doing it . . . you can make even the most natural and seemingly easy task sound unnecessarily convoluted and complicated.

So it is with golf: 'I can explain the grip, the set-up, the balance, the swing, the follow through. But in those critical moments of doing it, you're on your own, pal!'

Good advice and good grounding from Nick Lunn, one-time resident pro at Lavender Park golf range, Ascot. Nick, a man always concerned with the right things about golf, was the

Practice in front of a mirror

first to get me to practise in front of a mirror to see the full extent of the swing and the plane ('think of a cartwheel!') and the high finish.

He was a man who succeeded in giving credence to the efforts of many a hacker by patience and care, a man who could produce a gentle draw shot from people who I'd swear did not know how they did it even after they'd achieved it. No wonder Nick, who had that happy knack of getting the best out of other people and making them feel really good about it, has moved on to golf management, organisation and public relations.

As well as the pros and those born to teach, I've learnt important lessons from some of the greatest, from those born to play. Stars like Lee Trevino, who told me once, 'Tommy (why do Americans insist on calling me Tommy?) if you wake up with a slice, play to a slice . . . and most importantly, Tommy, if it ain't broke, don't fix it.'

And Sandy Lyle added, 'Try to slow your swing down to a blur . . .' I knew what he meant!

Then there was John Jacobs, the ex-Ryder Cup player and one of the best golf coaches around – a real golfing master. He can give lessons to any golfer and, merely by suggesting small refinements, improve any game in an

afternoon. John would tell me, for instance, 'There is a club in the bag for every shot. The driver is the only club you need to hit as hard as you can.'

On the practice ground one afternoon he showed me several things I was doing wrong and suggested simple remedies. Then I went out and had a round of golf with him – and beat him. As he handed over the fiver I won off him at the end of that round, he grinned, 'You wouldn't have won that without my help!' And he was right – I still have that fiver framed in my den.

So we've established that golf is there to be taught – although lessons seem to have a long-term wrecking effect on one's playing. Perhaps the best thing is to practise for six months but never actually to play. That at least would establish your natural game and 'groove in' the good habits.

After all, we all know how to play golf like Nicklaus and as long as we don't have to show we know, there's no problem. But golf is not like that – you can fool everybody except yourself and a good pro – 'If you swing like that and you say your handicap is 14, you must be the world's best putter, mate!'

Why can't we resemble computers and remember all the good advice while forgetting

all the useless stuff that's flying about? Computers have information punched into them – maybe they should punch it into us! Mind you, computers are also susceptible to bugs ... perhaps nobody or nothing is perfect after all!

I know from my days as a schoolmaster that good teachers give you two or three things to concentrate on, without confusing you with too much too soon.

So it is with golf. Concentrate on the set-up. 'Imagine an aircraft carrier,' I was told. 'A solid base made by the feet, the whole upper body pivoting on this, the arms and hands and club-head moving as one through the ball.'

An aircraft carrier? Yes – think about it. Anyone can land a plane on a runway. But try doing it when the runway is pitching and rolling, or even gently moving up and down. The art lies in the guy on the bridge keeping the *Ark Royal* as level as possible to aid the other guy trying to land the plane.

The take away: should be slow, deliberate – watch the shoulder go under the chin.

The follow through: our old friend the circle again! Maintain the swing and follow your hands through to watch the flight.

The head: down or up or whatever, the head should always be still.

14

The grip: too strong or too weak, watch the knuckles, the overlap, try it baseball style . . . whatever!

Most important, don't try to remember everything at once. Just like the man told to put his best foot forward, shoulder to the wheel, head up, chest out . . . you too could end up looking like Quasimodo and possibly suffering from 'golfers' droop', for which there is no known apothecary's cure.

The best lessons I have ever had consisted of 30 minutes on the practice ground followed by nine holes with the pro to experience real life situations – slopes, hanging lies, sand traps, trees, and so on.

And sometimes you can learn just by watching other golfers . . .

Trevino showed me an escape from under trees: take a six-iron, ball well back in the stance, a steady swing and the ball flies low and long. It looks good and feels even better if you call the shot before you play it.

Mike Burton, a great comic and a pal since our days together on *The Comedians*, showed me a wonderful sand shot: stance wide open, face wide open, swing out to in. The ball flies up and slices – a truly spectacular recovery shot!

Gil Dova, a brilliant juggler and a six-handicapper, on the first hole on the Burma

Road, all of 472 yards and a par four, told me, 'Tommy, call it a par five and try to birdie it.' It certainly saved the grey matter worrying about whether to 'lamp' it.

John Jacobs even taught me how to plan a hole backwards. It's no use smashing a ball as far as possible, leaving an indeterminate shot with the wedge. Better a controlled drive, possibly a three-wood, leaving a full wedge or a nine-iron to the green. I sometimes wish I knew half of what John knows – or even a tenth of what he's forgotten.

Stories of golf lessons and golf advice are legion. My all-time favourite golf lessons must be the ones given by Alan Egford, then resident pro at Torquay. Alan was the first pro I knew who used a video camera to demonstrate the rights and wrongs of swinging a club. Believe me, it's more effective than listening to comments like, 'You're still trying to hit from the top, you twit!'

Unfortunately, the funniest thing that happened to Alan happened on the day his video was on the blink. But just picture it ... 10.30 a.m. on a bright sunny June morning and into the car park at Torquay Golf Club glides a pale blue Rolls Royce driven by a man in pale blue trousers, hat, shirt, socks. As he emerges from the car it is apparent that he also owns a

Mr Pale Blue swung

pale blue golf bag with matching tees, towel, head covers and trolley.

Mr Pale Blue is in fact a scrap metal dealer, digital watch, sovereign ring, tattoos ('Love', 'Hate', 'Mum' and so on) – and he confesses to 'problems wiv me middle irons'.

On the practice ground with a six-iron, Alan ascertains that the problem lies in his swaying instead of turning his body in text-book style round the central pivot of his trunk.

Many, many efforts later and 'We are still swaying...' So Alan says it is time to concentrate on 'keeping our head still while we swing around it' and suggests, 'Let's pretend that the head is fastened by barbed wire to the nether regions – then it shouldn't move.' But still it doesn't stop Mr Pale Blue swaying.

In desperation Alan comes up with a possible solution. 'Look,' he says, 'I'll hold your head in my hands while you swing' – and if the video had been working, what happens next could have become a Jeremy Beadle *You've Been Framed!* classic!

With Alan's hand firmly gripping the man's head, Mr Pale Blue swings – and while the whole of his body sways to the right, his wig stays in Alan's hand! The head goes out, the club completes its swing and the head returns to the wig.

Oh, the fun the pros must have at our expense when they gather together . . . 'He'd be all right if he could get it in the air . . .' 'He asked me how to play a putt on the 18th. I told him to try and keep it low . . .' 'He's not the worst pupil I've ever had, but I can't remember who was . . .' and so on.

My undying memory of the ultimate 'harassed' teacher was an American pro I met on the QE2. He sat at the golf nets all day, tumbler of gin and tonic by his side, a carton of Lucky Strikes, and his back to the 'pupil'. From that relaxed position he would shout, 'Too close to the ball' or 'Swinging in to out' or 'Swaying . . . moved your head' or 'Breaking your wrists' – and the amazing thing was, he'd be right every time!

But then it is true – you too can 'hear' a bad swing. On the course it is accompanied by 'Oh no . . .' or 'What am I doing?' or 'Aaargh!' or even '*!@÷△f≈œ*'

Memorable shots, holes, scores, days . . . they're all a part of the rich tapestry that is the great game of golf. They are often things that only fellow golfers can share, moments that mean nothing to mere mortals ignorant of the finer art.

But more of this when we play 'The Game'.

19

THIRD HOLE

Playing the Game

IT'S THE GAME to beat all games, more attractive than any other to play, more religious than Sunday morning, more rewarding to play well, more punishing to play badly.

It arouses peaks of passion – I've seen rounds of drinks, and I've seen clubs round trees . . .

There is the story of the golfer who has butted a tree a dozen times in rage. As his head streams with blood, he is borne off the course on a stretcher, and still manages to call out to his playing partners, 'Same time next week, chaps?'

Golfers are said to be eternal pessimists – witness the man who walked on to the first tee, took a practice swing, tore his card up and went home.

21

Or again, witness the man who topped his drive, threw the driver down the fairway in disgust, walked after it, picked it up – and threw it again.

There is many a home truth spoken in jest. 'My best two shots are the practice swing and the conceded putt', 'What goes putt, putt, putt? Me!', 'I started well, then he threw a 91 at me . . .', 'I started 8, 8, 9, 8, then blew up . . .', 'The most difficult wood in my bag is the pencil'.

Being not so much a comedian as a reporter of life, I have had a great deal of fun playing 'The Game'. I have seen triumph, disaster, heartache, ecstasy – sometimes all on the same day!

And one lesson I have learnt, sometimes the hard way, is that in golf, if they give you anything, take it!

I couldn't believe it to begin with, but it's true. If they say this is a preferred lie, if it's winter conditions and you can put the ball where you like – do it. I used to think this was a little like cheating. I wanted to be a good golfer and I wanted to be able to hit myself out of trouble, to play from any position.

Rubbish – at the end of the day the important thing is to get your ball out of the trouble and drop it somewhere. If they say it's a rabbit scraping and you're allowed a free drop, take it

– because this guy won't be here tomorrow when you're trying to win his money and you're saying to no one in particular: 'Aren't I good – I played out of this hole!'

If you're murdering your opponent, if you've been given ten shots and you're knocking the stuffing out of them, don't say: 'I tell you what – don't give me any more shots. I'm playing well today.' Take 'em – drill the guy down, or as they say in Liverpool: 'Nail his hat on!'

Jimmy Mac is a big man, a builder, a Scouser and a steady ten handicapper.

I met Jimmy one Sunday morning at Childwall golf club in Liverpool. He helped me make up a four with two 18-handicappers, whose names should have been 'Butch' and 'Sundance'. Despite their obvious single figure ability, Jimmy and I had them neatly under control and were three up with three to play.

As he mounted the 16th tee, I said to Jimmy: 'We've got them. Now let's give them the *coup de grâce*.'

Jimmy shot me a withering look and said: 'Give them nothing!'

The game produces characters both good and bad. I've met the celebrity who had a pocket full of balls all the same number – the only man who never loses a ball in the trees but always

23

finds it teed up with a clear sight of the green.

I've also met the man who by rights should be the author of the book *101 Ways to Improve Your Lie*, and the player whose pencil won't write more than five no matter what he scores. But then they are all part of golf's rich tapestry.

Why is golf the only reason men will let you leave a bar at night? You can say, 'I'm not well' and they say, 'Sit down. You look all right . . .' Or 'I'm working tomorrow' and they'll say, 'Calm down, there's stacks of time.' Or you try, 'The wife's not well' and they say, 'You'll only be another 20 minutes.' Tell them you're on tablets and they'll say, 'This'll help to wash them down.'

But say, 'I must go. I'm on the first tee at eight in the morning' and watch them sympathise. 'You'd better get an early night then . . .'

The game is all, and all about the game is memorable. Bob Scholes is an estate agent, a golfer and the only partner I've come close to strangling on more than one occasion. He has a habit of saying, 'Take it away' (meaning the flag), but it has resulted in many an opponent saying, 'Thank you' and picking up his ball thinking we've conceded the hole.

We were nip and tuck with a pair at Waterlooville. Bob was in trouble but I had driven to the edge of the green on a short par

four. They were both out of bounds with their first drives, but one reached the green with his second and lay there for three.

As we approached the green, Bob opened his big mouth and said casually to our adversary, 'You're not going to putt that, are you?' He meant it as a joke, I suppose, but our surprised opponent said, 'No. Thank you very much' and picked up his ball for a conceded shot. That left me in rage to four putt, lose the hole and chase Bob nearly to the club house.

In my short golfing life span I suppose I must have tried every technique and every plastic-coated invention that's ever been produced to help me to play better.

It always amazes me whenever I play in a big Pro-Celeb-Am or the like that the pros don't have any of these things – the portable ballwasher, the combined score card, tee holder, pitch market, pencil and nail for taking things out of horses' hooves, the plastic-coated towel which never gets wet because it disappears up its own handle when not in use, the natty golf trolleys, motorised or transistorised or whatever, or the trolleys combined with bags that fold up to nothing and stack in the hold of an aeroplane . . . all of them wonders that make up the wonderful world of golfing gismos.

Golf doesn't finish on the 18th green. It only just begins . . . because that is when you go into the clubhouse and waffle on about your previous 18-hole exploits, or you go into the pro-shop and find out what else is new, the latest colour of sweater or golf shirt or glove, and thrill to the knowledge of the latest development. I'll never forget the first time I found out that FootJoy actually make golf gloves and gauge them by the size of your shoe. I couldn't believe it when the pro asked, 'What size shoe are you?' I said, 'Nine' and he said, 'This is the glove for you . . .' and it was! Whether that was a fluke or not I still don't know . . .

There are various implements to help you around the golf course – like the one for getting the ball out of the water. It looks like a ping-pong ball net at the end of a very long shaft, and it extends to scoop the ball out. There's the 'chipmaster club' which is basically a putter with a six- or seven-iron face. You take it away from the ball as a putter but when it strikes the ball it chips it, lifts it a foot or so off the floor and scuttles it along – a lovely pitch and run club for just off the green.

In my local golf club I have seen a driver which is actually supposed to correct a slice. In actual fact it looks like the rear light of a bike.

It costs about £600 and if you slice the ball as you hit it, this thing corrects the slice and hits it straight – which is fine except that it only corrects the drive. What you do if you slice your second shot, heaven only knows. Unless you are going to buy an alternative set of clubs to correct your slice all round the course, the odds are you are bound to slice with your wedge even though the 'super club' has corrected your drive.

I have seen clubs made totally of titanium, fashioned all in one piece and costing about £950. I've seen any number of weird and wonderful implements, all well worth the money, of course . . . but when it comes down to it, what does it matter? If you can't project the ball correctly in the air and send it forward in a specific line, give or take the odd yard, what is the point of having a fortune's worth of equipment?

At the end of the day, for a learner, a good half set of clubs – a three-, five-, seven-iron, maybe a wedge, possibly one or two woods, and a putter is all you need. The better you get, the better is the equipment you can buy.

It is always wise to know when to speak and when to stay silent on a golf course, as we have already seen, and this is certainly true where equipment is concerned. One of my more

embarrassing moments cropped up when I went to Anglia TV to prepare for a new game show called *The Zodiac Game*. I'd been told that the hierarchy at the station had a great love of golf and I was asked to make up a four with the producer, the programme controller and the head of light entertainment (otherwise known as God!).

The day dawned that we met on the first tee at Royal Norwich and to lighten the mood I decided to crash in with a funny. 'Have you heard,' said I, 'about the bloke on the first tee who said, "If anyone's interested, I'm playing a Commando 3", and his partner replied, "If you're playing a Commando, we don't need to know the number . . ." '

As I laughed, I realised God was unwrapping his own Commando 3! Fortunately, he and the others saw the funny side of it and the show still went on.

Frank Carson woke me once with a story about the hard-pressed hacker whose bogey hole was the 14th – a par three, 167 yards, pond in front of the green. Every Sunday he planted one, two, sometimes three balls in the water and he'd had enough.

The resident pro recommended a prayer. 'I don't believe in God,' said the hacker.

'Well, you've tried effing and blinding. You've

nothing to lose,' the pro told him.

So there he was on the 14th tee, three under his handicap, ball teed up and ready to go. And found himself muttering, 'If there is a God up there, will you help me?'

'Certainly my son,' said God. 'But first put away your four-iron and get out a three wood. You're playing into the wind.' And he did as he was told.

'Secondly, my child,' said God, 'you've teed up the ball too high. Lower it.' And again he did as he was told.

'While you're at it,' God added, 'that ball has more smiles than a clown. Use a different one.' Then as the hacker started to unpeel a Titleist, God said, 'Not a new one, you prat!'

Sometimes God's help may not be enough. Take the story I was told at the lovely Slaley Hall golf course just outside Newcastle.

That district was blessed with its own version of Mr Pale Blue of Torquay – but this man's problem was a massive hook. Every shot went left, all the time, sometimes like a batsman's pull to square leg. No amount of corrective therapy could cure this fault – opening the stance, weakening the grip, playing under- water – until it became obvious that our man was letting go of the club with his right hand, thus causing the left to pull everything round.

He swung it as he had seen the dustbin men do

It was clear that the only cure was rhythm, or at least some means of co-ordinating grace, tempo and a firm grip on the club. The pupil was instructed to watch other people's rhythms – kids on swings, ballet dancers, tennis players – anything to try to find that elusive flow.

He found it while watching a bin lorry pull up outside Curry's electrical shop and seeing a dustman swinging bins on to the truck.

Having begged, pleaded and eventually bribed permission, he proceeded to attempt a rhythmic practice swing. He picked up a dustbin, aimed it at the cart, swung as he had seen the dustbinmen do, let go with his right hand – and hooked it through Curry's window! Oh, I do hope that story is true!

The game is all, and it's all about the game I write.

When all else fails, who can I turn to? Of course – I can turn to the caddie.

FOURTH HOLE

The Curse of the Caddies

THE CADDIES . . . ah yes, the caddies. Where would we be without them? Languishing in the rough, among the trees, deep in the bunkers without their advice, encouragement, side bets . . .

The caddies are living legends as famous in their own way as the pros. I've met many and enjoyed their company, their banter and their idiosyncrasies.

For two or three years running I played in the Howard Keel Classic at Mere Golf Club, Manchester and there I came across Ben, a man whose grip of the English language was constantly slipping.

Ask him, 'How's this putt, Ben?' and he would say, 'Straight as a whistle!' (Pardon?)

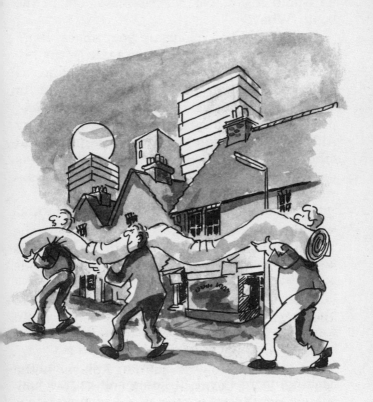

Ask him, 'What are you drinking Ben?' and he would insist, 'No, I'll get these. I'm in the boat.' (What?)

Ask him, 'What colour are your shoes, Ben?' and he'd say, 'Jet white!' (Come again?)

My first meeting with a real caddie as opposed to a mate who humped my bag, was in Southport. Drinking in the Fisherman's Rest pub, I made the acquaintance of the legendary Alfie Fyldes, caddie to Player, Watson and others. Alfie's knowledge of courses was unrivalled – yardages, traps, wind directions – would he ever caddy for me?

'As soon as you get a swing, lad,' he said – and he was right.

Alfie and his brother Albert had me in absolute hysterics with their tales. Albert had a stammer and apparently when Alfie first got him a job as a caddie he was teamed with a player who suffered from the same defect. They were asked before the competition, 'Name your ball' and neither of them could say 'Titleist'!

I had only recently moved into a house backing on to Royal Birkdale golf course just outside Southport, and we were enjoying a few drinks in a local hostelry. 'How big is your lounge?' Alfie asked me. I told him and he said, 'I've got just the Persian carpet for you!'

We agreed a price and they promised to

deliver it when the pub closed. It was one of those occasions when, your judgement clouded by the devil's brew, everything makes perfect sense . . .

So it was that at closing time, late night Southport revellers were treated to the sight of three grown men, the worse for wear, carrying a 40 ft by 30 ft Persian carpet from one side of the town to the other.

'Dog-leg here, Albert,' Alfie would shout as we turned a corner. 'Sh-sh-shut up. I-I-I can see . . .' he'd reply. I still laugh at the memory of that crazy night – and they are still my friends.

Scotland, bonnie Scotland, home of golf, the greatest courses and the ultimate in unique caddies.

It was pro-celebrity golf time on television, filmed at Turnberry, and I was to partner Sandy Lyle against Lee Trevino and Jimmy Tarbuck – very illustrious company.

To soften the blow of my first television golf appearance, it was suggested I play a practice round the day before to get accustomed to the nine holes, and introduce myself to Willie.

Now Willie (or 'Wullie' – where are you now?) was the archetypal Scottish caddie – purple nose, red cheeks, whites of the eyes brown, breath like kerosene, and an expert on the course.

I was with Kevin Keegan and a couple of friends, and a par three loomed, 157 yards, wind of gale force directly behind.

'Eight-iron, Willie,' I said.

'Seven,' came the reply.

'No, eight in this wind,' I insisted.

'Tack ma wurd, it's a seven.'

So I did – and I hit the ball with a seven. It was still climbing as it cleared the green.

'Well,' said Willie, 'it'll be a seven tomorrow . . .'

On another occasion, Rover Cars arranged a special corporate day and flew 14 top dealers and fleet buyers up to Scotland for a day's golf. First class air fares, hotel, all you can eat and caddies paid for. However, there was a small request: 'We thought it would be nice,' the party was told, 'if you clubbed together to bung the caddies a tip.'

'Nobody bungs me and I refuse to tip my caddie,' said a portly gent, who arrived in a Bentley and had a watch like Big Ben. 'I prefer to hire a trolley.'

And this he did for the princely sum of £2.

The day dawned and we all trooped off down to the first tee, five teams of three, including me. The portly gent's team teed off from the second and as they proceeded down the fairway, three players, two caddies and a trolley, one

player asked: 'What is it for me from here, caddie?' 'A five-iron, sir,' came the reply.

And the portly gent piped up, 'What is it for me?'

'Ask your trolley!' Ah, sweet retribution . . .

Have you ever wondered what caddies talk about when we can't hear them? Things like, 'I've had some awful players in my time, but this feller . . .'

Maybe they don't talk golf at all. They can certainly play the game, and they do give useful advice. More importantly, they can convince you they are right even when they are not.

Witness the irate golfer, who accuses, 'You said three iron – and it's short!' 'Ah yes,' says his caddie, 'but there's a lot of wind up there you can't see . . .'

Or the golfer and caddie watching a sliced drive. 'Is that in trouble?' asks the former. 'Not yet, sir.'

In the game of golf, there are no surprises and all stories are true . . . so they say.

Take the tale of the pro on the 18th hole, on the final day of the British Open. He is well down the fairway with his drive and only needs a par to win the championship.

'Five-iron, caddie.'

'Three.'

'Five-iron.'

'Three.'

'Are you sure?'

'Trust me . . .'

The three-iron is hit, just as the wind comes up, pulling the ball down on to the green three inches from the hole. The pro taps in the easy putt and the championship is won.

'Thanks caddie,' he beams. 'But how did you know it was a three-iron?'

'I didn't,' the caddie confesses, 'but I'd already cleaned all the others.'

Do the pros suffer the same live-wire chat from their caddies as the amateurs? 'Of course,' said a pal of mine. Witness the legendary tale of the pro playing at Royal Dornoch, having just won the Open.

He asks his caddie, 'What's the line on this dog-leg?'

The caddie tells him, 'We play out to the right with a wee bit of draw, and the wind from the sea brings it back.'

'But I play with a fade,' says the pro.

Nevertheless the caddie insists, 'Play out to the right with a wee bit of draw, and the wind from the sea brings it back.'

The pro persists. 'But I play with a fade, I tell you, so I'll cut the corner off, shall I?'

'You do what you like,' says the caddie, 'but have you a spare ball in your bag?'

Subtle sarcasm, but well meant. And the story must be true – because it's about golf.

FIFTH HOLE

The Ladies, God Bless 'em

WHY CAN'T WE be more pragmatic? Why can't we be more realistic? Why can't we be more like the ladies, God bless 'em? Nobody – usually – has such a blissful outlook on golf.

'I keep topping the ball . . . you know, catching the upper half,' the golfer says to his wife. 'Well, why don't you turn it over?' she advises.

'The motorised trolley won't go. The battery's flat,' he tells her. 'Oh dear, what shape should it be?' she asks.

And they are alive to all the excuses. 'Sorry I'm late, dear. I had a hole in one,' he says. 'Surely that meant you finished quicker,' she suggests. There's no answer to that.

In golf there should be a very special place for

Clubs to the tip

all the ladies – and I don't just mean on the forward tees. It is good to see clubhouses with whole families enjoying the fun. I look forward to mixed foursomes (who said 'gruesomes'?) – they are good for the game, part of the new face of golf.

But changes can be a long time coming in certain quarters. Who was it said: 'Golf means gentlemen only, ladies forbidden!' And who still believes it?

I heard a good story (and I have no reason to believe it's not true) from a snooty Home Counties club, where a party of ladies were sitting out on the verandah, watching a male four-ball coming up the 18th. One of the players obviously was heading for a very good score that only needed something like a par or a bogey to break the course record. But he duffed his second shot into the heather and it was totally unplayable. Understandably, he came out with a four-letter mouthful in sheer frustration.

On hearing this, one of the ladies got up and stormed into the secretary's office. 'This is disgusting,' she complained. 'I am out on the patio with a group of other ladies and we shouldn't have to put up with such disgraceful language from some of these so-called gentlemen – something should be done about it.'

The committee met and took it very seriously. After a long deliberation they decided the best

way to prevent this embarrassment happening again was to ban ladies from the verandah . . .

Playing at a well-known northern club, which, I might add, has its own ladies' course, and which you might think would be more liberal in its attitudes, Pat joined me as caddie and we had a very pleasant round. Coming off the 18th, my partner said, 'What's the round?'

'A pint, and a half of lager and lime, please,' I said.

'OK,' he said. 'See you in the bar. We'll pass Pat's out to her through the window.'

'What!!!!' Stand by for decibels from both of us.

'You see,' explained our flustered partner, 'I'm afraid the clubhouse is gents only. Ladies aren't allowed.'

'Well, you know what you and your club can do . . .' and we both exited, our smiles now a mere grimace.

I got a fortnight of earache after that experience. 'I don't know why you bother with such a chauvinistic shower!'

'They're not all like that, dear. Honest!'

'Don't give me that. For two pins I feel like taking your clubs down the tip!'

'Don't do that love . . . hey, you know that expensive dress you fancied last time we were in town . . .' Thanks a lot, guys. Never again!

Pat is never backward in coming forward and making her feelings known. There was the time I played at Portmarnock just outside Dublin. That was the day I bought a brand new golf ball from the caddie, hit it off the first tee and it broke in two. I had to walk down both sides of the fairway to retrieve the pieces and take it back. Pat meanwhile was having problems of her own.

In the clubhouse she discovered she wasn't allowed to have a drink because she couldn't go into the main room – it was 'gentlemen only' again. So she complained bitterly to an important-looking chap who, when he could get a word in, said, 'I do agree, madam. I'm very sorry – but what can I do?'

When he walked away, one of his party came across to Pat and said, 'Do you know who that was?' and she replied, 'No.'

'That was the President,' she was told.

'The President of the golf club?' she asked. 'No,' he replied. 'The President of Ireland . . .'

Ladies are capable of the most amazing feats on a golf course – and one I won't forget in a hurry occurred at Eastbourne, ideal for the 'in and out' golfer – a fine 18-hole course, and a short but equally good nine holes which can combine with 'the loop' to make a change whenever you

feel like it. Here on the ninth hole of the short course, I saw my first hole in one. The distance was about 106 yards and a steady sand wedge on a still day was all that was really required.

Leaving the green one Saturday morning, I turned to see a wonderful combination on the tee. He was a slimmish chap, in his mid 60s, told to play golf for exercise to help a heart condition. She was of a similar age but portly and wearing a mackintosh (honest!), accompanying hubby for the sake of his health and her sanity, I guess.

She must have won the eighth because she stood first on the tee with (I later learnt) a two-wood (for 106 yards, remember!).

I saw the swing, the ball left the club at a height of two or three inches and bobbled gently but inexorably towards the green. Then as if by magic, it was drawn straight into the hole.

'Where did it go?' cried hubby, obviously myopic.

'In the hole,' I answered.

'Don't be damned ridiculous, man . . .'

I moved away – never intervene between husband and wife, especially at times like these.

Later I saw the lady again in the pro shop, enquiring, 'I holed in one on the ninth. Do I get anything?'

'Yes – an eagle, luv,' replied the Scouse-born pro.

Truthfully, I have found that ladies love golf and I love the dignity they bring to it – steady swings, eagle-eyed putts, grace and, most importantly, competitive spirit.

I caddied once, and only once, for a lady in a club competition. We lost our drive on the fourth and spent ages searching heather and undergrowth while the opposition stood looking at her watch.

Eventually our opponent said, 'Your five minutes are up . . . and by the way, your ball is over there!' Wow! Never again . . .

On the other hand I had the great pleasure of playing a couple of holes with Mickey Walker, that lovely lady pro. It was at Foxhills in the Colonel Sanders Golf Classic.

Mickey was in great form – an elegant swing, no apparent effort. We played the first and waited on the second for the next team to come along – a trick I now use on corporate days. It makes for a long day but it is a great way to get to know the audience before the evening's speech.

It is a shame that we ask lady golfers to play on courses designed for men, and that to 'help' them we allow them to tee off nearer to the trouble.

I wonder if Mickey remembers the prize-giving at the Colonel Sanders Classic? I'll never forget it.

Having had one of those days when everything went right – I had recorded the longest drive, nearest the pin and best individual score – and not wishing to look too much of a 'smart alec' (remember Rudyard Kipling: 'Don't look too good, nor talk too wise') I offered a putter as a prize in the charity auction.

There had been a booby prize for the person who had lost the most balls and that had been 'won' by a man who claimed 22 balls adrift. Would you believe that this man bid for my putter! He'd never been near enough to a green to use one . . .

Mind you, that does pose an interesting question. Why reward the player who records the longest drive with a driver? Or the player who sinks the best putts with a putter? Seems there's a lot of 'Irish' logic to golf at times.

Prize-giving in golf to the amateur side always amuses me because they tend to give putters to the guy who has won. If he's won he's obviously putted very well, so what does he need a putter for? And they give drivers to the feller who has hit the longest drives. If he's hit the longest drive with the club he's got, why does he need another one?

47

On big golf days, the companies – Dunhills, Benson & Hedges – often give the celebrities and all partakers in the game a souvenir bag with Dunhill Masters on it or a golfing umbrella, or waterproofs and things, and these are as good a trophy as a celebrity would want because that's the kind of thing he's going to use as well as treasure.

You can tell how my golf has changed if you look in my trophy cupboard. Because when I started off, if I appeared in anything or even won anything, I got a little tiny cup, a shield or a plaque. That has since gone on through the phase of the pewter mug to the crystal glass – which naturally I am always afraid to use – now I'm waiting for the day of the Teflon frying pan golf trophy.

Syd and Eddie of Little and Large, when they stage their Golf Classic, tend to come up with some novel prizes. A few years ago it was a little pair of bronze golf shoes on a plaque. That's what I call original.

Giving a winning celeb a bottle of champagne is not as satisfying as giving him a little certificate or plaque, or indeed something completely different. Gradually the world of golf is realising that it has got the right kind of prizes to hand out. It only takes a bit of thought.

SIXTH HOLE

The Courses – Beside the Seaside

I HOPE my shows have entertained seaside audiences as much as their golf courses have entertained me.

Come back with me to Gorleston Golf Club, Great Yarmouth in the summer of 1977, with George Willard in charge of instruction and yours truly doing everything right – the right clubs, balls, a half decent swing and all day to practise and play. Here it was that I learned the value of the social side of golf – a good clubhouse and great members very tolerant of learners, particularly those who shout 'Fore' after every shot – just in case!

I remember my first par on the first – a

*Cracking a drive over the edge and
on to the beach below*

three-wood, wedge and two putts. George told me on the green, 'Always remember the bucket principle. Get as near as the rim of a bucket and even you can't miss with the second putt . . .' True enough, George, but the only putt I've ever been sure of was the fourth!

Gorleston's course runs along the seaside with the North Sea as a neighbour. Many is the time I've conceded defeat when cracking a drive over the edge and on to the beach below.

One of my favourite Gorleston stories features two of my heroes, not pro golfers but great amateur players and brilliant comedians. Arthur Askey and Ted Ray were allegedly playing at Gorleston one afternoon. (I'm told for the Town Hall clock!). Here were two Scousers locked in mortal combat and Arthur was trying to slot in a two-foot putt. Out at sea were yachts gently tacking in the breeze when Arthur over-borrowed and totally missed this simple putt. Staring wilfully at Ted, he pointed out to sea and remarked, 'How can I putt with all that racket going on?'

Ted Ray also features in a story I heard about Torquay Golf Club. Torquay to me is almost like going home. Some of my best golf, happiest days and most traumatic moments are bound up in that club. I spent one long hot summer playing that lovely course and many enjoyable hours

featuring in charity golf days with the members.

I learned never to have the honour when playing the sixth, because the climb is a real heart tester and you're better off losing the fifth in order to get your breath back.

Berni Flint, the much underrated singer and a golfer of very low handicap, had purloined an exploding ball from somewhere and while I was wheezing myself together again, switched it for mine on the tee.

Playing a three-iron for safety, I hit the ball straight and true, only to see a puff of blue smoke and the ball disintegrate about 150 yards away. I can't repeat my first expression (I think it was something like 'Golly heck!'). But my second was to ask for medical assistance.

'For you?' asked my partner.

'No,' I said. 'For Flint!'

But I digress. Ted Ray was playing a morning round at Torquay and striding down the superb 18th fairway following a good drive. To his left a mechanical digger was hard at work in the garden of a house, excavating a trench to lay drains. As he passed, Ted shouted to the digger driver: 'Don't bother on my account. It was only an old ball . . .'

After Yarmouth and my lessons and practice

with patient George, Blackpool Opera House loomed, but top of the bill status prevented serious golf in 1978 – just the odd knock and hope that the swing stayed together for another time.

The Old Links, Royal Lytham, Fairhaven . . . all lovely Lancashire courses and always a joy to play. Let me tell you, however, about Poulton-le-Fylde. I was staying out Poulton way in a sumptuous flat belonging to showbiz friends while entertaining the early holidaymakers at Blackpool's North Pier. The season included 2.30 p.m. matinées and thus prevented a full 18 holes. So we frequented Poulton-le-Fylde course, where a challenging nine holes was ideal for a comic seeking regular exercise.

The weather was good and the course so busy that it was imperative to book a starting time. So it was that I came across an amazing Scottish four-ball. They arrived fully clad for anything but golf – cut-away jeans, flip-flops, and no clubs.

Having been suitably equipped for the fray and provided with plenty of 'ammo', they enquired about the geography of the course. Obviously they were virtual beginners and the pro took kindly to them.

'Look,' he said, 'the chap in the green hat

knows the course. He and his partner are off just before you. Follow them!'

Off went the Green Cap and his pal, followed rapidly but very erratically by the Scots, balls flying in all directions.

After about 40 minutes, the head Scot was back at the clubhouse. 'We need more balls, pal.'

'How's it going?' he was asked.

'Great.'

'Are you finding your way OK?'

'No problem. My pals are waiting on the fifth tee, and we've got the guy in the green hat there till I get back!'

Obviously they were taking no prisoners that day . . .

Staying with summer seasons, let me drift north-east to Bridlington, a great little town full of warm-hearted folk and good steady golfers, always willing to make up a game, no matter what.

Here at the Belvedere Road, a cliff-top course, prone to be windy, I met David Owen, a ten-handicapper, photographer and producer of the best hand-out pics I have ever had. He is my only witness to the reactions of British folk to the unexpected.

The local trams and buses were carrying a

subtle advert for my summer show at the Spa Theatre – it involved a picture of me all of four feet tall.

The back nine holes at Bridlington pass the bus terminus at one point and on this summer morning David and I were teeing up, being watched by a dozen people on the upper deck of an open-topped bus. They looked at me, then over the side at the picture, then back to me again. And we could hear them arguing . . .

'Naw,' said the expert, 'it's not him. Too old and too poor. He's carrying his own clubs.'

As David took a practice swing, the expert exclaimed: 'God, he's missed it!'

We waited for the bus to pull away before drawing breath – and collapsing in a heap!

Golf was fun at Bridlington, and the fun began even before the season opened. I always arrive a couple of days early for a season or a panto, to 'bed in', sort out digs and parking, and make for the golf course – though not necessarily in that order.

I contacted the theatre on the Friday to see if anyone was available for a round of golf on Saturday morning and was put in touch with the captain of Flamborough Head Golf Club, who in turn put me on to the proprietor of a local hotel.

Mike was a two-handicapper, a great bloke

and heavily overworked in the catering trade. But he was delighted to oblige, and we agreed to meet at about 8.15 on the Saturday morning.

He was full of smiles when he arrived and after two or three holes of getting to know each other, he spilled the beans on the 'joke of the day'.

The night before, Mike had said to his wife, 'Give me a shout at seven in the morning, luv.'

She said, 'You never get up early on a Saturday. What's up tomorrow?'

'I'm playing a quick round of golf, that's all.'

'Oh yes, and who's free to spend three hours playing golf with you at peak booking time?'

'It's Tom O'Connor, luv!'

The good lady said nothing for a few minutes and then announced, 'When you come home, Mike, I may not be here. I'm going shopping.'

'Who are you going to the shops with, luv?'

'Barbra Streisand!' came the snappy reply.

We played Flamborough Head, a tricky course made even trickier by the fact that most of the morning it was covered in mist.

'The line is roughly there . . .'

'Can you see the lighthouse? Well, it's that way . . . about an eight-iron.'

'I've pulled that drive – where would you say it was?'

'Gone!'

We stopped for tea at a small café halfway

round the course. I still can't believe that the folk in that little village still left their doors unlocked. Was it ever like that where I lived?

Maybe this wasn't Flamborough after all. Maybe it was Brigadoon, and Mike was really Gene Kelly ... No, with that beautiful swing, he had to be for real!

Along the coast to Scarborough. The year is 1981 and I am playing the South Cliff golf course. Next to my home course, I have probably played this one more often than any other, so often, in fact, that I indulge in a mental round of golf at South Cliff if I can't get to sleep! It's much more interesting than counting sheep, or whatever ... I wonder if other golfers do the same! My best score on the first is a three – a three-wood, a nine-iron and one putt. On the second, another birdie ... It's amazing how you can break 60 by remembering only the good holes!

Denis Taylor was the pro at South Cliff in my day – a good teacher, Yorkshire born and proud of the fact that he'd never been out of the county!

'We're standing tall and we're remembering tempo,' he would stress. It was great to play a round with a man who could almost anticipate your next mistake.

He once admitted to me that when he first arrived at the club, he'd played a practice round and shanked three consecutive shots. 'I don't think I'm going to like it here!' he told the secretary. But thankfully he stayed. He was a good man and those were good days.

They were also days of practising with Alberto, a Spaniard, a collector of drivers and any gadget that would lengthen his drive.

'This driver hits the ball ten further yards,' he would enthuse; or 'This Pinnacle ball goes ten further yards.' Many a day I would see him with a bucket full of balls and half a dozen weird and wonderful woods lined up ready to be 'auditioned'.

'He's got all those drivers – he only needs a conductor,' I heard one wag say.

Alberto, in fact, was leader of a Latin singing group called Los Zafiros, a great support act, professional and very entertaining.

He was also the owner of the longest back swing I have ever seen. Only the ground or his left ankle prevented it going full circle. It was amazing to watch him play a weeny sand shot with the same action as his drive!

Here was a man who claimed he once won 60 (or was it 600) balls from Jimmy Tarbuck on the putting green. The story goes that Alberto turned up at a particular golf club looking for a

game and found Tarby on the putting green. 'Fancy a quick nine holes?' he suggested. 'Play you for a ball a hole . . .' And, of course, Alberto won. 'OK,' said Tarby. 'Double or quits' – probably not realising that double or quits can apply to each hole. It's amazing how it all adds up. Actually I've always been too scared to question Tarby about this tale . . .

Anyway, here at South Cliff, with Alberto, Denis and many other partners, I played some of the best golf of my life. How? Put it down to early nights, a two-mile jog in the morning to loosen up, 50 practice balls, ten minutes' putting practice and then off to the first tee. But why does it feel like cheating?

Probably because real golfers jump out of the car, change shoes in the car park with one foot on the bumper, then scurry to the tee, take a single practice swipe and lurch into the ball. Then, if their shoulder is still in its socket, they clump off round the course, attempting to shake off last night's hangover and lack of sleep.

It is possible to play 18 holes in that condition – and actually forget some of the holes you've played. How many times have you had to consult your card to see what happened back on the fourth? 'Did I really par that hole . . . surely I would have remembered!'

But golf is all about remembering, isn't it? At

rabbit level we remember only the good shots. At ten-handicap and below we only remember the bad ones . . . 'Did I really pull that five iron into a gale?' 'How? . . . Why? . . . What am I doing!'

And you are ready to blame everyone except yourself. 'What a brainless twit I was to let this guy talk himself into caddying for me! I asked for a six-iron, he gave me a nine and without checking I hit it. Now the gallery are playing a new game show – Spot the Prat!'

Incidentally, Scarborough was where I first heard of the Henry Cotton ploy of swinging a club against an old car tyre to strengthen the wrists. It works for sure, and I gained the nickname of 'Wristy O'Connor' for a long time, although the actual cause of my 'wristitis' was human, not inanimate.

At South Cliff club there was a young boy, maybe 17, who hung around the pro-shop practising day and night. It seemed he always had time to play a round and he hit the longest iron shot I'd ever seen.

His entire set-up was wrong (well, not 'wrong' really, just not orthodox. After all, what's 'right' in golf?) He kept his legs nearly together, his stance was high and gangly, his swing went nowhere – just up and down in a narrow wristy arc – but when he connected with an eight-iron it flew as far as my five.

All right – so he probably closed the face of the club, and I could have hit my five-iron better – but not much!

Purist members of the club would say: 'It's all very well, but it's all to do with split-second timing. He's got no margin of error. When his timing goes on a bad day he'll be all over the place.'

I was there 14 weeks and this lad never had a bad day. I even tried to copy his style because it was effortless, all wrist and no shoulder. I had many bad days – roughly seven a week.

But the lad gave me a little light relief during this period, except for the 'straw ball' incident.

I was playing down a long par four, hit a goodish drive and was looking for a five-wood to make the green. Unlike most of my efforts at that time, the five-wood flew 'straight out of the screws' (I think that's the expression) like a bullet, connecting just before its zenith with a baling machine crossing the fairway. The ball was baled in straw and never seen again – and no one could give me a ruling for laughing!

On my last day at the club I was presented with a bale of straw containing a golf ball – a Commando Cross-out as I recall. Very funny, lads!

SEVENTH HOLE

Hospitality and Hostilities

GANTON is a super course which would test the very best. It's the only place where I've seen a window cleaner's ladder in a bunker – boy, it's a deep one!

During my Scarborough summer season, I was lucky enough to get a game at Ganton, thanks to a kind fan who was also a member.

I was slotted into a four-ball with three of the 'youth club' – all over 75 and still steady golfers, but prevented from making a full shoulder turn by the attentions of Father Time. Direction and control had superseded length in their game, but at least it kept them together on the fairway.

My self-appointed coach was a lovely man called Cecil, who I swear was still using the

first ball he ever hit. He never missed a fairway, and never missed a green – albeit not in regulation – but he wasn't up to advising a young upstart comic who was knocking 'em long.

'What club is it here, Cecil?' I would ask.

'Four-iron,' he'd say confidently, and – whoosh! – I'd find myself clearing the green and landing in deadly serious undergrowth, Apache country as they say.

'I can't understand it. That's what I use!' Cecil would wail.

'In future,' I suggested, 'just give me the approximate yardage'; but it still did no good. I remember being in no fewer than 12 bunkers in 18 holes – must be some kind of record!

At least I finished on a par, which always looks good in front of the clubhouse. The knack is trying to look disappointed at only parring the hole. It's good for the ego – as long as no one asks to see your score card!

I really must play Ganton again one of these days. I hope the 'youth club' is still there. I'm sure they must be . . . good guys like that live forever, don't they?

On to The Belfry, and many more happy memories, not just of the golf but of the wonderful hotel facilities and the many conferences I have addressed. It is a great set-up there, complemented by smashing staff!

I will always remember the courses at The Belfry for the tragi-comic circumstances surrounding my performances. I remember the long par four dog-leg over the water, for instance. You may know the one I mean – it's where Sevvy once drove the green.

Did I drive it too? Did I heck! Under John Jacobs's instruction I played safe. It was the final day of the BMW Classic, always a day to remember. John and I were playing with the UK boss of BMW – and for money, as I recall.

'Do yourself a favour,' said John. 'Take a five-iron down the left, and then a nice little chip to the flag over the water.' Sure as eggs, I hit a blinding five-iron to the perfect spot. There was appreciative applause from the gallery accompanied by that heart-warming opinion from the great man: 'If you could have walked down and placed the ball, you couldn't have put it in a better spot. That's perfect!'

So down the fairway I strode, the epitome of Mr Cool, and took a quick look into the distance at the flag, before hatching my next plan. I reckoned it was a sand wedge, high in the air: plonk the ball by the stick and hope it grabs tight on the green and stays.

Action! I took a gentle swing with the sand wedge, and up went the ball. I lobbed it straight into the water! What was it the gods of golf once

decreed: 'There is absolutely nothing more embarrassing in the whole world than a duffed chip!'

Sorry John – your plan was perfect, but your pupil wasn't up to the job.

Let's fast forward to the Brabazon course on another day, and another corporate function. This time I am playing in a four-ball, and there is no particular problem, except that it is foggy, very foggy. A shotgun start, and we're off the 12th, or any hole we can actually find.

We tee off and follow the vague direction of our drives. Amazingly we find them all and most of our second shots too. Gradually it becomes easier, we think, to play in this grey shroud . . . or is it?

Suddenly, to coin a phrase, the wheel comes off the bike and we find ourselves scrambling round a dog-leg of uncertain length – and meeting another four-ball doing exactly the same, but coming the other way!

'Are you with our Society?' we call.

'No – we're with the Woolwich!' comes the jovial reply, a humorous topicality in those days but of absolutely no help to us, cast adrift and possibly lost forever.

Obviously we didn't die of exposure, though it was a close run thing. Eventually we contacted

friendly life and returned to the right track, several balls shorter and much wiser. In future, I decide, there is a simple weather rule – if helicopters don't fly what chance have golfers got?

The pros have to be part diplomat, part wise-guy, with the right answers for any number of awkward occasions. When I played at Moore Park, a super course, in the Coca Cola Classic, my caddie, a charming fellow called John who used to be caddie-master but has now retired and just comes out for celebrity events, gave us the lovely story about the lady who went up to the golf pro and said, 'I want a ruling and I want it now!' So the pro asked, 'What's the problem?' She said, 'I want to know what's the penalty for playing an air shot over somebody else's ball . . .' Now as far as I can see that penalty should be three – one for playing the air shot and two for someone else's ball. But the pro's problem is to determine whether she's asking on behalf of herself or her opponent. It's one of those occasions where you have to think twice before you answer.

It was a golf pro, I might add, who in my very early days shamed me into appearing in a charity tournament, the George Elrick Classic at Royal Eastbourne. George, the perennial Housewives' Choice, is a lovely man, much

talented and devoted to charitable works. Furthermore, he was just the spark I needed to get into golf for fund raising.

He had organised a great day complete with teams, sponsors, starter, media coverage, everything you could wish for – and more, as it turned out. For there were also watering holes at the ninth and 18th, and they were to be the source of my woes on this day.

Not being up to the standard of the bulk of players I chose to go off last with another 'rabbit' – but this guy had been practising! After eight I was eight down, the sort of situation that merited two more holes and an early bath, I thought. But no – he contrived to lose his ball on the ninth and somehow I scrambled a half in eight!

So we came to the café at the ninth – and what a difference a stop makes.

'I don't drink, but you have a jar,' insists the rabbit.

'I'm not fussy,' says I.

'Go on, do you good . . .' he urges.

'Really I'd rather play on,' I say truthfully.

'Look,' he persists. 'You have a quickie and I'll join you.'

'Oh all right. I'll have a can of lager please,' I say resignedly.

'In that case I'll have a wee treble Scotch,' says the rabbit.

Several wee trebles later I find myself assisting my 'oppo' to the tenth tee and winding him round a ball washer while I tee off, he having hit his drive 200 yards straight up, his ball dropping almost between his feet.

I coasted easily round to the 18th and a one-hole victory, only encumbered by having to drag a blathering partner from rough to rough in search of his ball.

Mentally I felt elated at my amazing comeback, physically I felt as if I'd gone 15 rounds with Muhammad Ali, and morally I was disturbed to discover I had helped pander to the cravings of a reformed alcoholic – whose wife still hasn't forgiven me . . .

A victory is still a victory, but so is a defeat, and I'll always remember Eastbourne for my most unusual one. George Elrick, by the way, did it to me. I was playing a few holes with him, feeling great and on the green in two, while he had duffed his second shot deep into the foliage and was snarling and calling on the Lord.

Suddenly, his shot fired out of the under-growth and, following two ricochets off trees, I realised his seven-iron had somehow guided his ball 140 yards or more – out of trouble, over sand, two bounces and into the hole for a birdie. What a fluke!

He had no idea what he had done, of course,

but the shot so unnerved me, I three-putted and took a five. Three holes later he was taking a fiver off me as coolly as if he knew what he'd been doing all the time. Watch the Scots – they are dangerous foes!

I have known good days, bad days, and special days. Days when you do something so amazing you desperately yearn for witnesses who will talk, or even live coverage on News at Ten.

I had such a moment while summer seasoning on the Isle of Wight, a quite incredible place, ideal for relaxing. In addition to beautiful scenery and genial residents, plus the best in yachting and boating, it has a self-imposed 14 mph speed limit, as the roads are dominated by tractors, caravans and most other vehicles that just can't be passed. It's a good thing that the Isle of Wight encourages dawdlers otherwise it would be a very frustrating place indeed.

It is, in any event, perfect territory for a memorable summer season – I can't recall opening as many garden fêtes before or since, but that's all part of the fun.

Sandown golf club is the venue for this tale. It is a summer's morning and there is time to play only the front nine, on my own . . .

The shot of the year, fortunately, comes on

the first and is witnessed by two roofers atop the clubhouse.

'We seen your oppo here last year, you know,' they tell me.

'Who?'

'Jimmy Tarbuck. He played great.'

'You ain't seen nothin' yet,' says I.

I have two chances now – either hit a good 'un and become a name worth quoting, or a duff one and hope they think it was a gag to impress them. I stand up to the ball, take three practice swings and – bang! I connect with one that almost reaches the green, a good 260 yards, starts low and climbs. You know the one – it looks like it's still climbing even as it stops. It has a nice bit of draw on it and is ideally positioned for the second shot.

'Wow,' comes the gasp from the roof.

I tell myself, 'Keep calm . . . try to look disappointed!' I say casually, aloud and to no one in particular, 'Too far. I really wanted a full wedge for my second. Must use an iron next time.'

'D'you hear that?' says the roof. 'He's not happy. What a player . . .'

Wait until you play there again, Tarby. I can just hear them . . . 'That grey-haired mate of yours! What a guy – knocks 'em out of sight!'

I just hope they aren't still watching as my

second goes into the bunker greenside, or when my third and fourth are also played from the same bunker.

EIGHTH HOLE

Scotland and Ireland

LET'S MOVE north of the border to bonnie Scotland – lovely scenery, exquisite courses, the home of golf and many a good player.

Those Scottish golf courses are really something else. Ray Floyd was in a light aircraft flying over the Firth of Forth one time and he asked a fellow passenger, 'What's that below?'

'That's the Forth,' he was told.

Ray thought for a moment, then said, 'Hell of a carry . . .'

Two consecutive winters I did pantomime in Inverness, and it gave me the chance to play at Nairn and Inverness golf clubs. In all those winter weeks, both years, I only failed to play on one day, and that because snow lay on the greens. I even played on New Year's Day,

despite the head that needed calming with many paracetamols and the stomach churning in the way that only whisky can make it churn. It was here I learned that Hogmanay means 'Help me up!'

I often long for the pleasures of northern Scotland and never miss a chance to visit. So it was that I came across the Boat of Garten club. Together with a pal, Jim, and his good lady, my wife Pat and I spent a week based in Inverness, touring the area playing golf.

We found Boat of Garten on a day when no one else was there. The clubhouse was empty, and there were no players in sight. There was just a note explaining the procedure – place the fee in an envelope, write your car number on the envelope and place it in the honesty box. Amazing!

It was an interesting day's golf. For a start, Jim lost his temper – I had never seen this before. He lay on the grass beside the ball screaming, 'Will you go into the hole!!' It didn't work – he three-putted.

So much for Mike Burton's belief that in every ball there is a little pilot steering it in and out of mischief. Why else does a ball do things for which there is no rational explanation? This uncertainty probably explains why it is more of an achievement to stop a ball inches away from the

pin on a par three rather than hole in one – which, as we have established, is a fluke shot anyway!

In Scotland I was questioned about my handicap. 'Ten,' I answered truthfully.

'Which course?' they demanded. So you can't talk a good game up there. You are judged, quite rightly, on ability and performance.

My solitary foray into entertaining the Scots was equally traumatic – not only on Hogmanay but also live on television!

In the early 1980s I was chosen to host *The Hogmanay Show* live from the beautiful Gleneagles Hotel. It may sound like a fairy tale, but it just about ended in nightmare for me!

We had a great cast: Moira Anderson, Maggie Moone, the late great Chic Murray, plus more singers, bands, raconteurs, a live and lively audience. It just couldn't go wrong – could it?

The rehearsals went OK, but I wasn't that happy about the sound level. To me it seemed too quiet for a room full of Hogmanay revellers. In retrospect, a lot of things were assumed to be in order, when today they would have been checked and rechecked. Items already recorded on video tape were intended as back-up – the 'belt and braces' approach, as they say, in case of emergency – and boy, did we need them!

The show opened with the Britannia Airways

Pipe Band outdoors, playing us in through the main doors and into the dining room, full of guests in great spirits.

After a song from Moira and a bit of opening chat, I already realised that the audience noise was louder than the sound system. But still we pressed on with various items, including some recorded material.

Then the pipe band came back. They sounded wonderful, but at the end of their piece, things began to go seriously awry. The mark for poor old Chic was covered by furniture which had been moved while the audience settled down, and consequently cameras were not at the correct angle to pick up the right shots, links started to go adrift and we began to race headlong into a mini-shambles.

I couldn't wait for the end of the show, but even then there was no relief. Sitting quietly with Pat, Maggie Moone and her husband, we found ourselves analysing our futures following this débâcle.

Hopefully, we convinced ourselves, nobody would have been watching: they would all have been out celebrating themselves. At least nobody important in the world of television would have been watching it ... would they? Eventually I admitted that Maggie might salvage some pride from the show, but I reckoned I

was doomed. There was only one thing for it – a round of early morning golf to lift the blues.

Somehow, at eight in the morning, despite much quaffing of the 'falling down liquid', I staggered out to play a very important 18 holes. For some reason, my head was in perfect shape for the game. I couldn't have cared less, I felt all was lost and I really wasn't bothered. If you could bottle that feeling, I reckon we'd all have a chance of winning the US Masters . . .

I clocked up a par, par, birdie, birdie, par, birdie. Maybe it was me keeping my head extra still – only because even the slightest excess movement sent it spinning. Or perhaps it was my slow deliberation over every shot – simply to prevent me falling asleep.

Up to the ninth it was the best round of golf I had ever played, but then human failure began to creep in. Suddenly the devil began: 'If you can protect this score you could be well under par at the finish.' Ah yes, when that little voice starts nagging at your brain, it's the kiss of death. That's when I took an iron off the tee for safety, topped the drive, duffed the second, three-putted on the green. Down for six – aargh!

Anyway, I still finished with a very good personal score and returned to the hotel delighted and relieved to learn I was not being made a scapegoat for the previous evening's

disaster. All in all, it was quite a weight off my shoulders!

But the formula for a great nine holes remains my legacy of that fateful Hogmanay. It is easy to set up: merely do something so chaotic that it puts your whole future, your entire career in jeopardy, then soften up the brain with the juice of the glen, assume all is lost – and relax! Even so, I wouldn't recommend it as a regular tonic.

I have played courses north and south of the border in Ireland, too, and find them just as relaxing in their own way.

I will never forget one time at Royal Portrush on a day that the heavens forgot. In seven holes we suffered hell, high water, hurricane and rain like bullets on the skin. Soon it was too cold to grip the bag, never mind the clubs, so we decided to creak back to the clubhouse.

As we stood there, wrapping our purple frames around large warming brandies, we watched a video of Sevvy doing endless tricks with a putter.

I said to my blue-nosed Irish partner, 'Isn't he just wonderful?'

Ken sniffed, and said, 'Ah yes – but can he tile a roof?'

Seemed, really, to put the day into some kind of perspective!

NINTH HOLE

Up in the World

BEAUTIFUL WOBURN is a regular date on my calendar, marking my yearly trip to play in the Dunhill Masters pro-celebrity tournament. To think that a kid from the back streets of Bootle could ever be invited to play each year on this stately course and join the likes of Berhard Gallagher, Sevvy, Ronan Rafferty – sometimes I just know I am a very lucky man.

The set-up is a Texas scramble with pros, celebrities and two or three amateurs connected with Dunhill or its sales groups. A Texas Scramble is one of those combinations designed to speed up the game on the day. In a four-ball, the team takes the best drive and each player hits his second shot from that spot. Then the third shot is taken from where the best second

lands. And so on. Theoretically you should be in with a birdie chance at each hole.

It is akin to playing a greensome, where each pair picks the better of their drives, then the partner plays the second shot, and so on in turn.

The best greensome story I heard involved Tony Jacklin playing with a little old lady. They teed off and took his drive. She hit the ball into the bushes, and he went across and hacked it out in line with the green. She slammed the ball into a bunker on the edge of the green. He chipped out of the bunker and luckily it went straight into the hole. So he said to her, 'Now look luv, we'll have to steady up. This is a par four and we took a five then,' to which she replied, 'Yes – but you played three of 'em.'

In Liverpool, instead of a greensome we play a yellowsome, where instead of you and your partner electing the better shot, the opposition has the choice. The legendary yellowsome story is of two guys: one who holed in one and the other who put his ball in the bushes. The opposition chose the ball in the bushes as the better shot – so the hole in one didn't count!

Anyway, back to Woburn, here it was, in my first year, that I met an unforgettable character – Peter Barnes.

Big Peter is the most genial of men with a

great sense of humour, brilliant wit and a perfect laugh for a struggling comic. Here is a man who eschews the niceties of the club maker – woods, long irons, short irons, and the rest. Peter hits everything with a five-iron. 'It saves a lot of messing,' he explains. I suppose he's right.

It was Peter who, coming back to England after a tournament abroad, bemused Customs officials who suspected him of bringing in a new full set of clubs, by showing them 'the trusty five' worn to a wafer with constant use.

But my all-time favourite memory of this great fellow, great friend and amazing sponsor of charity tournaments, was watching him actually playing the 18th at Woburn – and missing an 18 in putt.

Said the pro, who shall be nameless, 'My nine-year-old daughter would have holed that one!'

'Oh really,' remarked Peter, 'and how many cigarettes does she sell?'

Still at Woburn, and in another year of the Dunhill Masters, I was in the team with Ronan Rafferty, a nice guy and a very good golfer. I hit a screamer on the first and as it was Texas Scramble, I raced down the fairway to show the gallery that we were going to use my ball. Four chips (one each) and one putt and we were down in three – a birdie is always a good start.

Feeling really good, we moved to the second tee and as we prepared to tee off we heard the crowd behind us screaming approval as Sevvy chipped in for an eagle! Nothing else for it but to bite your lip and keep saying, 'But can he tile a roof?' Bah!

Moving house from Birkdale to Ascot was obviously time to break new ground. Although I had lived many years in the Southport area, it wasn't until I left that I really got into the golf swim up there. But the serious stuff began as I got used to my new home club, Royal Ascot. I guess I imagined it to be one of those clubs where you have to wear a collar and tie in the showers, but truthfully I have been very happy there and made quite a few down-to-earth friends.

I prepared myself with daily visits to local driving ranges and steady practice with a bag of balls and an upturned umbrella on the lawn before I ventured out for my first 18 holes.

Situated in the centre of Royal Ascot race course, the golf course has all a golfer can desire – heather, a water hazard, a cricket pitch, public rights of way all over the place – an ideal course to play a visitor for money!

I was introduced to the course by Dick Richardson, former European heavyweight

*He has a putter like Harry Lauder's
walking stick*

boxing champion and one of the hardest hitters of the ball I've seen – with no backswing!

Here I also met John O'Neill, then captain and for many years club chairman, a Dublin man who in those days never used any club larger than a four-iron. I believe he's matured now!

John has been a great friend and partner to me, so much so that he probably won't mind me saying that his is without doubt the worst swing in golf history. If Moses had seen his swing, there'd have been another commandment.

He also has a putter like Harry Lauder's walking stick . . . but he is in truth a great partner. Overall I think we've only lost once while playing together, and there's a secret to this.

I 'lamp' one a long way, hopefully, then John lays up with a four-iron, swung like no other. This has two effects: the opposition can't believe the swing contortions, and his effort makes mine look twice as long and demoralises the others.

We played together on the day that Royal Ascot launched its new par five hole (now the first, then the third) and the gods were kind to me.

Following a three-wood and a five-wood, I

holed a 12 ft putt for a three. Needless to say it was all I did all day, but I couldn't wait to tell the clubhouse.

I entered all smiles and announced, 'I've just eagled the par five.'

'So have I,' said old Bill, sat in the corner. Bill is a grand old character, 80 plus, so I ask him, 'What did you use?'

'Three three-woods.'

I've often mused how long it took him to realise his third shot was in the hole.

Bill was the first person I saw use an eleven-wood. In fact he had a bag full of woods, down to a thirteen I think. It looked like Sherwood Forest in there.

He was a steady player, always down the middle, landing just short of the green, always putting for par, but he was no help to a stranger, club-wise.

'What is it for me, Bill?'

'I don't know, but I use an eleven-wood with half a swing.'

Try converting that to an iron . . .

While we are rambling around Royal Ascot, let me tell you about my 'almost hole in one'. Some years ago, the second hole (now the seventh) was a short par three, and John O'Neill and I teed up on a bright summer's afternoon.

John hit an eight-iron and his ball landed 3 feet away from the pin, which brought a satisfied smile to his lips.

I also took an eight-iron and hit the ball beautifully, even if I say so myself. It flew right to the flag, striking it, and fell stone dead an inch from the rim of the hole.

As we both strode towards the green muttering something about, 'If Peter Alliss could see those shots he'd want to play a round with us!' we were approached by a charming lady clad in a mini-dress and sporting an advertising sash. She called out, 'Congratulations. You've won! You're the nearest!'

'Say nothing . . .' said John, preparing to walk on.

Apparently the Society before us had been sponsored by a well-known drinks company based in 'Varrington', and the 'nearest the pin' prize for the day was a giant bottle of vodka. Protesting (but ever so slightly), we accepted the prize and finished the round, subsequently joining the Society in the clubhouse and explaining everything. They pressed us to keep the prize, even though we weren't officially with their party (which, of course, we did, although secretly trading it for the equivalent in Scotch with the club steward!)

*

From my home these days I'm only a short distance from many great clubs – Sunningdale, Wentworth and so on. There is plenty of scope for golfing enjoyment and for meeting interesting people.

Take Paul, a long-time member of Wentworth, a good player and a gentleman, always polite and a marvellous teller of tales.

I'll never forget a 'friendly' we played when, after 13 holes, he'd kindly allowed me to be all square, such was his prowess. We were standing on the 14th tee of the west course facing 160 yards, all uphill – not an easy prospect.

Paul pointed out the green-keeper's hut on the right of the fairway and asked if I had heard the sad story about it. I fell for it and said, 'No, please tell me . . .'

Apparently, Paul went on, nine years before, in a Sunday morning mixed foursome, a man had teed off, duffed his shot and his ball had landed behind the shed.

'Play it out sideways to the fairway,' he told his wife, 'and I'll try to chip us somewhere near the flag.'

But she had other ideas. 'There's a door at this end,' she said. 'If there's one at the other end, open it and I'll try to play through . . .'

For some reason he complied, opened the far door and watched her strike an iron straight at the door frame. The richochet hit her between the eyes and killed her outright. Her husband understandably never played again.

Eight years later, however, he was persuaded to go out on another Sunday morning round, 'just to give it a try,' and by a billion to one chance his ball performed exactly the same feat on the 14th and landed behind the self-same shed again.

'Shall I try to play it through if you hold the door open?' enquired his new lady partner.

'Get lost!' he replied. 'Last time I took a seven . . .'

Good story, Paul – it had me fooled right up to the tag-line!

Wentworth is a fine club with fine courses and brings back many happy memories.

The first trophy I ever won, the Panasonic Pro-Celebrity-Am, partnering Bernard Hunt, another gentleman and a great player, was won with no help from me.

Among the many celebrities that day was the legendary wartime hero Douglas Bader, sadly no longer with us. I recall he played very well that day, his team losing to us by the odd point.

My lasting memory of that day is of a young

cub reporter covering the game and asking Douglas why he used a shooting stick when walking the course. Was it perhaps to keep his balance?

'No,' smiled the great man. 'It's to stop these legs running away from me on the slopes!' God bless him – he was a fierce competitor and it was a privilege to meet him.

Of the Wentworth courses, I guess the east course is my favourite; not so long as the Burma Road, but just as interesting and, I think, just as difficult.

Whenever I had time at home in the summer I would join Mike Burton, possibly Russ Abbot and Shakin' Stevens for a knock. It is a great way to relax with fellow artistes; plenty of gags, but no quarter asked or given.

However, in all my golfing days and in all the elite company I have enjoyed, the most remarkable and incredible incident happened to me at Wentworth.

It was a Saturday morning, members and guests only, first up, first served, with golf balls in the chute to determine pecking order. I'd been signed in by my ex-manager and had put in a monogrammed ball as our place in the queue.

When our turn came, I eagerly took my 'Won from Tom O'Connor' ball from the chute and proceeded to tee up.

A man raced to the tee and shouted, 'It's our turn!' I pointed out that he had no ball in the chute and he replied, 'I did have – it's down the fairway now!'

Apparently, several four-balls ago, he had played his drive down the first, then sat waiting for his partner to finish getting ready in the clubhouse. No thought that, as a member, he should have known the rule that all players in his party must be present before teeing off. No thought that many another player could have picked up his drive as a 'find'.

I prayed – as you would – that his ball was gone, but it was still there. Drat! It ruined my day!

TENTH HOLE

Golf, TV and Me

PROBABLY THE hardest thing to do in life is to make an extremely intricate task look easy. It's an art bestowed on very few people.

In soccer, Beckenbauer had the art, as did Pele and Gordon Banks.

In horse racing, Arkle, Red Rum, Millhouse were really special. In boxing, Sugar Ray Robinson and Muhammad Ali had the gift.

We can each compile our own special list of accomplished sporting folk, those who have given us pleasure simply watching what they do and watching them do it well.

In other fields of endeavour, too, we can find and appreciate people who make what they do seem so simple. Witness the ease with which Bruce Forsyth hosts a television show – such

Nothing to it!

professionalism, such dynamism, and yet apparently something you or I reckon we could do just as well because it looks so effortless.

Forget it! I've tried it and I have to tell you it is not as easy as it looks. For behind Bruce's easy-going smile, the funny banter and the seeming nonchalance there is a whole lifetime of experience, hard work, highs and lows – and most important of all, a special gift.

So it is with golf, our favourite sport (I guess that's right, otherwise I wouldn't be writing and you wouldn't be reading!). Golf looks deceptively simple when watched from a warm armchair with beer in one hand and the TV remote control in the other. A drive, a five-iron, two putts maximum . . . nothing to it. On to the next tee . . . easy game. No wind, no pressure, no problem . . . anyone can do it. Makes you feel it's hardly worth trying it for yourself. Better to find something tricky to play – like darts.

Television may have made sports such as snooker and golf more popular but it has also given people a false idea that they are easy to play. They see Steve Davis or Sevvy doing something fantastic and then hope to emulate them on the table or on the course the next day. Remember when you used to go for a suit to Burtons? If it needed altering they would do it while you waited and to pass the time, you

could go upstairs and have a game of snooker –
at least you could in Liverpool!

And if you think of it in terms of our very first
games of snooker, remember breaking off,
splitting the pack and scattering the reds
everywhere? Your mate would say, 'You twit!'
Yet if Steve Davis plays the same shot on
television, the commentator whispers things
like, 'There's an awful lot of pressure on the
game here at the Crucible. There has to be a
reason for that bold move . . .' So it's all a
matter of values.

Golf is a game of opposites really. You and I
can do things that make others exclaim, 'You
twit – what have you done that for!' Whereas if
Trevino does it there is obviously a deep hidden
meaning. But the one thing we must not do is
say to ourselves, 'If it's good enough for Trevino,
it's good enough for me!' As soon as you do that,
you start on the path to a round of 95.

Moreover, golf, like snooker, gives a totally
wrong impression when viewed on the small
box. There is no hint of the agonising hours of
practice required; the soul searching, the
bottling of emotions as a player stands over a
putt. It may be only 2 feet, but it could also be
the difference between abject failure and
glorious immortality.

If one man could be said to have changed the

way we see the game of golf, it must be Severiano Ballesteros.

You may agree with me that the future of TV coverage of golf, and the subsequent popularity of the game for spectator and player, was boosted enormously by the sight of a young Ballesteros in the British Open.

Here was a kid defying everything the text-books said should be done and playing as none of the 'correct' players had done before. He never played safe, he seemed hardly ever to be on the fairway, even playing one shot from the car park. You could hear the armchair critics saying to themselves, 'What is going on? Maybe this game isn't so easy after all. Maybe I'll go and try for myself . . . see if I can play straight all the time. Maybe I'll go and watch real-life golfers on the courses and get the proper feel of the game.'

Sevvy became everyman's hero, and TV became a major part of golf lore. By satellite we can now watch our favourite players all over the world. Videos help us learn from the greats. Videos of our own game can help us iron out faults.

Television is here to stay, and truthfully it can enable us to see the funny side sometimes too.

My daughter Anne Marie lives in Italy,

married to a charming Italian who thinks Nigel
Mansell is the second coming – poor chap, he
knows only cars.

Some years ago Christy O'Connor Jnr was
leading the Open overnight, and leading well.
Anne's husband Rocco was watching it on
satellite TV and all he saw was Christy's back
view, grey hair peeking from beneath his cap,
and the name O'Connor.

'Hey,' he called to Anne, 'your father's leading
the British Open.'

Before she could take stock of this astounding
feat, Christy turned round and Rocco added,
'Oh no, it's not your dad – this chap is far too
young and good looking.' One to you, Christy!

I must admit my own TV golfing debut (the
pro-celebrity event I already mentioned in
passing) was fraught with trepidation. Hosted
by Peter Alliss, I found myself partnering
Sandy Lyle, and playing against two legends,
Lee Trevino in golf and one of my showbiz
heroes, Jimmy Tarbuck.

You have got to remember that although I'd
worked many thousands of hours on TV, it did
not include any type of sport. In fact it only
covered my job as a comic and quiz show host.
Like everyone else, I am confident and cool
doing the things I'm trained for, but suddenly to
have my hobby, and my shortcomings, scruti-

nised at very short range was a nightmare.

Funnily enough, I wasn't too bothered about the cameras. 'They'll cut out the worst bits,' I thought. It was the gallery that frightened me.

But the gods were on my side. They gave us weather like only Turnberry can enjoy, a freezing, biting wind and torrential rain! Consequently there was no gallery – thank you, Lord!

We had a quick warm-up on the practice ground during which Trevino dropped a ball into sloppy earth and hit it with a one-iron more than 250 yards. It hardly left the ground all the way. 'Wind shot,' he explained. I thought to myself, 'It's no use making a note of that. I'll never be able to play it!'

On the first tee, Tarby attempted to keep us smiling, a herculean task in this weather even for the 'guv'nor'.

The cameras were set and ready to roll, and Trevino was over his ball. 'You know, Tommy,' he said to me, 'Americans never play a practice shot in the wet.' The next thing I know – bang! – he's hit the ball 290 yards.

'Ready when you are, Mr Trevino,' said camera one.

'He's already hit it!' I told the crew.

'While he was still talking?'

'Yes, and I swear while he wasn't even looking!'

We had a good day in bad weather . . . well, actually Sandy did. Apart from chipping from nowhere, hitting the flag at 100 mph and stopping dead for a four-inch putt, I did very little to help our win by four shots.

Lee Trevino was brilliant both with club and repartee while Tarby was also his usual entertaining self, and quite a wizard with the golf shot. On the day, however, Sandy was outstanding – he missed nothing! 'I can't be as funny as Lee,' he told me. 'Don't worry,' I replied. 'I'll do the funnies. You just keep playing out of your skin,' And he did.

The day remains a great memory of trepidation followed by exhilaration. How much we can receive when we dedicate ourselves to the 'great game'. It is truly a wonderful leveller, a marvellous soother of aches of all sorts, and a friend when all else seems lost.

There have been happier TV days for me – notably the time I was the victim for a Noel Edmonds's Gotcha Oscar.

What a set-up that was: it included my management team, my wife, my entire family – all involved in a ploy to hatch a plot to catch a poor unsuspecting comic.

I was working on a tour of Butlin's Holiday Worlds in 1991, travelling up to 1500 miles a

week, enough to guarantee to soften the brain and burn out the car. During this run I was told by Tom and Kevin, my managers, that I had been chosen to help present a TV show on the history of golf. Keith Chegwin was to be the interviewer. I would be playing in 1920s get-up, including period cap and clubs, and comment, as I went along, on how it felt using all this vintage gear.

After a journey from Minehead to Ealing, with little sleep, I was wide open to be picked on. Togged up in this 1920s costume, a stiff collar, studless shoes, plus fours and a monster cap reminiscent of the type the late Colin Crompton used to wear when hosting the Wheeltappers and Shunters Social Club, I strode out on to the first to be greeted by a normal-looking film crew. I chose a three-wood from a very old bag full of very old clubs, while trying to keep calm and 'start off with a good 'un'.

Almost immediately I found myself the centre of harassment. The sound man kept interrupting and walking into my line of fire. Cheggers dropped the golf bag behind me and talked all through my backswing.

Whack! I pulled the drive. It was no good for the film. 'Reload.'

I was unhappy with the club-face, and

decided it was not as square as it could be. This was confirmed when – whack! I duffed the next shot into a bunker. 'Reload!'

I was beginning to suspect the clubs, and changed the three-wood for a five. One good swing and – whack! This time we were off down the fairway, 220 yards or more. I decided the clubs were all right and began to relax.

While lining up the second shot and talking it through with Cheggers, Noel moved in back of me, heavily disguised, and as I swung he let off with both barrels of a shotgun at 'rabbits' in the shubbery.

'Golly heck,' I cried (or words to that effect). Suddenly I realised that the bushes he aimed at weren't moving. Could he be firing blanks? But why? Perhaps it was a wind-up. If it wasn't Noel Edmonds, it might be Jeremy Beadle. In any event I decided to play along.

Once I had sussed it, the result was great fun. They did their best to wind me up with duff advice, brought on noisy motorbikes, tractors – finally I was introduced to a 'Mr Heaney' who ostensibly owned a priceless golf ball which he brought out in a special wooden presentation box. Cheggers told me he was going to 'lend it to us for you to putt with'.

The gag was the ball would go into the hole in which there was a trick flap. The ball dropped

down, the flap came up and to all intents and purposes the hole appeared empty, the ball having disappeared. Good gag!

Twice I missed the putt, infuriating for the crew, but the third time I sank it and 'Mr Heaney' went raving bonkers looking for his ball. On came Noel again, still in disguise, to join in the argument.

I decided to keep out of it while the heated confab went on, and chose my moment to intervene.

'Excuse me, Noel,' I said, 'it's like this . . .' And the penny dropped all round.

The 'Gotcha Oscar' now stands in my snooker room as a memento of an unforgettable day – it looked good on telly too. I was very thankful to Noel, and to the rest of the team, for thinking of me.

TV is a great source of memories, but there have been times when I've wished I had a full blown crew, or even a camera, to record an event for posterity.

My mind goes back to a day at one of my favourite clubs, Penwortham near Preston. Over the years it has remained a club dear to my heart: the members, its secretary and the committee are all a great bunch.

Many a game I have played there – and many

a 'megameal' I have attempted! Joe, the steward, made the largest mixed grills in the world. Fry a dozen eggs, four pounds of sausages, one cow, one pig . . . only joking! But only just.

It was Thursday morning in July and a pal and I had arrived to play a quick 18 holes. John, the Penwortham secretary, had organised coffees and I had a brandy as a 'heart starter'. Then it rained heavily.

Discretion being the better part of valour, we decided to have another coffee and debate our prospects. Eventually the consensus was that we'd stay in the warm: no use catching cold.

That's when they started arriving . . . the Society, booked in for the full day. Thirty-six able-looking men who made much noise with their carefree banter and various modes of limbering up, none of which would have been recommended by Jane Fonda.

The first at Penwortham is a good par four, trees and trouble all down the left but nothing that a steady tee shot can't handle. From the clubhouse we watched 36 golfers tee off and counted them out. Unbelievably, only one player hit the fairway and that was with his second.

There should have been cameras that day! We were witnessing the worst collective group of golfers ever.

We watched them out of sight and sighed. Half

an hour later a two-ball strode out on to the first and played the hole beautifully. Obviously low handicappers and used to the course.

Suddenly our minds raced fast forward. What would happen when this two-ball caught up with the rear of the Society? They will be thinking, 'We'll just get through these three and we'll be clear . . .' Wait until they find they're behind twelve threesomes, all just as bad as each other! Welcome to my nightmare . . .

Ah yes, the funny side of golf . . . you can't beat it, you can join it, or you can have just as much fun watching it.

Who was the man in the crowd? He'll probably be forever anonymous, but for all that he'll be forever in my thoughts.

Witness Royal Birkdale, hosting the British Open in 1976. I had only recently become interested in the game and was watching Jack Nicklaus on the tee, hammering a ball out of sight down the first. 'Rubbish,' said a voice, quite distinctly in the crowd. 'His tee never went backwards!'

If it is unwise to open your mouth in the gallery, it is also unwise to be unwell. I recall a charity game at Torquay, and a very gentle-mannered celebrity on the tee, struggling not only with his shot but with a cougher in the crowd.

The golfer addressed the ball – Cough! He relaxed and addressed it again – Cough!

And so on. Eventually the quiet man of golf stared hard at the unhealthy fan. Silence fell and he played his shot. As he left the tee the quiet man turned to the unhealthy fan and said, 'You know that stare I gave you – I really meant it!' That was telling him!

If you are talking golf or talking about golf, you must know what you're saying. And if you are in any doubt, check with my dad – he knows!

Remember the controversy over the simple pronunciation of one player's name? The television commentators couldn't decide: was it 'Ola-tha-bal' or 'Olazz-abal', and which syllables should be stressed?

No one knew for sure until my dad said to me: 'That Josie Ozzleball is good, in'ne?'

Now we know. And yes, dad, he is good. I played with José in the Benson & Hedges – what a player. He has a great temperament and is a real gentleman. I'm a big Ozzleball fan.

ELEVENTH HOLE

Home and Away

PLAYING overseas and in unaccustomed
circumstances can be a pleasure, but it can also
throw up hazards all its own. There are
compensations ... the sun on your back,
beautifully manicured greens, fairways like a
front lawn. Nothing like it!

Each year Pat and I take a welcome break
and work two or three weeks for P&O aboard
one of their world cruise liners, among which I
claim the *Canberra* as my favourite. If ever a
man had a love affair with a ship, 'twas she and
me!

Acapulco is one of the main ports of call on
one leg of this cruise and I have been lucky
enough to visit it many times. The Princess
Hotel is an elegant residence and I have played

the beautiful course there on two occasions. On the first time out, accompanied by the ship's purser and two fellow entertainers, it was an idyllic day, with steady scores and easy on the feet – even the girls enjoyed the walk.

I only hit trouble once, and hit a 'shot of shots' to escape – in front of witnesses too! I'd driven a three-wood to the right. It went a long way but landed behind a tallish tree, maybe 15 feet back. A direct line to the green was blocked and I approached the ball with thinking cap in overdrive.

Out from a neighbouring condominium came a huge man, and I'm talking gross weight here! Seriously, he must have been 30 stones – at least he would have been in the UK. But as he was American, I shudder to think how many pounds he weighed.

Although only in his mid-30s, or possibly younger if his charming wife was any guide, he wheezed and lumbered like an old 'un. Oh, the penalties of being too overweight.

'Hi, young feller,' he called.

'My kind of bloke!' I thought, suddenly feeling a lot less than my 45 years.

'What do you plan doing with this shot?' he asked me.

'Tell me what the great Tom Watson would do,' I suggested.

'Well,' said 'my kind of bloke'. 'I guess he'd tickle a little three-iron off his back foot, draw it low around the tree and stiff it by the flag.'

Three-iron, back foot, swing and duck in case of the rebound, Tom – Whoosh! The ball flew like a bullet, drew round the tree and landed a foot from the stick. A dream of a shot!

'Remember,' I said to myself, 'keep cool, look disappointed, move away quickly . . .' I did.

'Gee, did you see that, Martha? He didn't like it! I tell you, I've seen some golf in my day, but . . .'

Keep talking pal, I ponder as I walk to the green. I can't stop now, I'm on a roll. Please God, the putt drops . . . and it did!

Another year, another cruise, and Pat and I are back in Acapulco, playing the Princess again in company with a fellow artiste called Neville, plus Joe O'Keefe, a retired Irish Army commandant, and Sam, a passenger of dubious credentials. We later decided he was probably a spy, but we didn't know for which side.

If you ever play the Princess course, take a tip from me. Don't listen to wifely advice!

'Why don't we hire a buggy and I'll drive us?' suggested Pat.

Bearing in mind that I usually play golf for exercise, I should have insisted on carrying my bag, but on this day I gave in. We hired two

buggies and set off in convoy to 'murder this course'. The problem with hiring a buggy, of course, is that you are never away from the ball. You have hardly hit it before you are beside it again. The buggy ride gives little time for thought and no conception of distance played.

The final drawback is the drinks buggy full of gin, tonic and ice which tends to dog you on courses like the Princess – and always serves large measures.

So it was that we partook of the devil's brew while playing the angels' game. The effect of cool gin in a hot climate is to make golf seem a very easy game, and adversaries are prone to come out with such friendly sympathetic comments.

A totally duffed tee shot brings, 'Not easy from there', and indifferent strokes all the way round are accompanied by, 'Good shot!' 'Bravo!' 'Well done!'

The truth is that too much of the falling down liquid can let you down just when you don't expect it.

There is a par four at Acapulco, easy enough on paper, with only two hazards of any note. In front of the tee is a lake, biggish, but nothing a seven-iron can't carry, and further up the fairway is a huge tree, impressive but no threat to the hole.

Playing last of the four that day, I watched my three 'chums' play successive shots straight into the lake. Three drives, three dives. Spectators were gathering to watch the course record being broken.

'You've got to do something to save face, Tom,' was the spluttered advice from the erstwhile pals, so I did some thinking, albeit scrambled.

'Three-wood for safety, easy swing, watch the right shoulder doesn't lurch through and smother the shot . . . head still, relax . . . slow take away . . .' When in doubt remember a tip I learned from a little old lady: 'Sing "Nellie the Elephant" to yourself for tempo!' (Mind you, it depends on how fast you sing it . . .)

All this procedure was put into practice; after all I was saving face on behalf of the whole of P&O. The ball flew sweet as a bird, over the lake, heading for the fairway.

Then the little pilot inside the ball did the unforgivable. He steered the thing to the left. Was it the gin? Did I breathe unfairly on the ball before teeing off?

Whatever the reason, my drive hit the tree front and centre, and, amidst screams of laughter and gurgles from the gallery, it ricocheted straight back into the lake. Four drives, four dives – an unbeatable record for that hole.

Then there was Kagoshima, Japan, a beautiful port and equally beautiful people, willing to show us around their city, and even their homes. When time came for us to leave, a huge choir of Japanese school children congregated at midnight on a cool evening, dressed in their uniforms and carrying candles, to sing 'Auld Lang Syne' in conjunction with a tannoyed record.

In the background tugs were hooting, and the *Canberra* was echoing their tribute while thousands of passengers sang, waved and cheered. Twenty minutes later, the novelty was beginning wear off. The children were beginning to shiver, the tannoy wavering and the waves from the passengers weaker as the cheers died away. Something was obviously wrong, but no – ten more minutes, and we began to inch away from the quay. 'Auld Lang Syne' came back to full strength and there was one last burst of spontaneous enjoyment.

But what caused the hiccup in the proceedings? The answer was Reg the Veg!

Reg was in charge of peeling vegetables and getting rid of the waste, which was usually bagged and weighted, then dumped at sea without trace. But not in Kagoshima.

Reg had decided to unload in the docks, so swung a surreptitious sack out from the ship's

loading bay – and forgot to let go. Out he went,
landing with the sack between the ship and the
quay. Panic ensued. Dockers tried to hold off
the ship with poles, while some wag shouted
'Shark!' Reg popped out in a trice!

Back on board he was asked for an
explanation, in other words, 'What the blankety
blank was going on?'

'It was like this,' explained Reg, 'I swung the
sack out of the loading bay and . . . argh!' And
out he flew again, repeating the operation as
before, keeping thousands waiting while he was
rescued a second time.

With the ship back at sea, I was to be found in
the golf practice nets, naturally. It was great for
posing in front of Japanese tourists! My swing
must be on dozens of Japanese home video films
. . . goodness knows what they think of the
hacker in the long shorts, flip-flops, white body
and red head. I must look like a golfing safety
match.

The *Canberra* is certainly a very special
cruise ship, and, as with golf, when you are on
her the years just roll away. I well recall
bidding farewell to her in 1982, in the midst of
the Falklands War. The whole crew volunteered for active service and I left the ship at
Southampton. Hours later she was being
re-equipped for the hostilities, a big white

target in the South Atlantic. Thankfully she returned intact.

I know the old saying that you make your own luck . . . 'The more you practise, the luckier you get, etc.' But I think my personal luck changes for the worse whenever I leave British shores.

Take Spain, home of great golfers, great courses, and beautiful weather – most of the time. Why can't I play well there? Maybe there is too much going for the golfer, no big worries or challenges. At least that's my pretty weak excuse.

Aloha golf course is a gem of a spot, with manicured fairways and greens, super company, very good, steady players. Here, one summer, I spent five days playing goodish golf, preferring early mornings when the greens were still damp with dew and easier to putt on than later in the day when they were like glass.

Kenny Lynch was a great partner on a couple of occasions, and so was a Geordie lad, a smashing character called Dan McKenzie. After a couple of days of blissful friendly games I was approached to play in a Celebrity-Am day for charity. All the lads were there – Tarby, Kenny, Kevin Keegan and so on. Of course I said I would take part: 'I'd be delighted, can't wait, hold me back, sure thing . . .' and all that.

But wait a minute . . .

I am picked to partner a chap who was over 75 at least. I decided it's no problem. There is good news – he plays off 28. Bad news – handicaps are only allowed up to 18. Even worse news – he can't carry a bag.

Good news – I'll hire a buggy. Bad news – all the buggies are accounted for.

Good news – I'll get a caddie. Bad news – 'Sorry señor, the caddies, they are all busy.'

So I have to hump the gear for both of us.

It wouldn't have been so bad if we'd kept our drives together but no way! I must have walked double the length of Aloha that day, feeling like a cross between Gunga Din and a pack-horse. In the end, the score became secondary to actually staying alive in the heat. I was delighted to break 100 and not break my back. The clubhouse loomed like a friendly oasis and the first three ice-cold lagers never touched the sides . . .

Who cares who won the money that day – I reckoned I'd found a new endurance test for the SAS!

But what of Dan McKenzie? He was a builder, a good golfer and splendid company, whom I met on my first day at Aloha. He has a place out there and speaks Spanish fluently. In fact, being a Geordie, he speaks Spanish

A new endurance test for the SAS

better than English.

He and his lovely wife royally entertained Pat and me both on and off the course, and I must relate one lovely anecdote which to me typifies the Geordie wit.

We went for a meal one night in Porto Buenos. The meal was enormous, but then so was the bill. It was too big, we reckoned, by about £60 or its Spanish equivalent.

'This bill's not right,' said Dan to the waiter.

'Que?' said Manuel's double.

'The bill is wrong,' persisted Dan. 'Bring the manager.'

Bearing in mind that while the waiters conversed, Dan could understand every word they said, he was ready when the manager arrived.

'Can I help you, señor?'

'Aye. This bill is not right. The bill is erroneous.' If the manager looked confused, I must admit Dan had me with that one too.

'We will have to negotiate this bill,' Dan told him.

'Negotiate? I do not understand, señor.'

'It's quite simple,' said our genial Geordie. 'You see this total at the bottom? This is what you're not getting!'

Ah, the logic of simplicity. I must catch up with Dan and his mates the next time I'm on

the Costa del Sol.

Talking of home and away, it reminds me that in golf, as in life, the unexpected can hit you right between the eyes at the most unlikely moment.

I remember Castletown Links on the Isle of Man, a good course, tricky on any day, difficult in the wind. The sort of course that makes you smile if you can keep within four of your handicap.

I have played Castletown on many occasions, and lost a few balls to the Irish Sea. I have met great companions there and shared their laughter. But once, just once, it was the scene of my worst ever golf day. Believe me, I have had a few bad 'uns, but this was the ultimate!

It all started miles away in Panama City . . . I've always said if you're going to the Isle of Man you should start in South America.

Pat and I were leaving the *Canberra* at Cristóbal, the port nearest to the Panama Canal. We'd had a great cruise, and finished off with a very long night entertaining the crew. As I recall, I was still playing my guitar at 5.30 am and at several different times through the night, for no reason at all, poured cold lager over my head to stay awake.

We crashed out in our cabin at about 6 am

and had hardly settled when the door opened and a chap in full chef's uniform wheeled in a silver salver on a trolley saying, 'Your order, sir!'

My God, where was I? What had I ordered? Normally when I'm in jolly vein I order Lobster Thermidor but hopefully not this time! Instead it was a full English breakfast – bacon, runny eggs, the works. Then I noticed the 'chef's' eyes: they were bloodshot. And I looked at the clock; it was 7 am. I knew then it was a wind-up. The 'chef' hadn't been to bed yet.

Never mind, the food was welcome. We ate heartily, then couldn't get back to sleep. Now we had to spend several hours wandering ashore before our flight home. But so what? Plenty of time to recover before I worked again . . .

The *Canberra* sailed off into the mist leaving Pat and me to face the rigours of the airport. The plane, it appeared, was not air-worthy and there would be a delay of fully 24 hours before it could be fixed. The alternative was a full week's wait before the next flight.

Nobody slept that night. We all just ambled zombie-like around the hotel in the steamy evening, wondering, just wondering. The next day at the airport – no joy, no plane! What now?

Out of the blue came our saviour, an amazing

chap called Major Peter Ball, a retired army man and an absolute wizard at organisation. He tackled the airport staff. 'Bring me the highest ranking person here who can speak English!' They did.

'Bring me an A-Z of flights.' They did.

'I want three seats on the next plane going east, first class, mind. And a taxi to take us back to the hotel where you will ensure we are re-accommodated.' They did.

Next morning, we took an Iberian flight to Madrid to link up with a BA flight to Heathrow, eternally grateful to the major. There was just time to unpack, repack and fly off to an after-dinner job on the Isle of Man. In three days we had had barely three and a half hours' sleep. My head was still banging, my fingers still raw from guitar strumming, my throat aching. Never mind, I reasoned, we can sleep all day at Castletown, take a shower, have a shave and a Strepsil and still be on about 11 pm for an hour.

It was not to be. We tottered off the plane at Ronaldsway and fell into a cab. At Castletown we checked in, went up to the bedroom and dropped into bed.

Then the phone rang. 'Who knows I'm here?' I thought, 'Must be a wrong number. Ignore it.' But it kept ringing so I eventually answered it

and it was the organiser of the 'do' at which I was due to speak.

'Where are you?' he demanded. 'We're waiting for you on the first tee. Hurry on down!'

'Sorry,' I said, 'I haven't brought my clubs.' No problem, they had a set they could lend me.

'No shoes?' What size, he asked. We'll find a pair.

Drat and double drat! There was no escape . . .

I staggered around the bedroom, bumping into almost everything, to make myself almost presentable – eye drops, breath freshener, after shave. Breathe in, shoulders back . . .

'I don't know how you can do it,' said Pat. 'You're so brave!' Nice words but they didn't cure my ills. So I ventured out into the breeze, all of 40 mph off the sea.

I do not believe I could have played a worse 18 holes if it had been pitch dark and myself handcuffed. 'Dreadful' would have been praise. 'Stinker' was nearer the truth.

Never will I forget one passing player, the third four to come through as I searched the countryside for my ball. He turned to his partner and remarked: 'Single figures and he plays like that! God knows how bad his jokes will be!'

Luckily they were better than we all thought

possible. In truth I wowed the late night crowd, more by good luck than skill. But I reckon that round of golf shortened my life by a full three years.

Why can't we keep our heads together and learn that life is a marathon and not a sprint? The ideal is to stay as fit as possible, and ration the good times. No need to cram everything into today. Well, up to a point.

Remember the story of the American billionaire who was so afraid of a nuclear holocaust that he spent millions of dollars building a fall-out shelter in the Nevada desert. He was just putting the last brick in the wall when an Indian shot him in the back with an arrow. So you see, you never know . . .

TWELFTH HOLE

Preparation and Practice

OH, HOW LUCKY I've been – to do a job I really enjoy and get well paid for being myself. No acting, no rehearsing.

Along with that, how lucky to have a hobby I enjoy as much as life itself. What more could a comic ask for? Well, good health and good friends, I guess, but then I have been amply blessed in those departments too.

From my early days as a singer in Liverpool pubs, teaching all day, singing all night and sleeping in shifts, it became quickly apparent that health and relaxation were vital to the job. It was no use spending the whole night carousing and then spend all the next day recovering . . . you know the sort of thing, eight paracetamols, mega-cups of Alka Seltzer, port

and brandy to settle the stomach . . . It's no use dreading going on again the following night because your head's not together.

It is more important to keep both body and head as fit as possible, while regularly honing the act, introducing new material and dropping the dead wood. You have to work at this job day after day.

I began by making notes in the working men's clubs. I bought a large 'page a day' diary and at a venue I would list the names of the doorman, the secretary, compère and all the people with whom I had direct contact. The next time it was easy to walk in and say, 'Hello Charlie. How's the wife's hip?' and get them to think, 'Blimey, he's remembered! What a nice guy!'

Another sharp move was to say to each concert secretary or booker, when they began complimenting me on my act, 'My agent doesn't know how good I am. No one ever tells him!'

That way I had my agent bombarded with complimentary letters and phone calls about me.

But most important of all, as I entered a new piece of comedy into the act, I would also note the date. This meant that at any time I could go back to a venue and have a list of all the material they hadn't heard before.

The only pitfall on the way was ignorance of new technology. I entered all the new material and dates I had carefully collated on to a computer disc. Then my son Stephen decided to use a microwave next to the computer and the 'wave spill' wiped the disc! It took me several days checking through envelopes, Woodbine packets and serviettes to recoup the details.

Still the system is tight now and works virtually all the time, given normal circumstances – mike, lights, audience still awake . . .

This strategy, believe it or not, has also helped to improve my golf, or at least prevent the worst aspects of my game recurring.

One of the earliest lessons I learned came from a smashing newspaper strip, and was from Gary Player, that golfing legend and bunker player par excellence. 'Always accept your punishment with the same eagerness you accept good luck,' he wrote. And how right that is.

Come on – how many times have we duffed a drive into the trees, and ended up blocked out to the green except for a possible needle-eyed gap ahead. All sense says, 'Play safe to the fairway and forego a shot', but the devil inside you is saying, 'Go for the gap. The pros would!' They probably wouldn't, you know.

Here's another great line that little devil

throws at you: 'Don't forget all trees are basically 90 per cent water!' Oh really? When was the last time you hit a tree and heard a splash!

How many good looking cards have been ruined by that totally over-ambitious shot. You've probably been there: it's a par five dog-leg, and the simple way is a three-wood, middle iron, wedge, and one or two putts – a safe par. Sounds so sensible one can feel the serenity and lack of pressure.

Contrast that to the actual situation, standing on the tee and listening to 'you know who'. The devilish voice is saying, 'Blast the driver hard as you can, smash a three-wood and we're on in two. Who knows – you could even be near the pin. Down for three or at worst four. Go on!' Hard to resist, isn't it?

Consistency will never come from a rush of blood, so why not be practical and face facts? The secret of consistency is knowing what you can't do, and never trying it. That's probably incorrect grammatically, but it's right enough in golf terms!

While on tour I like to make good use of driving ranges, which are becoming more and more popular. In Brighouse, West Yorkshire, for instance, there's a beautiful council-owned

driving range. The golf shop is attached to a small municipal course, all the equipment is in good repair, and it is floodlit – this obviously has to be the thing of the future if golf takes on the same value here as it has in, say, Japan, where they have multi-storey driving ranges. You have to possess a very good eye to determine which ball is actually yours, I guess, but it gives the Japanese something to do when there are so few golf courses.

Driving ranges are ideal for the likes of me. When I can't afford the time for a full round of golf I can spend a couple of hours knocking buckets of balls on the range. In fact it was at a driving range where I first had lessons to play golf properly. I have received lessons from various pros on my travels, but the major problem is that in order to go out and practise, you need a lot of grass, a lot of space between you and where you are actually knocking the ball, a lot of practice balls and a lot of time. At a driving range you just smack 'em into the distance and hours later a man picks 'em up in a machine! Can't be bad.

Another good thing about being at home on a range is that when you stand in your 'box' you are square on – everything is lined up, the angles are right, and when you hit the ball you know exactly where it should go. It is a totally

different feel to smacking one down a fairway and when you look up, the green is somewhere in the distance and all around is open space and wilderness.

Golfing ranges are therefore very handy to practise golf theory. And one of the great things I was taught on the range was to take the club-head away from the ball with my left hand – in fact, to make everything left-handed. You learn to put the club-face down with your left hand, with the blade facing in the direction you want to hit the ball, to stand square to the blade of the club and place your right hand to the club. In taking the club away you start with your left hand, which doesn't lurch it away but gives it a nice gentle swing, and this makes sure that when the club is taken away and the shoulder is turned, the head will come back in the same line to the ball. So you are not tempted into having a thrash, with your right shoulder coming in and trying to smash the ball with your right hand.

One of the first rules of golf, as far as I am concerned, is that you learn to play a golf stroke instead of a golf hit when you swing the club. As always, the major guiding principle is tempo. It doesn't matter how well you swing or how well in line everything is, if you swing at 150 mph, your chances of returning the club-head to the

ball at the same angle as it left it are virtually nil, because everything happens in such a blur of speed and anything could result. Your hands, your wrists, your ankles, your eyes, your head could move. I am not saying we should all swing at a funereal pace but it should be a gentle swing.

Think tempo – and think in terms of allowing the club-head to come away from the ball so that you can see its path, if need be, thus giving the body time to turn, because weight has to transfer from left foot to right foot and then back again. And remember, of course, that the most important six inches of any golf swing are the three inches just as you hit the ball and the three inches just after you've hit the ball as the club-head goes through it. That's the only point of the club swing that actually propels the ball. Anything that goes on behind your back or over your shoulder or above your head when you've finished is only frills. The essential moment is when the blade actually hits the ball and guides it away to the target.

The most important thing in golf, next to your swing when trying to hit a ball, is complete concentration. The really vital part of any golfer, so it is said, is the bit between the ears. If you don't think you are going to play well,

*A mental blind spot when it comes to
left and right*

then you won't play well.

I remember a pro telling me that he kept changing his putter. 'I am never happy with a putter for a long time. I might change it once a fortnight or once every three weeks. I have a wardrobe full of putters at home.' A fairly new putter that impressed him might not guarantee him holing every putt but it would give him the confidence to expect to hole every putt. Once that confidence had gone and he began to believe he was not going to hole putts with it, he would have to change it.

So a lot of the art of golf is in the mind, convincing yourself that your swing is right and that your choice of club is right. It is no good selecting a club from your golf bag and then thinking, 'I'm sure I should have picked another one.' Select a club, stick with it and hit with it – try not to smash it or be too gentle with it to compensate for selecting the 'wrong' club. Hit it quite normally, never stopping halfway through to say to yourself, 'This isn't going to work. I should never have picked an eight-iron'. As soon as you do that you are bound to duff the shot. You are thinking wrong, you're thinking anti-golf, you're resorting to power instead of technique, and you are 99 per cent certain to play a bad shot.

To be a good golfer, it helps to know right

from left – or at least be aware of the difference. It is amazing how many people have a mental blind spot in this area. My Pat still uses 'knife side' and 'fork side'!

If you are a right-handed person then golf is naturally a left-sided game. I think the nicest image of golf was given by a young assistant pro who said to me, 'There are mornings when I get up and I can see the picture. I can put the club-head to the ball and I can see where the ball is going to go, whether it is going away or coming back, flying to this point or that point . . . the picture is clear. If you can't visualise that picture then you can't play the shot.' And he was right. It is all a matter of composure and minimising the drawbacks.

It is fun to watch an opponent stagger into a pot bunker wielding a two-wood and it's great to be able to sympathise when he hits the face of the trap and buries himself deeper in the mire.

'Hard luck – two inches higher and you'd have been on the green.' Hopefully that will convince him to try the shot again if he finds himself in another trap.

Sometimes preparation for the game can include practising those extremely important comments on your opponent's game, and then getting the timing right.

I learnt from some great teachers ... 'On your back swing are you breathing out or breathing in?' That's a cracker!

Cardew 'The Cad' Robinson was responsible for the next beauty. He never did it to me, but I have it on good authority that he sometimes let his opponent play two or three good holes and then said, 'Now that last shot, you got everything right – arms, hands, legs, balance . . .'

The poor victim then spent the rest of the round trying to get 'everything right' again – and failing, naturally. It's another version of the 'gotcha' joke. If you don't know the 'gotcha' story, ask around!

I suppose the words about golf that have had the most lasting effect on me came from Gil Dova, my American friend, a golf fanatic whose greatest moment, he says, was actually dreaming he'd won the US Open. He could even remember the exact score on each hole. What a disappointment waking up must have been!

Gil said to me, 'The greatest thing about golf is the pride it gives you in your own ability. Shame alone prevents people giving wrong handicaps in order to win.'

And you know, all joking aside, that is true of most golfers. All right, there are bandits in the game and we get to know them over the years.

But generally, if anything, the handicap system works for us and against us because we are always trying to be better than we are.

The handicap system, after all, is probably the reason why golf is the only game in which you and I, scratch or 28 handicap, can take on the world's best and have half a chance.

There is no way you could take on a tennis player, even with three points start in each game. Or match a world class boxer even with one hand tied behind his back. Or a snooker pro, even with a four blacks start.

Yet play golf with a great player, he off the back tees and giving you shots, and who knows? The one sure thing is that the pro will be as helpful to you as possible, giving any advice that will help you improve your game. That's golf – a game for the fairest of the fair.

It is pride in personal ability that is the key to preparing and playing well. Winning really becomes secondary. Wouldn't you prefer to be six under par and lose than be ten over and win?

I recall the story of the old codger who at 75 had given a lifetime's leisure to playing a hacker's game at his local club. On the eve of his 76th birthday he was asked by the club captain what his one main ambition was.

'I've always dreamed of reducing my handicap to 27,' he mused.

'Aha . . .' thought the captain. 'Maybe, just maybe . . .'

On the morn of his 76th birthday, the old codger shuffled out of the car park into the clubhouse to be greeted by the chairman of the handicap committee.

'I'm sorry, Harry,' he tells him, 'but after much deliberation and observation, we have to say that we've decided to cut you to 27.'

'Yippee,' came the answer as Harry did an Irish jig and rushed to the bar for a celebratory drink.

After that a delirious Harry joined three lifelong chums for a birthday round of golf, all full of the joys of spring. Three hours later they trudged back in, heads down and wheezing.

'How'd it go, Harry?' asked the skipper.

'Rubbish,' said Harry. 'I played like a 28!'

THIRTEENTH HOLE

I'm Enjoying It, Honest . . .

WHAT IS THE classic chauvinistic golf gag? 'I'll never forget my wedding day. I holed a 32 ft putt.'

I suppose in all walks of life there are things that make unforgettable impressions, but only in the great game are there so many, many things . . .

Enjoyment, the main reason for playing golf, so they say, can be achieved through good performance or good results. Preparation, that vital cog in the performance wheel, is all – plus natural talent as well.

Witness the would-be golfer given this advice by the golf pro who said, 'If I were you, I'd go down the driving range, spend about three hours hitting about 200 golf balls and then pack

up altogether . . .'

Never dismiss the flippant golf gag. There could just be a glimmer of truth in it.

'Our club never play away matches 'cos the captain hasn't got a tie.'

'Ours is the only club where the putting green is cobbled.'

'I had to take up golf otherwise I'd never see my doctor.'

'Charlie says he's going to drown himself. What do you think?'

'No chance – he can't keep his head down long enough.'

'I'll tell you how bad our team was – we were only together on the tee. We were scattered around the course like shrapnel.'

Yes, all good stuff . . . and more to come, because in golf who knows what will happen next?

Two lifelong adversaries are out on a Sunday morning, scores level and more than 50p riding on the game.

Player A is in the semi-rough and not sitting too well.

'Three-wood, caddie.' Addresses ball – no.

'Five-wood, caddie.' Addresses ball again, jiggles club – no.

'Three-wood again.' Another jiggle.

'Five-wood again.' Jiggle, jiggle.

'Hmm. I don't think this is a wood shot . . .'

Player B chips in, 'No, but it soon will be!'

Then there is the expert ball marker – you must have met him. This fellow is more deft at sleight of hand than Paul Daniels.

Instead of marking behind the ball, he marks in front. Then, when replacing the ball, he puts it in front of the marker.

I watched one from close up one day and a member of our four said, 'Careful, pal. If you mark that ball once more, you'll be in the hole.'

See? There's fun even in adversity on a golf course. Surely those stories we pass on at golf dinners aren't all jokes . . .

'The way he played he didn't need a watch. He needed a compass.'

'A bloke with us cried "Fore!" and an auctioneer in the game ahead said, 'Do I hear four-fifty?'

'Did you hear about the bloke who won the Irish Open two up and six to play?'

What about the almighty row coming from the 18th green, lots of screaming, shouting and scuffling. 'What's going on?' asks the steward, sprinting towards the incident.

'My mate's just had a stroke,' said the player, 'and these two are trying to count it!' Ugh! Even I don't believe that one!

Although there was the tale of the three who

*The other three saw a hand rise
as if to grasp Excalibur*

came in saying, 'Poor old Percy passed away on the seventh green.'

'Oh dear,' said the steward. 'You must have been devastated.'

'Yes – particularly as we've had to carry him for 11 holes.'

If golf jokes are often a little macabre, they still show a healthy ability to poke fun at ourselves and our passion for the game.

Witness the bloke whose ball flew into a lake, infuriating him so much that he stormed in after it, his head gradually disappearing under the water, leaving only a floating cap.

After an interminable wait, the other three saw a hand rise as if grasping Excalibur and flicker gently.

'He's drowning for sure,' says one.

'Not necessarily,' says his partner. 'He could be calling for a five-iron.'

Then there is the bloke whose misfortune is to partner a fussy putter. You've all met this one – he stalks the hole for fully 20 minutes, looking for borrows, holding up the putter and aligning the head behind it. What are they looking for?

'When was this green cut, caddie?'

'This morning, sir.'

'Yes, but what time this morning?'

He's the one who finishes a foot from the hole

and waits a while before saying, 'I didn't hear anything . . .' No, and you won't, pal!

The first time I ever played an American was at the Foxhills, Chertsey course, and I found myself teeing up with a Texas magician, Jay, over here on tour and appearing in my TV series. He asked, 'Would you like to join me for a knock?' and of course I was delighted to accept.

The first hole was no problem for me. I played a nice easy three-wood down the middle just to show Jay the line. On the tee Jay took his driver and – whack! Goodbye ball. Reload.

'Oops, Tommy,' he said. 'I'll just play a Mulligan.'

OK, I thought. It's transatlantic good will, hands across the sea, Anglo-American relations stuff . . . all good reasons for allowing him a free ball.

He took the same driver and – whack! – same result. Reload.

'Oops, Tommy,' he said. 'I'll just play a Shapiro.'

'Shapiro?' I ask.

'Jewish Mulligan, son.'

There was no answer to that, other than to bite the bullet, and keep your head down. Jay won, by the way.

Another day, another course, this time Shawhill in Lancashire – a great club, with a hotel and a golf complex that's popular with societies and ideal for corporate days – and I'm not just saying that because I happen to be a vice-president . . .

Anyhow, I recall one particular morning when, being the celebrity guest, it was my brief to play a hole with each team, present the prizes and perform the cabaret. It makes for a long day but it can be very satisfying.

The first at Shawhill is a good par four. There's trouble to the left and right but only if you go looking for it. Legends abound that the hole is drivable on a good day: 'Just catch the top of the rise in the right position and down she rolls.'

There is a slight dog-leg left, with trees on the right and general nasties on the left. To lead the way I played a good three-iron safe and slightly right of centre. The next two went slightly more right, the first into the undergrowth and the other, a man whose swing was so fast it was impossible to tell whether it was out to in or not, belted his to the left and, as far as I could tell, was lost forever.

While I was lining up the next shot for his friend, this player was crashing around looking for the lost ball on the left. Soon he cried, 'I've

found it,' and a micro-second later – crump! – he'd smashed it out of Indian territory and as if by magic it plonked stiff by the pin. He was down for three the hard way.

We walked to the next hole where I had to wait for the next team, and I watched him assessing the hole. It's 142 yards, hardly any breeze and he took a two-wood.

'Look,' I said. 'It's never a two-wood from here. What did you use for your second on the last?'

'Five-iron,' he answered.

'Go for that, then,' I suggested.

He hit the five-iron as sweet as a nut and the ball had hole in one written all over it. One bounce and it disappeared into the hole for an eagle.

'What a start to a round,' I remarked.

'Better than that,' he beamed, 'I get a shot a hole as well.'

The last I saw of that team they were still trying to work out their partner's points to date. Surely I had just left the ultimate winner of the competition, but no! It transpired that after he left me he had tried to protect his gains and wrecked his card. So there is a God after all . . .

The 18th at Torquay (mentioned already in memory of the late, great Ted Ray) is a good-looking hole. It sweeps gently left to right, past

the clubhouse, across the first fairway and the
hole nestles by a wall below a school
playground. It's amazing how far the noise of
children playing can travel on a clear day.

Just to the right of the green is the practice
ground, but not so you'd notice, unless you
knew it was there.

A visiting celebrity, who shall be nameless,
was doing a Sunday concert at the theatre
where I was in summer season, and asked for a
knock on the Monday morning. So there we
were, me down the fairway left of centre, and
maybe a seven-iron from home, and he over by
the trees to the right, safe enough but short of
my ball.

Slowly I realised he was not making a
bee-line for his ball. Instead he would pause,
stoop, stand erect and move on. Then it dawned
– he had found a ball! No one about – a pick up!
And further along he found another one . . . and
another. Boy, this must be a nest of 'em!

Only the laughter borne on the wind brought
him back to reality. As he looked ahead, pockets
stuffed with Pinnacles, Titleists, Dunlops, he
saw the pro and a pupil in the practice area.
They'd been hitting all those balls he'd been
picking up! Laugh? Well, he had to – especially
as the entire clubhouse had witnessed it all.

Remember the apocryphal story about the

man who won the pools, moved to Southport to live and was persuaded by his wife to take up golf? Maybe you've heard it before, and maybe then it was set at another course, but anyway it's the one that goes like this . . .

He went to his local sports shop and said, 'I'm thinking of taking up golf so I'd like to buy some bats.'

'Certainly sir,' said the owner, and off went our hero to pay for his first round of Royal Birkdale, complete with a bag of bats and plenty of 'ammo'.

He proceeded to tear shreds out of the course, hitting everything but the ball and generally creating havoc.

Back in the clubhouse he ordered lunch and tucked in while the other members grumbled at the bar.

'It's absolutely disgraceful – the man's an idiot.' 'Quite so. He's destroying the place!' 'Someone should tell him.'

So a committee man was delegated. He strode over to the pools winner and said, 'I say, my man. I want to have a word with you. I'm responsible for the greens here.'

'That's good,' said our man. 'As it happens I want a word with you. These sprouts are awful!'

Not a true story, but a good one for all that.

There are plenty of rules in golf not printed in

any book – experience is the only way to learn them. How to sabotage the game of a person who is taking unfair advantage, for example. You know the sort – the one who is forever watching your club selection or listening to your request from the caddie. The simple solution is to have numbered head covers on the irons and put them on the wrong clubs. Boy, that soon stops their gallop!

Another ploy is to ignore their constant cries for relief from various lies. 'Is that a rabbit scraping?'

'Not unless he's got feet the size of a yeti!'

'Is there a ruling on this water?'

'Yes, get wet or drop a shot.'

We had a regular at Royal Ascot whom we used to call Dracula. They had planted some baby trees and put stakes round them for protection. If a young tree is staked you can get a drop ball a club length or two away, so you don't damage the tree. And they called him Dracula because every time he got near a tree he would ask, 'Is this a stake?'

The usual answer was, 'No, it's a pork chop!'

He's now retired to the course in the sky where I suppose he is still appealing against something!

FOURTEENTH HOLE

Golf? What Is Golf?

GOLF IS like the high jump – you never actually beat the game – there will eventually come the point whether it's a round of 60 or 55 or 50 or whatever, when you realise you are never going to go round a golf course in none!

All you can do to improve your own particular game is to remember your mistakes and learn from them, discover what your limitations are and play to them. And try to do the good things consistently well.

If you want to play a half decent game of golf, find a good golf pro. Ask around, check them out and stick with the one you choose. What with tours and summer seasons, this has been impossible for me. But the advantage of staying with one pro is that he will develop your game –

because you are not going to learn it all today or tomorrow or in two years – then gradually show you the good habits and iron out any faults.

It is important, too, to play with good partners, or against good opposition. Probably the best games of golf I have ever played have been with players far better than I will ever be. It forces you to concentrate! Rather than look a complete idiot, you are forced to think and play the best game you possible can.

Another prime lesson I've learned in playing golf is consideration for others. At my late stage of taking up the game (and probably the same goes for most people who take up golf late) we do it to for enjoyment, exercise and companionship. So you can show consideration in a variety of small ways – by raking out bunkers, replacing pitch marks, replacing divots and the like.

Equally important is consideration for other people's emotions, bearing in mind we can all be nervous, frustrated, tired, hot tempered – all the things that golf is *not* about. Golf should have a calming influence. The last thing you want to do is to play a game that winds you up so that you end up banging your head against the wall and breaking your clubs. Golf must be played serenely. Henry Cotton once criticised a well-known pro for practising when he was

tired, after doing an exhausting round of personal appearances and so on. We have to give golf our fullest attention when we play. It's no good steaming up to the club with two minutes to spare before you run on to the tee, slinging your shoes on and trying to smash the first ball 300 yards.

Golf is a way of life, a way of slowing you down, taking your mind off the problems of the day, helping you to relax in your own kind of company.

There are no short cuts. It's all down to serious effort and serious concentration – blood, sweat and tears, if you like – you only get out of golf what you put into it. If you play a fluffy shot, you get a fluffy result. If you concentrate on getting the correct weight of head through the ball at the right speed, you get the kind of shot that's as good as any pro could play – though you might not hit it so far.

You can get sentimentally attached to your equipment, sometimes to the detriment of your game. One girl who was a member at our club collected golf balls the way we used to collect conkers. She had one particular ball with which she had played 22 complete rounds of golf. It broke her heart when she lost it. I think she would have been happier if it had broken in

half. At least she could have said, 'Well, that's it finished, I can't use it again.' Just knowing this favourite ball was out there somewhere, lost in the bushes – she was still pining for it weeks later!

I mentioned that John O'Neill has a putter which he has had ages and it is almost as bent as Harry Lauder's walking stick – yet it works for him. And that's as it should be. If it works, stick with it. If you think it's helping you, then that's 30 per cent of the job. But many golfers prefer to resort to alternatives. If something goes wrong and they three-putt three holes in a row, they will probably drag out another putter. Because golfers will never blame themselves – they will always blame the club. 'The putter's too light, too heavy, the face is gone, it's worn . . . give me something new.' We're conning ourselves really.

Golfers also tend to have a weird selection of clubs in their bag. I would love to empty Trevino's bag and see what's in there. I know he has two different wedges. He may even have three, either to get the ball up or to get it up and knock it a long way as well. And apparently he has a couple of three-irons and a couple of three-woods. You and I buy a full set of clubs and we go out with one of each. The pros don't do that: they may have a couple of woods and

one iron, or a couple of three irons and no two-iron. Because the pros can make one club do another club's job.

One of the most amazing things I saw was Sevvy playing a round of golf with only one club. He just used the four-iron – as a driver, a wedge and a putter – and still parred the course!

Pros can adjust their drivers too. Those I have picked are a lot heavier than you expect them to be because they have lead weights underneath them. The basic rule is if it works for you, use it.

I try to have a complete set of clubs of the same make. I know guys who have the odd wedge that doesn't go with the set, or two woods of one set and one of another. That doesn't work for me. I try to concentrate on having all the clubs of the same weight and the same feel, all set up from the same manufacturer. That seems to make sense.

Sometimes, when you stand to a ball, the caddie can give you the wrong club. Once I asked for a nine-iron and he gave me a six. The ball was still climbing when it cleared the houses, never mind the green, because it was too much club. More recently it happened in reverse – I asked for a six and he gave me a nine – but I knew it was wrong the moment I got

hold of it. You must get used to the feel. I don't think I could adapt to a strange wedge, iron or whatever. For me they all have to slot in and all have the same 'feel'.

Golfers love gimmicks, but they are divided over the long-stemmed putter used by the likes of Sam Torrance. I have had a go at one and I must confess I can see the point, because putting is the only part of the game where the right hand takes over. Assuming you are a right-handed golfer, the left hand is the prime mover in playing all the shots, except in the case of the putter when the right hand tries to 'bowl' the ball along the green into the hole. It is a stroke and not a hit. A big putter makes sense because it is an obvious pendulum – but it looks unwieldy to me.

I do see that being so long it is easier to keep it straight. With a normal-sized putter sweeping from right to left through the ball there is a tendency to push or pull or cut it. But then again the long putters look and feel like the long rest at snooker, and I was never happy with that. My uncle Tom, who was good at snooker, used to refer to the long rest as 'the furniture' – 'Don't get the furniture out, son – forget it. I'd rather hit something else!' The long putter may be effective for Torrance but I couldn't be bothered.

The trouble is you look such a twit at our level, staggering on the green with one of them and then missing the putt. It looks good when Torrance does it, but out there on the midden – forget it!

I'm beginning to believe that the best way to putt is to copy my pal Stan, a stalwart golfer from way back, and the scourge of Bootle golf course.

Stan's motto is very simple: 'Assume all putts are dead straight and hit them at 100 mph – don't give them a chance to borrow.' Honestly, the number of his putts I've seen hit the back of the cup, fly a foot in the air and drop in. It's very spectacular but no good for the nerves when he's your partner. 'It's only a game, son,' he would say. 'Only a game . . .'

I love the nicknames that golf can produce. We have a guy, nameless for my own safety, who is called the Quizmaster. He keeps coming into the clubhouse saying, 'I've found the answer!' Well, he might think he has – until the next round!

I'll never forget the best lesson I ever had. David Lloyd is the pro at the West Lancs Club, a smashing bloke and one of my favourite teachers. He and Doug Currey, alias 'The Swing Doctor', from Filey have between them given me some semblance of a golf game.

Neither of them is overawed by fame or fortune and can gently 'bully' you into good habits.

David had me practising shots with the feet together, feeling the rhythm and gently learning how to 'groove in' the swing, controlling the right shoulder, careful not to lurch into the ball, holding it all back till the crucial moment.

If only he'd been six months earlier with this particular lesson he could have saved me a lot of pain. I was appearing in Blackpool and arranged a Saturday morning knock with two pals I hadn't seen since schooldays.

On the first I felt generous, giving them shots all round. Then I saw them tee off well and the devil inside was already saying, 'Wow! Never mind a steady start with a four-wood. You'll have to go for the big one!'

So it was the driver with no warm-up. A mighty heave and I hit the ball a good way but immediately felt a stabbing pain in my chest.

'Heart attack!' I panicked but no, thank God. It was only a pulled muscle in the diaphragm area, making it impossible to play even a second shot. 'Goodbye lads,' I said, 'see you in the bar!' The next thing I was being looked after by a football club physio in the clubhouse. 'Tell you what you've tried to do – knock the skin off it while your muscles were still cold. I bet it hurts!' He didn't have to tell me that.

Meantime what were my pals thinking? 'We haven't seen that O'Connor for 18 years . . . funny bloke. Shortest round I've ever seen anyone play. Mind you he always was a nutter at school . . .'

Ever had that desire to read people's minds and discover the real thoughts behind their outward reactions? Take the Wang Open, a Pro-Celebrity-Am tournament, and on the tee is Ian Woosnam, accompanied by my wife's hero, 'Wobbly' the caddie (these Yorkshire folk stick together, you know!)

Woosie hit a ball to the limit of my vision and Wobbly said 'Rubbish. Topped it!'

I paced out that drive – it was at least 280 yards. Were they just having me on?

FIFTEENTH HOLE

It Works For Me!

PEOPLE ASK ME, though not very often, what is the secret of my golfing success? I would not presume to set myself up as a good teacher of the game – I'm no Jacobs or Leadbetter – but I can tell you what works for me, what I have discovered through my own follies and foibles. You never know, you may discover it's simply a piece of cake! Read on . . .

No matter how good a swing you have, and no matter how good an eye for the ball, if your basic set-up isn't correct, you are not going to strike the ball properly. You will hit the ball, but its direction will be governed by luck and not by skill.

The basic skill, therefore, is to align yourself properly. Try to think in terms of, say, two

railway lines or two sides of the road. Standing on one railway line are your feet, and on the other, parallel to you of course, is the ball – and hence the back of the club. If that is not achieved immediately, no matter what else happens, the ball will not be struck correctly. If the lines diverge, the club-face will come in across the ball and knock it to a slice. If they converge, the result will be a hook. So the stance and the alignment are vital.

The grip is also very important. The best advice I ever had came from Peter Alliss, who recommended me to hold my hands together as if to clap them, and then put a club between them. The only way the hands can then hold the club is the correct way. So remember – clap hands, here comes the club . . .

After the stance and the grip comes timing. It matters a lot how fast or how slowly you take away the club and how correctly you turn your whole body. Remember the lady who taught me to sing 'Nellie the Elephant' to myself – anything to help the tempo. The slower you can swing the better, because the most important part of any swing is the last six inches, just prior to hitting the ball, then striking the ball and then following it through.

You can swing as hard as you like over your head – it might look good but that doesn't count

for anything. The most important speed of swing is right at the bottom of the pendulum. So if we think pendulum we grasp the fact that the only reason the club is going backward is to propel it forward. It's going back to be part of that smooth pendulum action.

Everything now should be a piece of cake; and in fact, it might help you to imagine you're standing vertically with your arms out at an angle to your body. The club is an extension of your arms and when the whole set-up swings it's like taking a slice out of that imaginary cake.

The swing isn't up and down: it's also around and across, a three-dimensional movement. It makes a plane at 45 degrees to your body. The speed at which you take away the club-face and, more importantly, the speed at which you return it will determine whereabouts the ball eventually lands. Because if the club-face is square, the only thing that can alter the ball going straight is if you bring it in too quickly and make it angle one way or the other. If you bring the club back slowly and return it along the same path every time, you should hit the ball straight – every time. The only things that change this are nerves, panic, anger, and all those other elements that have to be under control!

The only other way I can imagine the route a swing should take is to imagine a fat mayoress and think of the way her chain would lie across her chest.

Actually, one of the funniest sights is a man who has had a basic early lesson in golf and tries to do everything he has been told. We're back here to the 'nose to the grindstone, shoulder to the wheel' syndrome. Some look quite deformed as they swing because they are trying to improve on the pro's advice, carrying it to extremes.

When the pro says, 'You know why you're not getting the right result – it's because you're not standing near enough to the ball,' some folk over-compensate and actually stand on top of it. Instead of saying, 'I'll go forward a quarter of an inch and see if it helps,' some golfers think, 'If the remedy is getting near, let's see how near I can get. If I end up with the ball behind me I don't care . . .'

Don't exaggerate the pro's instructions. Instead, do whatever is comfortable for you, because at the end of the day there might be a thousand guys who look good when they swing but only a hundred of those who play well.

People say there is a correct way of doing things – but what is correct these days? If you look at Trevino's swing, it's not good according

You can't swing like Faldo, so that's it

to the purist. Nancy Lopez was the best lady golfer in the world but her swing was all her own. No one tries to make you imitate Trevino or Lopez – but they all try to make you copy Faldo with his immaculate swing. Who's to say you can swing like him anyway and feel right doing it? If you have a couple of stone more round the waist you haven't a hope – so that's it. 'Correctness', then, is whatever feels comfortable for you and whatever gives you consistency.

We're back to the maxim, 'Whatever suits you . . .' If you can get on to a driving range or a practice ground, develop a swing you are happy with and, say, eight times out of ten, hit the ball roughly in the direction and for the distance you want, then that's it. No need to improve on that because you aren't aiming to play in the Open anyhow. Alternatively, you could use the golf secretary's style – keep your head down and let the club do all the work!

As I said before, no one ever tells you how to drink a pint of lager. You just pick it up and drink it. But try to teach someone exactly how to do it – it's very difficult to explain – the way to grip the glass, the correct inclination of the arm, the right angle at the elbow, and at the last moment the split-second timing of when to open your mouth . . . never mind how to drink a

pint of lager on a ship that's pitching and rolling.

People can do it but they don't necessarily know how.

Apart from the basic shots taught by the pro, it is as well to have other shots in your locker, either worked out by yourself or copied from others. For instance, I watched Tom Kite at the American Open play a particular shot brilliantly. It's one I have mastered only because I play with old men – a pitch and run shot – which the guys I play with call a 'scuttery' shot. Trevino calls it a 'bump and run' shot.

Basically it's a stab with a seven- or eight-iron from about 40 yards off the green. You need to know how to play it because one of the hardest shots in golf, particularly if the wind is blowing, is a short one. A pro playing a 320-yard par four could, in theory, very nearly drive the green. But he wouldn't. He would play an iron short of the green and leave himself a full shot – a full sand wedge or a full wedge shot to throw the ball up and stop it on the green, near the hole.

You or I would get out the wood, hit the ball as hard as we could to get as near as possible, and be left with something like 60 yards – which is a really awkward shot. On a summer's

day it's hard to gauge how far 60 yards is and
stop the ball. I would rather have 100 yards to
go and hit it as hard as I could with a wedge,
knowing it would not go much further past the
flag, because that's roughly my distance with a
wedge. A pro would try to leave himself a full
shot with any club.

What we amateurs tend to do, because we
want to hit the first as hard as we can, is to
leave ourselves a shot so near the green that we
find ourselves playing a short second shot we're
not used to. So we try to play 40-50 yards,
throwing the ball up in the air, and hopefully
stopping it dead somewhere near the hole. If
the wind's blowing, the ball is going to go
anywhere. When Tom Kite was playing at
Pebble Beach, that's what was happening. The
hole was less than 150 yards. But because the
wind was so strong, players were hitting
everything into the rough, even into the sea.

The 'scuttery' shot, as played by the old boys,
particularly up north, stabs the ball a mere
three or four feet in the air. Then it bounces its
way on to the green. It's a bit six of one, half a
dozen of the other as to where it'll stop; but at
least if you pitch it up into the air and let it
bounce along it has some chance of staying on
the green. If you throw it higher in the air and
the wind gets it, it could go anywhere. This one

is unaffected by the wind because it keeps nice and low. And there is truly an art to it: if you play these old guys you will find when they are 50 yards out from the green, they are deadly. They are down in two with one of these little 'scuttery' chips; a pitch and run, and a putt and they're down.

Every golfer has a shot that he can play that may be new to everyone else! Think about it. I was once about 120 yards from the green and under a tree. I couldn't play any kind of ordinary shot. 'What are you going to do?' smiled my partner, thinking he 'had' me. I showed him with my trusty five-wood!

Normally with a five-wood, if I hit it well, the ball goes about 220 yards – twice as much club as I need. But a five-wood has a flat face and I can actually play it from beneath a tree very low because it doesn't need to be lifted up but swung around. With an iron you have to stand up to hit the ball, but you can play a wood, because it has plenty of face, by standing back and sweeping lower. To be truthful, it is hardly my secret weapon – I learnt it from Ozzleball when we were playing in the Benson & Hedges.

The other shot I play is again from beneath low-lying foliage. Trevino told me that if I was under a tree and had to keep the ball down for a

long way, I should play a six-iron off the back foot. It hits the ball not more than about a foot and a half off the ground, and it stays at that height. Same principle as the bump and run shot.

The unfortunate thing is that golfers of our ilk, unlike pros, need those shots simply to get us out of trouble!

Length of shot depends on strength and conditioning. For instance, John Jacobs's maxim, that there is a club in your bag for every shot – is true. A pro may take a six-iron to get to the green and you may take a three – but if you are both on the green, at the end of the day that's what it's all about. Golf is not a matter of how but how many. If you've taken four shots to the green and so has Sevvy Ballesteros, then who's to say he's any better than you are? (Well, probably everyone but you!)

I played in the Dunhill Masters with that marvellous South African player, Mark McNulty. Mark, unfortunately, was having a bit of a back problem, which is normal for golfers, even good golfers. He told me, 'Golf is one of those games where the more you think you know about it the more intricate it becomes.' I suppose that's right; it's all down to our concept of the game. When you're hitting the ball well it can be the easiest game in the

world. The irony is that when you've played a bad shot you know at least three reasons why you've played it. When you've played a good shot, you've no idea why it was a good one and what you did differently.

If you could harness or bottle the technique and the tempo when you've played a good shot, you'd have a world best-seller. It's one of those things: we play golf at our level not expecting to play the perfect shot, so when it comes we are not ready for it. Everything goes together – the hands, the wrists, the arms, the shoulder, the feet – everything is in perfect unison. Then for the rest of that day and maybe for the next week we are still trying to re-enact that exact move. It's to do, again, with our frame of mind.

Sevvy reckons he has about 20 different things he could try when he's playing badly, different techniques he can apply to put his game back together – all of them aimed at steadying the brain, and preventing him from panicking. Yet many pros I've met can't explain why they play well one day and not another; and that is encouraging to the honest hacker like you and me.

But then, isn't that always the way? I think it was George Gershwin who, when asked, 'How do you write a musical?', replied, 'I can't tell you.' The questioner pointed out, 'But you wrote

one when you were seven . . .' and he answered,
'Yes, but I didn't have to ask anybody how.'

Blessed are they who are naturally gifted at
golf, those who can pick up a club, let fly and
never have to worry about whether the line was
inside or outside the lie of the ball or whether
the swing was too hard or too soft. Blessed are
they who can swing a club and hit it like the old
codgers you see playing golf – the 70- and
80-year-olds who can still make a perfect swing,
don't try to knock the ball out of the screws of
the club and thoroughly enjoy their day.

It wasn't until my company decided to come
up with a TV game based on golf that we
realised the advances that have been made,
even since I started to play. Our basic idea was
to film contestants and their celebrity partners
actually playing a hole, like the ninth at
Carnoustie or the fourth at Turnberry or the
second at Wentworth or whatever. When we
approached a TV company with the idea, they
said, 'That's fine. We can do all that in the
studio.'

Of course they can – the whole thing can be
re-enacted on a video screen. You stand on a
teeing-off mat which is scanned by an infra-red
sensor. Depending on how you hit the ball, the
sensor can tell you how far it will go, and

whether it will hook or slice. The shot is then transferred to the major screen which tells you your position relative to the bunker, the fairway or the rough. Thanks to modern technology, which is there to help you eliminate any possible wrong shots, bad swings, and so on, you can now learn golf without even setting foot on a golf course!

The aids to the game that are around nowadays are unbelievable. Video screens can show you exactly how your swing will look and compute the plane, and you can see it all explained in graphic detail. All this points to a new generation of potential players who should be able to do nothing else except play perfect golf!

The only things we are not catering for here are the brain and the good old British weather. In 10 or 15 years' time we shall see exactly what these video tutors have passed on to the youngsters, and how they cope with the elements.

I guess I was lucky to live for a long while in an area which has to be the perfect breeding ground for golfers in all conditions: the north-west coast with its string of good links courses, like Royal Birkdale, Hillside (probably one of the most difficult courses), plus a club where I'd be delighted to be a member – West

Lancashire. That really is a different course if the wind is blowing. It can blow there for a long time and very strongly. Add that to the mix of brain power, arms, hands, wrists, ankles, club-face square to the ball, tempo of swing. As the ball leaves the club at whatever speed, it is hit by a 70 mph gale coming from left or right (or I swear in some cases, both ways at once!). And when the ball lands it can hit anything – a dry patch, a wet patch, a brick, somebody's foot, a watering nozzle on the edge of the green – and end up anywhere.

There are wonderful stories of balls doing the most amazing things. There was one ball that was lost and eventually found in the hood of somebody's anorak. Or you could hit a tree and the ball could ricochet anywhere. Generally, when the pros smack one into the trees it goes for good. With us amateurs, it usually just drops down, perhaps with a lucky bounce and within range – but who knows? All these elements have to be put into the pot before you can say, 'I've really got a grip of golf, I understand it all now – I've got it sussed!' And no video tutor is going to help you solve all the riddles and enigmas. For, when 99 per cent of things are going right for you, the shot can still be wrong. That's the astonishing thing.

Probably the greatest feeling in the game,

other than hitting a perfectly fine shot, is to be able to stand on a tee and call one. When you announce, 'I'm going to hit this with a six-iron and I'm going to fade it around the corner and it should land by that white marker over there,' and then actually land the ball within a couple of feet of it, the sense of achievement is total.

Such things, however, are easier said than done. I once read about two golfers, Neil Coles and Brian Barnes, I believe, who were asked to play a round of 70-plus, and to state honestly how many shots (excluding putts) went exactly where they intended. They came up with only four or so occasions when they could truly say the ball landed in the spot where they would have run up and dropped it, given half the chance.

One of my favourite golfing songs is called 'Straight Down the Middle'. It was written by Sammy Cahn and Jimmy van Heusen especially for Bing Crosby and he is one of only two people I have ever heard sing it well. The other was the late and great Dickie Henderson – and it is significant that both these fine entertainers gave their all for the game of golf.

It truly has such lovely lines in it . . . '*I aimed it at two but it bounced off nine. The caddie said "Wait – because if you're still in the State, it's OK!"*' (What a wonderfully optimistic point of view.)

Then it goes: *'The life of a golfer is not all gloom, there's always the lies in the locker room . . .'* and that's so true. No matter how well or how badly you've played, who can stop you talking a good game?

Golf is probably one of the few games you can talk about informatively without actually being able to perform. I have seen fellers duff shots all over the course and then go in and complain about the conditions – the wind and the greens weren't holding, and so on – and they could be right. There are good golfers sitting there agreeing with them. Who's to know these moaners didn't even get to the greens?

I sometimes used that as my opening gambit at after dinner speeches: 'I'd like to thank the ground staff for the condition of the bunkers. I'd like to thank them for the greens as well, but sadly I didn't get near enough to one to form an opinion.'

SIXTEENTH HOLE

The Shot That Got Away

THE SOCIAL SIDE of golf is a marvellous thing. I suppose when one gets to the end of one's career, when one is 70-plus, it's probably a good three-quarters of what the game is all about anyway. And we'll always be able to talk about the shot that did the business or the one that only just got away.

I have never had a hole in one but I always maintain that a very close hole in two is always better-looking than a fluke hole in one. It's the ball that stops dead about three inches from the pin, and gets your playing partners saying, 'God, isn't he good – see how near he put that!' It's the old adage of being a near hit rather than a near miss. I know which one I would call the better shot.

175

You *saw that didn't you, Lord?*

In every golfer's memory, and consequently in his armoury, there will always be The Story – the one where he hit the flag and it dropped down and nearly went in the hole, the two that would have been a one and broken the course record. Not to mention the one that would have been the longest drive on the day but unfortunately rolled into the rough and wasn't counted.

So golf is a game of 'if onlys', marvellous memories and indisputable facts. Unless someone has gone all the way round the course with you, how can they gainsay anything you claim?

There's the old tale of the guy who came into the clubhouse and said, 'You know that lake by the fifth – must be 300 yards or more from the tee. I hit a shot this morning that cleared the water and landed the ball in line with the pin. Great eagle shot – must have been all of 350 yards!' And one of his mates observed, 'Funny you should say that. I hit a ball down by the lake yesterday and do you know what I found – a lantern from an old Spanish galleon! And do you know the amazing thing – it was still alight!'

So his friend looked at him and said, 'I don't believe you . . .' and he replied, 'I'll tell you what. You knock 80 yards off your shot and I'll blow out my lantern . . .'

Then there was the sad tale about the parish priest who played a round of golf alone on a Sunday morning, sank a hole in one and had to keep it to himself. He stood there thinking, 'Who can I tell about this? I'm not supposed to be here in the first place!'

Probably the most enjoyable golf I ever played and a round I'm hoping to re-achieve sometime, was when I did a summer season in Scarborough. I had the whole health kick going – I gave up smoking, gave up drinking and tried to go on a strict diet all at the same time. It's amazing how much of a martyr that can make you feel. Every day is a minor triumph – no cigarette for so many hours, two pounds lost in a day, and so on. I also went into light training and used to jog a couple of miles before going on to the practice ground and hitting a bucket of balls, then went out to play the course. Surprisingly, that was the most consistently good golf I've ever played.

I suppose that's understandable because if the brain's sharp from the running and the fresh air, then the rest of the system is alert and warmed up before you start. If I had to give pointers to would-be successful golfers I would say be a 'rested' golfer. Don't play when you're tired because you have to get your head together and concentrate. And don't ever take a

mobile phone with you on a course – that is the kiss of death.

Be as loose as possible, do as much warming up as possible. Try not to play a serious game the day after a lesson. Remember the old gag: 'I couldn't play that well, I was seriously injured – I had a lesson yesterday.' Lessons are marvellous if you want to get your game right, but don't expect to play a match the next day for a fiver and still try to do all the things the pro told you, because when things start to go wrong you will return to your old habits and have wasted a lesson. You will have lost the game, and the fiver as well. Always keep a good perspective on your health and the game, and give any lesson time to sink in, time for you to practise it yourself before attempting to emulate it.

Fitness is essential, but not the ultimate. If fitness were everything, you wouldn't have any chubby golfers or chubby snooker players, would you?

The eye is a wonderful machine – so get your eye in! It will correct things for you. While the stance is very important, the eye will try to make you do what it can see. If the eye sees the shot as being straight, it will make you play straight, no matter what. If you are going to play at that tree, the eye knows where the tree is even though you're not facing it and will

make you pull away from the trouble, almost without your realising it.

The phrase 'Out of the corner of the eye' should be allied with the bad back syndrome. You are about to do one thing and the eye corrects your action subconsciously! Perhaps you spot an overhanging branch out of the corner of your eye. Even though it's only a twig, it can seem enormous and it can put you off – sometimes you have to overrule your eye – but it's hard, because you always know it's there.

If you think you're going to hit the tree, you are drawn to it. The head is saying, 'Go over there where it's safe' . . . and it's true. The eye will try to over-compensate for any trouble and you can't kid it. It says to the brain, 'The tree is over there – hit this way.' It's like the story of the vicar with the big nose. Everyone tried to ignore the fact except one old lady who said, 'Have a cup of tea, vicar. How many sugars would you like in your nose?'

A retired old pro once said to me, 'If you have swung correctly, when the head comes up your eye should follow the direction in which the ball has gone.' This is true because basically you are keeping your head down until the club has hit the ball and then the whole thing follows on . . . You can't kid the eye, therefore you have to gear everything else up so that when you hit the ball

it goes where the eye wants it to go.

It is very difficult on a wet day to play in glasses. I now play in contact lenses – I'm fortunate in that my eyes are equally short-sighted, so I can put one lens in for driving, and leave the other eye for putting. I've tried the other way – wearing the glasses for putting and taking them off for driving, but it doesn't work. So I drive with my right eye and putt with my left. I guess a cross-eyed golfer will always put it in the bunker: They said, 'Follow the ball with your eye,' and he said, 'It could have gone anywhere . . .'

When you are in trouble, out scouting in Apache country, it really is your own fault if you haven't read the guide book. We should absorb all the things that can help us. At least read the rules on the back of the card; more often than not they will give you a clue as to how to get out of a fix. Rabbit scrapings, ground under repair, various lies in various places, where you can move your ball without penalty – the rules are there to help you avoid trouble. It's no use saying the pros have all the advantages because they know all the rules; you should too. And the local rules as well – those adjustments that only apply to that particular course.

If your ball is in trouble, the first thing to do is get it safe. There's no point thinking, 'If I were to whack this and kept it a foot off the ground and drill it hard, just slightly right of that tree, it might get on the green.' That's a mighty big 'if' – if we could all play that shot we wouldn't be carrying our own bags. We'd all have a caddie and be playing in the Open.

Obviously you have to get the ball back on the fairway. And don't panic! If it's a par four and you're in the bushes off the tee, you could still be on the green in three and with a bit of luck be down in four, or take a five (if your partner is giving you a shot this hole so much the better). So swallow your pride, accept that luck evens itself out in the end, make the best of it, and get back to where you can play properly.

Assume that now and again in your golfing life you are going to land in a bunker. It really pays to practise getting out of bunkers. The keen golfer should start at the practice ground, hit 20 or 30 balls, continue on to the putting green or the chipping green, and then go into the practice bunker. If possible, spend five minutes in the bunker to get the feel of it. For a start, it matters what kind of sand is in there, whether it's wet or dry, thin or heavy. In some bunkers the sand is like sugar, in others it's like plasticine.

At Ascot I have known five different consistencies of sand in the bunkers! And you don't know until you are in, what you are up against. So don't forget to practise bunker shots – and try to assess how, if need be, you can get out within the rules. There are certain things you can't do and which you have to adjust to when playing out of a bunker. You can't ground your club, for instance, before you hit the ball; but you can walk in and just from your footfall and the feel of the sand you should gain some idea of what kind of trouble you are in. And depending on how you are lying depends on how you are going to play the shot – whether you will take a lot of sand or no sand or flick it off the top.

Wear comfortable clothes on the golf course, too. Don't buy a brand new pair of shoes and expect to play perfect golf in them first time out. If they pinch or rub, they are going to ruin your concentration, as will a sweater that is tight under the arms or whatever. No matter that your sweet Aunt Lily knitted it for you – wear what you feel comfy in.

I wear 32/31 (32 waist, 31 inside leg) but sometimes I see in golf shops trousers marked up at 56/24. I'd love to meet him – Cinderella in reverse! It doesn't matter how abnormal that guy looks, if he feels right that's all that matters.

Mia Carla, a bonny girl who could be mistaken

for a Roly Poly, is a great comedienne and a good singer as well. She has taken up golf and her biggest worry is how to swing a club around her chest – is it over or under?

A lady who is well endowed has to make this decision very early in her career, because it will determine whether she uses irons or woods. Mia has now sorted herself out with woods, which means she is swinging around herself – and that's fine. It works for her.

The saddest sight is the guy who, for one reason or another, usually for health, has been told by his doctor to diet and lose something like six stone. He has been conditioned all his life to swinging round this girth, this lump of lard in front of him. Now he finds he is swinging more upright and has to learn tempo all over again. With the weight gone, he virtually has to rejig his whole game to hit the ball as well as he did before.

You have to customise what you use to the way you play and the way you look.

SEVENTEENTH HOLE

Celebs and Showbiz Partners

BERNARD DELFONT once maintained we would never have had an American top of the bill in Britain if it hadn't been for our golf courses, and it's probably true. The likes of Bing Crosby and Bob Hope were lured over here by the prospect of playing golf – entertaining was probably a secondary consideration!

Don't forget it was in 1952 at Maidenhead that Bing and Bob Hope played the first ever showbiz celebrity challenge golf match in the British Isles; they challenged Ted Ray and Donald Peers. And so great was the crowd, it swamped the course so that the game had to be abandoned. There are wonderful pictures of Bing and Bob riding across this golf course in an open car being pursued by fans with the

other two players clinging to the running boards.

There is an apocryphal story about The Ink Spots, too, in their early days. Val Parnell and Bernard Delfont had both agreed on the maximum sum they could pay the group to work their respective venues – the Palladium and the Prince of Wales. Instead of outbidding each other to put them on, they played a game of golf to decide who would get them. So golf is very important to showbiz.

One of the best celebrity golfers, a man who in his time I believe played off scratch, is Christopher Lee. But then nobody is likely to mess with Christopher Lee!

Jimmy Tarbuck is a marvellous golfer with a handicap of five. He may not always win competitions but he will always be within a point or two of his handicap, and will always deliver the goods, which is pretty good going. I played with him once on a course he had never played, on a funny old day weather-wise, and he was a bit shattered. Yet he still came within a few points of his handicap, leaving me for dead!

Roy Walker is also a very low handicap golfer. Roy used to be a left-handed shot-putter but he plays golf with his right hand. If he is innately strong in his left arm, then he is

certainly going to have an advantage over the rest of us – and he uses his strength well.

The best celebrity striker of a golf ball was Val Doonican. I think he was off two at the time and he is a very fine player. But then you'd expect him to be on song. When a pro hits the ball it climbs and keeps on climbing even when it's falling. Doonican was the only celeb I ever saw do that – send his ball off the tee like a rocket and knock it a mile.

Of the fun-type golfers, Norman Collier is a lot of fun; and no matter what time of the day it is you'll know where Frank Carson is on a course because you can hear him – unless he's doing well. If he's building a good score he'll be silent. He's a grand Irishman, and wasn't it an Irish golf pro who actually said these marvellous words on a very wet day: 'D'you know, if it wasn't my job I wouldn't do this for money, even if you paid me!'

I won't say it's the worst swing in the world, but Stan Boardman's swing is certainly unique! I couldn't describe it but I'd advise people to go and see it in action. I know some golfers who have heard about it and travel for miles to see him swing. Yet the amazing thing is . . . it works. When he takes a practice swing, observers remark, 'Now that's funny!' Then he hits the ball the same way and they all do a

double take. 'Now wait a minute . . . did he really do that?' He's got a good eye for the ball though, has Stan – he used to be a footballer.

Bruce Forsyth is a good steady golfer and like Tarby, he will always deliver the goods. Little Ronnie Corbett, who uses specially shortened clubs, is proof that you don't have to be massive to hit the ball a long way, because he has timing and rhythm. The art in his case, being a small man, is to get everything he's got behind the ball – and he does it so well.

I have played quite a lot of golf with Russ Abbot, who's a good golfer – I think he's a twelve now, and he takes his golf very seriously. What I like about Russ is that he's a stickler for the etiquette of golf – very precise and dignified. Precision is the secret of his successful career and with his wonderful gift of inventing characters. He doesn't have to wait for whoever is next going to be popular on telly – he has a wealth of comic characters in his head.

Shakin' Stevens too is a consistent golfer – though he does tend to shake his knees even when he putts! He is a nice player and excellent company.

Of the ladies, Rachel Heyhoe Flint plays off eight and is a good steady player, a natural sportswoman. Another fine striker of the ball is

the actress Suzanne Danielle, who is married to Sam Torrance.

Lee Trevino reckons the best swing he has ever seen on a lady is Mary Parkinson. He says she is one of the few golfers whose practice swing is the same as her ordinary swing. Most people swing nice and steady in practice and then give it loads in their actual swing. But Mary gives them both the same treatment, which is ideal and what we all aim for. She is a lovely player. Parky's not bad either.

You would expect guys who play other sports to take to golf naturally. Nigel Mansell, Ian Botham, Fred Trueman, Richie Benaud and Ted Dexter for example, are all good players. For cricketers especially, golf is marvellous for keeping fit and enjoying later in life. They don't need to run at 100 mph and limber up. It's a good game for them to play and they can adjust accordingly.

Among many soccer players – Kenny Dalglish is a fine golfer. And I admire Alan Hansen, the Scots international. He is a very low golf handicapper, played rugby for Scotland as well as soccer and basketball. And he's a good-looking feller and a talker. Dammit!

One of the most amazing guys at golf is Brian Close – because he can play left or right-handed and has two different handicaps. It's true! He is

very low handicap, if not scratch, with one hand and four or five with the other. So it would be impossible to get him into trouble because there are shots where a right-hander would be stuck against a wall or a tree and he could play out left-handed! Maybe he keeps one or two left-handed clubs in his bag just in case. Not many can do that trick. Bernhard Langer, I believe, played one such amazing shot out of a tree with his wrong hand. If you only have a right-handed club you can end up performing some contortions on the course, where a left-handed club could help!

I always have a straight-faced putter in my bag – straight-faced on both sides – and I can use that when up against a wrong 'un. I am not saying other putters are no good, but for safety, I always have a straight-faced one.

A number of sterling characters form the backbone of the Variety Club's Golf Society and the Comedians' Golf Society as well as the Stage Golf Society. These clubs consist of people in the entertainment world who love the game of golf, and in one way or another, throughout the year, help to raise funds for many worthwhile charities or projects, like the Variety Club's Sunshine Coaches.

I could namedrop a whole roll call – Roger de

Courcy, Henry Cooper, Henry Kelly, Mike Reid and so on – as well as those already mentioned, who are willing to travel hundreds of miles at their own expense. They not only travel and play all day, but also do a little entertainment in the evening, all for the good of golf and in the name of charity.

Ask me who are the pros I love to watch, and Trevino has to be the man, because he has a gag for every hole; he's the funniest guy and he is the most all-round professional. He would have been a success at anything – even a very good stand-up comedian had he put his mind to it. Or in any other sport too, he would have excelled because he has such a good eye and such fine coordination. What with his sharp wit, plus being a top-class golfer, he is a terrific ambassador for the game.

Golfers are special people. Without exception they are probably the greatest sportsmen in the world, followed (with minor exceptions!) by snooker players. Golfers have enormous patience, too – even more so than cricketers. You may be 22 behind on the first day of a golf tournament, but you carry on because by the fourth day you could be back in the frame. It's a matter of waiting for your chance and taking that chance – not throwing your clubs on the floor and giving up in digust.

Trevino I could watch all day – but it's difficult to say who isn't a hero. I like Woosnam as a man and he is great when he is on form: he can knock a ball a mile. Sevvy is the people's favourite, good-looking and capable of playing shots that others wouldn't dare take on.

Sandy Lyle is coming back now. I have a feeling Sandy will be all right if he doesn't get too much advice! It's very easy for everyone to tell you what you are doing wrong and what you should do to put it right. Sandy is young enough to learn life's greatest lesson – you need to be down to be up.

To be a successful comic you have to die on your feet. The only way you're going to get better is to go in there and be shown that you ain't the business, that there's more to it than you. And if there's a salutary lesson to be had, then I reckon Sandy's had it. The deeper the trough has gone, the more strength you gain when the next high comes. I have a lot of confidence in Sandy – we'll hear a lot more of him, maybe more than we heard before. I have played with him when he was on song and the ball used to scream when it left the club. He could pinpoint shots – say, 'I'm going to put it there' – and he did.

It's like a snooker player, on a smaller field of course, saying, 'I'm going to hit the blue and

leave the white nestling behind the pink – for all you watching in black and white.' But when a guy can do that from 300 yards, it's really impressive.

Jacklin was the best hitter of the ball I've ever heard, the cleanest, sweetest hitter . . . in his time so I'm told, was Alliss, but I never saw or heard him. But when Jacklin hit the ball you knew it was hit.

I like watching lady pros because they are so graceful – the only man who comes close is Hale Irwin. At his peak he was the most graceful swinger. He didn't look as if he'd hit it very far but he was proof that if it looks good it must be good. If a golf swing finishes nicely then the ball must finish nicely as well. He sacrificed power for this grace and artistry, and he guided the ball more than he smashed it.

Nicklaus was graceful and natural and that's why he stayed at the top so long. I heard that as he got older he had to learn how to chip a ball – because he'd never had to do it before. He had to learn the 60-yard pitch and run – he'd never needed it before because he was so powerful. Then, as his power waned, he introduced new shots into his locker. The story goes that it was his son who taught him how to play one shot when he started finding himself 40 yards short of a target he would have hit at his peak. 'Come

here dad – let me show you . . .' Can you imagine that!

One of the last rounds of golf Henry Cotton played, bless him, was at Ascot. I sadly missed him, but I was told he could still hit the ball and was a hard man to beat even in old age. That's why it's such a good game – the only one where a pro can give you a start and still play you. McEnroe might give you three points every game – 40 love down and still win. Steve Davis could give you a 50-point start at snooker and batter you. But Trevino or Sevvy could give me a regulation handicap start – say seven shots – and with a fair wind and good putting I could have a darn good try at holding them. At the end of the day it's still a game we can all play and all enjoy without getting slaughtered.

Golf has always had a Brit in the top ten. The same applies to motor racing, of course, but that's not quite in the same league. As for summer sports, we can't do it in tennis, our cricket comes and goes – yet in golf we have Faldo, Woosnam, Lyle and many more capable of winning major tournaments. Why? Is it the range of courses available in Britain, or our temperament, our weather, our innate love of the game?

The short answer to all these questions has to

be 'Yes'. Certainly the Americans love playing over here. I think it's marvellous when Americans can adapt to our game. We enthuse when we win something in America, but when we go out and play in their conditions, the weather is generally a lot better, and the greens are slicker. The Yanks who come over here have a lot more to contend with – they end up almost playing in snow, often in howling rain and gales – and all credit to them.

We have so many different kinds of courses, and one thing you can't beat is healthy competition. In boxing, Frank Bruno can practise and spar for hundreds of rounds, but it's not like fighting a challenger over ten rounds. Competition is necessary. Generally there are enough golf competitions around for our pros to keep that edge, because you need that extra sharpness which you get when you don't play for fun. We have it, thankfully, in golfing terms. Wouldn't it be lovely if all the sports we played had that same competitive edge?

American courses, by and large, tend to be man-made and well manicured, whereas ours are mostly natural and range from the rugged Scottish courses to the lush greens of the south.

The greatest accolade I heard came from one of the record holders of the British Open, Tom

Watson, who maintains that one of the best courses in the world is Dornoch in Scotland. That is his favourite all-time course. Now he has played everywhere and even built courses, and if he is willing to pick Dornoch as his number one, it has to be right.

We tend to take our great courses for granted – yet Americans make pilgrimages. I was up at Turnberry once with Tony Jacklin and Brian Huggett for a big Pro-Celebrity-Am day and the weather was appalling. The flags were almost horizontal, and it was blowing a gale. Gordon Banks was there, Freddie Trueman, Peter Parfitt – we all came in and said 'Forget it.' It was that bad. So we had a Question of Sport session in the hotel instead.

Yet four Yanks played the course that day. They said, 'We've come 5000 miles and we ain't missing this.' They came in like snowmen at the end, freezing yet totally exhilarated. But then that's dedication: they'd come miles and they were willing to suffer anything to realise their dream!

The Japanese are the same – they come to Wentworth, buy everything in sight and sometimes don't play! Just take everything home with them to prove they've been here.

We love the Americans, but don't forget they tend to talk differently to us! John Jacobs,

apparently, when he went to America for the first time to do golf commentaries, didn't appreciate that Americans have different terminologies to ours. This guy had hit his ball out of the bunker and taken no sand, just flicked it off the top. Over here we would call that a 'pecker' (like chicken pecking corn), which of course has a totally different connotation in the States. So when John said, 'This man looks like a pecker,' they gave him some very odd looks. It all went very quiet in the box.

It was like the American GIs, when they came here during the war, and were told by the girls they met in the Forces canteens: 'Keep your pecker up!' – they thought to themselves: 'Boy, what a great country!'

Then John turned to his companion in the commentary box and confided, 'Can't wait for the commercial break. I'm dying for a fag.' That was his reputation gone up in smoke!

But we can get our own back if we want to. There's a story told of an American group in this country, over for a golfing tour and being treated after a day of golf and good company at a North Country club to a typical northern evening out – hot pot supper, red cabbage, the lot – no expense spared. There's even a waiter in what passes for an evening suit doing the rounds, giving out the pats of butter to

accompany the rolls. And this American says to him, 'I'll have two of those, please.' The waiter says, 'Look mate. I've got orders. One plate, one pat of butter.' The American insists, 'But I always have two.' Again the waiter answers, 'Listen mate, I don't care what you always have. I've been told – one plate, one pat of butter.'

So the American asks, 'Do you know who I am?' The waiter says, 'No.' So the American tells him: 'I am a multi-millionaire businessman in America, I have a business that goes into 48 states, I've got a 200,000-acre ranch. I've got five oil wells . . .' And the waiter replies, 'Do you know who I am?' And the American says, 'No.' And the waiter says, 'I'm the bloke with the butter.'

EIGHTEENTH HOLE

Around With O'Connor

THE GREATEST moment of my golfing life came when I played in a Celeb-Am tournament at Patshull Park near Wolverhampton, arranged by Rachel Heyhoe Flint. Nicholas Parsons and Roger de Courcy were there; so was Bernie Cribbins. Par for the course was 71 and I parred it. That is the only time I have parred a proper course. I have gone round the back nine of an eighteen-hole course and parred that, but I actually parred Patshull.

It was a lovely summer's day and the putts all went down. I was playing off eight, so I was basically eight shots better than my handicap. Even so, our team got 94 points. We were playing in a four-ball and you picked the best two scores on each hole – and we got 94, which

is massive. Theoretically, if we all played to handicap we should shoot 72. But with 94 we weren't even in the first three. No names will be mentioned – but Bernard Cribbins won it. He's a lovely man and he was mentioned in dispatches. I stood up at the dinner in the evening and said, 'I'd like to read you Bernard Cribbins's score card. It begins, "Once upon a time . . ." '

The only way to learn better golf is to play with better people. Just like the only way to look young is to hang around with old folk. You may think you're at the top of your sphere, but it is only when you play in Pro-Celeb-Ams with the likes of Lyle or Trevino that you appreciate there is a totally different dimension to the game. The things you think are important mean nothing to them.

They say, 'Never mind where you were taught to place your feet, stand like this . . .' It's like learning maths – you start with basic sums, adding up and taking away, dividing, multiplying. By the time you get to the sixth form, you are doing logarithms and calculus, and it all becomes one great experience; everything else is so elementary.

When you are playing with a pro who is saying, 'I am going to place the ball there because of this factor and that factor,' you worry about whether your toe is in line with

your other foot. Suddenly it's a totally different ball game – and yet it isn't. You learn more about priorities playing with better players.

So here are some of the tips I have learnt from players better than I will ever be! The first rule I was ever given for teeing off – and it still works for me today – is look at the tee, look at where you're aiming to put the ball. On most holes you should be able to see the flag, unless it's a dog-leg or over a hill or whatever. Generally speaking, you can see the flag or where the flag ought to be. Look at where you want the ball to be for your second shot.

On certain holes, like a par five, there's a certain amount of forgiveness. You can actually stray quite a way out on a par five and put yourself back again, because you're going to take three shots to get to the green – if the first shot is wayward, the second can rectify it. But on a par four where, for regulation, you have to be on in two, your first shot is all-important.

Now there's going to be trouble on one side of the hole, maybe even on both sides, and you have to decide whereabouts your ball will be best placed. You don't want it to be in or near the trouble, either for this or your second shot. On a dog-leg hole, if it's a dog-leg to the left, ideally you want to be at the apex of the bend on the right at the end of shot one, looking up the

rest of the fairway at the hole. The big hitter will try to go over the trees and land it short of the green, but it's a lot more risky for you. You want to have a clear shot at the flag for your second.

When you tee up you have to be aware of where the ball is going to go. I've always maintained – and it's worked for me every time – that you should play away from where you don't want to be! Sounds simple, but you'd be surprised how many rushes of blood to the head can occur out there on a golf course!

If you want to be on the right-hand side of the fairway, tee up on the left-hand side of the tee. And vice versa. This minimises the temptation of going over the trees and cutting the corner. The chances of you or I going over high trees is one in five – and that's praise. And if you do get over, you are only left with a shot that's too short for you to work out. It looks good for macho man if there is a group of female spectators he wants to impress, and who are going to coo, 'My God, can't he hit the ball!' But at the end of the day who cares? What counts is who's got the money. Drive for show, putt for dough!

You always tee up on the side where there's trouble; if it's on the left, tee up on the left and play away from it. Your eye will take you away from the trouble and your hands and your body will follow . . . it says here!

Secondly, you are thinking ahead and picking your second shot. All the pros play each hole backwards – they know what shots they are going to play to get them down in three on a par four. The best you can aim for is par, so do yourself a favour and think ahead. Leave yourself 100 yards for the second shot and work it out in your head. I've got 350 yards this hole . . . I need to hit 250 or so with a three-wood to that spot . . . then a nine-iron to the green. We should know within five yards how far we can hit each club – a seven-iron is 140 yards, a six-iron is 150 and so on. So we can work it back: to leave us a nice eight or nine to the green we need to take a three- or four-wood from the tee.

Also we have to be aware that the wind can play tricks: the easiest wind to play in is the one immediately behind you or the one right in your face. The hardest one is the one that's coming left or right, because goodness knows how strong it is. The trick there is to look up and see what the wind is doing to the treetops – it's no good looking at the distant flag drifting softly in the breeze. Look up into the trees and watch the branches swaying madly about – because up there is where the ball is going to go.

If you were going to pot the ball like a snooker shot, there would be no problem, because there would be no wind resistance along the ground.

But if you are about to hit an eight-iron 60/70 feet in the air you need to know what's happening up there. Try to do this all in the few minutes you are setting your stall out and preparing to hit the ball – it is all-important.

The second shot, assuming you are in a good position, will be to the green, and now you have to pick whereabouts on the green you want to be. The men who lay out greens are very crafty. On an ordinary day the hole will be easy, sited somewhere in the middle; so you just aim at the flag, and whatever happens you're safe. On competition days they will put the flag behind a bunker, or as near to the edge of the green as regulations allow – which I think is six feet. This time you can aim at the flag and maybe go just a little too far and find yourself rolling off the green and maybe into a bunker. Or into the water.

So the rule for hackers is: no matter where the flag is, go for the middle of the green. At least then you are on the green. A maxim I learnt from Gary Player years ago is always to play over the flag because all the trouble is usually to the front of the green. Certainly that used to be true but it isn't always so nowadays. People are beginning to put trouble at the back. There are places at the back of the greens now where Red Indians live!

Therefore we shouldn't really be wondering

*The hardest wind is the one coming
from left or right*

what side of the green we need to be on: we should be aiming for the middle.

Mind you, having said that about the trouble, have a look at where the bunkers are placed, because that will give you an idea of the lie of the hole. If the bunkers or the trees or the water are on the left, it must mean that the ground runs that way or the wind blows that way. There is usually a reason why they are sited there to grab your ball. And the maxim here is the same as for the fairway: play safe, protect your par to the centre of the green, and then it's between you and your putt.

Everything sounds simple when you hear it for the first time, and you wonder why you didn't think of it before! The best tip I ever learnt about putting was to imagine that the flag was really in the middle of a bucket. So when you are putting to the hole pretend you are actually aiming into a bucket about two feet in diameter. If you can get the ball into that diameter then with your next shot you are bound to sink it because from two feet you can't miss.

It's like the old gag of the feller baling out of the plane, isn't it? They told him, 'For the parachute you pull this first cord – and if that doesn't work you pull this second cord.' And the feller asked, 'What happens if the second one

doesn't work?' And they said, 'By that time you'll
be about ten feet off the ground – and you can
jump ten feet, can't you?' So get the ball within
the rim of that imaginary bucket. The principle
sounds simple – and it is – but it's so often forgotten. People play from about 20 feet trying to
hole the ball. An ace pro will sink a 22-foot putt,
but if you and I get it, it's a bonus. We simply aim
in that direction, hoping to get it near.

So no rush of blood on the putting – aim for the
bucket. If it's inside the bucket, it's a good three,
you've scored and earned yourself a birdie. If you
don't and you're still inside the bucket, you're
going to get a four, which can't be bad.

Peter Alliss always said that putting is
probably the most important part of anyone's
game and certainly the stroke that is played
most often, yet we seldom have a lesson on it.
People tell us how to putt, possibly show us how
to grip and suggest various tips, but no one
spends an hour watching you putt, or helping
you to putt properly when you are hitting drives
or sand wedges or whatever. It's a part of the
game we could all spend a little more time
working on.

Having said that, I must confess I have a
putting machine at home, where the ball rolls
in and is returned to you automatically for
another go. Actually the cat spends more time

playing with it than I do . . .

What wins matches at our level is not having to three-putt and always getting at least a three on a par three. The things that can ruin an amateur's card are bad par threes and lousy putts. And when you think about it, if you shoot an 85, and 25 of those are putts, you would have had a very good round. Two putts a hole (36) represents over a third of your shots — so putting is very important.

Playing par threes well boils down to knowing what you can do well yourself. It's the Liverpool FC principle. The essence of their success is that they know what they can't do, so they don't do it! Remember that apocryphal quote of Bill Shankly, probably the best football manager of his time: 'Football isn't life or death — it's more important than that!'

It summed up Liverpool's dedication, and it is true with the Liverpool team that they don't play a specific game of football because it looks good. They have a system and it works really well. In fact it goes right through their organisation. They must be the only team in the world who can sign a goalkeeper for a million quid and put him in the reserves! Can't be bad.

The same is true about golf. My son Stephen is a powerful hitter of the ball. He is a big lad, one of the ilk — and there are a lot of them

around in golf – who want to hit the ball a long way every time. So when I hit a five-iron he wants to hit a seven to show that he can hit a seven as far as I can hit a five. At the end of the day John Jacobs says, 'In every bag of clubs there is only one you have to hit as hard as you like and that's the driver. Everything else you can taper back.'

If Sevvy hits a four-iron 220 yards, I've got a four-wood that can do the same job. I don't have to use the same club as he does. As long as I have a club that will do the job, who cares? I don't have to be macho about it. At the end of the day if he gets a four and I get a four it doesn't matter that we did it using different techniques – even if I've hit a tree or someone on the head and the ball has rebounded and gone down the hole.

Yet there are people who psyche themselves out. Stephen used to be one of them, although he's mellowed now. When he took golf seriously, he had a massive driver – you have to be Rambo to pick it up let alone swing it – and he would hit it miles. But he would then rely on my judgement for the next shot. I would say I was going to use a five-iron – he would use a seven. In the end I stopped telling him what I was using. That made it difficult – now he had to guess which club I had taken out the bag.

So while I was hitting my shot, he would be looking in my bag. I sorted him out by getting head covers for all the irons – and putting them on the wrong clubs. He would see me take a club out with a seven-iron cover on it (it was really a five), pick a nine from his own bag and find he was nowhere near me – maybe 20 yards or more short.

And he couldn't fathom it for a long time.

But that was only because he wanted to play the game better than me. Instead of saying, 'This is my game and this is what I'm going to play,' he did what you see so many players doing. They'll stand on the tee and one will say to the other, 'What have you got there?' and the other says, 'A three-wood.' The first player then draws in his breath and says, 'I don't know so much . . .' and he's psyching his opponent out now. The basic rule of golf is once you've taken a club out of your bag – hit it! That's the end of it. Even if it goes up in the air or it goes too far or too short – hit the ball well.

Buy a yardage chart – some clubs even give you the yardage on their score-cards now. And play the game to suit yourself. We can't all hit a ball 300 yards or we'd all be on the circuit. We can't all sing 'Delilah' or we'd all be getting Tom Jones's money. So we play it the best way we can.

NINETEENTH HOLE

Golfers' Heaven

EVERY GOLFER at one time or another has got to dreaming what it would be like in Golfers' Heaven. Over a relaxing drink or two at the bar after an exhausting round, they'll map out their ideal round on their ideal course.

No wind, no rain, no bunkers, no tees, always on the green in regulation, every putt a birdie, no holes in one because a hole in one always looks a fluke, but lots of nice holes in two – the first shot always inside the bucket, of course!

There would be no queueing on the tee; you'd always tee off on time, and there would be no one holding you up in front, no one pushing you from behind. You'd always have the right selection of club, be able to call every shot – and be right every time.

There'd be no cheating and the prizes would be things you'd never won before and really wanted – no more flipping crystal! There'd be a free supply of golf balls, but if this was heaven you wouldn't need more than one. I'd also like a different coloured outfit for every day – a free wardrobe of clothes.

And there'd be ideal company. A heavenly four-ball would be Sevvy, Faldo and super coach David Leadbetter – and all three would be asking my advice!

You would also have first crack at any new gadget that came out, and in the clubhouse you would be able to open a door and there would be a tract of land where all the lost balls land up. And a pond full of broken clubs and bags thrown in by frustrated golfers.

But at the end of the day it's only a game . . . Oh really? Every golfer knows you can get too obsessive with golf – yet they still persevere. Once the bug has bit (and we've come full circle now) golf becomes more important than anything (well nearly everything). People move house, change countries, retire early to play more. It's good for you, that's for sure. It may not cure all but it can help people who are stressed. Who knows, if Elvis had played golf, he might be alive today.

For a golfer it's heavenly to sit at a table and

— *and heaven can wait*

talk golf. It's a great thing to be able to talk with pride about other people's achievements. You can say, 'I was standing behind Nicklaus when he hit this ball . . .' and you actually have pride in some other guy playing better than you.

Golf is one of the few sports where there is pride from the people within and true sportsmanship among the players. Ask Christy O'Connor about when we did the business in the Ryder Cup that time and he hit a two-iron to the green and he will tell you the greatest help he had was from Sevvy. And that's great – to think that players, sometimes on opposite sides – will share with one another in competition. Try to get a hardbitten businessman to show you his tricks – no way!

When in the clubhouse, the only round they are interested in is theirs – they all want to tell you how *they* did, but in an ideal world they wouldn't want to know anything except how *you* did.

'How did you get on with Faldo?'

'Well, I put him right . . .'

But coming back to golfing reality – if it really was no wind, no rain, it would be no fun, no challenge. So eventually the game has won anyway. It is the only game where you can't afford a rush of blood, the only game where you

play yourself, where when you win the prize, only you know if you were pleased with the way you won it. That time when Sevvy hit the ball twice and only he knew and he declared it – nobody else would have known but he admitted it. Amazing that, but natural to a golfing great.

That, and the very many other things I have not the wit to write about, are the reasons why you and I play the great game.

One day it will all be worth it. That'll be the day when the phone rings and Faldo is at the other end saying, 'Tom, I need a partner this afternoon. How about it?'

Wow! What a moment that will be. And heaven can wait . . .

Contents

PROLOGUE
Teeing Off   1
FIRST HOLE
When the Bug Bites   3
SECOND HOLE
Keep Taking the Lessons   10
THIRD HOLE
Playing the Game   20
FOURTH HOLE
The Curse of the Caddies   32
FIFTH HOLE
The Ladies, God Bless 'em   40
SIXTH HOLE
The Courses – Beside the Seaside   49
SEVENTH HOLE
Hospitality and Hostilities   63
EIGHTH HOLE
Scotland and Ireland   74

THIS BOOK is dedicated to my lovely Pat, the best wife and roadie in the business.

All the stories are true. Only the names have been changed to protect the wrongly handicapped.

A *Warner* Book

First published in Great Britain in 1992 by Robson Books Ltd
This edition published in 1993 by Warner Books
Reprinted 1993

Copyright © 1992 Tom O'Connor

Illustrated by Jim Hutchings

The moral right of the author has been asserted.

A CIP catalogue record for this book
is available from the British Library.

ISBN 0 7515 0735 0

Photoset in North Wales by
Derek Doyle & Associates, Mold, Clwyd.
Printed in England by Clays Ltd, St Ives plc

Warner Books
A Division of
Little, Brown and Company (UK) Limited
Brettenham House
Lancaster Place
London WC2E 7EN

From the Wood to the Tees

An Amusing Golf Companion

Tom O'Connor

Caddy: David Stuckey

WARNER BOOKS

Also by Tom O'Connor:

THE WORLD'S WORST JOKES

Tom O'Connor was bitten by the golf 'bug' in 1977 and, he says, life has never been the same since.

A household name through his highly successful television shows, including *London Night Out*, *Night Out at the Casino* and *The Tom O'Connor Show*, he is one of the most sought-after entertainers in the country and one of Britain's funniest comedians. With seven popular game shows, including *Name That Tune*, *Gambit*, *Password* and *Cross Wits*, to his credit, Tom continues to undertake a heavy schedule of concerts and cabaret engagements around the country.

He lives in Berkshire with his wife, Pat.

GERMAN PUBLISHER'S FOREWORD
TO THIS EDITION

Hans Fallada's penultimate work, *Der Alpdruck* [*Nightmare in Berlin*], appeared under the Aufbau imprint in the autumn of 1947, but the German publisher's warm commendation and sustained international lobbying elicited only a handful of foreign-language editions — in French, Norwegian, Italian, and Serbo-Croat — despite the countless translations that had been brought out earlier by Fallada's various foreign publishers. Contemporary publishing houses reacted to this novel in much the same way as Britain's Putnam had to *Jeder stirbt für sich allein* [*Alone in Berlin*]: it was felt to be a weaker product from a once successful writer, the author of *Little Man – What Now?* and other global bestsellers, whose demise was widely mourned, as he might well have produced further masterpieces had he been granted a longer span of life.

In the case of *Alone in Berlin*, posterity has already come to a very different conclusion. Sixty years on, this last work, which initially met with a rather muted response, has become what is probably his biggest international success, which has moreover significantly altered the perception of Fallada and, to some extent, of Germany itself. So the question is whether the same can be claimed for *Nightmare in Berlin*, the book that Fallada was working on in the immediate aftermath of the collapse of Nazi Germany, from February to August

1946 (for some of that time as a patient in various sanatoriums and hospitals), and which by his own account he needed to 'get out of the way' first before he could tackle the subject matter of his next book. He had already started to study the Gestapo files from which he drew the material for *Alone in Berlin*, but it was only after writing *Nightmare in Berlin* that he was able to turn these shocking and extraordinary documents into another novel.

But why, after the sensational late success of *Alone in Berlin*, in which Hans Fallada, through the story of the seemingly futile resistance of ordinary people, paints an unsparing picture of the moral ambivalence of an entire society, would one want to re-issue a book (or indeed read a book) which, in the words of reviewers at the time of its first publication, 'is a kind of thinly disguised autobiography which it is difficult to read with any great pleasure' (*Schwäbisches Tagblatt*), and which was seen as 'a confession of his own human weakness and a picture of life in Germany in the wake of its downfall' (*Leipziger Zeitung*), and as an 'account that is perhaps not yet sufficiently distanced from the horrendous events of Hitler's war' (*Freie Presse*)?

Well, Cossee for one, the distinguished Dutch publisher of Fallada's works, did not even ask itself this question prior to the recent publication of *Der Alpdruck* in a Dutch translation, along with the other important late works with which the book belongs by virtue of its subject matter and genesis: *In meinem fremden Land (Gefängnistagebuch 1944)* [published in English as *A Stranger in My Own Country: the 1944 prison diary*], *Der Trinker* [*The Drinker*], and *Jeder stirbt für sich allein* [*Alone in Berlin*]. Cossee's initiative is to be applauded: for with the directness of its observations from a long-suppressed phase of German history—that time between the end of the evil old order and the gradual emergence of a new one, when life was on hold, abandoned by the past and still in search of a future—this book fills a gap that far more comprehensive and ambitious works such as Kasimir Edschmid's *Das gute Recht* (published in 1946) had not been able to fill. This is true of provincial life (Mecklenburg, in this case), which was more or less marginalised anyway in the literary treatment of these times; but more especially is it true of Berlin, the setting for the last months of Fallada's life: the city punished for its historic guilt, where the local population and the author were both fighting for their survival—lost and adrift to begin with, but then increasingly with a single-minded determination born of necessity.

More especially, this child of his times, this writer caught up in a private battle for survival, for a firm stance, for a clear perspective on his own guilt, achieved something unique, which has perhaps been best summed up by his obituarist Johannes R. Becher (who appears in this book in the guise of Doll's advocate and champion, Granzow): 'The contradiction that he embodied was not just private and personal. He embodied and represented, in his mental and spiritual crises, a general German condition.' Nowhere in Fallada's work is this more true than it is here, in *Nightmare in Berlin*.

When the protagonist, the writer Dr. Doll—easily recognisable as a figure based on Fallada's own experience—tells us that he is filled with a 'feeling of utterly helpless shame', 'the malady of the age, a mixture of bottomless despair and apathy', this private mentality shared by Hans Fallada represents that of German society at large, which found itself in a state of crisis. It is hard to imagine a more striking or immediate insight into the psyche, the dawning realisation of a German living in those times who had not been a supporter of the Nazis, but who had also not done anything to oppose them, who had come to an accommodation of sorts with them, than the following scene. Doll thinks he can welcome the occupying Russian troops joyfully as long-awaited liberators, only to be confronted with a different reality: 'He was a German, and so belonged to the most hated and despised nation on earth. [...] Doll suddenly realised that he would probably not live long enough to see the day when the German name would be washed clean in the eyes of the world, and that perhaps his own children and grandchildren would still be bearing the burden of their fathers' guilt.'

Tragic episodes like the story of the chemist and his family who had survived all kinds of horrors, but now tried to take their own lives because they were afraid of the Russians, alternate with more mundane observations, such as the fact that nobody who had not seen Berlin for a while could find their way around any more, since all the familiar landmarks had disappeared under a uniform landscape of rubble. Fallada directs a pitiless gaze at the all-encompassing misery around him, which was also his own: 'But what Doll had not foreseen was a new loss of self-esteem. [...] They would be left naked and empty, and in letting go of the lies that had been drip-fed to them all their lives as the most profound truth and wisdom, they would be stripped of their inner resources of love and hate, memory, self-esteem, and dignity.' He paints a frank picture of Doll and Alma's drug addiction, clearly drawing on his own experiences in a series of touching, sometimes pathetic, and at other times supremely comic descriptions, as when Doll and Alma, cunning and brazen by turns, are forever angling for fresh supplies of their 'little remedies' from hospital doctors or GPs (and here Gottfried Benn puts in a guest appearance as Pernies, 'the doctor with the papery skin').

With the unique capacity for empathy that characterises his work, Fallada also describes the 'little people' here, such as the kindly and ever-helpful Mrs. Minus, who ('just this once') packs up bags of groceries for him in her shop when he has no ration cards to pay for them, while elsewhere he displays a no less typical penchant for euphemism, especially when it comes to Alma. On one occasion early on in the book, for example, she goes to get her 'medication for her bilious complaint' (in other words: the morphine addict goes in search of her next fix).

At the same time, this tendency to whitewash, which runs through virtually all of Fallada's quasi-autobiographical works, stands both the novelist and the reader in very good stead. The latter will certainly enjoy the little scene where Doll and Alma are on a tram together, and Doll is doggedly refusing to speak to his wife, who instead of trying to kick her drug habit is determined not to deny herself anything. The two of them find seats across the aisle from an old lady, who starts to get worked up because Alma is casually smoking on the tram. The old woman's remark — 'They're all the same, these dolled-up little tramps!' — is parried by Alma with: 'And they're all the same, these dried-up old bats!', whereupon the whole tram erupts in laughter, and one passenger is so tickled that he even drums his feet on the floor with glee. Then we read: 'After this little interlude, everything was sweetness and light again between the married couple.' Fallada's natural talent for storytelling finds an outlet even amidst the squalor and misery of a devastated Berlin.

What he does here is to make the depressing reality more bearable — for the reader, and perhaps for himself. There's no doubt that these times were hard for Fallada, hard for Doll to endure: 'We're probably going to die soon anyway, but you can do it more discreetly and comfortably in the big city. They have gas, for one thing!' Fallada is able to turn even this into a little tragicomedy: *How would we do it? We don't have access to poison. Water? We both swim too well. The noose? Couldn't face that! Gas? But we don't even have a kitchen with a gas stove any more.* And yet a little later, despite all this, a gleam of hope appears briefly on the horizon, a tiny shred of optimism: 'But the world out there, this vast, sprawling, chaotic Berlin, is so weird and wonderful, so full of wondrous things!'

Qualities of this kind, unique to Fallada, the qualities of a strong book about a weak human being, earned him the respect of contemporary arts reviewers, who were starting to find their feet again. Berlin's *Tagesspiegel* wrote: '*Nightmare in Berlin* is emblematic of what went on in Germany after the capitulation.' The *Berliner Zeitung* noted: 'A piece of concentrated contemporary history whose value transcends the personal [...]. It need hardly be said that the writing is both gripping and vivid.' The *Frankfurter Neue Presse* wrote: 'A supremely honest book, a human testament.' And the *Norddeutsche Zeitung*: '*Nightmare in Berlin* is the quintessence of Fallada's realisation that the ruins are not important, that the only thing that matters is life and living.' It is best summed up by the journal *Der Zwiebelfisch*: 'In his excellent book *Nightmare in Berlin*, Hans Fallada paints a picture of the despondency and apathy felt by Germans. The final months of wartime life are portrayed in masterly fashion, along with the end of the war, the entry of the Russian troops, the "respectable" bourgeois world as it adjusts to the new environment, and the moral decline of the population.'

Fallada himself achieved one of those wondrous things that Berlin, by his own account, was full of. In one last push he succeeded in producing the two late works, *Nightmare in Berlin* and *Alone in Berlin*, that have cemented his enduring literary reputation. But before these last two books could appear, the man behind the writer, Rudolf Ditzen, died of heart failure on 5 February 1947, his strength finally exhausted.

The *Schwäbisches Tageblatt* lamented the fact that when *Nightmare in Berlin* was first published, the moving obituary penned by Becher for his writer friend appeared at the end of the book: 'It would have been better as a foreword.' The present brief introduction is an attempt to make good that deficit—even if the passage of time has made it easier for today's reader to judge the book's merits and its place in the canon. The personal directness of this 'strong book, which tells us so much about the author' (to quote the then director of Aufbau Verlag, Erich Wendt), bridges the time gap as only literature of enduring relevance can do. It would be wrong to deny the reader access to such literature—even if it means that he or she may learn more about the dark side of an admired author than he or she is comfortable with. For this is the only way we can learn real answers to the basic question: how can we build a happy world again on the ruins of a world that has been defiled?

Berlin, April 2014
Nele Holdack & René Strien

AUTHOR'S FOREWORD

The author of this novel is far from satisfied with what he has written on the following pages, which is now laid before the reader in printed form. When he conceived the plan of writing this book, he imagined that alongside the reverses of everyday life — the depressions, illnesses, and general despondency — that alongside all these things which the end of this terrible war inevitably visited upon every German, there would also be more uplifting things to report, signal acts of courage, hours filled with hope. But it was not to be. The book remains essentially a medical report, telling the story of the apathy that descended upon a large part, and more especially the better part, of the German population in April 1945, an apathy that many have not managed to cast off to this day.

The fact that the author could not alter this, and could not introduce more elements of levity and gaiety into this novel, is not simply due to his own outlook on life, but has to do much more with the general situation of the German people, which today, fifteen months after the end of hostilities, remains grim.

The reasoning behind the decision to place the novel before the public despite this shortcoming is that it may perhaps be of some value as a *document humain*, a faithful and true account (to the best of the author's abilities) of what ordinary Germans felt, suffered, and did between April 1945 and the summer of that year. The time may soon come when people are no longer able to understand the paralysis that has blighted this first post-war year to such disastrous effect. A medical report, then, and not a work of art—I'm sorry to say. (The author, too, is a child of his times, afflicted by that same paralysis.)

I have just called the book 'a faithful and true account'. But nothing that is related in the following pages happened exactly as it is described here. For reasons of space alone, a book such as this cannot possibly record everything that happened; I had to be selective, to invent material, and things that were told to me could not just be set down verbatim, but had to be recast in a different form. None of this means that the book cannot—therefore—be 'true': everything related here *could* have happened in the manner described, but it is nonetheless a novel, or in other words a product of the imagination.

The same is true of the characters who appear here: none of them exists outside the pages of this book exactly as they are portrayed here. Just as the events described had to obey the laws of narration, so too did the characters. Some are pure invention; others are amalgams of several different people.

Writing this novel has not been an enjoyable experience, but to its author the book seemed important. Amidst the changing fortunes of life, the upturns and the reverses, what remained important to him throughout was what people went through after the end of the war, in mind and in body. How nearly everybody lost faith, yet in the end rediscovered a little bit of courage and hope—that is the story that these pages tell.

Berlin, August 1946

PART ONE

Downfall

CHAPTER ONE

The first illusion

Always, during those nights around the time of the great collapse, Dr. Doll, when he did eventually manage to get to sleep, was plagued by the same bad dream. They slept very little those first few nights, constantly fearful of some threat to body or soul. Well into the night, after a day filled with torment, they stayed sitting by the windows, peering out onto the little meadow, towards the bushes and the narrow cement path, to see if any of the enemy were coming—until their eyes ached, and everything became a blur and they could see nothing.

Then someone would often say: 'Why don't we just go to bed?'

But usually nobody answered, and they just carried on sitting there, staring out, and feeling afraid, until Dr. Doll was suddenly overcome by sleep, as if ambushed by some bandit clapping his great hand over his whole face to smother him. Or else it was like some tightly woven spider's web that went down his throat with every breath he took, overpowering his consciousness. A nightmare ...

It was bad enough, falling asleep like that, but, having fallen asleep in this hideous fashion, he was immediately visited by the same bad dream—always the same one. And this was Doll's dream:

He was lying at the bottom of a huge bomb crater, on his back, his arms pressed tightly against his sides, lying in the wet, yellow mud. Without moving his head, he was able to see the trunks of trees that had toppled into the crater, as well as the facades of houses with their empty window openings, and nothing behind them. Sometimes Doll was racked by the fear that these things might fall down deeper into the bomb crater and end up on top of him, but not one of these dangerously precarious ruins ever shifted its position.

He was still tormented by the thought that a thousand water veins and springs would inundate him and fill his mouth with the sloppy yellow mud. And there would be no escape, because Doll knew that he would never be able to get up out of this crater by his own strength. But this fear, too, was groundless; he never heard a sound from the springs or the trickling water veins, and all was deathly silence inside the huge bomb crater.

He was haunted by a third fear, and that was an illusion, too: vast flocks of ravens and crows flew in a constant stream across the sky above the bomb crater, and he was terrified that they might spot their victim lying down there in the mud. But no, the deathly silence continued unbroken; these vast flocks of birds existed only in Doll's imagination, otherwise he would at least have heard their cawing.

But two other things were not figments of his imagination, and he knew for certain they were true. One of them was that peace had finally come. No more bombs came screaming down through the air, no more shots were fired; peace had come, and silence reigned. One last huge explosion had flung him into the mud at the bottom of this crater. And he was not alone in this abyss. Although he never heard a sound, and saw nothing except what has been described, he knew that his whole family was lying here with him, and the whole German people, and all the nations of Europe—all just as helpless and defenceless as him, all tormented by the same fears as him.

But always, throughout the endless hours filled with anguished

4

dreams, when the busy and energetic Dr. Doll of the daytime was obliterated and he knew only fear—always in these harrowing interludes of sleep he saw something else. And what he saw was this:

Sitting on the edge of the crater, silent and motionless, were the Big Three. Even in his dreams he called them only by this name, which the war had seared into his brain. Then the names Churchill, Roosevelt, and Stalin came to mind, though he was sometimes tormented by the thought that something had changed there recently.

The Big Three sat close together, or at least not very far apart; they sat as if they had just turned up from their part of the world, and stared down in silent grief into the vast crater, at the bottom of which lay Doll and his family and the German people and all the peoples of Europe, defenceless and defiled. And as they sat there and stared, silent and full of grief, Doll knew with absolute certainty in the innermost depths of his heart that the Big Three were ceaselessly pondering how he, Doll, and everyone else with him could be helped back on their feet again, and how a happy world could be rebuilt from this ravaged one. They pondered this ceaselessly, the Big Three, while endless flocks of crows flew homewards over the pacified land, from the killing fields of the world to their old roosts, and while silent springs trickled inaudibly, their waters bringing the sloppy yellow mud ever more perilously close to his mouth.

But he, Doll, could do nothing; with his arms pressed tightly against his sides, he had to lie still and wait, until the Big Three, deep in mournful thought, had come to a decision. This was perhaps the worst thing about this bad dream for Doll, that although he was still threatened by many dangers, there was nothing he could do except to lie still and wait, for an endless eternity! The empty house fronts could still fall in on him, the flocks of crows, hungry for carrion, could still spot the defenceless figure, the yellow mud could still fill his mouth; but there was nothing he could do except wait, and maybe this waiting would make it too late for him and his family, whom he loved very much … Maybe they would all perish yet!

It took a long time for the last traces of this haunting bad dream to leave Doll, and he did not really break free until a change in his life forced him to stop brooding and busy himself with useful activity again. But it took a great deal longer for Doll to realise that this entire bad dream, rising up from within like a ghostly apparition, was only there to fool and delude him. As painful as this dream was, Doll had believed it was true.

It took a very long time for him to grasp that there was nobody out there who was prepared to help him up out of the mire into which he had plunged. Nobody, not the Big Three, much less any of his fellow countrymen, was remotely interested in Dr. Doll. If he died there in the wet mud, too bad for him—but only for him! Not a heart in the world would grow heavier on his account. If he really had a desire to work again and write things, then it was up to him and him alone to overcome this apathy, get up on his feet again, brush the dirt off, and get down to work.

But at that time Doll was still a long way from understanding this. Now that peace had finally come, he thought for a long time that the whole world was just waiting to help him back on his feet again.

CHAPTER TWO

The second illusion

On the morning of 26 April 1945, Doll had finally woken in a good mood again. After weeks and months of passively waiting for the war to end, the hour of liberation now seemed nigh. The town of Prenzlau had been taken, the Russians could arrive at any moment; in the morning, planes had been circling over the town — and they were not German planes!

But the best news had come to Doll's ears in the late evening: the SS was pulling out, the *Volkssturm* had been disbanded, and the little town would not be defended against the advancing Russians. That took a huge weight off his mind: for weeks now he had not ventured out of the house for fear of drawing attention to himself. Because he was absolutely determined not to fight in the *Volkssturm*.

But now, after this welcome news, he could venture outdoors again without worrying about what the neighbours would say — three of whom, at least, overlooked his house and garden. So he stepped outside with his young wife into the glorious spring day. The sun felt warm, and its warmth did them a power of good, especially down here by the water's edge. The leaves and grass were still fresh and bright with all the myriad hues of the season's first growth, and the ground beneath their feet seemed to heave and tremble with urgent fecundity.

As Doll was soaking up the sun outside the house with his wife, his gaze fell upon two long borders planted with shrubs, which lay either side of the narrow cement path that led to his door. There was new growth sprouting in these borders, too, and the first grape hyacinths, primroses, and anemones were starting to come into flower. But welcome as this sight was, it was spoilt by a tangle of wire, some of it hanging free, some of it still attached to ugly wooden stakes, which formed an untidy mess that was an affront to the young growth, while the loose ends of wire, dangling where they could catch you unawares, made it dangerous even to walk along the footpath.

No sooner had Doll's gaze taken in this untidy mess than he exclaimed: 'I've got my work cut out for me today! That hideous tangle of wire has been annoying me for ages!' And he fetched his pincers and mattock, and went to work with a will.

While he busied himself in the sun, he was finally able to see into his neighbours' gardens again. He soon noticed a lot of unusual activity there. Wherever he looked, there were people running back and forth, lugging suitcases and furniture out of their houses and into sheds—or the other way round—and others wandering about aimlessly (or so it appeared) with spades, which they drove into the ground here and there, seemingly at random.

One neighbour ran out along the jetty and then stood still, hands in pockets, as if he suddenly had all the time in the world. Then something plopped into the water, and after the neighbour had looked around in an elaborately oh-so-casual way to see if anyone was watching—Doll carried on swinging his mattock the while—he sauntered back to his house with a rolling gait, as if deep in thought, and then promptly threw himself into another round of frenetic activity.

8

Then, all of a sudden, everything came to a halt again. Groups of people gathered at the fences dividing their properties and whispered conspiratorially among themselves. Large packages changed hands over the wire, and then everybody scattered again, looking furtively about them, intent on more secret business.

Doll had only been living at this property, which belonged to his second wife, for a few months, and as an 'outsider' he remained excluded from all these busy comings and goings, which suited him just fine. The fact was that most of the people engaged in this blatantly surreptitious behaviour were women or very old men, which gave him licence to dismiss it all contemptuously as 'women's stuff'.

But he was not able to enjoy his isolation for long, because two women, ostensibly friends of his wife, now turned up at his property. These women, whom he had never been able to stand, hung around next to him and acted all surprised that he had time for that sort of work on a day like this—when the Russians would be arriving any minute!

Dr. Doll had now been joined by his wife, and with a slightly mocking smile he explained that that was just the point: he was clearing the paths for these long-awaited visitors. The ladies inquired with astonishment if he was planning to stay here and wait for the enemy to arrive, because that was surely not advisable, with two children, an aged grandmother, and a young wife? The people living out here on the edge of town, at any rate, had all got together and agreed to cross by boat to the other side of the lake when dusk fell, and to hide deep in the forest and await the next turn of events.

Doll's wife replied for her husband: 'Well, we won't be doing anything like that. We're not going anywhere, and we're not hiding anything away; my husband and I are going to welcome the long-

9

awaited liberators at the door of our house!'

The two ladies urged them strongly to reconsider, but the more forcefully they argued, the more they wavered in their own resolve, and the more doubtful they seemed about the safety of the forest retreat they had just been commending so warmly. When they finally left, Doll said to his wife with a smile: 'They won't do anything, you'll see. They'll poke around aimlessly for a couple of hours, like the hens when there's a storm brewing, picking things up and putting things down. But in the end they'll just flop down exhausted and do what we've all been doing for weeks: just wait for the liberators to arrive.'

As far as her friends were concerned, Alma was in complete agreement with her husband; but as for herself, she felt neither exhausted nor disposed to wait patiently. After lunch she told Doll, who planned to lie down on the couch for a while after his unaccustomed morning's labours, that she just wanted to cycle into town quickly to replenish her supply of gallbladder medicine, as there was unlikely to be much opportunity to do so in the coming days.

Doll had some concerns, as the Russians could arrive at any moment, and it would be best if they were there at home together to welcome them. But he knew from past experience that it was a waste of time to try and dissuade his young wife from some course of action by pointing out the possible risks. She had proved to him a dozen times — during the heaviest air raids, battling the firestorms of Berlin, under attack by low-flying enemy aircraft — that she was utterly fearless. So he gave a small sigh and said: 'If you must. Take care, my dear!', watched from the window as she cycled off, lay down on the couch with a smile on his face, and fell asleep.

Meanwhile Mrs. Alma Doll was pedalling hard uphill and

down, heading for the local small town. Her route took her initially along quiet tracks, where there were hardly any houses, then along an avenue lined on both sides with villas. It struck her here that the streets were completely empty, and that the villas — perhaps because every single window was shut — looked unoccupied and somehow ghostly. *Maybe they're all in the forest already*, thought Mrs. Doll, and felt even more excited about her little adventure.

At the junction of the avenue and the first street of the town proper, she finally encountered a sign of life, in the form of a large German army truck. A few SS men were helping some young women and girls to climb on board. 'Come quickly, young lady!' one of the SS men shouted to Mrs. Doll, and it sounded almost like an order. 'This is the last army vehicle leaving the town!'

Like her husband, Mrs. Doll had been very pleased to learn that the town was not going to be defended, but would be surrendered without a fight. But that didn't stop her answering back now: 'That's just like you bastards, to clear out now, when the Russians are coming! Ever since you've been here, you've acted like you owned the place, eating and drinking us out of house and home; but now, when the going gets tough, you just turn tail and run!'

If she had spoken to an SS man like that only the day before, the consequences for her and her family would have been very serious. The situation must have really changed dramatically in the last twenty-four hours, because the SS man replied quite calmly: 'Just get on the truck and don't talk rubbish! The leading Russian tank units are already up in the town!'

'Even better!' cried Mrs. Doll. 'I can go and say hello right now!'

And with that she stood on the pedals and rode off into the town, leaving behind the last German army truck that she hoped to see in her life.

Once again, it felt as if she was riding through an abandoned town — perhaps those few women by the army truck really were the last people living in the town, and everyone else had already gone. Not one person, not even a dog or a cat, was to be seen on the street. All the windows were shut, and all the doors looked like they had been barricaded. And yet, as she cycled on through the streets, approaching the town centre, she had the feeling that this creature with many hundreds of heads was just holding its breath, as if at any moment — behind her, beside her — it could suddenly erupt in a hideous scream, tormented beyond endurance by the agonizing wait. As if living behind all these blind windows were people driven almost mad with fear for what lay ahead, mad with hope that this horrendous war was finally coming to an end.

This feeling was reinforced by a few white rags, barely the size of small towels, that had been hung over some of the doors. In the ghostly atmosphere that had enveloped Mrs. Doll since she entered the town, it took a moment for her to realise that these white cloths were meant to signify unconditional surrender. This was the first time in twelve years that she had seen flags other than ones with swastikas on them hanging from the houses. She involuntarily quickened her pace.

She turned the corner of the street, and that sense of a pervasive unseen fear was gone in an instant. And she had to smile in spite of herself. On the uneven street of the small town, moving in all directions in a seemingly random way, were eight or ten tanks. From the uniforms and the headgear worn by the men standing in the open hatches, Mrs. Doll could tell at once that these were not German tanks; these were the leading Russian tank units she had just been warned about.

But this didn't seem like the sort of thing you needed to be warned about. There was nothing menacing about the way these tanks drove back and forth in the fine spring sunshine, effortlessly mounting the edge of a pavement, scraping past the line of lime trees and then dropping back onto the roadway. On the contrary: it seemed almost playful, as if they were just having fun. Not for one moment did she feel herself to be in any kind of danger. She wove in and out between the tanks and then, when she reached her destination, the chemist's shop, she jumped off her bicycle. In her sudden mood of relief she had failed to notice that the houses in this street, too, had been barricaded and closed up by their fearful occupants, and that she was the only German among all the Russians, some of whom were standing around in the street with submachine guns.

Mrs. Doll dragged her gaze away from this unusual street scene and turned her attention to the chemist's shop, whose doorway, like those of all the other houses, was securely barricaded and shut up. When banging and shouting failed to raise anyone, she hesitated only for a moment before walking straight up to a Russian soldier with a submachine gun who was standing close by. 'Listen, Vanya', she said to the Russian, smiling at him and pulling him by the sleeve in the direction of the chemist's shop, 'open up the shop for me there, will you?'

The Russian returned her smiling gaze with a look of stony indifference, and for a moment she had the slightly unsettling sensation of being looked at like a brick wall or an animal. But the sensation vanished as quickly as it had come, as the man offered no resistance and let himself be pulled over by her to the chemist's shop, where, quickly grasping her purpose, he hammered loudly on the panel of the door a few times with the butt of his weapon. The leonine head of the chemist, a man in his seventies, promptly appeared at a little glass window in the upper part of the door, anxiously peering out to see what all the noise was about. His face normally had a jovial, ruddy complexion, but now it looked grey and ashen.

Mrs. Doll nodded cheerily to the old man, and said to the Russian: 'It's fine, and thanks for your help. You can go now.'

The soldier's expression didn't change as he stepped back onto the street without so much as a backward glance. Now the key was turning in the lock, and Mrs. Doll was able to enter the chemist's shop, where the seventy-year-old was holed up with his much younger wife and her late-born child of two or three years. As soon as Mrs. Doll was inside, the door to the shop was locked again.

Though each individual memory of this first day of occupation was still fresh and vivid a long time after the events themselves, Mrs. Doll's recollection of what had been said inside the chemist's shop that day was unclear. Yes, she had her usual medication dispensed with the customary precision, and she knew, too, that when she went to pay for it her money was initially declined, and then accepted with a weary twinkle of the eye, like the playful antics of some silly child. After that, it was just casual talk; they told her, for instance, that she couldn't possibly set out on the long ride home with all those Russians about, and that she absolutely had to remain in the shop. And then, a few moments later, the same people who had urged her to stay were wondering if the house was still a safe place to be, or whether they would not have done better to go and hide in the forest after all. And they began to reproach themselves for not getting out much earlier and heading for the western part of Germany—in short, what Mrs. Doll heard here was the same wretched, pointless talk, the talk of people worn down by endless, anguished waiting, that could be heard in just about any German household around this time.

Here, however—given that Russian tanks were rolling past the windows of the chemist's shop—such talk was especially pointless. There were no more decisions to be made: everything had been decided, and the waiting was over! And anyway, Mrs. Doll had been outside, out in the sunny spring air, she had cycled in between the tanks, she had impulsively grabbed a Russian by the sleeve. The last vestige of that pervasive, unseen fear had left her—and she just couldn't bear to listen to any more of this talk. In the end, she asked the family rather abruptly to open the door for her again, and she stepped back out onto the street, into the bright daylight, mounted her bicycle, and rode off towards the town centre, weaving in and out between the growing number of tanks.

Mrs. Doll was presumably the last person to see the chemist and his wife and child alive that afternoon. A few hours later, he gave his wife and child poison, then took some himself, apparently in an act of senseless desperation; their nerves, stretched to breaking point, had finally snapped. They had endured so much over the years, and now, when it looked as if things were starting to get better, and nothing could be as bad as before, they refused to endure the uncertainty of even the briefest of waits.

But the same chemist's hand that had just now dispensed Mrs. Doll's medication for her bilious complaint with such practised precision proved less adroit in measuring out the poison for himself and his family. The very old man and the very young child, they both died. But the wife recovered after a protracted period of suffering, and although she was left alone in the world, she did not repeat the suicide attempt.

Alma Doll had not gone very far on her bicycle before a very different scene caught her attention and brought her to a halt again. Outside the small town's largest hotel, a group of about a dozen children had gathered, boys and girls aged around ten or twelve. They were watching the tanks rolling past, shouting and laughing, while the Russian soldiers seemed not to notice them at all.

The mood of wild abandon that had taken hold of these otherwise rather placid country children was explained by the wine bottles they had in their hands. Just as Mrs. Doll was getting off her bicycle, a boy slipped out of the front door of the hotel clutching an armful of new bottles. The children in the street greeted their companion with cries of joy that sounded almost like the howling of a pack of young wolves. They dropped the bottles they were holding, regardless of whether they were full, half-full, or empty, letting them smash on the pavement, while they grabbed the new bottles, knocked off the necks on the stone steps of the hotel, and raised the bottles to their childish mouths.

This spectacle immediately roused Mrs. Doll to fury. As a mother she had always abhorred the sight of a drunken child, but what made her even angrier now was that these children, not yet adolescents, were dishonouring the arrival of the Red Army by their drunkenness. She rushed forward and fell upon the children, snatching the wine bottles from their grasp, and handing out slaps and thumps with such gusto that the next minute the whole bunch had disappeared around the nearest corner.

Mrs. Doll stood quietly and breathed again. The fury of a moment ago had ebbed away, and her mood was almost sunny as she gazed upon the street, deserted by its residents, where apart from her there was nothing to be seen except tanks and a few Russian soldiers with submachine guns. Then she remembered that it was probably time to be heading home again, and with a soft sigh of contentment she turned to retrieve her bicycle. But before she could reach it, a Russian soldier stepped towards her, pointing to her hand, and pulled a little package from his pocket, which he tore open.

She looked at her hand, and only now realised that she had cut it when she was grabbing the bottles from the children. Blood was dripping from her fingers. With a smiling face she allowed the helpful Russian to bandage her hand, patted him on the shoulder by way of thanks—he looked through her blankly—got on her bicycle, and rode home without further incident. But at the very spot where the German army truck had been parked an hour earlier, Russian tanks were now rolling through. Had the truck got away in time? She didn't know, and would probably never know.

When Mrs. Doll reported back to her husband with this latest news, it only served to confirm his decision to await the victors and liberators at the door of his house. But as the Russians could turn up at any moment, even in this remote corner of the little town, Doll abruptly broke off his conversation with his wife and went back to his work on the shrub borders with a dogged determination that seemed almost beyond reason at such a momentous hour, intent on clearing the last tangles of wire and rolling them up neatly and removing the last of the ugly wooden stakes.

Neither the departure nor the return of the young woman had gone unnoticed on the neighbouring properties. It wasn't long before these neighbours came round looking for Doll—always on some plausible pretext, of course, such as wanting to borrow one of his tools—and, as they watched him work, they tried to find out in a roundabout way what Mrs. Doll had been doing in the town and what news she might have to report. If he'd been asked a direct question—which would have been entirely justified under the circumstances—Doll would have told them immediately what they wanted to know, but he hated this sort of mealy-mouthed beating about the bush, and he had no intention of satisfying their unspoken curiosity.

So the neighbours would have had to go away empty-handed, if Alma had not emerged from the house to join her husband. Like most young people, she couldn't wait to relate her adventures, all the more so as they had been highly enjoyable and reassuring.

And what the young woman had to tell them brought about a complete change of heart among the neighbours. There was no more talk of hiding in the forest. All of them now planned to follow the example of the Dolls and await their liberators in their homes. Indeed, some began to wonder quite openly whether it might not be better to retrieve items that had been hidden or buried, and put them back where they belonged, so as not to offend the victors by the appearance of mistrust. Such suggestions were greeted by other family members with much irritation and head-shaking: 'You wouldn't, Olga, surely!' — 'What nonsense you talk, Elisabeth, better safe than sorry!' Or even: 'I don't think we've hidden anything away, Minnie, you must be imagining things!'

This neighbourly exchange reached its climax when two old men, who must have been in their seventies, got really fired up over the account of the scene in front of the hotel with the drunken children. At first, the fury of the two old men was indescribable. Had they not, for weeks and months past, been beating a path to the door of this self-same hotelier, whose regular customers they had been since time immemorial—and making that journey almost daily, despite their advanced years and the distance involved—and had not this villain, this criminal, this traitor to his own people, refused their requests for a bottle, or indeed just a glass, of wine, nearly always with the same refrain: that he just didn't have anything left, because the SS had drunk the lot?! And now it turned out that he still had wine after all, lots of wine most likely, a cellarful, whole cellarfuls, which had been unlawfully denied them, and which children were now emptying onto the street!

And the two old men stood there looking at each other—their faces, which had been grey and careworn just a few minutes earlier, now flushed red to the roots of their white hair, as if bathed in the reflection of the wine. They patted each other on their bellies, which had grown so slack over the past year that they no longer filled out their trousers, and recited the names of their favourite grape varieties to each other in fond reminiscence. One of them was short, invariably clad in a green huntsman's suit, and a passionate devotee of Moselle wines; the other was tall, always in shirtsleeves, and tended to favour French wines. As they danced around each other, shouting and patting each other on the belly, they seemed to be drunk already on the wine they had not yet imbibed. The uncertainty of the hour, the war that was barely over yet, the danger that might be lurking round the corner, all this was forgotten, and every memory of long-endured suffering was blotted out by the prospect of a drink. And as they now resolved, each egging the other on, to head into town immediately with a couple of handcarts, and fetch the wine that had been wrongfully denied them, Doll compared them in his mind to people getting ready to dance on an erupting volcano.

Thank heavens they both had wives, and these wives now made sure that the day's planned foray into town came to nothing, especially as the roar of heavy vehicles passing through the town, which could be heard very clearly across the lake, was getting steadily louder. Turning back to his loose wire ends, Doll said: 'But if things don't turn out quite as expected, we'll be the ones to blame because they didn't go and hide in the forest. Just as we'll be the ones to blame for everything that happens from now on ...'

'Well, I didn't say anything to persuade them one way or the other', said his young wife defensively.

'It's not about what you said', replied Doll, and yanked a staple out of the stake with his pincers. 'The point is that our dear neighbours have now found a scapegoat for everything that goes wrong.' He coiled up a length of wire. 'They won't show us any mercy, you can be sure of that! For the last few years they've always tried to put the blame on others for everything that's happened, and never on themselves. What makes you think they've changed?'

'We'll get through it', replied his young wife with a defiant smile. 'We've always been the most hated people in the town—a little bit more or less won't make a lot of difference, will it?'

And with that she nodded to him and went back indoors.

The rest of the afternoon passed agonizingly slowly. Once again they were back to this dreadful waiting, which they had hoped was finally behind them—and how often in the coming days and months they would find themselves waiting again, waiting and forever waiting! From time to time Doll stopped what he was doing and went down to the shore of the lake, either alone or with his wife; across the water from here, they could see a line of houses in the main street of the town. All they could see were the empty shells of buildings, with not a sign of human life anywhere, but their ears were filled with the endless roar of heavy vehicles and the blare of horns—a huge supply train rolling unseen, ghostlike, through the town and heading west.

Eventually—it was approaching dusk by now—the young woman shouted from the house that supper was nearly ready. Doll, who had spent most of the last hour fiddling about rather than working, packed up his tools, put them in the shed, and washed himself off in the scullery. They sat in the corner, around the circular supper table: the old grandmother, Doll, his wife, and the two children. The conversation went constantly back and forth between the old grandmother and her daughter. The old woman, who, virtually paralyzed, was confined to her armchair, was hungry for news, and this evening her daughter was very happy to oblige (which was not always the case, by any means). The grandmother wanted to know everything in exact detail, and would rather hear a thing three times than once. She bombarded her daughter with questions such as: 'And what did she say then? — And what did you say to that? — And what did she say after that?'

Normally, Doll was happy to listen to this steady burble of female chitchat, always wondering how the story would have changed inside the grandmother's old head the next time it was related. But this evening, when his good mood from the early part of the day had completely dissipated, it took a huge effort on his part to sit and listen to this idle chatter without becoming argumentative. He knew he was being unfair; but then he was in the mood to be unfair.

Suddenly the boy at the table called out under his breath: 'Russians!!' A noise at the door made them all stop talking and stare, the door opened, and three Russians entered the room.

'Everyone stay where they are!' commanded Doll under his breath, and stepped towards the visitors, his clenched left fist raised in greeting, and with his young wife at his side, who didn't think the order to stay seated applied to her. Now Doll was able to smile again, the tension, the angry impatience, had all gone, the time of waiting was finally over, and a new page had been turned in the book of destiny … With a smile on his face, he said, '*Tovarich*!' and extended his right hand to welcome the three visitors.

Doll would never forget the manner and appearance of those first three Russians who entered his house that day. The one in front was a slim young man with a black bandage over his left eye. His movements were quick and nimble, there was an aura of brightness about him, and he wore a blue tunic and a sheepskin cap on his head.

The man behind him looked like a giant in comparison with this rather wiry and dainty figure, and seemed to tower all the way to the ceiling beams. He had a big, grey peasant's face with a huge drooping moustache, which was black but heavily streaked with grey. The most striking thing about this giant was the short, curved sabre in a black-leather scabbard that he wore at an angle across the front of his body, which was wrapped in a grey greatcoat. The third man, who was standing behind these two, was a simple, very young soldier, with a face that was only now starting to take on a character of its own. He was carrying a submachine gun with a curved, segmented ammunition clip under his arm.

Such were the three Russians, the long-awaited guests, whom Doll welcomed with his clenched left fist raised in greeting and right hand outstretched, the word '*Tovarich*!' — Comrade! — on his lips.

But as he did so, as he stood like this in front of the three men, something odd happened. The clenched left fist was lowered, Doll's right hand crept back into his pocket, and his mouth did not repeat the word that was meant to forge a bond between him and the three Russians. Nor was he smiling any more; instead, his face had taken on a dark, brooding expression. He suddenly dropped his gaze, which a moment earlier had been directed at the three, and looked at the ground.

How long they stayed like this — whether for two or three minutes, or just a few seconds — Doll was unable to say later. Suddenly the man in the blue tunic stepped forward between him and his wife and went on into the house, followed by the other two.

Neither Mr. nor Mrs. Doll followed them, but just stood there in silence, each avoiding the other's gaze. Then they heard the boy cry out: 'There they are again!'

Now they could see the three Russians at the back of the house. They had exited via the scullery; it had only taken them a moment to go through the entire house, which was basically a cabin with just four rooms. And now they were striding past the shed, without pausing or looking round, as if they knew exactly where they were going; they walked out on the jetty, climbed into the boat, cast off, and a few minutes later they had disappeared from sight behind the bushes that lined the shore.

'They've gone!' cried the boy again.

'There'll be more on their way!' said the young wife. 'That was probably just a first check to see who is living in each house.' She shot a glance at her husband, who was still standing there with his hands thrust into his pockets, brooding morosely. 'Come on!' she said. 'Let's go and eat before the soup goes completely cold. Then we'll put the children and grandmother to bed. We'll stay up for a bit longer; I've got a feeling that more of them will be coming this evening or during the night.'

'Fine', replied Doll, and went back to the supper table with her. As he did so he noted that even his wife's voice had changed completely: there was none of that bright, vivacious quality it had had when telling of her afternoon adventures. *She's noticed something, too*, he thought. *But she's like me—she doesn't want to talk about it. That's good.*

Later on, he preferred to tell himself that perhaps his wife had not noticed anything, that her voice had only sounded so different because a new time of waiting was then beginning, waiting for more Russian visitors to arrive. Waiting was now definitely the hardest

23

part of life for every German, and they had to wait for many things, nearly everything, in fact—for days, months, and possibly even years to come …

But thanks to the grandmother and the children, a lively conversation did now develop, to which the young wife also contributed. The main topic of interest, of course, was the three visitors, whose motley appearance was something they were not used to seeing in their own German troops (or else they were so used to seeing it, in fact, that they no longer noticed). Later on, they discussed at length whether they would get the boat back, whether the Russians would bring it back …

Doll took no part in this conversation, and didn't want to talk at all for the rest of the evening. He was feeling far too worked up inside for that. He spoke just once to ask his wife quietly: 'Did you see the way they looked at me?'

Alma answered him just as quietly and very quickly: 'Yes! It was the same way the Russian looked at me this afternoon outside the chemist's shop—as if I was a brick wall or an animal.' Doll nodded briefly, and nothing more was said about this incident by either of them, either that day or subsequently.

But Doll pictured himself standing there in front of the three men, with a grin on his face, the greeting '*Tovarich*!' on his lips, his fist raised and his right hand extended in greeting—how false it had all been, and how embarrassing it had been for him! He'd got it all so wrong; right from the start, when he had woken early that morning feeling so cheerful, and then thrown himself into his work on the shrub borders so as to make the path 'safe' for their liberators, he had completely misread the situation!

And then he of all people had gone and boasted to the neighbours that he was going to meet the Russians at the door of his house and welcome them as liberators. Instead of reflecting on what his wife had said that afternoon and taking it as a warning, he had simply seen it as an affirmation of his own blind and foolish attitude. Truly he had not learned a single thing these last twelve years, however firmly he had believed otherwise in many a time of suffering!

The Russians had been right to look upon him as a vicious and contemptible little creature, this fellow with his clumsy attempts to ingratiate himself, who seriously imagined that a friendly grin and a barely comprehensible word of Russian would suffice to wipe out everything the Germans had done to the world in the last twelve years.

He, Doll, was a German, and he knew, at least in theory, that ever since the Nazi seizure of power and the persecutions of the Jews, the name 'German', already badly damaged by the First World War, had become progressively more reviled and despised from week to week and month to month. How often had he said to himself: 'We will never be forgiven for this!' Or: 'One day we'll all have to pay for this!'

And although he knew this perfectly well, knew that the word 'German' had become a term of abuse throughout the world, he had still put himself forward like that in the fatuous hope of showing them that there were 'still some decent Germans'.

All his long-cherished hopes for the post-war future lay in ruins, crushed under the withering gaze of the three Russian soldiers. He was a German, and so belonged to the most hated and despised nation on earth, a nation lower than the most primitive tribe of the African interior, which could never visit so much destruction, bloodshed, tears, and misery on the planet as the German people had done. Doll suddenly realised that he would probably not live long enough to see the day when the German name would be washed clean in the eyes of the world, and that perhaps his own children and grandchildren would still be bearing the burden of their fathers' guilt. And the illusion that they could persuade people of other nations by a simple word or look that not all Germans were complicit — that illusion, too, was now shattered.

This feeling of utterly helpless shame, which frequently gave way to extended periods of profound apathy, did not diminish with the passing months, but instead was intensified by a hundred little things that happened. Later on, when the war criminals were put on trial in Nuremberg, when thousands of shocking details gradually emerged to reveal the full extent of Germany's crimes, his heart wanted to rebel, unwilling to bear any more, and he refused to let himself be pushed down deeper into the mire. *No!* he said to himself — *I didn't know that! I had no idea it was that bad! I'm not to blame for any of that!*

But then came the moment — always — when he reflected more deeply. He was determined not to fall prey a second time to a craven delusion, not to end up standing — again — in his own parlour as a spurned host, rightly despised. *It's true!* he said to himself then. *I saw it coming with the persecution of the Jews. Later I often heard things about the way they treated Russian prisoners of war. I was appalled by all this, yes, but I never actually did anything about it. Had I known then what I know today about all these horrors, I probably still wouldn't have done anything — beyond feeling this powerless hatred …*

This was the other thing that Doll had to come to terms with entirely on his own: that he bore his share of guilt, had made himself complicit, and had no right, as a German, to feel that he should be treated like people from any other nation. A man despised, a figure of contempt — when he had always been proud of himself, and had children furthermore, four of them, all still unprovided for, all not yet able to think for themselves, but all expecting a great deal from this life—and now to be facing a life such as this!

Doll understood only too well whenever he heard or read that a large part of the German population had lapsed into a state of total apathy. There must have been many people who were feeling just like him. He hoped that they, and he, would find the strength to bear the burden that had been laid upon them.

CHAPTER THREE

The deserted house

Outwardly, the life of the Dolls changed dramatically in the first few days after the entry of the victorious Red Army. They had always kept themselves to themselves, living quietly at home and going about their business; but now, following a public proclamation, they were forced to report for work duty like everyone else in order to earn bread—a very small piece of bread initially. Shortly after seven in the morning, the two of them had to make their way to the designated assembly area in the town. On the way they were often joined by neighbours, but usually they managed to shake them off and be on their own, as they had been accustomed throughout their married life.

They walked side by side in the fresh May morning, Doll normally deep in thought and only half listening to the chatter of his wife, who was quite content with the occasional interjection of 'Yes, quite' or 'I see'. His wife's ability to carry on talking endlessly had prompted Doll to dub her his 'sea surf'. He said she reminded him of long walks he had taken earlier along the beach, accompanied by the constant rush and roar of the sea next to him.

When they reached the assembly area—the school yard—the togetherness they were used to, and the sea surf, came to an abrupt end: men and women were lined up separately, counted, registered, and assigned to all kinds of different work duties. If they were lucky, they could at least call out to each other as they were leaving and tell each other what kind of work they'd been given, so that each would know what the other was doing all the time they were apart. 'I'm going cleaning!' she might call to him. And he would reply: 'Stacking sacks!' Later on, both were given a fixed job: he was sent to mind the cows, while she was put to work carrying sacks.

They often didn't see each other again until the late evening, both of them exhausted by the unaccustomed physical labour, but both doing their best not to let the other know. Then he would talk derisively of his labours as a cowherd, where a herd of over a thousand cows, which were not from the same farm and therefore had no sense of solidarity, had to be kept together and prevented from getting into the cornfields. There were eight cowherds on the job, but his colleagues were inclined to stand around in the same place and pass the time chatting. It was the usual men's talk: how long would things go on like this, and the meagre ration of bread they got wasn't enough to feed a single man, let alone an entire family, and peacetime had not turned out quite how they had imagined, and the Nazis were up to their old tricks again, making sure they landed all the cushy jobs — it was all just hot air from start to finish, and it bored Doll stiff.

Meanwhile the herd of cows was scattering far and wide, straying from the fields of vetch into the barley crop, while Doll charged about like a madman, trying to herd a thousand cows on his own, throwing stones at them, beating them with his stick, and finally sitting down on a stone, utterly exhausted and out of breath, nursing feelings of despair, anger, and dejection. At that very moment, a Russian horseman would often turn up to check on the work of the cowherds. The other cowherds, who had wisely positioned themselves while they chatted so that they could see the rider approaching from afar, were now busy about their work, while the exhausted Doll was given a dressing-down for being lazy. But he could never bring himself to behave like the others. This whole way of carrying on — only working when the people in charge were looking, and in actual fact doing nothing at all — he found abhorrent, and typical of the hated soldiering life, where of course 'cushy numbers' are highly prized.

The only good thing about this cow-minding job was that when the cows had been driven in for the evening, cowherds and gasbags alike could stand in line with a jug — big or small, it could be any size — and they would get it filled to the brim with milk by the Ukrainian milkers. Thanks to this, the Doll family in those days could enjoy a bowl of soup for supper, which did them all good, young and old alike.

When it came to this kind of thing — getting hold of supplies — Alma Doll's efforts were a good deal more successful than her husband's, and she was more ingenious, too. Along with thirty or forty other women and girls, she had been given the job of clearing the remaining supplies from a hut camp formerly occupied by the SS, and transferring them to a large shed by the railway line. It was quite a distance, and the sacks that the women had to carry were often filled with heavy goods, so that the weight was sometimes too much for them.

What really made them angry, though, was the fact that all these preserved meats, these tins of butter, cheese, milk, and sardines, these cans of ground coffee, these packs of premium pressed leaf tea, these cartons filled with powdered chocolate (not to mention the racks of bottles containing wine and cognac and countless packs of tobacco goods) — what really made the women's blood boil as they lugged all this stuff about was the thought that all this abundance had been withheld for years from starving women and children, including many children who had never tasted chocolate in their lives, only to be crammed into the greedy mouths of swaggering SS bully boys, who were directly responsible for much of Germany's misfortune.

Ever since the children, bottles of wine in hand, had got drunk outside the largest hotel in the town, most of the local population had taken a new line on property ownership: these were all goods to which they were actually entitled. The selfishness and greed of the merchants had kept these things from them—so it was only right that people should now take whatever they could get their hands on! It was a long way from the SS hut camp to the railway sheds, and the sacks were a heavy load to carry: every so often, a woman would disappear into the bushes that lined the path, and when she emerged again to join the tail end of the long, straggling column, having just now been at its head, her sack was only three-quarters full, and in the bushes was a nice little stash of supplies to be picked up that evening.

Alma Doll was no more scrupulous than the other women; like most of them, she had children at home who were not getting enough fats in their diet, and who would also like to find out what a cup of hot chocolate tasted like. Like the other women, she stockpiled supplies in the bushes, and when she discovered that these supplies were being plundered before the end of the working day, either by her fellow workers or by other people watching from a distance, she became even bolder. Hidden in the bushes, she waited until the tail end of the column had gone by. As soon as the last woman was out of sight, she hurried with her sack to a nearby house occupied by friends of hers, and left everything there, to be shared with them later. When it was time for the column to pass the spot again on its way back, she would get back into the bushes and then slip out, her empty sack over her arm, to rejoin the others.

Her absence had not gone unnoticed by the other women, of course, and they made free with their barbed remarks and innuendos; but as they were all doing more or less the same thing themselves, she had nothing worse to fear. As for the Russian sentries who marched at the head and tail end of the column, they either saw nothing of what was going on or chose not to see. More likely the latter: they doubtless all knew what real hunger felt like, and they behaved magnanimously, even towards a hated nation that had let the wives and children of those sentries starve to death without mercy.

In the evening, Alma would then sit with her husband, while their supper of milk soup heated up on the little makeshift stove, and the young wife would show him her latest acquisitions by candlelight—because the electricity had been cut off. They all ate tinned sardines on bread to start with, and then powdered chocolate was sprinkled into the milk soup. They didn't just eat the food—they devoured it, gorging themselves until they were fit to burst, all of them, from the five-year-old Petta to the old and virtually immobilised grandmother. They didn't care about overfilling their stomachs, or the effect this would have on their already disturbed night's sleep, nor did they ever think about keeping something back for the next day. They'd said goodbye to all such thoughts during the years of sustained aerial bombing. They had become children again, who live only for today, without a thought for the morrow; but they had nothing of the innocence of children any more. They were uprooted, the pair of them, this herder of cows and this carrier of sacks; the past had slipped away from them, and their future was too uncertain to be worth troubling their minds about it. They drifted along aimlessly on the tide of life—what was the point of living, really?

When Doll went to work with his young wife in the early morning, and when he hurried home on his own in the evening after tending the cows all day, his route took him past a large grey house with all its windows shut up, giving it a gloomy and forbidding air. On the door of the house was a very old brass plate, tarnished through neglect and stained with verdigris where the brass had been dented. Engraved on the plate were the words: 'Dr. Wilhelm—Veterinarian'.

When Doll and his wife walked past this gloomy house for the first time after the end of the war, she had said: 'He's topped himself, too—did you hear?'

'Yes …', Doll had replied, in a tone of voice intended to indicate to his wife that he did not wish to pursue the subject.

But Alma had ploughed on regardless, exclaiming angrily: 'Well, I'm glad the old boy's dead! If ever I hated anyone, it was him—in fact I hate him still …'

'Fine, fine', Doll had interrupted. 'He's dead, let's forget him. Don't let's talk about him again.'

And they didn't talk about him again. Whenever Dr. Doll approached the house, he fixed his gaze studiously on the other side of the street, while his wife kept on eyeing the house with a resentful or scornful look. Neither reaction suggested they had succeeded in forgetting, as Doll had wished, and they both knew—although they said nothing—that they neither could forget nor wanted to forget. The dead veterinarian Wilhelm had caused them too much heartache for that.

He called himself a veterinarian on his brass plate, but in truth he was such a coward that he had hardly ever dared to go near a sick horse or cow. The local farmers knew this so well that they only ever called him out to give injections to pigs with erysipelas, which is why he was known far and wide as 'Piglet Willem'. He was a big, heavily built man in his sixties, with a grey, sallow face that was twisted into a permanent grimace, as if he had the taste of bile in his mouth.

There was absolutely nothing about this vet to set him apart from the common run of men, except for one thing: he was a connoisseur of fine wine. He drank schnaps and beer as well, but only for its alcohol content, because he had been for a long time what one might term a 'moderate drinker'; he needed a certain amount of alcohol every day, but his intake could not be called excessive. Wine was his real passion, though, and the better the wine, the happier he was. At such times, the bilious wrinkles in his face would soften, and he was seen to smile. For a man of his means, it was a somewhat expensive passion, but he usually found a way to indulge it.

Shortly before five in the afternoon, nothing would keep him at home a moment longer, and not even the most urgent phone call could get him to attend a sick animal. He picked up his stick, put on his little Tyrolean hat with its badger-hair plume, and strolled sedately along the street, dressed invariably in knee breeches, and walking with his feet splayed out to the sides.

Dr. Wilhelm — Piglet Willem — was just a short walk away from his destination, a small hotel where at one time he had effectively had his own private supply of wine on tap. That was when the landlord was still alive, a man who dearly liked a drink himself. After his death, the establishment was run by his widow and then increasingly by their youngest daughter, a girl of mercurial temperament and fierce dislikes, one of which — and not the least of them — was the vet, Dr. Wilhelm.

To his profound dismay, the vet found that the daughter of the house now frequently refused to bring him the bottle of wine he had ordered, only bringing him a glass instead, though other tables were still getting their bottles often enough. If he then complained, speaking with his characteristic slow and measured delivery through that caustic, nutcracker mouth of his, she would cut him off as soon as he started with her quick, sharp tongue: 'You expect your wine every day. The others just come in occasionally—that's the difference! You'd drink us dry if I let you!'

Other times, she would not even deign to reply. Or else she would reach quickly for his glass and say: 'If you don't want the glass, I'll be happy to take it back again. You don't *have* to drink it!' In short, she took care to remind him every day that he was entirely dependent on her whims for the satisfaction of his drinking desires. He had to put up with her insults and her diminishing servings of wine with a grumpy sigh, but still he came back every day for more, without dignity or shame.

From the little hotel, the vet would then process sedately, with his curiously splay-footed gait, halfway across the town to the little railway station, where he generally entered the second-class waiting room shortly before six o'clock. Here he often had the good fortune to find the town's wealthy corn merchant sitting at the table reserved for regulars, where he himself had a seat, and this gentleman was always happy to share his wine with him. Sometimes the corn merchant would be sitting at a separate table with one or more of his customers, in which case the vet would go up to them, inquire gravely 'May I?', and was generally invited to join them. For here Dr. Wilhelm was able to trade on another side of his character: he had quite a repertoire of bawdy country jokes and stories, which he could recite in the authentic local dialect. His stories were frequently met with gales of laughter, their effect heightened by the fact that his sour expression didn't change at all—which put the corn merchant's customers in a sweeter mood.

Otherwise the vet generally did all right for himself in the station bar. He'd been a regular there for decades. For decades past, he had sat at the regulars' reserved table from around six to eight in the evening, accompanied by his wife in earlier years, but on his own since her death. The landlord, Kurz, kept him on a tight rein, but generally made sure that his old customer didn't go without.

Around suppertime, the waiting room emptied quickly, and Dr. Wilhelm also went on his way. What awaited him now in the little town's premier hotel was always an open question: it might be a lot, or it might be virtually nothing. The wine still flowed freely in this establishment, but the landlord was a man who liked to take his customers' money—and the more the better. Even when it made very little sense to take money off his customers, since there was hardly anything left to buy with money, the landlord kept on increasing the price of his wines sold by the bottle, so that the cost of even a single bottle was way beyond the means of a poor pig innoculator like him, whose daily earnings frequently amounted to less than five marks.

So here Dr. Wilhelm had to take potluck, and there were many times when he had to sit for hours over a glass of watered-down, wartime beer, while he morosely watched SS officers drinking one bottle after another. They never invited him over to their table: the SS always kept its distance from the ordinary German people. Or else there would be some Hitler Youth leader, not even twenty years old, knocking back dessert wines with his girlfriend—and no more interested than the others in the storytelling talents of the ageing vet.

So these were difficult times for an old alcoholic, for whom drinking was a necessity of life. As the hours went by and the night wore on, and the patrons became increasingly drunk and boisterous, and the white-haired landlord, ever smiling and full of bonhomie, called time on them … as it became quite clear that there was nothing for him this evening, even though so many others were thoroughly well-oiled … as he then, having paid for his beer, totted up the few miserable coins and notes in his pocket to see if he might have enough for a small schnaps at least, knowing full well that he didn't … as he finally picked up his stick and his hat with a heavy, bitter sigh and stepped out into the night to walk back to his house … and as he thought about the night ahead, in which he would have to summon up sleep with boring tablets instead of alcohol, which so divinely filled his sleep with sweet dreams … then his leathery face became, if possible, even more jaundiced than before, he was racked with envy for everyone and everything, and he would have gladly let the whole world go to hell without a thought, in return for a single bottle of wine!

But the old vet had better days, too. All of a sudden, this premier hotel on the town square would be frequented by summer visitors or anglers on a fishing trip, who always loved to hear stories about this remote area that had scarcely been touched by the war. Or else a farmer would see the old man sitting there, which made him think how long it was since he had called him out to his farm, and his bad conscience would prompt him to invite Piglet Willem to join him at his table, chat to him, and give him a drink—for everybody knew about his weakness.

The best times, though, were when all the regulars came together around their table in this hotel. Unfortunately this only happened once or twice a month at most, whenever the circuit judge came over from the district town to hold the appointed court session in the little town. Then the hotelier would get straight on the telephone and notify a local landowner, the dentist, an agricultural-products wholesaler, and also Dr. Doll—but not the old vet, who turned up anyway.

How Doll had become a part of this motley company he was hardly able to say himself in later years. To begin with—and this was years earlier, at the time of his first marriage, when he was working a smallholding near the little town—he had probably been intrigued by such a mixed bag of drinking companions, and more especially by the stories they had to tell. The old judge in particular excelled in this regard, and told a far better story than the vet, whose jokes were often rather too broad, not to say downright vulgar. But Doll had quickly realised that even these people were utterly mediocre. By the second evening, the old circuit judge had to repeat the same stories; he only knew ten or a dozen, but he was more than happy to tell them a hundred times. It also became increasingly obvious that he liked to be given food for free, and to short-change the staff when it came to handing over his ration coupons. The dentist's head was filled with stories about women; his day job was just a pretext for him to grope his female patients while they were lying back in the dentist's chair. And as for the old vet, he was just an old soak who became more greedy and tiresome with every passing day.

It was the same story with the others: a dull, commonplace bunch, along with their sly landlord, who was only interested in making money. So Doll didn't always take up the invitation when he was summoned by telephone to join the other regulars. But he came often enough, maybe just because he fancied a few drinks or because he was fond of good wine himself, and because village life at home was even more dull than this crowd. He came and drank and played the generous host, being still fairly well fixed for money at that time, and any freeloaders, from the greedy vet to the cautious circuit judge, did well by him. On particularly good nights, the fat, white-haired hotelier would crawl into the furthest recesses of his cellar and emerge with bottles of Burgundy lagged with dust, or bottles of 'Mumm extra dry'. To go with the red wine he would serve fine cheeses — no mention of ration coupons! — which they ate in little wedges straight out of their hands. These were blissful times for the old vet, and his friendship with Doll seemed firmly established.

But that changed, and as is usually the case when male friends have a falling-out, it was all because of a woman. Quite how the old circuit judge came to meet this radiant young woman was a mystery; at all events, when Dr. Doll arrived a little late one evening to join the assembled company, he met there the wife of a Berlin factory-owner who had built himself a cabin on the shore of one of the many lakes in the area, so that he could come and enjoy some weekend fishing.

But on this particular evening the husband had stayed behind in Berlin, and his young wife was sitting alone among the all-male regulars gathered around the table. She tossed her strawberry-blonde locks, and gazed attentively at whoever was speaking, with her long, slender face and her lovely blood-red mouth — it was just as if this mouth was actually looking at you. Then she would throw her head back, her little white throat seeming to dance with laughter — heavens above, how she could laugh, my God, how young she was! Doll shoved the old vet aside and sat down next to this amazing youthful apparition, who was now sitting on the long corner sofa in between Doll and the old circuit judge.

How young she was, how full of life, and how alluringly she laughed at the judge's stories, however witless and inane! Doll began to tell stories himself, and if anyone could tell a good story, it was him. Unlike the circuit judge and the vet, he didn't just repeat the same old anecdotes he'd wheeled out a hundred times before; Doll's stories just popped into his head, from different times in his life, as if he had never thought of them before. He spoke more quickly—it all came tumbling out, his tales trumping everybody else's—and in between times he ordered wine, and more wine, and kept it flowing freely.

It turned into a great evening. It makes quite an impression on a man in his late forties when a beautiful young woman in her twenties lets him know that she finds him interesting. But the youthful interest being shown in him did not rob Doll of his powers of critical observation, and they alerted him to the fact that while he was talking intently with his neighbour on his left, the old vet on his right was looking after his own needs. The vet had long since lost any interest in stories or women; all he cared about was alcohol. There was plenty of alcohol around the table, but to Piglet Willem's way of thinking it was being drunk too slowly. When he saw that all eyes were fixed on the young woman, the vet reached out and felt for the bottle. He quickly filled his glass, drained it, and promptly filled it again …

'Whoa there!' cried Doll, who appeared to have his back to him, but had seen everything. 'That's not on! As long as I'm buying, I'll be the one to say when!' And with that, he took the bottle from Wilhelm's hand, though not ungently.

Needless to say, everyone promptly rounded on the old freeloader and soak, teasing him unmercifully. They made fun of him, dredged up the most embarrassing stories about him, and accused him to his face in the meanest fashion. But it didn't bother him very much; he felt no shame. He was long accustomed to having his human dignity insulted as the price for every cadged drink. This had been happening for so long, and so often, that by now all his human dignity was long gone. He despised them all, of course, and they could all have dropped down dead before his eyes—he wouldn't have cared, because alcohol was all he cared about now. So he let them mock and bait him, it all fell on deaf ears, and as his podgy, age-spotted hand gripped the stem of the wine glass, he thought to himself: *I've had two more glasses of wine than you have!* And: *If I get the chance, I'll try it again!*

Nor did he have to wait very long for an opportunity. Sitting at their table was a beautiful, blooming young woman, and a terrible flirt—they could have old Piglet Willem any time they wanted, but as long as *she* was in their midst, they were determined to make the most of her. So the vet sat there, ignored by everyone. This time, Doll really did turn his back on him completely. Three times he reached out and touched the wine bottle, and then drew his hand back. The fourth time he grabbed hold of the bottle and poured himself some more wine ...

Immediately, Doll's head swivelled round over his shoulder, and this time he said, without any attempt at gentleness: 'If we're drinking too slowly for you on this table, maybe you'd like to go and sit somewhere else? There are plenty of tables free ...' And as the vet looked at him with a hesitant, incredulous, almost beseeching expression, he made his meaning even clearer: 'Did you not understand? I want you to leave the table, now! I've had enough of your cheek!!'

Slowly, the old man got to his feet. Slowly, he walked across the room to a table in the far corner. (As it was very late, long after closing time, the room was empty except for the regulars around their table.) For a moment he had hesitated, but then he had picked up the glass that had cost him so dear and bore it before him with infinite care, like some holy relic. It was, after all, the last glass of wine that he was likely to drink on this ill-fated evening that had started so well. Behind his back, these fat, well-oiled burghers were mocking him in the cruellest fashion, utterly beside themselves with glee and *schadenfreude*. Doll himself, of course, took no part in this further humiliation of a man who was already down, and perhaps he was even regretting his angry outburst—Wilhelm was an old man, after all. But if he did regret it, his regret didn't last, because the young woman suddenly said: 'Quite right, Mr. Doll, I've never been able to stand the old sneak either!'

The drinking and the lively talk around the table continued—talk that became increasingly drunken. The old vet was forgotten. But he was still sitting there at his little table, his hand still wrapped around the stem of his wine glass, which had been empty for a long time. He sat, he watched, he listened, he counted. He counted the bottles as they were brought to the table, he counted the glasses that each person drank, and with every glass that was drunk around the table, he thought to himself: *I should have been included in that round!*

Dr. Wilhelm waited until they had all finally had enough, and made to pay the bill. Then the vet slipped quietly out of the bar and took up his position on a dark street corner across from the hotel.

He had a long wait before the two of them appeared, both wheeling their bicycles. He saw the woman's white dress; she was wheeling her bike in a perfectly straight line, while the man kept veering off to the side, and frequently had to stop. Then he started off again, bumped into his companion's bicycle, and dropped his own. He broke into drunken laughter, and held onto the woman. Dr. Wilhelm also noted that they did not part company at the street corner where they should have gone their separate ways. Doll accompanied the young woman on her way home, stumbling, falling, cursing, and laughing. Nodding his head, and with his leathery face twisted into a grimace, as if he was eating pure bile, the vet set off for home, walking slowly and sedately, with his feet splayed out to the sides.

Next morning, rumours of the 'orgy' that had taken place at the town's premier hotel were flying through the streets and alleys, and were soon getting out into the surrounding countryside on the milk carts. Doll was summoned into town by a distraught phone call from the young woman, who told him that the hotelier's extremely straight-laced wife had banned her from the bar permanently 'because of her immoral behaviour'. The young woman was upset and angry; for the first time in her life, she had come up against small-town prejudice, which condemns the accused without a hearing, and against which there is no appeal or defence.

'But we've done nothing wrong! Nothing happened, not even a kiss! And this swine of a vet has been telling people I was sitting on your lap the whole evening, and that I took you home with me in the night! When the whole hotel knows full well that you stayed there overnight!'

This was true. When it became clear that Doll was in no condition to walk or ride a bicycle, his companion had brought him back to the hotel, where he had then taken a room.

'Mr. Doll, you've got to talk to the landlord! The ban on me must be lifted, and someone needs to put a stop to these vile rumours! You've got to help me, Doll. I'm very upset! How horrid it all is! People round here hate a woman just because she's good-looking and laughs a lot. For two pins, I'd sell our weekend house right now and never come back!'

Tears welled up in the young woman's eyes, and Doll promised to do everything she asked. He would have done it anyway without the tears, for he too was full of anger and hatred. But he was soon to find that rumours of this kind are easier to start than they are to stop.

The hotelier, whose straight-laced wife had him completely under her thumb, twisted and wriggled like a worm; in the end, when the argument grew more heated, he slipped quietly out of the room and was not seen again for the rest of the day. The circuit judge, called in as a witness for the defence, and obviously madly jealous of the younger, more successful Doll, gave an inconclusive account of events: in the bar itself he had not observed any lewd behaviour, but as to what happened in the night out on the street, well, he simply couldn't say. And he really preferred not to get involved in this sort of thing ...!

Doll responded furiously: 'What could possibly have happened out on the street? Everyone in the hotel knows that I spent the night here!'

The hotelier's wife bowed her head and quietly pointed out that between the time the two of them left together and the time that he, Mr. Doll, returned to the hotel, more than an hour had elapsed.

'That's a wild exaggeration!' cried Doll. 'A quarter of an hour, maybe—it can't have been more than half an hour at the absolute outside!'

The hotelier's wife and the circuit judge smiled, and then Mrs. Holier-than-thou opined that even half an hour was quite a long time, and a lot could happen in half an hour ...

At this point the circuit judge, too, edged his way out of the room, and he only heard Doll's angry response—where did she get the nerve to insinuate, without a shred of evidence, that two persons of blameless character could not spend half an hour together without getting up to something?—as he was retreating down the passageway. He didn't wait to hear more. It was already looking as if this might end up in court, and he had no desire to be called as a witness in a case of this sort.

45

After that, Doll began to run out of steam in this battle against a sanctimonious woman who responded to all his arguments and challenges with a weak smile and evasive, equivocal replies. She wouldn't even give a clear 'Yes' or 'No' answer when he asked her directly if she planned to enforce the ban on the young woman.

Then Doll abruptly broke into laughter and walked out on the hotelier's wife. What was he fighting against here? Arguing with this woman, who for certain had voted every time for her adored Führer, was about as pointless as Don Quixote tilting at windmills. No: if he was going to get anywhere in this matter, he had to tackle the man who had started all these rumours—that old gossip and scandalmonger in trousers, the freeloading, free-drinking vet. He'd soon give him what for! And so, swept along on a fresh wave of anger, he set out to find Dr. Wilhelm. But it was a fool's errand, because the vet wasn't to be found anywhere—not at home, not in the town, not in any saloon bar. It was as if the old man, suspecting what was in store for him, had gone into hiding—and perhaps he had done exactly that.

So Doll had no option but to go to a lawyer and have him write formal letters to the vet and the hotelier's wife. Doll learned from the lawyer that private actions for defamation could not be brought, now that there was a war on. But the others didn't need to know this, and so letters threatening them with such an action were duly despatched. Maybe they had lawyers, too, or else they knew the score; at all events, they didn't respond. The rumours continued.

All this only made him more bitter, just as the departure of the young woman only served to increase his anger. She had been forced to flee in the face of the jealous, rancorous talk of these small-town bigots. He felt like someone trying to fight his way through a wall of feathers and cotton wool: he could hit it as hard as he liked, but it made no difference. In his present state of mind, the letters written by his lawyer seemed to him far too mild and diplomatic, so he sat down and wrote a letter of his own to Dr. Wilhelm, in which he announced his intention of publicly slapping him in the face as a slanderer the next time their paths crossed ...

Having sent the letter, he was overcome with regret. This was unworthy of him; he had sunk to the level of his enemies, instead of just quietly despising them, which had been his stance up until now. But the time would come when he would regret this letter even more. One morning, he walked into the waiting room at the station—and there was Piglet Willem, sitting on the sofa, with a bottle of wine in front of him!

Doll wished he could have turned around in the doorway and left, and it would certainly have been better for his peace of mind if he had. But as well as many strangers, there were also quite a few locals in the room, who were now looking back and forth expectantly from him to the vet. Doll knew that Wilhelm, like all old gossips, had shown the letter to the bar-room regulars and half the town, and his enemy's threat—to slap him in the face when he saw him—was common knowledge. If Doll retreated now, the vet would have won, and the whole rumour mill would start up again.

So Doll entered the room and sat down opposite the other man. The landlord, normally so talkative, said nothing as he brought him the bottle he had ordered. All the locals were waiting for the strangers to leave the waiting room—their train was due to depart in a quarter of an hour. Meanwhile Doll sat clutching the stem of his wine glass, battling inwardly with himself. *He's not worth it*, a little voice said inside him. *He's just an old man, a gossip, and a scandalmonger. What's he got to do with your honour?* And with a quick glance at the other man, who was sitting there in silence, like him, clutching his wine glass: *But they'll think me a coward, all of them, and him especially, if I do nothing. I've got to show these people that I won't just take this lying down! I can't back out now!*

The strangers filed out of the waiting room, and only five or six locals were left. The room was completely silent. Then the landlord Kurz, who was polishing his glasses behind the counter and watching like a hawk, began to pass the time of day with a painter and decorator. 'They're in for another bad day in Berlin', Doll heard him say, as the drone of enemy bomber formations passing overhead came to their ears …

Now he got to his feet directly in front of his own enemy. Leaning on the edge of the table with both hands, he thrust his face into the odious, yellow, liverish visage of the other man, and asked in a whisper: 'So are you going to take back your vicious lies right now, in front of these people?'

The landlord was at his side now, and said in a tone that was half-plea, half-reprimand: 'Don't do that, Dr. Doll! I won't have any fighting in my establishment! Go outside, if you want to …'

Doll carried on regardless, speaking softly as before: 'Or do you want me to slap you in the face, right here in public? Punish you like a child who has been telling lies?'

The elderly, heavily built man had stayed sitting still in his seat on the sofa. Under Doll's menacing gaze, the yellowish colour of his face changed slowly to an ashen grey, while his fishy eye stared at his oppressor without blinking and without visible expression. When Doll finished speaking, it was as if he wanted to say something in reply: his lips moved, and the tip of his tongue came out as if to moisten them, but no sound emerged.

'Look, I think you should leave, Dr. Doll!' said the landlord with urgent insistence. 'You can see that Dr. Wilhelm is sorry …'

48

At this point, the old vet suddenly began to shake his head with a weirdly mechanical persistence, like some nodding Buddha.

'Pssst! Pssst!' said the landlord, as if he was shooing some hens away. 'Don't do it, Willem!'

For a moment Doll had stared fixedly at this Buddha-like figure shaking his head, but now he raised his hand and slapped the slanderer lightly in the face with his open palm.

At this, the witnesses to this scene vented their collective relief with a long-suppressed 'Ah!'

'That's it!' said the landlord, plainly relieved that the slap had not been harder—and that Wilhelm had not hit back.

For a moment Doll had gazed into the face of his enemy, with a look that was both menacing and relieved. The violent urges that fought within him had calmed down; he was finally free again, free from hatred and free from anger. But then something awful happened, something utterly unexpected: two large, clear tears welled up from the expressionless eyes of the old man. For a moment, they hung on the edge of his eyelids, then rolled slowly down his cheeks. More tears followed, more and more, until they were streaming down his leathery nutcracker face, making it all shiny. His throat began to heave and sob: 'Oh! Oh! Oh!' sobbed the old vet. 'Oh, my God, he hit me, he hit me in the face with his hand! What am I to do?! Oh! Oh! Oh! I can't look anyone in the face any more, I shall have to kill myself! Oh! Oh! Oh!'

When Doll struck him, the sympathies of everyone in the room were undoubtedly on his side, as attested by the deep sigh of relief that came from their throats. But the old vet's tears changed all that. Doll was convinced from the outset that they were only crocodile tears, carefully calculated to negate the effect of his chastisement and get the townsfolk on the victim's side.

'Oh! Oh! Oh!' sobbed Dr. Wilhelm, as the tears continued to flow. 'He hit me—today of all days, on my sixty-third birthday! And I've never done anything to him. I've always stood up for him when other people were speaking ill of him. I was so grateful to him for all the wine he gave me!'

At these last words, Doll felt all his anger and hatred flare up again. He vividly recalled the whole episode where he had forced the vet to leave the table because he was helping himself too freely to the wine. The slanderous rumours had begun, not because he had given him so much wine on so many occasions, but because he had once refused him wine. 'That's enough!' he cried angrily. 'You're just an old scandalmonger and gossip, and that's why I slapped you. And if you carry on with your lies here, I'll slap you again—never mind your fake tears!' And he raised his hand as if to strike.

But Doll had reckoned without the other people in the room. They should have known what kind of a man old Piglet Willem was, and indeed they knew him of old, and thought very little of him. But in the face of these tears and laments, they promptly cast experience aside and abandoned their reason. The sight of an old man breaking down in sobs always touches the emotions, and so they all now ganged up on Doll, led by the landlord of the station bar: 'Look here, that's enough now! Surely you're not going to hit the old man again! I think it's best if you leave now—you can take your open bottle of wine with you!'

And in an instant, Doll was hustled away from his enemy, he was handed his hat, the landlord quickly put a stopper in the wine bottle and placed it in his briefcase, and the next moment Doll found himself standing outside on the station forecourt. Looking troubled as he gazed at him through bloodshot eyes, the landlord said: 'You never should have done that, Mr. Doll. You'll turn the whole town against you now! A gentleman doesn't do that kind of thing—hitting people! Well, maybe it'll all come right in the end ...'

But unfortunately it didn't all come right. Instead it was the landlord who was right: Doll forfeited all remaining sympathy in the town, and he became what he would forever remain: the most hated man far and wide.

Dr. Wilhelm exploited the situation with devilish cunning; on this occasion, his bilious brain counselled him most wisely. After Doll's departure he had carried on weeping, and averred in a sobbing voice that he could not live with this dishonour. He would have to take his own life, and on his birthday, of all days ...

They gave him wine to drink to calm him down—a great deal of wine—and then they took him home. But the news of his public humiliation soon went round the whole town, and aroused sympathy even in places where he had never attracted any before. His reiterated lament—that it was all so much worse because it had happened on his birthday—was not without effect: days later, he was still getting presents, in the form of food, wine, and schnaps, from people who would never have dreamed of marking the old sponger's birthday, were it not for this incident.

Meanwhile the war dragged on—another year, another two years. People had more important things to worry about now than Doll and his despicable conduct.

Doll himself had other things to think about, too. This was the year in which his marriage was dissolved. He had many cares and worries, and so it was all the more painful to feel the old hatred, which he thought he had put behind him, welling up within him again at the sight of the vet, still as strong as ever, undiminished by the passage of time, still the same old feelings of humiliation ...

And then the young woman turned up in the town again after a long absence. This time, she was dressed in black. Doll learned that she had been a widow for quite some time. When people heard this news, they studied his face with eager curiosity, but failed to detect anything but indifference. And indifference was exactly what Doll felt. If he had felt something more for this woman two years previously, in a moment of passion, all that was long since forgotten, and he no longer remembered …

But life in a small town is lived according to different rules. In a city, people's paths cross and they never meet again. But here was this outsider, Doll, a man who, despite his money, only aroused suspicion with his high-handed ways. And now there was this young woman, clearly widowed, twenty-three years old, no more, though she was already the mother of a five-year-old child, wearing her widow's weeds with painted fingernails and dark-red lipstick. The small town knew what to make of such a woman, just as it knew all about Doll!

Faced with a united front against them, excluded from the life of the community, spied upon, suspected, maligned, they were bound to meet and find common cause sooner or later.

'Hello!' said Doll nervously. 'It's a long time since we last saw each other …'

'Yes', she replied. 'And a lot has happened since then.'

'Of course!' he remembered, and looked at the young woman. He thought her even more beautiful in her widow's weeds. 'You lost your husband …'

'Yes', she said. 'It's been very difficult at times. My husband was ill for more than a year, and I nursed him myself throughout. Every time the siren went, I had to get myself and him down to the basement, and him a sick man, the apartment half-gutted by fire …'

'Difficult times!' he agreed, and then laughed scornfully at the inquisitive look they got from a passing local, the wife of a naval lieutenant. 'But this place hasn't changed—by this evening, we'll be the talk of the town again.'

'Yes, I'm sure!' she agreed. 'Will you walk with me a little? If they're going to gossip, let's give them something to gossip about! Would you like to have lunch with me today? I've just got a chicken from a farmer—that way', she smiled, 'you won't need ration coupons.'

'All right!' he replied. 'Gladly. I don't have to answer to anyone any more.'

'I know', she said.

That was how it all began, and everything else followed on from that. They were drawn to each other out of defiance, protest, a sense of isolation within the community. *At last*, they thought, *someone I can really talk to, who won't betray me.* Over time, this became something more—genuine affection, love even. They had long since ceased to care about the small-town gossip. They moved in together, living in the little chalet that belonged to the young woman, putting two fingers up to the scandalised locals. Nor did Doll care any more that Wilhelm the vet—so everyone was saying—was now telling all and sundry 'I told you so', claiming that every word of what he'd said before had been 'right on the money'. Let his enemy crow: Doll couldn't care less.

But later on, after they had married, not in the little country town but in the big city of Berlin, and were sitting together in the kitchen of their badly fire-damaged apartment, writing out addresses for the wedding announcements—then the old hatred rose up again in both of them, and they did not forget a single one of their enemies. Every one of them received their wedding announcement, and Piglet Willem and the hotelier's sanctimonious wife were top of the list!

What effect they thought these announcements would have, they wouldn't have been able to say exactly. But to them it was something of a triumph just to have married—in defiance of them all, a poke in the eye for prudery!

From Berlin, they went back to the small town only on the odd occasion. They often forgot about the place for days on end in the chaos of the big city, in its gathering gloom, relieved only by the ghastly flickering firelight of whole streets in flames. They sat with each other in air-raid shelters that afforded little protection, heard the drone of the approaching bombers and the impacts of the bombs getting closer and closer ... They held each other tightly, and the young woman spoke words of reassurance: 'They've gone on!' Then there was a deafening cracking and crashing sound, the light flashed bright yellow and died ... They could taste plaster dust in their mouths, as if they were eating their own death.

But when they had fought their way out of Berlin again, passing railway tracks and stations destroyed by the bombing, when the train took them deeper and deeper into forests that appeared completely untouched by the war, and when in the evening, before embarking on the last homeward stretch, they entered the station bar again to have a quick beer, they found everything just as it had always been. The landlord had become a little more mean with his provisions and a little more insolent towards his patrons, but the leathery old vet was still sitting in his usual place on the sofa.

But the moment Doll saw this man again, the old hatred suddenly flared up within him once more. It erupted with elemental force, and it was only later that the memories of all the trouble this man had caused them came back to him, as if to rationalise the feeling after the event—for all the good that did him. This hatred seemed senseless to Doll, when there was so much hardship to be borne in these times, and when life itself felt like a new gift after every air raid. This mean-spirited hatred seemed senseless to him, and yet he had to deal with it somehow. He had made room for this hatred in his heart, had allowed it to lodge itself there—and now he had to live with it, probably for the rest of time.

For the rest of time—but, as it turned out, only for the rest of the other man's time. When he walked past the old vet's closed-up house now on his way to work with his young wife, the place looking so gloomy and forbidding, or when he passed the battered old brass plate, flecked with verdigris, on his way home by himself, he averted his gaze from the house—but not because he still hated the dead man. No: the hatred had gone when he died, and in its place was a kind of emptiness, a vague memory of a feeling that he had felt ashamed of. In this time of the country's collapse and defeat, no feelings lasted for long; the hatred passed away, leaving only emptiness, deadness, and indifference behind, and people seemed remote, out of reach. Never had he felt so alone. No man had ever felt so alone. Only the young woman was still with him. But he let her know, too: 'Let's leave it there. We won't talk about it again. The subject is closed.'

No: there was another reason why Doll averted his gaze from this house of the dead. There was one thing that he kept on turning over in his mind: *I saw him sitting there in the station bar, with tears streaming down his face, and telling everyone he would have to take his own life because of the humiliation he had suffered. But the old whinger hadn't taken his life: instead he had turned his humiliation into a business opportunity, without dignity or shame! He'd been a coward all his life, this Dr. Wilhelm, scared of being kicked by a horse, gored by a cow, or bitten by a dog, and reduced to giving injections to pigs when they were too young to be dangerous: Piglet Willem! The nickname was well-deserved, and he had never protested when they called him that and ribbed him mercilessly for filling his glass at somebody else's expense … he'd always been a man without dignity or courage.*

And yet, Doll brooded, *this same Dr. Wilhelm had the courage to do what I lack the courage to do — even though my own dignity and self-respect, shame, faith, and hope are ebbing away with every passing day. I can't do it, and yet I have always imagined myself to be a moderately courageous man. But he was able to do it, coward though he was. The coward whose face I slapped, he had the courage — and I don't.*

Such were Doll's thoughts as he walked past this house, painful thoughts that tormented him every time; he would have given anything to be free of them, but they wouldn't let him go, whether he averted his gaze or not. Then he would try to picture the room where this man had spent the last hour of his life, the room where he had done 'it'. Doll knew that at the end the old vet had owned virtually nothing apart from a bed, a table, and a chair. Everything else had gone to pay for alcohol. He tried to picture the man sitting on this solitary chair, the pistol lying on the table in front of him. Perhaps the tears had been streaming down his face again, and perhaps he had sat there sobbing 'Oh! Oh! Oh!' again …

Doll shook his head. He didn't want to picture the scene; it was just too painful.

But one thing was certain: the old man with the leathery skin had gone, and Doll was left behind, empty inside, filled with self-reproach and doubt. So many certainties had been thrown into doubt at this time, and because of the old vet, Doll now lost both his inveterate hatred and his belief in himself as a man of courage. In all probability he was nothing at all, an empty husk; he had nourished himself with self-delusions, and now it had all vanished into thin air! There was no Doll any more.

How gladly he would have taken a different route, avoiding this closed-up house altogether. But the position of the town, sitting as it did on a peninsula, forced him to walk past it every time. Forced him to revisit these painful thoughts. Forced from him the admission that he was nothing, had never amounted to anything, and for the rest of his life, however long or short that might be, would never be anything other than a nobody. A nobody, for all time!

So it really was best just to say to his young wife: 'Fine, he's dead. Let's forget him. Let's not talk about him ever again!'

It was a lie. Nothing was 'fine'; nothing could be forgotten. But what did a lie matter these days? Let the woman go on thinking that he hated the old boy as much as ever. He couldn't hate anybody any more, but lying—he could manage that. And anyway, lying was somehow more in keeping with his own mediocrity.

CHAPTER FOUR

What the Nazis did next

Doll's career as a cowherd was short-lived, because a sequence of chance events resulted in his being appointed mayor of the town, and of the whole surrounding district, by the Russian town commandant. This was the kind of thing that happened in these turbulent times: the most hated man in the town was put in charge of his fellow citizens.

The string of chance events began when a rucksack was tossed over the fence into the Dolls' garden one night. It was a Wehrmacht-issue rucksack, and it contained the uniform of a senior SS officer. No doubt the dear neighbours who had laid this cuckoo's egg in the Doll nest felt it was getting too dangerous to have these items of uniform in their possession, now that increasingly thorough house searches were being conducted. Why they didn't put a few stones in the rucksack along with the uniform, and drop it into the lake that was right on their doorstep, is another story, which says as much about the neighbours' decency as it does about Doll's popularity.

He, of course, had no idea about this morning gift that lay in his garden. He lay awake and eventually fell into the brief, troubled sleep that was now almost normal for him. On this occasion, he was roused from this brief sleep at the crack of dawn by a Russian patrol, which gave him a very hard time. At first he couldn't understand what they wanted from him, and he went through a very unpleasant quarter of an hour before he realised what the implications of this rucksack and SS uniform were: the Dolls were suspected of secretly harbouring an SS officer! The entire house, attic, and outbuildings were searched from top to bottom, and even though no trace of the fugitive (who didn't exist, of course) was found, Doll was put into a two-horse hunting carriage and driven off into town to the commandant's office. Soldiers with submachine guns sat on either side of him. Such was the sight that greeted his fellow citizens, who assuredly felt no sympathy for him — partly because they all had enough worries of their own, and partly because this was Dr. Doll, after all. And whatever kind of trouble he was in, it was fine by them!

But at the commandant's office his troubles were quickly ended. There was an officer who conducted the interrogation, and an interpreter in civilian dress who translated Doll's answers. Having by now fathomed the mystery of the rucksack so treacherously left in their garden, Doll had no qualms about directing the attention of the Russians to the house next door, where the wife of the SS officer lived — a woman who was as stupid as she was malicious, since the provenance of this uniform was always bound to come to light.

A quarter of an hour later, Doll was allowed to return home, into the arms of his anxiously waiting family.

The following day was the 'Day of Victory', and everyone was given the day off work. The entire population was ordered to assemble on the square in front of the town commandant's office and told that the Russian commandant was going to give a speech. When Doll entered the square with his wife, there stood the officer who had interrogated him the day before, accompanied by his interpreter. Doll greeted them politely, and the two of them, after returning his greeting, looked at him earnestly and had a whispered conversation with each other. Then Doll was beckoned over, and the interpreter asked him on behalf of the officer if he felt up to addressing the local German population on the significance of this Day of Victory.

Doll said that he didn't think he had addressed a public gathering like this before, but he felt sure that he would make as good a job of it as anyone else. Whereupon he was led into the town commandant's office — his wife had to remain outside, with the waiting crowd — and put in a room on the top floor. Through a glass door, he could see the commandant addressing the crowd from the balcony, and the interpreter whispered into Doll's ear, giving him a few pointers as to what sort of things he should say. Then it grew very quiet in the room, while outside the town commandant was still speaking. He was a short man with a pale, brownish, handsome face, the archetypal cavalryman. He had taken off the white gloves that he normally wore, and was holding them in one hand, occasionally gesturing with them to underline something he had said. The commandant would speak for two or three minutes at a time, then pause to allow the interpreter to translate. But the translation barely took a minute to say, which is usually the case with poor interpreters. An occasional 'Bravo!' could be heard from the invisible crowd below.

Just you wait! thought Doll angrily. *Barely three weeks ago you were still shouting 'Heil Hitler!' and kowtowing to the SS, and jockeying for rank and position in the* Volkssturm. *I'll be sure to tell you what I think of all your 'Bravos' now!*

All the same, he was finding the day plenty warm enough. It was a fine spring day in May, certainly, but it was only ten o'clock in the morning, and already his brow was beaded with sweat. The interpreter bent down to him again, and asked if Doll was feeling agitated. Would he like a glass of water, perhaps?

Doll opined, with a smile, that he would prefer a glass of schnaps. Whereupon he was whisked off to the officers' mess and given a whole tumbler of very strong vodka.

Five minutes later, he was standing at the balustrade of the balcony, the town commandant a couple of steps behind him with his interpreter, whose job it was to translate what Doll said. There were other officers besides on the balcony, officers whom Doll would get to know very well indeed in the coming weeks. But today he didn't even notice them; all he could see was the mass of people below him, a great crowd of his fellow citizens who were all gazing expectantly at him with upturned faces.

At first, all these faces merged into a single, pale-grey line above the darker, broader band of colour that was their clothing. Then, as he was speaking the opening sentences of his address, he could suddenly make out individual faces. While he was listening a little anxiously still to his own voice, which had never been very powerful, yet now seemed to fill the square beneath him quite easily, he suddenly caught sight of his wife, almost directly below him. There she stood, calmly smoking a cigarette with her accustomed nonchalance; the people around her kept their distance, while everywhere else in the square the crowd was packed tightly. Consciously or not, their demeanour reflected the isolation in which the Dolls had always lived in this small town, and in which Doll now found himself, plainly visible to all eyes, up on the balcony of the town commandant's office.

He gave her a slight nod, imperceptible to anyone except her, without interrupting the flow of his speech, and she smiled back and raised the hand that held the cigarette in greeting. His gaze moved on, and came to rest on the grey-bearded face of a National Socialist town elder, a building contractor by trade and a quiet man by nature, who had nevertheless cunningly abused his position in the Party to put all his competitors for miles around out of business. Not far from him stood another short man, with a face as sly as it was brutal: he had collected the Party subscriptions, and used the opportunity to spy for his masters, the Party bigwigs who had all fled to the Western zone ...

But there were enough of the smaller fry left in the town: over here, the mail clerk who had been a sergeant in the local *Volkssturm*; over there, a schoolmaster, a feared informer; Kurz, the landlord of the station bar, a bully and, as it now turned out, another Nazi spy; and then—Doll's eyes lit up—standing close together with a look almost of derision on their faces, as if they were watching some trashy theatre show, two women, the wife and daughter of that SS officer whose uniform had nearly been his undoing on the morning of the day before.

Doll leaned forward, speaking more quickly, more loudly, talking now about the times just past, the people who had profited from them, the guilty ones and the ones who had just gone along with it all. And as he continued to speak, and as they persisted in shouting 'Bravo!' and 'Quite right!' (as though he couldn't possibly be talking about any of them), it struck him how different these fellow citizens of his now looked. It was not just their pale faces, which were scarred by fear, worry, grief, and sleepless nights, and it was not just the ones who, in order to avoid the initial confrontation, had spent days lying in the forest, so that their clothes were now torn and faded—no, all of them suddenly had a tattered and beggarly air about them, all of them seemed to have slipped several rungs down the social ladder, had given up, for whatever reason, a position they had occupied all their lives, and now stood without shame among their equally shameless brethren. That's exactly how they looked now, plain for anyone to see, and that's how they had always looked when they were alone with themselves. For these people from a nation that bore its defeat without dignity of any kind, without a trace of greatness, there was nothing left worth hiding. There was the fat hotelier, whose plump, smiling face was normally flushed from drinking wine, but now was pale and ashen, darkened by a beard that had not been shaved in days. And there was his pious and parsimonious wife, who ran the hotel with him, who had wrung the last penny out of the poorest customer, and if she had had her way would have weighed every bag twice, a woman who had always gone around in shapeless black or grey frocks, and now had a dirty white cloth wrapped round her face, like the cloths worn by toothache sufferers in the cartoons of Wilhelm Busch. Her scrawny body was now covered by a blue apron, like the ones worn by washerwomen, and her hands were wrapped in grubby gauze bandages.

It's finished, this nation, thought Doll. *It's given up on itself.* But in the fervour of his speech, he had no time to think about himself, who privately was in a very similar situation, after all. He called for three cheers for the 7th of May, the Red Army and its supreme commander Stalin, and watched them shouting and cheering (for, as well as justice and freedom, they had also been promised bread and meat) and raising their arms — the right arm still, in many cases, raised in the salute that had been drilled into them over many years.

The speech seemed to have gone down well with the commandant and his officers, too. Doll was invited to come along to the officers' mess with his wife and have a drink with them. The vodka glasses now seemed to be even larger, the schnaps even stronger — and they didn't stop at one glass. As Doll and his wife made their way home along the sun-drenched streets, both of them were swaying a little, but Doll more so. Thank goodness the local residents were still eating their lunch, and all of them were condemning the man then walking past their windows as a traitor and defector on account of the speech he had made, yet there wasn't one of them who wouldn't gladly have swapped places with him!

By the time they reached the outskirts of town, where there were hardly any houses, along the stretch of road officially known only as the 'Cow Causeway' that ran through sparse, deciduous woodland, Doll began to stumble about. The vodka saw to it that a stumble quickly turned into a fall, and he lay where he landed. He fell asleep. Mrs. Doll did her best to coax him back up, but he just went on sleeping, and she didn't feel strong enough herself to bend down and try and get him back on his feet. She was feeling pretty unsteady on her own feet by now. So she tried kicking him in the side, but the kick she gave him, which nearly made her fall over herself, failed to rouse her sleeping husband.

It was a difficult situation. They were still a good ten minutes' walk from their house, and even though she thought she could make it on her own, she really didn't like the idea of leaving her husband lying in the road, which would give the small-town locals the perfect excuse for more gossip. Luckily for the Dolls, two Russian soldiers now came down the road. Alma beckoned them over and conveyed to them through a combination of words and gestures what had happened, and what now had to be done. Whether the two Russians understood her or not, they clearly understood the plight of the man lying in a drunken stupor. So they picked him up and carried him home. With much laughter, they took their leave of the young woman …

But if she thought they had successfully escaped the attentions of the local gossips, she was very much mistaken — again. In a small town like this, there are eyes everywhere, even on the 'Cow

Causeway', where 'there aren't really any houses', and whatever wasn't seen was just invented. A rumour now went from house to house, and was retold every time with mockery and relish: 'You know Doll, the fellow who tried to cosy up to the Russians with that speech of his? Well, he's come a real cropper! Have you heard? You don't know the story? Well, the thing is, the Russians were so upset by his speech that they gave him a right royal beating! They worked him over so thoroughly that he couldn't even walk, and two Russian soldiers had to carry him home! He won't be up and about in a hurry—and serve him right!'

This was the story that got around, and as is the way with small-town gossip, it was generally believed, even by those who had seen Mr. and Mrs. Doll staggering past their window at lunchtime that day. Great was the general rejoicing, and so it was all the more gutting when, less than a week later, they learned that the same Doll who had been so royally beaten up had now been appointed mayor by the Russian town commandant.

Of course, from this moment onwards it was hard to find anyone who didn't change his tune and discover that in actual fact he had always thought a great deal of Doll, and had always wished only the best for him. When they had said as much to their friends and neighbours half a dozen times, they really believed it themselves, and would have called anyone a liar and a slanderer who reminded them of what they had said earlier about this self-same Doll.

For his part, Doll had not wanted to take on the job of mayor, but he was given no choice in the matter. He'd never been someone who took part in public life, and he was certainly not cut out for officialdom; and just because he had given one speech, fired up by vodka, that did not mean he had any desire to pursue a career in public speaking. Moreover, as already noted, he was in a state of deep personal crisis at the time. He was tormented by doubt and lack of faith in himself and in the world around him; a profound despondency robbed him of all strength, and a wretched apathy prevented him from taking an interest in anything that was happening in the world. Furthermore, his instinct told him that this office, by virtue of which the fortunes of his fellow citizens were placed in his hands, would probably bring him nothing but worries and cares, and a lot of extra work. His wife said: 'If you become mayor, I'm going to jump in the lake!' When he took the job because he was ordered to, she didn't do it, of course; she stayed with him, lived only for him, and did her best to make the few hours he spent at home as comfortable as possible. But it was effectively the end of their normal family life together.

For Doll had been absolutely right in his prediction — his position as mayor would bring him little joy, but a whole load of trouble and care. He was inundated with work, more than he could really cope with, and while his area of jurisdiction was not that large, with the small town and some thirty or so rural parishes, he still had to work from the early morning until late at night — and even the mayor of the biggest city on earth can't put in more hours than that. There were an endless number of things that needed rebuilding, organizing, setting up and sorting out, and there were virtually no resources available: everything had been plundered and destroyed by the Nazis and the SS, including the spirit of cooperation among the local population. They were so mean-minded, petty, and self-centred that they had to be ordered, pushed around, and often threatened with punishment. Behind his back, they did everything they could to undermine the common cause and feather their own nests. In fact, they often wrecked things out of pure *schadenfreude*, without any benefit to themselves.

But Doll had more or less foreseen all this, and when they were obstructive and malicious it just made him more determined to get his way; and he could always rely on the support of the Red Army officers. They were planning and working for the long term, and not just thinking from one day to the next. But what Doll had not foreseen was a new loss of self-esteem, and even though he was doing this job, he felt somehow diminished in his inner being. That's what it felt like, and the longer this feeling persisted, the stronger it grew, even now when he was leading such a busy life, as if Doll—and no doubt many other Germans like him—was now to be stripped of his last remaining inner resources. They would be left naked and empty, and in letting go of the lies that had been drip-fed to them all their lives as the most profound truth and wisdom, they would be stripped of their inner resources of love and hate, memory, self-esteem, and dignity. In those days, Doll often doubted whether the empty space inside him would ever be filled up again.

For twelve years he had been bullied and persecuted by the Nazis: they had interrogated him, arrested him, banned his books some of the time, allowed them at other times, spied on his family life; in short, they had made his life a misery. But as a result of all these hurts, great and small, inflicted upon him, and as a result of all the vile, disgusting, and horrendous things he had seen and heard in those twelve years, and read between the lines of all the vainglorious news bulletins and swaggering editorials, a lasting feeling had grown up within him: an utter hatred of these people who had destroyed the German nation, a hatred so profound that he could no longer stomach the colour brown, or indeed any mention of the very word. If he saw anything brown around him, he had to paint it over, paint it out: it was an obsession with him.

How often he had said to his wife: 'Just be patient! Our turn will come again! But when that day comes, I won't have forgotten anything, and I won't be forgiving anyone. There is no way I'm going to be "magnanimous"—who is ever "magnanimous" to a poisonous snake?'

And he had described how he would haul the schoolmaster and his wife out of their house, how he would interrogate them, harass them, and finally punish them, this pair who had not scrupled to make children of seven or eight spy on their own parents! 'Where has your father hung his picture of the Führer? What does your mother say to your father when the man comes round collecting for the Winter Relief Organisation? What does your father say in the morning—does he say "Good morning" or does he say "Heil Hitler!"? Do you sometimes hear people speaking on the radio in a language that you don't understand?'

Oh yes, the hatred he felt for this educator of our youth, who had shown photos of horribly mutilated corpses to seven-year-old children, that hatred seemed to have taken permanent root.

And now this same Doll had become mayor, and a portion of that retribution of which he had so often spoken, feeding his hatred by imagining how it would be, had now become a duty laid upon him. It was his job—among his many other responsibilities—to classify these Nazis as harmless fellow travellers or guilty activists, to root them out from the bolt holes where they had been quick to hide themselves, to kick them out of the cushy jobs they had cleverly and shamelessly landed for themselves once again, to strip them of the possessions they had acquired by fraud, theft, or blackmail, to confiscate the stocks of food they had been hoarding, to quarter the homeless in their big houses—all of this had now become his bounden duty. The local Party bigwigs and principal culprits had, of course, fled west a long time ago, but the National Socialist small

fry were just as disgusting in their way. All of them claimed—either
with righteous indignation or with tears in their eyes—that they
had only joined the Party under duress, or at most for economic
reasons. All of them were willing to sign a statement under oath
to that effect, and if they'd had their way they would have sworn
it right there and then, before God and the whole world, with the
most sacred of oaths. Among these two or three hundred National
Socialists there was not a single one who claimed to have joined
the Party out of 'personal conviction'. 'Just sign the statement', Doll
would frequently snap impatiently. 'It doesn't alter anything, but if
it makes you happy …! Here in the office we've known for a long
time that there were only ever three National Socialists in the world:
Hitler, Göring, and Goebbels! Off you go—next, please!'

Mayor Doll would subsequently visit the houses and apartments
of these National Socialists with a few policemen (some of whom,
in those early days, were pretty dubious characters themselves) and a
clerk to take notes. He found cupboards piled high with linen, some
of it hardly used, while up in the attic a mother evacuated from
her bombed-out home in Berlin didn't know how she was going to
put clothes on her children's backs. Their sheds were stacked to the
ceiling with dry logs and coal, but the door was securely padlocked,
and none of it was shared with those who lacked the wherewithal
to warm a pot of soup. In the cellars of these brown hoarders they
found sacks of grain ('It's just feed for the chickens!'), meal ('For my
pig! Got it on a ration coupon from the Food Office!'), and flour
('It's not proper flour, just the sweepings from the mill floor!'). In
their pantries the shelves were packed with supplies, but for every
item they had a lie ready to hand. They feared for their precious
lives—it was clearly written in their faces—but even now that fear
could not stop them fighting to the bitter end for these supplies,

70

claiming that everything had been acquired by legal means. They would still be standing there, next to the cart, when their hoarded treasures were taken away. They didn't dare cut up rough, but their faces wore an expression of righteous indignation at the injustice visited upon them.

Doll's own expression when carrying out these confiscations was invariably one of anger and contempt, but inside all he felt was disgust and weariness. As someone who had always preferred to live quietly on his own, and who even within his marriage had defended his right to solitude as something sacrosanct, he now had to spend nearly the whole day with other people, talking to them, trying to wring something out of them, seeing tears, listening to sobs, protests, objections, pleas; his head often felt like an echoing abyss filled with noise.

Sometimes he thought fleetingly: *What happened to my hatred? These are the Nazis I swore to be revenged on, after all, whose vile deeds I said I would never forget and never forgive. And now I'm standing here, and the only thing I feel is disgust, and all I want is my bed, and the chance just to sleep and sleep and forget about all this—just so that I don't have to look at all this filth any more!*

But in these days and weeks when he was constantly overworked, he never had time for himself. He could never think his own thoughts through to the end, because his mind was constantly taken up with other things. Sometimes he had the unsettling feeling that his insides were leaking away, and that one day he would just be a hollow skeleton with a covering of skin and nothing else. But he had no time to dwell on this thought, and he couldn't decide whether he really had stopped hating the Nazis, or whether he was just too tired to feel any kind of strong emotion. He wasn't a human being any more; he was just a mayor, a machine for doing work.

There was only one case where the feelings of hatred seemed to come alive again in Doll. A certain Mr. Zaches had lived in the little town for as long as anyone could remember, like his parents and grandparents before him—a genuine local, therefore, and the only kind recognised as such by the natives. Now up until the time when the Nazis seized power, this Mr. Zaches had run a small, struggling beer wholesaling business, and also used to make fizzy drinks for children from spring water, carbon dioxide, and coloured flavourings; latterly he had also supplied wholesale tobacco goods to the hospitality trade. But all of this combined had not been enough to support Zaches and his family. So the two nags he kept to transport beer were also pressed into service for all kinds of other haulage jobs—fetching suitcases and crates from the station, hauling timber out of the forests, ploughing and working the fields of local smallholders. Yet even with all this, the family could barely make ends meet; Zaches was constantly on the brink of ruin, the loss of a customer was enough to put the whole business at risk, and the days when payments to the brewery became due were days of fear and trepidation for the Zaches household.

But when the Nazis came to power, all that changed completely. Like many businessmen threatened with ruin prior to 1933, Zaches had joined the Party, bedazzled by all the talk of 'smashing the tyranny of usury' and of the universal prosperity that would surely follow. He wasn't a bit interested in politics, of course, but only in doing well for himself—and in that he succeeded after 1933. Quietly at first, but then more and more brazenly, he set about stealing business from his competitors, who had not been smart enough to join the Party in good time. He put pressure on landlords to order goods only from him, and those who complied were rewarded with little favours. He made minor political difficulties disappear, secured advantages for them by having a word with the local mayor, and generally used his position on all manner of committees, boards, and councils to ruthlessly advance his own interests. If anyone opposed him, he secretly gathered evidence against that person, set his spies to work to listen and watch, and then either issued threats or drew the net closed, whichever best suited his own needs.

As a result, his business flourished. As well as the cart horses, he now kept a separate team that only hauled crates of beer and barrels. And Zaches, the obsequious, ever-courteous pauper had now turned into Mr. Zaches, the National Socialist Party member, a man with a finger in every pie and a sharp tongue in his head, who knew that he had a lot of money behind him, as well as a Party that could make or break its fellow citizens, and held the power of life and death over them. On the back of all this, Zaches had become big and fat, and only his unhealthy, sallow complexion and his dark, piercing eyes, which avoided the direct gaze of others, recalled the lean years of the past. When the war broke out and merchandise in his line of business became particularly scarce and sought-after, his substantial earnings were unaffected; on the contrary, he made more money from a limited supply of inferior merchandise than he had been making from the good stuff. On top of that, the departure of so many men to go and fight in the war brought him a number of new posts, and like all National Socialists he did not feel bound by the rules governing the rationing of food. He took whatever he needed from the land—bacon, eggs, poultry, butter, and flour—and what he couldn't eat himself he sold on at extortionate prices, secure in the knowledge that an old Party member was effectively untouchable.

And so he remained—until the Red Army arrived on the scene. Zaches was one of the first to be arrested. His sworn statement that he had only joined the Party for economic reasons was surely no less than the truth in his case, but for many years now he had been such a selfish parasite and enemy of the people that economic reasons were no mitigation whatsoever. Yet once again he had more luck than he deserved. The authorities soon had to grant him a measure of freedom again, because he was needed for work in the town's dairy. In his youth, Zaches had learned the dairy trade, and when times were tough he had helped out there from time to time—so now he was just the man to step in and lend a hand. For better or worse, it was necessary to employ him there, though nobody liked the idea—least of all Doll. But the pressing need to feed the mothers and children of the town meant that political interests had to take a back seat for now.

Things went on in this way for a while, until certain rumours began to reach the ears of the mayor, and he summoned the onetime beer wholesaler and now dairy manager Zaches to his office. 'Look here, Zaches!' he said to the sallow-faced and still portly man, who couldn't bring himself to look Doll in the eye, 'I'm hearing all kinds of stories about a big stockpile of goods you're supposed to have hidden somewhere. What's that all about?'

Not surprisingly, Zaches assured him that he had no such hidden stock of supplies. He freely admitted that he had had cases of wine and schnaps buried in his garden in seven different places. But these hiding places had all been discovered, he said, and now he had nothing more hidden away.

While Zaches was speaking thus, in all apparent honesty, Doll had been observing him closely, and now he said: 'Everyone in the town knows about the seven hiding places. But there's a persistent rumour going around that what they found was just a trifle compared with the big hoard that hasn't been found yet ...'

'There is no big hoard any more, Mr. Mayor', insisted Zaches.

'It's all been found. I don't have anything more.'

'Repeat what you just said, Zaches, and look me in the eye while you're talking!'

'Eh?' Zaches was thrown into confusion by such an unusual request. 'How do you mean— ?'

'Forget that I'm the mayor. I want you to look me in the eye and tell me again, man to man, that there is no big hoard anywhere!'

But Zaches couldn't do it. Before he'd said more than three or four words, his gaze slid away, and though he tried again, his eyes promptly wandered off once more. Zaches became confused, started stammering, then tailed off into silence …

'So', said the mayor slowly after a lengthy pause, 'now I *know* you're lying. There's some truth in the rumour.'

'Not at all, Mr. Mayor! On my mother's life …'

'Don't give me that, Zaches!' said Doll in disgust. 'Just think for a moment, use your brain … You've always been a Nazi—'

'I was never a real Nazi, Mr. Mayor! I only joined the stinking Party because I had a knife at my throat. I'd have had to file for bankruptcy otherwise, and that's the honest truth, Mr. Mayor!'

'You have absolutely no chance of getting your property back again, and as for enjoying the stuff you have hidden, you can forget it! But the fact of the matter is', Doll went on, appealing to his better nature, 'that any hidden goods I find as mayor are for distribution to us Germans, Zaches. You know as well as I do that there are hundreds of people in this town, Zaches, who lack the basic necessities of life. And then there's the newly established hospital—they've got eighty patients there already—just think how much good a glass of wine would do them, and how quickly their spirits would be lifted if we could hand out a few cigarettes! Be a man, Zaches, and don't think about yourself for once: think about all the people who are having a hard time, and do something to help them! Just think of it like this: you are making a generous donation. So tell me where you have hidden the stuff!'

'I'd love to help all those people', replied the fat man, and there were tears of emotion in his eyes. 'But I haven't got anything else, I really haven't, Mr. Mayor! May I be struck down dead if I have hidden anything else away …'

'You've lived a life of plenty for twelve years now, Zaches', continued Doll, appearing not to have heard the other man's impassioned assurances, 'and you've never thought about anyone else. Now you've found out for yourself—but only in the last six weeks, mind, only in the last six weeks!—what it's like to do heavy work you're not used to, and to feel the pangs of hunger. Just think about other people for once, who are having to go without everything. Prove to the town that you've been unjustly maligned, that you can do the decent thing! Tell me where you've hidden the stuff!'

For a moment, Zaches appeared to hesitate, but then he came out with all his protestations and beastly oaths again. The mayor kept on at the former beer wholesaler for another hour. The longer it went on, the more convinced he became that the man had hidden something else away, and possibly a great deal; but he couldn't get it out of him. He was rotten and corrupt to the core. And it made no difference when Doll told him how much trouble he'd be in if they did find something. Then the dairy would just have to manage without him; he would be thrown into a black hole and kept on bread and water, and they'd make him work all day long, lugging heavy sacks of grain. 'You wouldn't survive that for long, Zaches, all bloated with alcohol as you are! And I gather you have diabetes, too! You'll probably end up paying for this futile lie with your life!'

But it was no use: no amount of persuasion could get the man to reveal his hiding place. He sat on his hoard like a malevolent little hamster, and would rather be beaten to death than give it up. A wasted hour behind him, Doll shrugged his shoulders and had the man escorted back to the dairy. He didn't doubt for a moment that this hiding place existed, quite possibly stuffed with very valuable goods. And then, with a hundred other matters to attend to, the mayor gave no more thought to the beer wholesaler.

Just how large and well stocked the hoard in question was, Doll learned only a few days later from his police constable. 'You should get along to Seestrasse, Mr. Mayor, and see for yourself what the Russians are loading up from the cellar of Zaches' place!'

'Is that right?' replied Doll, acting all indifferent, although his heart was already aching with grief and anger. 'So they've found his hiding place, have they? I always knew there was one, as soon as I started questioning the man. I thought I might go and poke around over there myself, but I never got round to it ...'

'You wouldn't have found it anyway', said the police constable by way of consolation. 'Zaches bricked up an entire coal cellar over a year ago — those Nazis, it just goes to show you again how deeply they believed in their precious Führer's victory! But nobody would have found this hiding place — someone spilled the beans, of course.'

'Who was that?' asked Doll.

'A servant girl who used to work for Zaches. She thought the Russians would let her have some of it, of course. But they told her to get lost — they've got their own views about informers like her!'

But when Doll learned in the course of the day how large had been the stockpile of goods stashed away by this lowly, rank-and-file member of the National Socialist German Workers' Party, he was overcome with anger again, and he gave orders for Zaches to be fetched from the dairy there and then.

'Well, Zaches!' he said to the fellow, who knew everything by now, of course, since news like that travels fast in a small town. 'Your storehouse has been busted, and how many days ago is it since you were standing right there and swearing on your mother's life that you hadn't hidden anything away?! You've been lying through your teeth!'

Zaches said nothing; he stood there with bowed head, his gaze wandering back and forth, but never looking the mayor in the face. 'Do you realise how much damage you've done to the town and to all Germans everywhere?!' And the mayor began to list the haul: 'One van packed with tobacco, cigars, and cigarettes. Two vans filled with wine and schnaps—and those are all goods that have been stolen from the German people, because they were supplied to you for distribution to the trade. But you just lied about it, of course, and claimed you hadn't received any deliveries, and kept it all for yourself instead, true to the good old Party principle: private greed before public need!'

Looking even more sallow and ashen than usual, the man just stood there and let the tide of anger wash over him, saying nothing in reply. 'But that's not even all of it', said Doll, and went on with his list. 'One van full of linen—and I don't have a single sheet, a single towel, left for the hospital. Five large wireless sets, three typewriters, two sewing machines, one sun lamp—and a whole van full of clothing and other stuff. Shame on you, you degenerate, for betraying your own people like that. I can't believe all the stuff you've stolen and hoarded!'

Doll was getting more and more angry as he looked at the man, his impassive silence driving him to distraction. The time before, he had not succeeded in getting any reaction out of him, any sign of human feeling, and it was just the same this time.

'And another thing', Doll went on, collecting himself again, 'hasn't it occurred to you how much damage you have done to whatever might be left of Germany's reputation! If I have to go cap in hand to the town commandant because I've run out of food again for the babies, the tuberculosis patients and the seriously ill, or because I can't allocate any beds for the hospital, do you know what they'll say to me? "Mayor must go find himself! Germans still have everything, only hidden! All Germans lie and deceive. Mayor, go find!" And do you know what? The Russians are right! How are they supposed *not* to think that, when they find something like they did at your place, you scumbag?! And now hundreds of people will carry on freezing, because you didn't speak up at the right time, you scumbag!'

It was at this point that the man who had been hauled before him and berated opened his mouth for the first and only time, and what came out was a classic piece of National Socialist thinking, which perfectly exemplified the mindset of Party members: 'I *would* have told the mayor about my hiding place if he had let me keep a share of the stuff, however small ...'

Mayor Doll stood there motionless for a while, shocked by this shameless display of heartless egoism, which was not in the least bit troubled by the sufferings of others, just as long as it didn't have to suffer itself. And he was reminded of a conversation he had had recently with an adjutant in the town commandant's office. The adjutant had told him how the ordinary rank-and-file soldiers in the Red Army had pictured the German people living much like their own people: frequently enduring abject misery because of the war, facing starvation ... That was the only way they could explain the way the Germans had so ruthlessly despoiled the Russian homeland. But then, as their armies advanced, they had entered German territory and seen with their own eyes farming villages amply supplied and provisioned, the like of which simply didn't exist any more back home, cowsheds bursting with well-fed cattle, and a rural population that was healthy and well nourished. And in the solid stone-built houses of these farming families they had found not only huge wireless sets, refrigerators, all the comforts of life, but also, in among these things, cheap, basic sewing machines from Moscow, brightly coloured scarves from the Ukraine, icons from Russian churches, all of it stolen and plundered: the rich man, who had plenty, had robbed the poor, who had nothing. And the soldiers of the Red Army were consumed with rage at these Germans, and felt utter contempt for a nation that had no shame, that could not control its greed, that wanted to grab up everything, possess everything for itself, without caring whether others perished in consequence.

Here was a perfect example of that nation, standing before his mayor. And they were exactly as described — in the end, it was all the same to them whether Russians or Germans perished. The very people whose Party principles put the good of the nation first did not have an ounce of fellow feeling in their bodies. They had an eye to the main chance in everything, and didn't care if thousands perished as long as they got what they wanted. The man who was standing there now was just one of many. Doll told the police constable to take him away and bang him up in jail on bread and water; they'd find someone else to take his place at the dairy. He gave orders for him to be put to work carrying sacks all day long under strict supervision, and with any luck this creature who had betrayed his own people would soon be done for!

With that, the former beer wholesaler Zaches was led away. Doll never saw him again, and never found out what became of him.

Shortly afterwards, Doll became seriously ill, the outbreak of his illness brought on, or at least hastened, by this whole episode.

The man had been led away, and the mayor was sitting alone in his office. He was sitting at his desk, his head resting on his hand. He could feel that the anger inside him had completely subsided, and he was filled with a deep, nameless despair. The anger had been easier to bear than this despair, which was devoid of any hope. He suddenly realised that in this despair his hatred, too, had gone. He struggled to recall all the things the Nazis had done to him: years of persecution, arrest, surveillance, threats, countless prohibitions. But it made no difference; he felt no more hatred for them. And he also realised that he hadn't hated them for quite some time now. If he had come across as harsh and abrasive when carrying out these confiscations at the homes of Party members, it was only because he felt duty-bound to act like that. He was slightly shocked to realise that he wouldn't have behaved any differently in the homes of non-Party members. He found them all equally contemptible. He couldn't hate them any more, they were all just vicious little animals — which was exactly how the first Russian soldiers had looked upon him and his wife, and exactly how he now saw the Germans himself — all Germans.

But he was one of those Germans, he was born a German — a word that had now become a term of abuse throughout the world. He was one of them, and there was nothing that made him any better than all the others. It was an old saying, but no less true for that: if you fly with the crows, you'll get shot with the crows. He too had eaten of the bread stolen from nations they had plundered and looted: now it had come back to haunt him! Oh yes, it all made perfect sense: he couldn't hate them any more, for the very good reason that he was one of them. All that was left to him was a feeling of helpless contempt—contempt for himself as much as for anyone else.

What was it they had said to him in the town commandant's office? All Germans lie and deceive. A sequence of chance events had led to his appointment as mayor of this small town, and as mayor the truth of the remark about lying and deceiving was borne in upon him every day. The memories came flooding back: once again he saw that woman, mother of two small children, who'd come to see him during his consultation hour. Her face was streaming with tears, she'd lost everything in the bombing of Berlin, and she didn't have a bed, a cooking pot, or clothes to put on her children's backs: 'Have pity on me, Mr. Mayor, you can't send me away again like this! I can't go back to my children with nothing!'

The mayor had nothing either, but he went to see what he could find. He sought out Party comrades who had plenty and to spare, and he took from them to give to their 'fellow German citizen'—not an abundance, but a sufficiency. But the following day another woman stood before him in tears, the neighbour of the woman he had just provided for, likewise a mother of children, likewise living in abject poverty; and the woman who had just been given gifts and furnished with what she needed had stolen her neighbour's few pieces of tattered laundry from the washing line during the night! Germans against Germans, every man for himself, and every woman, too, keeping up the fight against the whole world and everyone else.

The mayor also recalled the carter who was given the job of taking the belongings of a paralyzed old man to the old people's home. But when he got there, anything worth keeping had been stolen from the cart, either by the carter himself or by passers-by, as he maintained. Germans against Germans ...!

He also thought about the despicable doctor who, in order to settle some wretched private score from earlier times, certified a sick woman as healthy, and indeed fit for heavy work—the same doctor who, when medicines were in short supply, always had plenty for his friends, but never any for his enemies or strangers. He was happy to let them suffer—serve them right, the more the better! Germans against Germans!

He remembered how they stole horses from each others' stables, and poultry, and the rabbits they had so painstakingly fattened up, how they broke into each others' gardens and tore the vegetables out of the ground and the under-ripe fruit from the trees, breaking off the fruit-bearing branches in the process, which caused a lot of damage and did nobody any good. It was as if a herd of madmen had been let loose and were now just behaving as their crazy instincts directed them. He also knew about their denunciations—often completely absurd accusations, so obviously false that they wouldn't bear any kind of scrutiny, made out of pure malice, just to scare their neighbour and put the fear of God into him. Germans against Germans ... !

So Doll sat there at his mayor's desk, his head in his hands, feeling completely drained. It had been an illusion, the idea that the world was just waiting to help the German people out of the mire, out of this huge bomb crater into which the war had flung them all. And it had also been an illusion that he, Mayor Doll, should be seen as any different from his fellow Germans: just like all the rest of them, he was nothing but a vicious little animal. Someone you didn't shake hands with, someone you looked straight through, like staring at a brick wall.

And they were right to hate and despise the German people, every last one of them. Doll had hated, too, after all—in private the old vet, Piglet Willem, and a good few others, but then more generally all the Nazis, every one of them. But his hatred, the small private one and the big general one, they had gone away, because he himself was just as hateful as the people he hated.

There was nothing left, Doll was drained and empty—and a profound apathy descended upon him. This apathy, which had been constantly lurking in the background in recent months, held at bay only temporarily because his duties as mayor had kept him so busy, now engulfed him completely. He looked over his desk, strewn with dozens of things that had to be dealt with as quickly as possible—but what did any of it matter any more? He was doomed, finished, he and all the rest of them! All effort was futile!

His secretary opened the door: 'There's someone from the town commandant's office here—they want you to go and see the commandant straightaway, Mr. Mayor!'

'All right', he replied. 'I'll go straight there ...'

But he didn't go straight there. He stayed sitting at his desk for a good while yet; his secretary had to remind him about the commandant a couple of times. Not that he was thinking any definite thoughts, or that he decided, in his state of apathy, that this too was a pointless errand, just as all errands were pointless, since all errands, for a German, just led nowhere ...

No, he simply sat there, thinking about nothing in particular. Had he wanted to describe what he felt like inside, he might have said that his head was filled with fog, a grey, opaque fog that nothing could penetrate—no gaze, no sound. And otherwise nothing ...

Eventually—when his secretary reminded him again with some urgency—he stood up and went to the commandant's office, just because he had been there a hundred times before. It was no worse, and no better, than anything else he could have done. It didn't matter. Nothing mattered any more—including Dr. Doll himself. He was wounded in his vital core, and had lost his instinct for survival.

Shortly after this, Mayor Doll fell seriously ill; now he was no longer mayor. His wife, who was also ill, went with him to the local district hospital.

CHAPTER FIVE

Arrival in Berlin

On 1 September of this pitiless year, 1945, Mr. and Mrs. Doll travelled to Berlin. They had lain in the local district hospital for nearly two months, and they were still far from well. But the worry that they might lose their apartment in Berlin altogether if they waited any longer had driven them from their hospital beds.

The train was supposed to leave at noon, but it had not been released until after dark; it was completely overcrowded, with its broken windows and dirty compartments. As they boarded the train and made a dash for the pitch-black compartments, all the passengers were in a foul mood, flying off the handle at the slightest provocation and viewing every rival for a seat as their personal enemy.

The Dolls had managed to bag two seats, where they sat squashed up by their seated neighbours and people standing in front of them. Boxes were shoved up against their legs, and rucksacks were dragged painfully across their faces. It was so dark that you couldn't see a thing, but the hatred that everyone felt for everyone else seemed to manifest itself in the stench that hung about the compartment, despite the shattered windows. It smelled to high heaven in there, and it just got worse as more people boarded the train during the journey, squeezing into the already packed compartment and cursing anyone who already had a seat.

These later arrivals were mostly Berliners who had been foraging for mushrooms, who simply parked their baskets of mushrooms on the laps of the people in the seats, sullenly muttering something about taking them away later. But since the compartment was already overfull to start with, the baskets stayed where they were: Mrs. Doll had four on her lap; Doll had three.

But they made no protest, spoke not a word to their fellow passengers, and kept themselves to themselves. They still felt far too weak and ill to get involved in these sorts of arguments. It was only the thought of at least hanging on to their apartment that kept them going, and especially the husband: to him it seemed the last opportunity they had to begin a new life again.

Doll knew, of course, that he was clutching at straws with his hopes for the apartment, but he wanted to give fate this opportunity at least of saving them—as he sometimes said ironically to his wife, whose constant gallbladder attacks had made her quite despondent and easily influenced by her husband's depressive moods. 'We're probably going to die soon anyway, but you can do it more discreetly and comfortably in the big city. They have gas, for one thing!'

If the others had too much luggage with them, perhaps the Dolls did not have quite enough. All they were carrying was a small weekend case, which contained a little bit of bread, a can of meat, and a quarter-pound of coffee beans wrapped in a twist of paper, plus two books and a few basic toiletries. Doll was wearing a lightweight summer suit, while Mrs. Doll had at least managed to borrow a pale summer coat from a friend before leaving. In his pocket, Doll had barely three hundred marks, which he had borrowed from an acquaintance; the only precious item they had with them was the young wife's diamond ring.

The train halted for ages at every station, and when it was

moving its progress was very slow. The Dolls could dimly see the fiery lines and dots shooting into the night sky from the chimney of the locomotive, which was burning brown coal. They had seen rather too much in the way of fireworks during the war to take any pleasure in the sight. The memories were still painful. But in the light of these dancing glow-worms, they could make out figures standing on the running boards, ducking down with their backs turned towards the dense shower of sparks. The contents of their rucksacks must have been very precious to justify burning and singeing their precious clothing, and hanging on precariously by one hand to the cold brass rail, at constant risk of falling off.

Most of the rucksacks probably held nothing more than a few potatoes, or a little bag of flour, or a few pounds of peas—enough food for a week, at most. But there they were, hanging on for dear life in the sparks and the cold, letting their clothes get singed with a kind of brutish resignation. They were doubtless all poor folk who used this mode of transport; there would be a wife and numerous children waiting somewhere for what these men were carrying. The black marketeers, who bartered items for more valuable commodities—butter, bacon, eggs—and who picked up potatoes and flour by the sackful, they didn't risk their lives when they travelled; they recruited truck drivers in return for a share of the goods, and they didn't have any starving children waiting at home …

But who was a black marketeer and who wasn't? When the Dolls ate some of their bread and tinned meat in the total darkness of their compartment, some of the others smelled it through all the stench and began to pass pointed remarks about the sort of people who could still get hold of meat to eat. There was definitely something funny going on, and it needed to be looked into, in the cold light of day!

The Dolls said nothing, but quickly ate up what they had in their hands, and put the rest back in the little case before snuggling up more closely together. Mrs. Doll draped her thin, borrowed coat around them both, as the temperature was dropping fast. They put their arms around each other and held each other tightly. Doll rolled himself a cigarette from the last of his tobacco, and immediately someone piped up in a shrill voice: 'That's the third one he's smoked! It's like I always say: some people have it all, and the rest never get a thing, no matter what happens!'

The conversation ranged more widely over the racketeering and petty officialdom that were just a fact of life, and for the moment the Dolls were forgotten. They had a whispered conversation about their Berlin apartment; now that they were getting closer to their goal, and indeed had a goal to aim for again, the fact that they had heard nothing more about the apartment since March weighed heavily on their minds. There had been fierce fighting in the city since then, which had caused a whole lot more destruction, apparently—maybe their apartment didn't even exist any more?

'Wouldn't that be just like it? All this travelling, half frozen to death, and when we get there, the apartment's gone! I'd die laughing …!'

'I have a feeling it's all still there, just as we left it. And it won't take much to get Petta's room sorted out—there wasn't a lot of damage.'

'I can always count on you to look on the bright side!'

'I've got lots of good friends in Berlin, you know! When my first husband was alive, we helped so many people—now they can do something for us in return! I'm pinning my hopes on Ben, in particular. Ben had an English mother, so he's bound to be doing very well now. Ernst'—the young woman's first husband—'got him out of the concentration camp, so he'll always owe me for that!'

'Let's hope so, Alma! Let's hope for all kinds of good things—but not take anything for granted. The only thing we can be sure of is that we have each other, and that we will always be together! And that nothing can ever separate us. Nothing!'

'That's right!' she said. Shivering, she snuggled up more closely to him. 'It's cold!' she whispered.

'Yes, it's cold', he agreed, and hugged her more tightly.

Berlin! Back in Berlin again, this beloved city where they had both grown up—he thirty years earlier than she, it's true—this bustling, restless place glittering with lights! Seemingly caught up in an endless frenzy of pleasures and delights—but only if you ignored the grim, sprawling suburbs where the workers lived. Berlin, the city of work! They were going back there again to start a new life: if there was anywhere on earth where there was a chance for them to start again, it was right here in Berlin, a city reduced to rubble, burnt out and bled to death.

It was half-past two in the morning when the Dolls left the train at the Gesundbrunnen underground station, with the curfew still in place until six o'clock. An icy wind whistled through the station; every pane of glass seemed to be broken, so there was nowhere to shelter from the cold and the wind. They tried various places, but everywhere they were frozen to the bone. Even the little waiting room on the platform, which had somehow survived, was no warmer. The wind rushed in through the broken windows; people were sitting bunched up together on the floor, waiting disconsolately or grimly for the morning.

Mrs. Doll squeezed in between them, seeking shelter from the icy gusts. But scarcely had she stood her little suitcase on the ground and sat down on it before she had to get up again: she was told she was blocking the passageway! And this woman who always had an answer for everything, who was normally so breezy and spoiling for a fight, now sat down without a word at the outer edge of the clump of people. She pulled her thin coat more tightly around her, trying to shelter from the icy wind that now struck her with full force.

Doll scraped together the last few strands of tobacco in his pockets, rolled a droopy little cigarette with hands that were trembling from the cold, and ran up and down. He stood for a moment in the ruins of the former station building and looked out at the darkened city, over which a half-moon cast a pale light. All he could make out were ruins.

'Don't go outside!' a voice warned him out of the darkness. 'The curfew hasn't ended yet. The patrols sometimes shoot without warning.'

'Don't worry, I'm not going out there!' replied Doll, and flicked the butt of his very last cigarette into the rubble.

And he thought to himself: *What a start! Things always turn out differently from what you expect. What you think is going to be hard is often easy, and something you don't even think about turns out to be difficult. Standing here for two freezing hours in a completely bombed-out station, with nothing more to smoke—and Alma is ill! Her face looked so yellow ...*

He turned round and went back to her.

'I can't stand it any more', she said. 'There must be a first-aid station or a doctor somewhere who can help me. Let's go and ask someone. I'm frozen stiff, and it hurts so much!'

'But we can't go into the city. The curfew's still in place! They say the patrols sometimes shoot without warning.'

'Let them shoot!' she replied in desperation. 'If they hit one of us, at least they'll take us somewhere warm where a doctor can help us.'

'Come on then, Alma', he replied gently. 'Let's see if we can find a first-aid station of some kind, or a doctor. You're quite right: anything is better than sitting here in the icy cold and freezing half to death.'

They walked out of the station and picked their way through the rubble. The pale moonlight was more of a hindrance than a help in lighting their path. Doll could see hardly anything with his poor eyes.

'Come on!' she said as she walked on ahead. 'That looks like a street turning over there! According to the description, that must be the one where there might be a first-aid station.'

He followed her, feeling unsure. Suddenly he tripped over an obstacle and fell forward into a dark cavity.

'Look out!' said his young wife. 'Have you hurt yourself?'

'Well, there's a thing!' an indignant voice called out of the total darkness, speaking in a strong Berlin accent. 'The wife just lets her husband fall in, and doesn't even fall in with him. Scandalous, is what I call it!'

'What good would it have done me', asked Doll, and found himself laughing despite the pain, 'if my wife had fallen in with me? Where are we, anyway?'

'Gesundbrunnen underground station', another voice piped up. 'But the first train isn't due until half-past six.'

'Thanks!' he replied, and they went on their way, arms linked now. 'That was a proper Berlin welcome, a bit painful, but the real deal. I've kissed the ground of this city like a conqueror and taken possession of it, and what Berlin had to say about it was pretty good, too.'

'Did you hurt yourself?'

'Not really—just took the skin off my hands a bit and bruised my legs.'

They dived into the dark sea of ruins, where the moonlight was unable to penetrate all the way down to the bottom of the street canyons. They picked their way slowly forward. The street was deserted; all was deathly silence, apart from their echoing footsteps.

'We'll hear any patrols coming from a long way off', said Doll. 'So we'll have plenty of time to hide.'

'Hang on', she replied. 'This looks like the first-aid station. Strike a match.'

It really was the first-aid station, but everything was in darkness, and although they rang the bell and knocked on the door, nothing stirred in the dark ground floor of the building.

'I expect the bell isn't working', said Doll eventually. 'What now? Shall we go back to the station?'

'No, no, anything but that! Maybe we can find a doctor, or a police station. A police station would be best. They'd surely let us sit inside so that we could warm up a bit.'

So they wandered on through the silent city, with not a single light to be seen at any of the windows, and eventually they did find a police station. After they had been ringing the doorbell for some time, a police officer came out.

'What do you want?' he asked brusquely.

'We travelled into town on the train a while ago, and my wife is ill. The first-aid station is shut. Could we come in and sit down until six o'clock, so we can warm up a bit?'

'I can't let you do that—that's not allowed', replied the policeman.

They resorted to pleading and begging, saying they wouldn't be in anyone's way, and would just sit quietly and wait.

But the policeman wouldn't budge: 'If it's not allowed, I can't let you do it! And anyway, what are you doing out on the street? There's still a curfew!'

'Well, in that case why don't you just arrest us for a bit, constable?' asked the young woman. 'Then we won't be breaking the rules by sitting inside!'

But the policeman didn't go for this suggestion either. Instead he shut the door in their faces, leaving the two of them standing on their own again in the dark street.

They looked at each other, their faces pale and bewildered. Suddenly they noticed that it was getting light, that it was nearly daybreak.

'Then it must be getting on for six. We'll just carry on walking. Maybe a tram will come along soon.'

Later on, they were sitting in a bus that was taking workers to a factory for the first shift. The bus wasn't passing very close to where they lived, but it did take them to a station on the city rail network, where the first train of the day was due to leave soon. But then they encountered a fresh obstacle: the woman in the ticket office had overslept, and the ticket collector on the barrier refused to let anybody through without a ticket: it was against the rules!

'And what if there's nobody on the ticket counter for another hour?'

'Then nobody goes through in the next hour! Rules are rules!'

'But we've got to get to work!' protested many of those waiting.

'That's not my problem! I have to stick to the rules!'

'We'll see about that!' cried a local. 'You lot, come with me!'

They all followed him through a side entrance, over a fence, across the tracks in semi-darkness, the electrified rails, and then another climb over a wall. The Dolls brought up the rear—she suddenly had pains in her leg, and he was still hurting all over from his tumble. They arrived on the platform out of breath, just in time to see the red taillights of the early train receding into the distance.

Then came more waiting in the freezing cold, sitting in the moving train feeling utterly exhausted, changing trains and waiting some more … How they longed just to get home at last! They went all dreamy at the mere thought of their couch! Just to lie there quietly, feeling warm again and falling asleep! Blissful oblivion! Dead to the world!

At last they were there: they got off the train. 'We'll be home in five minutes!' he said, jollying her along.

'At the rate we're going, it will take us another twenty minutes', she replied. 'I wish I knew what was wrong with my leg. It was only a little sore that had opened up a bit because I scratched it … Oh Lord, the bridge has gone, too. It was still there in March!'

And as they struggled along for what seemed an endless distance, forced by the destruction of the bridge to make a lengthy detour, suddenly all they saw was the destruction all around them—some of it from before that they already knew about, and some that had happened since they left Berlin. They fell silent, rendered speechless by the sight; so much more had been destroyed in the meantime. Doll thought: *What am I going to do with her, if the apartment has gone? She is ill and completely demoralised.*

Then they turned the last corner and peered intently. This time he was quicker off the mark: 'I can see the window boxes on our balcony! And the glazing bars are back in the windows! Alma, our apartment is still there!'

They looked at each other with a weary smile.

They had no keys, so had to go and see the caretaker first. Bad news—very bad news! The little caretaker had not been seen since April. Perhaps he had been killed in the fighting, or perhaps he'd been taken prisoner; his wife didn't know. Not a thing.

'Run off, you mean, done a bunk? No, my 'usband isn't the sort of man to run off and leave his wife and children, my 'usband's never been that way, Mr. Doll! And anyway, why should 'e? 'E never harmed anybody, 'e didn't! The keys to the apartment? No, I don't 'ave 'em any more. Somebody turned up from the 'ousing office a few days ago, a dancer or singer or something to do with the theatre, I don't rightly know. With mother and child—oh yes, there's a little one, too! She got the front room tidied up a bit. And the old lady's still livin' out the back, Mrs. Schulz, the one you used to let sleep there from time to time, when you went out to the country, so there'd be someone there to keep an eye on things. Well, you'll see for yourself 'ow well she's kept an eye on things, Mrs. Doll, I'm not goin' to speak out of turn. Anyway, your big cooking pot 'as gone, the 'ome Guard people came and fetched that. And if your vacuum cleaner 'as gone and your books and all your buckets and if the pantry is empty, then I know nothing about that, Mrs. Doll, and you'll 'ave to ask Mrs. Schulz—if you can get to see 'er, that is. She says she is livin' 'ere, but what do I know where she lives! I often don't see 'er for the 'ole week, and she's never paid a penny in rent!'

Slowly, ever so slowly, the Dolls climbed the four flights of stairs to their apartment. They hadn't said a word in response to all the bad news, which washed over them like a tidal wave, nor had they spoken a word to each other. It was just that their faces had turned a shade more pale, perhaps, than they were already from illness, a sleepless night on the train, and hours of sitting around in the freezing cold …

They had to press the doorbell for a long, long time before

anything stirred in the apartment—in their own apartment! And they had to be very patient before they were eventually let in by a swarthy young woman, who was scantily clad (but then it was only around eight in the morning).

'Your apartment? This here is *my* apartment, officially allocated to me by the housing office. I'm afraid there is nothing you can do about it, madam. The three rooms at the front belong to me, and I've already spent a few thousand marks to make the place more or less habitable. The other two rooms have been completely gutted by fire—but then you'll know that for yourself, madam, if this is your apartment! The big room at the back is occupied by Mrs. Schulz, but she's away at the moment, and I don't know if she'll be back today. But anyway, she's locked everything up. I'm sorry, madam, but it's very cold in here, and I'm standing around in my nightshirt, and I need to get back into bed. I suggest you go and talk to the housing office, madam. Good day!'

And with that the door closed, and the Dolls were left standing in the hallway on their own. He took his wife and led her slowly, leaning very heavily on his arm, into the interior of the apartment. But everything was locked up, and they couldn't get into any of the rooms. So he led her into the kitchen and sat her down on the only kitchen chair (surely there had been three there before?) between the gas stove and the kitchen table.

His young wife sat there, but she didn't look young right now, staring blankly ahead without seeing anything, her face a sickly, yellowish colour. Doll took her cold hands between his own, stroked them, and said: 'It's not a good start, Alma, I know! But we won't let it get us down, we'll find a way to get through it somehow. People like us don't give up that easily!'

At these words of encouragement, Mrs. Doll attempted a smile, but it was the feeblest, most pitiful, and heartrending smile Doll had ever seen from his wife. Then she lifted her head and gazed around the kitchen for a long, long time. She studied every single object, and then wailed: 'My kitchen! Just look around and see if you can see a single thing in this kitchen that doesn't belong to us! And now this female just gives me the brush-off in the hall and doesn't even offer me a chair to sit down on in my own apartment!' Alma seemed on the verge of tears, but her eyes were dry. 'And did you see? Through the open door I could see our radiogram parked there in her room, and the big yellow armchair you always liked to sit in! Just you wait—I'm off to the housing office right now!'

But she didn't go. She stayed sitting where she was, looking blankly into the distance again. She had always been a pampered, radiant woman. And now she was sitting there in her cheap little coat, which didn't remotely suit her, and which was borrowed anyway, her stockings were all snagged and torn from the mushroom baskets, and her hands and face still bore traces of the long, dirty train journey ...

Everything lost—drained and spent—like the rest of us! thought Doll bleakly, and went on patting her hands mechanically. But then he reflected that it was now up to him to do something; they couldn't just carry on sitting in the kitchen. A little while later, he took her downstairs again to the kindly caretaker's wife, and even if they were still sitting in the kitchen down here, at least this kitchen was warm. The last of the Dolls' coffee beans were roasted in a little skillet. Bread was sliced, and the remaining meat taken out of the tin and arranged neatly on a plate. With a spot of breakfast on the table, the future suddenly looked more hopeful.

But his young wife seemed not to share the feeling. She said that Doll should go now, right now, and seek out her friend Ben, the German who was half-English, and when Doll resisted, saying he would rather go after breakfast, she became very impatient: she knew for a fact that Ben was an early riser, and always left for work in good time. If he didn't go immediately he would miss Ben, and they wouldn't be able to reach him for the rest of the day—and she needed to speak to him *now*!

Doll could think of good reasons for refusing, but his young wife seemed so feverishly agitated and desperate, and he himself was so exhausted and keen to avoid an argument, that he did actually set out to find Ben's apartment. 'I'll expect you back in under half an hour!' cried the young woman, now quite animated again, 'and bring Ben with you. I'll have breakfast waiting for you!'

It was not possible to do the journey in under half an hour, because the trams that used to run there were not yet back in service. Doll had to walk the whole way—though 'crawl' would be a better word.

The house he was looking for was still standing, at least, but there was no nameplate on the apartment door, and when he rang the bell, nobody came. He finally discovered from the porter that the gentleman had moved out, just a few days earlier. (*Somebody moved into our apartment a few days ago, and now Ben has moved out: a promising start to our time in Berlin, I must say!*) The porter claimed not to know Ben's new address. *I can't go back to Alma with this*, thought Doll, and with some effort he managed to find an elderly gentleman in the building who knew where Ben was now living, somewhere way out in the city's smart, new west end. It would take hours to get there, and he had no intention of going now. Back to Alma, then—and breakfast!

She really had waited breakfast for them, and had even managed to drum up a few cigarettes, albeit at a cost of five marks apiece, which Doll, who had previously been kept well supplied with tobacco by the Russians, found staggering. The news that Ben had moved was received by Alma with composure. 'We'll go and see him after breakfast, even though it will be hard for me with my leg. Believe me, my instinct about this is right: Ben will help us in our hour of need, he'll never forget that business with the concentration camp! You'll see', his wife went on, growing steadily more animated, 'he's done very well for himself. The fact that he's moved out to the expensive west end proves it. He'll have a villa there, for sure. And he'll be pleased that he's able to help us!'

And so, refreshed by the breakfast and a good wash, they took their leave of the friendly but ever-despondent caretaker's wife. 'I'll be back again in the next few days', promised Mrs. Doll, 'and I'll go down to the housing office and sort out this business with that cheeky cow upstairs. Doesn't even offer me a chair in my own home — she's out on her ear!'

And how are we going to compensate her for the 'few thousand marks' she's spent on doing the place up? thought Doll. *And anyway, they'll never grant us the right to the whole seven-room apartment, not even if we include Petta and grandmother.*

But he didn't talk about any of this with his wife. Events would just have to take their course now. There was no point in getting worked up over anything, or making plans for the future. Things would turn out one way or the other — though hardly ever for the best.

The refreshing effects of the wash and the ground coffee had not lasted long, and his wife's leg must have been in a really bad way, because their progress was painfully slow. Time and time again, Doll resolved to hold back and walk with his sick wife, but before he knew it he was ten or twenty paces ahead of her. When he then turned round and went back to her, feeling guilty, she would give him a friendly smile. 'You go on!' she said. 'I'll whistle if I think I'm losing sight of you. It must be a pain to have to slow down for me—I'm like a snail today. You go on ahead!'

After the cold night, the sun shone warmly, with that pleasantly autumnal warmth that has nothing oppressive about it, but just feels good. Here in the streets lined with villas the trees had not yet lost their leaves. The foliage was paler and changing colour, but it was just good to see healthy trees again after all the ruins. Many of the villas here had also been destroyed, but nestling among shrubs and trees, and surrounded by green lawns and flowers, it didn't look so bad somehow.

Mrs. Doll said to her husband, who had just turned back again to rejoin his 'snail': 'Ben will have his own car by now, for certain, and I'm sure he'll take us out for a drive from time to time. Now we've got the whole of the lovely autumn ahead of us—let's just enjoy it for ourselves at last, without having to worry about anything. I expect Ben can arrange a truck for us, too, so we can pick up the furniture and your books from the sticks and set up house again properly. You wait and see what a wonderful home I'll make for you! We're sure to have lots of English visitors through Ben, and then you can invite your writer friends, too … I'll mix the most marvellous cocktails for you—I mix a mean cocktail, me! Ben will be able to supply the ingredients!'

Ben this, Ben that, Ben the other! What a child she was, the way she just pinned all the hopes of her innocent, child-like heart on a friend she hadn't thought about for weeks and months! A child in her faith and trust—so far, no disappointment had been able to eradicate this capacity for belief and hope from her heart.

Eventually, they really were sitting in the large drawing room of a huge villa, and from the windows they could see across the garden to the garage buildings, where a chauffeur was busy washing the car—Ben's car, and in that regard at least, Alma's expectations had been fulfilled. Her friend Ben had done surprisingly well for himself, and official plates on the garden gate indicated that Mr. Ben already held a senior position.

So far he had not yet appeared, having been detained for a few minutes by an important meeting on the ground floor. In the meantime, three interior decorators were busying themselves around the Dolls as they sat there amongst the antique furniture, looking lost in the magnificently appointed room; whispering among themselves, they were arranging diaphanous curtain fabrics in folds, climbing up and down ladders, and pulling on cords. And when Doll saw all this new splendour around him, such as he had not seen intact for months and years now, he felt his own down-at-heel appearance twice, ten times, as keenly. He looked from the snow-white tulle to the pale summer suit he was wearing, which showed dirty marks and streaks from the overnight train journey; and Alma's cheap little coat and torn stockings looked even worse against the rich brocade of the armchair in which she sat.

The truth was they had become beggars, and here in this house, which even in the best of times had been the villa of a *very* rich man, Doll felt this very acutely. It wasn't so long ago that he had thought of himself as a pretty prosperous man. But now he and his wife, as he suddenly saw very clearly, were no different from all those refugees whom he had only recently—when he was still mayor—had to direct through his little town in endless, wretched, starving columns. Now the Dolls, too, were down-and-out, with only a small suitcase to their name, homeless, dependent on the help of friends, strangers, maybe even public assistance. Mayor, property owner, an abundance of possessions, a bank account always in the black, decent food—and now suddenly nothing, zero, zilch!

Oh Lord! thought Doll. *Don't let Alma say too much! Please God she doesn't ask these two women for anything—I couldn't bear it, we're not reduced to begging just yet!*

The two women who had just entered the room were the wife of Alma's friend Ben and a woman friend of hers; they had eyed the two visitors with some surprise, but then Alma had started to explain ...

There was no risk of her saying too much. She didn't get a chance for that. What happened next was something that Doll was to observe quite often over the coming weeks and months. Alma had barely got into her stride before the two women became very restless and fidgety, and the reason was obvious: they were dying to tell their own story!

As soon as Alma paused in her tale, the other two jumped in immediately. In a breathless gush of words, taking it in turns to speak, they now told the story of how badly they had suffered, how they had nearly starved, how they had lost so much ... Sitting in this magnificent house, in an antique armchair covered in fine brocade, the Dolls learned what an awfully wretched time the owners had had of it, and indeed were still having.

Then the master of the house entered the room in a hurry; he could spare them just five minutes between two important meetings. He kissed Alma's hand, and said how sorry he was that life had become so very difficult. He could not even offer his guests a cigarette—that's how bad things were in his house! Mrs. Doll's leg really did look in a bad way; his guess was blood poisoning. He advised Doll to take her straight to a hospital.

A quarter of an hour later, they were both standing out on the street again, having got through the visit to Alma's truest and most grateful friend—thank God! The sun was still shining brightly and cheerily though the sparse foliage of the trees, the lawn in front of the villa was a deep green, and the Michaelmas daisies were in flower. Doll linked arms gently with his wife—she had such an alarmingly pale, ill-looking face—and said gaily: 'And you know what we're going to do now, Alma? Now we are going to look after our nerves, we're going to live the good life—and your poor leg will get better in the meantime. So where are we going? Well, it occurred to me, when there was mention of a hospital just now, that only a quarter of an hour from here there's a sanatorium where I have stayed a couple of times for my nerves. They know me there, and they'll admit us for certain.'

'Do what you want with me', answered Mrs. Doll. 'Just as long as I get to lie down soon!'

And so they set out for the sanatorium, but instead of a quarter of an hour it took them nearly an hour, because the woman found it such a struggle to walk. There was no more talk of best friend Ben during this veritable *via dolorosa*; deep in thought, Mrs. Doll merely observed once in passing: 'I'm never going to be decent and generous to people like I was before! Never again!'

'Thank God', he said, and gave her a tender look. 'Thank God, Alma, that's not something that depends solely on you. You'll always be a decent person, no matter how badly you've been let down!'

The sanatorium, a large, ugly building of red brick and cement, was still standing—it would have been almost unbearable if this had turned out to be another disappointment. They sat in the consulting room. 'Turn on all your charm, Alma', whispered Doll. 'They've got to take us in here. Where else are we going to go?'

Mrs. Doll quickly applied powder, rouge, and lipstick, intent on making the most of her charm. 'Of course we'll admit you, my dear!' said the white-haired lady doctor, and stroked Alma's hair. 'As far as your husband is concerned, we'll have to consult the privy councillor. But I've certainly got a bed free for you in my section.'

The privy councillor appeared. He looked a lot more jaundiced, wrinkled, and careworn, and a lot more intelligent, too, than before—or so it seemed to Doll. 'I've got a room free for Mr. Doll', he announced after brief reflection. 'But unfortunately not for the young lady at present—perhaps we'll be able to do something in three or four weeks.'

Having only just been relieved of their worst cares, the Dolls looked at each other in disbelief, then at the white-haired lady doctor, who now looked at her boss with a tight-lipped and submissive expression. Pointing out that she had just said something different was clearly a waste of time: fate was against the Dolls—end of story. Protest was futile. One disaster after another—they were headed for the streets …

'I'm not leaving my wife now', said Doll after a protracted silence. 'Come on, Alma. Goodbye, Councillor. Goodbye, Doctor!'

This time, out on the street, they didn't notice that the sun was shining, that the trees still had their leaves. The pressing question 'What now?' overshadowed everything else. They had other friends, of course, and they still had relatives living in the city, too, but with the young wife in her present condition, how could they think of walking halfway across Berlin only to find a bombed-out shell instead of a house?

'What now? What now?' And turning suddenly to look back at the sanatorium: 'How I hate that man with his polite weasel face! Of course they had spare beds—beds for both of us. But he knew your first wife—I could tell straightaway that he was comparing me to her, and took against me. But where are we going to go now? Dear God, I've got to lie down somewhere, just a couple of hours, and then I'll be all right again.'

'I think we'll just go back to the dear old caretaker's wife for now. She's sure to have a sofa or some sort of couch where you can lie down. And in the meantime I'll find something else.'

And since at that moment they couldn't think of any alternative, they decided to do just that. The endless return trek began: travelling in overcrowded underground trains, where it didn't occur to anybody to offer the sick woman a seat, toiling up and down stairs, being pushed, shoved, and berated because they were going so slowly. He had the little suitcase in his hand, with their last crust of bread inside — the meat and the coffee were all gone now. It was lunchtime, they had no apartment and no ration cards, and no immediate prospect of getting any. And after Alma's extravagant purchase of cigarettes, they had less than two hundred marks left to their name.

We're facing utter ruin, thought Doll. *How would we do it? We don't have access to poison. Water? We both swim too well. The noose? Couldn't face that! Gas? But we don't even have a kitchen with a gas stove any more.* And then aloud to his wife, who was leaning against him: 'You've nearly made it! We're nearly home!'

'Home', she answered with a smile, and just a hint of irony. Then she added with a sudden rush of remorse: 'But you'll see, I *will* make a wonderful home for us!'

'Of course you will', said he. 'A wonderful home — I'm already looking forward to it.'

CHAPTER SIX

A new burden to bear

And then it really was almost as if they were at home. Alma Doll lay on a couch that belonged to the caretaker's wife, covered with a duvet, because she suddenly felt very cold. Her teeth were chattering. He sat on the edge of the couch, held her hands, and gazed anxiously into her face, which had become so thin.

Then the shivering attack abated, and she lay still for a long time, as if utterly drained. Now she opened her eyes. 'Dearest', she said, 'will you mind very much if I send you off on another errand? I think I need a doctor …'

'Of course I'll go', he replied. 'And I don't mind one bit. I'll go and find a doctor right away.'

She pulled his face down to hers and kissed him. He felt her dry, cracked lips coming to life again under his kiss, filling with blood again, and becoming soft and pliable.

'I'm such a burden to you', she whispered. 'I know I am, I know. But I'll make it up to you—you know me. Just you wait till your Alma's back on her feet again, and I'll pamper you like before, you know that!'

'My wonderful pamperer!' he said tenderly. 'Yes, I know, I know you will.' He kissed her once more. 'And now I'm going.'

'You don't have to go far', she called after him. 'There are six or eight doctors living right here in this street.'

They had indeed lived there, or were living there still, but it turned out that none of them had time for a house call right now. One of them could not come until the late evening; another, not before the following day. He couldn't possibly leave his wife lying in pain for all that time. He went on further, trudging up and down stairs, semi-stupified with fatigue and hunger, his feet hot and sore ...

He did eventually find a doctor who was prepared to come with him immediately. Not exactly the right kind of doctor — this one specialised in dermato-venereal diseases — but right now he couldn't care less. All that mattered was that she was seen by a doctor. *I can't go back to her having failed again! We've had enough failures already today. Our whole life is just one long series of failures.*

The doctor had a face that appeared to be covered not with skin, but with thin parchment paper, stretched so taut that it looked about to tear. He had a ghostly air about him, with slow, careful movements, as if he might shatter into pieces at any moment, and with a soft, almost soundless way of speaking, as if he was speaking into fog ...

They walked along the street side by side. The doctor was carrying his case containing some medical instruments. Suddenly he asked: 'You are a writer, Mr. Doll?' Doll said that he was. 'I'm a writer myself', said the doctor, still speaking in the same soft, impersonal manner. 'Did you know?'

Doll tried to remember the name on the doctor's nameplate. But all he could remember was the reference to 'dermato-venereal diseases'. 'No', he replied. 'I didn't know that.'

'Oh yes!' the doctor insisted. 'I was even a very famous writer once. And it's not all that long ago.' He paused, and then added out of the blue: 'My wife killed herself out on the highway, by the way.'

What a spooky character! thought Doll, shocked by this revelation. *Of all the people I had to bring to Alma's sick-bed! I hope she doesn't find him too scary!*

But the doctor behaved quite normally at Alma's bedside. Something like a smile even flitted across his parchment features when he saw the pretty, childlike face of the young woman. 'Now then, what seems to be the trouble, my dear child?' he inquired gently. He examined her briefly, and then said, speaking more to Doll than to the young woman: 'The early stages of blood poisoning. The best thing would be for the young woman to go straight to hospital. I'll write you a referral.'

'And what's to become of my husband in the meantime?' cried Alma. 'I don't want to go into hospital. I'm not leaving my husband alone now!'

Doll tried to persuade her: 'You know our situation, my dear. It may be the best solution for the time being. In hospital, you will at least have a bed. And meals. And rest. And proper care. Please say yes, Alma!'

'And what about you? What about you?' she kept on asking. 'Where are you going to be, while I'm having rest and meals and a bed and proper care? Do you think I'm going to live a life of ease while you're struggling to get by? Never! Never!'

During this exchange, the strange doctor had sat with bowed head, not saying a word. Now he picked up his bag and said in a flat, toneless voice: 'I'm going to give you an injection for now, which will take away the pain and let you sleep for a bit. I'll call in again this evening.'

'But we have to vacate this couch before tonight!' countered

Doll. 'This is where the caretaker's wife sleeps. By this evening we might be sleeping on the street!'

The doctor didn't answer, but carried on with the injection. The effect was immediate: no sooner had the needle gone in than Doll saw the relaxed, almost happy, expression spread across his wife's face. (It wasn't her first morphine injection, of course. She'd had them before—for her bilious attacks.) She suddenly smiled, stretched herself out at her ease, and snuggled down into the sheets. 'God, that feels good', she whispered, and closed her eyes.

In the space of just five seconds, she had forgotten her husband, her pain and disappointments, and her hunger. She had forgotten a lot more besides. She had forgotten that she was married and had a child. She was completely alone with herself, in her own world. A smile played about her lips, and there it stayed. Doll watched her breathing gently, and understood that the very act of breathing was pleasurable for her now.

The doctor had packed his syringe away again. 'I'll walk a little way with you, Doctor', said Doll. For the moment, it seemed to him impossible to sit with this woman who was now so far away. Through all their differences over the past weeks and months, he had never once felt so alone as he did now.

'I'll call in again this evening', said the doctor, exactly as before, as if he had not heard a word Doll had said. 'Between eight and nine. Please make sure that the street door is not locked.'

Doll didn't bother to object again; there seemed no point with this doctor, who didn't listen anyway. For a while they walked along side by side in silence. Then the doctor started up again: 'It seems a very long time ago now, but back then I really was a very well-known writer.'

There was no hint of vanity; it sounded more like an observation from a train of thought that haunted him obsessively. And the observation he now came out with appeared to belong to the same train of thought: 'The injection I gave your wife came from my suicide pack. It contains scopolamine, around 30 per cent. She'll be asleep when you get back.'

And again after a further pause: 'Yes, I'll be committing suicide, maybe tomorrow, maybe in a year's time.' He extended a limp, damp hand to Doll. 'This is where I live. Thank you for walking with me. Of course, I didn't have a large readership like you. Anyway, I'll call in again this evening—don't forget about the street door.'

And as they took their leave of each other: 'I definitely won't be committing suicide today. You know, of course, that your wife is a real addict?'

Doll sat by his wife. She was sleeping soundly. Her face now looked carefree and happy; she was sleeping like a child. Through the open window came autumn sunshine and fresh air from the street, and the happy sound of children playing outside. Doll was not a happy man; he was feeling very tired and utterly despondent. He was also suffering the pangs of hunger. The last piece of bread had been eaten a long time ago. They had nothing left.

Why on earth, Doll thought to himself, *didn't I get him to give me an injection too? To forget it all for a while, just for once! That half-crazed doctor would have done it. So he's called Pernies. I remember, he* was *famous once. I don't think I've ever read anything by him; he was probably more someone who wrote about art than an actual artist himself. And now he's talking about suicide, and his wife killed herself out on the highway!*

Doll started up on his chair. He had nearly fallen asleep, and yet something had to be done. It would be dark in less than three hours, and the night afforded them no shelter.

He stood up. Even as he was leaving the apartment, he had no idea where he was going. So he climbed the stairs again to their old apartment.

This time, the door was opened as soon as he rang the bell. And it was not the snippy dancer who opened it, but Mrs. Schulz, the woman whom Alma had asked to look after their things while they were away, and whose honesty had now been called into question by the caretaker's wife.

The white and rather podgy face of Major Schulz's widow lit up when she saw Doll. 'There you are, Dr. Doll! I fought like a lion for your apartment — if only you had come two weeks earlier! Now you'll have trouble with the housing office and with that woman living at the front. So where is your wife? She's sleeping? That's good — if she's sleeping, that gives me time to get the room sorted out for you. You'll have to manage with *one* couch for the first night — the other one has gone, but you only need to go and ask for it back. Would you like a cigarette? What, you haven't got any more? Here, take the whole pack! Don't be silly, I can get as many as I want, even American brands, for five marks apiece, German money … Look, I was just brewing up a pot of coffee when you arrived, so you must have a cup of coffee with me. Not the artificial stuff, but real coffee! I got some for four hundred marks a pound. That's cheap, my dear, I only buy things cheap. We'll have some white bread with it, and I've also got a tin of cheese here, and I think there's a bit of butter left.

'You can talk! You say you've lost everything? Well, my dear, you've no idea what it's like for me, I literally don't have a thing! Just the clothes on my back. No, no, today you're my guest! Should we perhaps wake the young lady up? No, you're right, we'll put something back for her. But you eat up everything that's here; I'll be getting more later today. They all spoil me … And I never have to pay extortionate prices. Yes, the quilt has gone, stolen. I know who took it, too, but I can't prove it, so I'm not going to speak out of turn.

'You've heard that her husband has gone, I suppose? They came and took him away, of course—paid-up Nazi that he was. They should come and get the wife as well, she was worse than him! I've had the wall put up and plastered a bit—I've made a note of the cost somewhere, I'll let you know later. It wasn't much, a tradesman did it for me more as a favour. The two window frames with the cellophane and plywood are just borrowed, but there's no hurry, they can stay in the wall for the time being.

'But of course the room is available for you to use—it is your room, after all, and it's your furniture, too. The crockery and kitchen utensils belong to you as well. I can always sleep at a friend's place, and you'll get the housing office to evict the little singer and her family. They're decent enough people—but so what? These days, everyone has to look out for themselves. She's so scared of you! They've got nothing at all of their own, not so much as a spoon or a cup … By the way, the teapot I've just made the coffee in doesn't belong to you—all your teapots got smashed in the air raid. An old lady gave it to me; she doesn't want any money for it, of course. I thought I might give her a pound of sugar and a loaf of bread. That's not much, my dear: sugar is now going for a hundred, and a loaf of bread for eighty—and you must have a teapot! I can discuss it with your wife later.

'You can eat all of the white loaf, if you like; it tastes nice, but it doesn't fill you up. I'll go and get some fresh now. I might get some jam, too. If you'd come yesterday I'd have been able to offer you cake—proper butter cake with lots of sugar on the top. Pity. But I know what, I'll have a cake baked for you for Sunday. My baker will do it for you very cheaply …'

She prattled on. And on. All Doll had to do was sit there and listen. An occasional 'Yes', 'I see', or 'Thank you' were quite sufficient. He had found a safe haven; at long last, when he was on the point of giving up hope, a safe haven had been found for them both. He sat at his ease in an armchair, his weary legs and aching feet stretched out in front of him. He ate one slice of white bread to begin with, then three slices, then seven slices, drank coffee, smoked a cigarette, and started to eat again. Meanwhile, Mrs. Schulz was still in full flight.

There she sat before him, a woman in her forties, just starting to lose her looks—though she was in denial about it—her clothes a little crumpled and scruffy, but unquestionably a lady. Or someone who had once been a lady—for who today was still a 'lady' in the traditional sense of the word?

Then it got dark outside, the big electric standard lamp by Doll's bed was switched on, and dance music played softly on the radio. The doctor, that spectral figure with the papery skin, came and went again. He did say again that the young woman ought to be in hospital, but he didn't press the point, and gave them both an injection instead. Now they were both relaxed and calm, the morphine making them believe that all their difficulties were now behind them.

On the table next to the couch are plenty of cigarettes, a pot of real tea, condensed milk, and sugar—and a loaf of white bread, too. They are well provided for, with a home, choice music. On the walls are pictures, originals, nothing to get excited about exactly, but of decent, middling quality.

The Dolls are not yet asleep. This time it was pure morphine that the doctor gave them. They are chatting quietly, making plans for the future ... Plans? Now they have completely lost touch with reality: these are just flights of fancy, and every hope that springs to mind is immediately fulfilled. The apartment belongs to them, they have ration cards for food, a truck and trailer will fetch their child Petta and their things from the little town. Tomorrow he will begin to write books again, his head is suddenly full of plans, he will become an international bestselling author ...

The young woman's salon will be *the* salon in Berlin. The 'sea surf' talks of dresses she will have made, dresses that she once owned; he hardly needs to say anything in reply, and can pursue his own fantasies instead. Yes indeed, now he will travel the world with her and their child, just as he dreamed of doing before this war. Now the ghastly slaughter is ended, a few more months and they'll be able to leave this city of ruins behind and journey to brighter climes, where the sun always shines and southern fruits ripen on the trees ...

They lie there in a semi-waking dream, experiencing the euphoria, the rush; at last they have managed to escape the bitter reality. Both of them cherish a thousand hopes; no more obstacles bar their way. They gaze at each other and exchange tender smiles, not like a married couple, but as young lovers or children do ...

Sometimes the wind makes the slackly fitted cellophane chatter in the window frames, and a door slams in the burned-out courtyard building. There are all sorts of mysterious noises coming from outside. Trickling debris? Rats, looking for something unspeakable in the basements? A world in ruins, which will take everyone's determination, everyone's hands, to rebuild. But instead they are lying on their backs and dreaming. They have no love for anything any more, and they don't really have a life to live. They have nothing now, and they are nothing now. The smallest setback could tip them into the abyss and finish them off for good. But they are dreaming …

'Give me another cigarette! Don't worry, we'll soon get some more. I have a feeling that from now on things are going to go our way.'

But then — it is not yet midnight — they grow restless. The effect of the injection has worn off; the sweet illusion has vanished.

'I can't sleep!' And: 'I can't bear the pain any more! We must get the doctor back.' — 'Too late. Curfew! We can't go out on the street any more!' — 'It's crazy! What if I was having a baby? Or I was dying?' — 'Well, it's a good job you're not! I'll go and fetch the doctor first thing tomorrow!' — 'Tomorrow? I'll never last that long with this pain — I'll go and see him now!' — 'What, *now* Alma, and with that leg of yours? Let me go instead!' — 'No, it's better if I go. If a patrol does show up, they won't do anything to me, for certain!' — 'But the houses are all locked up now!' — 'I'll get in somehow. You know me! I'll find a way!'

And she went off, leaving him alone. The music was still playing, the lamp beside the couch was still burning brightly. But now the high was past, and he saw their situation for what it really was: without means, ill, lacking in energy, with no desire to work and no hope … a paper-skinned spectre and a dubious lady had made them forget for a few hours what their real situation was like, but now he knew again. Yes, for the moment they had a roof over their heads, but in the greater scheme of things nothing had changed for the better, and if anything it had changed for the worse: now his wife was running around on the streets at a dangerous hour looking for a shot of morphine! He remembered how, the night before, she had insisted on leaving Gesundbrunnen station to find a first-aid post. She had talked about bilious attacks, but now that she had this pain in her leg she hadn't mentioned her gallbladder trouble again. All day yesterday she must have been thinking only about getting this shot. An addict—so one more burden to bear, therefore!

One o'clock. She said she would be back straightaway, and now she had been gone a whole hour. He should get up and go and look for her, make sure she was all right. But he didn't get up. What could he do, after all? Perhaps she had been arrested and was sat in some guard post. Or she was with a doctor in one of these dark houses—how was he supposed to find her? All he could do was wait, all he ever did was wait, time after time—a whole life whiled away in waiting, with only death awaiting him at the end.

His thoughts wandered. Extreme exhaustion, and perhaps also the after-effects of the injection, caused him to fall asleep. Or rather, he fell into sleep as into some deadly abyss.

Later on, he was aware of her lying down on the couch beside him again. She was in excellent spirits. Yes, a patrol had stopped and detained her, but they had behaved very gallantly. 'Go and see your doctor', they had said. 'Hold a white handkerchief in your hand, and nobody will bother you!'

No, she had not been able to get into the house of the strange Dr. Pernies, but she had found another doctor, a most accommodating playboy type, who had opened the door to her in his pyjamas and given her a shot of morphine straightaway. She laughed merrily. And for him she had brought tablets—no, of course she had not forgotten her husband, never! He was to take these tablets right away, the doctor had said; they were as good as morphine, and very strong. She laughed again. 'Look, I've even got a few cigarettes. One of the soldiers in the patrol gave them to me. Let's see, eight, ten, twelve—wasn't that kind?'

This isn't right, Doll wanted to protest. *This is all heading in the wrong direction. We shouldn't be doing this kind of thing, getting hold of cigarettes like this, or the morphine. That business with Mrs. Schulz was already way out of order. We can't be doing this, even if I have thought to myself a hundred times that I'm all played out. We can't be doing this, otherwise we are completely finished. No more begging for cigarettes, no more running around after a shot of morphine ...*

But he said nothing. A leaden weariness had descended upon him, and the feeling of apathy had come back with renewed force. There was no point in talking to her: Alma would always do exactly as she pleased. She was so far away. It was as if he perceived and heard the world, and her, through a curtain; everything seemed somehow unconnected to him. Nothing mattered to him any more; as hard as he tried to be 'there', he couldn't do it. He had also taken the tablets, of course, the ones that had the same effect as morphine and were said to be very strong. Perhaps they would blot out these thoughts that haunted him, and transport him from this earthly abode for a while ...

He remained in this state for days on end—how many days? Later on, he couldn't say, and nor could she. At some point he awoke from an artificially induced deep sleep, and gazed at the little cellophane window. Then it was light or dark outside, day or night, but it was all the same, whatever it was—he stayed in bed anyway. What was there to get up for? He had nothing to do out there; he felt no sense of duty or responsibility.

He struggled to collect his thoughts, and then turned over slowly and looked beside him. Sometimes she was sleeping there next to him; sometimes she was gone. Sometimes he was gone, too (it sounded strange, but that was exactly the right way to put it!), and then she had nagged him to go and see a doctor. Yes, he did that, too, since she absolutely insisted, but the truth was that he stayed in bed and did nothing because he had no purpose or goal any more, was completely drained and empty ...

But generally she went herself, even though her leg was now constantly weeping pus, and all the doctors were saying she needed to be hospitalised immediately. They had quite a lot of doctors by now, but it was important that none of them knew about any of the others. Sometimes, when Alma had arranged for several of them to call on the same evening, she took fright in case they met up and it came out just how many shots she was getting every evening. But it always worked out all right. She usually got plenty of shots now, while he nearly always went without, but she made sure she got a good supply of sleeping pills for him. When the doctors came, he had to get dressed and play the healthy husband. In his own mind, he often felt like some sort of ghost, sitting there and making polite conversation about his sick wife's condition.

But if he was not able to get himself up and ready, he would go and hide in the little servants' toilet until they left, or else he squatted in the room that had been gutted by fire, and stared out at the ruins; their whole street consisted almost entirely of ruins. But they didn't depress him quite so much now; he and they seemed made for each other, somehow ...

When the doctors left, he went back to bed and soon fell asleep. Or else he lay there for hours, as if in a drugged stupor. And throughout this time, however many days it was, they did nothing, absolutely nothing at all. They didn't go to the housing office; they didn't apply for ration cards. They couldn't even be bothered to go and get the second couch. Their friends and relatives didn't hear a peep from them: they just lay there, as if struck down, stupefied, paralyzed, unable to think or do anything. The only thing that could rouse them briefly was the need to go and get more medicines, and maybe cigarettes …

They would have succumbed from weakness a long time ago, of course, if Mrs. Schulz had not looked after them, together with Dorle, a friend of the young wife's, who had turned up from somewhere—Doll didn't know where, or why. (Even in more normal times, he had never quite worked out who was who among his wife's many friends.)

But Mrs. Schulz would not have been Mrs. Schulz, always a dubious character even when she was doing good, if her ministrations for the sick couple had been in any way regular. She said she'd look in on them the next day, and then didn't show her face for two whole days. Not that it mattered that much to the Dolls—one day or three days or a week meant nothing to them now. If they got too hungry, Alma would sneak into the kitchen. A kind of friendship had developed between her and the little dancer—who was not a dancer at all, but an actress, and one of no small standing at that—and more especially with the woman's mother. Both parties had realised that the other was not as bad as they had initially thought. Alma usually returned from these trips to the kitchen with a little piece of bread, or even a jar of jam, but sometimes with only a plateful of cold potatoes or a few raw carrots. He no longer made any protest, but ate his share of whatever she'd got, before they both tried to sleep again and forget the world.

And now there was Dorle, this friend of his wife's. She was still a young girl, with a child and a mother. The mother had been in hospital since the fall of Berlin—she'd been shot in the leg, and the wound wouldn't heal. And the child had an insatiable appetite. So unlike Mrs. Schulz, Dorle was not able to help out with food for the Dolls; it was more a case of her sharing the food they had. But she cleaned the room, dusted, did the small amount of laundry there was, and dressed Mrs. Doll's wound as best she could. And she was always willing to go and fetch new doctors—more doctors in addition to the old ones. They could never have too many.

As for the Dolls' own financial situation, it would have been desperate without Mrs. Doll's diamond ring. Mrs. Schulz had managed to feed the Dolls for a week or two, but she couldn't keep it up for longer than that—presumably owing to lack of money. She hadn't said anything, but all of a sudden the white bread, decent coffee, and cigarettes stopped coming; instead of the mantra 'Cheap at the price!' the constant refrain that fell from Mrs. Schulz's lips now was: 'Dear me! The cost of everything these days!'

Then, one day, Mrs. Doll had said out of the blue that she intended to pawn her diamond ring—not sell it, she was too attached to it for that, but just pawn it. Doll had protested, but only feebly, because what other alternative did they have? They were just lying here, exhausted and ill; nobody was bringing them any money, but everything cost money—so there! Pawning was good, because it meant Alma could get her ring back again. One day, things would take a turn for the better, and they would be able to redeem the ring. (He knew very well that he was lying to himself and to her: there was not the remotest prospect of any turn for the better.) Mrs. Schulz was given the job of pawning the ring.

But the very next day she returned with the ring. She had found buyers for it, serious buyers who were prepared to pay handsomely, but nobody wanted to take it in pawn. Lending money was not a sound business proposition these days: you could earn more in a day on the black market than you could in a month from the interest payments on a loan. But there were people willing to buy the ring, and after a good deal of probing Mrs. Doll learned that twelve thousand marks had been offered for it. A good price, surely? But then it was a very fine ring: platinum setting, fiery white diamond, flawless, nearly one and a quarter carats.

In business matters, Mrs. Doll was always something of a surprise — not least to her own husband. She asked for the ring back. 'No', she said later to her husband, 'if they're offering twelve thousand, they can go to fifteen thousand, and they probably offered fifteen thousand anyway, and Schulz is planning to pocket the three thousand difference. No, I'll get Ben to sell the ring for me; he's much better connected than old mother Schulz ...'

Ben! The ring was unquestionably Alma's, a present from her first husband, and Doll had made up his mind to hold his tongue and not interfere in the matter of the sale. But now, briefly roused from his apathy and the stupor induced by too many sleeping pills, he expostulated: 'Ben, of all people! The man who treated us so shabbily!'

'That was just the two women!' countered Alma. 'Don't forget, he was really pushed for time that day.'

'He didn't even have a cigarette for you!' cried Doll.

'We often don't have any cigarettes', replied Alma. 'You leave it to me. You'll see — we'll get a much better price with Ben!'

'Do what you like!' And with that, Doll sank back into his apathy. 'I just hope Ben doesn't let you down again!'

As a result of this conversation, Mr. Ben turned up one day while the couple were still in bed, even though it was getting on for lunchtime. But Mr. Ben evinced no surprise; with greying hair but dark, fiery eyes, he kissed the young woman's hand, examined the ring closely, declared that he knew nothing about precious stones, but would see if it was possible to get the asking price of twenty thousand marks. At all events, he would certainly get the best price for it that he could — Alma could count on him. After Mr. Ben had handed over fifteen hundred marks he happened to have on him, to meet the Dolls' immediate needs, he disappeared again with the ring, kissing hands as he departed ...

Whether Mrs. Schulz was annoyed or not that the ring had been taken away from her again (and with it, perhaps, a substantial commission), the fact was she had an excellent nose for money. Mr. Ben's fifteen hundred marks had not been in the Dolls' possession for more than a few hours before Mrs. Schulz showed up with a little notebook, and it turned out that she believed she had a claim on the Dolls that exceeded this fifteen hundred by a fair amount. The Dolls listened in astonishment as she reeled off an endless litany of cigarettes, coffee, sugar, salt, cakes, and potatoes. Nor had the partition wall been forgotten, re-erected by a tradesman 'as a favour'—a favour for which he had charged handsomely. From the very first day, every item had been carefully recorded, including everything she had made out was a gift from her, and for which she had unblushingly received their heartfelt thanks. Now it was all listed here as goods supplied to order—and not 'cheap at the price', either! Indeed, they had a lurking suspicion that Mrs. Schulz had not only charged them for the cigarettes and coffee she had supplied, but also for quite a few cigarettes that had never been smoked, and quite a few cups of coffee that had never been drunk ...

Things might have come to a head on this occasion, with an almighty row that would at least have cleared the air, had it not been for the fact that neither of the Dolls could care less what happened to them. There was a brief eruption of anger—but even this took place only after Mrs. Schulz had gone (having dropped this bombshell, the good woman had had the good sense to withdraw and await the outcome from a distance)—and Alma swore they would never accept anything from old mother Schulz again, not so much as a single cigarette. So the fifteen hundred marks now changed hands again, and Ben was informed through Dorle that he needed to bring more money straightaway.

But this time Mr. Ben let a few days pass before doing anything. And when he did finally show up, he claimed that the ring had not yet been sold. He was very sorry to have to tell them that prices for gold and precious stones were falling, and that it was a bad time to be selling. He did have someone in prospect, however, who might be prepared to pay the asking price—maybe not the full twenty, but certainly nineteen or eighteen thousand. At all events: 'You know I'll do whatever I can for you, Alma!'

Meanwhile, he had brought two thousand marks with him, an advance taken out of his own pocket, and not without considerable sacrifice—as he mentioned several times.

But for now, the Dolls' boat was afloat again, the balance of their debt to Mrs. Schulz was paid off, and from then on Dorle took care of all the Dolls' shopping.

CHAPTER SEVEN

A parting of the ways

In terms of days and weeks, the Dolls would have found it impossible to say how long they had been lying on their couch. At all events, it seemed like an eternity, a time when they were never fully awake, never attending to anything beyond the most urgent necessities of life.

The young woman's need for injections of narcotics had increased in inverse proportion to the doctors' inclination to dispense them, and the abscess on her upper thigh, which had never been treated properly, was getting worse. The doctors were becoming ever more insistent: 'Either you get to hospital, or we stop treating you!'

The economic situation of the Dolls was also becoming steadily more impossible. Ben's visits became increasingly irregular, and he brought less and less money with him. The ring had still not been sold, he still had to 'make sacrifices' in order to advance them sums from his own pocket, and the amounts got steadily smaller — first a thousand marks, then only five hundred. The state of the market in precious stones was just too bad. It was not advisable to sell right now; one would not even make fifteen, and maybe a lot less than that. But he would keep on trying, true friend of Alma's that he was ...

Until one day the young woman suddenly made up her mind

and said: 'I'm going to get myself admitted to hospital today!' And a moment later she added: 'But first I'm going to take you to your sanatorium!'

This time she really meant it. The young woman displayed an energy that she had not shown for days or months past. She sorted out some underwear and toiletries for her husband, and when he asked: 'And what about you?' she just replied: 'Don't you worry about me, I can take care of myself!'

If Doll had been a little more alert and not so apathetic, he would not have ceased to wonder at his wife's sudden new-found energy; she even managed to get hold of their district mayor, and scrounged a car from him to drive her seriously ill husband to a sanatorium.

At some point, Doll awoke there from a sleep so deep that it had been more like death, without memories or dreams or any obvious sign of breathing ... Still feeling completely dazed, he turned his head with an effort, looking around him for someone to ask where he was, and where Alma was. He had always felt her presence next to him in bed, now she was gone, and he was all alone. This discovery made him very agitated, and helped to clear the fog in his brain (from the sleeping pills) more quickly; he sat up in bed and looked around him ...

The iron bedstead he was sitting in had once been painted white, but now the paint was chipped and battered; a blue check bedcover lay across his body. The room was very small, and contained nothing apart from this bedstead. The wall was painted to head height with green oil paint, and above that it was whitewashed like the ceiling, on which, very high above him, an electric light was burning. A section of the ceiling plaster had fallen off: he could see the exposed reed lathing and the boards to which it had been fixed ...

For a moment, he sat and stared at all this. He had to think where he had seen this damaged ceiling before. Then he suddenly remembered. Suddenly he recalled the night of 15–16 February 1944, when one of the worst air raids he ever experienced went on for fifty-five minutes over Berlin. For fifty-five minutes bombs had rained down in the immediate vicinity of the sanatorium, and in the next block everything had been completely flattened by an aerial mine. They—the patients and the nurses—were sitting in a completely inadequate air-raid shelter that was half above ground, and they had seen the glow of the fires in every direction. When they emerged after the all-clear, all the glass from the windows in the rooms lay scattered across the floor, most of the ceilings had collapsed, and some time that night the piece of plaster up there on the ceiling had fallen off.

He now remembered it again very clearly; suddenly it was as if he could feel the horror and the fear of that night all over again. Suddenly he had the feeling that the siren could go off any minute, and force him down into the basement for another terrible hour of torment.

But then he remembered: it was peacetime now, peacetime ... There were no more sirens going off. He could safely carry on sleeping in the sanatorium's padded cell until the morning, the padded cell that Sister Emerentia just called 'the little room'. But how had he, Mr. Doll, ended up in this little room? Had he been so disturbed? Had he been raving? Never once had he been put in here when he was staying at the sanatorium before! At least he wasn't just lying on mattresses on the floor; they had left the bedstead for him, so it couldn't have been that bad. And it was only now that he noticed they'd left the iron-lined door of the cell ajar, so he couldn't have been in a very bad way.

Doll sat up gingerly on the edge of the bed. He still felt a little shaky from the sleeping pills, but he thought he would be able to walk if he leaned against the wall now and then. He automatically looked around for his slippers and dressing gown, but then he remembered that he no longer possessed such things. So he draped the bed cover around his shoulders, stepped out into the corridor, and walked along to the lobby.

As always, sitting in the big plush armchair by the light of the little auxiliary lamp, was the night nurse. For a while, Doll observed him from a distance. No, it wasn't the nice Dutchman who had been on night duty here throughout the war, and who often enough had been dragging the last unwilling patients out of their beds and down to the basement even as the bombs were already falling. It was a nurse he didn't know. Still— !

Doll gave a small cough and walked forward. The startled nurse woke from his semi-sleep, peered into the gloom, and then leaned back, reassured, having recognised Doll. 'So, you're awake, too?' he asked. And then added: 'Mind you don't catch cold, walking around like that in your bare feet!'

'No way!' replied Doll, sitting down in a wicker chair opposite the nurse, and wrapping the bed cover around his legs. 'I never get colds. I'm a tough nut. Once I lay for half a day on the red floor tiles outside the tea kitchen back there, in winter, and it did me no harm.'

'Not my idea of fun!' said the nurse. 'What did you do that for?'

'Can't remember', said Doll. 'Probably to get some medication they wouldn't have given me otherwise. Did you come straight after Simon Boom?'

'Who's that? Oh yes, I know who you mean: the Dutch night porter. No, I didn't ever meet him. They got rid of him as soon as the war ended. I've only been here a few weeks.'

'Are any of the old staff still on the ward? I expect you've heard that I was here quite often — I'm more or less a regular on the ward.'

He said it with a touch of pride. This was a place where he had always gone when his overwrought nerves, never very strong, went completely to pieces. He'd gone through some difficult times in this place — bouts of depression when he had given up completely on himself, when he thought he was losing his mind — but always he had managed to pull himself together somehow. Suddenly, from one day to the next, he had declared himself fit again, and had gone back to his work …

He loved the place, but especially this ward with its long corridor leading to the toilets, echoing with the footsteps of patients at all hours of the day and night; this corridor with its rust-red linoleum, onto which so many white doors opened, but all without door handles — so they could only be opened by the nurses with their keys — and with big glass windows that allowed people to see into the room from outside, windows with glass so thick that even the most agitated patient could not smash it with a chair leg.

He loved the mysterious atmosphere that permeated the place after every 'exitus', the nurses standing around aimlessly, and repeatedly shuffling all the patients back into their rooms, since they were not supposed to find out about the death. It was always 'unfortunate' when someone in the sanatorium died, because all the staff felt that it reflected badly on them: people didn't come here to die; they came to get well! And generally the management were able to smuggle a dying patient out shortly before the end, and transfer him to a city hospital.

He loved the 'shock days', when the patients were treated with Cardiazol or insulin, or given electric shocks. From his room he would suddenly hear the screams of the patients being shocked as they lost consciousness, which sounded exactly like the cries of an epileptic. And then a deathly hush would descend, as if those who had been spared didn't dare move, lest they attract a similar fate.

He particularly loved sitting around—against the rules—in the 'tea kitchen', where nobody ever made tea any more but only washed up, and chatting for ages there with the nurse who had known him for many years … She gave him extra food whenever she could. He liked the woman, who was still quite young, still attractive, and had been living for twenty years now among these men who were slowly dying; despite the loss of all her illusions, she had retained her helpful disposition and mother wit.

And he loved the ward rounds, when the doctors came around in their long, spotlessly white coats; for them, each patient was just another case, which held no more interest for them once the illness had passed through the acute stage. He was quietly amused by these psychiatrists, who studied the slightest mood swings in their patients in minute detail, but for whom physical ailments simply didn't exist. He loved these doctors precisely because the older and more knowledgeable they became, the more they seemed to resemble their patients, because they seemed to be so disconnected from real life.

He loved the walks in the little, high-walled gardens, which looked nothing like gardens at all, being places of the utmost dreariness. He loved the sudden eruption of noise out in the corridor, when an agitated patient was being hustled into the padded cell or the bathroom. He loved the whole building with its dense, stifling atmosphere, its enveloping feeling of security, the life behind the narrow iron windows. It was like home to him.

'Tell me', he asked the night nurse Bachmann later, 'why am I in the bunker? Was I that agitated? Did I smash something up?'

'Not at all!' replied the nurse. 'You were as gentle as a lamb. But there were no rooms free when you arrived, so they put you in there.'

'Were you here when I arrived? Have you seen my wife?'

'No, you arrived before I came on duty, in the afternoon. I don't know anything about it. You were pretty well drugged up, I think, but then they gave you something more.'

'I see!' said Doll. And then again: 'I see!' But he didn't continue the conversation; he just sat there quietly, and drew the bed cover more tightly around him. He suddenly realised that he didn't even know which hospital Alma had been admitted to. He couldn't write to her, send her a message, or call her. He was alone: for the first time in ages, he was completely alone again, and suddenly he felt how weak he still was, and how unwell.

He stood up. Without even thinking about it, he began to walk up and down, the bed cover draped around his shoulders, just as he had spent many previous nights wandering up and down this long corridor, getting through the endless hours of insomnia.

And that was how the old night sister found him. She called out to him in her high-pitched old woman's voice, with no regard for the other patients who were sleeping: 'And here's our very own Dr. Doll again! So how are you, Doctor? How do you like it in our little room?' And with a little giggle: 'Sister Emerentia has been having a little joke, putting Mr. Doll in the little room, our old regular! Well, you needn't worry, Mr. Doll, we'll get that sorted out. It's just that we've had over two hundred notices of admission, and not a single bed free for weeks. So when someone turns up without any notification ...'

'But they did notify you', grunted Doll. It wasn't strictly true, but ...

'Of course they did!' cried the sister, becoming more and more animated and high-pitched. 'It's no disgrace to be put in the cell if you're as good and well-behaved as Dr. Doll, is it, Mr. Bachmann?'

The night nurse grunted in agreement. 'But now it's time to get back into bed. It's much too early to be running around like this—it's only half-past two … You'll catch cold otherwise!'

'Never get colds—'

'Of course you do; of course you catch cold! And if you can't sleep, I'll give you a little something to help you. What would you like to help you sleep?'

If he hadn't already been thinking it, this question was all it took to transport him back immediately to the old game they used to play there, namely to inveigle as many sleeping tablets out of the staff as they possibly could. He said dismissively: 'Look, just let me walk around for a bit! You're not going to give me anything that does any good—you're all out to cheat a poor, wretched, sick man!'

Night nurse Trudchen uttered a horrified shriek. 'Doctor, how can you say such a thing, an educated man like yourself! When have I ever cheated you? But of course', the night nurse went on, 'if someone constantly misbehaves and is always kicking up a racket, then I sometimes give him scopolamine instead of Luminal. But that's not cheating by any stretch—that's a medical procedure!'

'Aha!'

'But such a thing has never been necessary in your case, Doctor! I tell you what, I'll give you some paraldehyde. You always called that your tipple—you always liked taking that!'

'Well, yes, but how much are you going to give me?' asked Doll, now suddenly very interested. Paraldehyde was not a bad suggestion from Trudchen; she'd got the measure of her patients, having done night duty in the sanatorium for over thirty years now. She took the place of a fully qualified night-duty doctor, so the privy councillor gave her a free hand when it came to prescribing and dispensing drugs.

'How much am I going to let you have?' asked the night nurse, and gave Doll a quick, searching look to appraise how much he needed. 'Well, I'll give you a three-line dose of paral ...'

Doll yanked the bed cover around his shoulders again and made as if to carry on pacing up and down. 'You can keep your three lines, Sister Trudchen!' he replied contemptuously. 'I'd rather carry on walking all night than be fobbed off with kiddy portions.' And as he turned away, he said insistently: 'I want eight lines, at least!'

Squeals of protest, much babble, and earnest entreaties: 'You know very well, Dr. Doll, that five is the maximum dose!' But Mr. Doll was not a bit interested in such absurd made-up notions as a 'maximum dose': he was immune to poison! He'd had sixteen once (a complete fabrication). The negotiations began, with Sister Trudchen imploring and pleading, Doll acting like some stiff-backed Spaniard spurning beggarly gifts, ready to walk away at any moment, but inwardly pumped up with the excitement of the chase. He thought to himself: *You lot are pretty dumb! I'd sleep just fine without a sleeping draught—I'm still full of the stuff from before. But I'm not letting on!* In the end, they settled on a six-line dose. Doll promised to go straight to bed, and the sister agreed not to dilute the paraldehyde with water. 'And if it burns your throat, Doctor, it won't be me who's hurting!'

Doll lay in his bed again, in the little room. This hospital was all right; in its way, it was a terrific hospital. He lay in bed at his ease, hands clasped behind his head, waiting for his bitter-tasting sleeping draught. He thought briefly about Alma, but now without any sense of yearning, without feeling an urgent need to rush off and see her. That wasn't necessary. Alma was also lying in a hospital bed, her wound was being treated and dressed every day, so she too was in good hands, just like himself—no need to worry!

As always in this place, the sleeping draught was a long time coming. This was a ploy by the staff to make the drug seem like a really precious commodity—either that, or they were just slow and disorganised. The patients weren't going anywhere, after all: they could wait. Doll heard Sister Trudchen talking to the male night nurse in the nurses' room, making no attempt to keep her voice down. In the past, he had sometimes kicked up a fuss about this lack of consideration, which showed no regard for the patients' need of a good night's sleep. But now he just smiled. It was just part of life in this place. And kicking up a fuss only created problems for the management: it just meant that even more sleeping draughts had to be administered.

For a moment, Doll saw clearly that this had been a stupid conclusion to draw: it wasn't bad for the doctors if the patients were given too many drugs to make them sleep; it was only bad for the patients, who then went around all next day in a semi-stupor. In terms of Doll's case, Sister Trudchen couldn't care less whether Doll received three, eight, or sixteen lines of paraldehyde. In actual fact, he didn't need any more at all, and he felt very relaxed in bed. His limbs, which had been icy cold, were gradually warming up again; he only needed to turn over in bed and fall asleep.

But no, it was better to be knocked out all at once, to not be there any more.

There was a poem that was printed at the front of a collection of short stories by Irene Forbes-Mosse. It was called 'The little death', and began something like this: 'The little death, how gladly would I die, the little death as stars light up the sky ...'

The poet was undoubtedly talking about a very different kind of death, but Doll called this sensation of being knocked out quickly by drugs his 'Little Death'. He loved him. Recently he had thought so much about his big brother, 'Big Death': he had lived with him, cheek by jowl, so to speak; he had grown used to seeing him as the last remaining hope, which would surely not disappoint him. He just needed a little more resolve than he could summon up at the moment, and then it was done. And until he could muster that little bit more resolve, he had 'Little Death'. Right now, he was waiting for his six grams of paral, and as soon as they were inside him, he was done with all this reflection and analysis. He didn't have to torment himself any more, he didn't have to justify anything to himself any more, why Dr. Doll did this and didn't do that, because there was no Doll any more ...

All the same, it was high time they showed up with their sleeping draughts. Doll leapt out of bed and went across to the nurses' room. The door was open, and the night nurse had already seen him. 'Here's Dr. Doll again! Come on, Sister, give him his stuff now!'

The sister had already picked up the brown bottle, and said (still smarting from Mr. Doll's unwarranted suspicion): 'The Doctor can see for himself that I'm not cheating him! As if I ever would! I'm more likely to give you too much than too little!'

And she poured it out. The characteristic smell of paral wafted through the room — and a vile smell it is, if truth be told. But to Doll it smelt good, wonderful! He watched closely as she poured it out, and even nodded in agreement when the sister exclaimed: 'You see that, you've nearly got seven there! Now, aren't I good to you, Doctor?'

But he was no longer in the mood for talk. He had the little medicine glass in his hand; at last, at long last, he had deep sleep, Little Death, in his hand, and was completely enveloped by the scent. He was done with talking now. His face had taken on an earnest, almost sombre, expression: he was by himself now, just him and his sleep. He tipped the entire contents of the glass into his mouth at once. It burned his throat more fiercely than the strongest schnaps, it felt like it was eating into the lining of his mouth, and made it impossible to breathe. Much as he didn't want to, he had to take two little gulps of water to dilute this—wonderful—taste of death. Then he looked at his two companions again, murmured a brief 'Night!' and went back to his cell, into his bed. He lay there for a moment, hands clasped behind his head, gazing up at the light.

His head seemed to fill with moving clouds, he tried to focus his thoughts on this and that, but already he was gone from this world, into the arms of his beloved Little Death ...

At some point he would wake up again, and each time his mood was different. Sometimes he would lie sullenly in his cell for hours, hardly speaking at all, and when the doctor came on his ward round he refused to volunteer any information. Or else he would cry quietly to himself for hours on end; at such times, he felt full of pity for himself and his wasted life, and felt as if he was going to die. On days like these, he wouldn't eat or drink anything: let them watch him croak in his stinking cell ... And then on other days he was in a sunny mood, and with his bed cover wrapped around his shoulders he would scoot around all over the place, talking to the other patients.

The young ward doctor was friendly with him, tried to help him, and wanted to understand where this mixture of apathy and despair in Doll came from. But Doll didn't want to talk about it; maybe he would never be able to talk about it, not even to his wife, to Alma. Maybe he would be able to write himself free of it one day—but only when it was all behind them. Sometimes he believed he would get well again, that there would be something there again to fill up the emptiness inside him. But those times were the exception.

Mostly he tried to throw the young doctor off the scent; he would tell him something about his life, talk about books, encourage the young doctor to talk about himself—about the bad pay, the even worse food, the long hours he had to work, the arrogant way the privy councillor treated his staff. Or else he tried to winkle information out of the young doctor about the different ways of committing suicide. He was very clever at doing this: he found out about cyanide, morphine, scopolamine, about dosages that were guaranteed to be fatal; about how to inject air into the veins to cause an embolism; about insulin, which enabled someone to commit suicide in a way that was virtually undetectable later. He was gathering information: he wanted to be ready when the time came and he felt strong enough to do 'it', to take the only way out that was still left to a German today.

PART TWO

Recovery

CHAPTER EIGHT

Voluntary discharge

While Doll was leading a life of idleness up on 'Men's Ward III', albeit forced to be a little more wide-awake each day as the dosage of sleeping drugs was progressively reduced, it could not escape his attention as the ward's resident patient that the other patients on the ward were now a very different bunch from before. The paralytics and schizophrenics had given way completely to a relatively transitory clientele, which appeared to be neither mentally ill nor emotionally disturbed.

These patients generally arrived in the evening, and were rarely accompanied by relatives. There was often a kind of strange, unreal hilarity about them, and they were very ready to engage in conversation and to dispense the most expensive English and American cigarettes with a generous hand. Later on, they would be taken off to the bathroom, with some gentle persuasion, by two male nurses, and while they were sitting in the bathtub the ward sister and the female nurse would go through their belongings very thoroughly. Doll sometimes watched them, and saw how they checked every corner of the pockets and every envelope with meticulous care, whereas earlier they had been content just to remove anything with a blade or point, and perhaps the dressing-gown cord as well, which some depressives used to commit suicide.

When the new arrivals emerged from the bath they were put to bed immediately, despite all their protests. There was no more chatting with the other patients. A nurse stood guard by their bed, the young doctor appeared, usually an intravenous injection was given, and the patient fell asleep. He was usually kept in this comatose state for a week. But sometimes there would be a lot of noise coming from the room—shouting and screaming, and the sound of feet dragging across the floor—and through the window in the door, Doll would catch a glimpse of a figure in pyjamas, wrestling with the sister and a male nurse, and hear him saying: 'You're driving me crazy! I want to …' And the soothing voice of reason: 'If you could just hold on for a moment, Doctor!' (Nearly all these patients were addressed as 'Doctor'.) 'The doctor is on his way …'

And sure enough, the doctor summoned by telephone quickly arrived on the scene—quite often it was the privy councillor himself—fresh injections were given, different sleeping drugs administered, and everything quietened down again.

Once this first week was past, the patient appeared from time to time, leaning on the arm of the nurse. Puffy-faced and drugged up to the eyeballs, he would make his way to or from the toilet, and it was not uncommon for him to stop part-way, lean his head against the wall, and groan: 'I can't go on, I just can't go on! What an idiot I was to come here!'

Idiots or not, it was obvious even to a layman that these patients made rapid progress. By the third week, most of them were wandering up and down the corridor fully dressed, leaning against the window, gazing outside and declaring impatiently: 'It's high time I got out of this place!' And for the most part they did disappear again quite quickly, especially the ones who were actually entitled to be addressed as 'Doctor', and new patients of a similar sort moved into their rooms.

Even someone less familiar with such places than Doll would have worked out after three days what was going on with these patients. So when one of these 'Doctors' spoke quite openly to Doll one day, he wasn't telling him anything he did not already know: 'It's all right for you, my dear fellow, you can stay here as long as you like. But I've got to get out again as soon as possible. I don't want anyone outside to know that I'm here, or why I'm here.'

Of course they didn't want anyone to know. They were medical doctors, after all, doctors who'd become addicted to morphine, who came here to be cured of their addiction in complete secrecy, and in particular without the knowledge of the feared public health authority. The fact that most of them were doctors was due to the circumstance that they had ready access to morphine at a time when it was in very short supply. If the drug had been more widely available and easy to buy, then doubtless three-quarters of the German population would have used it to anaesthetise themselves against the malady of the age—a mixture of bottomless despair and apathy.

So it was mainly doctors or other people with plenty of money who could afford the black-market prices for morphine. They began with one or two injections. These were enough to take away their cares, so that cold, hunger, the pain of loss—whether of people or of things—no longer troubled them. But gradually they had to increase the dose. What had worked a week earlier no longer worked now. So it was a case of step up the dose, and then step it up some more. In the beginning, they had only injected themselves at night, before going to bed, and then the afternoons began to drag, and another shot was just the thing to help them get through that, and eventually they could no longer get up in the mornings to face an endless grey day. In the end, they had used so much morphine that either the chemists had become suspicious or they had completely lost their zest for work. Or else their wives, relatives, or friends began to distrust them, and their marriage, their whole social standing, and their livelihood were put at risk: a man addicted to morphine was no longer a doctor who brought healing, but a sick man who was a danger to others. So they quickly disappeared inside a sanatorium. To the outside world, they were suffering from angina, and a friendly colleague stepped in as a locum — just as long as the public health authority, the body to which they were answerable, didn't find out about it.

Doll looked upon this endless succession of addicts as companions in suffering, people just like himself, who despaired of themselves and of Germany, who had broken down under the weight of all the humiliations and obscenities, and sought refuge in some artificial paradise. Just like himself, they were all seeking their own 'Little Death'. Maybe they all still cherished a tiny hope that kept them from taking the ultimate step; maybe they all still needed — just like Doll — that last, final push. Everywhere people were escaping from the present, refusing to shoulder the burden that a shameful war had laid upon all Germans.

But behind his own person, behind all these transient visitors up on Men's Ward III, loomed a dark and menacing multitude: the entire German nation. There had been a time, a time of illusion it had been, but during this time Doll had known that he was not lying all alone in that huge bomb crater: the entire German nation was in there with him. As the morphine-addicted doctors had cut themselves off from this nation, so too had Doll. Walking up and down the rust-red linoleum of the corridor at night for hours on end, lying in bed in his cell for hours on end, staring up at the ceiling light, he reflected and pondered, looked back over the road he had travelled to get here, deeper and deeper into selfish isolation — running away like a coward from the job they were all called upon to do …

But the German nation was out there. It could not be denied or argued away; it was there, and he belonged to it. While he was sitting idly in here, featherbedding himself, living off the charity extended to him by this place, in consideration of the times he had stayed here before, the German people were hard at work. They had cleared away the tank traps and the rubble from the streets, and were now repairing roofs and winter-proofing people's homes. They retrieved burnt-out machinery and got it working again. They were hungry, they were cold, but they repaired the railway tracks, dug for potatoes in the icy October rain, and hiked along the highways in endless columns, making do with next to nothing.

While Doll was gazing enviously at the extra rations of the other patients, the milk was drying up in the breasts of mothers and children who were starving to death. While Doll was arguing with the night-duty nurse over an extra sleeping draught, old women and men, exhausted beyond endurance, were lying down in roadside ditches or in the rain-soaked forest to fall asleep for the last time. While soldiers returning home were looking for everything — their old home, their wives and children, food and work, week after week, never giving up hope — it was too much effort for Dr. Doll to go and speak to some official about their apartment and their ration cards. While Doll lived the life of a freeloader, supported by the proceeds from the sale of his wife's jewellery, and complained bitterly that the money wasn't falling into his lap fast enough, money that he promptly squandered anyway, frail girls were doing hard, physical labour, so poorly paid that they couldn't afford to buy a cigarette — at prices that Doll had long since come to regard as normal.

The fact of the matter was that he had lost his way completely, and had lapsed into a shamefully useless and idle, parasitic existence. He saw clearly the path that had led him to the padded cell in this place, sinking deeper and deeper into the swamp and quagmire since that day, 26 April. And yet he had no idea how he could have gone down this path. How had he got himself into such a state over a harmless schmuck like Piglet Willem? And how come he had let himself get so worked up about the beer wholesaler Zaches? He'd always known what these Nazis were like, after all. All this pointless running around after doctors and sleeping drugs and injections, which didn't change anything, and just made every decision that had to be taken even harder!

And then there was something else as well. This Dr. Doll who had just come to his senses a bit, this writer of books who had thought he had nothing more to write, this brooding self-doubter, who had thought himself completely empty and drained, this ex-mayor who had not been up to the job, this father and husband who had forgotten all about his wife and children — suddenly he thought about his children, and, full of concern, he thought about his wife, too. Now that Doll felt he was getting better, and that there might still be some sort of work for him to do in this life, in the midst of a population that was labouring with grim determination once more, he suddenly remembered his wife, and felt fearful on her account.

By this time, Doll was getting some news of his wife. She hadn't written, of course, but one day Dorle turned up to see him, his wife's loyal friend, and she had brought him a brand-new nightshirt, and cigarettes, and half a loaf of bread. Yes indeed, his wife was thinking of him, she never forgot him, she was worried about him, and she took care of him. She loved him, and he loved her — once more.

He'd just forgotten the fact while he was ill, that was all.

Doll smoked, and wolfed down half the white loaf at a single sitting. Dorle sat on the edge of the bed and talked. She told him that Alma was the darling of everyone at the hospital, even the strict, devout nuns, and that everyone there spoiled her, including the doctors. Her wound had been really bad; the infection had gone quite deep because of the delay in treatment. But now it was looking better; they had sprinkled sugar in the wound, an old home remedy, and since then it was a lot better ...

And Alma had a bit of money again. Ben had eventually—after many phone calls—turned up at the hospital and had brought money with him, though only two-and-a-half thousand. Apparently he had said that with the continuing fall in the market for diamonds he had only been able to get eleven thousand in total, and he just hadn't been able to make any more. Alma had been furious with Ben, and she had forbidden her, Dorle, to mention the matter to Doll; Dorle implored him not to let on to Alma that he knew. A woman who shared the room with Alma, and who was very knowledgeable about the black market, had apparently told Alma that a ring like the one she had described would easily fetch twenty-five thousand marks, maybe even thirty thousand. 'So you can just imagine how angry Alma was', said Dorle, and added that she was done with her good friend Ben once and for all.

Doll shared her anger, but his anger was mixed with mild gratification, since no husband can avoid feeling a little jealous of his wife's former men friends, and is always glad to see the back of them. He listened patiently, therefore, when Dorle diffidently, but understandably, sang her own praises—how she was such a good friend to Alma, willing to do anything for her, through thick and thin. And as he listened to her prattling on, he thought to himself:

My dear, good, stupid Dorle! You, too, will only be such a good friend to Alma for as long as you can still get something out of her. And Alma must know this herself. Do you think I haven't noticed that there you are, all innocent and unassuming, already lighting up the third of the ten cigarettes you brought me? I bet you do the same with Alma, even though she's very willing to share—much too willing, in fact, and quite extravagant; she wants to share rather than have her things pilfered from her. And one day it will be all over with her as far as the friendly feelings are concerned—and that includes you!

Such were Doll's thoughts, but he kept them to himself, asking instead how it was going with his wife's painkilling injections. Here again, Dorle had all the answers. To begin with, Alma had had quite a few injections, but then the senior consultant had laid down the law, and now the patient was allowed just one small shot at night, and not every night at that. So she had to stage an elaborate little routine first with the young night-duty doctor, which usually achieved the desired result, the young doctor readily succumbing to her charms when she begged, pouted, cried, wailed, laughed, turned her face to the wall, and sulked—then immediately leapt out of bed when the doctor turned to leave and clung on to him, only to go through the whole rigmarole all over again. And if that failed to do the trick, the doctor was very amenable to foreign cigarettes, which he could not afford on his small salary. So Alma usually ended up getting her evening shot—according to Dorle.

Having reflected on this news for a couple of days, Doll decided it was time for him to go and check on Alma for himself. And anyway, it would be very nice to see the look of joy and surprise on his young wife's face when her seriously ill husband suddenly appeared in the door of her room. Doll knew the privy councillor, and rightly doubted whether he would give him permission at this stage to go out on his own into the city. Doll was right in the middle of coming off his sleeping medication, and his moods had not yet quite stabilised; so the doctors were likely to suspect that if he went off into the city on his own, he would try to get hold of additional sedatives or other, more powerful drugs. That's what these doctors were like, or so their patients thought—and therefore Dr. Doll, too: always distrusting their patients, and never able to distinguish the goats from the sheep.

But if Doll was acquainted with the privy councillor and his suspicious ways, he was also familiar with the routines of the establishment, and it was around them that he now constructed his plan to slip out of the locked-down Men's Ward III for a city visit. After lunch, when one shift of nurses was going off for their break and the next shift was returning from theirs, in that moment of transition when nobody was really in charge on the ward, Doll audaciously claimed that someone had phoned through to say that he should report to the office briefly to discuss his account.

'Well, you'd better get along to the office then!' said the male nurse with casual indifference, and unlocked the door for him.

Doll descended the stairs. The stairs reminded him that he was still very unsteady on his feet, and that this outing into the city was really quite a bold undertaking. Steps now struck him as a funny sort of arrangement; they were never quite where you expected them to be. His knees wobbled, and a light sweat immediately broke out on his brow. But he had successfully got past the first obstacle, and now it was time to tackle the second one, the main door out of the building. Sitting in the porter's lodge was a girl who was always alert, and she would never press the button to open the door without good reason.

Doll tapped on the window of the lodge and then said amiably to the face that peered out: 'The privy councillor phoned through to the ward—he wants me to go and see him in the spa house.' (This was the main building of the sanatorium, where the privy councillor also resided.) 'I'm Doll, by the way, from Men's Ward III upstairs.'

The girl nodded, then gave him a searching look. She said 'I know', but this 'I know' was in reference only to Doll's name and ward number.

Doll smiled again. 'Maybe you should call the privy councillor', he said softly, 'just to check that it's OK.'

But even before he finished the sentence she had made up her mind. She pressed the button, and the door lock buzzed. Doll said 'Thanks!', and he was standing outside in the grounds. The gate to the grounds was unlocked, and beyond that the street was just a few steps away.

But he said to himself: *I mustn't go out into the street here—the girl might be watching me through the window. I must go through the grounds to the spa house, and use the exit there. She was a little bit suspicious, I thought. It's good that I'm only wearing my suit, and don't have my hat and coat. Nobody goes out dressed like this in late November. Lucky she doesn't know that I don't own a hat or coat!*

He smiled to himself. He strolled through the grounds, hands in pockets, expecting any minute to run into a doctor or nurse who would not be taken in so easily. But he was in luck, and he managed to get past the main villa unchallenged and on to the street, where he now quickened his pace and headed off towards the underground station.

It was damned cold, though. Hopefully, Alma would soon be up and about, and the first thing they needed to do was to go back to the small town and fetch some different clothes more suited to the time of year. Well, no, the first thing was to sort out the business with their apartment and the ration cards. They had a lot to do before he could settle down to work in earnest again!

It was really too cold for the summer suit he was wearing, and he was glad when he was finally sitting in the underground train, where it was a little warmer. Now his teeth weren't chattering quite so much. People couldn't stop staring at him because he was so lightly clad, but let them take him for a fitness fanatic if they wanted to ...

He sat on a bench, his hands between his knees, his face leaning forward slightly so that it stayed in the shadows. He felt dreadful, overcome with nausea, and the sweating he had experienced on the stairs started again. Those damned dried vegetables he'd had for lunch! It made him feel sick just to think of it. Had they gone through the whole war eating dried vegetables, just to have them dished up now in peacetime, with a helping of mouse droppings?! *It's outrageous—the noble privy councillor can't get rich quickly enough!*

But a moment later, Doll had to admit that it was not the dried vegetables that had made him feel ill. He did get two second helpings from the male nurse Franz, after all—and the mouse droppings may not have been mouse droppings at all, but perhaps a bit of burnt turnip. The truth is, it was just too soon for this little jaunt. He wasn't properly well again yet. And it was too cold!

He felt this especially keenly as he made his way slowly from the last underground station to the hospital. It was not very far—a ten-minute walk normally—but today it took him half an hour. He was no longer feeling cheerful, and not especially looking forward to seeing Alma again. Tripping over a granite paving slab that had been dislodged by a bomb, all he could think about on the wearisome trek to the hospital was the even more wearisome return journey afterwards—that, and the reception that awaited him at the sanatorium. They'd be looking for him by now. The male nurse and the girl in the porter's lodge who had let him out would be getting it in the neck. There would be big trouble when he got back! Well, he was already in the little room, so they could hardly put him anywhere worse by way of punishment. Was this endless road going to go on forever? And then it began to drizzle—just the sort of weather you wanted for a little jaunt like this!

But when he was taken to Alma by one of those nuns whose smile, like something lifted from a painting of the Madonna, always has a mysteriously unsettling quality about it, and he found himself standing in the door of Alma's hospital room, and saw her lying there in bed—her back turned towards him, her face to the wall, probably sleeping—and when the lady in the other bed said: 'Mrs. Doll, I think you have a visitor ...', then all that he had been through was suddenly forgotten.

He placed a finger on his lips, took three quick steps forward to her bed, and said softly: 'Alma! Alma! My very own Alma! My darling!'

She slowly turned over, and he could see that she literally doubted the evidence of her own eyes. But suddenly her face shone with joy, she beamed with delight, stretched out her arms towards him, and whispered: 'Where have you suddenly sprung from? I thought you were in the sanatorium!'

He was already on his knees at her bedside, and threw his arms around her, his head resting against her breast. He smelt the old familiar scent of his wife, which he'd been deprived of for so long, and whispered: 'I've run away from them, Alma! I was missing you so much, I couldn't stand it any more, so I just took off ...'

What bliss to be together again, and to feel that there was a place for him somewhere in this icy-cold world of loneliness and destruction! Bliss and happiness, he had found them again—when for so long he had thought that he could never be happy again! To hear how she introduced him with pride to her roommate: 'This is my husband!' And he knew he was just an ageing man in a crumpled and far from pristine summer suit, looking crumpled and anything but pristine himself. But she didn't see any of that, because she loved him, quite simply, and was blind to the rest.

Later on, he sat with her on the edge of the bed and they told each other what they had been doing—dear God, they had so much to tell! They talked about the doctors they had, and about the other patients and the nurses, and about the food, where Alma had had much better luck than him, the poor man! She made him eat some bread that she still had, and also the soup that she got instead of afternoon coffee. She waved some money in the air, and a nurse went off to fetch cigarettes. Oh yes, the money: the two-and-a-half thousand, the balance owing from Ben and the last money she had received, it was nearly all gone already. Money didn't last long with her. He needed a nightshirt, after all (five hundred marks!), she needed a nightshirt (seven hundred!)—and now these cigarettes! *The crooks around here charge her fifteen marks for American cigarettes! They know she is confined to a hospital bed, and can't do anything for herself.*

But she laughed about it, laughed about the extortionate prices, laughed about the money that was draining away: live for today, that was her motto! It would all work out somehow. She was twenty-four years old, and somehow it had always worked out so far, something had always turned up. And something would turn up now! Once they were back together again, they would do things differently this time. They would fetch their belongings from the small town; they still owned many things of value, so they could live on their hump for a whole year. They would set up home in a lovely apartment, and she would open a shop on the Kurfürstendamm, selling men's ties. Only very expensive merchandise, mind you, preferably from England! She knew a thing or two about the business—she'd once worked in the most exclusive men's outfitters, as he surely remembered? She would see to it that she only attracted a clientele with real money; she had a nose for such things.

Meanwhile, while she was earning money in this way, he would write a great book that would make him a household name again overnight. But he wouldn't only write, he would also spend some of his time looking after their child, Petta. The child must get used to being around him a lot more; she must learn to love him properly, and never to think of him as her stepfather.

She chattered on. She saw no obstacles anywhere, and could only imagine everything turning out well. He listened to her, and nodded or looked reflective, but none of it signified. She was a child; today's plans would be forgotten tomorrow, and tomorrow there would be other plans, other hopes. He was happy to let her concoct the most outlandish plans, because they would never come to anything. And yet he felt himself infected by her spirit and energy, by this bubbling youthful vitality: breaking out of the sanatorium like this might have been premature, but it was a first independent step, a nod to the future!

So they sat and chatted tenderly about the past and the future, until the light was switched on in the room, which by now was in darkness, and a nun was standing in the doorway, her hand resting on the switch; as their startled faces quickly drew apart, she smiled her Madonna's smile and said: 'Supper is about to be served! I think it's time for you to go home, Mr. Doll.'

They had been so absorbed in their long conversation that they were quite oblivious to everything around them. They hadn't noticed that the light was failing and that it had now become dark. The dance music on the radio had ended a long time ago, and now some man or other, speaking with a lisp, was giving a speech about the necessity for paying taxes. Even so, Doll didn't leave straightaway. He would be getting back to the sanatorium much too late now anyway. Maybe they wouldn't even save his supper for him, just to annoy him, but right now he couldn't care one way or the other.

The last cigarette, the very last one left, they now smoked together: 'You take three puffs, then I'll take three, then you take the next three. But hey, no cheating in my favour — that was only two puffs!'

'You must come back tomorrow!' insisted Alma as he was leaving.

'Tomorrow?' he replied with a smile. 'I doubt if I'll be able to come again tomorrow. They'll want to keep me under lock and key for a while as punishment.'

'Oh, you'll find a way!' she opined confidently. 'You can do anything if you put your mind to it.' He just smiled at this compliment. 'And', she added quickly, 'if you can't come tomorrow, then come in three or four days' time! Just keep thinking to yourself that I'm lying here just waiting for you to come.'

He kissed her. 'Bye for now, my dear! As soon as I can!'

'As soon as you can! Bye! Get back safely — oh you poor thing, you'll be frozen out there!'

And he was indeed chilled to the bone on the way home, and glad when he finally reached the sanatorium. From the moment he pressed the bell and the door lock started to buzz, all he could think about, despite the cold, was the reception that awaited him, and he fervently hoped they would go easy on him.

The girl who had opened the door for him, and who was now looking through the lodge window, was the same one who had opened up for him in the afternoon after he had told her a bare-faced lie. She was about to open up her little window, but then thought better of it. Doll climbed the stairs with a sigh of relief, and thought: *Well, I've got over the first hurdle …*

But what am I like? he thought to himself as he was going upstairs. *I'm acting as if I've been summoned to the headmaster's study for playing truant at school. Am I a boy of thirteen, or a man of fifty-two? It's exactly the same feeling I had back then, and now it even smells the same as it did in the Prinz Heinrich grammar school in Grunewaldstrasse! That tingling, expectant sensation of fear, that smell of dry, dead dust warmed by the sun … It's true: we never leave school for the rest of our lives. Not me at any rate. I am and always will be the old grammar-school boy, and I'm still doing the same stupid things I did back then!*

Now he pressed the bell button for Men's Ward III. As always, he had a long wait before somebody opened the door. The old senior nurse looked at him for a moment, as if about to say something, but then let him in without a word. *So that's hurdle No.2,* Doll thought to himself.

Many patients were sitting around in the lobby, as always during the hour between supper and bedtime, while others were marching up and down the long corridor with angry impatience. This was the time when even patients who had lain listlessly in bed all day now got up. Driven by a vague sense of restlessness, perhaps impelled by an unconscious yearning for freedom, they stood or wandered around aimlessly, hardly speaking, until sleep came — generally dispensed by the night nurse in the form of potions, tablets, or injections.

Doll made his way without a word through this gathering of fellow sufferers, and they in turn paid very little heed to him. That was the big advantage of this ward for 'difficult' patients, that you could behave just as you wanted: talking to all and sundry today, not saying a word to anybody tomorrow, being cheery today, and smashing the place up tomorrow. Nothing came as a surprise, and the staff took everything in their stride.

Doll found his little room, the cell, locked up. Not only the inner door with its little glass spyhole was shut, but also the padded, sound-absorbing outer door. This was an awful lot of trouble to take over the possessions of a man who owned next to nothing. All right, so they had secured a very small piece of soap, a nightshirt, and a comb against possible theft by a kleptomaniac colleague; but now he needed to get into his room! He was dead tired and hungry, and hopefully they had left his supper there in the cell for him, so that he wouldn't have to go off and find it.

'Mr. Ohnholz', said Doll politely to the male nurse who was then walking past obliviously, 'could you please unlock my cell for me?'

'Your cell?' replied the nurse with a faint grin, and proceeded to do nothing of the kind. 'Bartel from Room 14 has been in there since this afternoon. He was a bit agitated, if you follow me.'

'And where am I supposed to live now? In Room 14?' inquired Doll, and still couldn't quite believe what now seemed the most obvious inference.

'I couldn't tell you!' replied the male nurse with a shrug of his shoulders, and was already walking away. 'As far as I know, no other arrangements have been made.'

Very nice—just what I wanted to hear! thought Doll, and carried on to the tea kitchen. *Well, we'll see about that—time will tell ...*

Sitting in the tea kitchen was his old friend, Nurse Kleinschmidt. They'd sat together trembling with fear in the air-raid shelter a few dozen times, and shared the last cigarette and the last of the real coffee between them when the raid was over.

'Well?' inquired Kleinschmidt, as Doll sat down without a word on the wooden chair on the far side of the kitchen table. 'Well? I thought you'd discharged yourself, Mr. Doll?'

'Just a little unauthorised visit to see my sick wife', replied Doll. 'And in the meantime they've occupied my bunker! Just like the boss, playing God Almighty!'

'God Almighty is always right!' said the nurse, nodding in agreement. She had as little time for the privy councillor as Doll, and she had known her boss for nigh on twenty years. 'You know what, Mr. Doll', she went on, and looked at him meaningfully through narrowed eyes: 'If I were you, I would settle for voluntary discharge ...', and then after another pause: 'I wouldn't wait until they kick up a fuss and chuck me out of a place that has made so much money from me. I'd rather chuck myself out!'

Doll thought hard about this for a moment. It was getting on for eight o'clock. 'Have I still got time to catch a train into the city?' he asked.

'Plenty of time!'

I'll get into the house somehow. Mrs. Schulz won't be very pleased to see me again, but I'll straighten things out with her somehow. It's all happening a little faster than I had planned, my return to the world, to an active life, but Kleinschmidt is quite right: it's better to be doing than to get done!

'Well?' asked the nurse again, and gave him a searching look.

'Right you are!' he replied, and got to his feet as he spoke. 'I'll see you again, my dear, or rather I won't see you again — not in this place, anyway!'

'Hang on a moment!' cried the nurse, and didn't take his proffered hand. 'You haven't had your supper yet! Wait, I'll get you something!' And from the warming cabinet she took out a dish of potatoes with carrots. She added some bread, four or five slices.

'I can't take that!' protested Doll. 'That's more than my bread allowance. I don't want you to stint yourself on my account.'

'Don't talk such rubbish', said Kleinschmidt. 'I'm only giving you what's going spare.' And by way of explanation: 'Old Bartel had a little turn earlier, and now we've given him an injection that he won't wake up from before tomorrow. So he won't be needing any supper—that's why!'

'Well, in that case, thanks very much!' said Doll, and fell to eating like a ravenous wolf. While he was eating, the nurse slowly and deliberately rolled herself a cigarette from various butt ends, lit it from the gas flame in the warming cabinet, and began asking Doll questions about his wife's condition, where he planned to live, what sort of possessions he still had, and above all, what his prospects were …

'Well, there now', she said when he had finished, clearing away the plate and replacing it with a mug of milky coffee and a plate of bread and jam, 'now you can start all over again, like the rest of us. It can't do you any harm. And it'll put paid to any silly ideas!'

Doll protested: 'But this bread and jam don't come from here. Someone else has brought them in—they don't serve jam butties here. And anyway, I'm completely full up.'

'For a grown man, you don't half carry on!' she said in a gently teasing tone. 'Just be glad that you can eat your fill before the lean times come! Eat up, man!' she cried, now sounding piqued. 'Did I say anything when you gave me the last of your coffee and your last cigarette on the morning of 16 February 1944?! Well then', she went on, calming down now that he was eating, 'why do you men always have to make such a fuss? You're worse than a bunch of old maids!'

Later on, as he was getting ready to leave, she pushed a 'proper' cigarette — as opposed to the home-made variety — across the table towards him, together with a twenty-mark note. 'Now I hope', she said sternly, 'you're not going to act all coy again! And I won't object if you bring me back two cigarettes instead of one. I'll expect the money back by the end of the month — point of honour, okay? And now get the hell out of here! I've put your things in a cardboard box; there's still room in there for more. And by the way, the last underground train must have gone by now. But the walk to Wilmersdorf is nothing for a strong young man like yourself — especially at this time of year. You may catch pneumonia — which is no bad thing! The way things are, you'll save yourself a lot of trouble!'

CHAPTER NINE

Robinson Crusoe

The last underground train really had left, and the walk in the dark through a bombed-out Berlin was no bad thing—just as Kleinschmidt had said. Sometimes Doll, who knew Berlin like the back of his hand, actually had no idea where he was. There were hardly any people on the streets to ask, and those he did see hurried on past him so fast, as if they were afraid of him—which they very probably were. Sometimes Doll himself felt a kind of horror creep over him, so monstrous did this nocturnal stone jungle appear, across which a November wind was blowing dark storm clouds. And yet something had changed inside him. When he arrived in Berlin, he had thought: *I'll never be able to work in this city of the dead!* But now he thought to himself defiantly: *But I* will *work here, even so! In spite of everything! Or because of it!*

He had to wait a long time outside the locked building. The doorbell was disconnected, and nobody seemed to want to go inside. It was very cold, and Doll's teeth were chattering. But he steadfastly resisted the temptation to revive his spirits by choosing this moment to smoke the cigarette that Kleinschmidt had given him: he had decided to save it until he was lying in bed, when he was really 'at home', in the house that was actually going to become a home for them—if he had anything to do with it. He also dismissed the fear that he might be waiting all night for someone to turn up with a key to the front door, because everyone who lived there had already come home: *No,* he told himself, *I won't be standing here all night; there'll be someone still to come. Any time now — I can feel it in my bones!*

For a long time, it seemed that his bones were playing tricks on him. Then a tall, lanky young man came round the corner and said with surprise: 'Ah, Dr. Doll, it's you! Forgotten your front-door key? And here you are, standing in the freezing cold without a coat!'

They knew each other, the way Berliners got to know each other in the air-raid shelters — in passing, exchanging names, telling each other what they did for a living, and trying to decide whether the other was a rabid Nazi with whom one needed to guard one's tongue. Doll was about to respond with some pleasantry or other, but then said, since the young man was known to be 'a decent sort': 'To tell you the truth, I don't have a front-door key as yet, nor a coat. We arrived here in Berlin pretty much cleaned out — like so many others today!'

The stairwell, where all the broken windowpanes had been replaced with cardboard, felt pleasantly warm to him after standing outside in the cold and wind. 'Ah!' he said, 'it's nice to be in the warm!'

His companion murmured his slightly surprised assent, and inquired after his 'good lady wife'. Mr. Doll informed him that she was in hospital, unfortunately, but that he hoped to have her home again soon. The young man said that he hoped so, too, and looked forward to seeing the young lady again soon — she had always helped to boost morale in the air-raid shelter. He — along with all the other residents of the building — had always admired her steady nerve during the worst of the air raids. Her carefree cheeriness had been an example and a comfort to many — including him, as he freely confessed.

The two men parted with a handshake that was unexpectedly hearty. Then Doll climbed up the next flight of stairs and rang the bell by the door of Mrs. Schulz's apartment—or rather, his own apartment. He pushed the doorbell hard and repeatedly. He had the cardboard box with his things under his arm, and, despite the 'pleasantly warm' stairwell, he still felt a chill running down his back.

Eventually, the door was opened, just as he switched on the emergency lighting in the stairwell for the eighth time. And again it was the young actress who opened the door to him for this, the start of his second life in Berlin. Alma had since discovered, of course, that this young woman was not at all as mean-spirited and snippy as she had appeared that first morning. On the contrary, she had often displayed great generosity in helping out the Dolls when they were short of food.

Having opened the door, she said: 'Oh, it's you, Mr. Doll! And at such a late hour! Come into the kitchen with me for a moment; I'm just heating up some food for the baby on the stove, and anyway it's a bit warmer in there with the gas on!'

Doll sat down wearily on the kitchen chair between the gas stove and the table, the same chair on which his wife had sat so forlornly that September morning, and the bit of warmth from the gas stove really was very pleasant. Miss Gwenda stirred her pan of puréed food, and said: 'Are you really feeling better now, Mr. Doll? You don't look all that well, I have to say, and if I was going to collect firewood in the forest I wouldn't be taking you along, that's for sure!'

'Oh yes, I'm quite well again', replied Doll, not entirely truthfully, for at that precise moment he was feeling particularly wretched and low. 'It's the hospital air that's made me look so poorly', he added by way of explanation, not wishing Miss Gwenda to get the idea that their shambolic way of life, lying around and going without food and sponging off others, was going to start all over again. 'All these weeks I haven't been out in the fresh air at all until today. I also went to see my wife, and it was probably all a bit too much for me on my first outing.'

Miss Gwenda inquired solicitously after the health of his young wife, and so it was quite a while before Doll was able to ask about his room. Was Mrs. Schulz there today? Was she already in bed? Was it possible to speak to her?

Yes. Miss Gwenda reckoned 'yes'—Mrs. Schulz *was* sleeping here today, as far as she knew. But she couldn't say if she'd already switched her light off. So Doll crept along on tiptoe to the door of 'his' room and peered through the keyhole. Everything was in darkness. He listened at the door for a long time. He could hear someone breathing in their sleep—a soft, wheezing sort of sound followed by a gentle whistle—and he knew now for certain that tonight he could kiss goodbye to a good night's sleep. As for a warm bed ... It looked like he wouldn't get to enjoy that nice, quiet smoke, courtesy of Nurse Kleinschmidt.

When he got back to the kitchen, Miss Gwenda and her purée were gone, and the gas was turned off. Here, too, things had shut down for the day without him. He stood there for a while, looking round the kitchen. It was indubitably his, her, the Dolls' kitchen; every item in it belonged to them, not just the furniture, but also every spoon, whisk, pan, and plate. But when he went to look inside the big, wide kitchen dresser, he found every door locked and the keys removed.

It's a funny old world, he thought. *They really ought to ask us, at least, and they ought to be paying us a bit of rent, too. What* is *the position with the rent on the apartment?* he suddenly wondered. *Miss*

Gwenda and her little family have only been living here since the end of
August, but as for old Mother Schulz, who's so good at keeping accounts,
I'll be putting the screws on her first thing in the morning for the rent,
electricity, and gas. That'll bring some money in, and even if it's not a
lot of money when you're paying black-market prices, even a little money
is a lot of money to those who've got no money at all.

While he was thinking these thoughts, he had a look at the
locks to the pantries, of which there were two in this rather grand
kitchen—one on the right of the window and the other on the left.
But they were both locked. *Of course,* he said to himself with a gentle
sigh. *One is for Mrs. Schulz, the other for Miss Gwenda. They haven't*
reckoned on the Dolls. That'll have to change, too. Tomorrow morning,
I'm going straight down to the housing office to clarify our rights here.
Ah, no, the first thing I need to do is go to the Food Office and get our
ration cards; we simply can't go on as we are, begging and borrowing,
and buying stuff on the black market.

Now Doll was standing by the kitchen table, gazing at it
thoughtfully. But it looked too short and too hard to spend the night
on. Then he remembered the bathtub, but the chill that still lay in
his bones made him shiver at the mere thought of sleeping there,
so he dismissed the idea immediately. There was carpeting on the
floor of the little lobby, and in the hallway he had seen some sort
of woman's coat hanging on the coat stand. He could use these as
blankets.

But he still wasn't quite sure this was what he wanted—and
then he remembered that the apartment had six-and-a-half rooms,
and the half room was for the maid. He went inside and flicked
the light switch, but the light didn't come on, either because the
wiring was broken or because there was no bulb in the socket. So
he went back to the kitchen, fumbled around with the lighter to

get the gas stove lit again, found a newspaper in the waste bin, and rolled it up to make a torch. He used this to light up the maid's room.

Yes, the bedstead was still there, with the mattress on top and even the wedge pillow, but nothing else — no bed linen and no bed cover. And it was damned cold in this poky little hole! He used the last of the torchlight to light up the window, and saw that there were only a few shards of glass sticking out from the frame. There was nothing to keep the cool night air out. But he decided to make this his bedroom anyway — a bed was a bed. And, like a typical man, it never occurred to him that a bed could be moved somewhere else, into the kitchen, for example, which was warmer, and protected from the weather. But no, the thought never even occurred to Doll, for the simple reason that he was a man — or so Alma said later, after she had heard about this first night of his.

And now Doll suddenly felt qualms about just taking the woman's coat to use as a blanket. He spent ages taking up a threadbare runner in the back passageway, pulling it free from the tacks that held it down. He managed it eventually, but it was clear that this runner, now completely frayed and tattered along its edges, could never be relaid. In the kitchen, Doll quickly stripped off his suit, lit his cigarette on the gas stove, dragged the runner along behind him, and moved into his overnight quarters, folding the old, dusty carpet over and over on itself to cover him. He used the remains of a dressing gown that he had found in the bathroom to wrap around his feet, which were stiff with cold.

He lay like this in the dark, the tip of his cigarette glowing red from time to time; with the fiery glow so close to his face, he could no longer see the pale window opening, with the black silhouette of the courtyard building roof and the grey sky above it. When the red glow subsided, he could see the light of the sky again, and the air felt cooler on his face.

At first, despite the cigarette, he couldn't really relax because he couldn't get warm; the runner was heavy, and smelled unpleasantly of dust and all kinds of other things he couldn't quite identify, but it certainly wasn't warming. But when he had finished the cigarette and only the night sky above the black roof cast its pale light over Doll's face, he suddenly found himself, in that bitter cold, in an imaginary world between waking and sleeping, in a place to which he had always resorted ever since his earliest childhood at times when he was feeling particularly vulnerable.

In this imaginary world, he was Robinson Crusoe on the desert island, but a Robinson Crusoe without Man Friday, and a Robinson Crusoe who dreaded the arrival of white people, and felt only fear at the thought of being 'saved' by them. This latter-day Robinson Crusoe did everything possible to hide away completely from his fellow creatures. The vegetation around his cave could never be sufficiently dense, or the pathway through it sufficiently overgrown and concealed. His favourite fantasy was a deep valley basin between steep, towering cliffs, only accessible through a long, dark tunnel cut into the rock, which could be blocked up easily with stones. The valley basin itself was lightly planted with trees, but the tree cover was dense enough to ensure that this Robinson could not be detected from the air.

Even as a boy, Doll had sought refuge in such fantasies of hidden solitude, whenever the world and other people became too frightening, or when he had failed to grasp a proof in geometry, or when he had told a lie and been found out. As a grown man, he had taken refuge in the same escapist fantasy in times of depression, and in the last few years it had assumed a special importance for him, of course, during the constant heavy bombing raids over Berlin.

At bottom, though — and Doll knew this very well since reading the works of Freud — this rocky cave or the sheltered valley basin signified his mother's womb, to which he wished he could return when danger threatened. There and only there had he been safely at peace, and the southern sun that he always pictured shining down on Robinson's island was in fact his mother's great, warm heart, which graciously and tirelessly streamed its warm red blood down upon him.

With these and similar thoughts, Doll finally fell asleep, and when he woke, the fading night was still a dirty grey light in the empty window opening. But Mr. Doll leapt out of bed with alacrity and still feeling all warm, eager to begin the first real day of useful activity after the collapse of all his hopes. In the kitchen, under the electric light, he got a shock when he saw how filthy he was from the dusty old carpet runner. But there was nothing he could do about it, not having a change of clothes with him. Instead he took time and trouble over his ablutions in the bathroom, and felt fresh, if also very cold again, as he inspected himself in the large mirror in the hallway. It seemed to him that he was looking fresher and healthier than he had in a long time. He hurried down the stairs and through the front door, which was already open; but around the corner, the shop run by Mother Minus was still closed.

He could see a light inside, and began to knock, and he carried on knocking so persistently that eventually the familiar, big, white-haired head of Mother Minus was pressed up against the glass in the door; but she was shaking her head vigorously, to indicate that it was not yet opening time. Whereupon Doll knocked all the harder, so that the sound echoed through the empty street in the pale grey light of dawn, and when dear old Minus finally opened the door to get rid of the importunate caller, with all the irritation that only she could muster, he immediately grasped her hand in both of his, and said: 'Yes, it's really me, Dr. Doll! We last saw each other at the end of March, and I'm so glad you've come through it all safely, as have we. My wife's in the hospital at the moment, but I think she'll be back home again soon. And the reason I was kicking up such a terrible racket just now was that I absolutely must speak to you alone before your first customers arrive!'

While Doll was chatting away so cheerily to Mother Minus, he had been gradually inching his way forward, forcing her to take little steps backwards into her shop. Now he closed the door of the shop behind him as a precaution, in case anyone else might be cheeky enough to take similar liberties.

'Yes', said Mother Minus, no longer angry. 'Yes, I'd heard that you were both back again, and someone did tell me that you were not well. So what's on your mind now, Doctor?'

But before Doll could tell her about his needs and his prospects and promises, she broke in: 'But what am I even asking for? Why would anyone call on Mother Minus at this early hour, insisting on speaking with her alone? You want something to eat, don't you? A nice, tasty morsel, eh? Well now, Doctor, just this once, I'll do it without ration cards—but just this once, understand? Never again!'

'That's fantastic, Mrs. Minus!' cried Doll, delighted that it had been made so easy for him. 'You're an absolute star!'

'Get on with you!' replied Mrs. Minus, and she was already packing things up and filling bags, weighing, slicing, and slapping stuff onto greaseproof paper—while Doll's eyes grew steadily wider, since the best he had been hoping for was a loaf of bread and a bit of coffee substitute. 'Don't talk so much—and don't make any promises! But don't forget, I said "just this once", and I mean it. I know everyone says I'm too soft-hearted and can't say "no", but I can! You know it's not allowed, and they can shut me down just like that for such a thing. But just this once, I say: you've got to do right by people, and I've heard what the two of you have been through. So here you are, just take the stuff and shut up. It comes to twelve marks forty-seven, and if you've got the money, you can pay now; otherwise you can leave it. I can put it down in the book, and in your case I'm happy to go on doing that for a while—that's different. But not without ration cards!'

And having said this for the third time with as much emphasis as she could muster, as if she was trying to harden her soft heart, she pushed Doll, who was really touched by her generosity, out of the shop and back onto the street. He heard the key turning in the lock, and nodded vigorously in farewell, since his hands were full and he couldn't wave. Then he went home, feeling that he'd suddenly become a very rich man.

When he had left, he had taken the key out of the apartment door and kept it with him, which was a good thing, because when he got back, nobody was stirring as yet. This suited him fine, because now he could unpack his spoils undisturbed and unobserved. When it was all laid out before him on the kitchen table, he really did feel like a rich man who'd been poor Lazarus just a little while ago. Arrayed before him now were three loaves of bread—one white, two brown—a bag of coffee substitute, another bag containing sugar, one with noodles, another with white flour, a twist of paper with coffee beans, a parcel of greaseproof paper with butter and another with margarine, and a cardboard plate piled with jam.

If I'd had to buy that lot on the black market! thought Doll, and put some water on to heat in a pan—for the coffee substitute, of course: he was saving the real coffee beans for his reunion with Alma.

He found it quite difficult to scrape together enough crockery for his breakfast, since they had locked up his kitchen dresser. But he finally found what he needed in the sink, washed it as best he could with cold water, and said to himself once again: *All this has got to change—as of today!* And then he sat down to a veritable feast.

He was disturbed only twice. The first time, Mrs. Schulz came wandering into the kitchen like a ghost, albeit a distinctly unwashed ghost, looked aghast at the early-morning guest and rushed out again, with a cry that was more of a croak: 'Dear God, you might have told me, Dr. Doll!'

And she was gone again, with her untidy, tattered nightdress and her tousled head, her short locks in curlers. Doll hurried after her. 'Mrs. Schulz!' he cried beseechingly. 'Hang on a minute. I won't look, really I won't!'

The door was slammed in his face, and he was reluctant to barge into her room. So he called to her through the keyhole: 'Mrs. Schulz, I'm just going to pop down to the ration card office—can I speak to you later?'

A sigh, followed by an 'Oh Lord!', came back by way of reply.

'I absolutely must speak to you today! It's about something that's important for you, too!' A sigh, deeper than the first one, was the only reply. 'It wasn't that bad, you know', Doll whispered, piped, through the keyhole. 'I've got an attractive young wife myself, after all! So: we'll speak again later, Mrs. Schulz—in peace and friendship! Until later, then!'

Another sigh of 'Oh Lord!', but at least now it sounded like something that Doll could take for a 'Yes'. *You old bat!* he muttered under his breath. *Just you wait, I'll have you out of here so fast your feet won't touch the ground! Do you think I've forgotten how you rejoiced over the divine deliverance of your beloved Führer after the 20th of July?*

He hadn't been sitting eating his bread and jam for long before he was disturbed for the second time: somebody rang the bell to the door of the apartment. When he opened the door, there stood the tall young man from the previous evening—the one who had let him into the house and thereby brought him in out of the cold.

'Oh, it's you, Dr. Doll!' he said, momentarily wrong-footed, then quickly collected himself. 'I thought you'd still be asleep, and I just wanted to drop this off ...' He produced a large package. 'It's a coat', he explained quickly. 'Only a summer coat, I'm afraid, but there's a hat, too. I'm taller than you, but it might just fit. It's just a loan, of course—I hope you don't mind. But I thought you could wear it until you get something else ...'

'But Mr. —', Doll started to say, quite overcome. 'See, I've even forgotten your name ...'

'Oh, never mind the name! Anyway, even though it's only a summer coat, it's better than nothing ...' The package had meanwhile changed hands, and the two men had exchanged a vigorous handshake ...

'That is really so kind of you, Mr —', began Doll, but then interrupted himself again. 'Look, you really must tell me your name—'. Doll felt as if he couldn't really thank the man properly unless he knew his name ...

'Grundlos', he replied. 'Franz Xaver Grundlos. But look, I really must be going—I have to get to work. The underground—'

The last words echoed from the stairwell. Just when Doll could have thanked Mr. Grundlos properly, he was gone.

For the second time this morning, Doll found himself unpacking gifts. It was as if Christmas and his birthday had come on the same day. How wrongly he had judged the Germans in his depression! *Decency, plain old-fashioned integrity—they haven't died out yet;*

they will never die out. They will flourish and grow strong again, overwhelming and choking the rank weeds of Nazi denunciation, envy, and hatred!

Only a light summer coat, and too big for him — the man was right on both counts. But it was a smart, blue-grey cloth coat, partially lined with silk. *So people are helping each other out again, nobody is completely alone in the world, everyone can help, everyone can be helped.* The coat was a bit too long, certainly, but what of it?

He kept the coat on, and put on the hat as well — a little velvet number in the Bavarian style. There was a time when he wouldn't have been seen dead with such a thing on his head. But it wasn't so stiflingly warm in the kitchen that you couldn't wear a summer coat while eating your bread and jam. And he did not sit down to resume his meal. He suddenly felt a pressing need to get down to the ration card office. He'd put it off for months, but now he would show the major's lady wife that he too had ration cards, that he was no longer dependent on her! And today was the day he would show her!

There was one problem, though: where was he going to put his groceries while he was out? He didn't trust anyone. In the end, he crept along to the fire-ravaged front room, which was filled with rubble and general clutter, and hid the bags in a drawer of Petta's scorched changing table.

He inspected himself one more time in the mirror. *Good!* he said to himself. *Or at any rate, a thousand per cent better than I have looked in the last few months. And now it's time to get down to the Food Office with all guns blazing! I hope to God that some of the people down there are as decent as the three I've met in the last twenty-four hours. But this is my lucky day, and I can't go wrong!*

It was well before eight when Doll left the house, and it was way past noon when he returned — a very different Doll. He sat down without a word on the kitchen chair next to the gas stove. He was utterly exhausted. Miss Gwenda, who was keeping an eye on her potato soup on the stove — it had been sitting there for four hours, and should surely have come to the boil by now, but the gas pressure was so feeble — asked him for the key to the door of the apartment, which she assumed he had taken. Doll stood up without a word. He saw at a glance that the keys to both pantries and the kitchen dresser were now back in their locks. He took them out, put them in his pocket, and made to leave the kitchen.

The two women — Gwenda and the widow of Major Schulz — exchanged a quick glance and came to a mutual understanding: they should just let the poor lunatic have his way for now. Mrs. Schulz was all dolled up now, her hair in coquettishly tight little curls, and she said in honeyed tones: 'If you want to speak to me, Dr. Doll, I am at your disposal. I have come specially to see you.'

But he was not at her disposal. He went along the passageway to Mrs. Schulz's room. He entered, locked the door behind him, and sat down in an armchair. He was feeling really under the weather, dead tired and pretty desperate. The morning had been too much for the feeble strength of a man who was still convalescing. All he wanted to do now was rest ... He leaned back and closed his eyes. But he opened them again immediately. He felt cold — really, really cold! He was still wearing the coat, but ... He struggled to his feet again and moved the electric fire right next to his legs. He fetched the quilt from Mrs. Schulz's bed-settee and wrapped it tightly around him ...

He closed his eyes for a second time. Before nodding off, he thought to himself: *I mustn't sleep later than four o'clock. I need to be with Alma by five. Though I don't know what I'm going to tell her about my brilliantly successful brush with officialdom ... But I mustn't think about that now, otherwise I'll never get to sleep!*

He slowly drifted off. But he hadn't been asleep for more than five minutes before there was a knock at the door and Mrs. Schulz was chirping: 'Dr. Doll, have you got a minute? I thought you wanted to speak to me?'

He pretended not to hear. He was sleeping. He had to get some sleep.

'Be a dear, Dr. Doll, and open the door just for a minute, so that I can at least get my hat and bag! I have to go out!'

Doll slept on. But when she had pleaded with him for a third time, he jumped up, knocked the electric stove over, lunged towards the door, turned the key in the lock, flung the door open, and shouted angrily: 'Go to blazes! If you don't get away from this door right now, I'll move you myself, down all four flights of stairs — do you understand, woman?!'

This angry outburst was so effective that Mrs. Schulz fled before him down the passageway. 'I'm going, I'm going!' she shrieked in terror. 'I'm sorry I disturbed you! It won't happen again, I promise!'

Doll then slept soundly, falling into a deep, peaceful sleep immediately after his angry outburst, as if this storm had cleared the air. When he woke again, it was already getting dark in the room. He felt wonderfully rested and refreshed — better than for a long time. His first healthy sleep without any kind of sleeping aids! He stayed sitting quietly in the armchair, and was now able to reflect more calmly on the outcome of his morning visit to the ration card and housing offices.

He pictured himself again, standing along with so many others in a long line at the ration card office. Even though he had arrived early, there were nearly a hundred people there before him. Once again, he saw how the other people waiting with him were constantly bickering and needling each other. He saw people nearly come to blows over a single word, which was often just a simple misunderstanding, and the unbelievable outbursts of fury when they thought someone was trying to jump the queue. Waiting for three hours in this hate-filled atmosphere inevitably put paid to Doll's early-morning conviviality. He tried to fight it, but this depressing mood was all-pervasive.

Eventually, he was standing in the room, at a table, in front of a girl or a woman, with people talking behind him and beside him, and now it was Doll's turn to speak, to say what he had thought about and rehearsed in his head a hundred times …

But he didn't get beyond the third sentence. 'First you need to bring your police registration form and your housing referral form', explained the girl. 'Without them we can't issue any cards here. You'll have to go to the housing office first!—Next, please!'

'But Miss!' he cried. 'It's always been our apartment, we were never de-registered, so why do I need to go and register again? You can check in your card index!'

'Then you'll have to get confirmation from the housing office! And anyway …' She gave him a dismissive look. 'Next, please!'

Doll was wasting his breath. One thing she had learned at work was the knack of not hearing. His words were like the buzzing of a fly to her. He had to leave, and he'd wasted more than three hours and a lot of energy just to be told that!

He went off in search of the housing office, and found it. This time he didn't have to queue for so long. He was only waiting an hour and a half. But he got nowhere at the housing office either. Once again a lady listened to his story, and felt doubtful about his case. He should have registered before the 30th of September, and now it was almost December! The lady passed him on to a male colleague, a very excitable gentleman, who, as Doll noted from his treatment of a man before him in the queue, was not a great listener, and preferred to do the talking himself.

Doll placed various pieces of paper in front of this man: old rent receipts for his apartment, proof of his appointment as mayor of the small town, written confirmation that the Dolls had spent time in hospital in the district town …

The man behind the desk blinked briefly, then pushed all the papers together in a heap and said quickly: 'I'm not interested in any of that. You can put it all back in your pocket, though you might just as well toss it into the wastepaper basket! Next!'

'And what about my certificate of residence?' persisted Doll, now quite angry.

'Your certificate of residence? That's a good one!' cried the excitable gentleman, now in full flight. 'On what grounds? I can't think of any! I've no intention of issuing one of those! Next!'

'So what kind of documents do you want, then?' inquired Doll doggedly.

'I don't want anything! You're the one who wants something! Next, please, and quick about it!' This 'Next!' appeared to be a kind of linguistic tic, the way other people end every sentence with '… you see?' He added quickly: 'Bring me a sworn statement from your landlord that you've occupied the apartment since 1939. Bring me a notice of departure from your last address in the town you were evacuated to, plus confirmation that you are signed off the ration card register.'

'I was never evacuated. And there was nothing to sign off from, because they haven't got ration cards there.'

'Ridiculous!' cried the official. 'Stuff and nonsense, a bunch of excuses! You just want to worm your way into Berlin, that's all! But you're not getting anything from me, nothing at all, and I don't care how many certificates you produce!' He slammed his hand down on the table. He was getting more and more worked up. 'I know your sort as soon as I clap eyes on them—you'll never get anything from me. Next!'

Suddenly his tone of voice changed. Now it was just sullen: 'And anyway ...'

It was the second time this morning that Doll had heard the words 'And anyway', and it sounded like some kind of dark threat against him. After these absurd rantings and accusations, Doll's own blood was up now, and he asked sharply: '"And anyway"? What's that supposed to mean? What are you getting at?'

'Oh, come off it!' said the official, suddenly acting very bored, 'You know very well. Don't pretend you don't!' He studied his fingernails, then looked up at Doll: 'Or are you going to tell me what you and your family have been living off here in Berlin since the 1st of September?' He ploughed on triumphantly, and all the other people in the room were looking at Doll and enjoying his discomfiture as he got it in the neck. 'Either you didn't move here on 1 September, but only just now, in which case you have missed the deadline, and there is no way you are going to get a certificate out of me! Or you've been living off the black market since the 1st of September, in which case I have to report you to the police!'

Doll flared up angrily, failing to see in his agitation and his uncritical self-regard that the man was at least partly right: 'If you had looked at the paperwork properly, instead of just binning it without even reading it, you'd have seen that I was in hospital until yesterday—so I got all my meals there. And my wife is still in hospital, you can get written confirmation of that any time ...'

'I'm not interested in any of that! It's got nothing to do with me! Next! I've told you what paperwork I need from you. Right: next!'

This time, his final word was not just a verbal flourish tacked on to the end of a sentence: he really did turn his attention to the next man in the queue. Doll walked slowly out of the office. He could feel the other man's disdainful, taunting gaze in his back; he knew that he was relishing his triumph and thinking: *I gave him what for! He won't be back again in a hurry!* And Doll knew with equal certainty that the next man in line would have no trouble getting what he wanted, no matter how shaky his case might look. He would even receive friendly treatment, because the official was now keen to demonstrate to himself, his office, and the waiting public that he really was a decent sort of fellow. But he wasn't: he was one of the millions of petty tyrants who had wielded their sceptres in this land of commissars and corporals since the beginning of time.

On the way home Doll completely forgot that he was shielded from the November cold by a coat that had been generously given to him only a few hours earlier, and that his belly was full from a breakfast that had come to him the same way. Once again, he despaired completely of his fellow Germans. His buoyant mood of the morning had evaporated. Robinson felt very much alone on his island.

And so it was that Miss Gwenda, and more especially Mrs. Schulz, had to atone for the sins of the housing office. And so it was that Doll fell asleep feeling completely depressed. But now he was no longer the Doll of the recent past. An hour and a half of sleep had restored his confidence and spirits. *I'll get there!* he thought to himself. *And if I don't, Alma will succeed where I have failed. Maybe it would have been better to send her down there in the first place. She knows how to handle men much better than I do. And anyway, Alma is Alma ...!*

He had to grin, because here he was, resorting to 'And anyway ...' himself. Then he crept along quietly to the burned-out room to fetch his food supplies, and sat down to a late lunch.

CHAPTER TEN

Robinson at large

As quietly as Doll had crept along, the widow of Major Schulz had heard him anyway. He had hardly cut the first slice of bread before there was a gentle tapping on the door, and when he said, 'Come in', Mrs. Schulz's mop of curls appeared round the door. 'Oh, Dr. Doll, would it be all right if I fetched my things now—if I'm not disturbing you?'

'Take them, take them!' replied Doll. Then he remembered the angry outburst with which he had punished this woman for the sins of the housing office, and he said: 'By the way, I'm sorry I got so worked up earlier. They gave me a really hard time down at the government offices, and my nerves were in shreds. The fact is, I'm still not well again yet.'

The words were hardly out of his mouth before he regretted them. He could sense, indeed he could positively see, how Mrs. Schulz, all meekness just a moment before, now perked up again. It had been particularly unwise to mention the 'government offices', because she immediately asked: 'And what did they say down at the housing office? What did they decide about the apartment?'

'How the apartment will be divided up between me and Miss Gwenda', said Doll, rather more guarded now, 'has yet to be decided.

But you will understand, dear lady, that I cannot give up the use of this room.'

Mrs. Schulz grimaced. 'But Mr. Doll!' she cried plaintively, 'you can't put me out on the street at the start of winter! I'm happy to look for another room, but until then …'

'Until then we'll be living here together, and when my wife comes there will be three of us …' She made as if to speak. 'No, no, dear lady, it's out of the question. I know you've only ever made occasional use of this room …'

'That's a lie!' shrieked Mrs. Schulz, and her podgy white face quivered with anger and indignation. 'You shouldn't believe a word of what that Gwenda says! She's an actress—she tells lies for a living!'

'I've never said a word about you to Miss Gwenda, Mrs. Schulz!'

'No, of course you haven't. Please forgive me. I know who it was—that snake in the grass, the janitor's wife, that Nazi bitch! She's always trying to pin something on me! But I'll see her in jail yet! I can't tell you all the stuff she lifted from your apartment before I took the key away from her! Buckets and pans and pictures—your wife ought to take a good look round her rooms downstairs; there's enough stuff there to furnish half a house! Of course I've always lived here, every day!'

'So', said Doll, 'you've been using the room on a regular daily basis?'

'Yes, always! I've told you, since last year.'

'Then you'll agree that it's high time we settled up for the rent, etcetera. I haven't kept a written tally of everything, like you, so I'll make it very reasonable. Shall we say, for the rent and the furniture and use of the kitchen throughout that time, two hundred marks, and for the gas and electricity, another hundred, making three hundred marks in all? So, if you wouldn't mind, dear lady …?'

And he held out his hand.

Mrs. Schulz had involuntarily sat down, probably not so much because she wanted to get comfortable, but because the shock had made her unsteady on her feet. She hadn't been expecting such an assault. 'I've got no money!' she mumbled, holding on very tightly to her handbag. 'Barely twenty marks …'

'Oh well!' said Doll in a soothing tone, 'that doesn't matter. Give me the twenty marks for now. I'm quite happy to take instalment payments. And in the meantime, while you're getting the three hundred together, perhaps you could leave the quilt here for me! I could really use it at the moment.'

'No! No! No!' Major Schulz's widow was positively screaming now. 'I'm not paying that! That was never agreed! I arranged with your wife that I would look after your things here, and in return I was allowed to live here.'

'But you've just told me that so many of my things have been removed! How could that happen, if you were supposed to be looking after them? No, Mrs. Schulz, the three hundred marks have got to be paid. Maybe you recall that I didn't quibble when I settled your accounts for so and so many cigarettes, for this and that loaf of bread, for so many pounds of potatoes—no, my demands are very reasonable. And I'm quite certain my wife would take a different view; she would demand a lot more …'

'Your wife expressly told me I wouldn't have to pay anything here!'

'No, dear lady, that's not something she would have said. There's no point in discussing it further. That's how it is, and the money must be paid, and the sooner, the better!'

'And what about my quilt?' cried Mrs. Schulz. 'Doctor, dearest

Doctor, I've been bombed out of my house four times now, and all I've managed to rescue is this quilt. Doctor, you can't be that hard-hearted! I've got nothing left, I am a poor woman, and I'm getting old!' She had grabbed hold of his hand, and was looking at him with tears in her eyes. 'It's the cigarettes!' she whispered as if to herself. 'He's holding the cigarettes against me. I really didn't overcharge you—or only a tiny bit. You surely don't begrudge me my livelihood—the cigarettes are my living, after all, and I need to live, too! What was the point of struggling to survive for the last few years, only to die of hunger now? No, you can't hold the cigarettes against me, and you have to let me keep my quilt! You're not as hard-hearted as you make out. There is no way I can pay the three hundred. It would be a different matter if they paid me my pension. But nothing, not a bean! And yet the Führer said ...'

By now she had got herself into a complete state, and just looked imploringly at Doll with tears in her eyes. She was squeezing his hand in both of hers, which were unpleasantly warm and moist.

'Dear lady!' he said, and freed his hand with a sudden pull that was not polite. 'Dear lady, tears don't work with me; in fact, they generally just make me more annoyed. You've just admitted that you didn't charge me the correct amount for the cigarettes, so when you plead poverty I don't believe a word of it. You can keep your quilt if you pay me the three hundred. If you don't, the quilt stays here.'

'No!' said Major Schulz's widow, and her feverish agitation was gone in a flash. 'No, I'm not paying the money. You can take me to court if you want. Your claim won't stand up. Your wife expressly told me ...'

'We've been through all that, Mrs. Schulz. So the quilt stays here!'

'Fine', said Mrs. Schulz drily. 'In that case, you'll see where that gets you, you and your wife! Morphine addiction is against the law!'

'Not as serious as fraudulent trading in cigarettes.' But then he felt sickened by the turn this conversation was taking. 'Thank you, Mrs. Schulz, we have nothing more to discuss. Kindly remove your things from the kitchen dresser and the pantry. And give me your house keys.'

'I'm not giving you my keys! I won't be turfed out on the street like this!'

'Your handbag!' shouted Doll. He was suddenly angry again, to his own surprise. He snatched the bag from her hand. She squealed a little. 'Don't worry, I'm not going to take your things!' The bag was stuffed full of letters, all manner of toiletries, and cigarette packs. 'Where are the keys?' asked Doll, and burrowed down further into the bag. He came across a bundle of money—blue notes, hundred-mark notes, at least thirty of them, maybe even forty. He put them into her hand. 'Here are your twenty marks, you poor woman with nothing to your name, who has to wait until the Führer pays her pension ...' Finally he found the keys. 'Is one of these a private key of yours?'

She shook her head. 'I've got nothing ...', she whispered, holding the bundle of notes in her hand and still looking utterly bewildered.

'So I see!' said Doll, and gave her bag back to her. 'Thanks very much. Now if you could be on your way— ?'

She stood there for a moment, undecided, then suddenly placed three hundred-mark notes on the table—without looking at him, without saying a word. (Was she ashamed after all? Unlikely!) She walked out of the room ...

'Your quilt!' Doll called out after her. 'You've forgotten your quilt!'

She walked on down the passageway, past the kitchen. 'And your things in the kitchen dresser!' shouted Doll. But to no avail. The apartment door banged shut. Mrs. Schulz was gone.

Doll shrugged and went back to his loaf of bread. Despite the money, he was not really happy about the way their conversation had ended. The sight of the three hundred-mark notes made him feel a little uncomfortable, and in the end he put them in his pocket. Based on the prices that Alma was now paying in the hospital, they would only buy fifteen cigarettes or one pre-war mark. But they were worth a lot more than that to him, and not just because he had had to fight for them.

By now it had grown quite dark. He put the light on to eat his bread, and marvelled yet again how small a loaf of bread is when a man does indeed live by bread alone—and how quickly it is gone. He kept on saying to himself: *Now this really is the last slice!* And every time, after a moment of indecision, he cut himself another one. He ate the bread dry, keeping the jam and margarine until Alma came home.

Then he took his supplies, and was about to take them back to Petta's scorched changing table. Then he remembered that he'd had the keys to the pantry in his pocket since lunchtime, and went along to the kitchen.

There he found Miss Gwenda. She was now wearing a silver-grey fur and make-up, as if she was going straight from the kitchen to the stage. It turned out, however, that she had only been invited out by friends. Miss Gwenda started to moan about how cold it was now, and said that in the winter it would be so cold in the apartment that they wouldn't be able to stand it. So she had bought herself a little stove on the black market, and in the next few days she planned to get some briquettes on the black market, too, costing two-fifty apiece. She assured him that was cheap, incredibly cheap;

some people were paying four marks for a briquette. And what was he planning to do in the winter, she asked. He couldn't possibly run the electric fire all the time, otherwise they'd cut off the electricity, and they'd all be sitting in the dark!

'Listen, Miss Gwenda!' said Doll, interrupting her tale, which wasn't exactly gladdening his heart. 'Listen, Miss Gwenda, I've given Mrs. Schulz her marching orders and taken her keys away. So she's got no business here from now on. Just so that you know ...'

Miss Gwenda promptly twisted her painted face into a grimace that was doubtless an attempt at laughter, and she said: 'Ah, so you've rumbled her little game, too, have you?! I thought she wouldn't be able to keep it up much longer. Well, I won't be shedding any tears on her account.'

'So you've had problems, too', noted Doll. 'I think we'll leave the kitchen dresser open from now on, and each can take what he or she needs. There should be enough crockery for both of us. But we'll keep our supplies in separate pantries, and both hold on to our own keys. Which one would you like, the right or the left?'

Miss Gwenda preferred the left, and otherwise she was happy with the new arrangements. 'Well, let's both of us check what supplies Mrs. Schulz still has left, so that she can't accuse us of anything later on ...'

'Oh, you won't find much of hers here', said Miss Gwenda disdainfully. 'She always lived from hand to mouth, and just bought what she needed.'

Which must have been true, because they found nothing apart from a few spices, two onions, and a handful of potatoes. So Doll moved his things into the pantry, which was now considerably better stocked than during Mrs. Schulz's time.

Then he locked the door. Meanwhile it had grown late, and

it was already dark outside. The weather had turned rough; the wind pressed hard against the cellophane in the window, and squalls of driving rain rattled against it from time to time. But Doll was determined to go and see Alma in hospital anyway. He'd been thinking about this visit all day long. He pictured himself sitting on the edge of her bed again, with the radio playing softly in the background, and perhaps she'd have some smokes again … (Although, given their financial circumstances, it was a shocking waste of money!)

It would be best not to tell her that he had been discharged from the sanatorium, since that would only unsettle her. She would worry about how he was coping in the apartment on his own. She would then demand to be discharged herself, despite the fact that her leg was still not right. So he would act as if he had just given them the slip again at the sanatorium. He'd think of some little story he could tell her.

Turning these thoughts over in his mind, Doll went down the stairs and stepped out into the icy November wind, his face lashed by heavy rain. He shivered. *It's only a light summer coat*, he thought to himself. He came to a halt. Summer coat or not, he couldn't go to the hospital wearing that coat, because it would immediately give away the fact that he was no longer staying in the sanatorium. He would have to go in his thin summer suit, and the thought of this made Doll shiver even more. *I could drop the coat off at the porter's lodge*, he mused. But that wouldn't work either. Then she would feel sorry for him, and admire him for coming to see her in such weather—only to discover suddenly that his suit was dry, while outside it was pouring with rain.

No, he'd never get away with it—he would have to go in his jacket. Then he had a further thought: *I could say that somebody in the sanatorium had lent me the coat. But that's pretty darned unlikely—sneaking out on the quiet, and borrowing a coat to do so. And anyway, Alma might recognise the summer coat of Mr. Franz Xaver Grundlos—women have an eye for such things. No, there's nothing for it—I'll have to go in my jacket.*

The weather was really foul, wet and cold, and when Doll retreated into the stairwell, out of the wind, the still air once again felt pleasantly warm—just like the previous evening. But it was only when he got back to his room and saw the comforting red glow of the electric fire that it occurred to him he didn't really need to go at all. Alma would certainly not be expecting him. It was suppertime in the hospital now, so she had probably given up any hope of seeing him today. So there was no need to go out into the dark and the wet and the cold, and freeze half to death. He could just stay at home, climb into a warm bed, read for a bit, and then do his visit the next day, in the daylight, when hopefully the weather would be better.

But straightaway Doll shook his head and even stamped his foot, so determined was he. He'd planned to do this visit, and he did not want—did not ever want—to fall back into the old ways of the last few months, sinking into an apathetic stupor and letting himself go because he just didn't care. And quickly, as if he feared he might change his mind again, he tore off the coat, threw it over the armchair, and ran back down the stairs, out into the stormy blast and the ice-cold rain. And he ran on so fast that he didn't really notice how cold he was, or that he tripped over the same loose granite paving stone as before: all of this pretty much passed him by. All he could think about was the soft light of the hospital room, with the faint sounds of music on the radio, and in his mind he heard himself, still out of breath from running so fast, saying 'Good evening, Alma!' and saw her face light up with happiness.

And as he ran on, propelled by this joyous expectation, he felt as if he were escaping from his own broken, godless past, in which he had lived with a false and foolish pride in his solitary ways and his desert-island existence. And it felt as if this poor, bare man that he had become was now running towards a better, brighter future.

And so he entered the doors of the hospital as if effortlessly wafted there by the wind. He paused for a moment, dried his face off with his handkerchief, and wiped the rain off his glasses. Then he smoothed his hair with his hands — he'd forgotten his comb, of course, as he always did. Then, when he was breathing a little more easily again, he slowly climbed the stairs, reached the door of her room without anybody stopping him or even seeing him, knocked, and quickly entered.

He saw her face light up with joy, just as he had expected, and yet a thousand times lovelier than expected, and heard her cry: 'It's you, my dear, it's you! Have you run away from them again? I've had a feeling all day long that you would come!'

He went across to her bed at more of a run than a walk, bent down and kissed her, and whispered: 'No, Alma, I didn't run away this time. They kicked me out last night. I didn't really want to tell you, but when I saw your happy face, I knew straightaway I couldn't lie to you!'

He sat down beside her and told her everything that had happened to him since he had left her the day before, including his wasted trip to the government offices, which had almost dashed his spirits completely again, and his battle with Mrs. Schulz, and at the end he told her the tale of the coat he had so foolishly left behind. 'And now I've got myself frozen for nothing! Or maybe it wasn't quite for nothing. I don't know yet — the whole thing feels like some sort of conversion. And anyway, I wasn't actually all that cold, or at least I didn't have time to notice.'

He gazed at her as he spoke, in a way that made her reach up and pull his head down to her and whisper: 'What's that look on your face, you! You know that I love you terribly much, and that you suddenly look thirty years younger! If I had my way, I'd be out of here right now myself, and I'd come back with you this evening to our darling little home!'

In the instant that she spoke these words, he saw from the change in her expression that the sudden notion of coming home with him there and then was taking shape in her mind, and that the fleeting wish had quickly turned into a fervent desire and then, seconds later, into a firm intention. She had forgotten all about her leg wound. She murmured: 'I'll manage it somehow! And if they won't let me out, then I'll do what you did, and discharge myself!' She beamed: 'Think how nice that will be: this evening we'll be together again!'

He replied with some annoyance: 'Don't even think about it, Alma! Think about your bad leg, which still needs to be treated and dressed every day. You need to get properly well again first. I can manage by myself until then. The main thing is not to start lying around in bed all day again!'

She told him defiantly that she still had a mind of her own, and did what she wanted. And she would *definitely* be getting out of here this evening now!

He knew how stubborn she could be, so he had no choice but to change tack and try and win her over with soft words. But he got nowhere for a while, and she stuck to her decision to get herself discharged the same day. 'I'll soon talk that young doctor round ...!'

They carried on arguing, with no end or resolution in sight. The nun, with her Madonna-like smile, had already said a couple of times that it really was time for Mr. Doll to be leaving. Alma's supper had now been sitting on the bedside table for some while. In the end, when he did eventually leave, he got her to concede that she would not leave this evening at least, and that she would in any event check with the senior consultant first. The evening that had begun so happily ended on a sour note: neither of them had got what they wanted, and both were feeling upset in consequence.

As Doll was crossing the hallway, he looked through the open door of a room and saw a youngish man standing there in a white doctor's coat. *Aha*, he thought, *let's go and see about this!* He entered the room and made himself known. It turned out that the young, jaundiced-looking man was indeed the night-duty doctor. Doll, who had taken an instant dislike to the man, said: 'My wife has just told me she wants to be discharged immediately. I've managed to talk her out of it. I assume that meets with your approval? The condition of her wound—'

'Is excellent!' the doctor promptly chimed in, finishing Doll's sentence. He seemed to feel much the same about Doll as Doll felt about him. 'She no longer needs to be in hospital. Outpatient treatment is all she needs. If your wife comes to have her wound dressed twice a week, that will be quite sufficient.'

'I have asked my wife, and made her promise, to discuss her discharge with the senior consultant first', continued Doll undeterred, though there was a note of irritation in his voice. 'Apart from the wound, she needs a morphine injection more or less regularly every evening, surely? And before she is discharged, these injections would need to be discontinued completely, wouldn't they?'

There was no doubt about it: the young doctor had wilted under this assault, and his jaundiced face now looked pale and ashen. But he quickly collected himself and answered, laying it on thick as the medical professional who knows better than the ignorant layman: 'Oh, the injections — your wife has told you about those? Well,

I can put your mind at rest on that score, too: your wife *thinks* she has been getting morphine. In actual fact, I gave her harmless substitutes to start with, and more recently she's only had distilled water ...'

The doctor smiled so unpleasantly as he said this that Doll was tempted to reply: *And you let her give you expensive American cigarettes in return for distilled water! How very decent of you! Anyway, I don't believe a word of it. Alma can tell the difference between the effects of water and morphine. That's all just a smokescreen, to cover your back with your boss!*

But he said none of this, for what could be gained by turning it into an argument? Instead he observed: 'As far as I understand these things, she'll still need to be weaned off her faith in the water that she thinks is morphine, won't she?'

The doctor smiled unpleasantly again. 'Oh', he said, with a dismissive wave of the hand, 'these things are not as complicated as all that. I suggest we both go to your wife's bedside now, and I'll explain the necessary to her. You'll see that it won't come as a shock to the system — on the contrary, it's likely to produce a certain sense of relief.'

'No!' said Doll with a look of fury in his eyes. 'I haven't the slightest intention of going along with such a suggestion. All that would achieve is to make my wife angry with me instead of you. We'll do as I said: I'll discuss the matter first with the consultant, and I must insist that you don't mention this conversation to my wife in the meantime!'

Now the man in the white coat gave a superior smile. 'Don't worry, Dr. Doll!' he said, full of sardonic solace. 'I won't show you up in front of your wife — you won't get to feel the full force of her wrath! Needless to say, it was only a suggestion of mine that you should be present when I tell her. I can of course quite happily do it on my own ...'

'I don't want you to tell her anything this evening!'

'Well', said the doctor vaguely, 'I'll have to hear what your wife has to say about your visit. I will, of course, be guided entirely by the condition of the patient at the time.' He looked at the other man as if pondering what else to say. Then he reached into the pocket of his white coat and took out a little pack of American cigarettes. 'Please', he said to Doll, who was taken completely by surprise, 'do have one—'.

And Doll, defeated, wrong-footed and utterly taken aback, took the proffered cigarette ... An instant later, he could have kicked himself for this act of stupidity, this lack of presence of mind. Yes indeed, this cunning little schemer had got the better of him in every respect, and by accepting a cigarette he had cut the ground from under his own feet, making it impossible to speak of the matter again.

So the two men merely exchanged a few courteous pleasantries, and Doll went home filled with rage—rage at himself and his chronic inability to think on his feet and display presence of mind.

The only consolation was that Alma had given him a firm promise not to request her discharge today, but to wait until he or she had spoken to the senior consultant. But as Doll pondered the matter further, he could draw little comfort from this. For while he was sure that Alma would keep her word, it seemed to him entirely possible that the young doctor would talk, and thus bring about the very thing that Doll most wanted to avoid at the moment: Alma's premature discharge.

On his way to the hospital, the feeling of joyous anticipation had made him impervious to the cold and rain; on the way home, it was his gloomy thoughts that stopped him noticing the rain on this stormy November night. He was only shaken out of these thoughts when he ran straight into a man not far from his apartment, knocking him over. He promptly helped him up with profuse apologies, resigned to the prospect of being showered with abuse and threats by the man. But, to his surprise, this didn't happen; instead, the other man, who was completely unrecognizable in the dark, inquired in tones that were almost apologetic: 'Have you done anything about re-establishing yourself in the literary world, Mr. Doll?'

He was so startled by this completely unexpected question in the middle of the night that it took him a long time to work out who it was talking to him, and who it was he had knocked over in the dark: namely, the doctor with the papery skin, the first one to have attended his wife in Berlin. Eventually he said, somewhat fatuously: 'Oh, it's you, Doctor! I do beg your pardon. I hope I didn't hurt you …'

'I think', said the other, still a past master in the art of not hearing something that didn't interest him, 'I think one will have to move quickly now if one wants to play a real part. All sorts of complete unknowns seem to be jostling round the trough again now …'

This sounded not so much envious as simply disembodied, spoken into the fog, like everything else he said, without resonance for himself or those around him. They walked side by side towards their neighbouring homes. The spectral doctor went on: 'And there are all sorts of clubs and associations, leagues, chambers, groups being formed again—but not a single one has invited me to join. And yet at one time I was quite a well-known writer; not as well-known as you, Mr. Doll, but still, a well-respected figure.'

While he was talking, they had been approaching their

destination, and it seemed the obvious thing for Doll to accompany the doctor into his building and into his apartment and then into his tolerably warm surgery, where they sat down, again without preamble, on adjacent sides of his desk. The white-painted treatment chair with its stirrups for the legs looked just as spectral as its owner. There was something unreal about all of it, as though Doll were trapped in a dream from which he was about to awake.

The doctor went on: 'It's as if everyone thinks I'm dead — that's how forgotten I am. But I can't be entirely forgotten, because I'm reading the names of old friends in the newspapers. I haven't forgotten them, so they *can't* have forgotten me. But nothing! Not a peep! As if I were already dead — but I'm not dead, not yet!'

He fell silent for a moment, and gazed at Doll with his expressionless brown eyes, in a blank, unblinking stare. Thinking to make him feel better, Doll said: 'Nobody's got in touch with me either ...'

'No!' said the papery spectre, with a forcefulness that was quite unlike him. 'No! I have nothing to reproach myself for!' He answered a question that hadn't been asked: 'No, I was never a Nazi. Of course, I was a doctor in the Wehrmacht for a while, that was something that nobody could get out of. But I was never in the Party — and now this silence, as if they thought I was a Nazi. How do you deal with that?'

He looked at his companion with feverishly blinking eyes, and the paper-thin skin over his cheekbones appeared almost flushed. 'How do you deal with what?' inquired Doll. 'Being ignored? Why don't you get in touch with one of your old friends? They may not even know that you're still alive. So many people have perished in recent times ...'

'I've written letters, lots of letters!' replied the doctor. 'Look — half a drawerful! He opened a drawer in his desk, and showed Doll a little pile of letters, sealed in envelopes, addressed, and already franked with Berlin Bear stamps. The doctor quickly went on: 'A letter is like putting out a call—just by writing it, you are calling out to your correspondent.' He was silent for a moment. Then: 'Nobody can reproach me! Not when I was never a Nazi! Never! Really not!' He blinked even more fiercely.

Doll felt certain that this Dr. Pernies still partook sufficiently of this world to be tormented by something, and that he was even capable of lying in order to avert this torment. The reiterated assurance that he had never been a Nazi seemed suspicious, at the very least. It reminded him of that beer wholesaler, who had repeatedly sworn to his mayor that he honestly hadn't hidden a thing—until the hiding place was discovered.

Doll stood up. 'I would send the letters', he said.

But the doctor had become quite impenetrable and remote again. 'Of course!' he said in a toneless voice. 'Only, which one shall I send? And to whom? All those people are incredibly vain, and anyone I haven't contacted will feel ignored. I thank you for your visit!'

Doll stepped out into the night. Maybe Alma had talked to the young doctor in the meantime about her discharge, and was already at the apartment? He quickened his pace.

But when he entered the room, it was empty. There was no Alma; he was on his own again this evening, and it might be that for some days to come he would have to labour alone at building their future life together. His intention was to get back to his work, and thus to a meaningful life, as soon as possible. To do that he would have to seek out the people who were in the know today, and find out what sort of publishing opportunities there were now, and what there was in the way of newspapers, magazines, and publishers. But who could he turn to? He'd been in the city of Berlin for two months, but he knew nothing, absolutely nothing of what had happened here since Germany's collapse and defeat. He'd never looked at a newspaper—shameful as it was to have to admit it to himself!

While Doll was thinking these thoughts he had been tidying up his room and getting it into some sort of order. He had also laid out everything for his supper, and brewed up some coffee. Now he knocked softly on Miss Gwenda's door, which was opened by her mother, and he asked her politely if they had a few newspapers to hand—it didn't matter if they were out of date. He promised to return them the next morning.

He was given a whole stack of newspapers, and retired to his room with them. That evening he ate his bread and drank his coffee without even noticing, because he was reading—reading the newspapers, new ones and older ones, totally absorbed in the words on the page, the way he had been as a fifteen-year-old reading his Karl May adventures, without a thought for anything else. He read everything: domestic and foreign politics, letters to the editor and the features section, arts reviews and small ads. He devoured the newspapers from the first page to the last.

And as he did so, the world in which he had hitherto lived with his eyes closed now opened up before him, and everything became clear to see. He had walked through the streets of this city without once stopping to think who had removed the anti-tank barriers, cleared away the mountains of rubble, and got the transport system running again. He had seen them working in the streets, and his only thought at the time had been that it was a little odd to see people working again—what was the point? Or else he had thought: *These people are former Nazis, who are being* made *to work. The rest of us, who don't have to work, will just wait and see for now, the situation will change somehow …*

Yet these workers were people in the same situation as himself, no better and no worse; but while he had been lazing around and busily making himself ill, these people, who were just as disillusioned as he was, had got stuck in, and through sheer hard work had overcome their despair and disillusionment.

He read about theatres that were putting on plays again. About art exhibitions and concerts, about new films from all over the world. He read about the self-help initiatives for fetching timber from the forests, rebuilding homes that had been destroyed, repairing roofs, and getting burnt-out machinery working again. He read small ads where people were offering items for sale that for a long time had simply been unavailable. There weren't many of these, but at least it was a start—and that's all that could be expected for now.

He'd dismissed Berlin as a 'city of the dead', a 'sea of ruins', in which he would never be able to work: but just look how much work was being done in this city now! Anyone who wasn't doing their bit should feel ashamed of themselves. They had been living in a state of blind selfishness for the past few months—a parasitic, self-centred existence. All they had done was take, take, never stopping to think how they might give something back.

When Doll had put down the last newspaper that evening, that night, laid down on the couch and turned out the light, he didn't need to resort to some pathetic Robinson Crusoe fantasy in order to get off to sleep. Instead, all the things that he had read were going round and round in his head, and the more he went over in his mind all that had been achieved so far, the more incomprehensible it seemed to him that he had stood idly by, resentful and blank, while all this was happening. These reproaches pursued him into his dreams at dead of night.

CHAPTER ELEVEN

A stormy start

In spite of his tormenting dreams, Doll woke feeling fresh and rested, and, like the day before, he took a great deal of trouble over his toilet so that he wouldn't be distracted by thoughts about his unkempt appearance. He hoped very much that his planned errand would be successful, and that he wouldn't have his spirits dashed again by some other petty little tyrant like the one at the housing office.

Reading the newspaper the night before, Doll kept coming across the name of a man whom he remembered from pre-Nazi times. He had not had a great deal to do with him personally, but as publishing editor for a large publishing house, this man—Völger by name—had overseen the publication of several of his books. Doll now planned to track him down, and hoped that he might even find him at the editorial offices of that very newspaper.

Doll was just slipping his arms into the sleeves of his borrowed summer coat when the doorbell to his apartment was rung repeatedly, five or six times; and when he opened the door to see who was so impatient to be let in, who should it be but his own wife, Alma! She had a bulging shopping bag in each hand, her arms were festooned with items of clothing—dresses and skirts or something—and it was clear from the expression on her face that she was not in the best of moods.

Doll, who had been worried the night before that his wife might turn up, was now nonplussed by her sudden appearance. His newspaper reading and his planned visit to the publishing editor Völger had so preoccupied him that he had barely given a thought to his wife this morning, and certainly not to her arrival at the apartment. 'Alma, it's you!' he said, sounding genuinely flabbergasted.

'Yes, it's me, Alma!' she said, mimicking him with angry sarcasm. 'And if it was left to you, I certainly wouldn't be here—I'd be stuck in hospital for weeks on end! (Can you just shut that door and take some of these things from me? You can see I've got my hands full here!) That's a great way to keep a promise, turning that young doctor against me! And then you go and accept cigarettes from someone like that—well, thanks very much!'

As she spat out these words, she marched ahead of him into the room. Here she dumped her bags, tossed the armful of clothes over a dining chair, and sat down in an armchair. But she was on her feet again straightaway, dug a pack of cigarettes out of her pocket, and lit one up. Despite her anger, she showed that the spirit of comradeship was not something acquired or artificial with her, because she immediately proffered the pack and invited him to take one: 'Here!'

Doll, who the evening before, to his own annoyance, had not declined the offer of a cigarette from the young doctor, chose to do so now—another mistake!—with his wife, and said angrily: 'I didn't turn the doctor against you! And anyway, I didn't ask for cigarettes from him; he pressed them upon me and I took one, just one, just to be polite!'

'Is that so?' she replied angrily. 'But you won't take one from me? Then again, why be polite to your own wife? That makes it easier to go behind her back and persuade the doctor, contrary to a solemn promise, to keep me in hospital for God knows how long!'

'I didn't promise anything of the kind! But you promised *me* solemnly that you wouldn't leave there until you'd spoken to the senior consultant!'

'See—you've said it yourself: we were going to talk to the consultant, but you go and hide behind the ward doctor! Typical! All you were interested in was making sure I stayed there! Presumably you don't need me here!'

'Alma!' said Doll quietly. 'Alma, let's not quarrel. Let's think about the future instead. And I can't imagine a future without you. But you need to get well again first, that's all I care about here. I was reading the newspapers last night—Alma, there's so much been happening in the world during the two months we were lying around here doing nothing! From now on we need to do our bit again. When you arrived, I was just about to go and see Völger, my former editor, who always spoke up for my books. They've discharged you, all right; what's done is done. But now you need to lie down and look after that leg ...'

Her face had relaxed and become friendly, now that he had dropped the combative tone. But at his last suggestion she shook her head like a sulky child, and replied: 'I can't see why I shouldn't come with you. My leg is fine—or nearly. I don't want to lie around here and get bored!'

When he answered, his tone was still gentle: 'It's because we don't want to end up lying around again the whole time that I'm asking you to take care of yourself. If we go back to a life of idleness, there'll be no more getting out of bed in the mornings and going to work—or only to go and fetch morphine, and then Mrs. Schulz and Dorle will be running our lives again. Have a care, my dear, and look after yourself, before we end up like that again!'

But she shook her head and repeated stubbornly: 'I've looked after myself for long enough; now I want to do my bit again, too. Whatever you're doing, I want to be part of it!'

'You've been confined to bed the whole time until just this morning — you can't just start running around again as if nothing has happened!' he persisted. 'You've no idea how scared I am that we'll fall back into our old ways. And this time we have no reserves, no more diamond rings to sell. You've got to get used to the idea that we are poor now, Alma, and that there are lots of things we can no longer afford, such as doctors and expensive American cigarettes, and maybe not even white bread, which gets eaten much too quickly and doesn't fill you up anything like brown bread.'

'Is that so?' she cried, growing more heated herself. 'Is that why you wouldn't take a cigarette from me just now? So now you want to play the pauper? And then I won't be allowed to smoke cigarettes either, and I'll have to eat brown bread all the time, when you know it always plays havoc with my gall bladder! If that's how you want to live, be my guest, but you can count me out! For a start, I've still got lots of things I can sell, and when they're all gone I can still think of a better way out than rotting away in misery.'

He was now equally fired up with anger: 'Oh yes, it's easy to say you're not prepared to make any sacrifices and threaten to run away every time the going gets a little bit tough. But I'm not going to be threatened, even by you, and if you want to run away, then the sooner the better! I'll go my own way, on my own!'

'See!' she cried triumphantly. 'That's just what I thought — there was a reason why you tried to persuade me and the young doctor that I should stay in hospital as long as possible! I'm just a burden to you, and you want to get rid of me. Well, fine, I don't want to make things difficult for you, I can go whenever you like! I'll get on much better without you!'

'What rubbish you talk!' he cried. 'I haven't said anything about you being a burden and me being better off without you! You brought the subject up, not me! But that's not what it's all about! The question is simply whether you're prepared to be reasonable now and look after your health. Yes or no?'

'No — obviously!' she replied scornfully. 'If you'd asked me nicely, I might have done it. But not like that!'

'I asked you nicely enough at the beginning, but you just don't want to. So if you really don't want to …'

He looked at her expectantly, but her anger, if anything, was mounting.

'How many times do I have to tell you that I don't want to! And I'm certainly not going to be bullied by you! See, I'm lighting up another cigarette now, just to annoy you!'

And she lit a fresh cigarette.

'Fine, fine!' he said. 'At least I know now where we stand!'

And with that he walked straight past her. Her eyes had grown black with anger; but he walked out of the room, shut the door behind him, put on his coat in the hallway, put on his hat, and left the apartment.

It wasn't blowing a gale outside today, and it wasn't raining either, but never had the street they lived in, with its burnt-out ruins and huge piles of rubble, seemed to him so dark and menacing. Which is just what his life looked like: the war had destroyed everything, and all that was left to him were ruins and the ugly, incinerated detritus of former memories. And that's how it would probably always be; in this respect, it might even be that she was right: there was no escape from this scene of devastation. What he had just been through with his wife was enough to discourage anyone from going on. And he was right, but she was wrong. Reason was on his side, and everything she'd just been saying about not being prepared to do without was utter nonsense!

Yes, she was young, yes, she was pampered and spoilt, and he needn't have come down on her so hard; his comments about the cigarettes and the white bread would have kept until later. He could have been a bit more patient and circumspect. But he was only human, for heaven's sake, and these troubled times weighed heavily upon him, more heavily than they did on her, who lived free as a bird and forgot all her cares from one day to the next! Why did he always have to show consideration for everybody else, when nobody ever showed consideration for him?

No, it was probably just as well, the way things had turned out. The manner of their parting just now showed how things really stood between them, when infatuation didn't make them blind to their differences: at odds about everything; strangers, complete strangers; apart and alone. And now he would go his own way, alone; he wouldn't be telling her what to do any more — she could smoke and sell things off to her heart's content! Not another word! But nor would he be telling her anything about the outcome of his visit to the publishing editor Völger.

Absorbed in these thoughts, he had reached the underground station, bought a ticket, and was waiting for the train with other travellers. The train arrived, and the alighting passengers elbowed their way through the narrow gap grudgingly created for them by the people waiting on the platform. Then he squeezed into the overfilled carriage with the others.

Suddenly a voice beside him inquired in a mocking tone: 'Perhaps you'd care for a cigarette now?'

He spun round and gazed with bewilderment into the face of his wife, who eyed him with cool disdain. He didn't answer, but declined the proffered pack with an ill-tempered shake of his head. This was the last straw, and anger rose within him again. To have her follow him in secret after such a quarrel and now make fun of him in public—it was more than he could bear.

He was furious that she was coming along with him to what might be a crucial meeting, as if she really belonged there. She was a distraction. He wanted to reflect on what he needed to say to the publishing editor Völger, but all he could think about now was this wretched woman!

He had to change trains from the underground to the local commuter network, and then take a tram, but there was no shaking her off. He had to admit that his behaviour was not exactly gallant—as when he jumped onto the tram at the very last moment, when it was already moving. But she wasn't going to be caught out, and managed to jump aboard after him; enjoying her triumph at his expense, she even paid his fare. He put up a feeble protest, but neither she nor the conductor took any notice.

But it wasn't just about *schadenfreude* for her. Twice she had tried to let bygones be bygones and engage him in harmless conversation. But he had remained tight-lipped, and refused to say a single word.

Now that they had alighted from the tram and had to walk the last part of the way, she tried a third time. They were just crossing a temporary wooden bridge; alongside it, the broad iron bridge with its tarmac-covered carriageway lay in the water, dynamited by Hitler's minions in a futile gesture of defiance. She looked intently at the smooth roadway, which, still in one piece, dropped down steeply from the river bank to the water—which covered it to a depth of less than half a metre—and then rose steeply again to the other bank. Dreamily she said: 'It's a pity I'm not a child any more: I'd slide down there on the seat of my pants! I'd still do it now—you could do it on a sledge or a bike, too. Tell you what — for a hundred American cigarettes, I'd give it a go here and now!'

Her last words spoiled the impression made by her initial remark, at which he found himself smiling inwardly, despite himself. He could clearly picture her sliding down the slope, laughing and flashing her white teeth, her strawberry-blonde hair streaming out behind her. And she would have done it, too — she was quite capable of something like that. But her last remark about the American cigarettes promptly soured the mood of levity.

But her words had had the opposite effect on her. She took the pack of Chesterfields from her pocket, looked inside, and offered it to him: 'Well, how about it? The last chance! There are just two left — shall we share?'

He pressed his lips more tightly together and shook his head, even though his fingers were itching to reach out and take one, so badly did he crave a smoke.

'Have it your own way', she said evenly, and took out a cigarette for herself. As she lit it, she went on: 'If you insist on being silly and stubborn like a little child, be my guest! But I'm still going to enjoy my cigarette!'

She had drawn the smoke deep into her lungs with a sensual relish, and blew it out again in his direction, doubtless not entirely unintentionally. With the same mocking superiority as before, she said: 'You'll come round. You'll introduce me to your editor fellow, and you'll have to talk to me, however silly you're acting now!'

The whole time he had been thinking that her remark had struck home at the heart of his frustration. Stung by her words, he now broke his silence and said angrily: 'Instead of trotting along beside me and distracting me when I need to think, you'd have done better to get down to the housing office and the ration card office!

You were full of talk about how you could get it all sorted out in no time! But it never occurs to you to take the initiative, of course — it's so much easier just to leave it all to me!'

She replied scornfully: 'Don't you worry about the apartment or the ration cards! You think, because you didn't get anywhere, I won't do any better. Well, I'll go down there myself this afternoon, and I'll see that we get what we need!'

Full of feigned pity for her preening ignorance, he said: 'The offices are closed in the afternoons.'

And she shot back, even more sure of herself: 'Not for me, my friend, not for me! You'll be surprised!'

To which he replied: 'No I won't — because you won't get anywhere.'

And with that, this fresh argument was ended for now. They had arrived at the big publishing house, which had once been one of the largest and most imposing buildings in Berlin. On the outside, the towering building still looked impressive and, apart from the window openings — some with shattered glass, others empty or patched with cardboard — untouched by the war. The great heaps of rubble around the building were the only indication that it had probably not escaped unscathed on the inside.

And indeed, when they entered, they found themselves in a cavernous, smoke-blackened space, still reeking of fire, which had been created by the collapse of internal walls.

They then went through a low iron door, and suddenly the smell of burning was gone, and they breathed in the damp, acidic smell of fresh lime. A broad, dimly lit staircase rose before them, the paint on the walls seemingly only just applied by the decorators. Everything smelt new, though it had the smell of a rather cheap job. At any rate, this part of the building had only just been patched up.

On the second floor they entered the editorial office, where Doll hoped to find the publishing editor, Völger, or at least learn his whereabouts. His voice almost faltered as he inquired after the man who had formerly overseen the publication of his books; suddenly he felt as if he had been pressing towards this moment ever since the collapse of the regime, the moment that—hopefully!—would enable him to reconnect a broken past with a new and happy future. Suddenly, in the intervening second between question and answer, he trembled in fear of a 'No', or a 'No one of that name here', as if such an answer would definitively slam the door on a better future.

So he breathed a deep sigh of relief when he heard: 'I'll just go and see if Mr. Völger is free. Who shall I say is inquiring?' He felt a deadness in his limbs as he gave his name, and it was as if, overcome by vertigo, he had just been saved from falling into the abyss.

They were then led into a large, untidy-looking room, which looked more like the workplace of an engineer than a literary editor. Doll gazed into the old, careworn face of an elderly man with sparse white hair. *Good Lord!* he thought to himself in a daze, as he shook the proffered hand, *surely that can't be Völger, not this ancient old man! That can't be Völger!* And as he heard the other man start to speak, he was still thinking to himself: *Maybe he is just as shocked by my appearance. I would never have recognised him! This bloody war—what has it done to us all!*

Meanwhile he heard the other man say, visibly moved: 'Doll, I can't tell you how pleased I am to see you! You realise, don't you, that you were reported as dead? We all thought: so now he's gone, too! And now here you are, in my office! Take a seat, please, and you, too, madam! I'm sorry, it's such a mess in here ...'

And he heard himself answer, no less agitated and flurried: 'It doesn't matter if they said I was dead. As the saying goes, there's life in the old dog yet, and I intend to prove it!' As he spoke he felt Alma's eyes upon him, and was glad that she was sitting quietly, not trying to be the centre of attention at this particular moment, and so, quite contrary to his original intention, he introduced her: 'This is my wife, by the way, Mr. Völger!' And then added, sensing surprise in the other man: 'We married shortly before the end of the war.'

'Yes, indeed!' replied the man, and nodded his white-haired head. 'There've been big changes everywhere—and that includes me!' He glanced at the young woman, and it sounded almost as if his own marital circumstances had changed. But then he went on: 'And yet here I am, sitting here in this building again, like I was before the start of the Thousand-Year Reich, older and more bedraggled, doing my job like before. Sometimes it feels as if everything I've been through in the last twelve-and-a-half years is completely unreal, like a distant memory of a bad dream ...'

'Not me!' countered Doll. 'I haven't reached that point yet. For me, all these horrors are still very real. But then, of course, you've got your work again ...'

'And you? Have you not been able to do any work since the surrender?'

'No, nothing! But you have to remember, they made me mayor of the town. And then I was ill for a long time.' And he began to talk about the events of the previous months, about the hopelessness, the growing sense of apathy ...

The other man grew restless as he listened to this account, and he seized the first available opportunity to tell Doll what a dreadful time he'd had of it, and what bad experiences he'd had with other people.

Listening distractedly to the other man's story, Doll immediately thought of the far worse things that had happened to him. He barely heard what the other was saying until he had finished, and then promptly launched into his own tale of horrors.

Both men paused, each looking into the other's careworn face with a wan smile as they realised what they were doing. 'We're doing it', said Völger, smiling more broadly, 'just like our dear fellow men, whose foolishness we like to make fun of. Everyone has had it so much worse than anyone else!'

'Yes!' agreed Doll. 'And yet it turns out we've all been through pretty much the same things.'

'That's right', said Völger. 'Everyone has suffered about as much as they can take.'

'Absolutely!' agreed Doll.

And then they both fell silent. Doll was in two minds whether he should get up and leave now. Völger had not offered him the prospect of any work; he had not even asked if Doll wanted to write a piece for the newspaper he now helped to edit. Even if Völger didn't see it, Alma knew with what expectations her husband had come here. Perhaps Völger thought that Doll had simply dropped by to say hello to an old acquaintance. But she knew that this visit was meant to be the start of a new life ...

And yet ...! Precisely because Alma was there, he didn't want to ask Völger straight out if he knew of any work for him. He didn't want to beg in front of Alma. No, the only thing he could do after the other's long and unambiguous silence was to get up, say goodbye, and leave. *Moriturus te salutat!* He who is about to die salutes you! Leave now, and die quietly and with dignity! And Doll was instantly put in mind of another writer, the doctor, the doctor who had once been a writer, the fellow with a head like a skull, ignored and forgotten — how had he put it? *It's as if one were already dead*. And Doll stood up, stretching out his hand: 'Well, my dear Völger, I must be going. You must have a lot to do ...'

'Yes', said Völger, and took the proffered hand. 'Yes, there's always a lot to do, far too much! But it's really done me good to see you again—the man they said was dead! Granzow must have been pleased to see you, too. Do give him my regards. I take it he told you I was here?'

'No!' replied Doll, little suspecting what he was about to learn. Consequently he didn't inquire who this Granzow was, to whom Völger sent his regards. 'No, I read your name in the newspaper, Völger. I just came here on the off chance.'

'But you have seen Granzow?'

'No', said Doll, cautiously. 'Not yet.'

'Not yet!' cried the other. 'Maybe you didn't even know that Granzow has been trying to get hold of you for weeks now, ever since there was a rumour that you were in Berlin? Didn't you know that, Doll?'

'No', answered Doll again. 'And to tell you the truth, I don't even know who Granzow is.'

'What!' cried Völger, and was so genuinely shocked that he suddenly let go of Doll's hand, which he had still been clutching. 'You *must* know who Granzow is! You must know his poems, at the very least! Or his big novel, *Wendelin and the Sleepwalkers*? Well, of course ...', he went on, as Doll continued to shake his head, 'of course, Granzow *was* living in exile for twelve years, and the Nazis immediately banned all his books in '33, obviously. But all the same—you must know him from the time before '33!'

'I really don't!' insisted Doll. 'You have to remember that I've nearly always lived out in the country, and I know very few writers in person.'

'But you must have read about him lately in the newspapers', said Völger, trying another tack. 'He returned from exile back in May, and founded the big artists' association. You *must* have read about it, Doll!'

'I was the mayor of a small town, working an average of fourteen hours a day', said Doll, smiling at his persistent inquisitor. 'So I barely had time to read the letters I was sent, let alone a newspaper. The truth is, I looked at a newspaper last night for the first time since the end of the war, and the only name I came across that I knew was yours, Völger. That's why I'm here today. But perhaps you can tell me', he went on, 'why this Granzow is looking for me, when I don't know him and have certainly never met him?'

'But Doll!' said Völger, 'Granzow wants you to join his association, of course! People are expecting great things of you—you're just the man to write a popular novel about the last few years ...'

'No, no', said Doll in reply, and his face had suddenly darkened. 'I'm definitely not the right man for that, and I wouldn't go near the subject.' He shook his head again and went on: 'The thing is, Völger, I started off like everybody else, of course, down in the mire. But even later on, when I had clawed my way up out of it a bit, and started to think about what I might like to do later, it seemed to me impossible to write books like before, as if nothing had happened, as if our entire world had not collapsed around us. I thought we would have to write in a completely different way now, not pretending that the Thousand-Year Reich had never existed, and that one only needed to pick up again where one had left off writing before 1933. No, what was needed was a completely new beginning, new in terms of content, certainly, but also in terms of form ...'

He paused for a moment and looked a little uncertainly at Völger, who was listening closely. He ended abruptly: 'But I don't know—so far, I haven't found a way. Maybe I'll never write another book. Everything looks so bleak. Who are we any more, we Germans, in this world we have destroyed? Who should we be talking to? The Germans, who don't want to listen? Or people in other countries, who hate us?'

'Well', said Völger, 'if I were in your shoes I wouldn't worry about it, either about finding the right form or finding a readership. I am quite sure that one day you will write again, simply because you are compelled to write! And now you should go and see Granzow—I'll give you his address. The best time to catch him is around lunchtime.'

They parted shortly afterwards. The young wife had not contributed a single word to this memorable discussion, which was highly unusual for the 'sea surf'. And now, too, as they were walking back on their own, she was silent. This prolonged silence was making Doll feel uncomfortable. Even if he did feel unable to write the novel that had been suggested, and even if he had to disappoint the hopes that Völger, and presumably Granzow, too, had placed in him, he was still gratified by the reception accorded him, and by the fact that people were actually searching for him in the great metropolis of Berlin. (Though how exactly such a search could be conducted was something of a mystery to him.)

For months on end he had felt so small and dejected that the first little bit of interest anyone showed in him, the first sunshine ray of sympathy, warmed him and brightened his life. He felt different, he walked differently, he gazed with different eyes upon the burnt-out machinery lying in the fire-ravaged hall. *Perhaps one day you'll be working for me again after all*, he said to himself. *You look burnt-out and ruined now, but that can be put right—everything in life gets back on track sooner or later …*

He stepped out into the grey November day, making his way between the huge heaps of rubble. The wind whipped up evil clouds of dust and ash and scorched scraps of paper. But to him it felt like the wafting of a warm spring breeze, as if all the birds were singing, and the trees were just putting out their first green leaves. He was still somebody, after all! For so long he had felt like a nobody, he had let everyone push him around: but he was still somebody, after all! Völger had shown him it was so, and Granzow believed in him. He felt just like those machines: one day they would all be working again.

He looked across at his companion with an unspoken challenge. Why didn't she say something? Now would have been the time to let him know that she, too, was happy about the reception he had met with.

But she wasn't looking at him at all. Her gaze was directed at the windows of the shops and their pitiful displays, a meagre selection of overpriced substitute goods and showpiece items that were not for sale. All of a sudden, and without giving him any indication of her intentions, she had disappeared inside one of these shops, or rather not a shop but a pub.

Once again he was infuriated by her behaviour, the completely inconsiderate way she just left him standing there without a word of explanation, simply taking it for granted that he would wait for her. But she might be wrong about that: the tram stop was not far away, and when she emerged from the pub he might well be on the tram and on his way, and she would not be present when he had his crucial meeting with Granzow.

It upset him and fuelled his rising anger that his partner, of all people, had to sour this day when his luck was beginning to turn. So no sooner had her face appeared again than he strode off in the direction of the tram stop, not vouchsafing her so much as a glance or a word when she blithely took her place at his side as if nothing had happened.

She was smoking again, of course! So that's why she had gone into the pub—to buy more cigarettes! She was blowing the last of their money without a thought for the future. And now, of course, just when he might have had a cigarette to celebrate this special day, she hadn't offered him one.

The tram was not particularly full, and as luck would have it there were two free seats next to each other, on one of those benches by the door that face inwards rather than forwards. On the other side of the entry door, separated from them by the full width of the tram, sat a fat man with a pale but jowly face, and an old lady who was clearly not with him, whom Doll promptly dubbed 'the putrid baby' in his mind. This old maid, who had plainly never married, had the pink, innocent cheeks of a baby, but was so disfigured by age and the signs of approaching death that her childlike appearance had something vaguely obscene and sinister about it.

This old creature, decked out in frills, lace, and buttons, appeared to be irritated by the mere sight of Alma casually smoking a cigarette. She gave a couple of contemptuous snorts, looked at her jowly neighbour, then at the young woman again and finally at Doll, who revealed by the fact that he was now paying the conductor for himself and his wife that she was with him.

Doll returned her look with a cool, impassive stare, whereupon 'the putrid baby' began to mutter furiously. She directed the gaze of her pale-blue eyes now at Alma, now at the other passengers, as if inviting them to join in her protest. It was obvious that the old lady would not be able to contain her feelings for much longer. An explosion was imminent.

Perhaps Alma wanted to hasten the detonation, or perhaps she was simply oblivious of this entire dumb show. At all events, she suddenly took a comb from her handbag, tossed her hair to fluff it up, and began to comb her locks.

This was too much for the old lady. In a loud voice verging on a shriek, she called across to Alma: 'Kindly do that at home, young lady! You're not in a hairdressing salon here!'

The jowly man nodded involuntarily at these words, and indeed it seemed as if everyone on the tram who had observed the incident was on the old lady's side. But the young woman responded coolly and with controlled politeness: 'I'm sitting far enough away from you, madam, for it not to bother you!'

But when she saw the cantankerous look on the putrid baby's face, and the censorious or gleeful expressions of the other tram passengers, she suddenly handed the comb over to Doll. 'You need to use this, too, my dear. Your hair's a real mess.'

After a brief hesitation Doll took the comb and began to comb his hair. At Alma's impulsive action the gleeful faces of the onlookers had taken on an expectant or smiling expression. Even the jowly man sitting next to the old lady was smiling now. But the aggressor flushed crimson with rage, then her face suddenly turned a yellowish white, and she barked out a stinging reprimand: 'They're all the same, these dolled-up little tramps!' To which Alma coolly replied, while the whole tram waited silently with bated breath: 'And they're all the same, these dried-up old bats!'

Doll was not the only one who thought the term 'dried-up old bat' a priceless description of the old lady, because the whole tram was laughing. In fact, the jowly man was so tickled that he drummed his feet on the floor with glee—though he promptly shot an anxious glance at his neighbour. But there was nothing more to fear from her; she had lost the battle. She leaned back in the dark, grimy corner of the tram, and appeared to be wheezing her last, in the last stages of putrefaction, as Doll said to his wife.

After this little interlude, everything was sweetness and light again between the married couple. They chatted away as if they had never had the slightest falling-out. Doll now took a cigarette without hesitation, drew the smoke that he had denied himself for so long deep into his lungs with great relish, and even nodded in agreement when Alma said, almost apologetically: 'I've been reckless again — I wanted to celebrate today!'

An hour later the two of them were standing in a large, almost opulently appointed anteroom. The general state of the building and its furnishings were far superior to the place they had visited earlier. And just as this anteroom, with its old paintings on the walls, the deep-pile carpet underfoot, and the ordered efficiency of a well-run office, into which two female secretaries nonetheless injected a note of homely warmth, was far superior to Völger's place of work, so the reception they were given here far exceeded the one they got from Völger. Doll had only just said his name, and one of the two ladies had only just disappeared into the next room to announce him, when the door of this room was opened (it turned out to be a spacious salon, decorated throughout in white and blue) and a tall, fat, grey-haired man rushed out to greet Doll.

'Doll!' he cried, seizing his hand, and his entire body seemed to be shaking with excitement. 'Doll! You've finally come!'

Completely overwhelmed, Doll was tugged from the anteroom into the blue-and-white salon, while Mrs. Doll followed on silently behind. 'Doll! So you're not dead after all! You've no idea how worried we've been about you!'

And Doll, his hand clasped between the large, soft, moist hands of the other man, could think of nothing to say apart from the name that he had heard for the first time an hour and a half previously: 'Granzow! Yes, here we are, Granzow!'

They looked at each other with tears in their eyes. It was like a reunion of old friends. And there was nothing fake about these tears. They were overcome by emotion, and the memory of the past twelve years, spent in exile or in servitude, swept through them again. They were both survivors of a catastrophe, after all. Both felt the other's joy at seeing each other and getting acquainted. Under normal circumstances they would have got to know each other a long time ago.

Doll felt rather more conscience-stricken than Granzow, who did at least know Doll's books, and he was filled with a faint sense of guilt. As in: *I hope Völger never tells him that I hadn't even heard of him.* But this sense of guilt was quickly dissipated. Granzow was plainly quite uninterested in himself. He only wanted to hear about the Dolls, about what had happened to them in the last few years, where and how they had lived, where they were living now, and how they were doing. All Doll could see in the eyes of Granzow, who was listening attentively to every word he said, was joy, kindly joy. *And what am I, when all is said and done? A minor novelist, who had given up on himself a long time ago and gone into hopeless decline. But I can't let him see that, now I need to pull myself together again …*

As these thoughts were going through Doll's head, the three of them were already comfortably installed on the curved blue-velvet sofa around the big table. Lying on the table were packs of Granzow's cigarettes, to which the Dolls were free to help themselves. Coffee had also been ordered and brought in — not coffee substitute, but the real thing, even if it was a little weak: 'You'll have to excuse us, Doll. Our canteen is not quite up to scratch yet. But that will soon change, things are getting better now ...'

The 'now' almost sounded like a reference to Doll being found again, as though this moment marked the beginning of a new era—which in the present context could hardly be the intended meaning.

The conversation now took a quieter turn. The two Dolls did most of the talking, describing their experiences over the preceding months. It was very different from their meeting with Völger; here, Alma spoke, too, with no thought of demurely holding back. Which was only right and proper, for while Völger had taken no notice of Mrs. Doll apart from an initial surprised look, Granzow was visibly charmed by the vivacious young woman. He divided his attention equally between her and Doll himself, his expression by turns smiling or solicitous.

Granzow knew how to ask the right questions—and he was a great listener. What happened with Völger couldn't possibly happen here—that both parties couldn't wait to talk about their own sufferings. Granzow seemed to feel no need to talk about himself; he was, as the expression goes, all ears. He nodded eagerly when they talked about their decision to leave the small town for good. He shook his head with a worried look when he heard about the state in which they had found their Berlin apartment. He slapped the table with his hand when Doll was telling the tale of the tyrannical official at the housing office. In short, he appeared to take a lively interest in every phase of the Dolls' recent life, and they had the impression that he was not just listening for the sake of it—in one ear and out the other—but that he was already drawing conclusions and reaching decisions even as he listened ...

And they were correct in their impression, because, during a lull in the conversation, Granzow said: 'I think I've got the picture, and

I know what needs to happen next.' They looked at him expectantly. He went on: 'First, you need to get a decent apartment, ideally in an area that has not been too badly damaged. Secondly, we need to sort out a truck and trailer to fetch your things from the small town. And thirdly, you need to be issued with ration cards, preferably the No.1 card, but failing that, the No.2.'

He smiled in an affectionately fatherly way when he saw their astonished, incredulous expressions. They had only wanted to get things off their chest, after all; they were quite prepared to shift for themselves. All they wanted was a bit of sympathy, a bit of encouragement. And now it looked as if they were about to get something like real, practical help.

'Yes,' continued Granzow, still smiling, 'we can sort all that out. I'll just go and make some inquiries ...' And the big, heavy man stood up, hurried from the room, and left the two of them alone.

They looked at each other, and their faces had brightened. 'It's not possible', said Doll. 'And yet it is so. Someone's really going to help us again!'

And she replied: 'I've always liked my apartment, even though it's been wrecked—but if we can get a place of our own, just for us ...'

Doll said: 'It was that simple: we just needed to talk to this one man. And we were pretty much on our last legs, Alma!'

He felt a kind of trembling in his limbs, and she too was sitting quite still, thinking back on the journey that had led them here, to the blue-and-white salon. They had got through the bad times; now things were looking up again. At that moment it did not occur to Doll to think that maybe it wasn't that easy, that it would take more than having a place to live, food to eat, and their old things around them. He forgot now that there had been a war on, the time of suffering before that, that he was a burnt-out case, an empty shell devoid of content … That even the helpful Granzow could not give him this content, that he would have to create it for himself, finding a faith again, not only in himself, but more especially in his fellow Germans, in the entire world, in the meaning of work and perseverance, a firm belief in a bright future for mankind: he forgot that he had none of this in him.

Right now, all this was far from his thoughts. Instead he said, as he freed himself from her embrace: 'Now we have been given a chance, and God knows we'll make the most of it! We mustn't let Granzow down and make him regret it!'

'Definitely not', she agreed.

Granzow returned with a smile on his face. 'That's all arranged!' he said. 'The best thing would be to come by again the day after tomorrow, then I can tell you more. Would one o'clock, the day after tomorrow, suit you? Good, then let's say Thursday at one o'clock here!'

He looked at them both, smiling benignly, like a father who is well pleased with his children. The thought flashed through Doll's mind that Granzow could hardly be any older than him, and yet he felt so young, so boyish and immature by comparison. 'And there's one thing more I must ask you, Doll', continued Granzow after a pause. 'But you don't have to answer if you don't want to. So: how are you getting on with your work? You understand that we're all waiting for it … Have you written anything recently? Or have you got plans for a new work?'

'Well', said Doll hesitantly, 'The thing is—'

And Granzow cut in quickly: 'No, really, Doll, if you'd rather not talk about your plans … I'm not asking just to be nosy.'

'Oh, I understand', replied Doll, speaking more quickly. 'And it's not that I'm reluctant to talk about it. It's just that I'm afraid you'll be disappointed, Granzow. The fact is, I don't actually have any plans. It's true that in the last six months before the surrender, I started to write down my memories of the Nazis …'

'That's great!' cried Granzow.

'I don't know. I don't think it *is* great. Nothing really terrible happened to me, you see, and to note down in such detail all the little pinpricks that came my way … The book might have been of some interest, perhaps, because it shows how a person can be driven to the brink of suicide just by pinpricks …' Thus far, Doll had been speaking hesitantly, almost reluctantly. But now he went on more quickly: 'But it's all so long ago. Since then the war has ended, and so much has happened to me that my hatred for the Nazis has gone completely, and been replaced by a general hatred of mankind. For me, the Nazis have ceased to exist …'

'No, no!' protested Granzow. 'On the contrary, Mr. Doll, I think those Nazi gentlemen are still very much alive. There are times when I am acutely aware of that.'

'Well, yes, perhaps the odd one here and there, who will never learn and never change.' Granzow shook his head vigorously. 'But', Doll went on, 'be that as it may, the book is past history for me.' And when the other gestured as if to plead with him: 'I can't even bring myself to take a look at it or type it up—not for now anyway …'

He fell silent and looked at Granzow, who replied quickly: 'Look, my dear Doll, nobody is going to force you to do anything you don't want to. All in good time. And what about your own plans for the future?'

'Nothing!' said Doll, feeling guilty. 'I have thought about writing novels sometimes, and about particular themes. But none of it seemed of any consequence. After everything fell apart—including me—I've always had this feeling that I need to start all over again, and do things differently.' He was speaking more quickly now, only repeating what he had said to the publishing editor Völger an hour and a half previously. 'No', he said in conclusion, 'I'm sorry to disappoint you, Mr. Granzow, at our very first meeting. Maybe my appetite for work will come back again, once my outward circumstances have improved a little. I need a certain inner calm in order to produce anything, as well as peace and quiet in my outward life.'

'Of course!' agreed Granzow. They carried on talking for a few minutes, but not about Doll's work. The jovial mood of first acquaintance returned once more. Then they took their leave of each other, with the promise to reconvene at one o'clock in two days' time.

But as they were leaving the building, a chauffeur in grey uniform inquired: 'Mr. Granzow has asked me to drive you home. Where would you like me to take you?'

More kindness and courtesy, more indulgence! But more of an inward obligation, therefore, not to disappoint so much good faith.

For a while they sat in silence in the back of the car behind the driver, overwhelmed by happiness. Then the woman nudged her husband gently. 'You know—!' she whispered.

To which he replied: 'Yes, what then?'

'My dear', she said, 'I'm so happy I'm going to die! To think that someone is helping us out again! I want to shout—shout for joy!' And she babbled on like a spoilt child: 'And now you must be really nice to your little Alma! Now you must give her a lovely long kiss! A thousand kisses! Otherwise I'll scream!'

'The chauffeur!' he reminded her, and yet was happy to oblige her anyway.

'Chauffeur very old man!' she babbled. 'Chauffeur only drive car! Chauffeur see nothing! You young man, you give little Alma thousand kisses, otherwise I'll scream!'

And so the Dolls exchanged a long, lingering kiss … It was so long since they had sat in a car that it didn't even occur to them that a chauffeur has a rear-view mirror, in which he can see everything that's going on in the back of the car. Just like children, they thought that nobody was looking.

The chauffeur was not a discreet man, but he was a genuine Berliner. 'And do you know what, Mr. Granzow', he said, as he was driving his employer home that evening and had finished telling the tale, 'do you know what, they didn't just give each other a little peck, like an old married couple—they were all over each other, like a pair of young things. And as for him, he's getting on a bit, he must be our sort of age, Mr. Granzow. But he's all right, he is, and if he writes books the same way he kisses, then I might take up reading yet, Mr. Granzow!'

CHAPTER TWELVE

Restored to health

In a northern suburb of Berlin, a man is sitting by the window of a small room. It is high summer, July; to be precise, it is the fifth of July in the year 1946. Although it is only around nine in the morning, the air has lost the dewy freshness of the night. It is hot, and it is going to get a lot hotter still today, unless a thunderstorm cools things down a bit.

But for now the sky does not look as if a storm is brewing. It is radiant with sunshine, completely cloudless, and not so much blue as a dull, whitish silver with just a hint of blueness. Whenever the man looks up from his writing and gazes out of the window (which he does not infrequently; he appears to be not all that absorbed by his labours), he finds himself squinting a little to shield his eyes against the glare of the summer sky. But then beneath this sky shimmering with heat he sees something that gladdens the heart, even in a suburb of Berlin: green treetops, the gables of houses, and red roofs, but not a single ruin. There's not so much as a freshly repaired roof to be seen, and even the windows of the houses appear to be all intact. A real sight for sore eyes in this city of ruins!

The writer looks up frequently from his work. He sits there, pen in hand, poised to begin writing again. But first he listens out for the voices down in the yard. The voices he hears are invariably women's voices, and almost always those of young women, and they all speak in the easy, rather throwaway manner of native Berliners. More than once, somebody says: 'It's too 'ot indoors by 'alf today!' or: 'I'll tell you what *that's* all about, so I will!'

But the man doesn't smile at this, and he doesn't feel the slightest bit superior when he hears this kind of rough, 'uneducated' talk. He has learned that he has no reason to feel superior to anything or anyone.

Although the voices sound young, and although the man only needs to stand up and step over to the window to get a good view of the women as they speak, he doesn't do so. He knows that some of these girls and women are very pretty, and they are sunning themselves out there in the most casual state of undress, but he is not curious; instead he feels old, very old, and tired. During the last year, his hair has gone very grey; but given how old he feels, it ought to be snowy-white.

As he writes, the man frequently hears another sound apart from the chattering of the women. He lays the pen down and listens, straining hard to hear. It's a very strange sound that comes to his ears, a cross between the cooing of a dove and the fluting of a slightly out-of-tune blackbird. This strange sound, which he could not identify at all during the first few weeks of his stay here, is made by a large dog, half Doberman and half Alsatian. This creature was probably driven out of its mind by all the gunfire and the flames and the crazy commotion during the final assault on Berlin, and is now chained up somewhere down there beneath the green treetops, looked after by a halfwit who lives in this building at No.10 Elsastrasse. In the evening, Hermann — that's what everyone in the house calls her, though her real name is Hermine — lets the dog loose, and the creature then guards No.10 Elsastrasse through the night; and woe to the stranger who dares to climb over the fence! The dog would tear him apart without a moment's hesitation: it is a mad dog, and nothing could hold him back, not even his keeper Hermann.

The strange thing is that this dog—called 'Mucki', a name conferred on him in happier times that no longer suits him at all—can bark at night, but during the day, when he is chained up, he can only flute and coo like a bird. He just didn't have a good war. Wounded inside, he cries out in pain, is capable of murder, and is no use for anything. The man sometimes wonders, when he hears this strange sound, how many humans are in much the same place as this Mucki.

Yes, the man finds all kinds of reasons for looking up from his work and taking a break for a few minutes from the concentrated effort of writing in his scratchy hand. From time to time, he looks across at a loudly ticking wall clock to check the time and see if it is still too soon for him to stand up and tidy his papers away. This wall clock with its faded blue face and brass-coloured pendulum is the only item of furnishing in the small, cramped room that goes beyond the bare essentials. A table, a chair, a bed, a narrow wall closet, and an ancient, completely faded velvet armchair constitute the sum total of the room's furnishings.

Except—there is one object that should not be forgotten, even though it is generally tucked away out of sight. It is a black velvet cushion, decorated with a kind of painted scene. The scene depicts a castle with three turrets, lilac-coloured roofs, and lots of windows, which are red at the bottom and yellow at the top, while the walls of the castle are formed by the unpainted black velvet. One turret has a white flag on top of a long pole, the second has a cross, also in white, and the third just has a kind of very long white lance. Also in the picture are trees with white trunks and green leaves in many shades;

rocky crags in pink, lilac, and flame-red; and dotted about here and there, for no apparent reason, are white railings. Hanging over the whole scene is a circular, yellow orb, which might equally well be the moon or the sun.

The man loathes this cushion with a fierce hatred. He curses it just because it has survived this war undamaged in all its bovine ghastliness, while so much of beauty has been destroyed. He hides the cushion at the bottom of his bed or in the little wall closet, just so that he doesn't have to look at it all the time. But the cleaning lady keeps on finding it, and helpfully pats it out flat again on the faded velvet armchair, clearly delighting in this choice work of art. The man could ask the cleaning lady to leave the cushion where he has hidden it, but he refrains from doing so. He never says a word to this woman, even though she always announces in the same friendly manner, when she has finished cleaning the room: 'Now you can get back to your work!' or: 'Now you can have a cup of coffee.'

Not that one could really blame the writer all that much for pausing so often in his labours. He is only writing out of a sense of duty, without any real enthusiasm or belief in what he is doing, perhaps in part just to prove to himself and others that he is capable of finishing what he has started. Begun six months or so earlier, this piece of work at first seemed to be going well. Then came various interruptions, due to personal disagreements, illness, or simply a lack of appetite for work, and the more he delayed final completion, the less interest the writer himself took in the work he was doing.

But the situation on this fifth of July was a little different. On this morning, the man had awoken from a sound night's sleep and had suddenly realised how to steer the little ship of his writing out of the sea of facts and into a tranquil harbour at last. He could not yet say with certainty whether he would reach this harbour in two days, eight days, or twelve days, but even a voyage of twelve days held no more terrors for him, since he now knew that a safe harbour awaited. When he paused in his work today, he was just continuing the bad habits of previous days; he was not deliberately looking for excuses to be lazy.

The man glanced again at the wall clock with the faded blue face, and saw that it was late enough for him to stop writing with a clear conscience. He gathered up pen and paper, put them away in the wall closet, and picked up a block of wood with a key hanging from it. With this key and some toilet things, he crossed a forecourt towards a door on the far side, on which was hung a sign that said in large, clear letters: 'Not to be used by gon. or syph.!'

The man made to open the door when he saw that there was already a key in the lock, attached to a block of wood exactly like the one he was holding in his hand. He muttered something about 'bloody cheek!' and was about to place his hand on the door handle when the door was opened from the inside and a girl or young woman, dressed only in a very short shirt, brushed past him, obviously feeling guilty, and disappeared through the door of a nearby room.

The man gazed after her for a moment, in half a mind to kick up an almighty fuss over this unauthorised use of his toilet. The sign was clear enough, after all. But then he thought better of it. He had never yet sounded off since he had been living in this place, and he would adopt a different tactic. He withdrew the key from the lock, went into the toilet with both keys, and bolted the door behind him.

As he was having a thorough wash in there, he wondered whether he should complain to Mother Trüller about this blatant disregard for the no-entry sign, or whether it would not be simpler just to commandeer this second key, which was supposed to be for the sole use of the nursing staff, and had only been left in the door as a result of someone's carelessness. He decided on the second course of action: Mother Trüller had enough on her plate, and the effect of even the most severe dressing-down from her would last only for a day at most. As for the so-called patients here …

Yes, as for these so-called patients, who for the most part were not actually ill at all, as for these sixty women, with whom he shared this madhouse at No.10 Elsastrasse as the only male occupant, all warnings, tongue-lashings, pleas, and prohibitions were completely lost on them. On the contrary, they were all imbued with the best of bad intentions, determined to break all the rules and make trouble wherever they could.

When the man moved in here a good eight weeks previously, and suddenly found himself in the company of sixty women who were mostly young and pretty, he had expected to be living a highly entertaining and also instructive life. Not that he had any designs on these ladies, not at all: the nature of the diseases that had landed them in this place—usually under gentle pressure from the police—was such as to deter him from any such designs. The women had picked up these diseases, the names of which were spelled out with brutal clarity on the no-entry sign on the door of his toilet, out there in the city of Berlin, recklessly, knowingly, or—in a few cases—unknowingly. They had been diagnosed by doctors and put on a course of treatment.

But these women had given up on the treatment, either failing to turn up for their appointments at the doctor's surgery or choosing to ignore the doctor's instructions, so that they posed a constant threat to anyone who had anything to do with them. That's when the gentle police pressure was applied, and they were deposited at the door of this institution, which they were not allowed to leave until they were fully cured. Some of them had proved difficult to find; they knew what awaited them. They had changed their address, avoiding their treatment by devious cunning, only to be scooped up eventually in some police raid.

Well, despite all this, or perhaps precisely because of it, the man had hoped to derive some entertainment and instruction from these ladies, and hear some colourful life stories. Instead he soon realised that all these girls were hopelessly stupid and dishonest. To hear them talk, they had all ended up in this place through the dirty tricks of the doctors, the public health authorities, and the police, and it was only when they got here that they had been infected by the immoral women they had to share a room with!

It didn't take great powers of discernment to see that they were lying, and as for their laziness, it beggared belief. Although they were not confined to bed by illness, except on the days when they were given their injections or a crash course of pills, there were many among them who hardly got out of bed during the whole eight or twelve weeks of their treatment. There they lay, young and blooming, with strong, healthy limbs, but bone idle and not prepared to do any useful work. They were so lazy that if one of them felt sick from the large intake of pills, none of the others could be bothered to hold out the sick bowl for her. For all they cared, she could vomit all over the floor — that's what the nurse was there for, to clean it up afterwards. So they would ring for the nurse, and if she didn't come at once, the mess stayed where it was. The filth and smell didn't bother them, but the idea of doing any work at all was anathema to them.

That wasn't what they were here for, living in a world where it is so easy for a pretty young girl to clean a man out, like a nicely fattened Christmas goose! And they would boast to each other of their triumphs, telling of pockets daringly picked, of their magnetic charms as barmaids, of their whole wasted, useless lives — and the more useless, the more glorious in their eyes. And then they went and stole cigarettes from each other, and tossed their medical prescriptions out of the window or dropped them down the toilet (being too 'smart' to let themselves be poisoned by these doctors!); and when their relatives came to visit them on Sundays, they complained bitterly about how bad the food was here, and how they had to go hungry. Yet according to their regular weekly weight checks, they were growing steadily fatter from idleness and gluttony.

No indeed, the man's expectations had not been fulfilled. There was nothing romantic about these women; they were not bathed in some redemptive glow. He was not very patient with them, it is true. There had been great excitement among them when this man came to live in a house of women; they had been friendly and welcoming towards him, and in the first few weeks there had been no shortage of visitors who sought him out in his room under all manner of pretexts. But he had soon given up chatting to them. It annoyed him every time that they thought him stupid enough to believe their cock-and-bull stories.

And they were greedy. He could tell from the way they looked at the food on his plate, comparing it with their own portions. As a private patient of the senior consultant, who had not been able to find room for him anywhere else but here, he did enjoy something of a special position, but by and large he was given exactly the same food as they had. Mother Trüller could hardly cook separate meals for one man! But they eyed the size of his bread slices, gauged the thickness of the topping, and said: 'It's all right for some!' Or else: 'I couldn't care less!'

And then they always wanted something from him: a cigarette, or a light for a cigarette, or a book or a newspaper or fuel for their lighter—they took it to such extremes that he would refuse them the simplest favour.

Then came a stand-off period, when they no longer visited him and hardly gave him the time of day; after that, open war was declared on him. One day, a drunken lout had tried to climb over the garden railings and get into the house, whereupon the man declared that it could hardly come as a surprise to anyone who had observed how they shamelessly accosted or taunted every passing man from the balconies of their rooms, after the manner of whores, which of course is what most of them were. This had driven them to extremes of indignation at this liar and traitor. None of them had ever called out to anyone from their balcony—not so much as a word—and when the doctor gave instructions for the balcony doors to be locked anyway, they swore to the man that they would beat him one night until every bone in his body was broken!

Well, they hadn't beaten him. In fact, they had soon abandoned the silent treatment they gave him during the first few weeks following this incident. They were unreliable in everything—even their dislikes. They started speaking to him again, every now and then one of them would come and scrounge a cigarette, and if he couldn't spare a cigarette, then a couple of butt ends would do. But the man didn't forget so easily; he was finished with them for good, even if that meant casting out a few righteous souls for the sake of the many unrighteous.

The man finished his ablutions some time ago, and now he has tidied up his room a bit and locked the two keys to the toilet away in his wall closet. He grinned a little at the thought of Nurse Emma and Nurse Gertrud, who would soon be searching frantically for this key!

He now put on a coat, despite the blazing sun: he was ashamed to be seen on the street in his stained and crumpled suit. He went downstairs and made for the kitchen. In the kitchen, Mother Trüller and her acolytes were busy preparing lunch for the eighty or so residents. Her face was flushed a deep red; her stout chest, invariably covered by a yellow or lilac lace ruffle, heaved mightily as the heavy cooking pots became as light as feathers in her hands. She was working so hard that the sweat stood out on her brow in bright little beads, but she was in an excellent mood.

She smiled radiantly when she caught sight of the man, and said: 'Mr. Doll, are you leaving so early? You want to sign out now, I expect?'

'Yes, I'd like to sign out, Mother Trüller, I'm in good health, and ready to roam! And if the truck and trailer really do turn up today, I won't be back for lunch, either. I hope they do turn up.'

'I hope so, for your sake. But I won't hear of you missing lunch. I'm glad to think I've put twenty pounds on you! If you're not back by three, I'll send out some lunch for you—and enough for the whole family!'

'No, don't do that, Mother Trüller!' said the man. And in a quieter voice, so that the others wouldn't hear: 'You know I'm already too deeply in debt to you. Who knows when I'll ever be able to pay it all off again!' And he sighed deeply.

'Oh, you'll have paid it all off in six months!' announced Mother Trüller with a broad smile. 'A man like you—healthy again, full of energy, all you have to do is sit down and start working, and you'll be rolling in money! So what is there to sigh about, on a nice summer's day like this?'

While she was administering this good-natured rebuke, she had shepherded Doll to the door of the building, stopping at the threshold that the girls and women who lived here were only allowed to cross when they were fully recovered. 'Well, all the best, Mr. Doll! Maybe the truck really will come today. And if you should hear anything—you know what I mean—you'll let me know at once?'

'But of course, Mother Trüller', replied Doll, and stepped out onto the street, into the brilliant sunshine.

That's her all over, he said to himself as he walked on, *and she'll never change. She'll never forget to remind anyone leaving the house that they must tell her at once if they hear any news. It doesn't matter what they've been talking about—she always thinks to give them this reminder as a parting shot.*

In actual fact, she is always thinking about it, even when she's having a conversation about something completely different. The worry about her missing son is constantly eating away at her, underneath it all—the thought of him, her love for him. As the director and proprietor of this somewhat crazy hospital in Elsastrasse, an institution for women run by a woman, she thinks all the time only of her son, and thinks of herself only as his trustee. She has had no news of him for fifteen months now; Erdmann disappeared at the time of the battle for Berlin. He might have become a POW, or he might be lying somewhere on the streets of this vast sea of ruins, hit by a stray bullet, crushed under falling masonry, buried under rubble. And this might have happened a while back, fifteen months ago.

But his mother is still waiting for him, and she will carry on waiting if she has to, for years on end. And many other mothers and wives are waiting with her for their sons, their husbands—waiting for loved ones who may never return. Meanwhile this farmer's daughter from Hanover, who has worked her way up in the world by her own efforts, is tirelessly busy. She keeps her female patients, who are always up to mischief, on a tight leash, she works day and night, she has a friendly word for everyone, she has a sympathetic ear for everyone's troubles, and tries to help wherever she can. She really doesn't have time to feel depressed and fed up with work. With her plain, no-nonsense approach to life, she is an example to us all.

But she never forgets to say to anyone who is going out: 'If you hear anything—about my son Erdmann, that is—you must let me know at once.'

The outside world, beyond the neighbouring streets where all her tradesmen live, is a remote, alien world for Mother Trüller, who is always in her little hospital, constantly under pressure to keep people fed and attend to their other basic bodily needs. For her, the big wide world, where miracles can happen every day, begins a leisurely five-minute walk away from her front door—a world where one might run into her missing son Erdmann in the street, and say to him: 'Look here, Erdmann, it's high time you called in on your mother again. She's been waiting for you constantly, day and night, for fifteen months. She's still living at No. 10 Elsastrasse.'

Not that Erdmann is the kind of son who needs to be told to go and see his own mother. Quite the contrary: Erdmann would have got in touch with his mother without being told.

But the world out there, this vast, sprawling, chaotic Berlin, is so weird and wonderful, so full of wondrous things. The visitor might run across someone who has heard of the son, who has perhaps seen him somewhere. He might have heard news of the repatriation of POWs, the most astonishing and incredible rumours—Mother Trüller is ready to hear anything and everything. Her stout heart is not apt to flutter at the smallest thing; she is not that easily discouraged. Her hopes are kept alive by the story of one home-comer who turned up out of the blue.

So she waits and hopes. And waiting and hoping along with her are hundreds, thousands, of women that nobody talks about. In the war they were good enough to offer up their sons and husbands, and then quietly step into their shoes in the workplace. Now they are quietly waiting, getting on with their work, wherever they are. It's just that they say to anyone who is going out: 'You will let me know if you hear anything, won't you?'

Good, capable, indestructible Mother Trüller, mother of the people, eternal mother, eternal believer, who waits and faints not, who seeks to help wherever she can …!

As he was thinking these thoughts, the man in the shabby, crumpled, stained clothes under the pale summer coat, which was not exactly in pristine condition itself, walked past quite a few pubs, where—as he very well knew—cigarettes could be bought on the black market. He was dying for a smoke, but he restrained himself. Dear American cigarettes costing eleven marks apiece had been off-limits for a long time now in the Doll household—as he had rightly predicted to his wife. But even so-called 'cheap' German cigarettes at five marks each were strictly rationed to one a day, at most; one German cigarette only in the evening after supper, the smoke drawn deep into the lungs with sensuous relish—and then that was all for the next twenty-four hours.

All? Well, not quite. The Dolls were smokers; they would always be smokers. Even now, Doll had his pockets filled with something he could smoke. They collected the rose petals from Mother Trüller's garden—not just the ones that had fallen off, but the ones that were in full bloom as well—and dried them. They reasoned thus: 'This rose will drop its petals in the next few hours anyway!' and then they would pluck them, stuff Doll's pockets with the petals, and turn his room into a drying and curing plant. So the room smelled constantly of roses. They had also smoked the leaves of cherry trees, and, when they were really desperate, even a vile-tasting blood-cleansing tea, from which they first had to pick out the juniper berries and stalks.

That's how frugal they had become, even the young wife, who was so determined never to deny herself anything. They once owned a car—one each, in fact—and money, and all the things that money can buy; such commodities, the good things of this life, were no problem for them. But now the mantra that they were a defeated nation had become engrained in their thinking. They laughed at their foul-smelling 'tobacco', they were apt to cover up their stained clothing, but they were not ashamed any more. *What do people expect? We are a defeated nation, we have lost an all-out, total war, and now we are reduced to total beggars.* The suburb through which Doll was now walking had survived the war relatively unscathed. Here and there a roof had been blown in, even the odd house reduced completely to rubble, but by and large everything appeared intact and not too run-down amidst the abundant summer greenery. It was just the people on the streets: they could all have done with twenty pounds more weight on them, and fifty fewer wrinkles on their faces. They were still enduring unimaginable poverty, wearing rags instead of clothes, and shoes that were forever falling apart and being mended, held together with string, shoes that looked as if they had trailed the length and breadth of Europe.

For quite a while there was a young girl walking ahead of Doll, who had none of the charm that youth confers on even the most unprepossessing; she walked with difficulty on bloody, festering, dirty legs, as if barely dragging herself along. Her dress appeared to have been made from a couple of flour sacks. When the wearer made it, she still retained a little bit of hope, despite her wretched circumstances; she had added some crudely embroidered decorative trims and a little white collar, as if to say: 'I'm young, you can still look at me, even if I am only wearing a dress made from old sacking!'

But all these additions were now looking battered and crumpled, and so dirty that the white collar looked almost black, or at any rate no lighter than the sacking. In the course of her long travels she had lost all hope, given up on herself a long time ago. *These people I see walking the streets with me can be divided into two groups*, thought Doll: *the ones who cannot hope, and the ones who dare not hope.*

But all of them, whichever group they belonged to, were carting something around with them: a few wretched twigs snapped off the trees; burst suitcases, whose contents one would really rather not know; handbags stuffed full; and mysterious briefcases whose locks had long since broken because they had been overfilled too often, and which were now held together with a piece of string.

We're all going to perish anyway, thinks one group. *But first, let us eat our fill again! Eat until we are replete with good things, and contentment flows through our veins along with the bright blood, which has at last received some decent nutrients!*

Meanwhile the expressions on the faces of the other group are saying: *We have to gather our strength for our daily toil, so that we can survive these times in one piece.* But all of them were scarred by the war, and all of them shared a tendency to caution, a lingering doubt: *Maybe something terrible will suddenly happen to us, too — so it's good to have had our hopes, at least!* Doll himself was moderately pessimistic: he didn't believe that he or his family would perish, but he thought it entirely possible that the future could get extremely unpleasant.

He now turned off from a main thoroughfare into a quiet, green side street lined with villas. But his access to this street was blocked by a red-and-white barrier pole, with a sentry box next to it painted in diagonal red-and-white stripes, where a Russian sentry and a German policeman were standing guard to ensure that no unauthorised persons entered this area, where only officers of the occupying power were allowed to live. Doll had the necessary identification papers on him, and was let through without difficulty, but he still didn't like going through this barrier. Anything that reminded him too much of the war and the military was unwelcome. The sense of impatience he felt at the sight of this red-and-white sentry box could be more or less summed up thus: *It's time to be done with this kind of business—not just here, but across the whole world!*

At the same time, he knew very well that such feelings were foolish. All of this was still necessary: the world, and his fellow countrymen in particular, were not yet ready for a life without constant supervision, without the threat of force. For too long had reason been cast down from its throne. Especially as his dear fellow countrymen would doubtless smash each other's heads in if they were left unsupervised ...

By now, Doll was only twenty paces away from a pretty, yellow-painted villa, which looked very well maintained, with its flowerbeds out front (though they had potatoes growing in them now), and its windows all intact and fitted with blinds. This villa was not his final destination today—that lay three or four minutes further on—but he had made up his mind to call in briefly while he was passing. In it lived a man who had helped him a great deal during the previous, difficult year, a man whom he had repeatedly disappointed, and yet who remained unfailingly kindly and helpful. A good, true friend, and quite selfless—one of life's rare gifts even in normal times, and how much more so today!

Doll had neglected this man criminally in recent months, acting as if this man, who continued to worry about him, no longer existed. Doll had made absolutely no effort to contact him. Now it was high time to go and show his face again.

Even so, Doll was sorely tempted to walk on to the next street corner, and the one after that, to see if the truck and trailer had arrived yet from the small town. And if the truck was there, then he would have to help unload the things and set them up indoors. In which case, he would have to skip this visit.

He stood there hesitating for a moment, and then told himself to get a grip: *Never mind the truck and trailer—you've put it off for long enough!* He pressed the bell button, and a moment later the garden gate buzzed. He pushed it open, walked through the front garden, and said to the maid: 'Is Mr. Granzow at home?' And as it had been a long time since he was last there, he added by way of explanation: 'Doll.'

'Yes, I know!' said the maid, sounding slightly offended, and disappeared inside the house.

Doll didn't have to wait long. He didn't have to follow the maid through into the writer's study, feeling anxious as he crossed the threshold and trying to read his host's expression. As so often, it was made easy for him, easier than he probably deserved ...

Granzow appeared at the door of his house, dressed in dark trousers and a pristine white shirt, evidently having come straight from his desk, with a pen in one hand and a cigarette in the other. And just like before, he cried: 'Doll! How wonderful to see you here again! Are you well again now? Are you living over there now? So you're waiting for Alma, who's coming with the truck that's bringing your things? I say again: wonderful to see you! Now you're starting to get somewhere, and it's all happening for you! But come on in, don't stand out there in the blazing heat. You do smoke, don't you?

Here, take one! And here's a light. Now sit yourself down and tell me how you are! What are you all up to?'

And so the conversation began to flow—no word of reproach, not so much as a passing thought. Nothing but kindliness, interest, and an eagerness to help. And then, of course, the moment came when Granzow leaned forward and cautiously inquired in a soft voice (as though he didn't want to damage something fragile): 'And how's the work going? Have you started to write again? Are you making good progress?'

'Oh well, Granzow …' replied Doll, slightly embarrassed. 'Yes, I've started to write again. I'm doing my stint every day, but that's just it: I'm just going through the motions. Like a schoolboy doing his homework. But I don't have the spark or the drive, the inspiration that is really the best part of all. And as for my day job, writing short stories for newspapers just to bring some money in … Well, yes, sometimes I do actually enjoy it again. But I'm not really getting anywhere. We're saddled with debt from the time when we were struggling. We can just get by each day, but there's nothing left over. And now there's the hire of the truck to fetch our things from the country, and that's going to cost thousands!' He looked quizzically at Granzow.

He had been listening to this litany of sorrows with his customary attentive concern. 'Ah yes, your debts!' he interjected. 'I've heard about them. I'm also told that you've started to sell off your books. You shouldn't do that, Doll! You've sold enough already. Far too much, in fact. It's time to stop!'

'But what am I supposed to do?' cried Doll in despair. 'It's all very well to say "Stop selling off your things!" I'd like nothing more. You know how I love my books. It's taken me fifteen years to amass my collection. Every spare mark I had went on buying more books.

But now I simply have to sell them. These debts are starting to make life very difficult!'

'I understand, I understand!' said Granzow soothingly. 'But I still wouldn't sell the books. Why don't you have a frank talk with a publisher?'

'But I'm already in debt to Mertens!'

'I'm sure that won't matter, Doll', said Granzow. 'Mertens is a reasonable man. Talk to him—he can only say no, and even if he does, you won't be any worse off than you are now. But he won't say no. Most likely he's only waiting for you to ask. Do you want me to have a word with Mertens?'

'Absolutely not!' cried Doll, appalled. 'I can't let you do all my dirty work for me, Granzow! If anyone is going to talk to Mertens, it'll be me!'

'So you will speak to Mertens?'

'Probably. Very likely. Don't give me that sceptical smile! I expect I'll do it, really I will.'

'And if you don't do it, then I'll do it for you. Anyway: no more selling off books and other things, Doll! Forgive me for interfering like this. But the other way really is better.'

'Fine', said Doll, his mind now made up. 'I'll speak to Mertens. You can't imagine what it would be like, Granzow, to be free from all these worries at a stroke! I never had debts before—it's just awful!'

'And then you'll be able to write freely again', Granzow went on. 'You'll see, one day you'll write the book that everyone is waiting for! I'm absolutely sure of it, and you'll do a great job!'

And he wouldn't be persuaded otherwise, despite Doll's sceptical head-shaking. Then they talked about Granzow's trip down to the south of Germany. They told each other stories, they chatted, they were still the same old new friends from before, even if there had been disappointments. They didn't have a lot in common, but there was one thing that united them every time: the belief that they had to work, for themselves and for their nation. And they loved their work—for them, everything revolved around this work, which never became just a day job for them.

Doll found himself out on the street again, still smoking one of Granzow's 'proper' cigarettes. He turned a couple of corners and stood at the entrance to the little street of villas where he now lived. There was no truck and trailer parked outside his house. So it was good that he had called in to see Granzow without checking first, good that he had made the effort—otherwise he would be feeling ashamed now that he had ducked out of it.

He walked slowly up to the house, unlocked the door, and went in. The children were living here alone now, looked after by an elderly housekeeper, but at the moment they were at school. The whole place was deserted and empty. Worse than that: it all looked untidy and squalid, covered in dirt and dust. Nobody was lavishing any care or attention on this house, which could have been a proper home. In the little girl's room the bed had not yet been made, even though it was now getting on for midday. Items of laundry, some clean and some dirty, were draped over the furniture or lying on the floor. An outsize teddy bear, as big as a six-year-old child, was sitting in the corner and gazing blankly at the visitor with its brown eyes.

He stood in front of the gaping wardrobe, trying to decide whether he should try and tidy up a bit. But he abandoned the idea with a sigh even before he had begun. Tidying up involved more than just stuffing the scattered laundry into the tangled mess inside the wardrobe. Tidying up meant cleaning the wardrobe from top to bottom, inside and out, along with all the other furniture, and then scrubbing the entire room, cleaning the windows …

So he just shrugged his shoulders. What would have been the point of tidying up, since there was nobody in the house with an interest in keeping it tidy? He opened the windows, just for the sake of doing something ... Then he went upstairs to the top floor. *The boy's room is locked—and quite right, too! The lad keeps it tidy himself—and he doesn't want anybody poking about in there.*

The parental bedroom looked just as it did a week before, when Alma left to go to the small town. The bed was just as it was when she got up, with a few newspapers scattered around on the floor and a dirty ashtray, from which all the butt ends had been removed, leaving just the paper behind; a used washstand; and here, too, underwear and items of clothing scattered about on the furniture and on the floor, and the wardrobe gaping wide open.

It would be easy to blame the old housekeeper for doing nothing. But the few hours she was here each day were almost entirely taken up with shopping for food, waiting in queues, and cooking the meals. No, it wasn't the housekeeper's fault, but somebody else's ...

Once again, just like downstairs in the children's room, Doll shrugged his shoulders, but here he didn't even bother to open the windows. He walked across to the other room, the one that he had planned to make into his study. Something had come up in the meantime; but the plan was still to turn this light, airy room into a study for himself.

He sat down at the desk and looked around the room. A few bookshelves had been hastily placed against the wall at random, only half-filled. The desk was still standing in the middle of the room, where the removal men had left it. The top section of a large bookcase was standing on the floor, like a second desk, and like the desk itself it was piled with books, the books that he hadn't been able to sell. Doll's gaze fell upon a large, lidded Chinese vase, a magnificent piece in purple, green, and blue, which stood on a tall, black pedestal in a corner of the room.

Doll greeted it with a wave of his hand. The vase was the only item of value they had managed to salvage from a catastrophic world war. It was the last of many precious things that remained in their possession, for no apparent reason—probably only because they were too feeble and lazy to carry it all the way out to an antique shop in the west end of Berlin. Otherwise they had lost practically everything that they cared about, he and Alma both, and what was left was more like a den than a house, a bolthole to eat and sleep in, but not a place to live, not a home.

And yet at one time it had very nearly been a home for them. Back then, after that first meeting with Granzow, when Doll received so much help from an entirely unexpected quarter, when they were able to move out of the half-wrecked room with its cellophane window constantly fluttering and twittering and into this house, leaving behind the dubious Mrs. Schulz, and Gwenda the actress, and all the doctors they had exploited; back then, when they had not wanted for encouragement, food, and fuel; back then, when Doll made contact with the publisher Mertens, and wrote articles for newspapers and started a novel—back then, they had thrown themselves enthusiastically into the business of making a home for themselves. Back then, this house had looked quite cosy and inviting …

So how come everything had started to fall apart again, and hard-won gains had quickly turned to losses? Sitting at his desk, in the dusty den, Doll pondered this as he gazed out onto the street, which lay shimmering in the heat …

Perhaps the first setback had occurred when Alma travelled to the small town to fetch the things they needed urgently; when they discovered that they had been robbed and plundered, that they had been reduced to poverty. Those small-town people had certainly taken their revenge on their hated mayor! During his absence, they had not left him a single sock or shoe, not a shirt or a suit, and not a frock for his young wife to wear—all they had left hanging in the cupboard were the oldest, shabbiest rags. He had found out once again, and this time to his own cost, how feral and depraved this country had become: people felt they had a perfect right to plunder and steal, since the war had robbed them of so much. Who was going to stop them helping themselves? The mantra 'Public need before private greed'—never actually practised—had been supplanted by a different one: 'Help yourself—and don't hold back!'

In the case of a man as hated as their former mayor was, they didn't need to be told twice. They had paid him back for that speech he made from the balcony of the town commandant's office, when he settled scores with the Nazis among them. They had not forgotten his interrogations, the house searches, the confiscations; every request he had turned down had been added to the list of his crimes.

Well, the Dolls had made the best of it, telling themselves: *What would we have done if the place had been hit by a bomb? Then we would have lost everything! At least now we have salvaged the furniture, or what was left of it after the little darlings used some for firewood, and some of the carpets and your books, which have survived more or less unscathed.*

So they had made the best of it. They had started to set up their new home, and he had started to work again—but maybe they still carried some inner trauma that had not gone away. There was nothing of the old fire and energy. *I'm getting old*, Doll kept on thinking. Not that he mourned the valuables they had lost: *What was bought for money before can always be bought with money again.* Nor did he care very much that he only possessed two pairs of old socks, which had been darned a hundred times, and one very shabby-looking suit.

None of this bothered him much. But what did bother him, perhaps, was the discovery that evil continued to triumph, as it had for the previous twelve years, that everything was actually getting worse all the time. There seemed no possibility that this nation could ever mend its ways. He often had the feeling that deprivation and hardship were simply turning them into better Nazis than they were before. How often did he hear the words: 'Oh yes, under the Führer we had a lot more of this and a lot more of that ...!' To all of them, including many who had not been Nazis before, the years of the Hitler tyranny suddenly seemed like some sort of golden age. The horrors of the war, with the nightly bombing raids, husbands and sons sent off to bleed and die, the defilement of the innocent—all that had already been forgotten. They reckoned they had got a bit more bread or meat back then: end of story. They seemed beyond redemption, and sometimes it was almost unbearable to be living among them; for the first time, Doll thought seriously about emigrating—now, when the war was over!

But none of this was sufficient reason to sink into such a deep state of apathy again, to destroy their hard-won gains, to give up what they had struggled to hold on to. Perhaps the work also had something to do with it, this work that had become more of a duty than a pleasure: work that lacked any spark, any intuition, any love, work that his heart simply wasn't in. He had always loved his work, had seen it as the thing that gave his life meaning. And now he watched himself just going through the motions, and the feeling often came over him that he might never be able to work again like before, that the old fire had gone out of him for good.

That's where they were now, and a thousand minor adversities, impossible to avoid in these times, had added to their troubles. He had even lost the ability to manage money sensibly, it seemed. Money was a constant problem: it never went far enough, and since it didn't go far enough, despite all their economies, why bother to limit their smoking? Why not smoke English and American cigarettes? What did it matter, after all?

And right on cue, his young wife's gallbladder trouble had started up again, whether due to some physical cause or just psychosomatically induced. When this complaint returned to the Doll household, so did the 'little remedies', and this time Doll made no protest; this time, it was a case of share and share alike. Now they abandoned themselves to their dreams, the world appeared in a rose-tinted glow, all their troubles were forgotten, and they were barely aware of feeling hungry or cold; they only got out of bed in order to go and fetch more 'stuff'.

But getting hold of money became increasingly difficult. Doll was not working on anything—so the big sell-off began. First the furniture went out the door, and then Persian rugs, pictures, and books. They were pouring their lives into a bottomless pit. Their strength, their courage, their hopes, their last possessions, they all went the same way—out the door.

They hid their passion cunningly enough from the world; when they were talking to Granzow, the work was making great strides. Doll talked the talk, coming out with one project after another; he invented the most amazing stories, and then promptly forgot about it all again as soon as he stepped outside Granzow's house. They lived only for their dreams now, each dreaming their own dreams alone, lying in their bed-graves ...

Until the day came when it had to stop, until everything had been sold, until they had lost everything they owned and run up a mountain of debt besides, until the body barely responded even to the strongest dosage, until they so hated their stupid, pointless lives that they just wanted out. But they didn't get out, any more than the rest of their nation did, though there was reason enough to go. They eventually ended up in hospital again—in his case, in that strange women's refuge at No. 10 Elsastrasse. She, young as she was, successfully overcame her substance abuse after a short course of treatment; now she was back in the small country town again, where she had gone some time before to collect the rest of their things.

So they would make another attempt to start out all over again—another attempt, and under much more difficult circumstances than before. They had squandered a great deal of capital in terms of friendship, trust, property, and self-belief.

He stood up from his desk in this dusty, threadbare room, where the remnants of his library gazed back at him accusingly. He stretched his limbs, stepped out on the balcony, and looked out over the sunlit greenery. *The trees haven't been through a war,* he thought to himself, *nor the shrubs or the grass. Life goes on.* It was not much comfort, but it was comfort of a sort. Why shouldn't he write another book that everyone would read, that would be a success? Soon—perhaps it was happening at this very moment, as he stood there on the balcony—the truck and trailer carrying the rest of his books and furniture would be rounding the corner. They would make a new start once again—and this time they wouldn't stray from their course just when the goal was in sight.

He suddenly felt cold in the sun. He couldn't bear to remain in this house a moment longer; it reminded him of a tomb where so many hopes lay buried. He hurried out of the house, passed through the red-and-white barrier again, and a few minutes later was sitting in a tram.

Right, he thought to himself with sudden resolve. *I don't want Granzow thinking I shirk every decision and leave everything to others. I need to know one way or the other, and before the truck arrives.*

Later he was walking through the heart of the destruction, seeing few people on these streets, which seven years ago were absolutely packed and could barely cope with all the traffic. Now he was able to walk down the middle of the road, with no need to worry about the cars. When one did occasionally appear, it crept forward cautiously to avoid the deep holes in the road surface.

Doll's progress was likewise slow. The sun beat down on the ruins (it was all quiet around here), and the smell of dust and burnt debris was everywhere still. Many Berlin locals had happy visions of the ruins being grassed over in next to no time. But we are a long way from the nearest tropical jungle here, and anyway the topsoil was completely smothered by the fallen masonry; nothing was growing as yet. You hardly ever saw so much as a green shoot …

Yes, my friend, Doll said to himself, *and why are you surprised, aggrieved almost? Things just don't grow that quickly from ruins—and that applies to you, too, especially to you! You're no spring chicken yourself, and just think back to a year ago, how damaged you were then! Don't you remember how you were lying in that huge bomb crater, which was the world, or at least Germany, waiting for help from the Big Three? So there! But I think you've pulled yourself together a bit since then. There's a little bit of grass growing on the ruin. Don't be so impatient—just keep on going the way you are!*

So he kept on going the way he was, and that way led him, just a few hundred paces further on through all this destruction, to a large, fairly well preserved office building—the former headquarters of the

255

German Labour Front. He climbed the stairs; nobody asked him what he wanted, he didn't need to fill out a registration form stating whether he was born, baptised, or existent—he was going to see a truly modern businessman.

He opened a door, and there he was, standing in front of his publisher Mertens—no desk clerk, secretary, or receptionist.

Ten minutes later he left the former headquarters of the German Labour Front. Granzow had been right: this Mertens was not a small-minded man. No faffing around, no protracted discussion, no words of blame. Just questions, a few moments of reflection, and then a 'Yes'.

Under his arm Doll was clutching a package—new titles published by Mertens and dedicated to him—and his wallet was now stuffed with banknotes. He no longer needed to make the gaps on his bookshelves bigger, yet the burden of debt had been lifted from his shoulders. Now all he needed to do was to keep working steadily, stay lucky, and all would be well again.

Although Doll knew of a small, little-frequented post office next to the tram stop near his house, he headed off through the streets of ruins, asking people the way to another post office. He couldn't wait to do what now had to be done. It was a much longer walk to this city-centre post office, through the streets of ruins, and the post office itself was still badly damaged and very busy.

He had to wait in line for a long time before he was handed a pen and a sheaf of money orders and transfer forms. Then he went to one of the desks, and started to make out the money orders. They were for large amounts, and it would take a long time, many months of work, to earn back the money. He thought of all the good things they could have bought for that money; their home would look like a human habitation now instead of an animal's den, if they had not squandered the money so senselessly on this wretched 'stuff', this trash that had made them ill into the bargain.

But this was just a passing thought. Doll now filled out the money orders with genuine pleasure, and with a profound sense of relief he crossed off the names of his satisfied creditors from the list he always carried with him. He couldn't pay them all today, but in a week's time he would collect the rest of his advance from the publishers—and then he could draw a line under all this business.

When Doll stepped out into the street again a good hour later, his wallet had shrunk back to its normal size, but his heart seemed to have grown bigger and stronger, because he felt so easy in his mind. He no longer noticed that there was hardly anything green growing on the rubble; in fact, he didn't even see the rubble any more. He was free from the heavy cares that had so long tormented him, and he now saw a way forward ... Suddenly he was in a hurry to get home. That dreary, filthy den—suddenly he was calling it 'home'.

And lo and behold, as he turned the corner and could see to the end of the villa-lined street, a scene of lively activity met his gaze. A truck and trailer were parked outside his door, he saw the children helping the men to carry things in—and good heavens, there they were, just taking his books into the house! The shelves would be full again despite everything, the den would become a proper home, they'd managed to do it again! He practically ran the last bit ...

He found Alma sitting in an armchair and smoking, giving out instructions to the removal men. She had used the time he was away to remove the traces of her dusty truck journey, and now she was looking fresh and youthful again ...

'I bet you're surprised', she called out to him. 'Yes, I managed to fill up the truck and the trailer completely. Now it's all here. We don't need to make another trip. We've seen the back of that dreary little place for good. All your books are here—are you pleased? Haven't I done well?'

He was very pleased, of course, and gave her a kiss. Then he quickly asked Alma if she could spare a cigarette for him, too.

'You can have a whole pack if you want it!' she cried. 'You poor dear, are you feeling desperate? Here—take one! And I've got something else for you: there's two bottles of schnaps in my bag! We should let the men have some, they've worked really hard. And don't pull a face because you think I've spent too much money. Schnaps is cheap out there—less than forty marks a bottle! I've also come back with all my travel money. More, in fact!'

'You have?' he said. 'How come you've still got all your travel money? And more than you took with you! Do they let people travel for free on the railways now? Do the hotels pay you for sleeping in their rooms?'

'Oh, that's easy!' she cried. 'I quickly sold off all the useless junk that wouldn't fit on the truck—old stuff that we'd never have used: mattresses, plain wooden furniture. And now let's raise a glass—to a better future! Cheers!'

They clinked glasses and drank the schnaps. She stretched herself luxuriously. 'Oh, that went down well after the long, dusty drive! Am I glad to have that behind me! We were working until three o'clock in the morning loading up the truck. We worked hard, I can tell you, and now you can give me a kiss to say thank you! I'm feeling so happy!'

He kissed her, this spoilt child, who was now ready to walk the way of hard work and austerity with him. He gazed at her as she sat there, smiling in all her joy and wholesome youthfulness, pleased with her achievements.

In the late evening Doll returned to the hospital to spend his last night there. Next morning he would move into the villa-lined street and start to make a new home for himself. He was well again, he felt the desire to work, and he believed in his future. And one cannot believe in one's own future without thinking about family and friends, the nation at large, and humanity in general. Believing now that he would get back on his feet again, he believed that Europe, too, would endure and rise again.

The apathy had finally left him, and he was no longer lying in that bomb crater. The strength he needed to climb up out of the crater had come to him mysteriously from within — not from the Big Three — and now he was at the top. He applauded life — the life enduring, forever sullied, but magnificent. The nations would sort themselves out again. Even Germany, this beloved, wretched Germany, this diseased heart of Europe, would get well again.

And as Doll made his way through the streets of Berlin at this late evening hour, he felt for the first time that peace had truly come. He walked past undamaged houses, past ruins, under the leafy treetops, and felt happy. At one with himself. At rest. Restored to health — and fit for a life of peace.

Life goes on, and they would outlive these times, those who had been spared by the grace of God, the survivors. Life goes on, always, even beneath the ruins. The ruins are of no account; what counts is life — the life in a blade of grass in the middle of the city, in amongst a thousand lumps of shattered masonry. Life goes on, always.

And maybe people will learn something, after all. Learn from their suffering, their tears, their blood. Learn reluctantly, hesitantly, or with relish. Learn that things have to change, that we have to learn to think differently …

Doll, at any rate, was determined to be part of this learning process. He saw his path laid out before him, the next steps he had to take, and they meant work, work, and more work. Beyond these first steps, the darkness began again, the darkness that obscures the future for every German today; but he preferred not to think about that. In the last few years, people had learned so well how to live in the moment, from one day to the next: why should that lesson not be put to good use today? *Just get on with life and do your job*: that should be his watchword now.

A comforting late-evening breeze was wafting through the treetops. The breath of the big wide world was blowing upon him, the little man. He leaned against one of the trees for a while, listening to the wind whispering in the branches above. It was nothing, just the movement of air making the leaves rustle like that. Nothing. No more than that. But it sufficed. In the last few years he had never had time to stand under a tree and listen to its whisperings. Now he had time, for peace had come again—peace! *Know this in your heart, my friend: you are done with murdering and killing. Lay down your arms—peace has finally come!*

BRIEF BIOGRAPHY

1893 21 July: Rudolf Ditzen is born in Greifswald, the third child of Wilhelm and Elisabeth Ditzen.

1899 His father, a county court magistrate, is appointed a counsellor in the Court of Appeal in Berlin. The family moves to Berlin.

1909 His father is appointed to the Imperial Supreme Court in Leipzig. The family moves to Leipzig; he suffers a serious bicycle accident.

1911 Attends the grammar school in Rudolstadt, and is seriously injured in a suicide pact—made to look like a duel gone wrong—in which his friend Hanns Dietrich von Necker is killed.

1912 He is committed to Tannenfeld sanatorium in Saxony.

1913 Gets a job as an estate worker in Posterstein, Thuringia.

1914 Enlists as a volunteer in the German army, but is discharged a few days later as unfit for military service.

1915 Secures a position as deputy steward on the Heydebreck estate in Eastern Pomerania (until March 1916).

1916 Takes a job with the Chamber of Agriculture in Stettin, then joins the staff of a seed potato company in Berlin.

1919 He is re-admitted to Tannenfeld in August 1919, but soon leaves for Carlsfeld sanatorium in Brehna to be treated for drug addiction.

1920 Literary debut with the semi-autobiographical novel *Der junge Goedeschal* ['Young Goedeschal']; thereafter he adopts the pseudonym Hans Fallada. In November he takes a job as a bookkeeper on the Marzdorf estate in West Prussia (now Poland).

1921 Leaves Marzdorf in January. For the second half of the year he works as a bookkeeper on an estate near Doberan in Mecklenburg.

1922 From June to October he works as a bookkeeper on the Neuschönfeld estate near Bunzlau in Silesia (now Poland). Arrested in October for trading the estate's grain on the black market, he returns to Marzdorf for the last two months of the year.

1923 Publication of the novel *Anton und Gerda*. From the spring until October he is employed as a bookkeeper on the Radach estate near Drossen. In July he is sentenced to six months' imprisonment for embezzlement (deferred until 1924).

1924 Imprisoned in Greifswald from June to early November.

1925 Publication of three essays on social and political issues of the day in the liberal journal *Das Tage-Buch*. In the spring he goes to work as a bookkeeper on the Lübgust estate near Neustettin in Pomerania (now Poland); leaves Lübgust in July and takes a new job as senior bookkeeper on the Neuhaus estate near Lütjenburg in Schleswig-Holstein; in September he is caught stealing money from his employers again.

1926 Sentenced to two-and-a-half years in Neumünster prison for embezzlement.

1928 Earns a living addressing envelopes in Hamburg, joins the SPD (Social Democratic Party), and gets engaged to Anna 'Suse' Issel.

1929 Gets a job selling advertising space and reporting on local news for the *General-Anzeiger* in Neumünster; 5 April: marriage to Anna Issel; reports on the trial of the *Landvolk* movement agitators.

1930 Secures a position with Rowohlt Verlag; birth of son Ulrich.

1931 Publication of *Bauern, Bonzen, und Bomben* ['A Small Circus']; moves to Neuenhagen near Berlin.

1932 *Kleiner Mann – was nun?* ['Little Man – What Now?'] is published; he becomes a freelance writer. Moves to Berkenbrück in November.

1933 He is held in jail for eleven days after being denounced to the authorities; buys a house and smallholding in Carwitz near Feldberg; birth of daughter Lore.

1934–35 Publication of *Wer einmal aus dem Blechnapf frisst* ['Once a Jailbird'], *Wir hatten mal ein Kind* ['Once We Had a Child'], and *Das Märchen vom Stadtschreiber, der aufs Land flog* ['Sparrow Farm'].

1936 Publication of *Altes Herz geht auf die Reise* ['Old Heart Goes on a Journey'] and *Hoppelpoppel, wo bist du?* ['Hoppelpoppel, Where Are You?'].

1937 Publication of *Wolf unter Wölfen* ['Wolf Among Wolves'].

1938 Publication of *Der eiserne Gustav* ['Iron Gustav'] and *Geschichten aus der Murkelei* ['Stories from a Childhood'].

1940 Publication of *Kleiner Mann, grosser Mann — alles vertauscht* ['Little Man, Big Man — Roles Reversed'] and *Der ungeliebte Mann* ['The Unloved Man']; birth of son Achim.

1941 Publication of *Damals bei uns daheim* ['Our Home in Days Gone By'], *Die Stunde eh' du schlafen gehst* ['Before You Go to Sleep'], and *Der mutige Buchhändler* ['The Brave Bookseller'] (also published under the title *Die Abenteuer des Werner Quabs*).

1942 Publication of *Ein Mann will nach oben* (alternative title: *Ein Mann will hinauf*) ['A Man Wants to Get On'] and *Zwei zarte Lämmchen weiss wie Schnee* ['Two Tender Lambs White as Snow'].

1943 Publication of *Heute bei uns zu Haus* ['Our Home Today'] and *Der Jungherr von Strammin* (alternative title: *Junger Herr ganz gross*) ['The Master of Strammin']; at the invitation of the Wehrmacht, he undertakes fact-finding tours of the annexed territories of

Czechoslovakia and occupied France as a major in the Reich Labour Service; after Rowohlt Verlag is closed down by the Nazis and his general publishing agreement is cancelled, Fallada is left without any financial security.

1944 5 July: divorced from Anna Ditzen; during an argument he fires a shot from his pistol, and is committed to the Neustrelitz-Strelitz psychiatric prison, where the so-called *Drinker* manuscript with the 1944 prison diary is written (first published in 2009 under the title *In meinem fremden Land* ['A Stranger in My Own Country']); following his release he writes *Fridolin der freche Dachs* ['That Rascal, Fridolin'].

1945 Marriage in Berlin to the 22-year-old Ursula 'Ulla' Losch, who also has a history of morphine addiction; because of the ceaseless air raids they leave Ulla's apartment in Meraner Strasse (Berlin–Schöneberg) and move out to her wooden chalet in Klinkecken, on the outskirts of Feldberg; when the war ends, Fallada is made mayor of Feldberg by the occupying Red Army; in August the couple suffer a breakdown and are hospitalised; they return to their apartment in Berlin–Schöneberg, which is partly destroyed, partly occupied by others; first meeting with Johannes R. Becher, through whom he gets commissions to write pieces for the *Tägliche Rundschau*, and who arranges for him to move into a spacious house with a garden and garage in Eisenmengerweg (in the Pankow-Niederschönhausen district of Berlin), Fallada's last place of residence.

1946 Repeated admissions to hospital, including a spell in a private temporary infirmary specializing in female venereal diseases at 10 Marthastrasse, where Fallada is the only male patient; works on *Der Trinker* ['The Drinker'] (published in a reconstructed version in

1950/1953), *Nightmare in Berlin* (published in 1947), and *Alone in Berlin* (first published in 1947, although the book did not appear in its original version until 2011).

1947 5 February: Fallada dies in Berlin; he is cremated in a cemetery in Pankow, and his ashes are later moved to the cemetery in Carwitz at the instigation of Anna Ditzen.

EDITORIAL NOTE

The text of this edition is based on Volume 7 of the *Ausgewählte Werke in Einzelausgaben* ['Selected Works'], edited by Günter Caspar, Aufbau Verlag, Berlin and Weimar, 2nd edition, 1988. The 1988 text was in turn based on the first edition (Aufbau Verlag, Berlin, 1947), which contained two obvious slips that Caspar corrected: at the end of Chapter 8 the nurse talks of '16 February 1943', although she clearly means '1944', as mentioned at the beginning of Chapter 7. And towards the end of Chapter 12 there are two references to the 'Big Four', although this clearly refers back to Chapter 1 and the 'Big Three'. While preparing the new edition, Caspar also consulted Fallada's correspondence, the manuscripts, and other material relating to the novel, when the author's papers were still in the possession of the then copyright owner, Emma D. Hey (Braunschweig). Some of the material is now kept in the Hans Fallada Archive (Neubrandenburg/Carwitz), but the location of the manuscripts and typescripts, as well as the proofs for *Nightmare in Berlin*, is today unknown.

Günter Caspar assumed that Hans Fallada had read the proofs in full. But letters kept in the Aufbau company archive cast doubt on this. Based on three such letters (dated 17, 24, and 27 November 1946), it is safe to assume that he read 'the first 20 page proofs of *Nightmare*' as well as 'p. 21 to 127' ('page proofs 61 to 100 are missing'), and then returned them to his publisher (the first edition ran to 236 printed pages). The correspondence of the publishing director Kurt Wilhelm also contains a letter of 31 December 1946, in which he laments the fact that 'at the time of writing' he has still not received the corrected proofs back from Fallada. He reverts to the matter on 27 January: 'Our production department is still waiting for your proof corrections for *Nightmare*, and needs them very urgently now. Is it not possible for you to send me your copy of the proofs through an intermediary, as soon as possible after you receive this letter?' Wilhelm never received a reply to this request. Fallada died on 5 February 1947, in Berlin's Charité hospital.

As far as the preparation of the manuscript is concerned, it is clear from the correspondence that Fallada revised the text several times. On 27 September 1946, he wrote: 'Dear Mr. Wilhelm, with this letter my wife is bringing you the finished manuscript of my novel *Nightmare in Berlin*—unfortunately I am unable to come myself, owing to a bad attack of rheumatoid arthritis. / As you will see from a quick look through the copy, I have put a great deal of additional work into this novel, and I doubt if there is a single page that hasn't been revised, but the main thing is that I have cut the text substantially, probably by as much as a quarter. I hope that the book in its present definitive form is to your liking. [...] / Before the manuscript goes to print, I would like to look through it myself one more time, since all too often typing mistakes creep in that distort the meaning. I would also like to read the galley proofs myself.'

In October, further specific changes were agreed in an exchange of letters and sent on to Wilhelm by Fallada. The latter also expressed detailed views on the format and design of the book, took it upon himself to organise serialisation in the *Frankfurter Rundschau*, and announced his intention of placing the novel with three of his foreign publishers: Gyldendal in Copenhagen, Putnam in London, and Hökerberg in Stockholm: 'It would be really nice if you were the first German publisher able to announce the publication of a German book in a foreign country.'

What emerges clearly from all this is that even if Fallada was unable to deliver a full set of corrected proofs to his publisher before his death, he had meticulously prepared the text of *Nightmare in Berlin* for publication.

Dr Allan Blunden is a British translator who specialises in German literature. He is best known for his translation of Erhard Eppler's *The Return of the State?* which won a Schlegel-Tieck Prize. He has also translated biographies of Heidegger and Stefan Zweig, and the prison diary of Hans Fallada.